The
MX Book
of
New
Sherlock
Holmes
Stories
Part XLII – Further Untold Cases
(1894-1922)

THE MX BOOK OF NEW SHERLOCK HOLMES STORIES

PART XLII
FURTHER UNTOLD CASES
(1894-1922)

SOUTHAMPTON STREET

359

EDITED By David Marcum OFFICES

TRADITIONAL HOLMES ADVENTURES COMPILED FOR THE BENEFIT OF THE RESTORATION OF UNDERSHAW

ISBN Hardback 978-1-80424-365-7
ISBN Paperback 978-1-80424-366-4
AUK ePub ISBN 978-1-80424-367-1
AUK PDF ISBN 978-1-80424-368-8

Published in the UK by
MX Publishing
335 Princess Park Manor, Royal Drive,
London, N11 3GX
www.mxpublishing.co.uk

David Marcum can be reached at:
thepapersofsherlockholmes@gmail.com

Cover design by Brian Belanger
www.belangerbooks.com and *www.redbubble.com/people/zhahadun*

Internal Illustrations by Sidney Paget

CONTENTS

Forewords

Adventures

(Continued on the next page . . . .)

(Continued on the next page . . . .)

These additional adventures are contained in
Part XL: Further Untold Cases
(1879-1886)

The Case of the Cases of Vamberry Bergundy – Roger Riccard
The Adventure of the Aluminium Crutch – Tracy J. Revels
The Most Winning Woman – Liese Sherwood-Fabre
Mrs. Farintosh's Opal Tiara – Brenda Seabrooke
A Case of Duplicity – Gordon Linzner
The Adventure of the Fraudulent Benefactor – Mike Adamson
The Adventure of the Dead Rats – Hugh Ashton
The Laodicean Letters – David Marcum
A Case of Exceptional Brilliants – Jane Rubino
The True Account of the Dorrington Ruby Affair – Brett Fawcett
The Adventure of the Old Russian Woman – Susan Knight
The Adventure of the Silver Snail – Alan Dimes
The Adventure of the Invisible Weapon – Arthur Hall
The Backwater Affair – Paula Hammond
The Adventure of the Opening Eyes – Tracy J. Revels
The Man in the Rain with a Dog – Brenda
The Problem of the Grosvenor Square Moving Van – Tim Newton Anderson
The Dark Tavern – Robert Stapleton

Part XLI: Further Untold Cases
(1877-1892)

The Case of the Trepoff Murder – Stephen Herczeg
The Strange Case of the Disappearing Factor – Margaret Walsh
The Mystery of the Three Mendicants – Paul D. Gilbert
The Difficult Ordeal of the Paradol Chamber – Will Murray
The Amateur Mendicant Society – David MacGregor
The Amnesiac's Peril – Barry Clay
The Mystery of the Unstolen Document – Mike Chinn
The Adventure of the Infernal Philanthropist – Tim Newton Anderson
The Adventure of the Murdered Mistress – Ember Pepper
The Rouen Scandal – Martin Daley

(Continued on the next page . . . .)

(Continued on the next page . . . .)

(Continued on the next page . . . .)

PART V – Christmas Adventures

(Continued on the next page . . . .)

PART VI – 2017 Annual

(Continued on the next page . . . .)

(Continued on the next page . . . .)

Part IX – 2018 Annual (1879-1895)

(Continued on the next page . . . .)

The Lambeth Poisoner Case – Stephen Gaspar
The Confession of Anna Jarrow – S. F. Bennett
The Adventure of the Disappearing Dictionary – Sonia Fetherston
The Fairy Hills Horror – Geri Schear
A Loathsome and Remarkable Adventure – Marcia Wilson
The Adventure of the Multiple Moriartys – David Friend
The Influence Machine – Mark Mower

Part X – 2018 Annual (1896-1916)

Foreword – Nicholas Meyer
Foreword – Roger Johnson
Foreword – Melissa Farnham
Foreword – Steve Emecz
Foreword – David Marcum
A Man of Twice Exceptions (A Poem) – Derrick Belanger
The Horned God – Kelvin Jones
The Coughing Man – Jim French
The Adventure of Canal Reach – Arthur Hall
A Simple Case of Abduction – Mike Hogan
A Case of Embezzlement – Steven Ehrman
The Adventure of the Vanishing Diplomat – Greg Hatcher
The Adventure of the Perfidious Partner – Jayantika Ganguly
A Brush With Death – Dick Gillman
A Revenge Served Cold – Maurice Barkley
The Case of the Anonymous Client – Paul A. Freeman
Capitol Murder – Daniel D. Victor
The Case of the Dead Detective – Martin Rosenstock
The Musician Who Spoke From the Grave – Peter Coe Verbica
The Adventure of the Future Funeral – Hugh Ashton
The Problem of the Bruised Tongues – Will Murray
The Mystery of the Change of Art – Robert Perret
The Parsimonious Peacekeeper – Thaddeus Tuffentsamer
The Case of the Dirty Hand – G.L. Schulze
The Mystery of the Missing Artefacts – Tim Symonds

Part XI: Some Untold Cases (1880-1891)

Foreword – Lyndsay Faye
Foreword – Roger Johnson
Foreword – Melissa Grigsby
Foreword – Steve Emecz
Foreword – David Marcum
Unrecorded Holmes Cases (A Sonnet) – Arlene Mantin Levy and Mark Levy
The Most Repellant Man – Jayantika Ganguly
The Singular Adventure of the Extinguished Wicks – Will Murray
Mrs. Forrester's Complication – Roger Riccard
The Adventure of Vittoria, the Circus Belle – Tracy Revels

(Continued on the next page . . . .)

(Continued on the next page . . . .)

PART XIV: 2019 Annual (1891 -1897)

(Continued on the next page . . . .)

(Continued on the next page . . . .)

The Adventure of the Headless Lady – Tracy J. Revels
Angelus Domini Nuntiavit – Kevin P. Thornton
The Blue Lady of Dunraven – Andrew Bryant
The Adventure of the Ghoulish Grenadier – Josh Anderson and David Friend
The Curse of Barcombe Keep – Brenda Seabrooke
The Affair of the Regressive Man – David Marcum
The Adventure of the Giant's Wife – I.A. Watson
The Adventure of Miss Anna Truegrace – Arthur Hall
The Haunting of Bottomly's Grandmother – Tim Gambrell
The Adventure of the Intrusive Spirit – Shane Simmons
The Paddington Poltergeist – Bob Bishop
The Spectral Pterosaur – Mark Mower
The Weird of Caxton – Kelvin Jones
The Adventure of the Obsessive Ghost – Jayantika Ganguly

Part XVII – Whatever Remains . . . Must Be the Truth (1891-1898)
Foreword – Kareem Abdul-Jabbar
Foreword – Roger Johnson
Foreword – Steve Emecz
Foreword – David Marcum
The Violin Thief (*A Poem*) – Christopher James
The Spectre of Scarborough Castle – Charles Veley and Anna Elliott
The Case for Which the World is Not Yet Prepared – Steven Philip Jones
The Adventure of the Returning Spirit – Arthur Hall
The Adventure of the Bewitched Tenant – Michael Mallory
The Misadventures of the Bonnie Boy – Will Murray
The Adventure of the *Danse Macabre* – Paul D. Gilbert
The Strange Persecution of John Vincent Harden – S. Subramanian
The Dead Quiet Library – Roger Riccard
The Adventure of the Sugar Merchant – Stephen Herczeg
The Adventure of the Undertaker's Fetch – Tracy J. Revels
The Holloway Ghosts – Hugh Ashton
The Diogenes Club Poltergeist – Chris Chan
The Madness of Colonel Warburton – Bert Coules
The Return of the Noble Bachelor – Jane Rubino
The Reappearance of Mr. James Phillimore – David Marcum
The Miracle Worker – Geri Schear
The Hand of Mesmer – Dick Gillman

Part XVIII – Whatever Remains . . . Must Be the Truth (1899-1925)
Foreword – Kareem Abdul-Jabbar
Foreword – Roger Johnson
Foreword – Steve Emecz
Foreword – David Marcum
The Adventure of the Lighthouse on the Moor (*A Poem*) – Christopher James
The Witch of Ellenby – Thomas A. Burns, Jr.

(Continued on the next page . . . .)

Part XIX: 2020 Annual (1882-1890)

(Continued on the next page . . . .)

The Adventure of the Matched Set – Peter Coe Verbica
When the Prince First Dined at the Diogenes Club – Sean M. Wright
The Sweetenbury Safe Affair – Tim Gambrell

Part XX: 2020 Annual (1891-1897)
Foreword – John Lescroart
Foreword – Roger Johnson
Foreword – Lizzy Butler
Foreword – Steve Emecz
Foreword – David Marcum
The Sibling (*A Poem*) – Jacquelynn Morris
Blood and Gunpowder – Thomas A. Burns, Jr.
The Atelier of Death – Harry DeMaio
The Adventure of the Beauty Trap – Tracy Revels
A Case of Unfinished Business – Steven Philip Jones
The Case of the S.S. Bokhara – Mark Mower
The Adventure of the American Opera Singer – Deanna Baran
The Keadby Cross – David Marcum
The Adventure at Dead Man's Hole – Stephen Herczeg
The Elusive Mr. Chester – Arthur Hall
The Adventure of Old Black Duffel – Will Murray
The Blood-Spattered Bridge – Gayle Lange Puhl
The Tomorrow Man – S.F. Bennett
The Sweet Science of Bruising – Kevin P. Thornton
The Mystery of Sherlock Holmes – Christopher Todd
The Elusive Mr. Phillimore – Matthew J. Elliott
The Murders in the Maharajah's Railway Carriage – Charles Veley and Anna Elliott
The Ransomed Miracle – I.A. Watson
The Adventure of the Unkind Turn – Robert Perret
The Perplexing X'ing – Sonia Fetherston
The Case of the Short-Sighted Clown – Susan Knight

Part XXI: 2020 Annual (1898-1923)
Foreword – John Lescroart
Foreword – Roger Johnson
Foreword – Lizzy Butler
Foreword – Steve Emecz
Foreword – David Marcum
The Case of the Missing Rhyme (*A Poem*) – Joseph W. Svec III
The Problem of the St. Francis Parish Robbery – R.K. Radek
The Adventure of the Grand Vizier – Arthur Hall
The Mummy's Curse – DJ Tyrer
The Fractured Freemason of Fitzrovia – David L. Leal
The Bleeding Heart – Paula Hammond
The Secret Admirer – Jayantika Ganguly

(Continued on the next page . . . .)

Part XXII: Some More Untold Cases (1877-1887)

(Continued on the next page . . . .)

(Continued on the next page . . . .)

Part XXV: 2021 Annual (1881-1888)

(Continued on the next page . . . .)

(Continued on the next page . . . .)

Part XXVIII: More Christmas Adventures (1869-1888)

(Continued on the next page . . . .)

Part XXIX: More Christmas Adventures (1889-1896)

Part XXX: More Christmas Adventures (1897-1928)

(Continued on the next page . . . .)

(Continued on the next page . . . .)

Part XXXIII: 2022 Annual (1896-1919)

(Continued on the next page . . . .)

(Continued on the next page . . . .)

Part XXXVI: "However Improbable . . . ." (1897-1919)

(Continued on the next page . . . .)

(Continued on the next page . . . .)

Part XXXIX: 2023 Annual (1897-1923)

The following contributors appear in this volume:
The MX Book of New Sherlock Holmes Stories
Part XLII – Further Untold Cases (1894-1922)

The following contributors appear
in the companion volumes:
The MX Book of New Sherlock Holmes Stories
Part XL – Further Untold Cases (1879-1886)
Part XLI – Further Untold Cases (1887-1892)

Further Untold Cases – Parts XL, XLI, and XLII of
The MX Book of New Sherlock Holmes Stories
are dedicated to

Kelvin I. Jones

*I first became aware of Kelvin in the early 1980's, when I managed to
obtain a number of his expert Holmesian monographs. Little did I know
that one day I'd be able to be friends with him (even if we haven't met in
person) and that he would continue to contribute so ably. The world –
Sherlockian and otherwise – is a richer place because of him.*

Editor's Foreword:
Untold Infinite Possibilities
by David Marcum

In 1932, Edith Meiser did an amazing thing: By way of her Sherlock Holmes radio show starring Richard Gordon and Leigh Lovell as Holmes and Watson respectively, she related one of Holmes's *Untold Cases*. I may be wrong – I claim no expertise in Sherlock Holmes radio and film history, other than having a lot of reference books – but I think that this was the first time that anyone had done this – told an *Untold Case* – in any format.

For those who don't know what an *Untold Case* is, or believe that any post-Canonical Holmes adventure is an *Untold Case*, the term refers specifically to those *other* cases that Holmes solved (or some with which he was at least involved) that are mentioned in passing in The Canon. There are around 130 of them, some more famous than others, and – as seen with a few stories in this collection – other Untold Cases are being identified and related all the time. (More about that in a minute.)

I've been collecting and reading and studying Holmes's adventures since 1975, both those known as *The Canon* – those pitifully few sixty tales that came to us by way of the First Literary Agent's desk – and all the others that have been pulled from Watson's Tin Dispatch Box since then. And I'm pretty sure that "The Giant Rat of Sumatra", possibly the most famous of the Untold Cases, was the first one of those that were shared with the public. It was transcribed by Meiser from Watson's notes and broadcast on April 20th (although some sources say June 9th), 1932, and again on July 18th, 1936; and then on March 1st, 1942 (this time with Basil Rathbone as Holmes). Sadly, all of these versions are apparently lost, although I'd dearly love to hear – and read – them! (According to one source shared with me, Meiser's script for "The Giant Rat of Sumatra" is held within the Sherlockian collections at the University of Minnesota, but my attempts to see this – or any of her scripts that are kept there – have been unsuccessful.)

Meiser's "Giant Rat", though the first related Untold Case, wasn't her first post-Canonical tale. After numerous Canonical broadcasts, she approached the Doyle Heirs, who were in a non-litigious mood that week, about doing something different, and she was then allowed to present other Tin Dispatch Box-sourced adventures. The first of these was "The Hindoo in the Wicker Basket", broadcast on January 7th, 1932 (although one source I've seen shows some sort of Holmes *Christmas Carol* on

1

December 23rd, 1931.) During early 1932, there were a few more Canonical broadcasts – "The Yellow Face", "The *Gloria Scott*", and a six-part version of *The Hound*, but there were also a few others that people hadn't heard of before, such as "Murder in the Waxworks", "The Adventure of the Ace of Spades", "The Missing Leonardo da Vinci" – and then "The Giant Rat".

I would give much to hear (or read) some of these lost adventures (although some of the scripts aren't "lost", just hidden away). And of course there are many other cases from the Tin Box out there, also lost, would be just as interesting to read, see, or hear. Meiser wasn't the first to pull non-Canonical adventures from the Tin Box. For instance, not counting parodies, Kowo Films, a German concern, might have been the first, producing nine post-Canonical Holmes films between 1917 and 1919. (Apparently being on the losing side in an ongoing World War couldn't prevent the production of Holmes films by a German company about one of their enemy's greatest heroes.) These were fascinating titles like *The Earthquake Motor*, *The Indian Spider*, and *The Fate of Renate Yongh*. One of them, *The Cardinal's Snuff Box*, might possibly maybe could-have-been the actual first portrayal of an Untold Case – *The Sudden Death of Cardinal Tosca* – but as of now, we cannot know.

Now, assuming that one gives Meiser due credit for being the first to relate an Untold Case (as far as I can tell) with her version of "The Giant Rat of Sumatra", some might be inclined to think that she had staked that one as her own claim, and that there would be no need for someone else to find and publish an alternate version of "The Giant Rat". After all, Meiser had brought it forward first, and there's no reason to suppose that what she presented wasn't perfectly fine. But in truth, there have been lots of versions – all very different indeed – of this particular Untold Case. Over two-dozen of them, in fact, not counting irrelevant parodies, science fiction and fantasy attempts, and versions where the true Holmes is not present.

"The Giant Rat" is mentioned Canonically in "The Sussex Vampire":

> "Matilda Briggs *was not the name of a young woman, Watson,*" *said Holmes in a reminiscent voice.* "*It was a ship which is associated with the giant rat of Sumatra, a story for which the world is not yet prepared.*

That, and the fact that Morrison, Morrison, and Dodd said that Holmes's action in the case of the *Matilda Briggs* was successful, are all we officially know about the Giant Rat. We can speculate a few other things: Morrison, Morrison, and Dodd specialized in the assessment of

2

machinery – and yet they were somehow involved in the matter of the Giant Rat enough to know of Holmes's successful action. The fact that Holmes has to explain that the *Matilda Briggs* was a ship and not a young woman implies that Watson doesn't know about it – and that possibly this case occurred during some period when Watson wasn't involved in Holmes's cases – perhaps before they moved to Baker Street in January 1881, or during a period when Watson was married and living elsewhere. And we know that it was especially serious, and of a nature that might cause panic or with a solution that might stretch credulity. The world is not yet prepared. *The whole world? Not prepared?* That implies something that's seriously disturbing.

Or perhaps someone else might read this short description from "The Sussex Vampire" and interpret it an entirely different way. In fact, many have. Many of the different versions of "The Giant Rat" never even mention involvement of any sort by Morrison, Morrison, and Dodd. Instead of Watson being ignorant of details, all versions involve Watson right alongside Holmes. And he knows about the *Matilda Briggs* – except in some iterations, where the *Matilda Briggs* isn't mentioned at all.

The fact that there are so many versions of "The Giant Rat" might be a source of consternation for some, who think there can only be one, and that all others are simulacrums and distractions of greater or lesser quality. Just as some might think that because Edith Meiser was the first to describe Holmes's connection with the Giant Rat, and therefore no other descriptions are valid, others might prefer a different version. My personal favorite is the late Rick Boyer's *The Giant Rat of Sumatra*, published in 1976, one of those first post-Canonical adventures to ride the initial wave propagated by Nicholas Meyer's *The Seven-Per-Cent Solution* in 1974, beginning a Sherlockian Golden Age that has never faded since.

If I were to decide that my favorite "Giant Rat" by Boyer was the *only* "Giant Rat", I would have cheated myself of over two-dozen other versions, equally good in their own ways, and also any others that have yet to be revealed.

I play *The Game*, wherein Holmes and Watson are recognized as historical figures who lived and died – Yes, they're dead now, and have been for a long time. When doing that, one might be a bit wobbly when trying to figure out how one charmed and famous lifetime and notable career could have included over two-dozen encounters with a Giant Rat. Nearly everyone who has ever lived has never met a single Giant Rat. The easy answer is that these are all different encounters, and there just happened to be a lot of Giant Rat crimes across the decades between when Holmes commenced his career and when he and Watson discussed the Giant Rat in "The Sussex Vampire. It isn't as if Holmes solved the case

3

with a specific set of individuals, places, and circumstances, and then the deck was somehow cosmically reshuffled and the game replayed with the same individuals, places, and circumstances proceeding along different lines, (as were the characters in two Stephen King back-to-back companion novels, *The Regulators* and *Desperation*, both published on the same day in 1996.) The Giant Rat adventure related by Boyer is vastly different than the ones rescued from the Tin Dispatch Box by Paul Gilbert, Hugh Ashton, Amanda Knight, Alan Vanneman, David Stuart Davies, and many others.

And the Giant Rat is just an example, used because it is the Untold Case that has been related in the most versions. There are so many others that have also been told in multiple ways. The peculiar persecution of John Vincent Harden in 1895? Just keep in mind that there were a *lot* of tobacco millionaires in London during that time, all being peculiarly persecuted – but in very different ways – and Watson lumped them in his notes under the catch-all name of *John Vincent Harden.* Huret the Boulevard Assassin? There have been a number of different narratives telling how Holmes caught Huret – all completely different from one another, and all accurate and true and part of *The Great Holmes Tapestry*, that amazing mix of Canonical adventures, serving as the main cables, and the thousands of post-Canonical tales that make up fibers in between that fill in the details and provide all the color and nuance. The explanation for so many Huret narratives? There was a whole nest of Hurets to be rooted in out 1894, and each separate story relates how Holmes did it is just part of the bigger tapestry.

Since Meiser brought us the first Untold Case, there have been many others – far too many to list here. In *The MX Book of New Sherlock Holmes Stories*, we've had several volumes of them. In 2018, we presented Parts XI and XII – *Some Untold Cases*, and then in 2020, Parts XXII, XXIII, and XXIV returned to that theme with *Some More Untold Cases*. In the initial 2018 set, I required contributors to let me know beforehand which Untold Case they were going to choose, so that no one would provide more than one of them, and there would be no duplication. I only made one exception: Nick Cardillo had already signed up to bring us his version of "The Giant Rat" when Ian Dickerson made available the 1944 "Giant Rat" radio script written by Leslie Charteris and Denis Green – Rathbone and Bruce's *second* time telling that story, in a completely different script and investigation from the one by Edith Meiser which had been broadcast two years before. This worked out okay, because the 1944 script was set in the 1880's and included in Part XI, and Nick's story occurred in the 1890's and was in Part XII.

For the 2020 set, I had no requirement that anyone had to sign up and reserve an Untold Case. I was happy for people to send whatever Watson recorded, as long as it was traditional and Canonical. This was fortunate, because every story was excellent, even if there were some duplications of Untold Cases. For example, the matter of the Two Coptic Patriarchs occurs on a specific date in July 1898. Three contributors – John Davis, DJ Tyrer, and Harry DeMaio – all told versions of the Two Coptic Patriarchs, and since these books are arranged chronologically, these three stories were all presented side by side. There was no contradiction – they all told about different cases with Two Coptic Patriarchs that came to a head in that moment. (And of course, there have been a number of other narratives about these same Patriarchs in other books. Two, as a matter of fact, were by John Linwood Grant and Séamus Duffy and included in other parts of the MX Anthologies.)

In these new volumes, there are several versions of old intriguing favorites – *The Addleton Tragedy. The Sudden Death of Cardinal Tosca. The Most Repulsive Man. The Paradol Chamber. The Grosvenor Square Furniture Van* – all different, and all wonderful. Strangely, for all that I've mentioned it here, this time no one chose to provide any new revelations about one of the Giant Rats that Holmes faced during his career. But there are a few of Untold Cases described in these volumes by Alan Dimes and Chris Chan (and me) that no one had previously thought to add to the list. (My friend, the late Phil Jones, had a special passion for Untold Cases, and he would have been thrilled to see these.)

If you read Holmes adventures for very long – novels, themed or un-themed collections by one author or many, single magazine stories – chances are that someone will soon be telling you an Untold Case. And with so many of them, and with their mysteriously intriguing but often vague descriptions, one never knows what in what directions they'll jump.

In *The Valley of Fear* and "The Norwood Builder", Holmes used the phrase "*infinite possibilities.*" In "Wisteria Lodge" he also used the phrase "*a perfect jungle of possibilities*", and in "The Six Napoleons" he mentioned that "*There are no limits to the possibilities . . . .*"

Possibilities are what to expect when beginning any new Holmes adventure – reading one or writing one. As I've stated before, these can leap in any direction. One might find a comedy or a tragedy. A police procedural or gothic horror. The story might be set early in Holmes's career, or very late. It could be a city adventure or a country tale. Watson might be the narrator, or it could be Holmes, or someone else, or it might even be related in third person. And it might be long or short, taking just what it takes to tell what happened.

You may have read other versions of some of these Untold Cases before, and you may have favorites, but keep in mind that just because one version occurred in Holmes and Watson's life doesn't mean that it was the *only one* and that another didn't. They're *all* true, and they fit together like a most-intricate and complex puzzle, and in a vastly entertaining way.

In "The Sussex Vampire", Holmes states that Watson has *"unexplored possibilities"*. This, as well as *"infinite possibilities"*, is a good description of what one can expect when finding new adventures within Watson's Tin Dispatch Box – and also in the case of these volumes of *Further Untold Cases*.

* * * * *

"Of course, I could only stammer out my thanks."
– The unhappy John Hector McFarlane, "The Norwood Builder"

As always when one of these collections is finished, I want to thank with all my heart my incredible, patient, brilliant, kind, and beautiful wife of thirty-five years, Rebecca – Every day I count my blessings and realize how lucky I am! – and our amazing, funny, creative, and wonderful son, and my friend, Dan. I love you both, and you are everything to me!

With each new set of the MX anthologies, some things get easier, and there are also new challenges. For several years, the stresses of real life have been much greater than when this series started. Through all of this, the amazing contributors have once again pulled some amazing works from the Tin Dispatch Box. I'm more grateful than I can express to every contributor who has donated both time and royalties to this ongoing project. It's amazing what we've accomplished – over 860 stories in 42 volumes (so far), and over $116,000 raised for the Undershaw school for special needs children!

I also want to give special recognition to the multiple contributors of this set: Arthur Hall, Tracy Revels, Dan Rowley, Susan Knight, Alan Dimes, Brenda Seabrooke, Barry Clay, Ember Pepper, and Tim Newton Anderson. Finally, I cannot express how thankful I am to all of those who keep buying these books and making them the largest and most popular Sherlockian anthology ever.

I'm so glad to have gotten to know so many of you through this process – both contributors and readers. It's an undeniable fact that Sherlock Holmes people are the *best* people!

I wish especially thank the following:

- *Tom Mead* – Tom has burst on the scene as the new face of locked room mysteries in the best Golden Age style. We are all very fortunate that he's writing these type of stories, and also that we live in an age where social media, for all of its evil problems, also allows us to be in contact with authors in real time. When preparing these books, I realized that I wanted very much for Tom to be part of them. I'm still trying to recruit him to write a Holmes story – and what a Holmes story that would be! He's interested, but he's also very busy! – but in the meantime, he immediately agreed to provide a foreword to these latest books. I'm very grateful for that, and also the opportunity to have "met" him (though not yet in person) at the start of what promises to be his long and wonderful career. Thanks Tom!

- *Steve Emecz* – From my first association with MX in 2013, I observed that MX (under Steve Emecz's leadership) was *the* fast-rising superstar of the Sherlockian publishing world – and ten years later, that has not changed. Connecting with MX and Steve Emecz was personally an amazing life-changing event for me, as it has been for countless other Sherlockian authors. It has led me to write many more stories, and then to edit books, along with unexpected additional Holmes Pilgrimages to England – none of which might have happened otherwise. By way of my first email with Steve, I've had the chance to make some incredible Sherlockian friends and play in the Holmesian Sandbox in ways that I would have never dreamed possible.

  Through it all, Steve has been one of the most positive and supportive people that I've ever known.

  From the beginning, Steve has let me explore various Sherlockian projects and open up my own personal possibilities in ways that otherwise would have never happened. Thank you, Steve, for every opportunity!

- *Roger Johnson* – From his immediate support at the time of the first volumes in this series to the present, I can't imagine Roger not being part of these books. His Sherlockian knowledge is exceptional, as is the work that he does to further the cause of The Master. But even more than that, both Roger and his wife, Jean Upton, are simply the finest and best of people, and I'm very lucky to know both of them – even though I don't get to see them nearly as often as I'd like. I look forward to getting back over to the Holmesland sooner rather than later and visiting with them again, but in the meantime, many thanks for being part of this.

- *Brian Belanger* –I initially became acquainted with Brian when he took over the duties of creating the covers for MX Books, and I found him to be a great collaborator, and wonderfully creative too. I've worked with him on many projects with MX and Belanger Books, which he co-founded with his brother Derrick Belanger, also a good friend. Along with MX Publishing, Derrick and Brian have absolutely locked up the Sherlockian publishing field with a vast amount of amazing material. The old dinosaurs must be trembling to see every new and worthy Sherlockian project, one after another after another, that these two companies create. Luckily MX and Belanger Books work closely with one another, and I'm thrilled to be associated with both of them. Many thanks to Brian for all he does for both publishers, and for all he's done for me personally.

And finally, last but certainly *not* least, thanks to **Sir Arthur Conan Doyle**: Author, doctor, adventurer, and the Founder of the Sherlockian Feast. Honored, and present in spirit.

As I always note when putting together an anthology of Holmes stories, the effort has been a labor of love. These adventures are just more tiny threads woven into the ongoing Great Holmes Tapestry, continuing to grow and grow, for there can *never* be enough stories about the man whom Watson described as "*the best and wisest . . . whom I have ever known.*"

David Marcum
October 4th, 2023
The 123rd Anniversary of
the first day of
"The Problem of Thor Bridge"

Questions, comments, or story submissions
may be addressed to David Marcum at
thepapersofsherlockholmes@gmail.com

Foreword
by Tom Mead

It is perhaps notable that I'm writing this on Arthur Conan Doyle's birthday, and so I am thinking now about Conan Doyle as a man – as a human being, rather than a mere name embossed on leather spines. My image of him will always be the one conjured by John Dickson Carr in his excellently readable biography. Carr was a fervent Sherlockian, not to mention a *pasticheur* – his *The Exploits of Sherlock Holmes* collection, co-authored with Adrian Conan Doyle, is such a fascinating curio. So it's through the lens of Carr's admiration that I have recently revisited the Holmes stories.

My very first experience of Sherlock Holmes came courtesy of Basil Rathbone. They used to show those movies on Channel 5 here in the UK, padded out with commercials for a ninety-minute runtime. This was in the mid-to-late '90s, and I'd get my mum to record them on VHS while I was at school, to watch repeatedly at my leisure. To begin with, Holmes signified *adventure* rather than mystery: Espionage, the *Pursuit to Algiers*, the hunt for *The Scarlet Claw*, Gale Sondergaard as *The Spider Woman*.

Thus, when I actually sat down and *read* my first Holmes tale, it was certainly an eye-opener. It was the fabled "Adventure of the Speckled Band", not only a great mystery but a great *locked-room* mystery, a subgenre which has had a profound influence on my own writing – and which fascinates me still.

It was a slim illustrated edition with a colourful painted cover that completely gave away the solution to the mystery. But even that could not impair my enjoyment. The book was somewhat out of place on the shelf in my primary school's library – it was bigger than the other books (not thicker, but taller), and of course it had that weird title. What was a *speckled band*? The first image in my head was a marching band.

And the next Holmes I read was *The Hound of the Baskervilles*. Perhaps unsurprisingly, I was more interested in the hound when it was an entity of uncanny origin. And yet I remained enthralled by Holmes's unorthodox detection – his elaborate chains of deduction, his disguises which fooled Watson every single time.

I did not *devour* the Holmes stories the way I did those of other authors – Agatha Christie, for example. Rather, I eked them out over the years, and as I matured so did my appreciation of Conan Doyle's momentous accomplishment.

I read "The Man With the Twisted Lip" at university and found it to be a vivid, gothic portrait of psychological schism akin to Poe's "William Wilson". I read "The Red-Headed League" and found it to be a marvellous logic puzzle. And when I reread *Baskervilles*, I was surprised to find it was folk horror masquerading as detective fiction – a tale of rationality clashing with superstition in an uncertain world.

Now more than ever I see what a glorious sparkling gem each tale is, and what a towering figure Conan Doyle has always been. To have redefined a genre, but also to have gifted so many talented writers with so much scope to develop, to reimagine. I suppose you could say it took me a while to fully immerse myself in Conan Doyle's literary world – the world of the stories, which transcend the countless cliches they have spawned. I had to "find my way in", so to speak. But now I'm here, I have no intention of leaving any time soon.

Tom Mead
May 22nd, 2023

"What Is It That We Love in Sherlock Holmes?"
by Roger Johnson

Edgar W. Smith asked that question back in April 1946. It's the first line of his editorial in the second issue of *The Baker Street Journal*. The founder of the Baker Street Irregulars was, of course, Christopher Morley, but it was Smith who ensured the BSI's stability and viability. He was one of the great Holmesian scholars and commentators, so his creation and editorship of the *Journal* was surely natural.

I don't intend to discuss Edgar Smith's answers to his own question, except to say that they are intelligent and wise. (The two don't always go together.) [1]

However, it seems to me that the Great Detective is, on a superficial level, much easier to respect than to love. He can be remarkably churlish to those whose intellects are, by his standards, inferior to his own – particularly his professional rivals in the police, and on occasion he is more than waspish to the man he considers his only friend. Read "The Disappearance of Lady Francis Carfax" again, and note the words exchanged after Holmes has rescued Watson from his attacker:

> *"I cannot at the moment recall any possible blunder which you have omitted. The total effect of your proceeding has been to give the alarm everywhere and yet to discover nothing."*
>
> *"Perhaps you would have done no better," I answered bitterly.*
>
> *"There is no 'perhaps' about it. I have done better."*

Watson has every right to be bitter. In his admirable book *The Curious Case of 221B: The Secret Notebooks of John H Watson, MD*, Partha Basu imagines his unspoken response:

> *"It was I who tracked Lady Frances; it was I who discovered the Shlessingers, and their hold on her and the fact that they spirited her away to London. I did not raise any alarm with the Shlessingers or with Lady Frances because they had already left the Continent when I happened onto their trail. You, on the other hand, ignored my accurate deduction that*

11

the three were in London and not in Montpellier where you landed up in your ludicrous disguise . . . . "

Nowhere in the Canonical sixty records, fortunately, is Holmes's asperity as bluntly expressed as in one of the movies starring Basil Rathbone and Nigel Bruce. The exact context escapes me, but I remember the line exactly: *"No, no, Watson! D'you have to be so stupid?"*

Holmes's lack of manners and of friends does not inspire our affection, though it may amuse us. And, after all, that isn't the complete picture.

In "The Dying Detective", we learn that the faithful Mrs Hudson *"was fond of him . . . for he had a remarkable gentleness and courtesy in his dealings with women. He disliked and distrusted the sex, but he was always a chivalrous opponent."*

There are numerous instances throughout the Good Doctor's chronicles of Holmes's respect for women – or, more accurately, for those women who deserve his respect, from Mary Morstan to the tragic Eugenia Ronder. He even, most unexpectedly, refers to the wife of the missing Mr Neville St Clair as *"this dear little woman"*, and he treats Irene Adler with great respect, even while working against her. He is polite but cold towards Mary, niece of the unfortunate banker Alexander Holder, and he is necessarily harsh in dealing with Susan Stockdale and her employer Isadora Klein – though his manner towards both is naturally different.

After their first meeting with Mary Morstan, Watson exclaims, *"What a very attractive woman!"* To his surprise, Holmes languidly replies, *"Is she? I did not observe."* His friend's response is, I suspect, largely responsible for the image of the Great Detective as a man devoid of human emotions:

> *"You really are an automaton – a calculating-machine!" I cried. "There is something positively inhuman in you at times."*

In fact, however he might appear to the average person, Sherlock Holmes is one for whom Walt Whitman's famous words might have been written:

> *Do I contradict myself?*
> *Very well then I contradict myself,*
> *(I am large, I contain multitudes.)* [2]

Holmes is not a superhero. He is more intelligent than most, and he has developed his talents to an unusually high degree, but they are human talents, and he is a human being, who makes the occasional mistake. If we were to dedicate an immense amount of time and concentrated effort, a select few of us might actually be able to be something very like him. Would we really want to, though? Most of us, I suspect, would rather be a Watson – and in reading the accounts of Holmes's adventures, whether for the first time or the hundredth, we can effectively place ourselves in the Good Doctor's rôle, accompanying the Great Detective in his investigations, sharing the danger and the excitement, marvelling at his perspicacity and the almost magical moment when he reveals the truth, and perhaps relaxing with him afterwards, discussing the case over a glass of brandy and a cigar.

That is what we love in Sherlock Holmes!

Roger Johnson, BSI, ASH
Editor: *The Sherlock Holmes Journal*
September 2023

NOTES

1. If you don't have a copy, you can read the editorial online at:
   https://www.blackgate.com/2015/11/16/the-public-life-of-sherlock-holmes-edgar-smiths-the-implicit-holmes/.
2. "Song of Myself", Section 51, from *Leaves of Grass*, first published in 1855.

An Ongoing Legacy
for Sherlock Holmes
by Steve Emecz

Undershaw
Circa 1900

With over five hundred Sherlock Holmes books, it's been a fantastic fifteen years publishing novels, short story collections, graphic novels and more. *The MX Book of New Sherlock Holmes Stories* remains our greatest program and achievement – made possible by the authors, the editor, and the fans who support the series. The total raised for Undershaw school for children with learning disabilities has now passed $116,000.

In 2023, every book bought on our website means we donate a meal to a family in need through ShareTheMeal from The World Food Programme (WFP). I am proud to have been a member of the external advisory council and a mentor with the WFP for several years, and part of the team in 2020 that was awarded the Nobel Peace Prize.

You can find links to all our projects on our website:

14

https://mxpublishing.com/pages/about-us

As long as the fans want more Sherlock, we'll be here to publish it.

Steve Emecz
September 2023

The Doyle Room at Undershaw
Partially funded through royalties from
The MX Book of New Sherlock Holmes Stories

A Word from Undershaw
by Emma West

Undershaw
September 9, 2016
Grand Opening of the Stepping Stones School
(Now *Undershaw*)
(Photograph courtesy of Roger Johnson)

"Find a voice in a whisper."
– Martin Luther King, Jr.

Why is it so important to us that our students have a "voice" at Undershaw?

It seems like an obvious question, but all too often the very people for whom a school exists are not heard when it comes to decision-making. A healthy, inclusive, and inspirational seat of learning should have a whole-school approach to listening to the voices of everyone in the school community, including our children.

Our students offer us a unique insight into what it is like to be a learner at Undershaw and thus, involving them in the decision-making process makes perfect sense. We have made significant improvements to the curriculum, the pastoral care, and the learning environment over the last academic year. These evolutions often come about by listening to our children. We are here to ensure they have meaningful opportunities to share their views and their input features in every corner of our school life.

Our school vision clearly puts the child are at the heart of everything that we do, so what better way to achieve this then through listening to their voice.

> *Undershaw is an inclusive school where the best interests of the child are at the heart of everything that we do.*
> *Undershaw is a school where we empower students to aspire and achieve.*
> *Undershaw is a caring and safe environment which allows students to thrive and flourish, and prepares them to be socially and economically engaged in the future.*

If we are ever in doubt of our ethical centre, it is this. Our vision guides us, shapes us, and holds us to account. It is our conscience and our true North. Undershaw is a thriving centre of learning, friendships, noise, and bustle . . . and we will always strive to find a voice in a whisper.

As ever and on behalf of all our voices, my heartfelt thanks for being by our side during all of our evolutions. We have such a vibrant community here and we are very fortunate to have such a committed band of friends and supporters. Undershaw and MX Publishing have a friendship that spans a decade, and for that we are all incredibly grateful.

Until next time . . . .

Emma West
Headteacher, Undershaw
October 2023

"Undershaw," Hindhead, Conan Doyle's House.

Editor's *Caveats*

When these anthologies first began back in 2015, I noted that the authors were from all over the world – and thus, there would be British spelling and American spelling. As I explained then, I didn't want to take the responsibility of changing American spelling to British and vice-versa. I would undoubtedly miss something, leading to inconsistencies, or I'd change something incorrectly.

Some readers are bothered by this, made nervous and irate when encountering American spelling as written by Watson, and in stories set in England. However, here in America, the versions of The Canon that we read have long-ago has their spelling Americanized, so it isn't quite as shocking for us.

Additionally, I offer my apologies up front for any typographical errors that have slipped through. As a print-on-demand publisher, MX does not have squadrons of editors as some readers believe. The business consists of three part-time people who also have busy lives elsewhere – Steve Emecz, Sharon Emecz, and Timi Emecz – so the editing effort largely falls on the contributors. Some readers and consumers out there in the world are unhappy with this – apparently forgetting about all of those self-produced Holmes stories and volumes from decades ago (typed and Xeroxed) with awkward self-published formatting and loads of errors that are now prized as very expensive collector's items.

I'm personally mortified when errors slip through – ironically, there will probably be errors in these *caveats* – and I apologize now, but without a regiment of professional full-time editors looking over my shoulder, this is as good as it gets. Real life is more important than writing and editing – even in such a good cause as promoting the True and Traditional Canonical Holmes – and only so much time can be spent preparing these books before they're released into the wild. I hope that you can look past any errors, small or huge, and simply enjoy these stories, and appreciate the efforts of everyone involved, and the sincere desire to add to The Great Holmes Tapestry.

And in spite of any errors here, there are more Sherlock Holmes stories in the world than there were before, and that's a good thing.

David Marcum
Editor

Editor's Note:
Duplicate Untold Cases

In some instances, there are multiple versions of certain Untold Cases contained within this volume. Each of these are very different stories and do not contradict one another, in spite of their common jumping-off place. As explained in the Editor's Foreword, no traditional and Canonical versions of the Untold Cases are the definitive versions to the exclusion of the others. They simply require a bit of additional pondering and rationalization to consider what was going on in Watson's thinking, and why he chose to present them in this way.

In this volume, the reader will encounter several versions of The Old Russian Woman, The Grosvenor Square Furniture Van, The Amateur Mendicants, The Paradol Chamber, The Most Repulsive Man, the Blackmail Case (from *The Hound of the Baskervilles*), The Addleton Tragedy and the British Barrow, The Sudden Death of Cardinal Tosca, The Service for Sir James Saunders, and the interesting cases brought to Holmes by his brother Mycroft and Stanley Hopkins.

Enjoy!

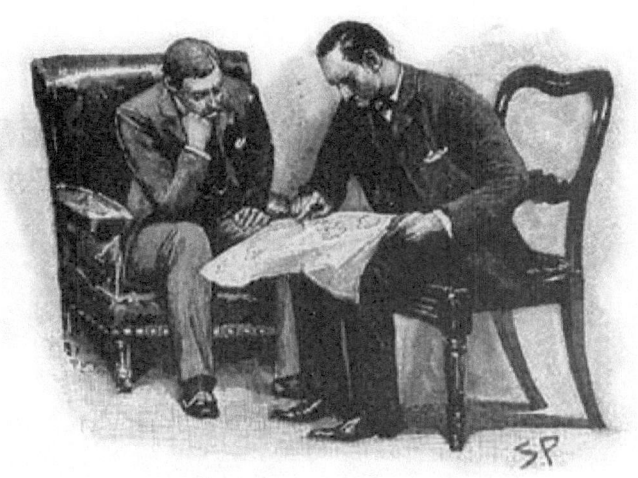

Sherlock Holmes (1854-1957) was born in Yorkshire, England, on 6 January, 1854. In the mid-1870's, he moved to 24 Montague Street, London, where he established himself as the world's first Consulting Detective. After meeting Dr. John H. Watson in early 1881, he and Watson moved to rooms at 221b Baker Street, where his reputation as the world's greatest detective grew for several decades. He was presumed to have died battling noted criminal Professor James Moriarty on 4 May, 1891, but he returned to London on 5 April, 1894, resuming his consulting practice in Baker Street. Retiring to the Sussex coast near Beachy Head in October 1903, he continued to be associated in various private and government investigations while giving the impression of being a reclusive apiarist. He was very involved in the events encompassing World War I, and to a lesser degree those of World War II. He passed away peacefully upon the cliffs above his Sussex home on his 103rd birthday, 6 January, 1957.

Dr. John Hamish Watson (1852-1929) was born in Stranraer, Scotland on 7 August, 1852. In 1878, he took his Doctor of Medicine Degree from the University of London, and later joined the army as a surgeon. Wounded at the Battle of Maiwand in Afghanistan (27 July, 1880), he returned to London late that same year. On New Year's Day, 1881, he was introduced to Sherlock Holmes in the chemical laboratory at Barts. Agreeing to share rooms with Holmes in Baker Street, Watson became invaluable to Holmes's consulting detective practice. Watson was married and widowed three times, and from the late 1880's onward, in addition to his participation in Holmes's investigations and his medical practice, he chronicled Holmes's adventures, with the assistance of his literary agent, Sir Arthur Conan Doyle, in a series of popular narratives, most of which were first published in *The Strand* magazine. Watson's later years were spent preparing a vast number of his notes of Holmes's cases for future publication. Following a final important investigation with Holmes, Watson contracted pneumonia and passed away on 24 July, 1929.

Photos of Sherlock Holmes and Dr. John H. Watson courtesy of Roger Johnson

The
MX Book
of
New
Sherlock
Holmes
Stories
Part XLII – Further Untold Cases
(1894-1922)

Gruner
by Kelvin I. Jones

His father named him Adelbert.
Even as a child, he loved to hurt;
Girls flocked to him like moths to a light;
But torturing women was his true delight.

Beneath his mansion
In respectable Kingston
He designed a room,
Dubbing it his "Pleasure Kingdom".

Celebrities, beauties,
Dukes' and barons' daughters,
They came to The Lodge
From every distant quarter.

At stately Vernon Lodge,
His salubrious London address,
Adelbert would watch
As they slowly undressed,

Then persuade them to pose
For a charming portrait,
Prior to a session
Of lust fuelled hate.

He'd kiss them
With those burgeoning white lips,
Caressing them gently
With his fingertips.

Their bodies were delicate
As the finest bone china,
Fired in the kilns of Asia Minor.

With those strong, supple fingers,
Gruner crushed and ravaged,

'Til their minds were drained and spent,
And their souls were savaged.

He loved to watch them there,
Lying on their backs,
Their soft limbs unadorned and bare,
Under attack.

Locked in his Inquisition machine;
He loved to hear them plead and scream,
Fine boned women of wit and charm;
His sole intent was to do them harm;

Adelbert kept a book in his safe,
Full of relics of his atrocious hate.
Locks of their hair he kept in there,
Images of cruelty,
Photos of mistresses he'd courted,
Later driven to despair.

Despite this litany
Of hatred,
And misogyny;
And the unforeseen attack
By the gang who wounded Holmes,
And beat him blue and black,

Gruner had not counted
On the scalding vitriol;

And now his face
Forever burns,
Like a brimstone river,
Straight from Hell.

The Addleton Tragedy
by Arthur Hall

On reviewing the many cases in which I was privileged to assist my friend, the consulting detective Mr. Sherlock Holmes, I must conclude that the circumstances surrounding more than a few bordered on the fantastic, if not the near-impossible. The example that immediately comes to mind is the extraordinary story of Professor Presbury, the account of which I have recorded elsewhere as "The Creeping Man". This, however, wasn't our only enquiry that developed in such a bizarre fashion.

I recall that Holmes and I had finished a magnificent luncheon at Simpson's, which I assumed was a favourite of my friend's since it was he that suggested that we eat there now and then, and especially when there was cause for celebration. On this fine late spring day, the occasion was his success in exposing Lord Verrimar, that most deceptive of opponents, as a card cheat, thus releasing the unfortunate young While-Jenkins from Newgate.

We had reclaimed our hats and coats and were taking our exit when we were accosted by an attractive young woman who had just entered the building. I scarcely had time to take in that she wore a costume of a delicate blue and that her blonde curls were arranged in a fashionable style before she addressed both Holmes and myself.

"Gentlemen, you must forgive me, but you are, I believe, Mr. Sherlock Holmes and Doctor Watson."

"At your service," my friend replied.

"Sirs, my name is Miss Julia Addleton. If I may presume, will you permit me to visit you in Baker Street later this afternoon? Since awakening this morning, I have been tortured by uncertainty, wondering whether I should take up your time. I finally decided that, after my meal with Mr. Peake, our family solicitor, I would either refer my difficulty to you or dismiss the notion. This chance meeting seems to have indicated my course."

"You wish to consult me on a professional matter?" Holmes enquired.

"I do, sir. It is a most strange occurrence that has terrified me. I know that Scotland Yard wouldn't believe me or would treat the matter lightly, but I have heard that you are able to throw light upon the darkest of human problems." She faltered and began to show signs of distress. I saw that her eyes were about to cloud with tears. "You are my only hope of discovering the truth. Please say that you will receive me."

"Pray calm yourself, Miss Addleton," my friend said gently. "What is the nature of this happening that has upset you so?"

"It is my father, who died two months past. Yet last night, as I walked home from the house of a friend, he approached me in Hyde Park and spoke to me."

I immediately became concerned because it was Holmes's custom, more often than not, to dismiss matters which appeared to contain an element of the supernatural. He believed, and indeed had proven before, that such events always had an ordinary explanation. But to treat this young woman's anxieties less-than-seriously would, I was certain, only increase the burden on her nerves. I was about to point this out to my friend when he answered her. I noted that his expression held no ridicule or indication of disbelief.

"I should make it clear that I have investigated many so-called mysteries involving the hereafter, and the result is invariably that the situation is in truth quite unexceptional. I have no doubt that your experience will not prove to be otherwise."

"Then you will help me?" she cried, immediately looking around her in embarrassment as she realised that her raised voice had attracted curious glances from the parade of others passing on their way to the dining room.

"If you will call on us at four o'clock, we will see what can be done."

"Could it not be that you spoke to someone resembling your father, and were deceived by the fading light?" I asked then.

I disregarded the scowl of disapproval that I knew I had earned from Holmes as she shook her head with certainty.

"Oh no, sir. That would be quite impossible. The resemblance was too great, the voice too familiar. I would swear on my life that it was he."

I was about to pose another question when my friend interrupted. "From the expression worn by the young man standing at the dining room entrance, Miss Addleton, it would appear that your solicitor is impatient to begin his meal. I can recommend the roast beef or the Dover sole. We will expect you at four. Until then, good afternoon."

She thanked us and we left as she hurried towards the waiting young man.

"From the way he looked at her, I do believe he has intentions," I remarked as Holmes raised his stick to attract a hansom.

"Then let us hope for her sake that they lie only within the boundaries of the legal matter on which he is representing her," Holmes said unsmilingly. "It's probably her father's will."

"Why do you say such a thing? What did you observe about him?"

"Nothing more than the annoyance that was written on his face. If waiting for Miss Addleton for a few minutes produces such anger, for that is how I perceived his expression, then how would he respond to a more intimate state, such as marriage? No, Watson, I fear that that young man, like myself, is destined to forego matrimony if he wishes a comfortable life."

I wished to avoid a discussion of marriage or the weaker sex, for I have long been familiar with his unchanging views, so it wasn't until we were well on the way to our lodgings before I spoke again.

"Holmes, I do apologise if my question to Miss Addleton was out of place."

"Not at all. It was an obvious starting point. I would have asked similarly had you not done so."

Back in our rooms, we enjoyed a glass of port and, after a short exchange, took up the latest editions of the various newspapers that we received daily. The doorbell rang at precisely four o'clock.

"Miss Addleton to see Mr. Holmes," our landlady announced a few minutes later.

We rose as one and welcomed her. Holmes guided her to a comfortable chair and offered refreshment, which she declined.

We settled ourselves in our usual armchairs. Holmes's expression was kindly and his voice sympathetic.

"Now, Miss Addleton, pray tell us more of your father and the extraordinary incident you described earlier. Be assured that Doctor Watson and myself will do everything within our power to put your mind at rest."

She hesitated, a little self-consciously I thought, before answering.

"It was as I said, gentlemen. Last night I left the house of my friend, Mrs. Gertrude Wellingham, whom I have known since our schooldays together. The shortest way back to Mayfair is through a corner of Hyde Park, but as it was such a lovely evening, I made a slight diversion which took me near the Serpentine. As I resumed my original path, I was approached by a man wearing a dark hooded cloak who, as he drew nearer, pushed back the hood to reveal himself as my father."

"One moment," interrupted Holmes. "Until that moment, had you any suspicion that you were being followed?"

She appeared confused by the question, and hesitated.

"Because your father knew where to intercept you." I clarified.

"I didn't notice anyone, but my thoughts were on the beauty that surrounded me, and there were many others strolling as I was."

"Please continue," Holmes said without glancing at me.

"Well, I was naturally both amazed and afraid since, as I explained, my father died two months ago. The shock was so great that I couldn't

37

speak until a moment later when he left me."

Holmes nodded. "Did this man appear different in any way, according to your memory of your father?"

"If you mean decomposition, Mr. Holmes, there was nothing that I could see. This cannot be, since I saw him buried in Highgate Cemetery, yet he was exactly as he had been in life."

"And he spoke to you?"

"Indeed he did, and in his normal voice, though he sounded weary. He said, 'You must obey my wishes, Julia. Give all that I left to The World Fellowship. Do it quickly. Their need is great and yours is so little'. He then turned away, and continued in the opposite direction, leaving me in a state of confusion and fear."

"Understandably. But tell me, was your father a wealthy man? I had assumed so, since your residence you have mentioned to be in Mayfair."

"He was, Mr. Holmes," she said then. "About ten years ago, he established a cotton import concern, which was very successful. I need hardly say that, since my mother died some years ago and there are no siblings or other relatives, I was the sole beneficiary of his will."

"So the reason behind this trickery – for that is what it is, although I cannot yet define its nature – is undoubtedly to deprive you of your inheritance."

Resting his chin upon steepled fingers, he sank abruptly into deep thought. After a while Miss Addleton gave me a questioning glance, as she doubtless wondered – as many clients had before her – whether Holmes had fallen asleep. I shook my head to indicate that we should remain still and silent, and she understood.

Minutes passed and the silence continued, except for faint sounds from Baker Street and a momentary clanging of pots and pans from below as Mrs. Hudson set about preparing dinner. I had begun to become conscious of the fragrance of tobacco that remained thick in the air from our earlier pipes, and hoped that Miss Addleton didn't find this distasteful, when my friend emerged suddenly from his reverie.

"Very well, the situation is quite clear. I must impress upon you, Miss Addleton, that there are but two possibilities: Either some as-yet unknown person or agency has discovered someone who closely resembles your late father, perhaps enhancing the likeness with theatrical make-up, or Mr. Addleton didn't actually die. You attended the funeral, I suppose?"

"Of course!" our client retorted in a manner that implied that not to have done so was unthinkable. "My father has always been very dear to me. I saw his coffin lowered into the earth, at Highgate Cemetery. It wasn't an occasion that I shall easily forget."

"Quite. Was his death certified at a hospital, or by a doctor known to you?"

"Doctor Sanderson has been our family physician for many years. He is elderly now, but his practice still thrives."

"Kindly give Doctor Watson his address along with your own, and any other details that seem relevant to you, at the conclusion of this interview," Holmes hesitated. "Pray tell us what you know of 'The World Fellowship'," he asked as an afterthought.

Miss Addleton shook her head slowly. "I didn't know of the existence of such an organisation, if that is what it is, before my father, or the man claiming to be he, spoke of it."

Holmes got to his feet unhurriedly. "Thank you, Miss Addleton, for bringing to my attention a most interesting case." Again he paused. "One more question, if I may: What was the cause of your father's death?"

That she was still grieving was apparent. "Doctor Sanderson confessed to having great difficulty identifying it. Eventually it was simply decided that my father's heart had given out."

"He had suffered from such attacks previously, then?"

"Not that I am aware of. If he did, he never confided them to me. That would have been most unlike him."

"Thank you. I must apologise if our discussion has upset you, but you will appreciate my need for knowledge before an investigation can begin."

"Of course." For the first time, a faint smile crept across her face. "I am immensely grateful to you gentlemen for allowing me to take up your time, and for your forthcoming efforts."

Holmes dismissed her with a little bow, and I asked for the details that he had requested. Putting my notebook aside, I descended with her to Baker Street, where I procured a passing hansom.

I returned to our sitting room to find that Mrs. Hudson had set out a meal of chicken pie and fresh vegetables. Holmes, as always when a new case presented itself, was distracted throughout dinner and ignored dessert entirely.

"I presume that in the morning we are to visit Doctor Sanderson in Harley Street," I said to break the silence.

His awareness came back to him as it does on awakening from sleep. "Not immediately. I cannot ignore the possibility that we might learn something at Highgate Cemetery."

With that, he pushed away his tea-cup and took up his violin. The unearthly sounds that followed were, I knew, his own composition. I had heard them played before at times when he was on the brink of falling into depression for want of a new problem, or when something had perplexed him. I concluded that he, like myself, was searching his mind to explain how a man, definitely identified, could return from the grave.

After almost an hour, he restored the instrument to its case. He mumbled a few words as he sat on the opposite side of the fireplace and lit his old briar. I resumed my reading and we smoked until the air became unbreathable, at which time he bade me goodnight and retired. I opened the window briefly to avoid Mrs. Hudson's rebukes and looked down on a deserted and darkened Baker Street before following Holmes's example and retreating to my room.

Surprisingly, I slept peacefully. Holmes seemed unaltered as I joined him at breakfast, and I wondered if he had slept at all. His food lay half-eaten on his plate, but the coffee pot was empty, so that I was obliged to call for another to conclude my meal. At the moment I drained my cup, he leapt to his feet with the enthusiasm of old, pulling his ear-flapped travelling cap onto his head and handing me my coat as he struggled into his own.

Upon arriving at Highgate Cemetery, we were fortunate enough to encounter a gravedigger hard at work. In response to Holmes's greeting, he put aside his shovel for a moment and wiped his brow with a red-spotted handkerchief before answering our question about Mr. Henry Allington's resting place with a vague wave of his hand.

"Over there, Guv'nor, I think. It's been a while now since I buried him, but I'm sure it was in the row next to the stone angel and that big old vault you see near the corner."

"My thanks to you," my friend said, reaching down to hand the man a half-sovereign before we struck out in the direction he had indicated.

We came upon the grave almost immediately. It had a stone surround with a heavy granite crucifix at its head, on which was inscribed the name of the departed. I read that of Mrs. Lisa Addleton, and then the newer addition of her husband.

"There seems to have been no disturbance," said I.

"Unless the desecration occurred soon after the burial, there will be none. In two months, all signs will have disappeared."

"Assuming the body was actually removed."

He nodded. "If our investigation proves to be unsatisfactory, it may be necessary to attempt to enlist Lestrade's aid to effect an exhumation, though I wouldn't wager much on our success."

"We have met this difficulty before," I reflected.

"There is always the unofficial course." He gave me a sly glance. "In that event, are you with me, Watson?"

"The exercise will probably be beneficial to us both."

That, I am glad to report, did not occur. To this day I don't know what Holmes expected to find there, unless he was seeking to confirm that the grave existed. As we left that place of eternal rest, we encountered two elderly women in the company of a young man, obviously visiting a departed loved one since they held bunches of flowers. We greeted them as we passed, and then replaced them in the hansom they had vacated. It bore us swiftly to Harley Street, the horse being young and energetic.

We encountered no difficulty in finding the address we sought. The stern-faced receptionist paused, temporarily abandoning her typewriting machine to ask our business. Holmes gave our names and requested to see Doctor Sanderson.

"That is quite impossible." Her expression was like flint, and I imagined she had repelled many callers before us. "The doctor is extremely busy."

"He is with a patient?"

"No, he has other work."

"Then kindly disturb him sufficiently to show him my card. I believe you will find that he will consent to see us."

"If you insist, sir." Grudgingly, the woman took the card from him. She glanced at it and looked up with surprised eyes. My friend allowed her a thin smile. "Very well," she said in a voice that had lost some of its assurance and got to her feet. She turned from us abruptly to approach the single door at the end of the room. After knocking once, she was bade to enter.

She reappeared moments later, and I immediately thought that Holmes's attempt had failed. Walking stiffly back to her desk, she resumed the operation of her machine without once looking in our direction. The man who followed her from the room was clean-shaven, white-haired, rotund, and elderly. His expression was friendly as he shook our hands.

"Mr. Holmes, Doctor Watson! I have heard of you, of course, and followed some of your exploits in the newspapers. Stirring stuff! Exciting! But I am intrigued, gentlemen, as to what could possibly have brought you to me. Pray come into my consulting room and we will discuss the matter. Lady Loxbury is due in a little over half-an-hour, but I'm certain our business can be concluded before then."

"My thanks to you, Doctor," Holmes responded. "We will not take up much of your time."

We found ourselves in a room that held no surprises for me: Two walls lined with books, leather chairs surrounding a polished desk – it was identical in content to many I had known at university and elsewhere.

Doctor Sanderson removed his stethoscope from where it lay on the desk and placed it in a drawer. "Well, gentlemen, how can I assist you?"

"Our investigation concerns a former patient of yours," Holmes began. "Mr. Henry Addleton."

Our host responded at once. "I knew him well. The poor fellow passed away a month or two ago. It was very distressing. A great tragedy."

"He was well known, then?"

"Indeed he was, sir. He was that rare person: A benevolent businessman. His contributions to aid the impoverished of the capital were many and legendary. Yes, a great tragedy to his daughter, and to us all."

"Can you recall the cause of his death?"

Doctor Sanderson appeared dismayed at the question for an instant. "Oh, yes, I see. You suspect something sinister here. No, gentlemen, I examined him thoroughly. I did have some trouble identifying the cause of his demise, it is true, but his heart had ceased to beat. Of that I am certain, although it was sudden."

"But there was no previous indication of this?" I asked.

"None, Doctor, but as a medical man you are aware that these attacks are often unexpected. Mr. Addleton's death was a shock to everyone who knew him, I think."

"Doubtless," Holmes agreed, "but was there anything unusual about it, anything at all? His daughter, Miss Julia Addleton, is still experiencing difficulty in coping with her loss."

Doctor Sanderson reflected, briefly. "No, I don't believe that I can say that there was any feature out of the ordinary involved. However, when you see Miss Addleton, please convey to her that I would be pleased to prescribe something to help her come to terms with her grief."

"I will certainly mention it to her. Tell me, Doctor, are you acquainted with a group known as 'The World Fellowship'?"

The physician hesitated, then shook his head. "Are they a charitable organisation? No, I cannot recall them at all." He took his pocket watch from his waistcoat then, and I remembered that he had mentioned that a patient was due. I believe that in any case Holmes was ready to leave, but at that moment the door opened and a tall man entered. His features were those of the African native, but his skin was the palest I have ever seen among such.

His look of surprise on seeing that Doctor Sanderson wasn't alone faded instantly, and he spoke with scarcely a trace of any foreign accent.

"My apologies for this intrusion, gentlemen. I was unaware that Doctor Sanderson was with patients." He placed some papers on the desk and made to leave, but our host got to his feet.

"Mr. Sherlock Holmes and Doctor Watson, may I introduce my assistant, Doctor Kalu Obuluku."

We stood up and were about to offer our hands, but Doctor Obuluku bowed across the short distance between us.

"I am most pleased to make your acquaintance, gentleman. Indeed,

Doctor Sanderson has spoken of you."

"We discuss items that take our fancy in the dailies, on occasion," explained the elder physician. He consulted his timepiece again. "Kalu, I believe that Mr. Quin-Bolton will be arriving at any moment."

"I will attend to him immediately." The African bowed again and excused himself.

"He has been a great asset to me during the last few years," Dr. Sanderson remarked.

"It is unusual to find such a one in practice here," I said.

"Indeed it is. In fact, I know of no other. I first met him before I established my practice here, while acting as medical officer to the South-East African expedition of Sir Randolph Burnham. Kalu had been taught English by a Christian missionary. He was skilled in the ways of his tribe, but I recognised his perceptiveness and potential and brought him back to England. I managed to arrange for him to study at one of our smaller universities, and he completed his course with flying colours." He smiled. "As I said, he has been invaluable."

"I'm glad to see that your practice is flourishing," I said.

We left Harley Street then and spoke little before our hansom had almost reached Baker Street.

"I'm not satisfied," Holmes began suddenly, "with Doctor Sanderson's assumption, for that is what it is as far as I can gather, of the cause of Mr. Henry Addleton's death."

"Nor am I."

"What has caused you to be of that opinion, Watson?"

"You will recall his removing the stethoscope from the desk as we entered his consulting room?"

He nodded. "What of it?"

"That instrument is an old tool, ancient, almost and long since superseded by more sensitive implements. I have the gravest doubt that, if Mr. Addleton had retained a faint heart-beat, it could have made itself heard if Doctor Sanderson had listened by means of it."

Holmes raised an eyebrow. "Are you suggesting that he could have been buried alive?"

"I am saying that, in those circumstances, that would have been a possibility. I also noticed that some of the charts on the walls of the consulting room display knowledge that has been disproved for some years. About our client's father, I suspect that we may never know the truth."

"That is most disquieting, but I cannot see that it would benefit Miss Addleton to be aware of such suspicions, so I suggest that nothing be said until our investigation has reached its conclusion. But now I see that we

43

have arrived back in Baker Street, and you are showing your usual signs of hunger. If you would be so good as to give our cabby his fare, we can turn our attention to the partridge that Mrs. Hudson will by now have prepared for our luncheon."

The meal was enjoyed by both of us. Indeed, Holmes surprised me by the relish with which he ate. Long experience of my friend has taught me that this is a sign that he has made some progress, if not attained a complete solution, to whatever problem lies before him. Several times as we finished the partridge and began our dessert, I enquired as to his conclusions, but he wouldn't be drawn.

"A ghost of a suspicion, Watson, that is all," he suddenly volunteered when I had accepted that I would learn nothing until he saw fit to confide in me. "But I will confirm it this afternoon. I am afraid I must leave you for a while, old friend, but I will return shortly. It shouldn't be necessary, I think, to instruct Mrs. Hudson to delay our dinner."

He departed swiftly, and I was left to peruse the ever-increasing accumulation of medical journals for which there never seemed enough time. I was startled by the noise of a thick periodical falling from my knee to the floor, and I realised that I must have fallen asleep. I decided against calling for coffee before Holmes's return and spent a further hour learning of two major outbreaks of malaria in the tropics before I heard his tread upon the stairs.

"Halloa, Watson!" he cried as he entered, and I knew instantly that whatever his afternoon's quest had been, it was successful.

He divested himself of his coat and settled his thin body in the armchair that faced mine, smiling in a conspiratorial fashion.

"Shall I call for coffee?" I asked him.

"I wouldn't bother Mrs. Hudson just now. In less than an hour, she'll be serving one of her excellent steak pies."

His apparent light-heartedness disturbed me.

"I take it that your theory was correct."

"In truth, I cannot say that I had much faith in it. I made a tenuous connection with an item I recalled from my index, with results that astounded me."

"What have you learned?"

"How to make dead bodies live again."

I regarded him incredulously. "That is preposterous!"

"So I believed until I consulted an old acquaintance, Professor Cyrus Palk, of the Department of African Customs and Religions at the British Museum. Our discussion was most illuminating."

"You indicated that you've discovered the true nature of Miss Addleton's strange experience."

"I believe that I have, and I've set in motion a series of events that may confirm this. After leaving Professor Palk, I went to St. James's to pay a visit to Langdale Pike, who you may remember. In exchange for some trifling facts about Lady Burringham that can do her no harm since her reputation is already in ruins, and some further indications of what may happen to the actor Arnold Trimbill after the courts have reached their verdict, he disclosed to me what is known about The World Fellowship."

He paused, I thought as much for effect as to await the passing of a coal cart along Baker Street. When the noise and vibration had ceased, I enquired of him, "Are they, in truth, some sort of criminal gang?"

"They could indeed be described as such, but not in the sense we've come to know. They present themselves as international saviours of the needy and impoverished, but in fact the money they obtain from extortion and blackmail and various other methods, such as that attempted in the case of Miss Addleton, is employed in financing wars and unrest in any country where it can profit their leaders."

"Good Heavens!" I took a moment to consider the enormity of the prospect. "What can be done?"

"On a large scale nothing, although I will certainly ensure that all I gather in the course of our enquiries reaches Mycroft's desk. I mentioned that I have embarked upon a path which seems likely to bring an end to this particular venture of theirs, and I expect to see some results this evening."

"Still, you have told me nothing of your discoveries regarding corpses returning to life, nor about what steps you have taken."

He sighed, a little impatiently. "Very well, Watson. You were never content to watch the game play out before hearing my explanation." He reached into his pocket for a scrap of paper, which he handed to me. "Perhaps this, a copy of the contents of the telegram which I sent as my final act before returning here, will go some way towards satisfying your curiosity."

I smoothed the sheet out upon the surface of a side-table. Holmes's pencil marks were barely legible.

My Dear Dr. Sanderson,

This is to convey my thanks for the most useful information regarding the organisation I enquired about that you supplied today. My investigation has now taken a new direction that will surely result in an early and satisfactory conclusion.

Holmes

"But Doctor Sanderson provided very little of any substance," I objected. "He will wonder what you are referring to."

"Precisely." Holmes inclined his head like an animal who has caught a scent. "But I hear Mrs. Hudson on the stairs." He laughed, and I realised that I must still be wearing a confused expression. "Cheer up, Watson! Tonight we eat like kings!"

His joviality persisted throughout our meal of which, despite his enthusiastic announcement, he didn't fully consume his portion. For my part, I did justice to it to the last. I noted that he seemed anxious for the clearing up to be completed, refusing our landlady's offer of a second pot of coffee and ushering her from our room quickly.

When we were settled in our armchairs, he began a conversation so different from before that he was obviously avoiding the subject. At the first opportunity, I broke into his tirade and asked him, "Holmes, do the arrangements that you have made for this evening include a visit from Miss Addleton, Doctor Sanderson, or someone else?"

"They do indeed. I must ask you, Watson: Are you armed?"

"My service weapon is never far from me." I felt the reassuring weight in my pocket. "We are expecting trouble, then?"

"It's possible, but by no means certain. Pray keep alert throughout the interview."

"But who is it that we are awaiting?"

At that moment the doorbell rang. I heard Mrs. Hudson answer, and then she ascended the stairs, accompanied by someone whose tread was unfamiliar.

The door opened. She stood there wearing a look of momentary dismay, and I realised that Holmes had been uncertain of this visit and therefore couldn't have warned her to expect it.

"A gentleman to see Mr. Holmes," she announced before withdrawing and closing the door behind Doctor Obuluku.

Our visitor seemed to have difficulty walking, since he leaned heavily on a stout walking-stick in the shape of a snake. As he leaned it against the wall, it struck me that he must have injured himself since we saw him earlier, as I could recall no such impediment to his movements then. He smiled, rather self-consciously I thought, and addressed us both.

"Gentlemen, forgive me for calling without an appointment, but I thought I might be of some assistance. Doctor Sanderson mentioned that you had spoken of a group known as 'The World Fellowship', and it so happens that I am slightly acquainted with their work. During my days in Africa, I encountered them on several occasions, and it struck me that to know of my experiences might aid your investigation."

"My dear fellow," Holmes enthused, "do come and sit with us. I am sure that what you have to tell us will be informative and interesting."

My friend's expression became a look of caution, a warning, as he glanced in my direction for a moment.

"Would you care for tea, coffee, or something stronger, perhaps?" he asked.

Our visitor held up a hand. "Thank you, gentlemen, but no. My time is short, but it occurred to me, bearing in mind your profession, Mr. Holmes, that you might suspect that The World Fellowship had some criminal purpose. I assure you this cannot be so, for their work is well-known and much respected in many parts of Africa, and I have brought what I can as evidence of this for you to examine." He unfastened a slim briefcase and extracted a bundle of papers, which he passed to Holmes. I rose to adopt a position where I also could see their content and found myself surprised by the praise and support that this organisation commanded. Many were the official documents from local dignitaries, the praising testimonials from missionaries and even, in childish scrawl, from tribal chiefs.

Holmes perused the documents carefully before returning them. "A very large area of the continent is represented here," he commented. "I thank you, Doctor Obuluku, for bringing these facts to my attention."

"I am glad to do so, for it would grieve me if your investigation took a false direction, when I could have prevented it." He withdrew his pocket watch and glanced at it quickly. "But now I fear I must leave you. As I said, I have little time, and two more patients to see this evening."

We all rose.

"Our thanks to you, for calling to inform us on this matter." Holmes walked with him to the door. "You have indeed thrown new light upon our enquiries."

Our visitor seemed pleased at this, and bid us good-night in a cheerful manner. We heard him descend the stairs and Holmes looked from the window, saying not a word until he saw that a cab had been summoned and was now departing.

"Very convincing statements, I think," I said. "I assume he saw your telegram to Doctor Sanderson and realised that we were on the wrong track."

"Ha! Surely, Watson, after all your time with me, you aren't so easily deceived."

"You believe that the papers are forgeries?"

"I am certain of it. Have you ever before seen a document dated a month ago, in a condition that you would expect after five years? Or one dated almost a decade past, with the vellum in pristine condition? Frankly, I'm disappointed, for I would have expected such a widespread and organised gang to produce something more convincing." He was suddenly silent, regarding me thoughtfully. "It would appear that our conversation with Doctor Sanderson worried them, and the subsequent visit with its 'evidence' were, of necessity, contrived rapidly. Watson, did you notice anything strange about Doctor Obuluku?"

I shook my head. "I cannot think that . . . Ah, there was one thing. He didn't limp as he left this room," I glanced towards the corner, "and he has forgotten his walking-stick."

In all my years with Holmes, I have rarely seen him move with such speed.

He ran across the room to the old gnarled bureau that serves as a writing desk and flung open a drawer. From it he extracted a short gleaming sword, which I recognised as that from a case which I have recorded elsewhere as "The Imposter Prince", but will never reach my publisher because my friend has refused his permission.

Holmes strode quickly across to where the stick leaned against the wall, and at that moment I believe that my eyes deceived me, for I would swear that it moved of its own accord. With five swift slashes it was severed repeatedly, and it was then that I saw, to my horror and disbelief, that it *bled*. The stain spread across the carpet, and somewhere in my mind I wondered what Mrs. Hudson would say of this. My friend put down the bloodstained weapon at last, looking fearfully exhausted, and I saw that the remains of the stick appeared to have lost the hardness of wood and taken on the softer texture of something that had lived.

"In God's name, Holmes! What devilry is this?" My voice was little more than a croak. I could hardly speak, such was the effect upon me.

"I must apologise, old friend. I should have told you of my discoveries earlier. A restorative, I think, is indicated. If you will return to your chair, I will pour us both a glass of brandy before furnishing you with an explanation."

We both drank deeply. I felt fire in my blood as the harsh spirit enabled me to accept what I had seen as real, although I had no understanding of it. Some of the fear and tension drained from me as I emptied my glass and awaited some sort of clarification from Holmes. I glanced across the room to where the mutilated remains of something evil had begun to congeal. I could now perceive two soulless eyes, staring sightlessly.

His gaze searched my face. "I see that your colour is returning, Watson. Do you feel able to listen to what I learned earlier today?"

"The shock has almost passed. Tell me, what was that thing that you cut into pieces?"

"It is as well, I think, that I hadn't yet consigned that sword to my tin box with the records of our earlier enquiries." He stared at me, apparently satisfied that I had recovered sufficiently. "Otherwise, I would have been forced to depend upon a firearm, and those creatures move with such speed."

"For Heaven's sake, what was it?"

"A mamba, one of Africa's most dangerous snakes. It is said that they are able to catch a man on horseback, and are possessed of a most vicious disposition."

I felt myself tremble, and heard it in my voice. "We faced such once before."

"We did, old friend, and I see that this has stirred your memories of that time. Calm yourself, Watson. The danger is past."

"How were you able to foresee it?"

"When Doctor Sanderson introduced his assistant to us, I recalled an insertion in my index, not long ago. The item concerned miraculous reappearances of tribesmen believed to be dead, in the African region that Doctor Sanderson mentioned. The similarity to our current problem was, I felt, too great to be anything but significant, but I had insufficient data either to understand what we are up against or to act."

I nodded. "That was why you consulted Professor Palk."

"Indeed. When I related our brief encounter with Doctor Obuluku, the professor was immediately familiar with the likely implications. He was able to tell me that the doctor's name is one common to a particular region of South-Eastern Africa, especially among tribal priests. One of their rituals concerns causing death to a selected subject, and then restoring him to life. This was for many years considered elsewhere as myth or trickery, but recent expeditions have discovered the process to be based on an ancient variation of mesmerism."

"Good Heavens!" I exclaimed, as the realisation of what had occurred came to me. "Does this mean that Doctor Obuluku's walking-stick was a real snake, hypnotised into rigidity until he released it in some way after he left?"

"It means precisely that." Holmes leaned forward in his chair. "Although how any of this is possible is still a mystery. It is one of the elements of the Dark Continent that we have yet to understand, but I have no doubt that it is the explanation also of the apparent death and resurrection of Mr. Henry Addleton."

"Then Doctor Obuluku must still have control of the unfortunate man, who was heard by our client to bequeath his wealth to The World Fellowship."

49

"I am quite certain of it. Concerning that unscrupulous organisation, Langdale Pike was a fountain of knowledge. It is known in the criminal underworld and, surprisingly, in some aristocratic circles, that the tentacles of it are widespread. Its resources have been used to the advantage of its adherents in many countries, but always with the eventual objective of fermenting conflict and upheaval."

"This is monstrous, Holmes! Who is behind all this?"

"That I cannot tell. Neither, I believe, can anyone in England, since the forces controlling the group's activities are remote from those who carry out their will. Doctor Obuluku we might view as a foot soldier, whereas his orders come from generals far away, if you will forgive the metaphor. However, it is him we have to deal with tomorrow."

"You have devised a strategy?"

"A simple one. We will keep watch on Doctor Sanderson's surgery – I don't believe, by the way, that he is in any way involved – until Doctor Obuluku leaves. If he is keeping Mr. Addleton prisoner, doubtless intending another eventually meeting with our client, then he must visit him from time to time, if only to supply food and drink. That is of course, assuming that Mr. Addleton's condition is as I have supposed. I am confident of this since, as I have postulated many times, the truly dead don't rise from their graves to be among the living, despite the assurances of those who would have many believe otherwise."

"We cannot be sure that Doctor Obuluku will visit Mr. Addleton. He may be visiting patients."

"Then we will pursue him regardless. When we have discovered his place of residence, where Mr. Addleton is most likely to be found, the opportunity to enter in his absence may present itself."

So it was that Holmes and I were already concealed in a waiting cab, as darkness fell the following evening. We had broken our journey only once after leaving Baker Street, briefly to allow Holmes to dispatch a telegram. I had never seen our driver before, an expressionless man of few words, but Holmes appeared to have trust in him and he obeyed without question.

We had waited near Harley Street, always within view of Doctor Sanderson's practice and changing our position several times, since consuming an early dinner and leaving our lodgings immediately after. Neither Holmes nor our driver uttered a word as the hansom moved nearer to where we were in shadow, yet retained a good viewpoint.

At last the front door opened, the brass knocker glinting momentarily beneath the street-light. Dr. Obuluku stepped out quickly, glancing in both directions before walking towards us. I felt myself growing tense although Holmes seemed unaffected, until another hansom arrived and was engaged.

"That was a close thing," I said in a low voice. "If he had approached and seen us, it would have been all up."

"Surely you cannot imagine that I hadn't foreseen that situation," he answered as our driver set off in slow pursuit. "But he seems in rather a hurry, which means he could be attending a seriously ill patient."

"Or that he is seeking to ensure the welfare of a captive left alone far too long."

"We shall see. Our driver is proficient in following without detection, so we may be able to keep the doctor in sight until he returns to his residence. A little patience is called for, I think."

We left Marylebone in the direction of Oxford Circus. Doctor Obuluku's conveyance soon turned off abruptly and entered a street which appeared to contain a row of offices on either side. At the far end it turned sharply to the right and disappeared.

"He'll be onto us if we follow him there, Mr. Holmes," our driver said as he brought the horse to a halt. "There's no way out, you see. It's a dead-end."

"Thank you, Gerrard," my friend acknowledged. "We will proceed on foot. Payment will reach you as usual."

We alighted and waited while the hansom departed. Moments later the cab that had brought Doctor Obuluku passed us on its return journey. The street was now silent and we were alone.

The corner was no more than a few yards away, and we turned it cautiously. One side of this short lane was mostly made up of a blank wall, the rear of a public building I supposed, while the other was a row of dark houses that extended to its end. It seemed deserted until Holmes's sharp eyes picked out movement.

"There," he whispered, as I saw him point in the meagre light.

Doctor Obuluku stood before a tall gate, possibly a place of storage, that appeared to be a later addition to one of the buildings. It stood between two identical houses and had no equivalent elsewhere. He was experiencing difficulty with the lock, and I heard faintly his curses and oaths in a foreign language.

"Not yet, Watson." I had unconsciously moved forward, but Holmes put a hand on my arm.

We watched as our quarry finally freed the lock, flinging it to the ground in frustration and anger. He entered the building and slammed the gate behind him, before we moved closer. After a minute or two we continued our advance, until we were able to tread silently along the short path. Against the gate we could hear his voice, first persuasive, then threatening.

51

"You cannot die! How could you? I have more work for you. Awaken!"

Holmes opened the gate noiselessly. Our entrance was undetected until he spoke.

"Good evening, Doctor Obuluku."

The African was poised over a body that was strapped to an iron cot. At the sound of Holmes's voice his head snapped up, and I saw at once that his expression was quite different to that we had seen before.

"So, Mr. Sherlock Holmes, you and your companion survived the little gift I left."

"The mamba lies in pieces. It can do no more harm."

The doctor raised his dark eyebrows, his eyes flashed white in the light of the single oil lamp. "I am most surprised. The snake hasn't failed before now. My colleague, from whom I borrowed it for the occasion, will be inconvenienced by the need for a replacement."

"He is, I presume, a dealer in exotic creatures."

"It was on his recommendation that I used the black variety, although the green snake is almost as venomous. They are peculiar in that they manifest anger when placed in unfamiliar surroundings. I would have wagered on your lives ending in less than ten minutes."

"What have you done to Mr. Henry Addleton?" I interrupted.

"I would have expected you to have found the answer to that by now. The art of inducing what you would call a 'hypnotic state' has long been known among the priests and shamans of my people, and I was able to use the ritual to great advantage here. The effect deceived his family and friends easily, and he was thought to be deceased. Together with a helper, I was able to recover his still living body soon after the funeral was concluded. Unfortunately, my influence wasn't great enough to preserve Mr. Addleton through his subsequent confinement, and he has now died." His expression hardened, becoming a cruel and evil mask. "A great pity, for his daughter needs further persuasion to obey her father and relinquish his wealth to us. Were it not for your intervention, my work would be done, and that gullible fool Doctor Sanderson would be wondering how his pleasant and obedient assistant could have disappeared so suddenly. The Fellowship will not forget your interference."

"We will await whatever steps they choose to take," Holmes replied. "But for now, I think we will all repair to Scotland Yard."

"I think not." Doctor Obuluku produced a slightly flattened spherical object from his pocket. "Put away your revolvers, gentlemen, or this explosive device will blow this house and others to dust. If you shoot me, I will let it fall to the floor, and we will know nothing more. I will leave you now, and you will be wise not to seek to prevent me."

I felt my body tense, but Holmes shook his head. "Let him go, Watson. There is nothing we can do."

"But he will escape and remain unpunished."

"I think not."

A moment later we heard a cry of surprise, and then the familiar voice of Inspector Lestrade.

"Holmes!" I cried. "The inspector will be killed."

"That I seriously doubt."

No explosion followed, and I shot my friend a confused glance.

"Lestrade and whoever accompanies him are perfectly safe," he explained. "No one would treat explosives with the clumsy cavalier attitude that Doctor Obuluku has just displayed. I knew instantly that he held nothing more dangerous than some sort of metal container. His deception failed, but I was certain that his apprehension was imminent."

"You notified Scotland Yard by telegram, shortly after we left Baker Street," I surmised. "But how did Lestrade know where we would be?"

"Gerrard had his instructions. As soon as we had discovered Doctor Obuluku's destination, he went directly to the nearest telegraph office."

We emerged to see Inspector Lestrade, with a tall and heavily-built constable to either side, in the act of placing police handcuffs on Doctor Obuluku's wrists.

"You may protest as long as it pleases you, and you may occupy an important position as you say, but the law is the law." He glanced in our direction. "Here are Mr. Sherlock Holmes and Doctor Watson now, so we can all go to the Yard together to get this matter made clear."

I saw that a two-horsed police coach waited near the corner and the metal container, Doctor Obuluku's "explosive device", lay abandoned at our feet.

"It is murder, Lestrade," Holmes said then. "Beyond that gate lies the body of Mr. Henry Addleton, who your prisoner appears to have starved to death. An examination, I have no doubt, will confirm this."

The official detective's expression became more serious. He turned to one of the constables. "Becket, take this man to the coach and sit beside him, with Seager on the other side. He will be charged when the extent of his villainy is known."

The remainder of the tale will doubtless be remembered from the many reports in the dailies. Doctor Obuluku cursed Holmes and myself bitterly as we all rode together. At Scotland Yard, he was held overnight while pathologists and others conducted a thorough examination of the body and the premises where Mr. Addleton had passed away.

Charges were brought the following day and he was found guilty of murder shortly after – despite Doctor Obuluku's assertion that he had deprived his victim of food and water to reduce him to a more ready state of obedience, rather than to cause his death. The execution date was set for six weeks hence but the defence lawyer, who had been retained by money from an unknown source, was able to obtain a postponement on the strength of new evidence. The nature of this was never revealed, but Doctor Obuluku grew fearful and desperate enough to reveal certain facts about The World Fellowship in an attempt perhaps, to avoid the hangman. As it was, he was found fatally wounded in his cell before the case progressed further. His murderer was never identified.

As Holmes later remarked, the supposed death of Mr. Henry Addleton had been described as a tragedy by many of those who knew of his generous nature, but perhaps the true tragedy was the death of his daughter, our client, whose delicate disposition could not support the grief of losing her father for a second time.

She was discovered in her home, having hung herself from an oak beam. Both Holmes and Lestrade have wondered since why no investigation was ever allowed to proceed.

"Here also I find an account of the Addleton tragedy . . . ."
– Dr. John Watson
"The Golden Pince-Nez"

The Book of Lucifer
by Alan Dimes

My readers may remember the sensational trial of The Legion of Lucifer, some years ago, which resulted in the execution of the leader and several members of that repellant organization. It may also be recalled that the judge praised the efforts of those Scotland Yard officials who had been instrumental in bringing the culprits to justice. What went unsaid, as is so frequently the case, was the aid given them by my friend and colleague, Mr. Sherlock Holmes. It is true that the matter did not afford him much opportunity to exercise his outstanding powers of logic and deduction, but it is equally true that, without his knowledge and insight, the official force would have had little to work with. On this basis, and considering the intrinsic interest of the case, I have decided, with Holmes's consent, to lay the full story of his involvement before the reading public.

During his three-year absence from London, there had been, as he pointed out to Inspector Lestrade upon his return in 1894, three unsolved murders.

"Perhaps you'd like to take a look at them, Mr. Holmes," the inspector remarked when he called on us one evening a few days later, "and see if you can make anything of them."

Holmes agreed, with the proviso that he would naturally give priority to any current case of interest or importance on which he was consulted. He was given access to the Scotland Yard files, from which I am not permitted to quote, but after Holmes's supposed death I had maintained a keen interest in crime and kept a scrapbook of newspaper clippings concerning those I considered of most importance. I draw on these to provide a brief outline of each case as it was seen by the public.

John Cooper Whitney was regarded by all who knew him as an upstanding member of society. A lifelong Liberal and a personal friend of Lord Bellinger, he was also a member of the Methodist Church and an early and active supporter of the National Temperance Foundation. His large personal fortune came from his ownership of several cotton mills in the north of England, where his teetotal principles were strictly adhered to – any worker who was found drinking at work was summarily dismissed, and any worker who brought alcohol onto the premises was fined, and suspended from work for a period of two weeks. Any worker who was

55

found guilty of offences involving alcohol outside the factory gates was also subject to dismissal, even though he had already been fined by the authorities.

Whitney had a large house in Rochdale, but spent most of his time at his spacious flat in Victoria Street, which he preferred for its proximity to the Houses of Parliament. He was unmarried and lived alone. He had three servants, a cook, butler, and maid who did not live in, but were employed under the same conditions as his mill hands, and liable to be out of their situation if they were caught drinking or in possession of alcohol. On the morning of April 27th, 1893, his current servants arrived at the flat to find their employer lying dead on the carpet of his living room, clad only in his nightshirt. His throat had been cut. The servants immediately went out into the street to find a constable, and within an hour two detectives and the medical examiner were present. There were no signs of a forced entry.

The murder was, of course, reported in the newspapers, and while he was well known within his own circles, there can be no doubt that, in the south of England at least, he became better known in death than he had been in life. As his life came under public scrutiny, it became clear that opinion on John Cooper Whitney was sharply divided. For every person who had come to the conclusion that he was a man of steely principle who had worked hard to rescue the labouring classes from the evils of drink, there was another who thought he was a damned interfering busybody who had no right to attempt to deprive the workers of one of the few pleasures they could afford. But could someone who held the latter view have hated him enough, or thought him enough of a threat to personal freedom, to have somehow entered – or been let into – his house to kill him?

With the assistance of the Lancashire police, Scotland Yard attempted to draw up a list of everyone who might have had a grudge against Whitney. I use the word "attempted" because he had been in charge of the family mills for forty-five years, and the number of people who had been fired because of his draconian attitudes ran into the hundreds. He had owned the flat in Westminster for twenty years, and in that time he had dismissed four cooks, three maids, and five butlers for alcoholic offences. The two police forces visited as many people on their list as they could, but found no one who didn't have an alibi, or was dead or had left the country. The three servants, and especially the butler, Lawson, fell under suspicion. The butler because he, other than Whitney himself, alone had a key to the flat, so he could have arrived earlier than usual and surprised his master in bed. Both cook and maid testified that he had in fact arrived last that morning, and that they had had to wait to be let in. Perhaps all three had conspired to kill him?

Witnesses came forward who had seen all the servants riding on the bus or underground after the time which the medical examiner determined to be that of Whitney's death. The suggestion was made in one of the more sensational newspapers that he had been done away with by someone hired by a cabal of disgruntled brewers whose livelihood he threatened.

"Despite the high profile of the National Temperance Foundation," said Holmes as we discussed the case one afternoon, *"it is doubtful that their influence, and especially that of one member, would be strong enough to spread fear amongst the brewers and distillers, nor that they would have resorted to murder had it been so. There are advocates of temperance in Parliament who would surely have been a more important target for an alcohol advocating assassin. You realize, of course, Watson, that despite the evidence of the other servants, and those who saw him on public transport, the butler is not exonerated."*

"Why do you say so?"

"He held one of the two keys, and keys can be copied. While it seems unlikely that he struck the blow himself, he may have facilitated the entry of the person who did. I shall recommend to Lestrade that he question Lawson further."

During the summer months, it was common for Martin Eastwick and his wife Joan to cross the small stretch of Hampstead Heath that separated their house in Spaniards Road from the Vale of Health, where Mrs. Eastwick's parents, Michael and Susannah Pope, lived, and, after their visit, return home by the same route. On June 22nd, 1893, Mrs. Eastwick made the short journey on her own as her husband was away on a business trip. According to Mr. and Mrs. Pope, their daughter stayed rather later than usual. She refused their offer of her old room and set off for her home in the dark.

An elderly gentleman who was out on his morning constitutional found her body at seven a.m. the next day. She had been strangled. As her rings, necklace, earrings, and purse were missing, the police concluded that robbery had been the motive. The value of the jewellery and money amounted to about forty-five pounds, a sum for which someone living rough on the heath (of whom there were several) might be prepared to kill. All the tramps known to be sleeping on the heath were rounded up and subjected to intense interrogation, but none confessed.

"Really, Watson, if you were homeless and sleeping on the heath, would you stay there after you had killed a woman and stolen forty-five pounds?"

"What should Lestrade have done, then?"

"He should have asked all the other tramps on the heath if one of their number was missing, and if so, whether they knew his name."

"Such people tend not to stay in one place for long," I said, "so it's unlikely that they are still all there to question."

"True. But then he should have gone to all the hotels and boarding houses in the immediate vicinity to see if any had rented a room to a obvious tramp with the unexpected ability to pay for it. That avenue of enquiry still remains."

"Supposing someone had another motive for killing the woman, and a tramp merely found her and took the money from her dead body?"

"That is a definite possibility, yet you will agree that in either case, a tramp must at least be looked for. Another possibility of course is that, as you say, someone had a motive other than theft, but took the money and jewelry to make it seem the work of a thief. There are certainly difficulties there. Mr. and Mrs. Eastwick, and Mrs. Eastwick's parents, all appear to be upstanding citizens with no enemies in the world."

Since the death of his only child, his son David, Abraham Weston, a widower, had become increasingly reclusive, until he took this tendency to an extreme, selling his house in Camberwell and moving to a lonely little cottage on a remote promontory on the west coast of Scotland. His only human contact was with a middle-aged lady, Mrs. Laurie, who cycled to his home from the nearest village once a week, bringing him groceries and staying to clean the cottage. Every other week she took his laundry and returned it the following week. She testified that while he paid her generously for these services, he spoke to her very little during her visits, preferring either to closet himself in his study with his books or go for a walk across the windswept terrain while she attended to the housework.

She arrived at about half-past-ten on the morning of July 24th that same year and found Weston in his study, dead from a single gunshot wound to the head. A sturdy, sensible woman, Mrs. Laurie didn't succumb to hysteria, but immediately jumped on her bicycle and pedalled swiftly home and reported the death to the village constable, who then sent a message to the authorities in Lillapool. From there, the responsibility for investigation was handed over to the police in Edinburgh, and then to the Scotland Yarders, who in truth stood little better chance of finding the culprit. They questioned the folk in the village to see if any strangers had been seen in the area at the time, but none had. No one amongst the villagers had any motive, and indeed, the only item in the cottage of any obvious value, a silver teapot, hadn't been removed. The detectives then switched their inquiries to Camberwell, where their efforts proved equally fruitless.

"The fact that no one in the village saw any strangers hardly proves anything," said Holmes. "According to the medical report, the murder must have taken place in the hours of darkness. When we combine this with the fact that Weston's house was on a promontory, we can at least surmise that the killer arrived at night in a boat, committed the deed, then left by the way he came."

Holmes looked at the cases from time to time when the steady stream of new clients which attended his return to active practice permitted, but in the end was forced to confess that while he could get a little further than the official force, he was still unable to produce anything conclusive.

The situation would have remained thus, had it not been for the occurrence of five more murders which were equally baffling and seemingly insoluble . . . .

"Ali Ben Abou" was the stage name of Norman Waters, the forty-two-year-old son of a lighterman from Bermondsey, who had been an entertainer in the music halls, in various capacities, after starting as a stagehand at the age of fifteen. By the time he was twenty-nine, he had established himself as a magician.

At the climax of his act, a marked bullet appeared to be placed in a gun and fired at Ali, who seemed to catch it in his teeth. A member of the audience was called up on stage to mark the bullet, fire the gun, and identify the bullet when the magician removed it from his mouth. Despite the loud report and the large puff of smoke, it was of course a blank that was fired. The conjuror palmed the marked bullet, held his hand up to his teeth and produced it as if he had caught it in them. On this occasion, however, the young woman Ali called to assist him was horrified when she fired the gun and he fell forward with a cry, shot through the heart. As the blood spread across the front of his silken tunic, his unwitting killer fainted. The audience sat in stunned silence for a few moments. Then there was uproar.

The curtain was dropped, and a minute or two later the manager came from behind it to assure the crowd that an ambulance had been called, and under the circumstances could the auditorium please be cleared.

Waters' dressing room was locked, and when the police arrived they insisted that it be unlocked. The master key was obtained from the theatre's doorkeeper and entry effected. There, on the dressing table, they found an open box of blanks, or at any rate, a box proclaiming itself to be such. In fact, it contained real live bullets. The murderer must have emptied the box and made the substitution.

Waters was a notorious womaniser, and had been married three times, on all three occasions to women working in his act, which he had been doing for thirteen years. Such was his easy charm that his two previous wives seemed to have accepted their situation with equanimity and bore him no malice, as far as one could tell. Indeed, one of them had carried on acting as one of his assistants even after she had been replaced in his affections. There was always a possibility that a jealous husband or fiancé or a slighted lover had killed him, and the police investigated that line thoroughly.

The obvious suspect, the only conspicuous enemy that Waters had, was another magician, "Mehemet the Magnificent", (born Alfred Leaman in Stockwell, 1853) who had been loud in his claims that Waters had stolen some of his tricks, and had based the Middle Eastern flavour of his identity on Leaman's act. On the night that Waters was killed, Leaman was himself on the stage, in the middle of his own act at the Camden Palais. It was of course possible that he had hired someone to kill Waters. The police investigated this aspect and could find no evidence for it.

Waters' assistants, including his wife, were all questioned by the police, along with the magician's behind-the-scenes staff. The regular Empire stagehands could be ruled out because they weren't privy to the magician's secrets, and Ali was strict about keeping his dressing room door locked when he wasn't in it. A thorough investigation of Waters' employees revealed that none of them had anything against him. They had all been with him for years, and he was a fair and conscientious employer.

The doorkeeper was briefly suspected, as his master key gave him access to Waters' dressing room at all times, but he could account for all his movements on that last day of Waters' life and hadn't been out of anybody's sight long enough to effect the substitution. His wife confirmed that he had come home at the usual time the previous evening and had been at home the entire night.

Quentin Maltravers was in his seventieth year and had sat on the bench for twenty, after a successful career as a Q.C. During his time as a barrister he had specialized in prosecution, and so it came as little surprise that when he was elevated to the High Court, he quickly became noted for the severity of his judgements. In his personal life, he was a bachelor of ascetic tastes, whose principal vice appeared to be the occasional pinch of snuff. He belonged to only one club, the Solomon, whose membership was restricted to sitting and retired judges.

It came as a great surprise and shock, then, when this pillar of society was found beaten to death in one of the least salubrious back alleys in Whitechapel. Had he been a secret participant in the various forbidden pleasures afforded by London's East End? Whether that were true or not, there was no doubt that the number of people who had a motive for his murder ran into the hundreds.

When Lady Violet Cantwell, the youngest daughter of Lord Caithness, was presented at court, there had been general agreement that she was the most beautiful debutante of her season, and now, some fifteen years later, it couldn't be denied that maturity had only increased her charms. As well as her physical attractions, she had an open-hearted and forgiving nature, which won her friends of all religious and political persuasions.

In those days of her youth, there had been much competition for her hand. Eventually it seemed clear to all that John Allingham, a subaltern in the Household Cavalry and the only son and heir of Sir Walter Allingham, had won her heart, and that their marriage would soon be announced. There was much surprise, then, when she became the second wife of Lord Kilgarriff, a widower eighteen years her senior. In some quarters, there was speculation that she was marrying the wealthy aristocrat because Lord Caithness was deep in debt, and that she was sacrificing her own happiness to keep her parents from penury and disgrace.

Whatever the truth of the matter, it soon became obvious that the marriage was far from happy. After thirteen years, Lady Violet had failed to produce an heir, a fact which Kilgarriff continually threw in her face. He embarked on a series of liaisons with other women, and didn't attempt to conceal them from her.

John Allingham, now Sir John since the death of his father, had remained unmarried. Lady Violet at first sought him out as a friend, and a sympathetic ear for her troubles, but, inevitably, the passionate love which had once existed between them was rekindled. So deep was that love that it couldn't be hidden from society at large, and both Lady Violet and Sir John were prepared to face scandal and divorce if it meant that they could finally be together. Lord Kilgarriff refused to grant a divorce, and there the matter stood, until one morning the bodies of Sir John and Lady Violet were found floating in the Grand Union Canal.

Lord Kilgarriff was the most obvious suspect, but at the time their drowned corpses were discovered, he had been at his estate in the Scottish Highlands for ten days, in the company of a young local woman, and his staff could bear witness to the fact.

There was a suggestion that the lovers had had a mutual suicide pact due to the intractability of their situation, but friends of both denied that this could be so. The couple, they said, had been determined to live through the situation, come what might.

Giuseppe Parisi arrived in London from the seaport of Gioia Tauro in Calabria, in southern Italy, and went straight to that little triangle formed by Rosebery Avenue, Farringdon Road, and the Clerkenwell Road which is variously known as the Italian Quarter, Little Italy, or Italian Hill. Parisi had no marketable skills – at least, none that were legal, other than his great strength. He soon became known in the area as a man to go to when heavy lifting was needed, and this provided him with a reasonable income. He became engaged to one Theresa Prezzemoli, daughter of a local trader, and it must have seemed to him that he had an opportunity to lead an honest, safe, and productive life. Then, six months after his arrival, Theresa, worried that she hadn't seen her fiancé for three days, went to his landlady, Signora Barbieri, and asked her to unlock the door to Giuseppe's room. Inside, the two women were horrified to find him hanging upside down from a gas fitting on the ceiling, his body naked and his skin a ghastly white. His throat had been cut and he had been allowed to bleed to death like a slaughtered pig.

Theresa fell into uncontrollable hysteria. Signora Barbieri did her best to look after her and sent another of her lodgers, Franco Vitale, to fetch the police. It transpired that Franco and Giuseppe had become friends, and that one evening, after they had shared a bottle or two of wine, Giuseppe had told Franco the full story of his life – that he wasn't, as he told everybody, Guiseppe Parisi from Salerno, who had been a sailor all his life, but Giuseppe Baldini of Naples, bandit and assassin. He had sworn Vitale to secrecy, on pain of his life, but now, as Baldini could no longer harm him, nor be harmed by the disclosure, Vitale told the police all that he knew.

There was one thing about the crime that Vitale and all the Italian community knew, which was that hanging a man upside down after his death was a sign that he had been killed because he was a traitor. Had an avenger followed Baldini's trail, all the way from Calabria to Little Italy? It seemed the only solution, and yet extensive questioning of virtually everyone in the district yielded up no clues.

Like many young aristocrats of the time, the Honourable Harold Hamilton-Acott devoted most of his time to the pursuit of pleasure. He was a frequenter of the music hall and the racetrack, but was most often to be seen playing roulette at Porter's, his club in Pall Mall. Porter's facilities included bedrooms for those of its members who could not, or did not wish to travel home after a late night at the club. So great was Hamilton-Acott's devotion to the wheel that he sometimes spent an entire week there, remaining awake until three or four in the morning, repairing to an available bedroom and then emerging in time for a lavish meal before returning to the tables. According to fellow habitues, and the club's staff, he was merely a fair player, neither winning nor losing a great deal of money on most evenings. The family fortune was considerable, and the allowance supplied by his father, the sixth duke of Conway, was extremely generous, so he might have been a far worse player and still able to carry on with his obsession.

His lack of large wins meant that he made no enemies among his fellow players due to deprivation or envy. His erotic liaisons tended to be either paying encounters with high-class courtesans, or love affairs with unattached women of his own social circle who shared his easygoing attitude towards the whole business of *l'amour*. It was unlikely, therefore, that when he was fatally stabbed outside his rooms at the Albany, his murderer had been either another gambler or a jealous husband or fiancé. After several days at Porter's, Hamilton-Acott decided it was time to go home, because the next day was the Derby Stakes at Epsom and he wished to attend. He took a cab from Porter's at five in the morning and was found dead in the foyer about an hour later, with seven knife wounds in his back. None of the other occupants of the Albany heard anything suspicious.

Scotland Yard did not come to Sherlock Holmes with these matters. It was their belief that their usual methods – the application of more detectives to the case, and the extensive questioning of witnesses – would yield whatever solutions were possible.

Nevertheless, Holmes was deeply interested in them, and followed the progress of the investigations with avidity, returning to them whenever his current cases allowed. Then one morning as we sat reading the newspapers, he threw *The Daily Chronicle* down on the table with an exclamation of impatience.

"What is it?" I asked.

He made no reply, but reached over to his pipe rack and took out the cherry-wood. I remained silent, as I knew that this meant he was in a contentious mood. He stood and went over to the mantelpiece, where he filled the pipe from his Persian slipper, pressing tobacco into the bowl with his long thin fingers.

"Those murders are connected," he said, tossing his spent match into the grate.

"Which murders?"

"Why, man, the murders of Waters, Judge Maltravers, Giuseppe Baldini. Hamilton-Acott and Sir John Allingham and Lady Kilgarriff."

The notion seemed so absurd to me that although I had determined not to engage in conversation with him while he was in a disputatious frame of mind, I exclaimed, "Really, Holmes, how can they be? Waters was shot, Maltravers was beaten to death, Baldini's throat was cut, Hamilton-Acott was stabbed, and Sir John and Lady Violet were drowned. It isn't even sure if the last two really were murdered. Waters and Baldini came from a different social class. Surely all they have in common is that their killings are unsolved and, as far as I can see, likely to remain so."

"Nevertheless, I am convinced that there is a thread that binds them together."

"Until you can tell me what it is, you can hardly expect me to believe that. You have said yourself, there are unsolved crimes aplenty, and for all your powers, you are only one man."

"The knowledge is somewhere in my brain. I merely need to find it and bring it to bear. Will you give me your gift of silence for an hour or two?"

"Certainly. I'll do better than that: I shall go for a walk in the park."

When I returned at eleven o'clock, Holmes sprang from his armchair with a smile.

"You have found a connection then?"

"Yes, old friend. Does this mean anything to you?"

He handed me a piece of paper on which he had written:

John Cooper Whitney: Temperance
Joan Eastwick: The Female Pope
Abraham Weston: The Hermit
Norman Waters: The Magician
Quentin Maltravers: Judgement
Lady Kilgarriff and Sir John Allingham: The Lovers
Giuseppe Baldini: The Hanged Man
Harold Hamilton-Acott: The Wheel of Fortune

"The three previous murders are also part of this? I'm sorry, Holmes, but I am none the wiser. What does all this mean?"

"Have you heard of the Tarot?"

"Something to do with fortune telling, isn't it? Like tea leaves and palmistry. Stuff and nonsense. We are men of science, Holmes."

"Agreed, but as men of science, we must acknowledge the existence of other methods of thought and accept that there are those who follow them, no matter how unscientific they may seem to us. Such a system is the Tarot. You are correct in saying that it is often used as a device for fortune telling, but I suspect that our murderer thinks that he has found something more profound within it."

"Murderer? Singular? One man has perpetrated all these atrocities?"

"I think that one person is ultimately responsible for these crimes, though I don't doubt he has agents who do much of the work, the investigation . . . and sometimes the killing."

So saying, he reached into the pocket of his mouse-grey dressing gown and took out a deck of cards. He pulled out eight and placed them on the table between us. *Temperance, The Hermit, The Magician, Judgement, The Wheel of Fortune, The Hanged Man, The Lovers,* and *The High Priestess*. He pointed to the last.

"In most decks this card is known as The High Priestess, but it is sometimes called *La Papesse* – the female Pope, a reference to the mediaeval legend of Pope Joan, who supposedly reigned as pontiff from 855 to 857. You will recall that Mrs. Eastwick's maiden name was *Pope*."

"Joan Pope – Pope Joan. And for that fact alone she was killed? That's insane."

"These are eight of what are known as the *Major Arcana*. In all, there are twenty-two, so if nothing is done, we may expect fourteen more killings, each of them somehow reflecting one of the cards."

And he spread them out in front of me.

The Emperor, The Hierophant, The Chariot, Strength, Death, The Devil, The Tower, The Star, The Moon, The Sun, Justice, The World, The Fool, and *The Empress*.

I confess that my imagination ran riot, wondering who our mysterious antagonist might kill for each card. Strength – a circus strongman? The Fool – a clown, or a music hall comedian? Justice – a barrister? Someone else on the Bench? The Tower – would he have someone thrown from one, or destroy one, as in the picture on the card? Perhaps even The Tower of London itself? I shuddered as I looked at the picture of The Empress. Might he even attempt the assassination of Queen Victoria, the Empress of India?

As so often, Holmes, who knew me so well, divined my thought.

"We will stop him before he has time to perpetrate any more of the horrors these crude pictures may suggest, old friend."

"I certainly hope so. What is our first move?"

"We are going to visit a member of The Order of Thoth."

The Hermetic Order of Thoth, as my companion informed me en route, was founded in 1865 by three Freemasons called William Henry

Archer, Hartley Frobisher, and Michael Drax-Morton. A number of celebrated names were involved, or alleged to be involved with the organization. The rituals of The Order were influenced by a mixture of so-called magical disciplines: The Hermetic *Qabbalah*, geomancy, alchemy, astrology, and the occult interpretation of the Tarot.

"How did you come to be interested in any of this?" I asked Holmes.

"It does seem a little out of character, does it not? I came to this knowledge by a circuitous route. As you know, before we began sharing rooms in Baker Street, I lodged for some time in Montague Street, near the British Museum. Pickings were thin, and it occurred to me that if I couldn't always use my abilities in the field, I might at least make a little money by writing monographs on subjects which were germane to the profession. I have mentioned before my studies of the different types of tobacco ash and the effect of different types of labour on the contours of the human hand. Both of these were produced doing this period. There were others which I started, but, for various reasons, did not complete.

"One of these was on the subject of the different methods of cheating at cards. There would be no point in finishing it now because Maskelyne has since written the definitive text on the subject. As to the Tarot, I learned, while studying the history of cards in the Reading Room, that despite some claims that it has its origins back in the mists of antiquity, in actuality the deck can only be traced back with any certainty to mid-fifteenth century Italy. First known as '*Trionfo*', then '*Taroccho*', the cards were used to play various games. The name *Tarot* comes from the French. It wasn't until about 1780 that it began to be used as cartomancy, using the fall of the cards to predict the future."

"And this fellow that we are going to see – ?"

"Is an expert on the Tarot. In fact, he has written a book on the subject. His name is Sebastian Childe."

"You don't think he is the author of these crimes?"

"I think it extremely unlikely, but he may be able to guide us to the person who is."

After Holmes rang the bell at 23 Holland Park Grove, the door was answered by Sebastian Childe himself. He was a tall, thin man of about thirty-five with a pale face, watery blue eyes, and light blond hair. Perhaps the most notable thing about him was his air of abstraction, which evoked the feeling that he wasn't entirely engaged with mundane reality, but lived half on another more-rarified plane of existence. I could agree with Holmes that he seemed unlikely to have anything to do with anything so base as murder.

"Yes?" he inquired in a reedy voice.

66

"Mr. Sebastian Childe?"

"I am he, and you are – ?"

"I am Sherlock Holmes, and this is Dr. John Watson, my colleague and friend."

An expression of pure joy spread across Childe's sharp features and he seized my companion's hand and shook it.

"Mr. Holmes! Why, this is indeed an honour!"

I hadn't expected a practitioner of the occult to be so pleased to meet the foremost practical logician of his day, but Childe continued, "A positive pleasure to meet another seeker after truth, for that is what we both are, in our own ways, though we travel to it via different paths. And Dr. Watson! I have read everything you have written, and with great enjoyment. Please, please, come in, and tell me how I may assist you."

Childe ushered us into his living room. Although it was still day, the gas lamps were lit, as the tall windows were masked by thick, colourful tapestries. A piece of some lightly scented incense was burning in a metal bowl set on a tripod in the corner. The walls were covered in bookshelves which were stacked with heavy old tomes, and here and there some obviously more recent publications, all doubtless concerned with mysticism and similar topics. On almost every other flat surface – the mantelpiece, the tables, and part of the floor – there were various artifacts which reflected the occupant's interests: A foot-high Buddha which appeared to have been carved from ebony, a bronze statuette of the goddess Kali, several African idols, a nine-inch replica of the Diana of the Ephesians, and, on a small metal stand, an icon of Isis, Osiris, and Horus. Amidst all this, only one modern thing stood out: A typewriter at a small desk, which Childe, or his secretary (if he had one), doubtless used to transcribe his various writings.

At his bidding, we sat down in two capacious armchairs opposite a chaise longue.

"Would you care for some tea?" he asked, ringing the bell. "I generally take some at this time. I trust oolong is to your taste?"

A neatly dressed, petite young maid brought the tea, and Childe said, as I took my first tentative sip, "So, how may I be of assistance to the Great Detective and his associate?"

"You are an acknowledged expert on the Tarot," Holmes began.

"Thank you. I take it you have read my book, *The Tarot Explained*?"

"Yes."

"Do you have a copy? You must let me give you a signed one before you leave, if you have not."

"That is gracious of you, but let me come straight to the point. Your interpretation of the deck is that it goes back to ancient Egypt, and that it is a guide to spiritual growth."

"Yes. I spent many years researching the subject before I first put pen to paper, and I am convinced that that interpretation is the only correct one."

"That may be so, but what other interpretations are you aware of? Are there any, for example, that might countenance or encourage the use of violence?"

"A strange question. Why do you ask?"

"You are unaware of the recent rash of murders?"

"I never read newspapers, Mr. Holmes. The mundane trivialities they deal in can only distract one from contemplation of the eternal verities. But since you ask, yes, I do know of one such. Have you heard of Valentine Athlone?"

"Never."

"The better for you. It is a lamentable aspect of occult groups that they are inclined to factionalism. Individuals will disagree over the meaning of texts, the correct conduct of this or that ritual, or the necessity of keeping the workings of the group a secret from outsiders. Fortunately, The Order of Thoth was free from such divisions – or, that is, it was until the coming of Valentine Athlone. My reading of the Tarot was accepted by most of the members of The Order, except him and a few others. It became clear that he was a Satanist, that he saw the Tarot as a guide to the liberation of Lucifer and his elevation to the Lord of the Universe. He was expelled from The Order and began his own group, The Legion of Lucifer. Our Order has a distinguished membership of artists, writers, and actors. He managed to convince a few of us, the weaker ones, the ones less sure in our truth, to join him, but for the most part his Legion is a cesspool of drug addicts and criminals. Let me show you a copy of his book, in which I believe he advocates human sacrifice."

He stood, went over to one of the crowded bookshelves, and took out a slim volume which bore the title *The Book of Lucifer*.

"It is an almost unreadable mixture of bad poetry, prose poems, and tortuous Satanic utterances, but look at this page."

He opened the book and handed it to Holmes. I leaned over to look. It read:

The Coming Age is The Age of Lucifer!
Tremble, O ye Christians, mired in repression and fear!
Tremble, O ye Muslims, in your base servitude!
Tremble, O ye Jews, in your temples of greed!

Tremble, O ye Hindus, in your dark and childish ways!
Tremble, O ye Atheists, deniers of His light!
For the Coming Age is The Age of Lucifer!
He rises once more from the ancient prison!
All earth shall bow to His thought!
Intellect shall rule over base emotion!
For His way is the way of the mind!
What must be done shall be done!
O, the Coming Age is The Age of Lucifer! "
On the Tarot

The ancient Tarot, first formed by the sages of Egypt and passed down the centuries to us, is more, has more power, than any other single talisman on earth. Some have called it a mere game, others a guidebook for the progress of the soul. I alone have uncovered its true secret. When the Catholic Church dubbed it the Devil's Picture Book, they were more correct than they knew. By the correct use of the Tarot, we can expedite the ascension of Lucifer to His rightful place on the glorious throne.

The way will be hard and bloody, and beset by the dull morality of the unbelievers. It will mean sacrifice for each of the twenty-two cards of the Major Arcana, *but when it is done and we are steeped in blood, then shall Lucifer return, for the Coming Age is The Age of Lucifer!*

The superior man shall rise, and the inferior man shall fall, for the Coming Age is The Age of Lucifer!

"These are the ravings of a madman!" I cried.

"Perhaps," said Holmes, "but there is nothing more dangerous than a madman who believes himself to be sane – saner, indeed, than all others. Mr. Childe, do you have Athlone's address?"

"You will find it in the book."

"May we take it?"

"Certainly, but – "

"I rather fear that Athlone has already begun his campaign of death. Come, Watson, there's no time to lose!"

"Your signed copy of my book – " Childe began.

"Send it to me. I think you know the address."

We rushed out into the street and hailed the first passing hansom.

"Scotland Yard!" cried Holmes as we clambered inside.

As may be imagined, the prosaic, stolid Scotland Yarders at first found it difficult to believe that the unprepossessing, badly printed little volume that Holmes presented to them could possibly contain the key to a series of unsolved murders. But during his long absence, it had become clear how valuable his methods were, and how keenly he was missed. His stock among the Force was high, and it wasn't long before a detective and two constables were dispatched to bring Valentine Athlone in for questioning. He proved to be a tall, dark-haired young man whose characteristic expression was a sneer of aristocratic disdain.

While he was being held at Bow Street Police Station, Inspectors Gregson and Lestrade acquired a warrant to search Athlone's house in Highgate. Holmes and I were permitted to accompany them, and there the four of us found ample evidence of Athlone's guilt.

The house, as well as having rooms adapted for various Satanic rituals, also contained information gathered by Athlone's Legion regarding the victims – newspaper clippings, transcriptions of gossip, names copied from electoral registers, dates and times, theatrical programmes, legal reports, and more. All evidence that the victims had been meticulously researched and chosen.

It was then that the diligence of the professionals came into play. By unstinting hard work, they eventually had the names and addresses of all the members of The Legion of Lucifer and a good grasp of the extent to which each one was involved in The Legion's terrible crimes. So the praise they received from the judge was well deserved, but as so often, without the help of Mr. Sherlock Holmes, they would have remained forever in the dark.

"I think you want a little unofficial help. Three undetected murders in one year won't do, Lestrade . . . ."

– Sherlock Holmes
"The Empty House"

The Adventure of the Curious Mother
by Tracy Revels

"Thank you for agreeing to see me, Mr. Holmes, especially on such short notice." The beautiful woman, who had just swept into our chambers with the regal dignity of a queen, offered her hand. "I hope I'm not preventing you from attending to some more important business."

"My friend, Doctor Watson, can assure you that I have been the laziest of men for the last week," Holmes replied, "and that I am in need of a puzzle or conundrum to exercise my brain. Please feel free to speak openly before him, as his assistance to me has been invaluable in my work. And now, Miss Agner, how may I help you?"

"Dear me, you remind me that I must go to the stationer's and have new cards made." The young woman sighed. "We are so informal at home. I hadn't thought of them." She was clad in a fashionable, amber-colored walking dress, with lovely fawn-leather gloves, and a rather saucy hat with a fake bird attached, its wings spread to one side. She was perhaps twenty-five years of age and exceptionally lovely, but there was something about her eyes and mouth, an expression of fierce determination, that implied a hardness within her soul. This was no blushing maiden, but a young woman of purpose and resolution. "I was married five months ago in America. My name is now Tabitha Carson. My problem, I suppose, concerns the marriage and its consequences. I will strive to be precise, sir, and not try your patience."

Holmes nodded his willingness to listen. I could tell, from a half-dozen little clues, that he had immediately found his new client intriguing.

"My late father was Mr. Alexander Agner. You have probably never heard of him – "

"The empresario of Agner's Ladies Accoutrements?"

Mrs. Carson nodded. A slight smile of pride momentarily softened her features. "Indeed, sir. Father took a small millinery business which he inherited from his mother and developed it into a network of shops specializing in items which are necessary to ladies and, with a bit of imagination, can be made stylish at very little cost. I doubt we have ever counted duchesses or countesses among our clients, but father earned a tidy fortune from making sure that the wives of store clerks and station agents didn't need to feel dowdy or provincial when they went visiting or

71

attended the theater." Here she tapped her delightful hat. "One advantage of being his daughter and his only child, I have always had first pick of the merchandise.

"Mine was a charmed life until Father passed away when I was fifteen. Mother instantly summoned me home from the school I was attending in Switzerland, and from that moment forward, my life wasn't my own. Mother had always been somewhat protective and nervous, but Father tempered her demands while he lived, insisting that I be well-educated and prepared for whatever future I desired. Upon his passing, Mother withdrew into her widowhood, and insisted that I entomb myself with her. Whenever I protested that our period of mourning was completed, and that I wished to return to school, or travel, she scolded and fussed, reminding me that even one of the Queen's daughters was a 'good girl' who 'never abandoned her poor mother'.

"I hope I don't sound petulant when I state, without hesitation, that her treatment of me was domestic cruelty. I was never allowed a moment alone or contact with friends and peers. Mother censored my mail – she read any letters that came for me, and threw so many in the fire without allowing me to read them, that my little classmates gave up hope and cut ties with me because they thought I had thrown them over and wouldn't answer their missives. I kept a locked diary to assuage my loneliness, until I realized Mother had made a duplicate of the book's key and was reading it! My only outings were to the market with her, or to church, but I wasn't allowed to step across the threshold without first swathing myself in black and lowering a heavy veil. I felt like a living ghost.

"I was forced to tolerate this imprisonment until I turned twenty-one. Father's business was managed by a colleague, Mr. Jones. When I came of age, he began giving me an allowance from a trust which Father had established for me. It would be mine to command when I turned thirty, or upon my marriage. With my own money in my purse, Mother could no longer keep me under lock and key, though of course she protested mightily when I went out in pretty dresses or met one of my few remaining friends for tea in a shop. She continued her exasperating habit of snooping through my possessions, and reading any mail of mine she snatched up before I returned home. She was particularly insistent that I shouldn't marry while she lived, reminding me daily that my first duty was to her. When I protested and said I wanted a husband and eventually a family, she acted as if I had announced my intention to become a pagan and perform blood sacrifices! She would theatrically insist she had a weak heart, and I would be 'free soon enough' to pursue my dreadful ambitions.

"A year ago, I turned twenty-six, and the situation became so intolerable that I packed my bags and left home. A distant cousin, who resides in Tucson, in the American state of Arizona, was getting married. I used her wedding as an excuse, claiming – Here, I confess my duplicity, though surely you understand it. – that Elizabeth wished me to be a bridesmaid. Mother would never think of making such a journey and forbid me to go, but I drew a large advance upon my allowance and simply vanished in the night. I knew Mother might never forgive me, that she might even disinherit me, but gentlemen, even direst poverty would be better than living under her oppressive thumb.

"While I was in Tucson, I met Mr. Quintin Carson. He was a former 'cowboy', as they are often dismissively called, a man who had spent almost twenty years riding the range and driving cattle across the vast plains. When he was thirty-five, he was thrown from his horse and received a grievous injury, so that he was forced to abandon the life of a herder. Fortunately, he possesses an amazing talent for illustration and is a keen observer of native wildlife. Some sketches he produced caught the eye of a travelling professor, who hired him to illustrate a volume on western fauna. This and other commissions made him comfortable, if not wealthy.

"I cannot tell you why I fell in love with him, sir. It isn't easy for a woman to speak of things which her heart knows to be true, even when her head finds them ludicrous. Quintin is nearly twenty years my senior, a man who has endured a harsh life, and who is often taciturn and moody, preferring to sit on some dusty mesa for hours, sketching a snake or a rodent, than engaging in society. Yet we were instantly drawn to each other, and within a month were deeply in love. We married quietly, and for a time made our home there in the desert, as happy as a pair of hawks surveying our vast, wild kingdom."

"Did you keep this from your mother?" Holmes asked.

"No, for my conscience plagued me. I wrote to her soon after arriving in America. She was none too pleased, but over the weeks, when we corresponded, I began to hope that she had softened, and that my absence had taught her a lesson. I told her and Mr. Jones of my marriage, and shortly thereafter I received a letter from Mr. Jones urging me to return home and claim my patrimony. I decided we could surprise Mother with an extended visit, so that she might come to know and love Quintin. He wasn't, as you might imagine, overly enthusiastic – but he agreed to it both to make me happy and to secure our financial future. As we travelled, we spent our time talking of the big house we would someday build and the children we hoped would eventually fill its many rooms.

"I was adamant that we shouldn't, however, reside under Mother's roof in London. Instead, through connections with Mr. Jones (who was amenable to keeping our secret) we found an agent who rented a home for us that was just a street away from Mother's. We took the place for six months. Yesterday morning, we arrived, had our luggage brought inside, brushed off our clothes, and then went down to street to knock on Mother's door.

"What followed wasn't the warm reunion I had hoped for, but a terrible, embarrassing scene. Mother had a wild look in her eyes. No harpy from Hell could have been more frightening. She absolutely forbade Quintin from crossing her threshold. He bowed himself away, never making a complaint, never raising his voice to her despite the horrible names she flung at him. I stomped into the parlor and was gathering my courage to make a final break with Mother when she thrust the following into my hand."

The lady opened her reticule and pulled out several folded papers, passing them to Holmes. I rose and moved to read over his shoulder.

The items were clippings from newspapers. The headlines read *"Vicious Murder"* and *"Sheriff Seeks Gang!"*. A quick perusal told the story – that a prominent farmer in the territory of New Mexico had been killed by a quartet of rustlers, men who had been hired by a rival infuriated that the victim had staked a claim to the best grazing land in the county and was fencing it for his sole use. Three of the killers and their employer had been captured and tried, with the gunslingers hanged and the rancher imprisoned for life. The last villain, however, had managed to elude the lawmen. The final paper was a small poster, one that proclaimed *"Wanted: Dead or Alive"*, along with a drawing of the criminal's face. The man's countenance was long and cragged, with a scar across his forehead and great walrus-style mustaches drooping over his mouth.

"I take it this is your new husband?" Holmes said.

"Indeed, sir. That picture is exact, though of course the name is different. I didn't knowingly wed anyone known as Red 'Dirt' Rogers."

The lady rose suddenly, and began to pace, her arms drawn tight across her chest.

"Mother said she 'had a premonition' when I wrote to her that I had married, and therefore she hired private detectives, American men known as 'Pinkertons', to investigate my spouse. This is what they sent her."

Holmes sat straighter in his chair. "I have some experience with that agency. Have you shown this to your husband?"

The lady shook her head. "Mother's revelation to me was made at around five in the afternoon. I returned to our house immediately, only to find that Quintin had gone off somewhere. He didn't reappear at home until almost six this morning, much the worse for drink. I left him unconscious upon the sofa, which was still covered with a cloth, and came straight to you.

"And now you understand my problem. Is it true, Mr. Holmes? Have I married a murderer? Was my mother correct about me? That I am such a weak judge of character I should have been grateful to have stayed under her wing, protected, for the rest of my life?" The poor woman dropped back onto the sofa. I now saw how diligently she had worked to maintain her composure, and the raging emotions she was strongly suppressing. "Quintin has shown me only kindness and love. How could I be so wrong about him?"

"He never spoke of his past?"

"Very little. He told me he was orphaned as a small boy and began riding the trails when he was just thirteen. I know that his work with Professor Rodrick is authentic, for I have met the distinguished gentleman and seen the books they collaborated upon – but Quintin doesn't willingly talk about himself and his past. The few times I have asked, his reply is that there is nothing more boring than a cattle drive."

"What does your mother wish you to do?"

"To leave him, Mr. Holmes – immediately – and come back to live with her."

Holmes frowned and went to his desk, removing his lens and examining the papers closely. "Hmm. I am certain that your spouse isn't the only American, especially in the western regions, to bear a deep scar and wear a set of prominent mustaches. It's a pity we don't have his statement yet." He gave his client a very serious look. "Is your husband prone to alcoholic binges?"

"No, Mr. Holmes, never. He likes his whisky, naturally, but I have never seen him in the condition he was this morning."

"Then I would advise – Well, hello Inspector! What brings you over this morning?"

Our friend Inspector Lestrade had, with some gusto, thrown open the door to the sitting room. He was clearly in a hurry, his coat flapping about him. At the sight of the lady, he snatched off his bowler hat.

"I beg your pardon, Miss. I have urgent business with Mr. Holmes."

I sensed my friend's annoyance at the interruption. He folded his hands behind his back.

"And I assure you, Lestrade, that Mrs. Carson's concerns are equally important to me. But quickly, what is your problem?"

"A murder, and a diabolical one. An elderly lady ran into her home shouting that she was being burned alive. Not five minutes later, she was dead, screaming to her maid that her evil son-in-law had killed her. The address is 14 Amwell Street."

Mrs. Carson gave a startled cry and dropped senseless to our bearskin rug.

It was almost an hour before I joined Holmes and Lestrade at the mother's home. Holmes asked me to first escort Mrs. Carson – who had recovered from her swoon and was weeping copiously into her handkerchief – to the residence of Mr. Jones, the family friend and trustee. The gentleman wasn't at home, but his good wife took our client in with great care and sympathy, and I promised Holmes would report to her as soon as he had news. I then hurried to rejoin my friends, thinking that the case, while tragic, would be a simple one for Holmes to resolve.

Mrs. Agner's home was on a street of similar terraced houses. My knock was answered by a young maid, her face pale and her hands shaking. She directed me to the front parlor, and the piteous scene within, which Holmes and Lestrade were examining.

An elderly lady reclined on her back, her limbs contorted and her face frozen in a rictus of pain and terror. Her long white hair was loose from its pins and had spread like greasy tenacles around her head and shoulders. She was small and frail in figure, but there were no obvious marks of violence upon her person, and no blood except on her lips, where she appeared to have worried the flesh in the moments of *extremis*. She had clearly not been shot, stabbed, or strangled. Holmes gestured for me to make my own quick inspection of the corpse. I was careful to sniff for any whiff of poison, but detected nothing, not even the scent of powder or perfume.

"The maid's statement was very clear," Holmes said, closing the door to ensure our privacy. "At eight a.m., roughly the time Mrs. Carson abandoned her drunken husband to seek our council, Mrs. Agner announced her intention to go over to her daughter's temporary residence and 'speak plainly to her'. Of course, such a resolution couldn't be followed through until the lady had finished her breakfast, which she did sometime between eight-thirty and nine. The maid believed her mistress departed a few minutes after the hour.

"Mrs. Agner was absent for some time. Just after ten, the maid happened to glance through the window and saw her employer running up the street, her hair loose, her hat missing, and her features contorted in pain. The maid threw open the door and . . . Let us call the girl back, Watson. I wish you to hear it from her lips. Lestrade, if you would, for the young lady's sake?"

Holmes motioned toward a sheet, which was flung over a sofa. The inspector quickly draped it about the body, hiding it from view. Holmes coaxed the little maid back to the threshold of the parlor.

"Jessica – please tell my friend what you said occurred as Mrs. Agner came into the house. He is a doctor, and your statement will help him understand what killed her."

The girl knotted her apron in her hands. "It was terrible, sir. She looked wild. She was groaning and twisting and screaming that she was on fire. She was holding her hands up against her chest, like this, the way she always did when she was distressed about Miss Tabitha. She ran right into the parlor, gave a terrible cry, and fell to the floor in a fit. I tried to grab her, and she threw out one arm, pointing down the street. Her voice was suddenly a whisper, and I heard her cry '*He killed me, that monster!*' And then her entire body went rigid, and she passed from this earth."

"You are certain those were her exact words?" Holmes asked.

"Yes, sir."

"And you believe she meant her son-in-law?"

The maid sniffled. "She was very angry with him. There was a terrible scene last night when she refused to let him come inside. It is the truth that ever since Miss Tabitha married, Mrs. Agner has referred to Mr. Carson as an outlaw, a killer, and a monster. And she pointed in the direction of her daughter's rented house, which she had gone to visit."

Holmes thanked the girl and sent her away. Lestrade pulled back the curtain of the window that fronted the street.

"I see the police ambulance is here. Well, I think we have all that we need."

Holmes knelt by the body, lifted the sheet, and motioned for me to look over his shoulder. He directed my attention to several incisions along the woman's right hand, between her thumb and pointer finger.

"What do you make of these, Watson?"

"Cat scratches. Quite recent."

Lestrade walked over, rubbing his chin. "Shall we arrest Puss for her murder then? Ha! Come, Mr. Holmes – you'll want to see this to the finish, I am certain. The killer's home is just down the street."

Lestrade led the way. I followed, and only when I reached the pavement did I realize that my friend hadn't come along beside me. I looked back to find him whispering a few words to the maid, who was shaking her head. He then plucked his hat from the hallway stand and hurried to catch up with us.

"A trifling matter," he said in reaction to my inquisitive face, "that may yet prove essential."

The Carson's rented house was only a minute's walk and appeared identical to all the homes on the street. As we approached, however, we noted the front door was slightly ajar. Lestrade made a show of removing his revolver from his pocket.

"Quintin Carson is surely a desperate character, to poison an old lady so savagely. I think we'd best not take chances."

"You think it's poison, then?"

"What else could it be?"

Lestrade leaned forward and kicked the door completely open with his foot, barking for Carson to come out with his hands up. The demand was met by complete silence. Several more shouts went unanswered.

"He's run away!"

"A possible explanation, but not the only one," my friend noted, in the driest of tones. "Let us have a look about the place," Holmes suggested. "It may have much to tell us. We know that Mrs. Agner stated her intention of coming here, so we may safely assume that she did. We know that her daughter wasn't in residence, for that young lady was in Baker Street at the time."

"And the girl's husband is the only one with a motive to do the old woman in!" Lestrade growled. "He may be hiding in a closet somewhere. I'll check."

Lestrade began darting from room to room. Holmes sighed, and I followed him at a slower pace.

"Does it stand to reason that a western desperado would cower in a cupboard or beneath a bed after assassinating his mother-in-law?" Holmes chuckled. "Let us allow Lestrade to have his fun and move at a more leisurely pace."

Slowly we began walking from room to room. I quickly noted something that Lestrade, in his eagerness to confront the villain, was missing.

Someone had searched the house before us. Many drawers were open, and a pair of carpet bags were unfastened, their contents strewn about on a bedroom floor. Lestrade returned from his unsuccessful hunt, scowling when Holmes pointed out the debris.

"The house has been burgled!"

"If Mrs. Agner flew out of this home in a fit," I said, "failing to lock the door, then it would have been easy for some criminal to slip inside and help himself."

Holmes shook his head. "Watson, Lestrade, pay closer attention. Here, for example!" He pointed to a lady's jewelry box, which had been overturned upon a dresser. Its contents twinkled in the light coming through the window. Holmes lifted a necklace with a stunning pendant. "This is obviously a diamond, not a bit of paste. I note several other valuable baubles, yet our thief has left them behind. And here are train and omnibus tickets, items that are useful and impossible to trace."

"Why, this is a man's pocketbook!" I said, opening a leather folder that rested upon a crumpled rug. "It is filled with money."

"What fool leaves such a treasure behind?" Lestrade muttered. "What is the purpose of it?"

"I have the advantage of richer data," Holmes admitted, "as Mrs. Carson described the character of her mother to us. The elder lady was afflicted with an immoderate curiosity. Indeed, she could well be depicted as nosey and intrusive. She came to this dwelling to confront her daughter, but – finding no one at home – she gave reign to her desire to inspect the dwelling and learn all that she could about her daughter's new life." Holmes picked a book from the floor, flipping through its pages. "The couple had barely begun to unpack, yet somehow the mother discovered the daughter's journal. Perhaps she was reading through it, an invasion of privacy she never hesitated to commit in the past."

"But where was Carson while she was doing this?"

"I cannot tell you. However, a man might be brave as a lion on the battlefield, but once he finds himself in trouble with both his wife and his mother-in-law, he is reliably reduced to the status of a quivering mouse. Would you not agree with me, Watson?"

I found myself chuckling despite the horrible circumstances. "I certainly wouldn't wish to find myself in that predicament."

"We know that Carson's immediate response to the accusations of his in-law was to take himself to a public house and become intoxicated. His spouse described him as comatose upon her departure."

"He might have awakened!" Lestrade said.

"Or never been asleep," Holmes replied. "Slumber is easy to feign. I have done it many times myself."

I bit my lip to keep from chortling. Lestrade glared at Holmes.

"Your point?"

"I believe Carson abandoned this dwelling immediately following his wife's departure. Perhaps fearful his spouse had gone away without her key, he left the front door unlocked. Mrs. Carson found the dwelling open and unattended upon her arrival. Therefore, she gave way to her instinct to search the place, and in the process met her death." Holmes shrugged. "It is a theory we can test."

"How?" Lestrade demanded.

"By being cautious not to encounter our own demise," Holmes warned. "Let us continue to investigate."

I noticed that Lestrade turned pale, but resolutely followed in my friend's wake. We moved from bedchamber to bathroom, and into a vacant room which seemed to be designated as a study. The couple had placed an easel and other artistic supplies inside, as well as several bundles of heavy books and three trunks. Two of these were open, with papers and rough clothes – dungarees, boots, and leather jackets – thrown about. Lestrade and I were going through the assortment of attire when Holmes drew a sharp breath.

"That trunk," he said, gesturing to the box in the corner. It was small and brightly painted with playful western scenes. My immediate thought was that it held children's garments, and perhaps our client hadn't been honest with us or was covering a painful loss. "Do you not see it?"

Lestrade snorted. "They must have a baby."

Holmes rolled his eyes. "One that they keep locked inside a travelling case? There are holes in this trunk, allowing something to breathe. I doubt very seriously that an infant is confined within."

"Holmes, be careful," I hissed, as my friend leaned down. The trunk was closed but unlatched. Gently, Holmes lifted the lid.

The bottom of the luggage was filled with straw, and emitted a foul stench, but there was nothing inside.

"A snake!" Lestrade said. "The villain attacked her with a viper."

"No. The wounds are wrong," Holmes replied. "The swollen marks on her hands were the only sign of violence, but they aren't the pinpricks of a serpent. Nor the scratches of a cat," he quickly added. "The lady didn't own one, and this isn't the smell of a feline. It is more . . . *reptilian*."

"Then what could it – ?"

I gave a startled cry. Something had rustled the pile of socks and shirts behind us. For a ludicrous moment we were all frozen, waiting to see what horror might emerge. Holmes put his finger to his lips and eased forward, using his walking stick to lift the clothing.

A creature unlike any I had ever seen was revealed, its tongue flicking back and forth, its squat head weaving from side to side. Its hide appeared to be covered in bright orange-and-black pebbles arranged in stripes across its nearly two-foot length. It opened a bluish mouth, giving a hiss of warning.

"What in the devil!" Lestrade cried. He fumbled with his gun, while Holmes raised his stick high enough for a fatal strike. A loud shout stopped them before they could attempt to eliminate the strange beast.

"Stop! No – Don't kill Charlie!"

The warning came from a man who had suddenly appeared in the doorway. He was a tall and cragged fellow, with long mustaches and a sunbaked, deeply lined face. His jacket and trousers were of an American cut, and he wore oddly pointed boots and a sombrero-style hat. He waved us back, then went to another chest and pulled out a pair of massive leather gloves.

"Here now, Charlie," he muttered. "Who in blazes let you out? Come on, rascal."

Quick as a flash, he seized the animal by its tail and dropped it back into the painted trunk, slamming the lid and fastening the latches. He turned, still crouching.

"He didn't bite any of you, did he? Good, good. He's quite venomous – not enough to kill a strong fellow, but enough to make you wish you were in your grave. I've been chomped on once, and that was enough for a lifetime." Slowly, as if struggling against pain in his hips, he rose to his impressive height. His words were spoken in the strange accent of an American from the western regions. "And who might you gentlemen be, to be snooping about my homestead?"

"Inspector Lestrade of Scotland Yard!" our official friend barked. "And you are Quintin Carson?"

"I'll not deny it."

"Then you are under arrest for the murder of Mrs. Judith Agner."

The tall man blinked, as if cold water had just been cast into his face. "The old lady is dead?"

"No need to play coy, my man. Clearly, you used that terrible beast to kill her."

Holmes raised a hand. "One minute – Mr. Carson, my name is Sherlock Holmes. I am a consulting detective who provides occasional advice to my friends among the police. Can you give an account of your actions this morning?"

The man continued to stare blankly. "My wife's mother? Dead? *Murdered?* My God, poor Tabby! She'll be all to pieces, she will. And she'll blame me! Sir, if you'll give me that pistol, I'll gladly blow out my brains, rather than face her."

"So you confess?" Lestrade demanded.

"To what? I've done nothing! But if the old woman is gone, Tabby will be upset. She said she hated her ma, but I knew better. She loved the lady, for all her faults and meanness. Tabby was a good daughter. She just wanted to have her freedom for a bit, like a wild mustang in a canyon. My poor little girl!"

The man began to weep. Holmes put a hand on his shoulder.

"Let us go to Baker Street, where there is food and drink and more comfortable chairs, and no venomous lizards lurking in the corners. If you would, Mr. Carson, please place something atop the trunk, or secure it with a lock. Charlie mustn't be allowed to cause more trouble."

Lestrade reluctantly agreed, and we hired a four-wheeler to transport us back to our residence. Once assured that his wife was safe with friends,

Carson came along quietly. He never protested his treatment, but instead spoke quiet words of gratitude when Holmes placed a glass in his hands.

"I will tell you everything, sirs. I have no reason to lie, and I am a stranger in your country, so I have little understanding of how things are done here. But with God as my witness, here is the truth.

"I met Tabitha Agner in Tucson, at the Oriental Hotel, where she was staying for the occasion of her cousin's wedding. I'm an old cowhand. I'm not educated or refined, but working for Professor Rodrick has taught me enough manners not to embarrass myself in polite company. When I saw Tabby across the dining room, I thought she was the finest little filly I had ever laid eyes upon. You could see her spirit, her fire. Some local ruffians came in and started making crude comments about her, loud enough that she could hear their rough talk. I rose from my table, walked over, and gave them a taste of my knuckles, then apologized to her for the scene. She didn't run sobbing to her room, but instead took my arm and suggested a walk in the hotel's arcade. That's how I got to know her, gentleman. You need to understand that I never expected anything sweet or gentle in my life, so it was like I struck gold when I found her.

"She told me about her pa's business, and how her ma had made her life a living Hell, until she rebelled and crossed the ocean. I told her none of it mattered, that I would love and care for her until the end of our days. We married five months ago, and shortly after she telegraphed home with the happy news, we got a letter that she should come and claim her inheritance. I was all for keeping the wide Atlantic and half of America between Tabby and her ma, but Tabby felt she had a right to what her pa had put aside for her. And, in truth, she wanted to make things square with the old lady. Tabby couldn't be so cruel as to say she would never see her ma again. And so, we packed up and came over."

"With a dangerous animal," Lestrade snapped.

Carson shrugged. "Dangerous only if someone tried to handle him. I've had him for years, caught him on my last trail drive. I thought maybe some zoo or museum might like to have him, that I would make a gift of him, a kind of 'Thank you, pardner' for sending me my little wife."

"Your spouse approved of the creature?" I asked.

"Well, she never touched him or fed him. I can't say she's overly fond of the Charlie, but she never whined or begged me to abandon him. That's what I liked about her. She has good sense, unlike most women."

"What happened when you arrived in London?" Holmes asked.

"Our boat docked at Southampton the day before yesterday, and we came into the city very early the next morning. We spent most of yesterday getting the house in a bit of order, though as you could tell we didn't have

82

time to finish our chores. The last thing I did was to open Charlie's chest and drop in some food for him before closing the lid."

"Did you lock the chest?" Holmes interjected. The man shook his head.

"Didn't see no cause to. We went over just before five. Tabby thought it would be a nice surprise and a happy reunion, but the old lady . . . Well, gentlemen, I won't sugar-coat it for you. She was stark-raving mad. She started screaming when we were standing on the doorstep. I won't even repeat the vile words she used – at her own daughter. If she'd been a man, I would have had taken my bullwhip to her for the awful things she said. Then she lit into me, saying that I was some kind of outlaw, that I'd been the leader of a gang of murderers, and that I should be hanged. Tabby told me to go on home, let her handle her ma, and I did."

"But you immediately left your dwelling and later returned intoxicated," Holmes said. "Why?"

The man's lean cheeks turned dusky with embarrassment. "I'm right ashamed of it, sir, but . . . I sat there, wondering how I could explain to Tabby that I hadn't told her everything about myself. I was a rough fellow in my youth. I did things I'm not proud of. I gambled. I jumped a claim, and I rustled my share of cows. I've known the company of soiled doves. But I swear upon my immortal soul I never killed any man, nor rode with any gang. I nearly died when my horse threw me, years ago, and I promised God if he'd let me live and walk again, I'd change my ways.

"I have, gentlemen, and so there was no need for me to share all that bad business with Tabby, the purest angel who ever walked the earth. But it seems like her ma might have somehow learned some of those bad things, and now who was Tabby fixing to believe? I needed a drink to give me courage, and one thing led to another. I went to The Bear and Fox, if you want to know the name of the place where I drank until I could barely stand. Then I wandered on home, but I knew Tabby would be asleep, so I just fell over on the sofa.

"I heard her about this morning. She was talking up a storm, and I figured it might be best for me to play possum and listen to what she was saying. She kept muttering that her ma had got information from some detectives in America, and she was going to go hire her own detective to see if it was true or not." Our guest turned mournful eyes upon Holmes. "I take it that would be you, sir?"

My friend bowed.

"Well, I thought that was a darned good plan. I figured I should just let her go ahead with it, not say anything, that way no one could ever accuse me of influencing her. I waited until I heard her leave in a cab and then I figured I needed to giddy-up myself."

"What did you do?" Holmes asked.

"I wanted to go stick my head in a watering trough," he said, "because it was pounding so hard. Plus, I figured a good scrubbing wouldn't hurt me none. We hadn't set up the bathroom yet, didn't have so much as soap and towels, so I walked out and hailed a cab. The driver had a spotted horse, white and black like an Injun pony, and I told him to take me somewhere I could get a bath. He carried me off to a place on – let me see, I think I remember the name – Northumberland Avenue."

Holmes nodded. "It is a familiar establishment."

"You should have seen the looks on those fellows faces when they saw my boots. Weren't sure how to go about polishing them, I guess. Anyway, I was more than an hour there, and then I visited a little shop and got some grub. I figured maybe by the time I got home Tabby would have returned. I didn't lock the house because I saw she'd left her key on the mantel."

Holmes nodded at this verification of his deduction.

"A likely story," Lestrade grumbled.

"Did you just call me a liar?" Carson asked, with such soft menace Holmes immediately stepped between them.

"It will be a simple matter to find the cab driver with the unique horse, and to make inquiries at the Turkish bath and the place where you took refreshment."

"It was called The Crown and Biscuit," our guest muttered, with an unfriendly glare at Lestrade. "I recollect the name because I thought, 'I bet the Queen ain't never had to eat an old trail biscuit.' I suspect they'll remember me at the place."

"Indeed, an American in unique attire will definitely be vivid in the memories of the attendants and waitress," Holmes said. "Mr. Carson, would you be willing to give Inspector Lestrade your passport?"

The man reached into his coat pocket, handing it over. "I have nothing to hide, and I've told you the truth. Now please – I can't imagine how broke up Tabby must be. Let me go to her."

Reluctantly, and with a stern warning not to leave London, Lestrade allowed him to depart, and I told him where to go. The inspector went to the window, watching as the man hailed a cab.

"I still think he killed the lady."

"If his alibis prove false, we will follow your theory, Inspector."

Lestrade turned with a scowl.

"What do you believe happened?"

"It is most elementary: The mother, having been deprived of the daughter she once held power over, schemed to get her back. When she learned, perhaps through the indiscretion of the business partner, that Mrs.

Carson was planning to return to claim her inheritance, she sought a way to discredit the husband. Ask any Englishmen about the character of western Americans, and they will assert such individuals are all outlaws and desperados. Whether our American detectives erred in their identification remains to be seen – a simple telegram to my contacts in their ranks should suffice." Holmes picked up the papers Mrs. Carson had left with us, showing them to Lestrade. "I suspect it more likely that Mrs. Agner hired a London detective firm to create the illusion that her son-in-law was a wanted man. It is an act of forgery which I can easily imagine one of my disreputable counterparts committing."

"Then who killed Mrs. Agner?"

"Charlie did, but certainly not out of malice. One consistent factor in this case is the old woman's curiosity. She went to her daughter's dwelling to confront the young woman. Finding the house unlocked and unoccupied, she immediately began to riffle through it, looking for something she might hold over her daughter's head. Like a man drawn to drink, she simply couldn't resist the urge to snoop and pry. After pilfering through papers and clothing, she turned her attention to the room where the art supplies and chests were piled. Charlie's trunk wasn't locked. The creature wasn't powerful enough to push the box open, and Mrs. Carson wasn't inclined to meddle with him. But when Mrs. Agner saw the trunk, she opened it. The lizard had buried itself within the straw, and when she reached inside to see what the straw concealed – "

"She was savagely bitten," I said. "The pain must have been intense."

"Exactly! Recall what she said to the maid – that she was being burned alive. The bite isn't deadly to a strong man, but to an elderly woman, who ran shrieking down the street, the effect was enhanced. The reptile's poison no doubt flooded her system even more vigorously and caused her demise."

"But she said Quintin killed her," Lestrade argued.

"According to Mrs. Agner's maid, her exact words were, '*He killed me, that monster!*' The maid assumed, too quickly, that such was a reference to Quintin, who Mrs. Agner had referred to as a monster. But in fact, her statement was the literal truth – She had been killed by a monster."

"So, it was an accident?"

"It was. I imagine that when Mrs. Agner fled, the beast crawled out of its trunk, perhaps striking the trunk's lid in its progress, which dropped shut. Deprived of his refuge, Charlie sought another burrow, digging down into the pile of clothing. Watson, you are fortunate not to have been harmed. You as well, Lestrade."

"And Mrs. Carson – ?"

"Had perhaps the greatest motive to kill her unbearable mother – but she was here, in this very room, when it happened."

"She could have known her mother's curiosity would lead to tragedy," Lestrade snorted.

Holmes picked up his pipe and lit it. "True, but she believed her husband to be asleep on the sofa when she departed. If she anticipated her mother's visit in any way, she would have assumed Mr. Carson's presence – even if unconscious – would have deterred her." My friend gave a short puff, smiling at the frustrated inspector. "Clearly, Lestrade, you wish to make an arrest, but unless you feel like slapping the cuffs on our lizard friend, I would advise you to wait until we have confirmation of the husband's movements, and an answer from the Pinkertons."

Less than a day later, all was made clear. The cab driver was tracked down by the Irregulars and readily told us that not only that he had driven Carson to the Turkish baths, but that Carson had commented upon the beauty of his horse. The attendants likewise recalled the stranger for his unusual clothes, and the waitress of the café for both his attire and his generous tip. Holmes's friends in the Pinkertons revealed that there was no such outlaw as Red "Dirt" Rogers, and Holmes later learned that the false newspaper clippings and the wanted poster were manufactured by a sinister agent in Soho, who specialized in false items used in divorce proceedings. I am proud to report my friend made it so hot for this fellow that he was forced to take his ugly business elsewhere. The Coroner's Jury ruled that Mrs. Agner had met her death by misadventure, and Charlie – who was properly identified as a specimen of *Heloderma suspectum*, or "Gila monster" – was sentenced to serve his time in a glass case at the London Reptile Exposition.

Mr. Carson made a full confession of his youthful sins to his lady, who – after consultation with both her business advisor and Holmes – forgave him his faults. Her family business and her mother's London home were sold at great profit, and the couple now make their home in Santa Fe, where they are said to be very happy and very private people.

I leaned back and took down the great index volume to which he referred. Holmes balanced it on his knee and his eyes moved slowly and lovingly over the record of old cases, mixed with the accumulated information of a lifetime . . . "Venomous lizard or gila. Remarkable case, that!"

– Dr. John H. Watson and Sherlock Holmes
"The Sussex Vampire"

The Mulberry Frock-Coat Mystery
by DJ Tyrer

The tragedy had already come to pass by the time my good friend, Sherlock Holmes, and I reached the barrow on the outskirts of the Sussex village of High Dean, too late to intervene to stop it. And though it was always the singular contents of that ancient British barrow that, frequently misreported, caught the imagination of the pressmen and their readership, for us the case shall always be dominated by our failure to prevent the awful unfolding of events that occurred there.

Our involvement in the sad affair began on a dreary evening at the end of October 1894, when a gentleman arrived at 221b Baker Street. Mrs. Hudson showed him in and took his rain-dampened coat as he introduced himself.

"My name is Gustave Addleton," he said.

"Please be seated," said my friend. "I am Sherlock Holmes, and this is my colleague, Doctor Watson."

"Thank you," he said as he accepted my friend's invitation. His movements were controlled and his voice level, yet the set of his jaw and the look of his eyes were of a man wrestling with some awful truth.

"As I say, my name is Gustave Addleton, and I am an antiquarian."

"Ah, yes," said Holmes, "I believe I have read one of your monographs – something to do with the prehistory of these islands. I was particularly interested in a digression you made concerning soil types in the southern counties."

Addleton nodded. "Yes, I have written a number of pieces about the true history of our nation, as revealed by my study of early sources and the monuments and ephemera left behind by its earliest inhabitants."

"True history?" enquired I, forgetting myself.

"Yes, the *true* history, largely obscured and forgotten." He leaned towards us, his eyes now shining with the intensity of the true believer and all tension vanished from his features. I could see my friend watching him intently, divining something about him that was beyond my ability to perceive.

"You see, Doctor Watson," Addleton said, "the myriad events that we ascribe to early Biblical, Greek, and Egyptian history all happened not in the east, but *here* – in the British Isles and northern France."

I scoffed at the notion.

"No, it is true. You see – "

"Sir," interjected Holmes, silencing him, "you came here with a mystery, yes?"

Addleton nodded and reached into the pocket of his jacket.

"Here," he said as he produced a bracelet comprising pale-blue sections of what I believe is termed *faïence*, which he handed to Holmes.

"I uncovered that, no more than two weeks ago, from a shaft I sank into a barrow outside the Sussex village of High Dean. Tell me, does that not appear to be Egyptian?"

Holmes nodded. "I am no expert, of course, but it strikes me that it does resemble examples of ancient Egyptian craftwork I have seen pictured in magazines."

As my friend continued to turn it over in his hands, I, unable to help myself, countered that it might have reached the Sussex shore by way of trade from Egypt.

"After all, don't several authorities contend that the Phoenicians once sailed from Tyre to Cornwall in search of tin? Might they not have brought such a trinket with them as an item of trade?"

Addleton started to argue against this, but Holmes held up one hand to silence him.

"I dare say," said Holmes, "that the subject is one which the two of you might discuss all night and yet reach no agreement, but I don't believe you came all this way just to discuss your thoughts on ancient history."

Our guest looked slightly abashed and nodded. The tenseness returned to him.

"Not as such," he admitted, "although that bracelet is the very reason I have come to see you. Or, rather, it is at the root of the reason why I am here . . . ."

He took a breath, then said, "Sirs, you may think me a fool, but I swear that I am not . . . Since digging up this bracelet, I have come to believe that I am haunted. *Cursed!*"

Holmes didn't blink. "I shall not think you a fool if you have some reason to believe yourself so haunted."

Addleton nodded. "Three months ago," he said, seemingly incapable of speaking succinctly, "I rented a property in High Dean with the intention of carrying out a number of excavations at promising sites in the locality, of which the barrow was one. Preliminary to a substantial dig, I sank three shafts into it, partly to understand the composition of the mound prior to excavating it, partly to see if any artifacts of interest might be discovered. One of the shafts broke through into a chamber of some sort within the barrow and the bracelet was fished out."

He looked towards the ceiling. "Ah, I was so . . . so *delighted* . . . Not now. No, not now . . . ."

After a moment's silence, he continued. "After I brought it home, it began. Footsteps and knocking sounds in the night when nobody was there. Items would be moved from one place to another or vanish altogether. This – " He gestured at the bracelet in my friend's hands. " – would appear outside my bedroom door or at the foot of the stairs, despite having been locked in a drawer. My favourite coat, a rather-worn mulberry frock-coat that nobody would have any interest in stealing when they could take the silver, vanished from the back of my bedroom door, never to be seen again.

"Call me mad if you will, sirs, but I swear it's all true, and I am becoming convinced that it is the ghost of a dead pharaoh or the curse of ancient gods that is bearing down upon me and my family."

"Did you not think," I asked, "to return the bracelet to the mound?"

The antiquarian looked at me as if I were a mad man.

"Return the bracelet? Return it? Where then would be my proof?"

I wasn't sure how to argue with him, but Holmes asked him if he'd commenced excavating the barrow.

"I did. Slow work, of course, as you don't wish to damage the real ruins hidden within. But with all the strangeness going on, the labourers I'd hired – local men, simple folk – refused to keep working and the attempt stalled."

"So, why come to me?" asked Holmes. "I am, after all, no exorcist."

"A friend of a friend recommended you to me – said that you can get to the bottom of any mystery, no matter how strange. I have little doubt that I am cursed, but maybe a man of your intellect can see the way to understanding and resolving these occurrences. The night the Keltic people knew as *Samhain* draws near, the night of All Hallows Eve, a date drawn from the beliefs of the Egyptians and Israelites, a time when dark powers are said to be strongest.

"If I am not freed of the curse by then, I fear it shall be too late."

Holmes gave a slight nod. "Very well, we shall investigate. May I retain hold of this?" He raised the bracelet.

"Yes, yes, do. But I warn you that it is cursed – any evil that falls from it upon you shall not be blamed on me."

"I understand," said Holmes, as if the talk of curses were the most reasonable thing in the world. "You shall return home?"

"First thing in the morning. I daren't leave my family alone when evil stalks our home."

"Watson shall go with you and begin on our investigation. I shall follow in a day or two, for I am otherwise detained for now."

89

Addleton nodded and rose. "Good night to you both, and thank you. Doctor Watson – until tomorrow."

"Yes," said I, a little bemused at the sudden announcement of my errand.

"Mrs. Hudson will show you out," Holmes, said, summoning her to take charge of the man.

Once Addleton was gone, my friend turned to me and said, "Well, Watson, what do you think?"

"Of him, or your volunteering me to accompany him?"

"Him."

"A mad man, Holmes. Hidden histories? Curses? Ghosts? And all he has as proof is a bracelet?

He chuckled and passed the bracelet to me.

"Superstitious, perhaps, but honest, I think."

"You believe he really is being tormented?"

"Yes," said Holmes, "but not by some ancient Egyptian imp, nor the ghost of some ancient burial. The theft of a favourite coat seems too prosaic to me. Not, of course, that I am an expert in the thought processes of ancient gods, but it seems to me the action of a mortal man."

"But why?" I asked.

"That of course," said he, "is the pertinent question. What does somebody gain by playing upon the gullibility of an antiquarian?"

I considered. "He must be a man of some means, to be able to dedicate his life to investigating such theories, so perhaps there is an inheritance. Or maybe someone wants him out of the house he is renting."

"Perhaps," said my friend, "but the supposed haunting began after he found that." He nodded at the bracelet in my hands. "Perhaps it was just convenient, offering something to latch a haunting onto, but I suspect a causal relationship."

"Someone wanted the bracelet?" I asked, then corrected course. "No, not when they were able to remove it from a locked drawer . . . The barrow, then? They wanted to stop him excavating the barrow?"

Holmes gave a nod. "Based on what little we know, that would be my first guess."

"Which is why you want me to accompany him to High Dean tomorrow."

"Correct, Watson. Go. Take a look. See what you can learn."

I rose with a sigh and handed the bracelet back to him. "Then I had better be away to bed."

Holmes continued to stare at the bracelet as I absented myself.

I rose early the next morning and fortified myself with a cup of strong tea, courtesy of Mrs. Hudson, for it was raining and the wind was picking up. Holmes was still seated in the same position, still examining the bracelet, as if he'd never gone to bed. Quite possibly, he hadn't.

"I shall see you in a day or two, once I have followed where this little treasure leads," he told me, enigmatically.

I shrugged and bade him farewell, for I was due at the station to meet Mr. Addleton and board the early train to Sussex.

"You said, last night, that all the early history of the Israelites and Egyptians and Greeks took place in Britain," I said as we seated ourselves and the train began to pull away from the station. "But I cannot see how such a thing could be true. If that were so, how could their lands be located, now, in the east? Why is it every learned opinion says that is where history happened?"

Addleton gave a weary shake of his head, as if I were a child pestering a parent over some trivial detail, but his general downcast demeanour lifted as he began to speak.

"Let me explain," he said. "The peoples of the northern lands, the first civilised peoples of the world, were forced to undergo an exodus from their homes to the shores of the balmy Mediterranean by an intense chilling of the land – what some geologists refer to as an *Eiszeit*, or 'Ice Age', that left the northern parts of Europe quite uninhabitable for a thousand years or more, until the glaciers receded, allowing the arrival upon these shores of the Keltik ancestors of the Britons and Gaels, and later still the Saxons and Jutes.

"Having removed to their new domains," he continued, "the Hebrew, Copt, and Hellene sought to recreate their lost homelands, building their cities anew. Thus, for example, we have columned Karnak in Egypt and the standing stones of Carnac in Brittany, from which it draws its name. Over the centuries, the nature of their migration was forgotten, reduced to occasional legends such as that of the Exodus and the Dorian Invasion of Greece, and the inhabitants of those lands came to believe they had ever lived there.

"Not so! No, they came from *here*, and it is *here*, upon these shores, that we shall find their greatest precincts. Stonehenge and the barrow tombs are their remnants."

"I have been to Egypt," said I, "and I have to say that Stonehenge bears little similarity to the ruins I saw there."

Addleton scoffed now. "Standing stones, such as those there, are *obelisks*, just like Cleopatra's Needle, save much worn by passing through centuries of excessive weathering during the years of ice. The barrow domes are merely the accretion of earth over millennia, concealing the ruins of the tombs and temples beneath, in the same way that Egyptian ruins must be dug from the grasp of the desert sands. Uncover them and you would see the similarity. Even the mighty pyramid has its origin here, concealed within Silbury Hill in Wiltshire."

I understood, now, what the antiquarian had meant by "the real ruins" when he'd spoken of uncovering the barrow.

Addleton spoke at length about his theories, proffering the times and dates of the events he believed had happened here and not in distant lands, while I attempted to feign a polite interest in his words. I received the impression that his obsession was his life, and that any enemies he might have were academic and unlikely to resort to the sort of torments he claimed to have suffered.

When we arrived at High Dean, Addleton took me to his home, where his wife and two young children, a boy named for his father and a girl, Alice, were waiting. I spoke briefly to Mrs. Addleton, who confirmed her husband's account of the peculiar events that had overtaken them recently, and also to a few of the servants. Then he led me across the fields to the barrow.

All the talk of ancient monuments had primed me to expect something impressive, tall and striking, but coming upon it on the edge of a muddy meadow, seen through a veil of drizzle, the barrow was anything but – just a hump of grassy earth with a squarish wound in its side where Addleton had commenced his dig. It was barely a hill. If the antiquarian were correct, anything of splendour was hidden within.

He spoke of it for a few minutes, explaining some of his theories about it, but as he did so, he grew more and more agitated, casting quick glances at the barrow, and then looking away again.

"I'm sorry," he said. "I just can't help feeling as if . . . Oh, I don't know!"

I clapped him on the shoulder, but I had been casting my gaze about myself. I had the sense we were observed, and not by any supernatural inhabitant of the mound. I'd thought I'd seen someone standing in the shadow of some trees on a distant hillside, but had anyone been there, they appeared now to have slipped away.

I looked at Addleton.

"Would you like to go?" I prompted.

He nodded.

I considered for a moment. Should I accompany him and observe events at his home, or should I remain here and watch the barrow? I recalled what Holmes had said and reached a decision: If the barrow were the cause of the events, the barrow was what I must watch.

Nodding Addleton off, I walked the field in search of a place to secrete myself, locating a hollow tree that would serve as a hide from which I could observe without being seen.

The day passed miserably, for it was damp with a chill wind blowing, and there was nothing for me to see, save the occasional crow.

Then, as darkness fell across the scene, I saw movement and a shuffling, scarecrow figure crept across the field to the barrow. He carried no light, making it difficult to discern what he was doing, but it seemed to me that he was probing at the pit in the side of the barrow with a stick.

After a few minutes, he slipped his way down the side of the barrow and headed towards the lane.

I waited a minute and then followed him, pushing through a gap in the hedge out of the field. I caught sight of him some distance along the lane, disappearing around a bend, but by the time I reached it, he was gone.

After walking up and down that stretch of lane and finding no clue as to where he had gone – the first cottages were here and he might have slipped into any of them, or down some half-hidden footpath shadowed by high hedges – I had to admit defeat.

Heading a little further along the lane, I found myself by the village green and spied the public house, The Grapes. Wet from the drizzle, I made the decision to step inside and avail myself of a restorative drink.

As warmth returned to my limbs, I observed the crowd and was surprised to catch sight of a man in a rather-worn mulberry-coloured frock-coat. Although it wasn't impossible that some local peasant had received an old jacket from a kindly master, it did seem somewhat unlikely that it would be in the same colour as that which had vanished from Addleton's home.

Although it was difficult to get a good view across the bar, I managed to make a general assessment of him as red-headed and stoop-shouldered. He appeared to be in conversation with a short, stocky man whom, I was almost certain, was one of the servants I'd spoken to that morning, a man named Box, which only served to make the presence of the frock-coat all the more unlikely a coincidence.

The man finished his ale and headed for the door. Trying to avoid being spotted by Box, I followed after him. As he stepped outside, I got a clear look at his face and saw that the man had a prominent scar running across his cheek and down his chin.

Outside, the wind was picking up and the drizzle had turned to rain, which lashed my face painfully. Holding onto my hat and pulling the brim low to protect my face, it was difficult to keep the man in sight. At least I could reassure myself that, if I lost him, I would recognise him again with ease.

It seemed that whatever his role in events, he wasn't based in High Dean itself, but somewhere outside the village proper, for he took a narrow lane out between the fields. My only comfort was that the weather that made it difficult for me to keep him in sight also meant that he was keeping his head bent against the onslaught and unlikely to spot me if he did turn about for any reason.

The lane twisted its way between hedges and I wondered just how far it was to his hideout. Then, a sudden loud creaking noise, like the timbers of a ship caught in a storm, caught my attention and I paused.

I started to turn, and that is when something struck me and I found myself pitched forwards into black oblivion.

My eyes fluttered open to sunlight and I winced. I was sprawled, face down, half in a ditch with a branch laying across my back. I stood, a little shakily, and looked down at myself, my clothes splattered in mud. My head felt as delicate as a china teacup and my hat, which had blown some distance down the lane, was crumpled and the crown broken, having clearly taken the force of the blow from the falling limb. I was reassured that my vision was fine, knowing that a blow to the head has the potential to render serious injury.

No bones felt to be broken and my skull was, as best I could tell, in one piece, but I resolved to locate the local medical man, whether a physician or general practitioner, to ensure my period of unconsciousness hadn't resulted in any problems I'd missed.

Spotting a local, and having reassured them that I hadn't been waylaid by a band of thugs, I received directions to the house of Doctor Stannage, where I knocked upon the door and was directed through into his study.

"Whatever happened to you?" he asked as I entered. He was an older man, close, I guessed, to retirement, genial and solicitous in his manner.

"A dispute with a tree branch," said I with a chuckle that became a groan. "I do believe I lost."

He smiled and told me to sit down upon a stool.

"I'm Doctor William Stannage," he said, "and you are?"

"Doctor John Watson."

"A fellow doctor?" He laughed. "Physician, heal thyself!"

"I would, but I cannot see the back of my head."

"A common failing in our profession," he observed, "but you have the wisdom to know it. Good. Very well." He leaned forward to examine me. "Let's take a look."

He ran his fingers over my scalp, then pronounced, "Your skull remains solid, sir."

"That's reassuring," I said.

After checking my vision and confirming my only other injury was to my pride, he told me that I was in tolerably good health and would soon mend.

"Thank you," I said, before enquiring of the fee for his services.

"Pish! For a fellow medical man, nothing. We fellows must look out for one another. But," he said, "what is it that had you taking a stroll about our village last night during the storm?"

I considered him for a moment, before answering. From his demeanour, I was willing to trust him with a little of my business in High Dean.

"I was following a rascal in a mulberry frock-coat," I said.

"Not Mr. Addleton!" he asked, incredulous.

I smiled. Addleton wasn't the sort of man anyone was likely to call a rascal.

"No," said I. "Although I do believe the frock-coat may have been his, stolen from his home a short time ago. You are aware of his travails?"

The doctor nodded. "Yes, I have heard something. We are merely nodding acquaintances – Mr. Addleton is a healthy man without need of my services, although I have seen his wife and children on occasion, but there is gossip all about the village concerning him – the haunting that is supposed to have taken hold of his house, and the treasure-laden barrow that the curse protects."

"Treasure-laden?"

"Yes, all sorts of rumours. You're aware of his theories?" I nodded. "Well, those have the local peasantry talking of Pharaonic gold and the Treasure of Solomon, while less-credulous minds imagine Roman or Viking loot buried there. Only the stories of ghosts and ill-doings keep anyone from resuming the dig for themselves."

"But you give it no credence?"

Doctor Stannage shook his head. "Goodness me, no. I see no reason to believe Mr. Addleton's wild claims, nor to imagine that there is any treasure buried there at all. That barrow is the resting place of some primitive chieftain and nothing more."

"And the curse?"

"Twattle and balderdash," he said with a smile, "though I'm sure he believes it all most sincerely."

"Just like his theories," I said, matching his smile.

We chatted a little longer and I asked if he knew much about Addleton's servants, in particular the man called Box, but his observations were limited to medical matters and of no help to me. Our conversation then turned to medicine and I was revived by some warm tea and toast.

"Well," I said at last, rising, "I really ought to go and change out of these clothes."

Doctor Stannage bade me good day and I set off back to Addleton's.

I found the antiquarian in a state of agitation upon my return, striding through the house in a condition almost as dishevelled as my own.

"Tomorrow is *Samhain* Eve," he snapped at me. "When night falls, it is *Samhain* itself, according to the manner in which the ancients measured time. The doom ordained by the old gods shall fall then, I am certain."

"Goodness, man," I responded, "there's no reason to think such a thing!"

I tried to tell him of the person I'd seen – how I thought he was in league with his man Box, that the entire situation was a cruel trick upon him, but he wouldn't listen. He just kept ranting about his fate and listing the Egyptian gods one by one that he believed had cursed him.

Shaking my head, I retreated from his presence and sought out the servant, Box.

"Sorry, sir," said one of the maids. "He was here earlier, but he left just after you arrived. Said he had an errand to run."

Coincidence? I doubted it. Had he seen me at The Grapes? Or perhaps he'd heard me mention his name to his master and had resolved to absent himself.

The weather was growing worse again. Having changed my outfit, I had no desire to undergo another soaking. We were bound to have a storm. Instead, I chose to keep an eye on Addleton, rather than resume my watch over the barrow. The man's agitation seemed to worsen as the wind picked up.

Although Addleton continued to claim he was actively being persecuted, I'd seen no sign of further trouble and, with Box gone from the house, I doubted more was likely – at least, not until night had fallen, and I planned to be ready for them then.

For now, I watched over my host, almost mesmerised by his mania.

The maid's voice pulled me out of my reverie.

"A telegram for you, sir."

I took it from her and read it. It was from Holmes: He would be arriving in the morning.

"Osiris shall take my soul!" cried Addleton as thunder rumbled about the house. "Anubis shall devour it!"

The maid looked at me, wide-eyed.

"Run and fetch Doctor Stannage," I said. "There's a good girl."

Addleton would need to be sedated before he harmed himself or others.

Come morning, the storm was over, though it was still raining fitfully. Even had the thunderous noise not shaken the house through the night, I would've had no sleep, for I was on watch for any mischief from Box or his red-headed ally. But I'd seen nothing untoward. Possibly the storm had encouraged them to stay in shelter.

Satisfied that Addleton was still sedated, I set out to the train station to meet my friend – but there was no train and no Holmes.

I approached the stationmaster and asked what the problem was.

"The storm," he said. "It brought down a mudslide in a cutting and blocked the track. The train won't be through until this afternoon, if not later. Takes time to shift mud."

"Can I get a telegram off?" I asked.

The stationmaster shook his head. "Dear me, no! The storm brought some trees down and they took the telegraph lines with them. We're cut off for now."

"Please send a message to the Addleton house when the train is due," I said, and headed back there.

The antiquarian was awake when I arrived back at the house and sitting calmly in his study.

"I am well enough," he said in response to my query as to his health.

Even though this was the eve of *Samhain* that he'd so feared, he gave no sign of his earlier terror and mania. Sedating him, it appeared, had broken the hold of it upon him and, though I watched him closely, he gave no further sign of being affected by his superstition. I allowed myself to relax a little, certain that, once my friend arrived, the case could be brought to a satisfactory conclusion. Outside, the rain finally ceased to fall.

A boy arrived with word that the line was finally clear and that the train was expected to arrive soon. I pressed a penny on him and set out to the station.

The train steamed up to the platform and Holmes leapt down even before it had quite halted, a sense of urgency enveloping him.

"I must speak to Addleton immediately," he declared, "lest he succumb to his fear of the supernatural and enter a fury of madness."

"He's fine," I told Holmes as we exited the station. "I had the local physician, Doctor Stannage, sedate him last night – he was in a mania – and this morning, he is a different man, calm and self-possessed."

"Perhaps," said Holmes, "but I want to tell him what I've learned, and confirm for him that there is nothing supernatural about his troubles." He looked to the sky. "Tonight is the night he fears."

"He's fine," I repeated, but Holmes didn't seem convinced and strode through the village in the direction I'd indicated to him.

"I should have been here yesterday," he said. "Had I been, there would be no risk."

"Where have you been?" I asked. "You never said."

My friend didn't slow, but turned his head a little to me. "The more I examined the bracelet that Addleton said he uncovered in the barrow, the more it seemed to me that I recalled seeing something similar. While you slept, I checked my files and confirmed that it was a close match to the description of a piece of jewellery stolen from a private collector."

"You mean Addleton is a fraud?"

Holmes shook his head. "No, Watson. A dupe, perhaps. Gullible, maybe. But an honest man, I have no doubt. I checked, and it seemed the theft occurred maybe a month before Addleton sank his first shaft."

"Somebody concealed the stolen items within the barrow?"

He nodded. "Yes. And then panicked when it seemed that Addleton might uncover them."

"Which would explain the campaign waged against him . . . ."

"Indeed. So while you came here to High Dean, I went to Hampshire to visit the home of Augustus Harrow, the man who was the victim of the theft. I showed him the bracelet and he confirmed that it was the very one stolen from him.

"He then told me of a man, a Robert Bligh, who was briefly in his service and who then vanished shortly after he items were stolen, and before the police could adequately interview him. He described Bligh as a tall redhead with a stooped posture, and – "

" – A distinctive scar?" I interrupted him.

"Why, yes!" said Holmes.

"I believe he is here in High Dean." I quickly told him of what had I had seen and Holmes nodded at my account. I couldn't help but allow my chest to swell at the thought that I was actually a step ahead of Holmes for a change.

"Here it is," I said, pointing to the house.

As we approached, I was surprised to see the front door was open wide.

"Something's wrong!" I cried, and we ran inside.

"Where is he?" demanded Holmes of a flustered maid.

"Gone, sir."

"Gone? What do you mean 'gone'?"

"Left the house in a state of upset, sir," exclaimed the maid. "He was having a right fit. Dragged his family off with him. Like a proper lunatic, sir."

"Where?" I asked. "Which way did he go?"

The maid pointed.

"The barrow – " said I.

We began to run.

The tragedy had already come to pass by the time we reached the barrow, too late to intervene or stop it.

Indeed, even before we reached it, we met Doctor Stannage on the path and he halted us with the horrendous news.

"They're dead," he said.

I was dumbstruck and even Holmes was silent a moment before he said, "All of them?"

Stannage nodded. "All of them. It seems he killed them, and then took his own life."

Holmes had a grim look on his face as he declared, "I was too late."

The doctor shook his head. "Doctor Watson and I did what we could to prevent this, but when a man is determined to destroy himself – "

"No," said Holmes. "I am to blame. I could have shown him he was under no curse – that he was a victim of a cruel trickster – but I arrived too late."

I had to disagree. "No," I said. "You are not. The ones who are to blame are those who tricked him into this madness."

Holmes looked to the sky. "Perhaps you're right . . . ."

The bodies had been removed to Stannage's house by the time the three of us arrived at the barrow.

It seemed that a labourer had been passing by when he saw a man dash away from the barrow, whom he took to be Gustave Addleton on account of the distinctive colour of his coat. The coat, of course, was the one that had been stolen and which I'd seen being worn by the man that Augustus Harrow had named Robert Bligh. The subsequent investigation into Addleton's death would confirm he'd been dead for at least an hour prior to the sighting. Naturally, some of the locals reached the conclusion that the man had seen the antiquarian's ghost, adding to the nonsense surrounding the events.

"They were found here," said Stannage, indicating a site a short distance away from the partially-dug pit in the side of the barrow.

Holmes showed little interest in where they'd fallen. He was instead examining the pit.

He gestured to it and said, "Watson, tell me what you can observe."

I looked at it and had to admit I could see nothing more than a hole in the ground.

"No," he said, "look closely. Observe the sides."

It took me a moment to see it, but then I saw it: The sides of the pit were slick and muddy from the rain, except for an area at the bottom which appeared relatively dry, save for a puddling of water in its bottom.

"That area is freshly dug," I said, "since the rain ended."

Holmes gave a curt nod. "And?"

"And – " Then, it struck me. "Someone was digging here while the Addleton family lay dead or dying."

"Exactly," Holmes said with venom.

Somebody, and I had no doubt it was Robert Bligh, had come and attempted to dig into the barrow, ignoring the family nearby, only to be disturbed by the passing labourer. Of course, we would never know if he could have done anything to help them, or if summoning Doctor Stannage might have saved the lives of Mrs. Addleton or her children, but it seemed that the villain had just not cared, focused as he was on regaining his stolen treasure.

"Vile," said Stannage, and I could do nought but agree.

If the tragedy that had befallen the Addleton family was, for Holmes and me, the terrible conclusion of our tale, the opening of the barrow was the denouement that caught the public imagination and fostered any number of ridiculous theories.

Holmes had Stannage summon a number of local peasants to dig into the barrow, opening a passage into its hollow interior.

A lantern in his hand, Holmes led the way inside.

I must admit, given that having mentioned the nonsense propagated in newspapers and magazines, that I had a similar credulous reaction when I saw what the barrow tomb contained. A mummified body, wrapped in bandages, lay at its centre. No mere dried husk, its head was covered by an ornate mask of gold and blue, and golden threads glittered as they ran in a web through the bandages. The mummy was surrounded by a variety of bowls, items of jewellery, jars that I subsequently learned are called *Canopic*, and golden statues of Egyptian gods.

"Could it be that Addleton was right after all?" I gasped.

"Oh, Watson," said Holmes with a sigh, "surely you haven't abandoned the path of logic?"

He proceeded to point out certain objects that matched the descriptions of ones stolen from Harrow's collection.

"Doubtless these others will be matched to other thefts," said Holmes. "Then, consider the mummy, laying there, and the damp conditions in this tomb."

"You're right," I said. "If that mummy was here for any length of time, its wrappings would have grown mouldy and started to rot."

"Exactly," he said. "While the ancient Egyptians perfected the art of mummification through the use of ingenious chemical processes, the preservation of the bodies owes just as much to the dryness of the Egyptian climate. In this place, as you say, it would rot."

"But," asked Stannage, "haven't there been reports of perfectly-preserved corpses retrieved from the bogs of Ireland and Denmark? Hardly dry!"

"Indeed," said Holmes. "Going back as far as the seventeenth century, such bodies have been found, but there the preservation is due to the acidity of the water, much like pickling fruit. They appear to be tanned like leather, rather than desiccated like mummies such as this. It's a very different process."

Then, in conclusion, he showed us where the earth of the side of the barrow had been disturbed, doubtless dug out then filled back in by Bligh and Box.

"It may be," Holmes said, "that the thieves chose the barrow to hide their booty because it was easy to locate, compared to burying it elsewhere in the ground. Or it could be that they thought superstition would deter anyone from probing their hiding place."

"Or," I suggested, "they might have found it a morbid jest to conceal a body and grave goods in a tomb."

"Perhaps," said Holmes. "But unfortunately for them, Addleton came along and began sinking shafts and planning to excavate the barrow and the thieves, now unable to retrieve their treasure without being observed, panicked."

"Then they tried to scare him off," said I. "But Addleton was neurotic and . . . ."

I left the rest of the sentence hanging. Holmes nodded.

While the men had been digging, Holmes had arranged for a message to go out to the Sussex Police with a description of Bligh and Box. It was no more than two hours later that we received word that the pair had been picked up at a train station, Bligh recognised thanks to the stolen coat he'd continued to wear.

Once the items found within the barrow had been crated up and taken away to be identified and reunited with their rightful owners, Holmes and

I journeyed with a detective to the police station where the two villains were being held.

The men looked defeated and downcast, a pair of fools rather than master criminals.

Holmes fixed them with a hard stare.

"If I could have my way and rearrange the workings of justice," he told them, "I would hang the pair of you for murder. But as it is, you cannot be held accountable for the actions of a man you sent into a fit of madness.

"Be assured, however, that I shall see to it that your fellow inmates know that you are, ultimately, responsible for the deaths of an innocent woman and her children, and I am certain I am correct in saying that they shan't allow the niceties of the law to impede them in expressing their opinion of you."

Then, he turned and stalked away, leaving the men ashen-faced and trembling.

When I look at the three massive manuscript volumes which contain our work for the year 1894 I confess that it is very difficult for me, out of such a wealth of material, to select the cases which are most interesting in themselves and at the same time most conducive to a display of those peculiar powers for which my friend was famous. As I turn over the pages . . . find an account of the Addleton tragedy and the singular contents of the ancient British barrow.

– Dr. John Watson
"The Golden Pince-Nez"

The Tracking and Arrest of
a Cold-Blooded Scoundrel
by David Marcum

The year 1894 presented Sherlock Holmes with a wealth of investigations, the records of which were enough to fill three massive manuscript volumes which rested on my desk in our shared sitting room. This level of activity was even more impressive when considering the fact that Holmes was away from London for the entire first quarter of that year, spending the last days of his supposed death upon the Continent, involved in a number of investigations which still remain largely unrecorded, while awaiting indications that he could finally return to England.

After his unexpected reappearance on the fifth of April, and the subsequent arrest of Colonel Moran later that evening, he immediately resumed both his residence and professional practice in his old Baker Street rooms. The following weeks were spent routing out the pale phoenix that had attempted to rise from the charred bones of Professor Moriarty's wrecked organization, as both the Professor's wicked but more-inept brothers – the Colonel and the station master – had each made their own plays to become the new spider at the center of London's criminal web.

I had known the Colonel from long before I met Holmes – in both India and Afghanistan, as a matter of fact – and he had devoted a great deal of effort during the past three years when Holmes was believed to be dead harrying me personally, before I was able, with the much-appreciated help of a number of Scotland Yarders, to put an end to those schemes. Meanwhile, the youngest Moriarty, curiously named James like the other two, had concocted his own bizarre plan where he disguised himself as his dead academic brother using makeup and a false bald pate, and a truly peculiar structure of straps and harnesses buckled around his body to change how he carried himself, attempting to convince the Professor's former creatures that he was their vanished leader, risen from the dead and ready to take up the reins anew, his argument being that since a body had never been found downstream from the Reichenbach Falls, then he surely must be the real Professor. Within days of Holmes's return, the youngest James Moriarty ended up fleeing to the Continent in disgrace and defeat.

With that business sorted, Holmes settled down to the resumption of his consulting practice, although in many ways it was much different than that of the earlier days of the 1880's, before his "death". Then, he was still

103

unknown to the greater portions of the capital, although the public and the professionals who needed his services managed to find their way to the upstairs sitting room to seek his aid. He regularly eschewed public praise, preferring to let the solution of the puzzle or the thrill of the chase serve as the source of his satisfaction – although fees to pay the rent were never unwelcome. But during those years when he was presumed dead, I had taken it upon myself to record and publish many of his adventures, revealing not necessarily the most complex or serious of cases, but instead providing a cross-sectional representation of both his abilities and his personality. A round two-dozen of these had appeared in a popular periodical before drawing to a close in late 1893, at which time the manner of Holmes's presumed death was revealed to the greater audience who had previously been unaware of it.

The general grief-filled reaction was overwhelming and surprising, and gratifying to me, as I was able to bring about a previously unimagined awareness and admiration for my friend. And then, just a few months after the details of Holmes's "death" were published, and when people were still greatly aware of the "fresh" news that he was dead, he returned to London and resumed his life.

He was not initially pleased to learn that he had become something of a legendary character in his absence, and people unnecessarily noticing him in public was distasteful, but he couldn't argue that his post-death fame did result in a noticeable increase in the number of visitors to his resumed practice. The spring and summer of '94 saw cases both large and small, such as the affair of the Borehamwood Typhon, an example of the former, and the peculiar matter of the red leech, the latter. Holmes did a most-workmanlike job organizing the facts in a succession case that had international implications (as the scion of the Smith and Mortimer union was the heir to a vast munitions fortune), and there were several matters related to discovery of hidden chambers in old houses used for nefarious purposes, such as the well-deserved ignominious end of Sean Harrison, the bulky abuser of women and children who hid in a defiled priest hole with his little white dog, and that of Jonas Oldacre, one of Moriarty's little fish who had escaped the net, and the shabby chamber he constructed as a hidey-hole in his Norwood residence. But one of the most important of the cases in that busy period, lasting as it did for much of the year, was that of the Huret assassins.

I had come down to breakfast on a rainy morning in early November to find that a visitor had just been admitted to the sitting room. The chances were almost certain that he was there to see Holmes, but it was just possible that he was seeking medical help, for sometimes patients still sought me. Several months earlier, I had sold my rather unfulfilling

104

practice and returned to Baker Street, settling into the old routine rather easily. I quickly determined, however, that the fellow was indeed there for Holmes.

He was still in his dressing gown, and his breakfast plate, pushed back on the table near one of the two tall windows, indicated that he'd been up for a while and had begun his day with an appetite – something that was not always the case. Before entering the sitting room, I'd called down to Mrs. Hudson from the landing that I was up and ready to eat, and I could already hear her starting up the steps as I opened the door to the sitting room and paused to examine the small man standing near the fireplace, rubbing his hands and seeming appreciative of the fire that was drying his damp clothing.

He was probably about thirty but looked quite a bit older. His features were pinched, and his careworn body was small, not much over five feet, and clearly a product of those regions of the capital where poor nutrition, meagre resources, and heredity combined to limit his opportunities for growth. The ideal British man is often presented as something resembling a tall, strong knight of old, but too often, what we produce, due to neglect and harsh circumstances, is something like this smaller specimen, held back from his or her full potential by hunger and ignorance, and the necessity of working in terribly unhealthy conditions while the country's industrialization requires more and more raw labor to grind forward yet another day. The city is always filled with men such as the one that stood before our fireplace that day, but there was something about his eyes that showed a shifty intelligence, as if he were cornered in an alley instead of a sitting room, considering which side he might run in order to have the better chance of escape. His eyes were dark and shadowed under a low brow, but a spark of interest was apparent when Mrs. Hudson came in with the breakfast tray.

"Would you care for something, sir?" I asked, moving to help Mrs. Hudson make room on the table. I saw that she'd brought more scrambled eggs than were typical for just my portion, and I understood that she had already taken the opportunity to prepare the fellow some food, should we choose to offer. I caught her eye, and she nodded with a small smile.

The man didn't answer, but I heard that he was already in motion toward the table. As Mrs. Hudson departed, pulling the door shut behind her, I did make sure to get my own portion first, before leaving our guest the remaning goodly amount.

"This is Simon Radlett," explained Holmes from behind us, sitting in his armchair and going through the complex operations of lighting his first morning pipe. From the time it was taking, the previous day's dottles weren't quite dry. "He has brought something of interest."

By this point I was seated at the table, eating my bacon, eggs, and toast a bit quicker than I would have preferred, but failing to match Radlett's speed. He'd claimed what food I hadn't, more than half of what Mrs. Hudson had carried up. For her to have had extra amounts ready so quickly, she had apparently begun preparing it while Radlett was first speaking with Holmes, and also while realizing that I would be down soon. Radlett finished quicker than I, with signs of satisfaction before my plate was halfway cleaned. Placing his own plate on the table – for he had never sat down – he wiped his mouth along his dark sleeve and turned back toward Holmes, "That's right. Ran across it this morning, and knew that it was important. Came right over." He lowered his voice and glanced back my way. "It's related to that *Hoo-ray* we've been hearing about."

He finished the statement by giving an exaggerated nod to punctuate its importance. I pondered his pronunciation of *Huret* – the name of the mysterious French assassin whose rumored deeds had been the subject of so much of Holmes's attention since his return to London in the spring. A terrible assassination had occurred at mid-year, and since then, there had been a number of other attempts, all prevented by Holmes, but some of them quite narrowly.

On the twenty-fifth of June, French President Sadi Carnot had been assassinated in Lyon, following a public speech. He'd entered his carriage and was getting seated when an Italian named Caserio, young and well-dressed, had rushed from the crowd, pulled a dagger from within a rolled newspaper, and plunged it into the President's back. Carnot collapsed, bleeding profusely, and he was driven away immediately to seek medical help. But there was no hope, as his liver had been pierced and the internal haemorrhage was too great.

Meanwhile, Caserio, just twenty-one years of age, had been immediately seized by French officers and rushed away to protect him from the crowd's vengeance. When their efforts to lynch the assassin failed, the angry citizens turned upon businesses and residences owned by Italians, and wreaked further vengeance on the Italian Consulate. It was later learned that Caserio had committed the crime in retaliation against the 1892 execution of the anarchist Ravachol. Initially there was no question that he had acted alone – but then, a few days later after the assassination, a letter had arrived, addressed to the editor of *The Times*, from a man identifying himself as *Huret*, mysteriously stating that he was behind the crime that had occurred in Rue du Pré Botté. There was no specific reference to Carnot, but a sharp reporter had quickly realized that this was the street in Lyons where the Palais du Commerce was located – the site of the Carnot's speech and subsequent murder.

The letter stated simply:

106

The death in Rue du Pré Botté was accomplished by another's hand, but it was my mind that controlled him – as I do a number of other hands, all in place at the sides of other notable men.

When I say so, these men will die. I ask for no payment of any sort to prevent this. It will happen.

You have been informed.

Huret

Inspector Gregson immediately consulted Holmes, who examined the letter, but he provided no specific assistance other than a brief analysis: The envelope had been mailed in Aldgate. The envelope was new and plain. The paper inside, upon which the message was written, was old and yellowed. It had likely been quarto-sized, but the top of the sheet had been trimmed away. Even I could see that had been done to remove the letterhead, done with two strokes of long-bladed shears.

The body of text and the signature were typewritten, and Holmes noted with interest that there were a number of distinctive characteristics that could be used to identify the machine when it was eventually located. Likewise, the typist also had distinctive traits, emphasizing his right hand, and certain letters as well, by the strength in which they had been imprinted upon the page.

Holmes was of the opinion that the letter was genuine, and not the attempt of some crank to generate panic. Likewise, he was certain that the reporter hadn't produced it for the purposes of creating a story, although he declined to explain the basis of his belief. He pointed out the trimmed-away letterhead, and the fact that a new envelope had likely been used because an envelope to match the stationery probably had the same identifying information that was on the letter. It was curious, he noted, that a letter relating to a French assassination was mailed in London. He indicated to Gregson that he had some thoughts about that, but that he would keep those to himself for now, and that he was available to assist them further, should additional information be discovered or letters be received, which pleased the inspector. Then he wanted to keep the letter, which did not. In the end, however, based on the vast number of services that he had provided to the police in the past, the document was left in his custody.

Soon after Gregson departed, Holmes began searching through his files, humming to himself. Clearly he wasn't frustrated at not immediately finding what he sought. Instead, he seemed certain that eventually it would be – and it was. He finally pulled a manila folder from beneath a stack of others just like it, opened it to reveal several documents (the contents of which were not shared with me), dropped in the Huret letter with them, and then turned toward the door. "As usual, Watson," he joked, "it was in the last place I looked!" Then he burst into one of his peculiar fits of laughter, the sort that always boded ill for someone.

"I'm off to see Mycroft," he added. "I have a little notion . . . ." And that was the last I heard of that letter for many months, although the rest of the year brought with it a number of encounters with the hands that Huret claimed to control.

When the police had left that day in late June, I had gathered that the official force expected a bit more from the famed resurrected consultant, but that was as far as he would commit publicly. However, I knew that Holmes continued to make inquiries. Unfortunately before the short note could be properly quashed by the authorities, it was mentioned in *The Times* – only once, but enough to generate a great deal of short-lived interest. The reporter irresponsibly referred to Huret as "*the Boulevard Assassin*", perhaps trying to provide something to fire the public's imagination in the same way that the Whitechapel murderers of 1888 had come to be lumped under the general *sobriquet* of *Jack the Ripper* after one of those myriad killers sent a letter to the press signed with that name.

The Government's quick suppression of the story only served to feed the public's curiosity, as evidenced by successive days filled with rising fear of conspiracies and the possibility of further imminent assassinations on a wide scale. Soon after being consulted by the police, Holmes was also approached by a *Times* reporter asking him his thoughts on the matter. Despite Holmes's own private inquiries, he publically scoffed, stating that, "There are a hundred other agents – A thousand! – all muddling about, crossing one another's paths, questioning their sources and secret contacts. They're probably all offering payments for bits of information, and before long, there will be a dozen different sightings of this 'Huret' – A dozen dozen! – based on whatever tale is bold enough to earn the price of a whisky. No, the field is too crowded for my talents."

Over the next several months, in between his many other investigations, Holmes was responsible for preventing nearly a dozen other assassination attempts, some in England, and others in Paris. All were carried out by men who initially called themselves *Huret*, but in the end, after substantial interrogation, were found to be someone else. They each had the same story: They were either members of various radical groups, or lone wolves who had worked themselves into violent anarchistic frenzies. Each had been approached by a mysterious figure – identifying himself only as "Huret", who offered planning and the means to carry out different murders. They couldn't describe this figure, as their meetings were always in shadows. Huret spoke either French or English as needed, based on the killer he was grooming, and his appearance was always concealed by dark clothing, and a melodramatic hood that hid his features. He had the resources and information to place them in a position to commit murder, and all he asked was that they claim the name "Huret" when the crime was committed.

Holmes's successes in catching the various lesser Hurets had brought him the gratitude of two governments, but he seemed no closer to catching the elusive master. Then, in mid-October, he had, seemingly without reason, begun to spread the word that he was closing in on his prey. I'd seen no indications of it, but as always, there was much that Holmes didn't share with me.

And now a fellow had shown up speaking of *Hoo-ray*. I didn't yet know what information that Radlett had brought, but he'd already earned a free breakfast for his trouble.

I finished my own meal, refreshed my coffee, and moved to my chair by the fireplace. On the way, Holmes reached across to hand me a visiting card, the front of which stated:

Gerald Fenton Westhouse
Westhouse & Marbank
Wine and Spirits Merchants
Fenchurch Street

The card was stiff and thick, with a warm tan color and clearly containing a great deal of rag content. The text was embossed, with the name of the company darkened and thickened for emphasis. I had some vague memory of the place, perhaps from an advertisement, as I knew I'd never personally visited a spirit merchant in Fenchurch Street.

Turning the card over, I saw that there was a handwritten message. The black ink wasn't unusual, and the words had clearly written in ornate script by a right hand using a new pen with a wide nib: *Huret – 5 November, 11 a.m. Fenchurch office.* I looked up at Holmes with surprise. He gave a slight nod and said to Simon Radlett, "Sit down, there in the basket chair, and tell us how you came by this card."

Radlett, who had been standing halfway across the room, centered evenly between the chairs, the dining table, and the door, looked suspicious, as if he were a stray dog that was being enticed into a trap with bits of food and gentle voices that would all go away when the cage door slammed shut. And yet, despite his instinct to flee, he had willingly brought the card to Holmes, so in the end it was his decision to stay and explain, likely hoping for some sort of reward beyond a plate of bacon and eggs. He warily sidled to the chair, first standing behind it, and then slithering around to the front. He sat down on the front edge, his short legs resting on the floor as if he might still roll forward and bolt at any second.

His mouth tightened as if considering what to say. Then: "I'll admit it – I pulled it from a gentleman's pocket. A man has to eat, don't he? I spotted him this morning in Leadenhall Street as he ran some errands, and saw that he was careless with his wallet. I came up behind him to lift it, but it went wrong – he felt my hand – and the card was all I could grab before he turned and tried to stop me. He swung his stick, but I ran away. In a few minutes, when I was alone, I looked at what I had – that card and nothing else. I was about to toss it away when I saw what was written on the back. I've heard that you were asking questions about that *Hoo-ray* gent, so I came here, the very next thing." He leaned forward, pointing a finger to the card still in my hand. "You'll notice that the man works in Fenchurch Street – just around the corner from Leadenhall Street."

"That had not escaped my attention," said Holmes. "Although presuming that the card belongs to the man you robbed isn't certain. It could be his, with the appointment written on the back to remind him. He could be someone else, and the card was given to him by Westhouse – or he could have found it on the ground and picked it up out of curiosity." Holmes's words diminished the possible importance of the man, but at the same time, I could see that he was most interested.

Holmes was leaning forward now as well, looking toward our visitor. "Tell us more about this man you tried to rob," he said.

Radlett frowned. "I only took the card, Mr. Holmes. Nothing else. He wasn't *robbed*." He seemed offended as he rubbed a dirty hand across his whiskers. Then he looked into the fire, ruminating. "About fifty, I suppose. Dressed like a toff – expensive-looking clothes and hat. Shiny boots and shiny stick. And fat – he doesn't miss any meals."

"And he raised his stick to threaten you when he felt you reaching into his pocket?"

"That's right."

"Show me." Holmes abruptly stood. "Come up behind Watson and try to take something from his pocket. There – grab your stick, Watson. Now, stand there while Radlett robs you."

I rose more slowly, uncertain as to the purpose of this exercise. I retrieved my stick from the stand by the door and returned to the center of the room, awaiting further instructions.

110

"Now," said Holmes to Radlett, who had also risen, "was this man walking or paused?"

Radlett, confused, seemed to visualize the scene. "Um, he was stopped – looking into a window."

"Was he holding the stick, or leaning upon it? And you approached him from behind? Good. Which direction? Show me."

I pantomimed a man looking into a shop window, holding the stick vertically and gripping it at the top as directed. I was aware of Radlett stealthily nearing my right side, where the stick rested, and then I felt his hand slipping around from behind and into my coat pocket. If he was demonstrating his typical pick-pocketing technique, it was no wonder that the man on the street had perceived his clumsy intrusion. Holmes hadn't given further instructions, but I played my part, turning toward Radlett, crying *"Stop!"* and raising the stick threateningly as I did so. The small man jumped backward, as if this were real and he was in actual danger. Then, after a few hurried steps, he stopped, recalling that this was simply a pantomime, and looked expectantly at Holmes. "It was just like that," he confirmed.

"Thank you. And after he raised his stick, you fled."

"I did. And then, when I was around the corner, I read what was written on the card and came here." He looked from one of us to the other. "Today is November 5th," he added, as if we didn't understand, "and it isn't that long until eleven o'clock, you know."

Holmes nodded. "Then it seems that the next logical step is that we should obtain a cab and visit Westhouse and Marbank in Fenchurch Street."

I saw that Radlett gave a small nod, almost involuntarily. But did I also see the merest shadow of a smile play upon his lips?

"Watson, will you go downstairs and summon a growler? And will you let Mrs. Hudson know that we'll need to miss our appointment with Desmond Wagenaar later this morning? Are you ready, Radlett?"

I nodded, now puzzled, but racing to catch up. Radlett seemed to be in a similar state.

"You don't need a growler, Mr. Holmes," he said. "I'm not going with you."

"Of course you are," replied Holmes, his tone tolerating no disagreement as he strode across the room to where his hat and coat were hanging. "How else will we identify the man from whom you lifted the card?"

"I described him for you."

"A fat man in his fifties, well dressed? Pshaw! I could put forth my hand and have five-dozen such as that here in Baker Street within an hour. No, your identification will be invaluable. Now Watson – about that cab?"

He looked directly at me to see if I understood, and I nodded, grabbed my coat and hat, and walked out to the landing, pulling the door shut behind me. But instead of immediately going downstairs and out to the street, I took the upper treads up one floor to my room, so recently vacated, in order to retrieve my service revolver – for surely this was what Holmes was indirectly reminding me to do. I knew that there was no other reason for him to tell anything about an appointment with Desmond Wagenaar, because the man had died five years earlier. I had killed him . . . .

Wagenaar was a good coiner and a bad man. His skills were of such quality that the security of the national currency was threatened. Mycroft Holmes had enlisted his brother to track Wagenaar to his lair and stop what he was doing. Extra caution was advised, as the coiner was also known to be a murderer may times over several decades.

At that time, I was newly married, living in Paddington with my bride and establishing a practice. Thus, while I had regular contact with Holmes and some knowledge of his activities, I was not fully informed of the current status of every case. I was making my rounds on that day when I received a terse message from Holmes seeking my help – or so I believed. I knew enough to be suspicious, for it was a single sheet thrust into my hand on the street by a boy I didn't know, simply stating, *Mr. Holmes needs your help – Baker Street. Urgent!* Before I could question the boy, he had run away. I responded to the summons by immediately changing direction and hurrying toward our old rooms, but it was one of the few times that I'd foolishly gone out without a weapon.

I knew better. I suppose that, in my newly married bliss, I'd foolishly forgotten that being associated with Holmes was a dangerous business. From the early days when Holmes had started inviting me to join him in his investigations, when my health permitted, I had seen that seemingly routine situations could unexpectedly pivot into danger with stunning immediacy. Additionally, Holmes's activities during the years before I met him had generated a truly impressive number of enemies who wished to do him all sorts of harm, from physical damage to taking his life. This had continued into the 1880's when I started working with him, and the longer our association continued, the more enemies that I made as well. Therefore, it had become my policy to go armed – but there were still times when circumstances prevented it, or I simply forgot or chose to do otherwise, and that morning was one of those, when leaving my service revolver behind was a serious mistake.

I hadn't walked far before I was taken from behind, pulled into the mews immediately past Dorset Square, just as one reaches Park Street. A bag was thrown over my head, and two men held me from either side as I was tossed into a carriage. Five minutes later, I was dragged into the back of an empty house north of Regent's Park and the bag was removed. I found myself facing Wagenaar – then simply a menacing stranger, completely unknown to me. He was standing alongside Holmes, who was bruised and bleeding, gagged and tied thoroughly to a chair.

Wagenaar had a gun, pointing it toward Holmes's head. "Doctor," he said, avoiding any delays, "tell me where Holmes keeps his important papers, or he dies now."

I had no knowledge of what was occurring, and no time consider. Without thinking, and with no cry of warning or signal of my intentions, I pulled loose from the two nonplussed and careless men who were holding my arms and rushed directly toward the man with the gun.

It was a distance of just ten feet, and even as I covered it, I could see Holmes's eyes widen in surprise. Wagenaar was caught unaware as well, having certainly pictured the events he'd orchestrated playing out in a much different manner.

It was over in seconds. I slammed into the man, outweighing him by twenty or thirty pounds, without mercy, as if I were still a young Rugby player. I violently raised my knee into his groin, even as I felt some of the ribs at his sternum snap underneath my driving shoulder – medical experience gives one a good sense of just where to aim. It was a matter of physics, with my mass and forward motion driving him backward into the unforgiving wall, even as my left hand reached for the wrist holding the gun, forcing it up and away.

Wagenaar was surprised, but only for a second or two, and then, despite his injuries, he began to fight back. His strength must have been immense, although he had seemed only average size. Perhaps he felt a desperation, aware that he was suddenly and unexpectedly in a life-and-death struggle. I got my other hand up and across his body, now using it to further grasp his wrist, attempting to make him drop the gun, or at least direct it away from me or Holmes. Meanwhile, he hit me in the back with his other hand, balled into a fist, but not very effective against the thickness of my wool coat. Then, he managed to pull the trigger. The gunshot sounded like an exploding naval shell in the small room, but thank Heavens the gun was aimed toward the ceiling.

Behind me, I could hear the two other men yelling, and I feared that at any moment they would come forward to assist their leader, possibly to put an effective bullet in my skull, but perhaps they were too fearful of where Wagenaar's gun might end up pointing when the next shot was fired. Meanwhile, Wagenaar was fighting to turn his hand and use the weapon upon me, and I could see that his finger had wound tightly around the trigger. He would fire as soon as he was able.

I gave no further thought to the men who had been holding me, for whatever happened now would be finshed soon. For an instant, my entire universe was reduced to Wagenaar's hand and that gun. And in spite of my advantages in weight and surprise, he was accomplishing his intention. The gun was turning, and he was ready to fire.

Then, at the very last, I shifted my right hand further up, grabbing the barrel and turning it away from me and toward him. I pulled the barrel up toward his head just as he fired, a deafening blast. Perhaps my tug on the gun contributed to his pull upon the trigger. Between me and the wall against which he was pressed, he spasmodically jerked, his sour breath making an involuntary groan as the air escaped his dying lungs past his vocal cords, already relaxing in death. He went limp. The tunneled vision I'd had of the gun shifted, widening, and I looked into his eyes, no more than inches from my own. Blood was already pouring down his brow around them, as he'd fired the gun straight up through his own head, tearing off the top of his skull and spattering the wall behind.

So much for my Hippocratic Oath.

But I had also been a soldier.

I watched as the hate-filled and awful awareness of what he'd done, boring into me, vanished as he focused on something else far away and eternal, and far more important. Then I released him and he slid down the wall, out of my view.

When he dropped, I turned. The two men were gone, having fled when death entered the room. I freed Holmes, who immediately and profusely apologized for my involvement, but I waved it away, instead asking, rather shakily, about the men who had brought me here. "Will they return?" I glanced at the gun, now on the ground, still in the dead man's hand, wondering if I ought to quickly retrieve it.

Holmes shook his head. "Griggs and Barton. I know them. Cowards – the both of them. They'll be easy to retrieve when I'm ready. First, let's check the house to make sure that everything has been recovered."

As we explored, he explained just who the dead man was, what he'd been doing, and how his death was not a tragedy in the least. I found, having just been responsible Wagenaar's demise, in spite of the fact that it occurred in a situation of his own making, that I didn't want to know too much about him. Holmes also told how his own carelessness had allowed for his capture not an hour earlier, and how, when he'd refused to reveal where he kept his accumulated evidence, the idea of finding out through me had surfaced, with a plan to collect me soon put into motion.

Holmes explained that we were in Wagenaar's own home, boldly used for his illicit activities, and we found all of the coiner's tools in the cellar, along with the wasted fruits of the dead man's labors. As we climbed back to the ground floor, Holmes thanked me again for my unexpected reaction, leading to his rescue. "I never get your limits, Watson," he said. "There is always something to be said for the direct and unexpected approach . . . ."

Years later, I could still only wonder at how such a spontaneous action on my part could have easily gone so very wrong. Rushing the man had been madness, I realized, and Holmes or I could have easily been killed during the wild events of the short struggle. As the passing minutes removed us from the event, I vowed that I'd never go out without being armed. Holmes knew that I had followed this rule ever since, but just now, as we prepared to depart with Radlett, he'd still felt the need to subtly remind me to bring my gun in a way that Radlett wouldn't understand. For some reason, there was danger associated with our upcoming journey. But in truth, it was rare that danger wasn't associated in some degree during any journey taken with Holmes.

Having retrieved my service revolver and stepped outside to hail a growler, I returned to the entryway, where Holmes and Radlett had just descended. Holmes knocked on the door to Mrs. Hudson's parlor, and when it opened, he handed her several telegram forms, asking that she have them dispatched immediately. Then he led us outside to the waiting cab, where Holmes murmured instructions the driver to head toward Fenchurch Street along a specific route. There was more, but his voice dropped too low to hear.

Radlett seemed nervous, much more so than when he had spoken to us upstairs. I had sensed that he was glad that we were taking action, as based on the card that he'd delivered, but that he'd expected nothing further afterwards, except perhaps some form of remuneration. Now he was being pulled further into the affair. I was also more nervous than I would have expected, stemming from Holmes's cryptic reminder to make sure that I was armed. I stayed alert to pick up on any other cues that he might direct my way.

We were moving west along Marylebone Street, each keeping to our own thoughts. It was only as we were turning into Tottenham Court Road that Holmes finally spoke.

"Did you know, Watson, that Simon here was once an Irregular? Just for a short time, in the late seventies, when I still resided in Montague Street. How old were you then, Simon? Not quite fifteen, I expect."

115

Radlett frowned. "That's right," he replied, his tone suddenly rather terse, I thought, for such a simple question.

"You were only involved in a few errands, as I recall," continued Holmes, seemingly oblivious to Radlett's change of mood. "Following a few people, or keeping watch on their houses. The last time was . . . Who was that? Whaley, I believe? Or was it Tibbles?"

"I don't really remember. As you said, it was a long time ago – half-a-lifetime for me." His tone was level. There was no enthusiasm for him about reminiscing.

Holmes nodded. "Indeed it was. Much has happened since then. Do you still keep up with any of the others from those days?"

Radlett shook his head. "That was too long ago. Everyone went their separate ways – those of us that survived, in any case."

Holmes started to say something else, but stopped himself. He then seemed to lose focus, his eyes drifting from inside the carriage to the passing street, as if he were tired of speaking about the past, and instead viewing something from those long-ago days. Radlett, meanwhile, seemed to pull inward, crossing his arms as if to ward off a blow and staring down toward his feet.

There was something happening here that I did not understand.

We had reached the intersection with New Oxford Street and turned east, following the thoroughfare toward our destination. The random changes in London street names were often a cause of consternation for visitors to the capital, with New Oxford turning into to High Holborn, Holborn, Newgate, and Cheapside, before finally becoming Fenchurch Street – each segment of the same thoroughfare lasting just a few hundred feet, or possibly just a thousand, before transitioning to the next. Our cab plodded steadily onward, and I wondered at Holmes's seeming indifference, headed as we were to follow up a clue to the mysterious assassin. He wasn't hunched forward, using every minute between now and the end of the journey to consider possibilities and plan strategies. Instead, he was idly watching the passing buildings with little interest. At one point, over the street noise, I heard that he was softly humming "*La Donna è Mobile*". I was certainly more tense than he was, having been forewarned to go armed, and Radlett was the most strained of all, the condition becoming more noted with each passing mile.

We weren't long past Lincoln's Inn Fields when Holmes stirred, now more alert, his eyes on Radlett. Aware that something had changed, I sat up a bit straighter, aware of the weight of my revolver in my coat pocket.

The cabbie gently gigged the horse to the left, turning us smoothly toward Gray's Inn. Radlett was suddenly alert, as if sensing some sort of danger. Holmes raised a hand.

"I asked the cabbie to stop here, on our way to Fenchurch Street," he explained. "There is someone who I hope to question before we go further."

"Who?" Radlett asked, his voice a high tight whisper. He cleared his throat."It's getting on toward eleven."

Holmes didn't answer. The cab slipped to a halt and I recognized the doorway. We were at the offices of my attorney, Marchmont. What on earth could Huret have to do with the lawyer?

We stepped down, and I kept an eye on Radlett, should he choose to run. I think he considered it, looking speculatively at both Holmes and me. I'm sure that he realized he could outdistance me in a footrace, especially as he'd be able to dodge into the narrow alleys that formed the rabbit's warren of this neighborhood. But he certainly also understood that he'd have no such luck when testing himself against Holmes.

We entered the building to encounter Marchmont's taciturn secretary. I hadn't seen him or the lawyer for several months – since selling my Kensington practice, as a matter of fact. As expected, nothing had changed, for it never did in these quiet austere chambers.

The secretary seemed as if he'd expected us. He led us through a door into a short hallway, where we found Marchmont, a heavy-set middle-aged man, standing in a hallway. He greeted us all, shaking our hands, and then, without comment or questions, he directed us into the small conference room where in the past I'd conducted several bits of my own business, and where I'd also been either an observer or participant when Holmes cleared up one or the other of his cases. When we were in the room, Marchmont nodded and walked back out, and the secretary closed the door behind him, leaving the three of us alone to find seats around the long rectangular table.

Holmes removed his hat and coat, laying the former at the head of the table, and placing the folded coat on top of a nearby cabinet. Then he stood behind the chair usually reserved for Marchmont. Meanwhile, I also removed my hat and coat (for there was no coat stand, and in the hurry to get us placed in the conference room, the secretary had neglected to offer to take them) and laid them on the same cabinet. I then chose a chair near the door, pulled it back from the table, and sat, and leaving the other seats, those farther from the exit, for Radlett's choosing. He kept his coat and hat on, and seemed inclined to stand.

"What's going on here?" he growled, his short figure tense as he sensed the implied threat. He glanced from the closed door to the tall curtained window, as if considering which was a better chance for his escape: Getting past me or defenestrating himself. "I brought you the card. There ain't no need for you to force me to go to Fenchurch Street, let alone stopping here. What is this place?"

117

"Didn't you read the sign upon the door?" Holmes countered. "That should have answered your question."

"I can't – " Radlett stopped himself, his mouth popping shut before he could let anything slip. Holmes advised him to have a seat.

"I expect that our visitors will arrive soon," Holmes added, apparently ignoring Radlett's aborted comment, "but they may be delayed."

At first the little man ignored him, but finally he pulled out a chair, several down the table and across from where I sat, and perched himself on the front edge, much as he'd done not so long before in Baker Street.

"Visitors?" asked Radlett. "Who?" But again Holmes didn't answer.

There was a low shelf near where Holmes stood, containing a variety of volumes. Some appeared to be thick and ancient, bound in cracked black leather – surely legal tomes from bygone days, perhaps left over from when Marchmont had acquired the practice from the original founder, now long dead. There were other books there, too, including a copy of *Whitaker's Almanac*, easily recognizable by its green boards and red spine, which was marked with the curious circular symbol at the top and the trident at the base.

Holmes had been studying the book shelf, which caused me to notice it as well. Then he leaned down and retrieved the *Whitaker's* before placing it on the table by his fore-and-aft cap and taking a seat.

"Watson," he asked, his fingers resting lightly on the almanac. "Do you recall several years ago, when the cat-and-mouse game against the Professor was escalating? There was a fellow, one of Moriarty's mid-level agents, who sent me information as he was able."

I nodded. "Porlock – or so he called himself. He was able to let you know about the White Hart plot, in time to save Calvin Thurlow – the poor man who needed a job. There were other instances, as I recall. He sent the message about where the grape leaves were picked when we were tracking the Rippers, and he tried to prevent the murder of that rich American at the moated house in North Sussex. I'm sure that I have other instances recorded in my notes."

Holmes tapped the book, drawing attention to it. "Porlock was a very clever fellow. You'll recall that back in '88, he used the *Whitaker's* to send us a message warning us of the Birlstone murder. It wasn't something that he and I had worked out before. He came up with that method on his own for that particular event, although he and I used it afterwards."

He tapped the book again. "The *Almanac* was quite useful for that sort of thing – something that the original creators never envisioned." Suddenly he slid it across the table, where it came to rest across from Radlett. "Don't you agree, Simon?"

118

Radlett jumped as if Holmes had pushed a swamp adder toward him. Then he nodded, warily. "I suppose so."

"Do you make much use of the *Almanac*?" Holmes asked. Even as Radlett shook his head, Holmes added, "Open it up and tell us some of the most useful parts."

Radlett looked from him to the book, and then again, before reaching and pulling it closer. He flipped it open and turned a few pages, staring at it. From where I sat, I could see that it was upside down. Then he closed it and said, "All of it is important, I suppose."

Holmes nodded, and then looked at me. "Even in 1879, Simon couldn't read. And yet, somehow he read that card this morning and recognized the French name when he lifted it from the man in Leadenhall Street."

Radlett, who had never relaxed, seemed even more tense, but he didn't rise, nor did he say a word. Holmes continued speaking to me.

"You'll recall that Porlock was killed – tortured by Moriarty and then thrown into the Thames." Simon Radlett gasped, and Holmes continued. "Just another of the many crimes that were draped like heavy chains to Moriarty's black soul." He glanced toward Radlett. "Of course, Porlock's death occurred many years after you and I parted ways, didn't it, Simon?"

The man didn't speak, his eyes fixed on upon my friend with seering intensity. Even more did he now appear to be a cornered animal.

Holmes looked back my way. "Porlock's murder was – I was outraged. But it only served to show just how malevolent Moriarty was. When he learned that Porlock was assisting me, he killed him – because of the betrayal, and also to send me a message, and as a lesson to his creatures. I was never able to determine just how he learned what Porlock was doing. But by then the specifics didn't matter. Events were crowding fast upon us, and he was one more casualty in the escalating war."

Then Holmes stopped for a moment, glanced over at the almanac, and then back up to Radlett. "You couldn't read fifteen years ago, Simon, and you can't read the book that Porlock used – can you?"

Radlett's suspicious mien was starting to crumble. He didn't look angry or trapped now. Instead, he began to chew at his lower lip, looking back and forth from Holmes to the book. Then he shifted in the chair and leaned forward, putting his head closer to the cover, staring intently. He raised his hand, apparently to once more touch the almanac, but then he dropped it back to his lap. Then with something between a sob and a sigh he leaned back, looking up toward Holmes. His face was now marked by grief.

119

"You're right!" he whispered. "I can't read it! What does it matter? Can you tell me what happened to my brother? To Alf? I was never able to find out."

Holmes nodded, his face marked by compassion.

"I can tell you, Simon. It's a terrible story, and your brother was very brave. But now is not the time. As you said, it's getting on toward eleven, and we have other matters to discuss – namely, the true reason that you brought that card to Baker Street."

Holmes stood and walked back around the table, retrieved the *Whitaker's*, replaced it on the low shelf, and then resumed his place at the head of the table.

"As you've perceived, Watson," he said, "Alfred Bassick, known to us as 'Porlock', was Simon's brother – actually half-brother, I believe. They were both Irregulars for a short period in the late seventies, but as often happened with many of them, they were seduced away by better pay, despite the fact that they migrated to the wrong side of the law. But while they were Irregulars, they had both been my responsibility for a while, and that did not end. I kept in touch with Alfred, the brother later known as 'Porlock', and at one point was able to do him a great favor – getting you, Simon, out of a hole in which you'd found yourself."

Radlett's eyes widened. Clearly, he'd been completely unaware of this.

"Your brother never wanted you to know what we'd done for you. Afterwards, he felt himself to be in my debt, and the best way that he could repay it was to provide information as he wormed deeper into Professor Moriarty's organization. I'll forever regret how he was eventually rewarded – with his own death."

Radlett cleared his throat. "But what about the book?" he asked. "Why did you trick me? Why are we here?"

Holmes shook his head. "I recalled that in the old days, you couldn't read, and I suspected that it was still true. I've followed your rather dubious 'career' over the years, and I've seen no signs that you have improved yourself. Certainly you weren't learning to read on your own, and no one was requiring it of you. Things might have changed in that regard during the three years I was away from London, but I doubted it. When you showed up this morning with that card, claiming to have read both the message, written in cursive, and the information on the front, I thought that you might be lying. Therefore, I contrived the little reading test just now with the almanac."

"But . . . but surely you didn't come here to this office just to trap me – to read a book?"

120

"No. I could have had you try to read while we were still in Baker Street, but I didn't want you suspicious any sooner than you had to be. After spotting the false note of your visit this morning, I contrived to take control of the situation. Apparently you wanted me – and Watson as well, I suppose – to race off to Fenchurch Street about Gerald Fenton Westhouse at eleven o'clock, which meant that we should *not* do that. Instead, as we left, I had our landlady send telegrams to Marchmont, asking if we could use his office as a wayside for a while, and also to the police, requesting, among other things, that they have Westhouse brought here to meet us, assuming that he's available. Based on what I've discovered over the last few months, and more through recent developments, I'm not surprised that he's been pulled into this, but I want to determine the full extent of his involvement – if any – with the so-called 'Boulevard Assassin'."

I tried to recall specifics regarding the little I knew about Holmes's recent inquiries. His association with the affair had begun with the arrival of Inspector Gregson to show him the letter, written by Huret and sent to *The Times*. He'd made some observations then but offered nothing of great value – or so I thought. He'd consulted with Mycroft, and he'd averted a number of other Huret-connected assassination attempts, but as far as I knew otherwise, he hadn't heard anything from the agents he'd set in to motion – certainly nothing that would cause him to leap up and rush forth upon the hue-and-cry in which we were now engaged.

"It had to be the original letter," I speculated softly, almost tentatively, thinking hard and trying to make a connection. "You saw something in the original letter that intrigued you – for I'm unaware that you've received further information since then."

Holmes nodded. "Good, Watson! And correct. There *was* something familiar about the letter, something that I chose for the moment to keep to myself, and a bit of focused research confirmed my conclusions well enough to proceed. From the beginning, I knew who wrote it, but Mycroft and I decided to set plans in motion to let events play out, and see where Huret led us – and he's revealed a lot since mid-year. You might be interested to know that soon after we began, your own writings – particularly an issue of *The Strand* from September 1891 – provided me with a most-important confirmatory clue."

"September – ?" I asked, trying to remember to which entry he was referencing. That fall had been a difficult period for me, just four months after Holmes's supposed death, and Mary's health sliding downward to a new level of seriousness and concern. I still had a medical practice for which I cared nothing, as my mood deteriorated and I recognized that my wife's condition was steadily and inevitably deteriorating. I found distraction and solace only by writing, and from my extensive notes and

121

journals, maintained over many years, I had a plethora of Holmes's cases from which to choose.

Every night, I wrote ceaselessly after Mary had been put to bed, recording one account after another, in much the same way that I'd written with such focused dedication following my return to London after being injured in the Afghan War. As the months passed, I accumulated more and more completed records of Holmes's adventures, one after another piling up along one side of my desk, and I only managed to tear myself away from the writing long enough to evince a limited interest and involvement regarding which of those was chosen for publication. By the time one of the stories would appear in *The Strand*, I had already written many more, and was working on yet another. *What was significant about the story from September 1891?*

"I have no recollection of which particular narrative you mean," I finally said, my confusion apparent.

Holmes smiled. "No matter. All will be clear soon enough – for I believe that I hear the arrival of visitors, and Gregson's authoritative tones."

The door opened to reveal the secretary. He stepped back, allowing Inspector Gregson and a heavy-set man, about ten years older than Holmes and me, to enter the room. Holmes and I stood, and Holmes asked, "Is he under observation?"

Gregson nodded. "As he has been these last four months. He'll be ready when you are."

My immediate reaction was to ask who "*he*" was, but I knew that Holmes would reveal that fact only when he was ready.

"Excellent!" Holmes turned to the man, who was looking most confused and unsettled. "Mr. Gerald Fenton Westhouse?" he asked. The man nodded. "Thank you for coming. Please take a seat."

The man seemed to find a little fortitude. "You act as if I had a choice. This policeman – " He glanced sourly at Gregson. " – collected me at my workplace as if I were under arrest. *Am* I under arrest, Inspector?"

"No, sir. As I explained, we wanted to remove you to a place where we could speak in confidence."

"By making it appear as if I were being detained?"

"There was a purpose to that, as I'm sure Mr. Holmes will explain."

"I will," said Holmes. "Please, sit down. This won't take long."

When we had settled, Holmes pointed at Simon Radlett, asking, "Have you ever seen this man before?"

Westhouse glanced that way. "Never."

"He didn't try to rob you this morning in Leadenhall Street? You didn't raise your stick to him and chase him away?"

Westhouse reddened. "Of course not! What is this? What are you trying to involve me in?"

"Is this your card?" Holmes pushed the one given to him by Radlett across the table. Westhouse took it and read the front. "It is."

"And the back? Did you write that? Or was it written by someone else and provided to you?"

The wine merchant turned the card over and glanced at the inscribed words. "Never seen it before," He said, tossing it back toward Holmes. He seemed to have no recognition of the assassin's name.

I glanced at Radlett. His face was pale, and he seemed to quiver with tension.

"Gentlemen," said Holmes, "please note that Mr. Westhouse picked up the card with his *left* – and dominant – hand. Earlier today, Mr. Radlett here demonstrated to Dr. Watson and me earlier this morning that when he robbed you, sir – when he *said* that he robbed you – you defended yourself by holding your cane in your *right* hand, and that when he approached you from your right, he found that card in your right coat pocket, where a right-handed man would have placed it."

"Ridiculous!" Westhouse snarled. He hit the table with his fist – his left fist – for emphasis. "What is this nonsense? I've never seen this man before, or you either, sir! No one tried to rob me, and I've never before seen what was written on that card!"

Holmes nodded. "So I thought, and as I'm sure Mr. Radlett would have admitted the same to us soon enough. And I already knew that you were left handed, for you and I met once before, seven years ago. In October 1887, as a matter of fact, although you wouldn't recognize me now. I was in disguise."

Westhouse frowned. "Disguise? What nonsense is that? Why would anyone want to visit me in disguise?"

"So that I could get a look at one of your employees while I asked you a few general questions, and so that he wouldn't recognize me when he came to visit my rooms a few days later."

"Employee? Which one? What is this about?"

"I manufactured an excuse to meet with you so that I could get a look at one of your salesmen – Mr. James Windibank."

Suddenly, as if bright sunlight blew away the fog of my confusion, I recalled the case to which Holmes had earlier referred, the story that had appeared in the September 1891 edition of *The Strand*. I had happened to visiting Baker Street that day in October 1887, discussing with Holmes a wide variety of topics, when a new client had arrived – Miss Mary Sutherland, whose fiancé, one curiously named *Hosmer Angel*, had vanished.

Holmes had recognized the similarity between those circumstances and several other cases, leading him to the suspicion that Angel was actually someone else in disguise, disingenuously courting the girl as a way to her money. She had provided Holmes with a number of typewritten letters from Angel, all of which had given him a number of clues as to the specific machine upon which they'd been written. He'd also noted that the girl's stepfather, James Windibank, a claret salesman for Westhouse and Marbank, conveniently took business trips to France and was gone whenever Hosmer walked out with the girl.

He'd immediately suspected that Windibank was posing as Angel. He'd corresponded with Windibank, and the return letter, typewritten on Westhouse and Marbank's stationery, had shown the same wearing and defects as those on the letters to the unfortunate girl from Hosmer Angel. Holmes was then able to confront the man, exposing that Windibank, by promising the girl marriage and disappearing before the ceremony, hoped to be able to keep her at home as a sad lonely spinster, forever bound to the mysteriously vanished Hosmer, while he remained in control of her substantial inheritance. It was a diabolical plot, and Windibank had proved himself to be a true villain.

I looked up to see that Holmes was watching me, smiling. He knew that I was now caught up.

"Windibank?" asked Westhouse. "What about him?"

"Has his work been satisfactory of late?"

"Why – No, it has not. His sales have dropped, and his traveling expenses have increased with very little return. He's been put on notice that he'll need to do better, or be sacked. He isn't happy with me right now, but I'm running a business."

"Interesting. And when did this trend begin?"

"What? Oh, I suppose in the spring sometime. He became rather insolent as well. Something the matter at home, I suppose. I'd heard that there was trouble – that his wife had left him."

Holmes glanced toward Radlett. "Simon – How did you become involved in this?"

The little man lowered his eyes. "I was introduced to a man," he mumbled.

"Who? Windibank?"

"I don't know that name."

"No, I don't suppose so. Was he about thirty-seven? Five-feet-seven inches in height? Strongly built, sallow complexion? Black hair, a little bald in the centre?"

I recognized that description of Windibank that I'd recorded in my original narrative, adjusted forward seven years from his then-age of thirty or so. Westhouse confirmed it. "That's him – that's Windibank!"

Radlett nodded. "That's right. They – this man knew that I . . . that I have no use for you, Mr. Holmes. After Alf died while working for you. I've done some things for him before – for Windibank – and a few days ago, he approached me with a simple task: He knew that you've been looking for this *Hoo-ray*, and that the word is going around that you're getting close to finding him. He said for me to take that card to Baker Street and get you interested in this man here – to tell you that I'd found the card in his pocket. You were supposed to charge off to the office in Fenchurch Street and then arrest him . . . but I have the idea that something else is supposed to happen when you get there."

Holmes looked toward Gregson. "*Did* anything happen when you arrived?"

"Not a thing."

"Hmm. Then perhaps whatever happens requires my presence." He looked back to Radlett. "When were you introduced to this man?"

"Last spring."

"You started to mention 'they'," asked Holmes. "Who might 'they' be?"

Radlett's eyes widened, and he involuntarily shook his head.

"It was in the spring. Might I theorize that it was in that same period when there were some thwarted attempts to restart the Professor's broken organization?"

I wondered if Radlett would be able to follow Holmes's thought, using words like "thwarted", but Holmes had more faith in him. Radlett knew what he meant, and he gave a small nod, without offering any explanation.

Holmes continued.

"This man you met – who we have identified now as Windibank – was he working with Colonel Moriarty, or the other one – the youngest brother who oddly disguised himself as the dead Professor?"

"Him," said Radlett softly. "The younger one. I don't know who he thought he was fooling with the bald wig and into the waterfall. Everyone knew that he wasn't the Professor – but it didn't matter, for we were all still afraid of him. He's a little crazy, he is. He had come from France last spring to try and take over, and that's where he met the other man – this Windibank – who was over in France a lot as well. They were working together, and had big plans. But then you came back to London, Mr. Holmes, and the two Moriarty brothers ran away – but Windibank was still

125

here, and he went ahead with whatever he was doing. I've run errands for him ever since."

"And it didn't bother you to work for the youngest Moriarty, even though the Professor murdered your half-brother."

"He wasn't the Professor," Radlett countered with a shrug, "and he was working against you, which suited me."

"I see. And what do you know about Windibank's plans?"

"Nothing. He was gone to France a great deal, but he paid me to run his errands when he was here. I suppose he trusted me as much as anyone."

"Do you know anything about a letter he wrote to the newspapers last summer?"

"Not much – just that he did it, and then right after, he said he'd made a mistake, and that he wouldn't do anything like that again."

Holmes nodded and spoke to Gregson. "That fits with our assumption that he realized that I might recognize the Huret letter came from the same typewriter as Windibank's, and he refrained from providing any further emphasis to it, hoping it would be forgotten." He included me in the thought, looking my way. "And that's what we let him think, giving him more and more rope while we learned about the organization he and the younger Moriarty have constructed, while preventing additional murders that they arranged.

"And Mr. Westhouse?" Holmes looked back at the now-much-puzzled merchant. "Do you know anything about Mr. Windibank's plan?"

Westhouse had gone pale as he realized that something was going on, involving him, beyond what was easily understood. "Plan? I do not. I . . . I'm just a businessman, a wine and spirits importer. Windibank has worked for us for a number of years. His performance has fallen off, but he's been a trusted employee for a long time. He would have to be, wouldn't he? He travels for us, making regular trips over to France. Even though his sales have declined, he's never given us a reason to distrust him. I just thought . . . thought that he was going through a low spot. I didn't – Just what has he gotten us into?"

Holmes didn't answer him, instead turning to Gregson.

"Well," he asked, "have we allowed this to go on just about long enough?"

Gregson nodded. "I was in a meeting with your brother this morning, Mr. Holmes, and now that Windibank seems to be spooked, it's probably time to shut him down. We don't think we'll get anything else useful by letting him run loose."

"I agree. Where is he now?"

"Still at the spirits office in Fenchurch Street. I observed him there when we picked up Mr. Westhouse an hour ago, sitting at his desk off to one side. If it surprised him that you weren't with us as intended when we staged the arrest, he might have bolted, but even so, he's being watched from a half-dozen directions – some of my best men who've had experience tracking the Dynamiters, as well as your brother's agents, and even those slippery children you employ. He won't get far."

"Then let's go retrieve him." Holmes stood. "Can you have your men keep Misters Westhouse and Radlett in isolation for another hour or so?"

"I can," replied the inspector. "Here?"

"I think not. We've intruded on Mr. Marchbank too much already. Take them to Baker Street. Watson and I will explain to them later what has happened. We owe them that much."

Westhouse sputtered, especially as Holmes had talked about him as if he wasn't there, but Simon Radlett simply hung his head. I could only wonder at what thoughts were crossing his mind.

Gregson opened the door and murmured a few words to a waiting constable. Then the officer, with four more of them, came in and took custody of the merchant and thief.

Not long after, we were back in our cab, this time with Gregson instead of Radlett. Another group of constables were following behind us. Holmes looked at me. "What needs to be explained?"

I ordered my thoughts. "I believe that I generally understand. When you saw the Huret letter, something about it reminded you of the letters Windibank had typed to his step-daughter, back in 1887. You recognized the defects in the typeface, and possibly the you saw a similarity in the paper." Holmes nodded. "You still had the old letters – I remember you searching for and finding some documents in a folder – and a comparison showed they'd been written by the same man."

"Remarkable," Gregson murmured.

"From there," I continued, "you worked out a long-range plan with Mycroft and the police to keep Windibank under observation – to see about his involvement, if any, with Carnot's assassination."

Holmes nodded. "The operation has grown over the last months as more aspects were discovered. After the youngest James Moriarty fled last spring to the Continent, still strapped into his outlandish Professor costume, we kept an eye on him. When Windibank tied himself to the Carnot assassination with his careless Huret letter, and drew our gaze in his direction as well, it wasn't long before we saw the two of them associating. Neither is a master criminal, although both are consumed with ambition and pleased with their own cleverness.

"It wasn't difficult to scotch their various planned assassinations as the year has progressed. But as their activities have flattened, it was decided that enough is enough, so we intentninally spooked Windibank by putting out word that I was getting close to identifying Huret. He knew that he'd made a mistake sending the letter, so he's likely been anxious ever since. His response, apparently, was to frame Westhouse, or at least involve him, and draw me in at the same time – two birds with one stone, as they say, since Westhouse was apparently going to sack him any day now. Soon we'll know specifically what he intended."

Westhouse's establishment was near the eastern end of Fenchurch Street, where it joins with Leadenhall Street to become the short stretch of Aldgate High Street, which in turn becomes the Whitechapel High Street. It's a narrow but bustling road, and the wine and spirit merchant's building was rather more prosperous-looking that its neighbors. Holmes informed me that the partner, Marbank, had died years earlier, so we didn't have to worry about any interruption by a second irate owner.

We had stopped just up the street, and once we'd alighted, Gregson raised a hand and waved twice. Without any hint as to what was coming, a dozen men, both in and out uniform, bled from nearby buildings, all armed and moving with the air of silent danger hanging about them. These weren't plodding constables, their Size Twelves broken down from endless repetitive rounds. Instead, we saw highly skilled and trained agents of various government branches, and it was good to know that they existed.

A few terse words from Gregson sent two of his men around behind the building, where they would give instructions to the others already waiting there. Then, without any drama at all, we walked quickly into the building.

It was one large room, with a pair of offices at the back, their doors closed. The entire front space was filled with desks, most with a number of men that were either bent over their work or engaged in conversations. To the right, a couple of desks back from the center aisle, was one man who stared straight toward us, even as we approached him at great speed. The initial conversation that was chattering throughout as we entered quickly died, shock filliling the room upon seeing so many grim men, all charging in one direction, with weapons pulled and aiming directly at James Windibank.

The object of our interest was glaring, singularly focused, upon Sherlock Holmes, instantly recognizable in his fore-and-aft cap and Inverness. Then, with a snarling curse, Windibank tried to pull open his desk drawer and reach a hand inside, but Holmes increased his speed and with a single graceful sweep, laid his weighted stick alongside Windibank's jaw, snapping the man's head back and causing his chair to flip over, throwing him to the floor alongside the next desk.

128

There is always something to be said for the direct and unexpected approach.

Holmes's motion carried forward, and he had Windibank jerked upright and in a wrestling hold before the evil little man could gather his wits. His face was swelling, and the skin had split, letting blood run onto his collar. No one made a move to aid him, in the way that a mad dog is to be avoided. Instead, half-a-dozen constables took him from Holmes and confined him immediately in wrist and ankle shackles. Then he was tossed onto the center aisle floor, surrounded by men who either faced him, weapons drawn, or faced outward, similarly armed and holding back any others who might choose to become involved. No one did.

Windibank's thin hair fell over his eyes and stuck to his sweaty face. He fought his bonds while shrieking like a hopeless Bedlam maniac, bloodying his wrists. It became apparent that he was crawling across the floor, bucking up and down like a land-trapped shark, trying to get to Holmes. One of Gregson's men grabbed him by the feet and yanked him back. Windibank suddenly bent double, trying to sink his teeth into the man's hands. After that, he was given a wide berth.

Inside the top drawer of Windibank's desk, we found a button, with wires leading down and under the floor, thence over to Westhouse's office, where an electrically devised dynamite bomb had been cleverly concealed in the man's desk.

Presumably when Holmes came to see Westhouse at eleven, based on the card that Radlett had brought to Baker Street just an hour or so before, Windibank would have detonated the device, killing both the man who was likely going to fire him, as well as the detective who had long served as his nemesis. It didn't matter that many others would have died as well. Windibank, knowing that he was setting off the explosion, had planned to duck and take cover behind his own desk and protect himself. Possibly afterwards, he could have even helped the wounded, presenting himself as a hero.

A handwritten note was found in his desk, implicating Westhouse as the master assassin. It seemed that he planned to toss it somewhere in the rubble just after the explosion.

Windibank twisted around on the floor, always so that he could see Holmes, cursing and promising my friend a painful death for crossing him – or so we assumed, because no one could truly understand his raging bleats by way of his shattered jaw.

"*Holmessss!*" he hissed. "*Holmesessssss . . . .*"

After Windibank was brought to Scotland Yard, he was treated and questioned thoroughly. Like so many men of his wicked ilk, he couldn't help but brag after enough pressure was brought to bear. It always seemed as if that type believed that their clever and boastful explanations would sway the authorities into somehow agreeing with them – as if we would all lean back, once we'd heard it all explained in the *correct* way, and look at one another, nodding at the previously unrealized wisdom and cleverness, and then laughingly step forward and unlock the handcuffs, and possibly shake his hand and apologize

After hearing James Windibank, no one was laughing.

He boasted of crimes that none of us, even Sherlock Holmes, had suspected, from even before Holmes aided the evil man's step-daughter. He explained how he had become more and more bold with his own plans, using the cover of his traveling job to commit a number of crimes in multiple countries, accumulating funds as he did so, but finding that simple riches were not enough. He liked the challenge of operating in the shadows, and he liked bragging about it.

He'd met the youngest James Moriarty in Paris, and they'd found ways in which they might benefit one another. Moriarty had a venture wherein he could make investments based on periods when the markets were destabilized – especially after the shattering events of a string of assassinations. Carnot was a trial run, from which both Moriarty and Windibank made a small fortune.

Afterwards, it was Windibank's idea to propose that the assassinations were being carried out by one man, the fictional Huret, when in fact he would recruit a number of other killers working under that name to confuse the issue – an entire *nest of Hurets*. He'd set this in motion by writing to *The Times*, using old Westfield and Marbank stationery – and only afterwards realizing that the newly returned Holmes, whom he hadn't previously considered, might somehow recall the typewritten letters he'd sent to his step-daughter years before. He knew that Holmes had originally found him then based on the fact that the girl's letters had been written on the wine merchant's typewriter, so he sent no more of them. But he'd been correct in his fears: Though he hadn't known it, and after he finally came to believe that it hadn't been noticed, Holmes was indeed on his scent, and he stayed that way throughout the subsequent months.

When it seemed that Holmes suddenly might be getting closer, according to the recent stories spreading through the underworld, Windibank had the idea to throw Westhouse, whom he greatly disliked, into the fire, using him as lure to kill Holmes, and also chalk up another killing by Huret. He boasted that he had tied some of the false Huret's activities to when Westhouse was visiting the Continent, in the hope of lending further confusion that the business owner might be involved.

Once the affair was completed, and the prevention of a number of crimes throughout the latter half of 1894 could be acknowledged, thanks for Holmes poured in from all quarters. Our sitting room was nearly as deep in congratulatory telegrams as had been Holmes's hotel room in Lyons following the defeat of Baron Maupertuis, also back in '87. After Windibank was hanged, following the much-argued decision of whether he would die in England or France, Holmes even received the French Order of the Legion of Honour, as well as an autographed letter of thanks from the new French President. As was typical of him, they were tossed into a drawer in his desk.

Back in Baker Street on that eventful Guy Fawkes Day, Holmes explained to Westhouse and Simon Radlett just what had happened. Westhouse, suddenly drawn into the affair, cared about nothing besides returning to his business in order to set things right. As quickly as he was involved, he departed. But Radlett seemed to have no interest in leaving, instead remaining seated with his head down.

Holmes retreated to his room for a moment, returning with a bottle. "I bought this last spring, intending to drink it to celebrate when the matter was concluded." He handed it to me. It was a labeled *Champagne Huret*.

"Imported by Westhouse and Marbank," he explained. "Windibank really is a rather arrogant and careless fellow. It didn't initially occur to him that writing Huret's letter on his firm's typewriter might be a poor idea. And he apparently took the assassin's name from one of the primary wines that they sell."

He shook his head and asked if I wanted a glass, but I declined. He then nodded in agreement. "I find that I'm also rather not in the mood myself just now."

Putting it aside, he and I instead settled back with lit pipes, whereupon Holmes asked, "Is there something else, Simon?"

He looked up. "Why am I not under arrest?"

Holmes didn't immediately answer, instead taking several draws upon his pipe.

"I suppose," he finally said, "that I owe a debt – to your half-brother, Alfred. But since he isn't here, I can repay you – and offer you a different path now, if you want it. Alfred was very brave, and did a great deal to help defeat Professor Moriarty, and after all that, I wasn't able to protect him when he . . . when the Professor killed him."

Radlett had been looking at Holmes, perhaps hoping for more, but my friend fell silent once again, lost in his own memories. Those months leading up to Reichenbach had been terrible, the worst that Holmes and I had faced since the battle against the Rippers in the Autumn of Terror.

131

He'd grasped so many ropes during that time, each with its own special aspects and dangers, and no one could fault him when his grip had slipped on a few and something had gone wrong. The matter was so complex, and he'd sacrificed so much to wrest a victory. During his struggle with the Professor, he'd nearly died a dozen times over, but when someone else had perished as part of the struggle, he'd punished himself terribly. I knew that the death of Porlock, and the guilt he carried because of it, would always haunt him.

And perhaps Simon Radlett now realized it too.

"Tell me," said Radlett, his voice little more than a rough whisper. "About what Alf did, and how he helped. And what made it so important for him to choose to be on *your* side."

And Holmes did tell him, including many things that I had not heard before. I tried to listen well, because it wouldn't have been suitable just then for me to take notes, and I wanted to remember all of it for when I had the chance later that night to record yet another chapter in the great ongoing battle when Sherlock Holmes had vanquished the dragon of our age.

When I look at the three massive manuscript volumes which contain our work for the year 1894, I confess that it is very difficult for me, out of such a wealth of material, to select the cases which are most interesting in themselves, and at the same time most conducive to a display of those peculiar powers for which my friend was famous. As I turn over the pages, I see . . . the tracking and arrest of Huret, the Boulevard assassin – an exploit which won for Holmes an autograph letter of thanks from the French President and the Order of the Legion of Honour.
– Dr. John H. Watson
"The Golden Pince-Nez"

"There's a cold-blooded scoundrel!" said Holmes, laughing, as he threw himself down into his chair once more. "That fellow will rise from crime to crime until he does something very bad, and ends on a gallows.
– Sherlock Holmes
"A Case of Identity"

NOTES

The Other Moriartys

Colonel Moriarty's vicious attacks on Watson during Holmes's supposed death were brilliantly retrieved from the Tin Dispatch Box by Marcia Wilson and presented as five novel-length adventures: *The MoonCursers*, *A Sword for Defense*, *The Narrow Path*, *The End of All Things*, and *A Fanged and Bitter Thing*.

The narratives describing the youngest Moriarty, who oddly tried to fool everyone into thinking he was his older brother by way of an elaborate disguise and harnesses and straps, were edited by John Gardner: *Moriarty's Return*, *Moriarty's Revenge*, and *Moriarty*.

The Other Hurets

Some of the cases in the latter half of 1894 in which Holmes defeated the other Hurets include:

- "The Adventure of the Boulevard Assassin" *1894: Some Cases of Mr. Sherlock Holmes* – Hugh Ashton
- "The Boulevard Assassin", *The Confidential Casebook of Sherlock Holmes* – Kathleen Brady
- "The Adventure of the Boulevard Assassin", [Internet Fan Fiction] – Sarah G. Hadley
- *Sherlock Holmes and the Boulevard Assassin* – John Hall
- "Huret, the Boulevard Assassin", *My Dear Holmes* – David Hammer
- "The Case of the Unseen Assassin", *Sherlock Holmes & Mr. Mac* – Gary Lovisi
- "The Boulevard Assassin", *The Continued Casebook of Sherlock Holmes* – J.A. Roberts
- "The Boulevard Assassin", *The Secret Documents of Sherlock Holmes* – June Thomson
- "The Adventure of the Parisian Gentleman", *The Mammoth Book of New Sherlock Holmes Stories* – Robert Weinberg and Lois H. Gresh

The following adventure, while not specifically about the Boulevard Assassin, provides peripheral details about one of the other Hurets:

- "The Adventure of the Red Barrow Horror", *Sherlock Holmes: The Impossible Cases* – Daniel McGachey

Holmes's bottle of *Champagne Huret* should not be confused with the current company manufacturing *Champagne Huret Colas*, as the latter apparently went into business in 1960. Their association with the name *Huret* is unknown.

https://www.champagne-huret-colas.com/la-maison

A Sudden Death
at the Savoy
by Dan Rowley and Don Baxter

"Well, well, if it isn't the esteemed author indeed!" said Mycroft Holmes. "Allow me to shake your hand, Doctor, if I may be so bold as to offer my 'flipper'."

My friend, Sherlock Holmes at that moment entered our sitting room from his adjacent sleeping quarters. He looked over at our visitor.

"Mycroft, what have you said to Watson?"

"What makes you think such a thing?"

"He is completely flushed. His eyes are roving around the room, and his mouth is agape, as if he is at a loss for words. The obvious conclusion is that you said something to disconcert him."

"I was merely complementing him once more upon his literary efforts," replied Mycroft, with an attempted air of innocence.

"You must have made some reference, yet again, to his somewhat unflattering description of you. It was published two years ago, and as I've repeatedly told you, he embellished for melodramatic effect. Don't be so sensitive. After all, he did include my admission that you are the superior in observation and deduction. And I stand by my statement that those qualities, without ambition and energy, are insufficient to bring wrong-doers to justice. In any event, you obviously didn't venture out from your normal haunts to hold a literary forum. Come, Watson, let us sit down. I see that Mrs. Hudson has brought coffee, and that Mycroft has helped himself. Let us do the same."

Throughout the conversation, from the time of Mycroft's unexpected entrance, I had been silent, once again regretting the description of the man that I'd published in 1893 while relating the problem presented to us by Mr. Melas. Mycroft occasionally teased me about it, and appeared to be unconcerned, but I wondered . . . .

Once we had settled ourselves, Mycroft Holmes (who, I must say, looks exactly as I have described him, if I might be indulged in a moment of authorial defense) cleared his throat. "It requires no great deductive ability to divine that I have come to enlist your services. You probably have read of the visit of Cardinal Tosca to our shores, but you may not know why he is here."

"I suspect he is here," repeated Holmes, "to hold discussion with certain Anglo-Catholics over the question of whether Church of England clerical orders might be absorbed into or approved by the Catholic Church."

I must admit I was a bit startled by Holmes's familiarity with such an esoteric subject, but his brother placidly continued. "Yes. Doctor. You may be unaware, but some prominent Anglo-Catholics, including Lord Halifax, wrote to the Pope asking that he rule that Anglican ordinations are valid as a first step to attempting to move England closer to the See of Rome. The Pope formed a commission to study the matter, and sent Cardinal Tosca here to explore the sentiment of certain members of the Catholic faith.

"Because of the domestic and foreign policy implications of this situation, I was given the working brief of Her Majesty's Government to keep a discreet eye on the Cardinal."

Holmes nodded. "The domestic ramifications are obvious for Her Majesty as head of the Church. And I assume the Vatican's recent strengthening of ties with Italy, France, Scotland, and Ireland have the attention of your colleagues in the Foreign Office."

"Obviously. In any event, the Cardinal had dinner last evening with four men in a private room at the Savoy. At the conclusion of the meal, during brandy and cigars, the Cardinal suddenly dropped dead, apparently of a heart attack."

"Is there any indication of foul play?" I asked.

"Not yet. And I fear we may not be able to perform an autopsy, as the Vatican is demanding the immediate return of the body."

"Mycroft, I have no desire to become involved in such an ambiguous matter – especially when surely any relevant physical evidence is long gone."

"Well, you see, there you are wrong. I had the foresight to have a young chap from the Home Office at the dinner last night, posing as a waiter. I had given him rather strict instructions not only to report what he heard, but be on the watch for anything unusual. Fortunately, once he realized the Cardinal was dead, he was smart enough to reveal his identity and order the room sealed. He had a letter from me informing anyone official to cooperate with him. He used that to summon the police to guard the room."

"I'm still not sure this is a matter for me, rather than the police, unless you suspect something of interest."

"It is more complex than that. The young man immediately notified me. Because the Vatican was aware of my role, I sent them a telegram last night. Here is the reply I received several hours ago."

136

He handed a paper to Holmes, who studied it with an increasingly serious regard. He handed it over to me. I reproduce the contents here:

Signor Holmes,

I have discussed this matter with His Holiness, who appreciates your discretion and sense of delicacy. So that there is no cause for tension between the Holy See and your country, His Holiness politely requests that you have your brother, Sherlock Holmes, look into this matter. His Holiness will pray for the success of your brother's efforts, whatever the facts may be (God willing).

Sincerely,
Cardinal M.

When I had finished, I looked at my friend. He was sitting with his eyes closed, and his brother and I knew what this portended. Finally, he opened them and sighed. "I cannot refuse such a request as that. Please provide what details you have."

"The dinner was held in the Wellington Room at the Savoy. There are only two entrances to it, and both were under watch by Home Office men. The only persons to enter were Wright, the man posing as a waiter, and the five guests."

"And the kitchen staff?"

"We investigated all of them. None has a whiff of suspicion."

"I will be the judge of that, if necessary. Tell me about the five men who dined last night."

"Cardinal Tosca, of course. He worked his way through the clerical ranks and has been serving at the Curia in the Vatican for some time. He and the current Pope apparently didn't agree with some of the more extreme statements of the previous pope, especially those regarding social matters such as the rights of workers. He was a close adviser and ally of Pope Leo, by whom he was elevated to his current position as a member of the cardinalate.

"Three of the other guests were Anglo-Catholics: Adam Clough is a solicitor, but also something of an intellectual. He never had met Tosca before this trip, but was included last night for his many writings on religious topics, particularly the potential acceptance of the Anglican Church hierarchy by the Vatican. Robert Ramsay is a merchant who served many years abroad in places such as Marseille and Saint Petersburg. At one time, he was stationed in Bologna, where he was converted to Catholicism by Tosca, who was bishop there at the time. They are quite close. The third Anglo-Catholic is Quentin Hunter, a banker here in the City. He had ties with advisors to the former pope, so we believe Tosca viewed him as a representative figure in that regard. Tosca and Hunter may have met during one or more of Hunter's trips to Rome after Tosca moved to the Curia.

"The final guest was Thomas Smythe, who handles European affairs at the Foreign Office. He is somewhere between High and Low Church Anglican. Tosca knew him from Smythe's involvement in certain Vatican matters, and felt Smythe was a way to take the temperature of Anglican opinion. Naturally, Smythe also could keep watch on any foreign affairs implications of the discussions. Is there anything else you would like to know, Sherlock?"

"I believe that will be all for now. I want to consult my indices first. Then I shall change, and Watson and I will proceed to the Savoy. Please notify the men on guard we are coming. I also want to interview the four guests and the Home Office man. I'm not sure of the order as yet, so can you arrange for them to come to the Savoy and be placed in a room with a man on guard so that they don't attempt to communicate with one another."

"Certainly."

"I may also have questions as I proceed."

"As the Good Doctor so diligently noted in his writings, I shall be in my office, and then at the Diogenes Club."

"Fine. I will contact you as needed." Mycroft Holmes bade us goodbye with no further references to my writing. Holmes went over to the shelves and withdrew one of his scrapbooks, the compilation of clippings and other material related to matters that might be required in one of his investigations. While he was deeply engrossed in that, I slipped upstairs to my room to change into more suitable attire, as the weather was quite blustery and cold this early in the year. When I returned, Holmes had also changed and was putting on his hat and coat, as did I. We went downstairs to hail a cab, which proceeded by way of Soho and past Trafalgar Square. We pulled into the entry way between the Hotel and the Theatre, coming to the magnificent entrance. I was frankly excited to be here, as the Hotel was only six years old, the first to be fully equipped with the new electric lights. We passed through the opulent lobby, after obtaining directions from the supercilious doorman.

After identifying ourselves to the man on guard, he unlocked the door and allowed us to enter. The Wellington Room was rectangular in shape, but quite large. We entered through one of the shorter sides, and the doorway was near the corner. To our left was a large fireplace. The room was richly furnished with mahogany, elegant chandeliers, deep red velvet, and Persian rugs scattered around the hardwood floor. There were two chairs in front of the fireplace, but most of the remainder of the furniture, chairs, and occasional tables had been placed along the walls to accommodate the circular table in the center of the room, where presumably the five guests had dined the previous evening. There were several small tables between the large table and the fireplace. On them rested ash trays with partially smoked cigars and glasses, each containing what appeared to be the dregs of brandy.

As we stood with our backs to the door, I noticed on the right hand wall a number of hangings and cases that held memorabilia, presumably from the Duke of Wellington. At the other end of that wall was another door, likely a service entrance. That supposition was strengthened by a large service table against the short wall opposite us. On the long wall to the left there were three windows, and between the window closest to the fireplace and the wall was a sideboard with several decanters and an open box of cigars. I saw a partially smoked cigar lying on the floor near the sideboard, which seemed to have fallen while lit, given the carpet beneath evidenced some scorching.

"Any initial observations, Watson?"

"I would say they had dinner over there at the large table. After that, as Mycroft had stated, they stood and obtained drinks and cigars from the nearby sideboard. They then stood around chatting, using the small tables to rest their drinks and dispose of the cigar ash. The cigar lying on the floor there may be where the Cardinal collapsed."

"Excellent. Your exposure to my methods has begun to bear fruit. With that in mind, I shall conduct a more minute inspection."

Holmes then slowly walked around the room, peering intensely at everything. He went down on his hands and knees to examine things even more closely. Being long familiar with this process and how long it would take, I decided to amuse myself by looking over the memorabilia along the right hand wall. It proved to be a treasure trove, including Wellington's uniform and a sword, a diorama of the Waterloo battlefield, and a large number of documents signed by him, including the dispatch to the Government announcing his famous victory.

I was so absorbed in all this that I didn't notice Holmes had finished and walked over to me. "My friend, if you can tear yourself away, I'm ready to commence. Could you kindly tell the guard to send in Wright, the Home Office man? I believe the large table will serve our purpose admirably."

I did so, and we were soon joined by a young man in his twenties with nondescript features, dull eyes, and fair hair. An altogether forgettable

139

personage, which suited the Home Office's purposes in posting him here. After introductions were made, we took our seats, and Holmes began his questioning.

"I understand you were posted here by the Her Majesty's Government. Were you the only servant to enter the room after the guests arrived?"

"Yes, sir. I also set the table before they arrived."

"Did you notice anything odd about the appearance of the glasses, the plates, or the cutlery?"

"No, sir. It all appeared normal to me. It also was fine to the touch. I would have noticed had anyone tampered with any of it, if that is what you are asking, as I have had special training."

"Very well. Please describe the events of the evening. Leave nothing out, however trivial it may seem." Holmes leaned back and closed his eyes, but I knew he heard and was picturing everything with his powerful mind.

"Well, after they arrived, they sat at the table. The Cardinal was directly across from the window there. Going clockwise, Mister Ramsay was to his left, then Mister Hunter, Mister Clough, and lastly Mister Smythe on the Cardinal's right. I then brought over the first platter, which was already on the serving table."

"Platter? You mean you didn't serve each guest with individual portions?"

"No, sir. Apparently it was some kind of Italian tradition to honor the Cardinal. I brought each platter over and placed it before the Cardinal. He then served each of the guests, with himself being last. He did the same with each bottle of wine, which I uncorked and decanted for him."

"I will explore that with the guests later. How many courses were there?"

"Six, sir. First some cured meats and cheeses. That was followed by soup, some type of what I think they referred to as 'pasta' (which looked like macaroni to me), veal, a salad, and finally fruit."

"I believe that is a typical Italian repast."

I couldn't refrain. "But that is extraordinary! The great Escoffier has been hired here to showcase the finest French cuisine. I cannot imagine he would agree to such a menu."

"Sir, they brought in an Italian cook to do the meal – I guess to honor the Cardinal."

Holmes continued. "We will also inquire into that. What took place after dinner?"

"They all stood up from the table and went over to the sideboard. The Cardinal served everyone a drink, and then opened a box of cigars and handed them out to all the guests."

140

"Just a few more questions. Did the Cardinal serve everyone brandy from the same decanter?"

"Yes, sir."

"Could you see if the cigar box was sealed?"

"The Cardinal unwrapped it and broke the seal. He went around and offered the box to each guest, and then took one for himself."

"Were you in the room while they were having brandy and cigars?"

"No, sir. While the Cardinal was serving them, I stood by the service door. When he was finished, I made sure they needed nothing further and left the room. I did come back in when I heard a commotion. The Cardinal was lying on the floor by the sideboard, and Mister Ramsay ran out the main entrance."

"Does everything appear to be the same now as when you came back in the room?"

Wright carefully looked around the room. ""Yes."

"Did you hear anything of interest in the conversation during the evening?"

"No, sir. I'd been instructed what to listen for regarding Vatican politics, foreign affairs, and so forth. There was none of that. Just general chatting about people's family, business affairs, the quality of the food, and such."

"If you will indulge me, I've made a study of regional dialects, and I like to test my knowledge. The guests might not appreciate it, but I assume you don't mind."

"Not at all, sir."

"You are, I take it, from Manchester."

"Why, that is amazing. Yes, my family has lived there for several generations."

"As I thought. You have been quite helpful, Wright. You may go now."

After he had left, Holmes looked inquiringly at me. "What say you, Watson?"

"I assume we must talk to the others, given the nature of your commission, but it certainly sounds to me that the Cardinal died of natural causes. The staff was investigated, and the condition of the service ware on the table and the method of serving the food, drinks, and cigars would rule out any administration of poison. Unless you can divine any other way of disposing of the Cardinal, such as a poison dart, I would say this is fairly straightforward."

Holmes chuckled. "You have been writing too many stories. Poisoned darts indeed! We'll speak to Ramsay next, but first I want to send a note to Mycroft." Holmes withdrew some paper and a pen from his pocket and scribbled several lines. He carefully folded the paper, went to the door, and spoke briefly to the guard.

About five minutes later, Robert Ramsay, the merchant, entered. He wasn't quite as tall as Holmes, slim, handsome, with a broad smile and bright eyes. Although in his early fifties, he had what some might consider a boyish charm, which probably helped him in his business dealings.

Ramsay sat down with us. "It is a pleasure to meet both of you. This is a most distressing situation, so anything I can do help, I will, although frankly, I'm not sure why you're here."

Holmes nodded. "An understandable question. I was asked by the highest authority in Rome to conduct an inquiry to ensure the Cardinal's sudden death doesn't create any diplomatic tensions."

"Of course, that makes sense. Terrible rumors are always afloat, especially when it come to us Catholics – plotters who will stop at nothing, and all that rot. Ask away."

"I understand you have known the Cardinal for some time."

"Yes. We met in Bologna some twenty years ago when he was Bishop there."

"How did you come to meet?"

"I had always been interested in the Catholic faith. He had somehow heard that and asked me to visit him. We began to meet rather regularly, and then he suggested I should convert. I began the normal inquiry, where he taught me basic Catholic doctrine to ensure I had a deep enough understanding, and I moved quickly to studying the catechism with him. That, of course, is a deeper reflection on the sacraments, and so forth. He and I then went on a retreat together. I had to accomplish another phase of reflection, until he was satisfied and baptized me, heard my confession, and then administered communion."

"How long did all that take?"

"A little over a year."

"Very interesting. I take it you two were quite close."

"Oh, yes. After I left Bologna for my next posting, we continued to correspond. Of course, once he achieved elevation, that became more infrequent, but we kept in touch."

"Can you describe for us your involvement in the current visit."

"When the Cardinal knew he was coming to London, he asked to see me. Shortly after he arrived, we met here in his suite at the Savoy. He expressed his desire to hold a small, informal dinner with individuals who represented a range of views on the Anglo-Catholic situation. He'd read some of the writings of Adam Clough and suggested him. I'm not sure if he ever met Quentin Hunter, but he probably had, and suggested him. I thought it would be useful to have someone from the Government here, so

142

that he could see the issues in a more sympathetic and less-polemic setting. He knew Thomas Smythe, so we included him to get a non-Catholic viewpoint."

"We'll return to the other attendees in a moment. Who made the decision to have the meal conducted the way it was?"

Ramsay smiled wistfully. "Mister Holmes, that typified the Cardinal. In addition to being wise and almost saintly, he was jovial and quite sociable. He wanted to have an Italian meal where he could act as *pater familias*, serving everything himself to show to the guests how he cared for them and wished to provide for their needs, physical and spiritual. There was a certain symbolism in it that, to him, might ease the course of future discussions.

"At first, the kitchen here refused to cook Italian food. I went to Charles Ritz, the manager, and explained the situation. He seemed quite amused, and we agreed to bring in the great chef, Cesare Montini, to prepare the meal. I'm sure Ritz had to mollify Escoffier in some manner. When I told the Cardinal, his response was typical: 'Robert, the Good Lord always provides for his servants'."

"How involved was the Cardinal in the selection of the food, drinks, cigars, and so forth?"

"He chose everything – all his favorites. To be honest, I was a bit concerned. You may not be aware, but the Cardinal had a heart condition that required regular medication. I worried that the rich food, alcohol, and tobacco wouldn't be good for him. In fact, before he arrived and the rest of us were here, Clough asked me if the Cardinal should be having a meal like this, and both Hunter and Smythe indicated their agreement. I told them the Cardinal had assured me he would be fine as long as I didn't tell his doctor."

"So, this condition was fairly well known."

"I believe so."

"Let us return to the guests and their views on the Anglo-Catholic situation. How would you characterize them?"

"Starting with Clough, he is what would be called a 'liberal' on the question. By that, I mean he felt the Church should be as lenient as possible on the question of whether Anglican ordination and similar questions were consonant with Catholic structure and doctrine. If I were to speculate based on some oblique phrases in his writings, he might have been worried that Pope Leo, guided by the Cardinal, might not go far enough.

"Ironically, Hunter might also have been concerned from the opposite perspective. As a 'conservative', he would want strict adherence to every Catholic nuance. He has made some remarks to me that suggest the

Cardinal was too 'soft', in his words, and would unduly influence the Pope to be conciliatory.

"As to Smythe, you probably know more than I do. The Foreign Office likely has views, but where Smythe stands I have no idea."

"And what of you?"

"I am more moderate. I would rather Lord Halifax hadn't suggested this entire enquiry. As long as Anglo-Catholics have no civil encumbrances and can worship in peace, I would let the whole thing go. The history and position of the Anglican faith is rather unique, and I see no good from this exercise."

"We're almost finished. During the course of the evening, did you see anyone tamper with the Cardinal's food or drink, such as dropping anything into it?"

"Of course not."

"Were you the first to arrive, and if so, was there any food or drink on the serving table or the sideboard?"

"Smythe and I arrived together a bit early. We were in the lobby at the same moment and came up. There was no food in the room. After the Cardinal arrived, the waiter started putting wine and food on the serving table."

"And the brandy?"

"About halfway through the meal, the waiter brought the bottle out, showed it to the Cardinal, and then decanted it."

"What about the cigars?"

"After unsealing the box, the Cardinal handed them out to us, and we all smoked the ones he gave us."

"Did anyone jostle or touch the Cardinal, especially after dinner?"

"No. When he entered, each of us bowed in turn and he blessed us. I don't think anyone touched him at all."

"Do you see anything out of place in the room, or different from when the Cardinal collapsed?"

"Well, of course my main focus was the Cardinal. But as I look around, I don't see anything different."

"Thank you, Mister Ramsay. You have been quite helpful. Please remain here at the Savoy in the event we have more questions. Kindly asked Smythe to join us."

Several minutes went by, during which Holmes closed his eyes and pursed his lips. He became alert when there was a soft knock on the door and it opened. Thomas Smythe was almost the parody of a career Foreign Office official – early sixties, bald, bland features, near-sighted, with an ingratiating look about him. He made some innocuous murmurings about the honor of meeting Mycroft Holmes's illustrious brother. As he took his seat, Holmes commenced.

"We have been informed that you have had dealings with Cardinal Tosca prior to his current trip here."

"Yes. I am tasked with European affairs at the Office. Pope Leo is quite conversant with diplomacy, having for example once served as Nuncio in Belgium. As you may know, he has been concerned to temper the views of his predecessor about the relationship of the Catholic Church to modern trends. That includes how he interacts with other powers. He has made conciliatory gestures to Russia and Germany, urged French Catholics to support the Republic, and defended the Church against the attempted encroachments of the Italian government. That naturally has required me to interact with him and his representatives. I've made several trips to Rome to hold discussions with both Pope Leo and Cardinal Tosca."

"What are your views on all that?"

"Of course, I follow official Government policy. We believe in a stance of cautious neutrality."

"And your personal views? They will remain between us."

"It is hard to penetrate the Vatican. Pope Leo has a mixed record. He tends to support the *status quo*, as he has done in France. But I did worry that the Cardinal tended to take a more activist line."

"Can you give me an example or two?"

"Well, take Ireland. There, the Vatican ordered priests not to become involved in anti-English activity. But in India, they established a complete hierarchy for the Church, which I believe sends a mixed signal to the local populace, in the sense that it suggests England, and its own hierarchy, may not be a suitable adjunct to colonial rule. We have heard rumors that similar doings may be attempted in Scotland. If I had to guess, Ireland demonstrates Pope Leo's hand, and India and Scotland the Cardinal's."

Holmes nodded, and then proceeded to review the events of the prior evening. Smythe's recollections matched those of Ransom: They arrived together, Smythe observed no opportunity to add anything to food or drink, the Cardinal served everyone from common sources, no one had touched him, and so forth. Holmes sat for a moment. "How did the Cardinal seem to you last night?"

"Very jovial. He was a quite-gracious host."

"While you were all enjoying brandy and cigars, where was everyone?"

"We were all mingling with each other. I would say there was fairly constant movement."

"Did everyone at one time or another come over to speak to the Cardinal?"

"Yes. He was mostly over by the large table, enjoying his cigar and brandy. We all went over in one's or two's to chat with him."

"Where were you and the others when the Cardinal fell to the ground?"

"I was over by the fireplace with Ramsay. Hunter and Clough were near that small table over by where we ate. The Cardinal had walked over to the sideboard, and it appeared he was going to replenish his brandy. He suddenly grasped his chest and fell over."

"And then what happened?"

"We all rushed over. Ramsay and I got there first. He knelt down to feel the Cardinal's pulse. He quickly got up, said he was going to find a doctor, then rushed from the room by the main door. He returned shortly with a small, stout man who appeared to be the hotel physician. He examined the Cardinal and told us he was dead. At that point, the waiter, who must have come in through the service door during the commotion, announced that he was from the Home Office and we should touch nothing. He sent Ramsay to fetch a constable."

"Were you aware that the Cardinal had a heart condition?"

"Yes, I believe it was common knowledge. There has been speculation in the press what Pope Leo would do if he were deprived of the services of his closest advisor."

"Thank you for your time. I realize you may need to return to the Foreign Office to report to your superiors. You may tell them that the Doctor and I have a bit more to do, but we will call you back when we are done." As Smythe reached the door, the officer on guard motioned that he had something for us. I went over to retrieve an envelope addressed to Holmes, which I brought to him. It contained two sheets of paper. My friend scrutinized them carefully, then gazed for some time into the fire. He had the distant look that I knew meant his brain was absorbing, rearranging, and analyzing whatever the two sheets contained.

"Watson, I begin to see the end. Let us speak to the last two guests, then I'll want to hear your views. Please have Clough brought in." I spoke to the officer and returned to my seat. Holmes had lit his pipe and was contentedly puffing on his favorite shag. He made no motion when there was a knock on the door, and a thin, bird-like man with a sharp face, darting eyes, and brown hair entered the room. He was in his mid-forties, and it seemed that today was a day for men who fit the stereotype of their profession. Like Smythe, the prototypical Foreign Office Mandarin, Clough exuded "solicitor" from every pore.

Holmes nodded solemnly and began with the chronology the previous evening's dinner. Clough was the fourth to arrive, after Ramsay, Smythe, and Hunter were already present. Holmes painstakingly took him through all the questions he had put to our first two witnesses, and Clough's account didn't vary in any significant way.

"Very good, Clough. Precise and detailed, as one would expect from your profession. Please enlighten us as to why you were invited."

"Ahem, rather. I didn't know the Cardinal other than by reputation. I believe he knew me by mine. If I might be permitted a bit of immodesty (which I normally eschew), I have written somewhat extensively on the question of whether Anglican orders – that is to say, its hierarchy – comply with the canons of the Catholic Church. As an avocation, I have made a rather extensive study of theology, canon law, and church history."

"In another life, you might have been a professor of religion."

"Er, well. I have tried to increase my talent, in the sense the good Lord Christ meant, so as to help others. I was quite flattered that my views had reached such an important personage as the Cardinal – Dare I venture to hope even His Holiness himself."

"Would you share with us the nature of your views?"

Clough leaned forward, eyes shining. I hoped Holmes hadn't opened the door to a lengthy and tedious disquisition. "Ahem. The simplest way to explain is that I believe the Anglican orders are fully consonant with the principles of Catholicism. You see – "

Holmes thankfully intervened. "I would be delighted to explore this further with you at a future time. As I am sure you can appreciate, I must remain focused on the task to which the Pope has commanded me. Do you believe the Cardinal shared your views? I sense you are reluctant. Given the source of my authority, please be frank."

"*Hrrumph.* I suspect the Cardinal did not agree with me. He likely was willing to broker some compromise, but that would require alterations to the Anglican structure. Those may not be acceptable to the Established Church here in England. Pope Leo might be more accommodating. I have written on the situation under Henry VIII that clearly demonstrates – "

"Yes, yes, I am sure. I must apologize, but we still need to talk to Mister Hunter."

A look of disdain passed over Clough's countenance. He spoke without, for once, clearing his throat. "He and I don't see eye-to-eye, but then he hasn't spent the time I have in the necessary scholarship. I will inform the officer you wish to see Hunter. Please don't hesitate to call on me for any further assistance that you may require."

We sat companionably in silence until the door burst open. In strode the banker, Quentin Hunter, a man in his fifties with grey hair, a stout figure, and a plump face with fiery eyes and a scowling mouth. Here was a man used to having his every command obeyed. "I say, this is a d-----

nuisance! I have fortunes to look after, and my associates require constant supervision."

"I am sorry to impose on your valuable time, sir. Had anyone other than the Pope asked for my help, I wouldn't have bothered you. But like you, I must be thorough and attend to every detail. Now I'm sure that a man of your ability can recall the events of last night in perfect detail. As you do with your accounts, leave nothing out."

Hunter glared at Holmes but took a seat. He brusquely recounted what had transpired. It coincided with what the other four had relayed.

"Perfect. Just a few questions. Did you know Cardinal before this trip."

"I had met him and Pope Leo when my wife and I visited Rome. We had a very pleasant discussion of the policies of his predecessor, Pius IX, of blessed memory."

"So, you are more aligned with the thoughts and policies of Pope Pius?"

"There would be none of this folderol about the Anglican orders under him. The idea that those orders are acceptable to a true Catholic is absurd! Pope Leo was too swayed by Cardinal Tosca, if you want my opinion. They need some good, blunt English common sense, and to stop bothering with this whole issue."

"One final question: Were you aware that the Cardinal had a heart problem?"

"Of course. Everyone knew. After dinner, that fool, Clough, was nattering on about how the Cardinal needed to be careful of his consumption of what was on offer. Kept asking everyone if they knew. Even when we said we did, he wouldn't stop. Once the man gets on a subject, he will not budge."

"Thank you, Mister Hunter. We should be done shortly. Please join the others, but we'll try and get you back to the bank as quickly as possible." Holmes accompanied him to the door and, once he was out of hearing, gave some instructions to the officer. He returned to the table, relit his pipe, and looked over. "Well, who do you see as having a motive here."

"Motive! So you believe it was murder? But how? Everyone agreed that no one could have tampered with the food, drink, or cigars. The Cardinal served everything from the same source, which would be relatively random and rules out anything being added at some other location. No one brushed against him or otherwise touched him. The man had a known heart condition and was indulging in rich food and drink and using tobacco. All that, it seems to me, points to a natural death by heart failure."

"Let us leave that aside for the moment. Who has motive?"

"That is more troublesome, I will admit. Ramsay, Clough, and Hunter all – for very different reasons – disagree with the purpose of Tosca's mission here in London. Clough believes Tosca was more conservative than himself and thus might have influenced the Pope in a stricter approach than Clough would prefer. Somewhat paradoxically, Hunter believed Tosca was more liberal than his views and might persuade the Pope to be too lenient to the Anglican hierarchy. And Ramsay prefers the issue of the relation of the Anglican orders to those of the Catholic Church not be raised at all. As to Smythe, I infer he disagrees with certain portions of the Vatican's foreign policy and the role of the Cardinal in that. But to me, any of those varying views would lead to murder only if held by a fanatic. None of the four gentleman strikes me as being fanatical, although you likely are a better judge of that."

"What of Wright?"

"The waiter from the Home Office? I detected nothing in him that points to motive."

"Watson, you *hear*, but at times don't *comprehend* the significance of what you have heard. Read this." He handed me one of the pieces of paper he'd had received earlier from his brother. I was stupefied.

"So, Wright's family has been heavily involved in anti-Catholic activities."

"Yes, I wondered about that when I heard his accent. As you may know, there was a large influx of Irish immigrants in Manchester following the potato famine. Because of resentment over the threat of lost jobs to these Irish Catholics, and general religious prejudice, Manchester has become a seed bed of anti-Catholicism, often of a violent nature. I asked Mycroft to look into Wright's family. The paper you have presents his findings."

"Well, I suppose that's another motive. And one might say he wasn't as forthcoming as the others as to this matter."

"True, but a clever villain might go out of his way to state something, especially if it is easily discoverable, on the assumption that such openness itself could divert suspicion. The mind of a criminal often can exhibit such deviousness."

"There is still the question of whether Wright is fanatical enough to want to murder a Prince of the Church merely to fulfill some blood lust. And the same objections as to how a murder was carried out apply to him as well."

At that moment, before Holmes could comment, his brother knocked and entered. "Well, Sherlock, I have followed your instructions. Extra Home Office men have accompanied me. Two are stationed behind the service door, and the others are discretely concealed in adjacent rooms. What would you like to do now?"

"Watson, help me arrange these chairs into a semi-circle of five facing the fireplace. We will also place two more off to the side for you and Mycroft. Please make sure that you and he are positioned so that you can observe the five men's expressions and bodily movements. "

"Sherlock, this seems quite melodramatic." He smiled. "You have apparently been associating with the Doctor too long."

Holmes ignored his brother, and we proceeded to arrange the room as he wished. He then went over to the service door and spoke softly with the two men on the other side. He crossed to the main door and again held a low conversation.

A few minutes later, Clough, Hunter, Ramsay, Smythe, and Wright entered the room, and Holmes invited them to take chairs in the semi-circle. Four of them looked perplexed, and Hunter began to bluster. "What is the meaning of this charade? You assured me you were finished and we could leave soon."

"I didn't say I was finished. If you will be seated, that will expedite this process, and then indeed we shall be finished."

After the five were seated, and Mycroft Holmes and I took our places, Sherlock Holmes sternly surveyed the five, and then commenced to speak.

"As you know, the Pope asked me to come here and determine whether there was anything suspicious about the sudden death of Cardinal Tosca. Apparently, he was concerned that rumors might begin to circulate that could damage the relations of the Vatican and Great Britain."

Clough interrupted. "Ahem, we understand the caution of His Holiness, but I fail to see anything suspicious about last night. As one trained in the law, I am attuned to be keenly aware of any situation."

Sherlock Holmes smiled slightly. "Yes, the Good Doctor correctly pointed out that it seemed there was no way anyone could have caused the Cardinal's demise. He served everyone their food, drink, and cigars. The beverages were opened in front of all of you. The cigars were sealed up, and he opened them. Only by sheer luck could a murderer trust that mere chance would kill the Cardinal rather than one of the four guests. And no one touched him, and no one heard or saw anything unusual. It appeared that the Cardinal's death was natural – but perhaps that is exactly what a clever murderer would intend."

Smythe interjected, "And I would add that none of us have the slightest motive to commit such a dastardly deed."

"Let us look at that. Please don't interrupt, but bear with me as I walk us through this. The three Catholic guests all have very different views, ranging from liberal desire that the Pope will accommodate the Anglican

150

orders, to a conservative hope that he will not, to a more moderate desire that the entire issue not be raised at all. But all three of you share one thing: The notion that Cardinal Tosca was influential enough to sway the Pope away from your own point of view. As illogical as that might seem on the face of it, my long study of human nature persuades me that such is the all-too-frequent result of strongly held beliefs.

"You, Smythe, share the same commonality with the other three guests in your fear that the Cardinal would persuade the Pope against policies you favor, although the root of those policies is political rather than religious. Of course, history is replete with examples of murderers motivated by political beliefs as strong as any religious tenet.

"There are several objections to these four motives, however. As Doctor Watson correctly pointed out to me, such motives would almost necessarily have to rise to the level of fanaticism to drive a man to murder. None of the four of you strike me as a fanatic. It's almost impossible to conceal such zeal, and the Doctor and I surely would have picked up on it, which we did not.

"A second objection is that these motives rest on the premise that eliminating the Cardinal would ensure that the Pope would make the decision the murderer desired. From all evidence, Pope Leo has a mind of his own. However influential the Cardinal was, only a fool would believe his elimination would alter the Pope's course. I doubt that even the Pope's repugnance at the murder of his advisor would sway him from his course, given his strongly held beliefs. Indeed, it might even strengthen his determination.

"That does leave one other motive along this line: Sheer hatred and a desire to make a statement by killing the Cardinal, regardless of the impact that had on the Pope. In parts of this country there are, unfortunately, strong currents of anti-Catholicism that might lead a man to such an act – for example, in Manchester."

Wright turned a bright red and began to rise from his seat. "Why, of all the – !"

Holmes gestured to him to sit, although he remained standing, looking with disgust at my friend. "Yes, Wright, the vetting process at the Home Office isn't as thorough as they think. My brother confirmed your family background. Please resume your seat."

One of the Home Office men took Wright by the arm and pushed him down. Wright stared sullenly at Holmes. Hunter once again began to bluster. "This is all well and good, but you have told us nothing to show us a murder was in fact committed."

"*Four* cigars, not *five*. That is what first pointed in the correct direction." The five men all looked at each other. At what must have been a prearranged signal, the service door opened and two men entered the room and advanced toward the semi-circle.

"Allow me to explain: You all have confirmed that this room is still arranged as it was shortly after the Cardinal collapsed." They all nodded. "Do not just see the room – *observe it*." I didn't perceive what Holmes was getting at, but his brother stirred next to me, about to say something. Then he thought better of breaking Holmes's hold over the five men.

"There are five brandy snifters – four on the occasional tables, and one, the Cardinal's, on the sideboard where he had gone to refill it. I examined all five, even taking a bit of the contents of each on my finger to smell and taste it. Nothing untoward.

"Now the cigars. There is one by where the Cardinal fell, and only *three* on the occasional tables. I also examined them, again nothing untoward.

"Where, though, is the fifth cigar? I carefully looked over the fireplace and discovered a cigar lying beside the andiron, away from the fire. Here it is." He reached into his pocket and extracted an envelope. I realized he must have found it while I had my back to him examining the memorabilia.

"I have made a study of cigar ash, and the temperature point at which certain potentially poisonous substances can be inhaled through smoke. The ash on the end of this cigar has slight traces of dark brown streaked with white – not what one expects in tobacco of this quality – where there is an even burn and uniformly colored ash. I tasted the ash, and could detect a bit of bitter fishiness, along with a slight floral odor. The cigar is rather long, so that the smoker wouldn't notice this, especially when imbibing strong brandy – at least until the cigar had burned down further away from the tip.

"All that tells me that someone injected cocaine and nicotine with a rather long needle through the tip of the cigar into a position several inches from the tip. A cigar burns at about twice the temperature required to convert cocaine and nicotine to smoke, but that temperature only extends about an inch down the cigar from the burning end. Thus, it would take a while for the higher temperature to reach any poison injected by a long needle.

"Cocaine leaves white residue, has a floral odor, and a slightly bitter taste. Nicotine is dark brown, has a smoky odor, and a slight fishy taste. Both can be inhaled. Cocaine can result in heart failure, nicotine in heart irregularity. Both work very quickly, almost instantaneously, especially on a smoker with a heart condition. Both are easily obtainable, and can be purified by, for example, soaking tobacco in water and then allowing the residue to remain after evaporation. Cocaine is readily available at any chemist and can be purified to a powder by heat treatment.

"So our murderer prepared such a solution and injected it into a cigar of the type he knew would be here. After the cigars were handed out, he quickly pocketed the one he had received and substituted the poisoned cigar he had concealed on his person. He likely didn't inhale after it was lit. Perhaps he had experimented some on another cigar to ensure it wouldn't harm himself or others. He waited until the Cardinal placed his cigar in an ash tray, came over to talk to him, placed his poisoned cigar into the ash tray, then picked up the Cardinal's cigar. Tosca unwittingly picked up the poisoned cigar and began smoking it. As the heat moved toward the poisoned portion, he began to inhale cocaine and nicotine fumes, inevitably causing his heart to fail.

"The murderer then managed to switch the cigar he was holding, the Cardinal's original cigar, with the poisoned one lying on the floor. The murderer then sought to dispose of the murder weapon by throwing it into the fireplace. Unluckily for him, it didn't fall into the fire but rather alongside it. Thus *four* cigars, not *five*, here in the room, and the fifth I have here."

All but one of the men began talking at once, demanding to know how that could have been accomplished. The fifth was staring at Holmes.

"Let me repeat if I haven't been clear enough, and I believe the repetition should make it manifest who is the murderer. The murderer injected a cigar with poison and brought that with him to the dinner last evening. When he received a normal cigar from the Cardinal, he pocketed that and retrieved the poisoned cigar hidden upon his person. He then substituted the poisoned cigar for the Cardinal's cigar, most likely when they were talking, and the Cardinal placed his cigar in an ashtray. After the Cardinal collapsed, the murderer replaced the poisoned cigar that had fallen next to him with the Cardinal's original cigar, then threw the poisoned cigar into the fireplace.

"As I said, this chain of events should tell you the identity of the murderer. Who helped with the arrangements and knew what cigars would be here? Who bent over the Cardinal to check on his condition, giving him an opportunity to switch cigars? Who rushed from the room to find a doctor by the quickest route from the sideboard to the main door right past the fireplace?"

Ramsay at last spoke. "You have eliminated, though, any motive on my part."

"But you see, I know about the other murders." There was stunned silence, and the two Home Office men moved directly behind Ramsay.

"This morning, my brother mentioned in passing various locations you have been posted. It jogged something in my mind, so I consulted the indices I keep concerning various crimes and similar activities. I had kept my eye on a series of murders of young women that bore remarkable similarities to one another: Red hair, mid-twenties, shop workers, living alone, and so forth. All had been strangled in a very similar manner. And three of them occurred in places you had worked: Bologna, Marseille, Saint Petersburg. There were several others, but my interest was aroused.

"After examining the room, I was sure that a murder had been committed here. Once I interviewed Wright, I knew the murderer was clever enough to make this appear as a natural death, but likely had to know of the arrangements before the dinner.

"I sent a note to my brother asking when you had been posted. I also asked about Wright's background, as a diversion to confuse the murderer. I knew Wright couldn't have done it, because he wasn't in the room when the cigars were being smoked, and thus had no opportunity to make a substitution. That's why I instructed the man at the door here to go to the room where you were all located and mention to his colleague that he had heard me talking about some city up north, where you had never been posted. Wright, I apologize for this, but I wanted Ramsay to relax and not be on his guard.

"Mycroft sent me a note back confirming the locations of your various postings. Every one of them matched a date when a murder I have described was committed. I suspect that as part of your conversion, you confessed to Tosca the first murder which, based on the date of it and your description of the process with Tosca, seems to have occurred before that process began.

"So, the Cardinal knew what you had done, but the seal of the confessional kept him from revealing your secret. But you stated you kept in touch with him, so he knew where you were. The killings were in the papers at the time, so he must have kept track of you and them. Perhaps he learned you were wooing a young woman here in London – it will not be hard to find her. The Yard also can coordinate with its various counterparts in the jurisdictions where you committed these heinous crimes. Perhaps the Cardinal felt a burden on his conscience and decided to relieve it by warning you to stop, even threatening you with exposure. In any event, you saw this dinner as an opportunity to silence him and make it appear a natural death. You didn't foresee that I would be asked to intervene.

"Mycroft, I am finished. You may take him away and start the wheels of justice turning."

The Home Office men pulled Ramsay to his feet. He said not a word, merely looking at Holmes with a chilling mixture of contempt and hatred such as I hope never to see again. It was as if a mask had slipped revealing his true, evil self.

The other four men gathered around Holmes offering thanks and congratulations. He accepted it with a quiet graciousness, slightly bowing to them. They left in a group, relieved their ordeal was over.

After that, Mycroft Holmes came over. "I don't think you needed all this show. The cigar was obvious."

"Certainly."

"Well, this should satisfy the Vatican and Her Majesty's Government. Religion had nothing to do with it, so there is no impact, domestic or foreign. I'm going now for a short meeting with the Home Secretary and the Attorney General, as they wish to hear my thoughts on appropriate next steps. May I suggest we meet in an hour at the Stranger's Room at the Club."

"Certainly. Watson and I will repair to one of the bars here for a preliminary celebratory libation and then join you."

Mycroft Holmes left, and the two of us found comfortable seats in a quiet corner of one of the Savoy's many fine bars.

"I say, Holmes, not bad for a day's work. You avoided an international incident, and brought to heel a vicious killing maniac."

"Yes, yes, but I will admit that isn't the best part of it."

"What might that be?"

"If you listened carefully to Mycroft's jibes just now, it was clear: He really had no idea about the other murders."

In this memorable year '95 a curious and incongruous succession of cases had engaged his attention, [including] his famous investigation of the sudden death of Cardinal Tosca – an inquiry which was carried out by him at the express desire of his Holiness the Pope . . . .

– Dr. John H. Watson
"Black Peter"

155

The Adventure of the Cardinal's Notebook
by Deanna Baran

To celebrate the anniversary of Their Majesties Umberto and Margherita, the City of Venice arranged for an international art exhibition. The populace responded with enthusiasm, turning out in droves to view it, but it naturally excited the attention of the criminal community as well. It was for this reason that I spent a good part of the spring of 1895 amongst the canals and gondoliers, the palazzos and the bridges, the winged lions and the living members of the old families. Although Watson had the good fortune to share the first part of my Venetian adventures with myself, and will assuredly relate them elsewhere in his own manner, circumstances compelled him to effect an early return to London. As for myself, those living members of old families continued to prolong my visit to the Continent with tasks beyond my original scope, and I allowed myself to be coaxed with liberal applications of Italian opera and Italian food, but remuneration was always in Italian gold.

Word spread, as word does, to dizzying heights, but even I was surprised upon the arrival of a request, written in a clear and graceful Italian hand by some anonymous Vatican secretary, with a modestly small signature in the lower right-hand corner. Needless to say, I preserved that missive for inclusion within my great scrapbook upon my own return to Baker Street – but that came much later, and only after many additional adventures had passed.

But those summons were summons enough that few men on the planet would ignore, and I found myself journeying to Rome in response. Doors and gates that would normally be secured were opened to admit me, and it was but a matter of time before I found myself ensconced in a small, intimate room, very different from the vast public spaces where citizens and pilgrims alike would congregate for even a glimpse of the one who now desired my services.

There were others. When dealing with dignitaries, there are always witnesses: Secretaries and guards, attendants and officials. But they gave us the illusion of privacy as we performed the ceremonial greetings, and then settled ourselves in, He to speak, and I to listen and respond.

"You have come a long way. I am sorry for the inconvenience," my host explained good-naturedly, "but you understand, I have not been permitted to leave these walls for the last twenty-five years. Otherwise, I would have been pleased to have visited you instead, and saved you the trouble of traveling so far.

"But there may be more travels in the future, should you choose to indulge an old man like me. On the shores of the Black Sea, there is the estate of the Toscas. As you can guess, it is an old Tuscan family. They originated as merchants, and amassed great wealth, controlling trade between the East and the West, from Odessa and Sebastopol, through Constantinople, to Naples and Livorno. You comprehend?

"Many branches of the Tosca family can be found in all those places, but the most important thing they dealt with was not in goods, but in *information*. It was through information that they became as wealthy and as powerful as they were at their peak, although they have suffered significant losses in the decades after the conclusion of the recent war. They still have much in the way of material possessions, understand, but many of the younger generations have died prematurely, so the family itself has grown smaller than it should. A family without a large pool of talent from which to select the leadership of its future generations. You can imagine the effects on the clan as a whole.

"I tell you this as background information so you understand the environment. The man I am concerned about was not interested in politics, and not interested in statesmen, but was drawn to serve others from within the church. He was a member of my Curia, and rose to the rank of Cardinal. Because of his family history in dealing with Slavic countries, and his familiarity with the languages of those places, he performed a number of important tasks that few men could be entrusted with. But because he performed those tasks, he has accumulated many enemies. He understood the dangers, and accepted them. The red that a cardinal wears is not for beauty, but a visible reminder that one may be called to shed one's blood as a martyr.

"Cardinal Tosca had enemies within the government, of course. That is a given. Many governments do not care for the people to serve a King beyond their own selves. They do not understand that we can tell the difference between that which is due to Caesar, and that which is due to God. They wish for it all. There are those who will persecute the faithful as a way to curry favor with their own superiors. Cardinal Tosca was good at dealing with these men.

"Cardinal Tosca had enemies amongst the religious as well. As you know, in the West, there are Catholics, and in the East, there are the Orthodox. At the same time of dealing with the problems of the State, there were those who wished to bring the Catholics under control and extend Orthodoxy in its place. But at the same time, there are others who

157

recognize that we are all members of one flock, and there is only one Shepherd. Cardinal Tosca's most important work was his efforts on a reunification between East and West. He was discussing these future movements with several men of influence in the area who had control of many monasteries and parishes, big and small, and they were listening and considering with interest.

"Somebody stabbed Cardinal Tosca to death while he visited his family's estate on the coast of the Black Sea. His body was found in the garden, but he was clearly killed elsewhere. I do not know if it was a member of the government, or someone who did not wish to lose power and control of these communities. It would only be idle curiosity if I were to ask you to find the exact circumstances of his death, for I know that the identity and motivations of his murderer are already known by the Just Judge. All I can do is pray for the conversion of his heart and his soul. It is not to be wondered at that it happened – only that it does not happen more often. Men forget that they are children of God and brethren in Christ. There are no remedies in legislation, or in penalties, or in any other human devices for the evils we perpetuate against each other. Arrogance, oppression, fraud, envy – they are everywhere. But when mankind's charity towards God has cooled, what else will happen except for man's charity towards each other to also cool? But my thoughts on that subject are for elsewhere.

"Instead, there is something very tangible that is the reason for my calling you here: When Cardinal Tosca went to visit his family's estate, it was because he was meeting a number of important contacts for his reunification efforts. Their names are recorded in a small black notebook, which looks much like this one." A gesture, and an aide passed an ordinary pocket-sized blank notebook into my hands. "If that list of names was to fall into the hands of the wrong people, dozens of people and their families would certainly face death, confiscation, and more. It is for their sakes and their well-being that I ask you to please find a way to discover that which is hidden, and bring it away to safety, so that no harm will befall the innocent whose only crime is desiring to reestablish a lost unity."

In reality, it was an organic and friendly conversation, and not a monologue, and we spoke of other things as well, and I don't remember how we got onto the subject of riddles in Latin, which he proposed to anonymously publish in the Vatican newspaper – but how *does* Watson write dialogue without making it tedious and drawn-out? But you understand the relevant parts of the facts at hand, and why it was that I found myself traveling to the Tosca estate upon the Black Sea, where the eminent Cardinal had met his decease, imposing upon his family's hospitality under the pretext of joining the Cardinal's secretary to assist him in wrapping up the Cardinal's affairs, and all under a hidden identity.

Preceded by communications to smooth my welcome, I arrived at the Tosca estate. The head of the Tosca family was away on business, but his wife was a gracious hostess, and introduced me to Monsignor Novac, the former Cardinal's secretary. He himself had already been apprised of my confidential task, and was glad to see me. I suspected he was growing tired of stalling his departure, and that my presence was a signal that his return to Rome was imminent.

"I'm not sure what you can find," he said doubtfully, as we stood in the Cardinal's private suite. "I understand that you would have preferred the door to be locked and the room to have been preserved as it was before the tragedy. But, you see, we were both living in these chambers, and I have continued to do so. And the servants have continued to clean, and life has continued to progress. His personal items are still quite present, you understand, but his presence is fading more and more every day."

"I expect you have already searched for it?" I inquired, observing a large desk with few papers, before making my way to the window that illuminated the workspace and admiring the view of the Black Sea at the base of the cliffs. There was little beach, and the rocky headlands would be exposed to storms. It was pleasant enough on a sunny day such as today, but I felt it would be gloomy and atmospheric should the weather shift.

"As you understand, His Eminence did not live here permanently. This was his childhood home. This suite of rooms was given to him by his father when he was a young man, and have been kept for his personal usage ever since. He actually lived in Rome, in small and humble quarters. Most of his books from his private collection stayed here. He would come here two or three times a year and switch out whatever books he missed, although of course, as a member of the Curia, there was no lack of local material to which he might have had access. So when we would visit the family estate, he would only bring a minimal amount of materials. Because of that, it was fairly easy to see that that which I sought was not located amongst his other traveling papers."

"And yet at the same time, I take it, such a sensitive item wouldn't be left unsupervised in an unsecured location, such as his chambers in between his visits?"

"Indeed," agreed Msgr. Novac, looking fretful. "I know for a fact that it traveled with us, in a secure dispatch box, where he kept his other sensitive and private work-related documents. I have his key. But as you can see – " And he took a moment to remove from a shelf a beautifully worked box in scarlet and gold. " – his papers were preserved untouched, but that which we seek isn't where it ought to be."

I looked through the papers tied together with ribbons and seals as I set them aside. "And the false bottom?"

"Not there either." Msgr. Novac obligingly removed the false bottom and showed me an additional shallow compartment within the box. It was completely empty.

I examined the dimensions, pressing and prying experimentally. After some effort, I found that which I sought, and we heard a clicking sound as I touched the spring. The bottom of the false bottom compartment was now slightly at an angle, and a thin-bladed knife helped me remove it completely to reveal yet another hidden compartment beneath. Msgr. Novac's exclamation of surprise indicated that he was unaware of the box's second secret. The compartment had a few sheets of paper, which I passed over to him for his perusal, but it was too thin to have contained an item even as small as a black memorandum book.

"These are – *important*," said Msgr. Novac, looking soberly at me. "Thank you very much." He carried them over to his own smaller desk to read them more thoroughly.

"I'm glad to hear," I said, reassembling the components of the dispatch box, relocking it with the key, and placing it back in its spot on the bookcase. The next several hours were spent with far fewer results, as I systematically investigated the office and its furniture for likely hiding spots. Each book was pulled from the shelf to see if the pages were hollowed. The upholstery of the chair was examined to see if it had been secretly slit. The drawers of the desk were examined, and three hidden compartments were found, their contents passed over to Msgr. Novac for his investigation, but still no black book.

We paused to join the family for dinnertime, although it only consisted of Simona, the Cardinal's unmarried younger sister, Elena, the wife of the family head, and an elderly maiden aunt, Sofia Tosca. The family head's children ate in their own wing of the house. The head was away on business in Theodosia for at least a week, and the three other cousins who were normally in residence were in business in St. Petersburg and hadn't returned.

I used the opportunity to encourage them to speak freely about the Cardinal, painting a picture of him as a man instead of a memory.

"Corneliu was the eldest, you see," said Simona, the sister. "Under normal circumstances, he would have inherited the leadership of the family, along with the business and the estates and everything else. But he had other plans for himself. He argued terribly with Father about it, but eventually, Corneliu prevailed and got his way. He always did, you see. Mihail was the second son, and ended up carrying on everything after Father passed. But Corneliu was definitely the more talented brother."

160

In someone less ladylike, the sound emitted by the elderly Aunt Sofia might have been called a snort. "Even Simona would have been a better family head than Mihail. He works hard, granted, but he doesn't have a good heart. He thinks too much about money, and doesn't think enough about the people around him."

Elena didn't seem too perturbed by the criticism from her husband's relations. Instead, she gently reminded them, "He asked us to remember Corneliu, not speak poorly of Mihail."

"It's always been hard for Mihail," explained Simona. "Corneliu always had what was called the 'Young Master's Suite', the rooms intended for the next head of the family. Even after it was clear that Corneliu rejected leadership of the family, Mihail was not promoted to that set of rooms where you are currently staying. They were kept empty for Corneliu's visits. Can you imagine how insulted he must have felt?" She didn't seem to have much sympathy for the younger brother's permanent relegation to secondary status.

"Corneliu always had a quick mind," agreed Aunt Sofia, "but was always kept in check by scruples. Mihail is not nearly as sharp, and not nearly as scrupulous. He wants to resurrect this family's fortunes, but sometimes, I'm afraid he's going about it the wrong way."

"That isn't to say that Corneliu was easy to manipulate," agreed Simona. "He was very obstinate about getting his way when he thought his way was the right one, and that someone else was abusing his or her power. He would have made an excellent nobleman, if only he had been born into it. As it was, he did the best he could do to protect those beneath him, only armed with what God had given him."

"Do you remember the time in the early days when he was patron of that seminary?" said Aunt Sofia, except, in the way of elderly aunts, she was not nearly so concise, and Msgr. Novac broke his careful silence to pitch in minor details to help color the anecdote.

"Some of the officials in the area were determined to close it down upon some pretext. Instead of closing down the seminary, he added additional secular classes and opened it up to non-theologians."

"He was upright, determined, and relentless," agreed Simona. "I remember when the Ottoman slavers were operating in these waters between Sebastopol and Istanbul – much more than they do now. Corneliu brought so much pressure upon our father regarding that matter to discourage the trade. It came at significant personal cost, both financially and in terms of relationships, but Corneliu was very unyielding on the subject and wouldn't give Father an ounce of rest until he had agreed and complied. Then he made sure Father stayed in agreement and compliance."

161

"That's one of the things about merchants," said Elena. "As you say, even nowadays, the Ottoman slavers still ply their trade on their routes past our very door here. But there are other things that are trafficked as well, both secretly and openly. Narcotics and arms and all manner of items. Corneliu was perpetually frustrated by the thought of the family profiting, even indirectly, from its involvement with vice. And yet, it's as Mihail perpetually tells me: If one wants to do business in a certain environment, one cannot be too particular about one's business partners or project one's own values upon them. Cargo is cargo, and customers are customers, and it is a merchant's duty to deliver the goods entrusted to it from one place to another place, regardless of one's personal feelings about the cargo itself."

"Is that not problematic in its own way, though?" inquired Simona. "To presume that millions of people are unable to improve their thinking, merely because they are Ottoman, and that the Ottomans have always been a certain way?"

"Is it not equally problematic," came the cool response, "to determine that one's self is the standard for enlightened civilization, and others are barbaric rather than merely holding different values?"

"In that case, you would be arguing that morality is dependent upon feelings," said Msgr. Novac. "The ancient Scots used to hold that charity to the poor was wealth twice squandered. Your brother held that we are ultimately measured with our own measure, and whatsoever we do to the least of his people, so we do unto our Master. You would hold both philosophies as equally meritorious?"

"If you've lived as long as I have and seen the things I have seen, you would know a thing or two about the Ottomans!" said Aunt Sofia ominously.

Msgr. Novac added his own helpful observations about the tribulations of his own people under the Ottoman authorities, and expressed gratitude that things were much better in Slavic territories, although there were troubling trends in the government and amongst officials. My dinner partners thoroughly explored this topic until the conclusion of the meal, and although Cardinal Tosca figured in a few additional anecdotes, no new information to change my perception of him was uncovered.

The Monsignor retired to slumber upon his long, narrow couch in the bedroom shortly after our return to the former Cardinal's quarters, but I stayed seated at the desk, immersed in thought as my candle wavered and flickered in its holder. I idly watched the shadows leap and bound as I imagined the former occupant going about his business, and wondered what sort of secrets he was privy to that so many lives depended upon. I

162

eventually resigned myself to sleep, and leaned forward to make my way to the Cardinal's bed, when the thought occurred: The candle was remarkably active in a room that had no discernable draught. The windows were tightly closed and the curtains drawn. I began to prowl about in search of that which caused the flame to react, and discovered an air current flowing through a section of what looked like solid wall.

Intrigued at yet another puzzle, for this room had seemed to be full of secret crevasses and compartments, I began to explore more thoroughly. It was only a matter of time before I discovered the secret button, which, when pressed, resulted in a segment of the wall opening up. A staircase led steeply down into the inky blackness, and I lost little time in awakening Msgr. Novac to convey this new discovery to him. With great excitement, we armed ourselves with sticks and light, and made the descent.

Our passage transitioned from a narrow corridor within the finished stone walls of a castle, with stairs cut from living rock, and now took the form of a massive natural cavern intruded upon by the sea. A dock followed alongside the waterline, and various small craft were tethered to it. Long, thin crates were stacked away from the water's edge. Lit lanterns illuminated the area. Due to the uncertain light and the presence of nightfall beyond, it was impossible to perceive precisely how the harbour within connected to the sea without.

We had but scarcely had time to take in the scene before us before a trio of ruffians jumped upon us from behind with violence. My baritsu training gave me an advantage I would not have otherwise possessed in fending off our attackers, but Msgr. Novac was less fortunate. A smart knock across the head, and he lay upon the ground. I held the three men at bay with my weighted stick, praying they had no firearms upon them, although I saw the light glinting upon two drawn blades and one stout length of wood.

"Is it not enough to intrude upon my hospitality, that you must also pry into my affairs?" came a voice from the darkness.

"Mihail Tosca, I presume?" I asked. Our invisible host, who was presumably away on business, emerged from a shadowy niche.

He neither assented nor denied. "I have met many meddlesome churchmen in my time, but they do not meddle for long when they try to meddle here."

"You refer to your brother, Cardinal Tosca," I said. "He knew of this cavern and discovered the use to which it was being put during your leadership of the family business. He attempted to dissuade you from your endeavours. You grew tired of his morality and committed the oldest crime one man can perpetrate against his brother."

163

"It was only small arms," said Mihail. "Hardly a thing to waste one's life over. A lucrative trade, especially after the prohibitions put in place after the war ended. But Corneliu didn't know how to accept the fact that if he wanted to control the family's business, he needed to have accepted his role as Father's heir. If he rejected that role, he couldn't complain about my management of the affairs of our clan."

I eyed him coolly, judging the distance between us. It was too far to take him by surprise, especially with his three henchmen standing between us. Yet if I dawdled, neither Msgr. Novac nor I would ever again see the light of day.

With a snap of my wrist, my weighted stick connected with the side of the closest ruffian's head. He dropped to the ground. A step, and I hit the elbow of his companion. His fingers reflexively flew open and his knife clattered to the ground. A kick sent it flying towards the water's edge, and I heard a splash as it fell, but I was already feinting towards the third ruffian's head. He stepped back without thinking, raising his arms to defend himself – but my stick switched directions in midair and connected with the side of his knee. He buckled to the ground. I whirled to confront Tosca.

In the time I had taken to eliminate the most immediate threat, he had managed to retrieve a gaff hook – a pole with a wicked-looking hook at one end. His reach was now superior to mine, but I couldn't afford to lose a moment to allow him to collect his wits. In the space of a breath, I closed the distance between the two of us, so that the length of his weapon was a liability rather than an asset, and used both my momentum and my weighted stick to smash the breath from his body and knock him from his feet over the edge of the dock, hook and all. Weighted down by clothes and weaponry, the water closed above his head with unyielding finality. I stood at the edge, ready to give a hand, waiting for him to struggle to break the surface. It was only after the passage of several moments which stretched into an eternity that I realized something prevented him, and I belatedly moved into action to look for a long pole with which to assist him. But the lantern light was dim, and the hook he had taken to the bottom of the harbor was the only one of its kind in the immediate area, and nothing remained with any chance of penetrating the depth. If he had been unarmed, I might have chanced the dive, but I didn't trust to be in unknown waters of unknown depth with the knowledge my enemy could still be in possession of a blade that could both pierce and slice, and little reason for gratitude.

I couldn't afford to remain fixed upon his fate for much longer, and turned back to survey my initial opponents. The first was unconscious. The second was injured and angry, the third was temporarily crippled. The ones who still had their wits about them, however, knew they had lost the upper hand, and submitted begrudgingly to me as I secured them with a coil of rope, to prevent further mischief while my back was turned. I then turned my attention to Msgr. Novac, who was coming to with painful groans. I extended a kindly hand, assisted him to his feet, examined his head for a wound, and asked him the usual questions. He sat on the edge of the steps to gather himself.

The rest of the evening was a blur as I alerted both the household and the authorities. I offered Cardinal Tosca's vacated bed to Msgr. Novac, but he expressed a preference for the long, narrow couch which he had inhabited during his stay at the Tosca estate. Thus it was that as night fled and dawn approached, I found myself amongst the elaborate fringed velvet hangings of the Cardinal's bed, designed to block both the early rays of summer sun and the winter chill. Despite my fatigue, sleep eluded me. I had solved the wrong problem. His Eminence hadn't been interested in the identity of the murderer of his colleague, yet it would interest him to know that man had been summoned before the Just Judge rather sooner than usual for an account of his weakness and cruelty. But where was the logical hiding place for such a sensitive document as a notebook? At first, upon discovering the secret passage, I had thought to find it hidden somewhere in that corridor, but after our encounter with the smugglers, I realized that it was far less secure than the Cardinal's own chambers. Yet I was positive it wasn't in his office. But what place would be even more private than one's private office?

I stared unseeingly at the bed-hangings, until I saw them.

A man's bed was a thousand times more private than a man's desk.

Within moments, I had stripped the bed of its sheets and pillows. The notebook was not there. I turned the mattress and examined it, but there were no signs of having been secreted and then restitched. Beneath the bed, there was dust upon the stone flags, but nothing else. I turned my attention to the canopy and the hangings, and thus it was that I found a small, handmade pocket on the inner fold of a drape – and within that pocket was that which I had come so far to seek.

In this memorable year '95 a curious and incongruous succession of cases had engaged his attention, [including] his famous investigation of the sudden death of Cardinal Tosca – an inquiry which was carried out by him at the express desire of his Holiness the Pope . . . .

– Dr. John H. Watson
"Black Peter"

Death in the Workhouse
by Thomas A. Burns, Jr.

By 1895, the name of Sherlock Holmes was well-nigh a household word in London, if not all of England. I would like to think that the publication of these little tales in the popular press had much to do with that, but Holmes averred that it was mostly due to his consummate skill as an investigator.

"No one pays much attention to the mundane or the mediocre, Watson. It is merely the backdrop against which we play out the script that is our lives. Were my abilities not truly extraordinary, no one would be interested in or even notice them." He smiled. "I daresay that you would not even be moved to chronicle them."

"Perhaps not," I agreed. "Although returning from the dead has also been a time-tested way of attracting attention." I referred to Holmes's re-appearance in London the previous year after a well-publicised hiatus during which many thought him gone for good.

"Indeed it has. Although let me assure you that I have no intention of founding a religion. I eschew belief in the absence of evidence, and I've always found worshippers rather tawdry."

Not with that immense ego of yours, I thought, but didn't say so.

It was late summer in the above-mentioned year, and our landlady Mrs. Hudson had just cleared the luncheon dishes from the table. Holmes and I were lounging about in post-prandial bliss with little to occupy ourselves. Changeable and showery weather had been forecast for that day, and as neither of us had anything of import pending, we had little reason to brave the elements. I still retained the old soldier's proclivity to take my leisure while I could, but Holmes was as prone as ever to that crushing *ennui* that could drive him to ill-considered action or even outright self-destructive behaviour. Sometimes I could forestall that by engaging him in verbal trysts in which I usually came out second-best, but it was a small price to pay to assure my friend's well-being. However, I was rapidly running out of witty rejoinders to keep him amused. So it was that the sound of the downstairs bell sparked a wave of relief in my soul.

A moment later, a knock came at our door, and I opened it to reveal a rotund fellow who appeared to be in his forties, holding a battered straw boater in one hand and a folded piece of paper in the other. He extended the latter to me, saying, "Mr. Holmes?"

I didn't bother denying it. I simply plucked the letter from his hand and handed it to the detective. He perused it, smiled, and passed it back. It ran:

Mr. Holmes:

This letter is to introduce Mr. Joseph Pepler, who has come to me with a problem with which I am unable to help. Since it involves the death of his older brother, it is of sufficient gravity that I thought it best to refer him to you. Please do not consider it cheeky of me if I ask that you give him a hearing.

Yrs truly,
Inspector Stanley Hopkins
Metropolitan Police

"Do come in, Mr. Pepler," invited Holmes, "and take the chair with the window at your back so the dreary weather doesn't exacerbate your grief. Surely it isn't too early for a little spot of brandy or a whisky-soda on such a grey and dismal day?"

"I'll just take you up on that brandy with much thanks, sir, as the dampness seems to have seeped into my bones."

Holmes glanced at me, then at the cellaret, so I rose to pour a tot of the *Hors d'âge* Armagnac that the detective had recently received from a grateful client. As I delivered it to Mr. Pepler, Holmes said, "Beyond the obvious facts that you are a cheesemonger with a shop near a railway station and married with a large family, I can observe little else. Please tell us the tale of your unfortunate brother."

Pepler sipped his drink and raised his eyebrows, doubtless a reaction to quality of the *liqueur* he had been served. "Mr. Hopkins told me your detective skills were unparalleled when he referred me to you, and I can see he didn't exaggerate. I guess my ring told you I am married, but please tell me how you know about my family and my profession. As you said, I have a cheese shop in Stonecutter Street next to the Farringdon Market near Holborn Station."

Smiling, Holmes replied, "It is my nose that informs me of your calling and the location of your establishment. And on your shoulder, I observe stains that could have come from nothing but an infant spitting up as you held it to expel gas after feeding. A married man of your age surely would have more than one child. Couple that with the fact that, if you don't mind my saying so, your clothing and shoes are somewhat dated. Surely a successful shop owner should have a sufficient income to support a wife and a child or two and to keep himself in new clothing. Hence, a large family."

"Little Nathan makes it six, and if another little one comes along, I may have to go into the workhouse myself. And speaking thereof, it was in that sort of establishment where Henry, my unfortunate brother, met his death."

The state of the poor has been a persistent and recalcitrant issue in Britain for centuries. The prevailing wisdom holds that destitution is largely the result of indolence, and many people opine that the poor deserve their fate with no obligation for the government to ameliorate it. However, poverty has long been recognized as a factor that undermines the social order, so others argue that the mitigation of its effects is for the good of all. To that end, the workhouse system was created by the passage of the so-called Poor Laws.

These laws required a person who sought relief to seek entry to a workhouse where he would receive food and shelter, but in turn would be required to work for no pay. The overseers, known as *Guardians*, were often local businessmen whom reformers described as pitiless, profit-seeking leeches exploiting the destitute. This was, of course, an overreaction – some Guardians were genuinely compassionate and charitable people. Nevertheless, their power was such that the inmates were at the mercy of their personal foibles.

Families who sought aid were necessarily separated by sex and age, with wives and children housed in different establishments from their husbands and fathers. Conditions were deliberately harsh, to serve as a deterrent to so-called persistent idlers who were capable of working but refused to do so. A workhouse inmate had to wear a uniform, was prohibited from conversing with the other inmates, and had to perform long hours of tedious, manual labor.

"Specifics, please, Mr. Pepler," entreated Holmes. "Which workhouse did your brother enter? When did he die? How was it that he met his end?"

"It was two weeks ago, at St. Luke's Workhouse in Hoxton. The Coroner's Jury ruled that Henry died from swallowing potassium cyanide, and that suicide was strongly indicated, which is why Mr. Hopkins said he couldn't help me. But I know that my brother would never take his own life, Mr. Holmes. He was a religious man who would never jeopardise his immortal soul."

"Quite," said Holmes. "It's unfortunate that so much time has passed since your brother's death. Please tell me as much as you know about it."

"Well, Henry was fifty-three when he passed away. He had made his living for many years as a French polisher, but a while ago his mind began deteriorating, possibly because of all the fumes he inhaled at his labours. His employer had to let him go because the quality of his work had declined. Henry knew no other trade. He tried to support himself with odd jobs, but that was no good. In short order, he lost his flat and was living rough. I would have helped him if I could, even taken him in, but it was simply impossible given my own financial status. So he applied to the workhouse and was taken in."

"When was this?"

"Last autumn. Given his age and his health, he knew he couldn't survive the winter on the streets." Pepler drained his snifter and set it down. "After he entered the workhouse, I went to visit him as often as I could. The Guardians discouraged such visits because they said they reminded the inmates of their former lives and affected their work. Anyway, I went to visit Henry after dinner on the day he died, and when I arrived, they told me he had passed." Pepler's voice broke at that last. Holmes glanced at me again, so I poured the grieving man another little bit of spirits. Sometimes a little alcohol will facilitate the telling of a sad tale.

"Please tell us what happened, sir. Omit no detail, however insignificant it may seem to you."

"It was awful, Mr. Holmes. They said they found him dying in the W.C. after luncheon. They tried to save him, but failed. They wouldn't have even told me about it if I hadn't come to visit – they would have simply buried my brother in Potter's Field as someone who died a natural death. Against their wishes, I called for the police, who referred the case to the Coroner to determine if there had been foul play."

"With whom at the workhouse did you speak?" Holmes asked. "Was there no mention of poisoning?"

"I spoke with a Dr. Harris, who said he was their Chief Medical Officer. No, he didn't mention poison. He did tell me that Henry had been ill and was in hospital."

"Which hospital?" I asked.

"St. Luke's. It's a hospital for indigents as well as a workhouse. I later learned at the coroner's inquest that Henry had actually been seeing three different doctors there, but none were able to help him."

"What was the matter with him?" I asked.

"Dr. Harris said he wasn't sure. Apparently, it was some kind of intestinal blockage."

"That wouldn't be unusual, given the poor diet in those places." I averred. I knew that the inmates were fed a lot of starches and hard-to-digest meat scraps.

"When did you find out about the prussic acid?" Holmes asked.

169

"At the inquest when the medical examiner testified. Some of Henry's organs were delivered to him because I called the police, and he found out how my brother died." Pepler drained his glass and set it down again. This time, the look on his face informed me that he'd had enough.

Everyone was quiet for a moment, immersed in his own thoughts. Holmes stared out the window to the damp street below, doubtless wondering if this was an actual crime, or merely a senseless tragedy of the sort that occurred in London every day. Finally, he said, "So, we have a coroner's verdict that strongly suggests suicide, and all you can offer to dispute it is a religious argument." Pepler's face fell at that statement. "However," Holmes continued, "I think we have sufficient grounds to investigate the matter further. You knew your brother better than most, sir, and religious convictions often provide very strong motives. I'll look into this for you, and see if I can find anything tangible that might expand upon the coroner's verdict."

Pepler rose from his chair and approached Holmes, taking both of the detective's hands in his own. "Oh, thank you, sir, thank you! I'm sure you'll find that Henry didn't do this awful thing to himself, although I'm at a loss to say why anyone would wish to hurt him."

After leaving us information as to where we could get in touch with him, Pepler left us. I inquired of Holmes, "Well, where will you start?"

"Where would you begin?" he asked.

"The workhouse, I suppose."

"You are truly the soldier, Watson," Holmes said. "Always the man of action. No, I think I shall begin with the coroner's report, to review the evidence that led to the inquest to call this death a suicide. We shall see where we shall go from there. If anywhere."

Later that day, we found ourselves in the mortuary at St. Bartholomew's Hospital, affectionately known as Barts. I had to catch my breath when we entered the dank basement because the odours of carbolic, formaldehyde, and decomposition assaulted my olfactory system in turn. As a practicing physician, I've concerned myself with the maladies of the living, so I've always found this place depressing – a reminder that our noble battle against mortality is ultimately doomed to failure. It proved even more dismal today, because the wet garments clinging to me added to the chill of the place.

Dr. Harold Latheby was the assistant medical examiner in charge that day. A young man, seemingly in his early thirties, he was neatly tonsured and wore a pencil moustache. He appeared more suited for an office in Harley Street than lurking about in this ghoulish den. But it was he who had done the autopsy on Henry Pepler – or rather, on parts of him.

170

"Dr. Chumley Harris of St. Luke's sent over a heart, two kidneys, and a stomach from Mr. Pepler after his brother requested an investigation of his death," he said in response to Holmes's inquiry.

The detective grimaced. "What about the rest of him?"

"Delivered to Potter's Field for burial, I'll be bound. We don't assume the responsibility for that if we don't have to. Finances, you know."

Holmes's disappointment at being unable to examine the body itself was apparent. "What did you ascertain from your examination of the organs?"

"The heart appeared quite healthy, but the kidneys were congested," Latheby said. "The stomach was intact and had a violent purple colour."

"Diagnostic of prussic acid poisoning," Holmes observed.

"Quite. I opened the stomach and found the mucosa inflamed. An analysis of the contents revealed nearly two grains of prussic acid and ten of carbonate of potash. I confirmed that the decedent had consumed a fatal dose of the cyanide of potassium."

"Anything else?"

"Remnants of bread, likely from his last meal. I put all of this in my report for the coroner."

"Then the coroner should be our next stop," Holmes observed.

The coroner was Mr. John Humphries, who held court at The Eagle public house in City Road in Hoxton. The effluvium of beer and sausage that permeated the place eradicated the last of the mortuary stench from my nose when we entered, and made my mouth water.

"At least if we don't find Mr. Humphries," I said to Holmes, "we can hopefully have luncheon."

"Oh, he's here," replied Holmes. "He always is."

I didn't bother to ask. Holmes seemed to know the locations of half of the important people in the city at any time.

The detective led the way to a rear booth occupied by a rotund fellow in his sixties, who greeted us with a broad, toothy smile.

"Begawd if it ain't Sherlock 'Olmes!" he said in a strong London accent. "To what do I owe the pleasure?"

"I'd like a few minutes of your time to discuss the Pepler case," Holmes rejoined.

"Ah. The brother brought you in on it, did 'e? I wouldn't 'ave known of it if 'e 'adn't gone to Scotland Yard."

Holmes motioned me to slide into the booth across from Humphries, then took the seat next to me. He always preferred to be on the aisle to effect a rapid departure if the need arose.

171

Humphries went on. "I 'ope the time will come when the work'ouses are required to report the circumstances of every death that occurs therein to the coroner, as the insane asylums currently are."

"Thousands of questionable deaths could be concealed behind those walls," Holmes agreed. "Yet your inquiry concluded there was neither evidence to suggest suicide nor homicide."

"Well, it 'ad to be one or the other, now didn't it?" Humphries averred, "But beyond the fact that the blighter 'ad p'ison inside him, there was nothing to say 'ow it got there. Suicide seems likely, but 'is brother patently refused to consider it. And Chumley 'Arris, the work'ouse doctor, affirmed that Mr. Pepler seemed obsessed wit' 'is health. 'Ardly someone who would deliberately ingest rat poison, ain't 'e?."

"An accident, then," I suggested.

"Possibly," the coroner agreed, "but again, 'ow? The gent was seen by three doctors for 'is ills. Doctor 'Arris testified that there was no prussic acid in any of 'is med'cins. The jury 'ad no choice but to return the verdict it did."

"Which tells us nothing," Holmes sighed. "Well, I suppose if this business was easy, I wouldn't enjoy it so much. Come, Watson, we're off to see Dr. Harris at St. Luke's." The detective must have seen my face fall, because he continued, "Don't worry. We'll have a spot of lunch when we're finished."

"Good luck with that one," said the coroner.

"What do you mean, Humphries?"

"Just that Dr. 'Arris didn't seem too 'appy to be on the spot at the inquest. Oh, the bloke answered all the questions I put to 'im all right, but he sure didn't volunteer anythin'. Seemed put out that 'e 'ad to talk about it at all."

We left the pub to find that the weather had deteriorated. A fine mist blanketed the city, causing the cobblestones to shine like glass, making the pavement slippery and treacherous. Fortunately, St. Luke's was only across the way from The Eagle in Shepherdess Walk – a four-storey brown-brick edifice that spanned fully a hundred yards, with twin steeples equidistant from the central main entrance reaching heavenward. Passing a line of raggedy people outside, we pushed through double doors into the receiving area and found ourselves between the officers' entrance on the right and the paupers' on the left. A white-coated orderly in front of the latter ran his eyes over us, then asked in a somewhat deferential tone, "Who might ye be, and wot's yer business here?"

Holmes removed a calling card from a pocket and scrawled on the back with the stub of a pencil, then handed it to the functionary. "Please deliver this to Doctor Harris."

172

Taking it, the man glanced at the writing, then said, "I'll see if he's taking callers." He vanished through a doorway into the bowels of the building.

The man returned in a few minutes time. "Doctor Harris has nothing to say to ye."

The detective looked as if he was going to argue, then apparently thought better of it. "Very well," he said. "Come, Watson."

When we were outside once more, I said, "You aren't just going to leave it there?"

"Of course not," Holmes replied.

A middle-aged, middle-sized man stood holding his battered hat in his hands before a tableful of men in business suits, like a penitent in front of his confessor. His coat was tattered, and scraps of a multi-coloured plaid shirt peeped through the holes in his outer garment. Baggy trousers, ineffectually held up by a rope 'round his waist, covered his shoes. His clothes and exposed skin were extremely grimy – several of the gentlemen at the table regarded the ceiling, or stared at the wall behind the fellow, presumably to avoid observing him too closely. A pretty sight he was not, with an ancient scar running obliquely across his visage from forehead to chin, as if he'd once been slashed by a broken bottle. One side his mouth hung perpetually agape, revealing dark, pitted teeth, his tongue lolling between them, and stream of drool ran down his chin. A shock of very vivid orange hair fell over his eyes.

A rotund gentleman at the front of the table consulted a journal open before him. "You are Mr. Hugh Boone, are you not?" he said to the wretched chap in an accusatory tone.

"Yesh, Yer Worship," answered the man, slurring his words because of his facial deformity.

"Speak up, please. You are applying to this workhouse as a pauper?"

"A what, Yer Worship?"

"A *pauper*. That means that you have no money. No family who can take you in. No way to support yourself. And you may call me '*Sir*', not '*Your Worship*'."

"Yesh, yer – ah, *Sorr*. That's me, *Sorr*. No money, no food, and nobody wants me. I needs me a place to be."

"Are you prepared to work for your keep if we admit you to St. Luke's? To follow our rules on pain of expulsion if you do not?"

"Yesh, *Sorr*. I'll be good. I promise."

The speaker looked at the other men at the table, saying, "Do any of you Guardians object to the admission of Mr. Boone to St. Luke's."

173

"I suppose we can't keep 'im out 'cause he's so godawful ugly?" a younger man snickered.

"We can keep him out for any reason," the first man said, "for we be the Guardians of St. Luke's, and our word is the Law."

The beggar's face fell at the prospect of refusal. He dropped to his knees, his hands raised in entreaty. "Please, yer highnesses! I ain't et in a week! Please don't make me live on the streets no more!"

"For God's sake man, get up!" the first Guardian said. "Show some dignity! We'll approve your application for admission."

Boone struggled to his feet and approached the table as if to throw his arms around his rescuer, but the Guardian put up a hand to stop him in his tracks.

"Come no closer!" he said, wrinkling his nose. "Abbott! Charles! Come and take this fellow to Admissions."

Two large, white-coated attendants appeared on either side of Boone, gripped him by the arms, and hustled him away.

"We'll never get the smell of that one out of here," the younger Guardian said.

Boone was taken to a bare stone room containing a wooden bench and a tub of water where his clothes were taken away, and he was scrubbed with coarse cloths and strong soap until the redolence that accompanied him was mostly gone, as were the majority of legged creatures who were his erstwhile companions. He was then given a new uniform consisting of cotton underdrawers and a striped shirt, a stout woollen jacket and trousers, a pillbox cap, and a pair of cheap leather shoes. He was reminded that his clothing was the property of the State – if he absconded from the workhouse while wearing it, he would be guilty of theft.

An attendant then brought the pauper to another room in which a group of similarly clad men squatted on stools unknotting thick, heavy ropes, then picking apart the fibres with a spike and throwing them into a tub. This task, known as "picking oakum", served to provide material for the manufacture of new ropes that could be sold for a profit – a profit that none of the workers would share in. It was an onerous chore that quickly shredded the pickers' fingertips, covering the ropes with blood that made them doubly difficult to disassemble. Boone was kept at this job for several hours until the overseer announced it was time for the evening meal.

The odours of porridge and rancid fat filled Boone's head as he shambled into a huge room with a high, vaulted ceiling. Tall, narrow windows lining the walls on two sides admitted light, which illuminated row after row of slender tables spanning the width of the chamber. Rows of straight-back wooden chairs were interspersed between the tables, all facing the same direction and placed so close together as to be nearly touching. The hollow feeling in Boone's stomach intensified as he noted that all of the seats seemed to be filled. Then he noticed some empty places scattered about, usually near the centre of the room. He scanned the chamber for an open seat, then made his way to the end of the row containing it, but the fellow who stood there seemed not to notice him, refusing to move so Boone could make his way to the centre of the room. Boone nudged him so he would allow access to the empty seat, but the churl turned to snarl at him continuing to block him, but upon seeing Boone's horrible visage the fellow recoiled, enabling Boone to get by.

The workhouse master faced the inmates from a table in front of the room. Once they had all taken a place, the master led grace, then the men were released row-by-row to proceed to the kitchen to get food. The kitchen staff consisted of female inmates who were assigned to housekeeping rather than to the odious tasks that the men performed. Dinner was a stew of potatoes and salt pork on a pewter plates, accompanied by a thick piece of hard brown bread – there was no tea nor even water with which to wash it down. Boone was offered a plate by a short, mousy woman who had her long brown hair tied up in a bun. She smiled at him, saying, 'Ere, darlin'. I'm Rosie. I've given youse an extra scoop." She invited punishment from the Guardians by speaking to him, because workhouse rules prohibited conversation amongst inmates. She looked hurt as Boone snatched the plate from her hands, not acknowledging her kindness in any manner.

By the time he returned to his place, Boone's dinner was cold, with congealed fat binding the potatoes to the plate like glue, but he was so famished he cared not. No one paid attention to him anyway, because much of his food fell on to the table from his injured mouth as he ate, and he had to scoop it back onto his plate to try again.

After he had finished his meagre fare, and the inmates were released from the dining hall, Boone sought out an attendant and inquired as to the location of a W.C. The attendant told him. Then Boone said, "It isn't the one where that feller killed hisself, issit? I want no truck with spirits."

"How do you know about that?" The attendant asked. Assuming a guilty expression, Boone didn't answer. Finally, the attendant said, "No, that was the one over in the west wing. And you have been told that speaking with the other inmates is forbidden. I'll overlook it this time, since it's your first day."

"Yes, Yer Worship. Thank'ee, Yer Worship." Boone went off in the direction of the W.C. that the attendant told him about, but as soon as he ascertained he wasn't being watched, he headed for the west wing instead.

The W.C.'s were long, narrow, unlit rooms with a door that could be closed for purposes of modesty, but not locked. Boone found a bank of three adjacent to each other in the area where Pepler presumably had died. Very well then. He'd have to search all of them.

It was a nasty, smelly job, with the details best left undescribed. However, Boone found what he was looking for in the last stall he searched. It was a crumpled square of waxed paper, residing in a corner. When he brought it outside, unfolded it, and sniffed it, he found that it smelled strongly of almonds.

Droning snores echoed throughout the steamy, sweat-laced atmosphere of the men's dormitory. Hugh Boone sprawled atop his lumpy wooden bed, still wearing his woollen workhouse uniform, as did others who were loath to have their fellow inmates see them unclad. He quietly sat upright, looking about to see who else might be awake at this hour. Standing, he made his way through the labyrinth of beds to the corner where the chamber-pots were located, but perceiving no untoward scrutiny, he slipped over to the exit instead and quietly stepped into the hallway. He stood in the cool, empty corridor for a moment, every sense alert, but detecting no danger, he cautiously proceeded to the ground floor and found the registrar's office, which he'd been careful to mark on his admittance.

It took but a minute to gain entry by plying lockpicks plucked from a pocket. Once inside, he relocked the door and found a candle and some matches to provide light for his search. The door was solid wood, so the glow wouldn't be noticed from the hallway, but it could be seen from outside, through the window that opened onto Shepherdess Walk. He hoped that anyone who noticed would think it a busy staff member, working late. Picking the lock on the desk, he located some foolscap, a quill, and ink, and then went to the shelves and found the workhouse daybooks: Folio-sized, leather-bound journals in which all the important events that occurred each day were recorded. He began a methodical search. When he discovered a piece of information of interest, he dutifully transcribed it to his paper, all the while emitting little grunts and groans of interest and satisfaction as he worked. After an hour or so, he ceased his labours, sat back, and surveyed his foolscap, which he had filled with notations on both sides.

"The pattern is clear," he purred. "Now, my only challenge is to snare the miscreant."

The following morning, when work began in the oakum room at seven o'clock, Hugh Boone wasn't there. Upon inquiry, the overseer learned that the misshapen man hadn't been seen at breakfast either.

"Lazy lout is prolly still in bed," one of his fellow pickers opined.

An attendant sent to investigate found that this was indeed the case. An attempt was made to rouse the shirker, to no avail. "Best send for Doctor Harris," the fellow averred.

The doctor arrived, and after a quick examination, summoned a couple of aides. He ticked off the symptoms on his fingers. "Xeroderma with erythema, mydriasis, pyrexia, tachycardia. Take this man to hospital at once!" he told the flunkies.

The men in the white coats loaded the hapless Boone onto a stretcher and bore him off.

Boone lay abed in the hospital ward, the smells of carbolic, alcohol, and humanity filling his head. He was indeed sick, but he was letting on that he was much more incapacitated than was actually the case. He knew he must be vigilant, lest he end up dead. When a nurse came around with a couple of tablets in a little glass cup, he mimed swallowing them, but palmed them expertly instead.

He drowsed after the nurse left. It was hellishly hot and the windows were kept closed, according to the prevailing belief that fresh air was deleterious to convalescence because of all the toxins it might carry. He roused as he sensed a presence next to his bed. It was Rosie, the short, mousy woman who had served him his food and said kind words the other day.

Stroking his brow with her cool, white hand, she murmured, "'Ere now, ye poor troubled soul. 'Ere's a little treat for youse, to make yer time 'ere a bit sweeter." She handed him a biscuit wrapped in white waxed paper. The scent of almonds wafted to his nostrils.

His hands lashed out and closed like steely shackles on her wrists. "Help! Murder!" he cried, not in the rheumy voice of Hugh Boone, the pauper, but in the rich baritone of Sherlock Holmes of Baker Street.

Some days later, Holmes, Inspector Stanley Hopkins, and I sat in Baker Street with snifters of Holmes's precious Armagnac.

"I shall never forgive you for this, Holmes," I sniffed, but I knew that was a lie. Hadn't I already forgiven him for so much more?

"It really couldn't be helped," Holmes replied. "Would you have supported my plan to have myself admitted to St. Luke's to hunt a poisoner had you known?"

177

I didn't answer – I didn't need to. Instead, I asked, "How was it that you weren't concerned about the doctors discovering that you were malingering when they examined you in hospital? You said you wouldn't let me within four yards of you during the Culverton Smith affair."

"Then I was just faking, and feared you would expose me if you found out, but this time I was truly sick. I knew that I would never be admitted to hospital without Doctor Harris's *imprimatur*, so I took a sub-lethal dose of belladonna upon returning to my quarters after examining the day-books. By the time I was found, I had a fever, red, dry skin, dilated pupils, and a heart rate over one-twenty."

"If you suspected a poisoner at work in St. Luke's," Hopkins asked, "how could you risk being poisoned yourself during treatment?"

"I resolved not to take anything they gave me, and palm the pills instead. I fervently hoped no one would come at me with a hypodermic syringe. I knew that they would think that their treatment was effective because my condition would improve in time. I had sipped from a vial of physostigmine, an antidote to the atropine in belladonna, as the workhouse personnel were loading me onto the stretcher to carry me to hospital."

"And how did you know to smuggle all that truck in with you, including the lockpicks, when you were admitted to the workhouse?" I inquired. "You must have known you would be stripped and searched before you were let in."

"The lockpicks were in my mouth when they searched me. I cached the drugs outside before I entered the building. It was a workhouse, not a prison, so it was no great feat to slip out when I needed to."

I shook my head in disbelief. "And how the devil did you know that you would require such things in the first place?"

Holmes smiled at the question. "I knew that I was dealing with a poisoner if Henry Pepler had indeed not committed suicide. How else would he have come to ingest cyanide? And something that Coroner Humphries said impacted me: That the workhouses weren't required to report deaths that occurred therein. If a poisoner were active in St. Luke's, the odds were favourable that Henry Pepler wasn't the first victim. I would have to search the workhouse records to identify other suspected cases. Since Chumley Harris refused to speak with me, surely the lockpicks were a necessity. And it was also likely I would need to get into the hospital wing at some juncture. Hence, the belladonna.

"My perusal of the day-books was illuminating. I identified no less than fifteen deaths at St. Luke's in the past year that could have been poisonings, and in a dozen cases, the putative victim was either in hospital or had just been released. Doubtless, that accounted for Doctor Harris's reluctance to endure further scrutiny. My search of the W.C. in which poor

Mr. Pepler expired turned up a piece of waxed paper smelling heavily of almonds. I inferred that someone may have given him a treat that he was loath to consume where hungry eyes might notice – it made sense that he would seek privacy to enjoy it. So I arranged to have myself admitted to hospital in the hope that the poisoner would show me the same thoughtfulness."

"And if she had not?" Hopkins asked.

"Then I would have had to come up with another scheme, wouldn't I, Inspector?" he replied testily.

"One more thing I don't understand," I said. "Why did this Miss Rosie want to murder these men? Had they offended her in some way?"

"Just the opposite," replied Holmes. "She told Scotland Yard that she did it out of pity for what she perceived as their wretched state. She took their hospitalization as a sign from the Almighty that they were not long for this world, and thought she was doing them a mercy by hastening their departure from it. I shall write a monograph someday on the classification of mass murderers. Miss Rosie was of a class I shall call an 'Angel of Death', similar to a Teutonic Valkyrie who delivers a deserving soul to paradise.

"Mysticism possesses both good and evil aspects" he went on, "and when some well-meaning mystics find themselves out of their depth concerning matters which seem overwhelmingly important to them, those two aspects can become horribly confused, leading to actions which would be unthinkable to a logical mind. This phenomenon isn't specific to any one sect. Rather, it stems from an obsession to understand that which can never be understood, only believed. Such is the pitfall of blind faith in the absence of facts."

"But our faith never justifies the wanton slaughter of the innocent," I observed.

"No, it doesn't," Holmes agreed, "but for some, it can be exceedingly difficult to discern that which arises from God from the artefacts of their own diseased minds."

"Then what's the solution?" Hopkins asked.

"I am," smiled Holmes. "And yourself, and Watson, and others like us, who cannot abide such transgressions in this world."

I swirled the excellent spirit in my glass before taking a sip and allowing the liquid to trickle down my throat and the bouquet to pervade my sinuses. Perhaps my great friend was right. As long as those of us who live to combat the evil in the world exist, things are as they should be. I found great comfort in that thought.

Life was indeed grand.

"Hopkins has called me in seven times, and on each occasion his summons has been entirely justified," said Holmes.

– Sherlock Holmes
"The Abbey Grange"

The Crimson Trail
by Brenda Seabrooke

"*Tha' must mind out for that 'un,*" *Peters said.* "*He's a right bad 'un.*"

"*Aren't they all bad 'uns?*" *asked Biggins.*

"*Some may be, but most in the big house ha' mental problems and can't help tha'selves,*" *Peters nodded at the imposing metal door, located deep within the Fairfield Asylum.* "*That 'un knows what he's doin', an' likes it.*"

"*You mean killin' an' all?*"

"*Aye. And robbin'. His kind don' want to work like ordinary folk. They feel like the world owes 'em sumpin', and woe to him who gets in his path.*" *Peters opened the small peephole door.*

Biggins peered inside. The prisoner lay curled on his bed facing the wall. He didn't react to their voices or give any sign he heard them.

"*Is he breathin'?*"

"*He's breathin', all right,*" *Peters said.* "*Nobody down here is as bad as this 'un, or as smart. He's a right brain, he is.*""

"*Not smart enough not ta get caught,*" *Biggins said with a grin.*

"*Tha' won't believe what he did ta get caught. I heard he's a' 'arch-criminal', as they say, an' a admitted murderer. He killed eight people in Lunnon alone!*"

"*What's his name?*"

"*We don't say his real name, you understand, but down here he goes by 'Roy Smith' He's some kind of kin to the Royal Family. He's right royal, he is – but keep that ta yerself.*"

"*Kin to the Queen?*" *Biggins' eyes widened.*

"*Aye. Sumpin' like that, he sez.*

"*What's he doing locked in here then, 'stead of with other criminals?*"

"*He's more dangerous than those. He's a real cold-blooded killer, he is.*"

Biggins looked thrilled. "*Do you think I could get his auty-graph?*"

"*Ask him – but be polite-like. He don't like people making fun at him.*"

Biggins opened the larger observation door. "*Mr. Smith, sir,*" *he said, his voice louder,* "*my name's Biggins. Could I please get your auty-graph?*"

No reply. Mr. 'Smith' didn't move.

181

"He isn't in a good mood," explained Peters, "but then, he never is. Just shove the tray through the slot and let's go now. Woodyard can pick it up in the morning. We got work ta do . . . ."

"You are the worst patient I have ever encountered," I said as Holmes leapt from chair to table to chair again, looking for entertainment in the form of a monograph, a newspaper, a chemistry problem – anything to pique his interest.

"I need a case."

"You won't find any in this room. Stop moving around. It jars your ankle. Sit down and stay in your chair. You're resting for a while until that ankle heals."

He had awakened me in the early morning hours when he hopped up the steps to our sitting room. I then spent the next few hours alternating cold and warm packs on his ankle, wrenched on dark ice when he returned from an investigation. "Take a nap. You must be sleepy after traveling all night."

He slapped a newspaper off the table. "I'm not tired. On the contrary, I'm full of energy and bored. I need something to distract me. You know how I hate to be mentally idle."

"Well, you're not going out on that ankle, and that's that." I tried to loom menacingly, but only made him laugh.

"I don't have any weight on it, see?" He crouched on one leg over a tangle of newspapers, his injured leg stuck out behind him while his right leg bore his weight, which wasn't as much as it should be for his tall frame.

He teetered and would've fallen had I not grabbed his shoulder and strong-armed him back into his chair. I propped the damaged limb on an ottoman and tossed a plaid rug over his legs as he settled his features into morosity. "Now you look the proper invalid," I said with satisfaction, "but remember to move your toes to keep the circulation going."

We were interrupted by the sound of the doorbell downstairs. Holmes perked up.

"You aren't going out of this house until your ankle is healed," I reminded him. "And don't think you can sneak out if I leave to see a patient. Mrs. Hudson will take over. There is no eluding her. She wields a mean broom."

As if in reply to her name, Mrs. Hudson knocked on the door. "Inspector Hopkins and two other gentlemen to see you, Mr. Holmes."

Holmes looked as thrilled as I've ever seen him. "Thank you, Mrs. Hudson. Send them in, please."

182

She disappeared for a moment and then returned with three men whose coats and hats had already been deposited in the downstairs hall. "Go right in."

"Come in, gentlemen. Hopkins." Holmes nodded at the inspector. "What can we do for you?"

The two strangers were well-dressed and bore the marks of the middle-class in their speech and manner. Hopkins was his usual self, with his thrown-together look in a brown suit, maroon tie slightly askew, and his narrow face home to a sharp nose and a sharper pair of eyes.

"This is Mr. Ogden-Truitt, Director of the Fairfield Asylum in Yorkshire, and Dr. Bennet, who is the – "

"Your famed prisoner has escaped from the asylum," Holmes interrupted.

They looked surprised, more so than Hopkins who was accustomed to Holmes's astounding powers. The inspector tried, but couldn't contain his snort.

Dr. Bennet recovered first. "How did you know?"

"Why else would you have come here at this time of day? Your special prisoner has escaped, and you believe him to be headed to, or perhaps already in, London. I can think of no other reason for your visit. Eliminate the impossible, and whatever is left must be the solution. Gentlemen, sit down and tell me about your concerns."

As they were being seated, I explained what happened to Holmes's ankle. They looked disappointed.

"We were hoping you could help us," Hopkins said.

"Because William Maugham has escaped," I said. It wasn't a question. I wasn't surprised it had happened. I don't have Holmes's powers of deduction, but after working with him, I've learned something of his methods.

Ogden-Truitt nodded. "We're trying to keep it quiet. We don't want to give the situation any more publicity than we have to, but we can't find a trace of him. It's as if he disappeared from the earth."

Recalling how Maugham's trial had been covered in the newspapers, I asked, "Does anyone know just many murders Maugham has committed?"

"Not for sure," Bennet said. "When questioned, Maugham just laughed."

"Scotland Yard attributes eight in London alone to him," Hopkins said. "No doubt that's a conservative figure. We have no idea what he may have done in the Shires."

"How long has he been missing?" I asked.

"Two days," Hopkins said.

183

"Two?" Holmes said, with not quite a sneer. "And you're just now seeking help?"

"We notified police in the area of the asylum," Ogden-Truitt said, "but they've turned up no traces of him. It's as if he's vanished."

This time Holmes snorted.

"We're sorry we took up your time," Ogden-Truitt said, his porcine features stiffening. He was about my height, but of considerably more weight and with large protruding blue eyes. The doctor was taller with dark hair and eyes, and an air of understanding that many in that profession aquire from observations of their fellow man.

"You're incapacitated," Dr. Bennet said. "We didn't know."

The party stood to leave, but Holmes stopped them. "Wait!"

They turned back to him in puzzlement – hoping, no doubt, for words of wisdom from the famed detective. I didn't expect him to give them much. How could he know anything from just now hearing about the escape? He surprised me.

"Just a run-in with a bit of ice," Holmes said. "I can manage with a cane – "

"You will not," I said.

"Watson, this is a gift! I'm between investigations, gentlemen. I shall be glad to take it."

"You're staying right here. Walking on that ankle now will only worsen the wrench and lengthen the healing time."

"Then I shall solve it for you from this room," Holmes said with certainty.

"Holmes . . . ." I warned.

"How can you?" Bennet was skeptical, and didn't try to hide it.

"I'll not leave this room. Watson, you'll see. Now, gentlemen, please be seated again." They returned to their chairs. This time, Ogden-Truitt took mine directly across from Holmes. His knees almost touched the ottoman bearing Holmes's s blanket-clad feet.

"Watson," Holmes directed, "a spot of brandy for this cold, dreary barely April morning."

I poured brandy into four glasses and handed them around. Then I poured one for myself and pulled up another chair to listen to Holmes spin a tale on this blustery London day. I was confident he wouldn't be able to do more than give the men direction, and wished I'd made a wager with him as Bennet recounted the little they knew about the escape.

When we were all settled, Holmes said, "Tell me everything. Leave out nothing, no matter how trivial or inconsequential you may think it."

Dr. Bennet cleared his throat.

"Two days ago – the day before yesterday – the guard delivered Maugham's morning meal and found him lying curled in his bed, facing the wall, as was his habit of late. He removed the evening meal tray and slid the breakfast tray through the slot. When he returned with the noon meal, the morning tray was untouched. Maugham hadn't moved, and he was unresponsive to commands. The guard returned and reported Maugham's condition. I called on another guard to accompany us and we went to examine the prisoner.

"I unlocked the door and we entered. Still no response from Maugham. I reached and felt for a pulse and, finding none, turned him over onto his back. His face was covered in blood that spilled onto the front of his nightshirt – or what we took at the time to be blood. Our first thought was that Maugham had been attacked with a cudgel of some sort and bludgeoned to death. I sent a guard to bring the director as I searched for wounds. I hadn't found any when they returned and, using the prisoner's carafe of water, I cleaned his face. That's when we made the discovery."

"The face didn't belong to the prisoner," Holmes said.

Ogden-Truitt looked surprised. Hopkins smiled and nodded to himself.

"How, sir, can you know that?" Ogden-Truitt asked.

"It is my business to know that."

Bennet nodded. He understood now he was in the presence of a razor-sharp intellect. "The dead man was the night guard," he explained.

"And the blood?" I asked.

Bennet consulted his notes as if to assure himself. "The blood on the face and the nightshirt proved to be dye of some sort, and didn't come from any wounds on the body."

"A theatrical touch consistent with his personality," Holmes said with a nod.

"I determined the cause of death was strangulation," continued the doctor.

"*Petechiae*?" I asked.

"Yes," Bennet confirmed. "His face exhibited *petechiae* due to manual strangulation."

"I questioned the guards," Ogden Pruitt added, "and assured myself that none had given the prisoner anything to aid in his escape. We can only surmise at this point what happened when the guard took the evening meal on the previous night. Maugham must've been lying in his customary position, but respiration couldn't be discerned. Against training regulations, the guard entered with his key to check on the unresponsive prisoner. As he turned him over, Maugham must then have clamped his hands around the man's throat and strangled him. It would've taken about three minutes.

"He then exchanged clothing with the guard and smeared his face with the red dye," Bennet concluded.

"And put him in the curled position in which you found him," Holmes added.

"He must have consumed the contents of the evening tray," Ogden-Truitt said, taking over the narrative. "It was clean the next morning when the guard brought the prisoner's breakfast. Then Maugham, using the dead guard's keys, walked out unnoticed."

"Wasn't the evening guard missed?" I asked.

Ogden-Truitt shook his head. "It was his last duty of the day to deliver the prisoner's meal, so if he didn't return afterwards, he wouldn't have been missed."

"And what happened when the escape was discovered?"

"There isn't much more to tell," Ogden-Truitt said. "We searched the buildings and the grounds and found nothing. We spent the rest of that day, and yesterday as well, hoping to pick up some sign of the man, but with no success. This morning we came to consult you."

I leaned forward. "Did you use dogs?"

"We did," Ogden-Truitt said. "The hunt continued with the dogs, but the problem was that Maugham had donned all of the guard's clothing and left his own on the dead man. They were about the same size. Some time passed before we could procure something of the guard's. The dogs were confused by the double scents and couldn't find a trail."

"There is also some indication," Bennet added, "that Maugham had saved pepper from his meals in order to put it outside the cell door so that the dogs' noses would be confused."

"And you informed the local police?" Holmes asked.

Hopkins glanced at Ogden-Truitt and said, "They did, and then in turn called in the Yard, but to prevent any public panic, we've simply put it about that a lunatic has escaped. We announced that it was '*Roy Smith*'. No one knows yet that it was Maugham who escaped."

"When the public perceives the massive efforts made to recapture him," Holmes said, "it won't take long for them to guess who is really at large. Was it wise to hide the fact that such a man is on the loose?"

Ogden-Truitt flushed. "We also let it be known that this man is dangerous and may be posing as royalty." He glanced toward Holmes's ankle. "And we had hoped you might help us catch him."

"And so I shall," Holmes promised once again.

"But how can you say that?" Ogden-Truitt said. "You're confined to your chair!"

186

"I repeat, I shall solve your case without leaving this flat." Holmes waved his hand. "Now continue. Tell me more about Maugham, beginning with his stay at Fairfield, from the beginning."

"He arrived six months ago, almost to the day," explained Dr. Bennet, "William Maugham, clad in women's garments to prevent any public knowledge that he was there, was brought to the institute as 'Miss Joanna Cane', dangerous and delusional."

"How was he conveyed to the asylum?" I asked. "By closed coach or by train?"

"Coach," Ogden-Pruitt said. "He wouldn't have been able to see much if any of the countryside, so he won't know a great deal about his surroundings."

"Upon his arrival," Bennet continued, "Maugham was issued men's clothing, *sans* belt, suspenders, or necktie. His shoes were carpet slippers. He was lodged in a part of the building formerly used for storage of things that needed to be kept cool. This was decided because the only way in or out is through a separate entrance. A grated stone fireplace along one wall is the only heat source. The room is furnished with an – " Bennet pulled a little book out of his vest pocket and turned several pages. " – iron bed against the far wall, horizontal to the door, a deal writing table, and chair on one side, a necessary with a basin and ewer on the other, and a rug on the floor. A narrow barred transom over the door is the only light source besides the fire. Coal was doled out to him through the slot where he receives his meal trays, a few small pieces at a time."

"Meals are served three times a day," Ogden-Truitt said. "At seven in the morning, at noon, and at five in the afternoon, and a pitcher of water daily."

"He also seemed to use a lot of soap," Dr. Bennet added. "More than the usual pris – er, more than the usual *patient* in the asylum, and he's asked for a second pitcher of water of late."

"Shaving apparatus?" Holmes asked.

"A razor contrived in a box attached to a chain held by the guard was allowed every other morning," Bennet said. "His hair was cut once a month on the first, while he's shackled. He'd last shaved the morning before his escape."

"And today is the third morning," Holmes said, "so his hair won't be disheveled from length, and he was freshly shaved and won't look to the untrained eye like a mental patient. Maugham thought of everything. All he had to do was await his opportunity."

Bennet nodded.

"You mentioned a deal writing table," said Holmes. "Was he allowed books and writing materials? Be specific," Holmes leaned back in his chair and closed his eyes.

"He was allowed books, periodicals, and newspapers," Ogden-Truitt answered, "and a few pieces of writing paper at a time, along with a soft stub of a pencil."

"I approved his reading lists," Bennet said. "The tomes all seemed time-consuming. They would keep him occupied."

"Did you choose the books provided to him?" Holmes asked.

"No," Dr. Bennet replied. "He made requests."

"And this consisted of – ?"

"Well, there were no lurid yellow books, I assure you," Bennet replied. "His list was most edifying: Historicals. A few novels – Dickens mainly."

"I need a specific list of the books in his possession at the time of his escape," Holmes stated, "and a drawing of his cell as it was when you found him. Show everything in it, including the vessels in which his food was brought, and the tray."

"Is that necessary?" Ogden-Truitt asked with obvious skepticism.

"Everything is necessary if you wish to apprehend him before he kills again," Holmes said neutrally.

Dr. Bennet looked slightly exasperated, but he consulted his notebook and spent a moment scribbling before he tore out several pages. He handed them to Holmes.

"This is everything?"

"Yes, it is."

"These are the books he requested?"

"Yes."

Holmes scanned the list. "Ah yes, Fitch's *Castilian Conquest of the Canary Islands*. Can you tell me if the edition of *Romola* was published in 1891?" he asked.

"I don't have that information," Bennet said flipping through his notes. "Is it important?"

"Yes," Holmes said, controlling his sibilance.

"Come, come, Mr. Holmes." Hopkins was impatient. "What difference does it make which edition the man read? The book didn't have information in it to help him break out of his prison."

Ogden-Truitt turned to Holmes. "Did it?"

"Not to the naked eye. Nevertheless, I need that information. Hopkins, please send a telegram to ascertain that fact. In addition, send wires to all the train stations near the asylum and beyond, asking if a man of Maugham's description boarded a train. That information is crucial to determine his route and possible destination."

"We've already done that, Mr. Holmes," replied the inspector. "No one reported seeing a uniformed man purchasing a ticket or boarding the train."

"What does the guard's uniform look like?" Holmes asked.

"Not too different from a police constable's," Ogden-Truitt said. "Dark blue coat and trousers, black shoes, a cap with a bill."

"Any insignias?"

"Yes, the initials of the Fairchild Asylum on the cap, and an insignia of rank on the collar devices – "

"Both of which can be easily removed and the cap discarded," Holmes said. "The uniform then could pass for ordinary clothing, especially if the wearer was perusing a newspaper."

Bennet nodded. "We didn't consider that."

"Maugham would've had no difficulty boarding a train surreptitiously. Ask the station masters you've already queried for descriptions of everyone boarding the trains – women or men – and not just to the south, but in any direction on that evening. And send telegrams to the next stations on the line as well."

Hopkins nodded and slipped downstairs to send the messages by way of a waiting constable.

"Did Maugham have the means to purchase a ticket?" Holmes asked as we awaited the inspector's return. "How much money would the deceased guard have carried with him?"

"Very little," Bennet said. "He hadn't been paid. The guards are discouraged from carrying more than a few pence with them in case some of the patients have light fingers."

"There is one way that Maugham may have obtained some money," Ogden-Truitt said. "He charged one of the guards ten pence for his autograph. He may have done the same for others we don't know about."

When neither Bennet nor Ogden-Truitt offered more, Holmes prompted them to continue.

"It seems that to the guards," Bennet explained, "Maugham was something of a celebrity – particularly to two of them named Peters and Biggins." He went on to explain how Biggins had, on several occasions and against all the rules, begun to pester the prisoner for an autograph. At first there was no response, but apparently Maugham finally agreed.

"Several days ago," explained Bennet, "Maugham agreed to sell an autograph. Biggins left the payment, and when he next delivered the prisoner's food tray, an autographed piece of paper was stuck in the slot."

189

"And which of the two guards was found dead in Maugham's cot?" asked Holmes. "Peters or Biggins? Surely it wasn't Biggins, who had requested the autograph. Or perhaps it was – with Maugham's twisted mind, he might have considered it an honor for Biggins to be known as one of his victims."

"No, it wasn't Biggins," said Bennet.

"I'm glad of that," I said.

"Nor was it Peters," Ogden-Truitt added. "It was a new fellow – Woodyard was his name – who went to the cell by himself before he was checked out to do so. New guards are to be accompanied by a seasoned man for a month. This man was cocky from all accounts. And he paid for it with his life."

As the afternoon progressed, Holmes – by way of Hopkins – sent and received various telegrams as ideas occurred to him. Bennet completed his drawings of the cell and the countryside around Fairview. Meanwhile, time passed slowly as we awaited answers. The mantel clock seemed to tick louder than usual. I poured another round of brandy for everyone. Holmes asked Hopkins what else had been done to capture Maugham.

"The nets are fixed, Mr. Holmes." The inspector rubbed his hands as if he'd been working in china clay. "Figuring that he'd head this way, officers are stationed in pairs all over Paddington Station. Maugham will not get past them."

"How long have they been in place?" Holmes asked.

"Since we were notified of his escape," Hopkins said.

I glanced at Holmes. I could, for once, tell what he was thinking. "If the escape was only discovered the next morning," I said, "then Maugham already had ample opportunity to go in any direction. You don't know the exact time he made his escape or the direction he was traveling, or his destination, or by which station he might enter London. Guarding Paddington isn't enough. If Maugham took a fast train immediately after his escape, he could have hidden himself anywhere in London long before your men positioned themselves."

Holmes gave me a nod. "Excellent assessment, Watson."

"The job now is to recapture the criminal," Hopkins argued. "The route he took can be established after we have him. Do you agree that London is his mostly likely destination?"

"Indeed," said Holmes, "but knowing the route he took could help us recapture him before he harms anyone – if he hasn't already done so. We have to consider his targets. In the past, they have always been members of the upper classes, but he was never averse to killing anyone else who got in his way."

190

Holmes asked me to retrieve the relevant scrapbook from the shelf behind my chair. He flipped through it until he found his entry for Maugham.

"In London he has killed a coachman, a baron, two elderly widows, an admiral, the niece of a member of Parliament and her maid, and Lady Tillson. I don't see much pattern there, but he seems to prefer members of society and their servants. The guard's death was necessary to cover the fact of his escape as long as possible." He looked to Hopkins. "No new reports of thefts or murders outside of the asylum grounds so far, I assume?"

"None reported as of noon today by the local constabulary."

Holmes nodded. "Then I think we can rule out his hiding in the local countryside or forting up somewhere on the moors." He turned to Ogden-Truitt. "Has he any relatives who would aid and abet?"

"None that we know about," explained Ogden-Truitt. "There is some truth to his claims of royal blood. The Royal Family has never acknowledged his existence publicly and wants him to go away and stay away – hence the Fairfield Asylum cell. They can't stop him from claiming royal blood, but many criminals have been known to do that. They don't want him hanged because then his royal status would be revealed. The publicity would be damaging to the Crown.

"They also don't want him housed with common criminals or mental patients for much the same reason. Hence his solitary cell. The staff hasn't specifically been told that he is a royal. They have heard rumors, of course, but only Dr. Bennet and I have this knowledge with certainty.

"The crimes and murders he has committed are known, but he is 'Roy Smith' at Fairfield." Ogden-Truitt finished his brandy.

"More?" I asked him.

"Not now, thank you."

Fortuitously at that moment, Mrs. Hudson – sensing, no doubt, the urgency of the situation without knowing the facts – brought us trays, with Daisy, the temporary maid, assisting her. They poured tea for all of us and left us replenishing ourselves with scones, sandwiches, and biscuits – a welcome respite after so much brandy.

I poured a cup of tea, buttered a scone, and topped it with jam. Meanwhile, our visitors also helped themselves. Holmes's appetite was also hearty now that he had something to occupy his mind. Mental activity would speed his healing as he forgot that he was staying off his feet. An immobile Holmes was difficult at the best of times.

Holmes continued to study the sketches as he ate whatever I put on his plate, without seeming to notice the difference between a scone or a biscuit or a sandwich.

"Any further thoughts?" Ogden-Truitt finally asked.

"None that I care to share at this point."

"Surely Maugham would've taken the easiest route," Ogden-Truitt theorized, not for the first time as the day dragged on. "And he wouldn't be able to travel far on foot, because he hasn't been exercising during the months he's been incarcerated."

"Not necessarily," replied Holmes. "He would know we would think of that. Maugham is smart, a wily criminal, or he would've been captured long before he was. Also, we don't know what he did at night. He could've lifted his iron bedstead a hundred times a night, run miles in place, and walked the distance to a distant railway station within the parameters of his cell. In short, gentlemen, he most likely has been planning and preparing for this escape since the day he arrived, half-a-year ago. He would have noted the uniforms which, with moderations, could pass for an ordinary man's coat. When he was brought in, did anyone check his mouth for anything he might have carried with him – Coins? A small penknife?"

"No," Ogden-Truitt said with noticeable exasperation, as if we were challenging his administration of the institution. "That's never been required at the asylum. I received the procedural manuals when I was named director. We followed them for Maugham, just as for the other patients."

Holmes gave him a sharp look. I knew what that meant: A new manual should've been written for this singular prisoner.

Ogden-Truitt must have understood Holmes's thoughts. "We were cautioned not to put any directives concerning this specific prisoner into writing, as something might embarrass the Queen should they be stolen or copied.

Holmes raised an eyebrow. Obviously something had gone awry, or we wouldn't be discussing the escaped killer.

Holmes continued to study the notes that Odgen-Truitt had provided. "Not much of a life for a man such as William Maugham," he mused. "I do wish the Royals would take care of their messes." He looked up. "All Maugham had to do in that cave-like cell was plan his escape and decide which of the guards he preferred to kill."

Holmes held up the drawing of the prisoner's cell and the food utensils. "The cups and bowls and plates are tin, you say?"

"That's right," Bennet said, "and all accounted for after every meal."

"The meals are left on trays at the cell and retrieved at the next meal."

"It simplifies the guards' duties. Breakfast is delivered at seven. Then at noon, that tray is retrieved when the noon meal is served, and then that tray retrieved at the evening meal."

"His morning meal tray was still there when the guard went to deliver the mid-day meal?" I asked.

"Yes."

"The tin tray's edge forms a lip?"

"Yes," answered Bennet. "In case of spillage. The spoons he used are carved from pine by one of the guards, as well as a crude fork."

"No wooden knives?"

A smile twitched at the corners of Holmes's mouth.

"None. His meat is always cut before leaving the kitchen."

"That must have been a great trial to the descendant of a Royal Duke," I said with a bit of sarcasm.

Hopkins laughed. He apparently had no great liking for many of the upper class. "Maugham probably told himself that having his food cut up is part of the service to his Royal Highness, like food tasting and embroidered underclothing."

Dr. Bennet turned away to hide his smile.

The doorbell sounded downstairs. "That will be Carstairs with answers to some of the telegrams," Hopkins said.

The constable was admitted by Daisy, who let him come up without being announced. No time for niceties now. I opened the door to the landing as soon as his knuckles grazed it. He held a sheaf of telegrams which he handed to me, and which I then passed to Hopkins.

"Thank you, Constable," he said. "You may wait downstairs." He glanced through them and then said, "These are lists of passengers – all that could be determined. Names, when known, and descriptions."

"Hand them around." Holmes said, and Hopkins parceled them out to the five of us.

"What are we looking for?" Ogden-Truitt asked.

"Anything that can give us a clue to the escapee," Holmes said. "Take out a pencil and cross out any passengers that cannot possibly be Maugham. When you're finished, pass them to someone else to double-check."

We quickly scanned the wire messages. I crossed out three short women, a family, and two couples. My possibles were two tall women traveling on a west-bound line.

"Let's report," Holmes finally said. "Watson?"

"Two tall women headed west," I began.

"We can rule them out," Ogden-Truitt said.

"Not necessarily," Holmes said. "The crucial factor is their status as travelers. Were they together or separate?"

"The ticket master says together."

"Dr. Bennet?"

"Three single men, but they were on the short side. Maugham isn't as tall as you, Mr. Holmes, but neither is he considered short."

"Director?"

"None to report."

"Hopkins?"

"Families – Short women, two short men."

"I have none either," Holmes said. "Director, are you sure?"

"Well, there was one tallish man, but he appears to be a Scot headed home on the north-bound train, instead of toward London."

"'Appears to be'?" I asked.

"Red-headed with a strong Scot's burr."

"Please pass me all of the telegrams," said Holmes, "so that I may scan them."

I collected them and deposited them into his outstretched hand. He was silent as he looked at each one, before then discarding each into a pile on the floor. He kept one in his hand. "I don't see a reply about the book edition," he said.

Exasperation flitted across Ogden-Truitt's ample features. "I fail to see the importance of one edition of a book or another."

Holmes curbed his impatience. "It is important to look at everything for clues."

The downstairs bell sounded and the constable returned with another telegram for Hopkins. In the meantime, Holmes scribbled a message on a scrap of paper and bade the constable to send it immediately. At Hopkins's nod, he took it. Hopkins wrote one of his own and gave it to him as well.

When we heard the downstairs door close, Hopkins said, "We have a problem. The Queen has been confined to Buckingham Palace by the weather for four days. She now wishes to go for a late afternoon drive in Hyde Park for fresh air. The departments who protect her cannot stop her, but we have warned her guards that today isn't the best time and to tell her the weather is uncertain – that it may rain or even snow."

"Can't you tell her the real reason?" I asked. "That a killer who likes murdering the upper classes is likely on the loose in London? She seems reasonable for a queen."

"She is also stubborn and has a calm, cool character after surviving eight assassination attempts," Hopkins replied. 'We shall not be ruled by the unhinged,' she is reported to have said. And Maugham is her relative, though publicly unclaimed. Apparently she feels he would not harm her."

"She may actually believe that as queen she is immune to death by assassination," Holmes mused, "but it would be prudent not to drive her carriage into face of it."

"The last assassination attempt was over fourteen years ago," Hopkins said. "And one of her past attackers actually hit her in the head with a cane. She sustained an enormous swelling and bruising of her face and eye."

"We must work faster," Holmes said. "I feel the need for a pipe. Will anyone join me?"

Ogden-Truitt accepted a Cuban cigar, but Bennet declined. Holmes filled his pipe with black shag and soon the room filled with the pungent smoke. I opened the far window an inch or two. Would this be a one-pipe problem? The most I'd seen Holmes smoke when mulling a case was three, but those cases didn't have the consequences this one now promised. While he smoked, Holmes continued to study Bennet's drawings of the cell and the grounds of the asylum, along with nearby railway stations. Once he consulted his *Bradshaw*, but made no explanation. He seemed lost in his musings when the bell sounded yet again downstairs. I met the constable at the door and accepted the telegrams he brought. I gave several to Holmes and another to Ogden-Truitt who opened it, took a look, and passed it to Holmes.

"Here is the further information on those books you seem to think is so important," he said.

Holmes read the telegram, along with his own. Then he stated, "I thought as much. Gentlemen, I can now tell you that the Scot who was headed north was William Maugham."

"Thank goodness the Queen is safe!" Ogden-Truitt said. "Hopkins, you can tell your men to stand down now. Maugham is fleeing the away from the capital."

Hopkins didn't react. He'd worked with Holmes enough to know something was afoot.

"I think not," Holmes said, pulling out one of his own telegrams from the stack. "Last night, a railway porter in his velveteen uniform was waylaid on that line and found locked in a lady's trunk in Berwick. When discovered, he was wearing only his underclothing."

"Did he say who did it?" Hopkins asked.

"He was hit from behind. Maugham didn't go to Edinburgh, but dressed as a porter and, without doubt, boarded a train at the next station headed south to London. Hopkins, you must telegraph the Yard to step up the constables on the grounds of the parks and palace, because the assassin may be headed for the Queen. Have them clothed in ordinary dress as much as is possible on such short notice, and watch for a tall red-haired man, most likely still wearing the porter's uniform – but he could also have affected another disguise acquired on the train or in London: A chimney sweep, a clerk, even a hansom driver. He may still have the red hair, and he'll likely be wearing a hat or cap."

Hopkins didn't wait around for explanations, but leapt to his feet and rushed downstairs, giving orders to the constable as he ran.

"Let us hope he's in time," Holmes said. "If Queen Victoria is his target . . . ."

The next two hours were excruciating as we awaited word on the capture of the criminal, but at half-after-five, Hopkins returned.

From the look on his face, like a man after a satisfying meal, I knew he'd been in time.

"Come in, Hopkins," Holmes said, "and tell us how it went."

The inspector didn't bother removing his topcoat, but he did take off his hat. He accepted the cup of coffee I poured for him. He was exhilarated by the successful capture, but he would soon begin to fade. I put in extra sugar. He nodded his thanks as he took a long swallow.

"It was just as you suspected, Mr. Holmes," he said. "The red-haired Scot *was* William Maugham. Since his escape, he acquired a pistol from some unknown source and a workman's clothing, but he isn't talking. When the Queen's carriage approached, he took aim. One of the disguised constables, hobbling along with a cane, saw him and raised it, bringing it down on Maugham's arm so hard that the cane cracked. Maugham was immediately apprehended by constables in the area and hustled away to the Yard. I doubt the Queen even knew what happened."

"God save the Queen," Ogden-Pruitt murmured.

"I rather think Scotland Yard did that," Holmes said.

"Tell us, Mr. Holmes," Dr. Bennet asked, "how did you know the red-haired man headed for Scotland was the culprit?"

"It was the two books I inquired about," Holmes said.

"Books!" Ogden-Truitt sputtered. "How could those two books tell you anything?"

Bennet gave him a look. He might have had an inkling of the part those books played. I had a glimmer, but it was far-fetched in my opinion.

"Here is how it had to have happened," Holmes said. "When Woodyard brought the evening tray, he found, as you surmised, the prisoner curled up in a fetal position, apparent blood staining his nightwear, possibly even some on his face. Woodyard entered with his key, which is against regulations for new guards, but he was startled and thought something had happened to the prisoner. He, no doubt, bent over to examine the prisoner, and that's when Maugham grabbed his neck and strangled him. He exchanged clothing with Woodyard and put red dye on

196

the man's face before turning him to the wall to delay his discovery longer."

"But – "

Holmes held up his hand to Ogden-Truitt. "A moment. Those two books are the key. Maugham requested them because the backing of the Canary Island history is *yellow* and the 1891 edition of *Romola's* cover is *red*. Maugham likely poured water onto his tray and used it to soak the backing of the book and make red and yellow dyes. He probably had already used his noon tray to make the red dye and put it on his nightshirt ahead of time. In the evening food tray, he soaked the yellow one while he exchanged clothing with the deceased guard and ate his meal. He mixed the red and yellow and applied the result to his fair hair, thus disguising himself as red-haired. He cleaned the trays and returned the dishes to them.

"He removed the insignias from the coat, possibly as he walked to the railway station, where he boarded the north-bound train, making us think he was a homeward-bound Scot. He attacked a porter, donned his velveteen uniform and got off at the next station to catch the London-bound train. He wouldn't need money for a ticket while wearing the uniform, and if questioned he could say he was on his way somewhere. When he arrived in London, he acquired a gun from some source and his workman's disguise which no doubt included a cap to cover his dyed hair Was he wearing one when you caught him?" he asked Hopkins.

"Yes, he was," Hopkins said, "but it didn't cover all of his red hair, and it fell off in the scuffle."

"He loitered unobserved, he thought, near the palace watching for opportunity. When the gates opened and the carriage drove out, the chance was his to kill the Queen. He is full of rage because the Royal Family won't include him or acknowledge his rightful place as a royal. Unbeknownst to him, the Queen has prevented him from hanging like the killer deserves."

"There's rotten apples in every barrel," Hopkins said.

Ogden-Truitt's face was a picture of amazement. "And you deduced all of that from a book cover?"

"*Two* book covers," Holmes said. "I knew that the Canary Island volume's cover was yellow because only one edition of that tale has been printed. I needed to know if *Romola* was the red-backed 1891 edition to proceed."

"Where will they incarcerate him this time?" Ogden-Truitt asked. "I hope not at Fairfield."

"Perhaps on an island somewhere," Holmes said with a smile. "I hear St. Helena is lovely this time of year."

They took their leave after thanking Holmes profusely.

197

Hopkins lingered. "A book, Mr. Holmes! This case depended on a book! Who would've ever suspected?" He left, shaking his head.

I refrained from saying *A book! A book! My kingdom for a book!* "This was an interesting afternoon."

"Indeed it was."

"I think Hopkins was wrong about the Queen, however. I'm sure she was aware of what was happening. Anyone who has survived eight known assassination attempts would perforce be acutely aware of what was going on around her."

"No doubt, Watson, no doubt."

A few days later, a courier arrived at 221b Baker Street. Mrs. Hudson brought him up the stairs herself. She was so excited she could hardly speak. "He's from the Palace."

The courier, a footman in Palace livery, presented a small box to Holmes. "With Her Majesty's deepest appreciation," he said and took his leave.

Mrs. Hudson was torn between escorting him down the stairs or staying to see what was in the box.

"I'll wait until you're back to open it, Mrs. Hudson," Holmes said with a smile.

No sooner had the downstairs door closed than she flew back up the stairs. "What did she send you?"

Holmes removed the silk wrapping. He opened the Windsor-blue enameled box, a treasure in itself, to find a small medal with a ruby imbedded. "It's a *'Personal Service to Her Majesty'* Medal," he said, taking it out.

The ruby caught the firelight and flashed red.

"Most appropriate," I said. "You followed a crimson trail from the Fairfield Asylum to Buckingham Palace, without ever leaving 221b Baker Street."

"Hopkins has called me in seven times, and on each occasion his summons has been entirely justified," said Holmes.

– Sherlock Holmes
"The Abbey Grange"

The Three Archers
by Alan Dimes

Those who have followed my chronicles of the exploits of Mr. Sherlock Holmes from their earliest publication will be aware that the first of them, *A Study in Scarlet*, is described, in part, as being *"A Reprint from The Reminiscences of John H. Watson, M.D., Late of the Army Medical Department"*. This has led some of my readers to inquire if it is possible to also obtain a copy of that book. The answer, alas, is no.

Any aspiring author can tell the tale of his or her early frustrations: The return of one's manuscript by publisher after publisher, the loss of a book in transit, (making it necessary to choose between rewriting the entire story and abandoning the enterprise altogether), or acceptance of one's manuscript accompanied by a demand for drastic cutting or revision.

My *Reminiscences* fall into the last category. My publishers determined that the public would not be interested in the story of my upbringing, my schooldays, and my early visits to the United States and Australia, and that the narrative really begins with my meeting Holmes, the main interest being our pursuit and capture of Jefferson Hope. The second section, "The Country of the Saints", while it is based on the experiences of Hope and the Ferriers, contains a strong element of fiction, as I was required to concoct a narrative using the meagre information on the subject I had to hand.

So while *A Study in Scarlet* drew on my manuscript, it cannot truly be described as a "reprint", since the original was never printed, and so does not exist as a separate entity. No doubt the publishers thought that it made the narrative appear more authoritative. I must admit that in all probability, they made the right decision, although I did not believe that to be the case at the time.

Another point which correspondents frequently raise in connection with that first book is: Why does Holmes's practice seem to consist, in those early days, entirely of cases which he can solve without leaving the confines of 221b Baker Street? Was the Lauriston Gardens mystery the first time he solved a case by visiting the location of the crime and questioning witnesses?

Certainly, it was the first occasion on which he asked *me* to accompany him, but from conversations with him over many years. It is clear that both the police and clients had summoned him to various locations during his time in Montague Street. It must also be remembered that during those first weeks during which we shared rooms, I was still in the last stages of a long convalescence, and thus unable in any event to accompany him on cases which demanded that he leave our lodgings.

As time went on, and Holmes's reputation grew, he could both command higher fees and be more selective about which cases in which he would become involved. The number which he could solve without leaving his armchair dwindled, but didn't disappear altogether. I have already related he stories of Mary Sutherland and her duplicitous stepfather, and that of John Openshaw and the five orange pips. The following narrative takes place some years later, but falls into a similar category.

By the year 1896, the popularity of archery had gone a little into decline. It had been surpassed as a fashionable pastime for the middle classes by sports such as croquet and tennis. Nevertheless, some fifty archery clubs still remained in Britain. In 1894, the first Olympics committee, headed by Baron Pierre de Coubertin, announced that the 1900 Games would take place in Paris, and that archery would be among the events. This provoked a fierce atmosphere of competition among that group of practitioners who made up the members of the remaining clubs. The fact that six years must elapse before the British team was chosen seemed to have intensified that atmosphere rather than dissipated it.

The Fernfield Archery Club near High Barnet in north London was one of the oldest in the country, having been founded in 1863, only two years after the formation of the Grand National Archery Society. The GNAS organized the Annual National Championship competitions, and would also have a considerable say in who was chosen to represent the country in the first British Olympic archery team. Fernfield's reputation was good. Only two of its members had ever won the championship, but they were always well represented in the semi- and quarter-finals.

In the year 1896, the club had three outstanding archers: W.H. Cullen, D.N. Edginton, and R.H. McNeil. In June, the month before that year's championship, it appeared certain that one of them would win the competition, though it was difficult to say which, since they seemed equally adept. Under those circumstances, it was understandable that there was a great rivalry amongst them, but that rivalry took different forms in each of the three men, who had starkly contrasting personalities. Robert Hugh McNeil was the most popular of the three among the hundred or so members of the club. A sandy-haired Scot from Edinburgh, he was a lawyer who had moved his practice to London when he married a woman from Hampstead. Fond of a drink, but not to excess, he was easy-going, and while he trained hard, he wasn't obsessive. Archery came naturally to him – he was good at it – but he didn't allow it to interfere with the attention he paid to his wife and child. If Edginton or Cullen beat him, he would be disappointed, but no more.

Dennis Noel Edginton counted McNeil among his friends, and it was as if he saw in the affable Scot the image of what he would like to be, but felt he never could. He was moody and insecure and spent virtually all his free time on his sport. McNeil alone was able to coax him out of his bouts of sullenness with some amicable teasing and a few drinks in the club bar. If Robbie McNeil was the most amiable of the three, Walter Henry Cullen was the most disliked. He was a braggart, and continually sought to undermine his rivals with insults and sneering assertions as to their lack of skill. McNeil had no problem laughing this off, but Edginton's sensitive soul was mauled by it. On one occasion, after some drinks in the bar, Cullen went over to his table and whispered something in Edginton's ear which was so offensive – no one ever discovered what it was – that Edginton stood and was about to take a swing at Cullen. McNeil restrained his friend, and surprised everyone by threatening to hit Cullen himself if he didn't leave.

Cullen's indisputable ability was the only thing that prevented the club committee from expelling him. Not long after he provoked Edginton, he tried to force his attentions on one of the club waitresses, and this, along with his general habit of treating them as grossly inferior, encouraged the entire catering staff to refuse to serve him unless he gave an apology. This was duly given, but thereafter Cullen stopped dining or drinking at the bar and restaurant. Any time he spent at the club was mostly occupied with archery.

A description of the club buildings is necessary at this point, based on photographs taken by the police. At the front of the clubhouse were two doors. The larger one, on the right, led into a hall leading to the reception room, while a smaller door on the left was to a room where equipment could be stored in personal lockers. This also contained small changing rooms for men and women members. Another door at the far end of the room opened onto the club restaurant, which could also be accessed by a side door.

Next to the restaurant was the bar, the only place where smoking was allowed. It was accessed by another door. Connecting to the bar, the restaurant, and the reception area was a large room which also contained the kitchen and a separate seating area for the staff. A door led into reception and, as part of the same wall, there was a space with a reception desk with a curtain behind it so that visitors couldn't see into the room.

The reception area had two windows, both of which looked out onto the large, square flat lawn to the right of the building where the practice of archery was actually carried out. The rest of the clubhouse consisted of two offices and a committee room which shared walls with the kitchen and the bar, but were only accessible by a door at the back of the building.

It was seven o'clock on the evening of June 16th, and because of the heat, many of the doors and windows, including those of the reception room, were fully open. Cullen, Edginton, and McNeil were the only members still out on the butts, and the other members who had been present that day, twenty in all, being either in the bar or at dinner. Cullen was the first to stop. He walked back to the clubhouse and went and sat in the reception area.

A few minutes later one of the staff went into reception and found Cullen dead, lying down with an arrow sticking in the nape of his neck. He kept his head and left the corpse, and the scene, untouched, and then went into the restaurant via the kitchen and informed the Club Treasurer, Mr. Lionel Harris, what he had found. Harris instantly went 'round into his office and telephoned the local constabulary, who, as was common in murder cases, notified Scotland Yard. He then had the main door to the club locked and allowed the rest of the members to finish their meals and drinks (the club closed at nine), and leave. He was later criticised for this action, but defended himself on the grounds that he had been in the restaurant and had seen no one leave.

The door to the bar had been closed, but he knew there were only three people in there and none had passed by the open restaurant windows. His immediate concern had been to neither upset nor panic the members, particularly the female ones. As McNeil had only just come into the restaurant, Harris told him to remain. He asked him if there was anyone else on the butts. McNeil replied that Cullen had just come off but Edginton was either still out there or in the locker room. Edginton had in fact gone into the reception area, and was there when the door was locked as per Harris's instructions.

When the police arrived, Edginton was seated in a chair, gazing down at his rival's corpse with an unfathomable expression. He was still dressed as he had been at the butts and had his bow and arrows. Inspector Stanley Hopkins of Scotland Yard arrived at about half-past-nine, accompanied by the medical examiner, a sergeant, and a police photographer. Hopkins apologised for his late arrival. The examiner, Dr. James Cardew, had been delayed by another murder in Camden Town and none of his colleagues had been available.

The site of the murder was photographed from several angles. Cardew then confirmed that Cullen's death was caused by the arrow in the back of his neck, and that death would have occurred instantaneously, or within two or three seconds at most, and had taken place in the last two to two-and-a-half hours. Hopkins then questioned McNeil, Edginton, and Huggins, the man who had discovered the body, in the Treasurer's office. Notes were taken in shorthand by Sergeant Griffiths.

These were the facts, as they were presented to us by Inspector Hopkins one evening as we sat with the Scotland Yarder in our rooms in Baker Street

"And what did those three gentlemen have to say for themselves?" asked Sherlock Holmes, leaning forward, the expression on his sharp features akin to that of the hound who catches the far-off scent of the fox.

The case had reached an impasse, so the inspector had swallowed his pride and come to ask for assistance from the one man in London who could help him with his investigation.

"McNeil says the three of them – that is, himself, Cullen, and Edginton – were out at the butts for about two hours. Cullen left first. McNeil was going to keep Edginton company, but decided to go to the restaurant and get something to eat."

"Did McNeil see Cullen in the reception area?" asked Holmes.

"He said that the door was open and Cullen was sitting in a chair about halfway between the door and the reception desk."

"Why did he go into the reception area rather than the restaurant?"

"He hadn't been in the bar or restaurant for a while, but he was prepared to pay a bit extra for someone to bring him a drink there. Apparently he would have one or two on his own there, and then get changed and leave."

"So, what did McNeil do after he saw Cullen?"

"He says he went and changed his clothes, put his bow and arrows away, then went into the restaurant. He ordered a meal, but before it arrived Mr. Harris asked him to stay after the club closed. He didn't find out why until we arrived. He took his time over his meal and then went into the bar, where he had a couple of drinks and read the newspapers."

"Did you ask him if he saw Edginton at any point after leaving the butts?"

"He said he hadn't. When I asked him if he had got on with the dead man, he admitted that Cullen was a first-class archer, but he was too arrogant about it, and that if he were honest, he wouldn't miss him.

"I let McNeil go and spoke to Edginton. He said the last time he had seen Cullen alive was when McNeil was leaving the butts to get something to eat. Edginton turned to tell McNeil he'd join him in a little while, and saw Cullen sitting in an armchair near the reception desk. Both windows were open, and he saw him through the right-hand one. That was about thirty yards from where he was standing."

203

"And Edginton was sure it was him?"

"So he said. Edginton then stayed and took a few more shots, gathered his arrows, and started for the clubhouse. When he got to the main door, he looked in and saw someone lying on the floor with an arrow in his neck. He went along the hall and saw it was Cullen.

"I asked him why he had stayed there, and he said he needed to sit down because he was in shock. There was no one else in the room. I was told later that Huggins had already discovered the body, and informed Mr. Harris before Edginton claims to have seen it. Then one of the staff locked the main door, not realizing that Edginton was in there, as the whole of the reception area isn't visible from the door. It was unlocked when we arrived. McNeil took Edginton to the bar and went behind it and got him a drink. Edginton admitted that plenty of the members had a motive for killing Cullen, but that he was high on the list. He denied being the murderer, but I felt he was uncomfortable because by saying he hadn't done it, he might be incriminating his friend.

"The last to be interviewed was Huggins, the staff member who had found Cullen. He was a virtual giant of a man, and I had to remind myself that the idea that big strong men were lacking in intellect was a dangerous cliche. Huggins's face displayed little emotion, but there was intelligence in those brown eyes.

"He stated that he had been working at the club for seven years. He was a little reluctant at first to give his opinion of Cullen, but when pressed described him as 'a bad'un', and said they should've kicked him out when he tried it on with Sarah – that was the waitress he had insulted – and would have been, if it wasn't for the National Championships and "their precious Olympics". He had joined the rest of the staff when they boycotted Cullen. According to Mr. McNeil, one of the staff was supplying him with drinks in the reception room for an inflated price. I asked Huggins if he had any idea who that might be.

"Huggins squirmed in his chair, a strange movement for so large a man, and admitted that it was him.

"'Money is money, sir,' he said. 'A bit extra always comes in handy. Please don't tell the committee, sir. I won't do it again. I mean, I can't do it again now, can I? Not now he's dead.'

"'All right, we'll pass over that,' I said. 'Just tell me what happened.'

"There wasn't much to tell. Cullen came in and rang the reception bell. Huggins went and answered it, and when Cullen saw it was him, he ordered a drink. Huggins went to get it, and when he came back, there Cullen was, dead, with that arrow sticking out of his neck. Huggins went for Mr. Harris, and the rest is as I have said."

"What do you make of it, then, Hopkins?" Holmes asked.

"Well, sir, it has to be either Edginton or McNeil, doesn't it? Both were excellent with the bow, and both hated Cullen. Ezdginton could have shot him through the open window, and McNeil could have stood at the open door and shot an arrow along the length of the hall into the reception room. It's a question of deciding which one. Edginton seems too nervous and sensitive to have done it, and McNeil seems too amiable – at first glance, anyway. We all know from experience that everyone has hidden depths, and that murder can find a home in what seems the softest of hearts."

"True," I said.

"It doesn't seem premeditated," Hopkins continued. "Edginton could have simply given in to a sudden impulse, and what we saw wasn't simply shock, but genuine remorse, and maybe horror at discovering that he was capable of murder. He doesn't seem the type who can live with guilt for any length of time. As to McNeil, Harris told us that McNeil uncharacteristically threatened Cullen when Cullen insulted Edginton. Was his friendship for Edginton so great that he'd kill to get Cullen off his friend's back?"

"You could look at it from a different angle," I said. "From what you've told us, McNeil and Cullen were polar opposites. They were bound to come into conflict."

"To the point of murder? And again, it seems unpremeditated, so we fall back on the idea that it was the result of a momentary impulse. McNeil saw Cullen, he had the weapons to hand, and *Whoosh!* Cullen's dead. McNeil then acted with fantastic coolness, went to his locker, got changed, and strolled into the restaurant, ordered a meal, and showed no sign of stress when Harris asked him to stay after the club closed."

"While these speculations are interesting, and no doubt of importance," said Holmes, "let us look first at what facts we have. Was the type of the arrow that killed Cullen the same as those used by Edginton or McNeil?"

"That was one of the first things I thought of, Mr. Holmes. Unfortunately, it is of the most common make, which is used by virtually everyone in the club."

"What was the exact position of the body when it was found?"

Hopkins reached into a small briefcase he had brought with him and produced a manila folder.

"These are the photographs of the murder scene, taken by our man, Atkinson. He's very thorough, and took them from every possible point of view."

The pictures showed a tall, dark-haired man of middle height, in his early thirties, dressed in archery gear, on his face on the floor with his head pointing in the direction of the door and the fatal arrow protruding from his neck. His bow and quiver of arrows lay on a chair.

"What do you make of them, Watson?" asked Holmes.

"I'm afraid these give no indication of the direction the arrow came from. As Cardew said, death would have been virtually instantaneous, but that doesn't mean that in his last moment Cullen's body might not have twisted, either in agony or from the force of the blow."

Holmes leafed through the photographs and after a minute or so gave a little smile of triumph.

"Nevertheless, gentlemen, these give us clear pointers as to the identity of the murderer."

"Then who should I arrest – Edginton or McNeil?"

"Neither. Your culprit, Inspector, is Huggins."

"Huggins? But he reported the crime!"

"Of course he reported it. Suspicion would have instantly fallen on him if he hadn't. As an intelligent man, he would have realized that."

"But the murder must have been committed by an archer, and Huggins was a member of the staff, not of the club."

"Really, my friend, you must learn to look at the facts, and not rely upon your assumptions. The fact that the man was killed by an arrow doesn't necessarily mean that it was shot from a bow."

Holmes spread the photographs across the small table around which we were sitting. I picked up each one and scrutinised it, but could find nothing to support Holmes's assertions.

"Our first indication that Huggins was lying can be clearly seen," began Holmes. "Or rather, clearly *not* seen. No?" he continued after a few seconds. "You still don't understand? According to Huggins, Cullen ordered a drink. Huggins went to fetch it, and when he returned, found Cullen dead and instantly went to inform Harris, who had the door closed. Where, then, is the drink? Had Huggins really brought one in, he would have put it down somewhere before going to tell Harris. But it is nowhere to be seen.

"Our second and third points may both be inferred from the arrow wound. Any arrow fired from a bow would have had sufficient force to not merely enter the back of the neck, but to go right through it. Then there is the angle of the wound. Again, if fired from a bow, it would enter at an angle of ninety degrees. The angle here is closer to forty-five degrees, which is consistent with the arrow being stabbed down *into* the neck by someone somewhat taller than the victim, and possessed of considerable strength.

"So, Cullen comes into the reception area, puts his bow and quiver on the nearest chair and rings the reception bell. When Huggins appears, he orders a drink and then turns his back, Huggins takes one of the arrows from the quiver and stabs it downwards into Cullen's neck."

"That's all very neat and logical, Mr. Holmes, but why did Huggins do it? He needed the extra money he made from supplying Cullen with drinks."

"From what you've said, Huggins is a large, powerful man. In my experience, such men may be divided into two broad categories. There are those who use their strength unscrupulously to gain whatever may be achieved by it, and those who have been taught from an early age, usually by their mothers, that their strength must be used carefully and responsibly, particularly where the weak are concerned. As the weaker sex, women are especially to be protected. As a manifestation of this tendency, consider how often one sees large men married to much smaller women.

"Yes, Huggins was dependent on Cullen for extra money. But he was also aware that Cullen had mistreated Sarah, for whom it is possible that Huggins has paternal, or even romantic, feelings. He may have loathed himself for accepting payment from such a man. These passions warred within him until – in one moment – he snapped. Casting self-restraint aside, he seized the nearest weapon to hand and dealt the fatal blow. I also think it entirely possible that had you arrested either Edginton or McNeil, Huggins would have come forward and confessed."

Hopkins stood up.

"Well, I shall certainly arrest him, and we shall see whether your speculations are correct. Thank you, Mr. Holmes. A very neat piece of work."

Huggins was tried at the Old Bailey some weeks later, and Holmes's theories turned out to be true in every particular. Among the witnesses was Sarah Crowden, a petite young woman who testified that she was sure that Huggins was in love with her, but hadn't spoken due to the twenty-five-year difference in age between them.

The jury found Huggins guilty after a very brief consultation, but submitted a recommendation for mercy, the mitigating circumstances being Huggins' previous good character, the bad character of the victim, exemplified by his mistreatment of the girl, and the fact that the act hadn't been premeditated. The judge concurred, and gave Huggins a custodial sentence with the possibility of parole, instead of sending him to the gallows.

"Hopkins has called me in seven times, and on each occasion his summons has been entirely justified."

– Sherlock Holmes
"The Abbey Grange"

The Three Maids
by I.A. Watson

"Tell me, Watson," Holmes asked me as the two large bullies blocked our way, "on a league table of all the various thugs and bravos who have threatened us, where would you rank these two specimens?"

I estimated the size and bulk of the two rough-looking street toughs that barred our path through Scuddall Passage in the East End, regarding their demeanour, fitness, scarring, and posture. "I would put them towards the lower end of the listings," I admitted. "We have encountered a much better class of lowlife before now. And dealt with them, of course."

"I agree," my friend replied. "The fellow on the left, with the unshaved stubble on a jaw which has been broken more than once, has the telltale marks of an unsuccessful pugilist. Moreover, his left knuckles have been damaged beyond full repair, which means he will favour striking from the right. His colleague is fleshier than in his youth, with fallen arches from his army days and a weakness in his right eye. He has taken a recent knife-wound in the left shoulder at the acromioclavicular that still pains him. Their coshes are of the cheap sort resorted to by rather impoverished criminals-for-hire."

"Get out of 'ere, flatties," one of our assailants warned us. "Y' can leave your note-cases and watches behind."

"They are certainly a little slow on the uptake," I noted. "They have paused long enough before following through on their threats of violence for us to – "

At that point I hit the thug on the left on his weak eye and then folded him over with a left to the belly. Holmes took the other chap, scientifically planting his fist on the fellow's stitched-up rotator cuff.

Our attempted robbers shied back, chastened – but they were not alone.

There was more movement in the darkened courtyard behind us. We weren't far from London Docks where great warehouses held sea-goods from all over the world, but nearer still was the waste-land that had once been Wapping Fair and still housed a ramshackle community of show-wagons and travelling men. [1] From the clothing and coloured scarves of our assailants, I judged we were being threatened by burly roustabouts from the adjacent campsite.

Whoever they were, more of the denizens of Scuddall Passage emerged from the shadows. Some carried bats or knives instead of coshes, intent on more harm than a simple robbery. I drew my service revolver to even the odds, but Holmes did one better and sounded a police whistle.

"*Ultray cativa slum*," Holmes told the lurkers gnomically. "Best you run before the *charfering-homa* arrives." I later discovered that this was the parlance of the travelling showfolk, telling them that it wasn't a good idea to continue with their plans and that a "talking man" – a police constable – was on his way.[2]

Our assailants, recognising that their time had passed, hastened away. The two that had been subject of our evaluation staggered and limped after their fellows as best they could.

"Should we apprehend them?" I asked. "If they are part of our investigation . . . ."

"They are the regular members of the Scuddall Passage Mutual Support Society," my companion answered, meaning that they were criminal *habitués* of this small corner of the great cluster of cheap housing around Wapping. I had learned enough from Holmes to know that each interconnected yard and alley in this part of London has a gang like this, fiercely territorial and violent. Two well-dressed gentlemen entering their locale by night were tempting prey.

"I thought that they might be from the caravans," I ventured.

"Oh, they were," my friend assured me. "The brass ear-rings and gaudy scarves distinguish them. But what were once travellers have somewhat settled now on the former campground and in the slums around it, such as the alley we now seek. You will find no greater collection of rogues, robbers, confidence men, tinkers, and good-time girls anywhere in London, or any closer-organised community intent on self-preservation. That makes our quarry's choice of location even more curious."

The last of the showfolk toughs had scarcely vanished when a bobby came trotting up, truncheon in hand. He eased up when he saw us standing beneath the only working gas lamp in the alley to which Scuddall Passage led.

"Mr. 'Olmes," he said, recognising my comrade. "I saw you at work during that business with the venomous lizard.[3] Can I be of assistance?"

"You may be able to bear witness," Holmes assured the constable. "Dr. Watson and I are seeking a missing silversmith named Edwin Morrow. His nephew consulted us when other investigation failed to discover where Morrow might have disappeared to. According to Morrow's account books, the silversmith evidently kept a store-house down here which I intend to discover."

"A store-house?" P.C. Bagley puzzled. "Around here? A silversmith's stock wouldn't last five minutes in this neighbourhood."

"Indeed not," Holmes agreed. "Nor would it be sensible for him to transport such valuable materials through these dark alleys. However, Morrow leased property hereabouts, and we intend to examine it."

"The smith disappeared two weeks ago, without any word to his apprentices," I explained, since Bagley seemed both intelligent and interested. "The nephew is his nearest relative except for an invalid wife in Brighton, so the live-in juniors contacted him about their master's disappearance."

The constable asked where Morrow's workplace and home were, and on being informed that the silversmith had an establishment on Angel Street off St. Martin's le Grande, [4] he whistled respectfully and responded, "Any complaint wouldn't come to *our* station, then." Exclusive St. Martin's le Grande was but two miles west, but it might as well have been a different world from this troubled rookery.

"There are some irregularities in Mr. Morrow's affairs," Holmes admitted. "He was often absent from his business, and there are sums of money and certain of his goods unaccounted for."

"And you think he might have come here?" Bagley apprehended. "And 'ad some kind of mishap?"

"It is a likely outcome which we must investigate," Holmes replied. He didn't need to add that if criminals were holding the silversmith, then time was of the essence, which was why we had elected to risk the seedy Wapping warrens after dark.

The three of us skirted the edge of the darkened showground, aware that many eyes watched us carefully from the lean-tos and gypsy wagons as we passed. Legislation to curb the migration of the Showpeople and the Didicoys has managed only to cause such rough camps as this, filled with poverty and misery, adding to the stew of desperate people in the shadows of our capital.

We made our way up the alley until we came upon the heavily reinforced doorway to a thirties brick row-dwelling that was Morrow's "store-house". Holmes showed our constable the letter of permission from Morrow's nephew that authorised us to enter the premises, and since no keys had been discovered amongst Morrow's belongings, my friend treated Bagley to a rare display of the use of burglar's tools for legitimate police work.

Two mortise locks and a stout padlock secured the way in, but it took Holmes less than two minutes to overcome them. The door creaked open onto a dingy entrance hall with a frosted-glass partition door before the main interior. Bagley obligingly hefted his night-lamp and we ventured in.

Past the seedy lobby everything changed. The walls were plastered and papered, the floors polished and rugged. Sporting prints were framed

211

on the walls. A quality coat-stand held three outdoor coats and three hats. The interior was in all ways as pleasant as any townhouse or club might be, except that closed curtains disguised bricked up windows. A gay banner hung upon the stair arch, embroidered with the legend "*The Fayre*".

"What does this mean, sirs?" Bagley wondered. "This is more like the West End, but hidden inside a slum."

"Has someone attempted to form another Amateur Mendicant Society?" I speculated, remembering the association of fake beggars who had plagued Holmes in our salad years. [5]

There were full-length standing candelabras around the stairwell and inner hall, but the candles had burned out, dripping wax over the varnished floor. The rest of the room looked, as well as felt, abandoned. A light coating of dust covered all.

A sound startled us, but when Bagley shined his lamp it was only a large brown rat that scuttled off.

Holmes sniffed the air. "That stench has attracted it," he told us. We sniffed along with him, discerning a corrupt aroma of decay from further within the house.

"May I call out a caution, sirs?" the constable sought permission, and on receiving assent cried out in a loud voice. "Is there anybody there? I am an officer of the law. Come out now!"

There was no response except the scratching of disturbed rodents beyond our sight.

"We shall progress further in," Holmes decided. "Watson, secure the front door again. Let us control what variables we may. Constable, kindly remain on patrol here at the base of the stairs, where anyone above or below must pass to exit. Doctor, the unpleasant miasma seems strongest in the rear parlour."

The whole of the back of the house had been knocked open into one large room, appointed with lush carpets and divans at one end and a huge bronze bathing tub at the other, with red velvet curtains between the two halves presently tied back. A folding dressing-screen was set around the bath for privacy. The walls were decorated with watercolours and charcoals of the Parisian style, featuring unclad young women in a variety of poses. Large potted plants were withered for lack of watering and light.

Holmes examined one of the spent candlesticks, noting the hallmark upon its base. "This is Morrow's work. He has stamped it."

"There is a drinks cabinet here with some choice vintages," I observed. The selection on the racks was somewhat above my budget.

Holmes paused to play his lamp over the floor and furniture before allowing us to approach the screened bath. Only when we could see behind the barriers did we discover the source of the rank decay: Three dead men rested hip-deep in the scummy red water.

The rats had found them long before we had.

The corpses were all naked, equidistant from each other in the circular tub, their arms spread out along the rim in attitudes of relaxed contentment. Within easy reach were a tantalus, a cigar case, and a silver platter that had presumably once contained delicacies for nibbling. Six fluted glasses and a pair of wine bottles around the bath's edge suggested that at one time the bathers hadn't been the only occupants.

"I must send for my sergeant," P.C. Bagley declared when we told him of our find. He stayed for a brief confirmatory glimpse, turned somewhat green, and retreated quickly with his urgent account of half-devoured corpses and their disgusting odour.

"Have word sent to Scotland Yard," Holmes advised the departing beat bobby. "Doubtless they will wish to send somebody down here to trample the evidence, but this time they will be too late."

Bagley hastened off to summon assistance. The denizens of Scuddall Passage and the silent showground would find their domain further invaded by more than one "*charfering-homa*" tonight.

"We shall examine what we can before the forces of Law and Order obscure the evidence," Holmes told me.

"This is a gristly business to examine," I pointed out. "Might we assume that one of the men in that bath our missing Mr. Morrow?"

As usual, Holmes would draw no conclusion ahead of his data.

We made a hasty check of the rest of the premises. In addition to the luxury suite, the ground floor also contained a serviceable kitchen that had been well-stocked with quality cuts of meat and jars of preserves, along with many confectionaries and desert delicacies. From their state of staleness, they had been neglected for several days. The china was of excellent make, and the silverware was first class. The kitchen hearth hadn't been cleaned or relaid. Its small fire had burned down to grey ash without being otherwise doused. The rear entrance had been bricked shut like the windows.

The upper floor also had blocked windows, though the profusion of silver candlesticks and lamps must have allowed for plenty of light. The candles, mostly burned to the base now, were of best beeswax rather than common tallow. The table lamps had used up their oil reservoirs before they were extinguished. There were three bedrooms, each containing a luxury four-poster with goosedown mattresses and pillows. Large wardrobes in each chamber were empty.

An attic that might once have contained servants' quarters was completely unfurnished, cobwebbed and mouldy where the roof had begun to fail. The cellars were mostly unused too, dusty and damp, except for two more racks of fine wines and spirits, and many discarded packing cases that must once have been stuffed with the finest wares.

We found no lurking murderers. If Holmes saw tell-tale traces, then he didn't point them out to me at that time.

"There's a lot of wealth here," I pointed out. "If those men were killed for robbery, then why were silver candlesticks and expensive vintages not removed?"

"It is a distinct point," Holmes agreed. "I am also curious as to who has kept this house in order prior to recent events. Hearths were laid. Beds had clean linen. Food was prepared. Yet the servants' rooms above were vacant and unused."

We returned to the opulent lounge to review the three cadavers. "Their throats were cut," I saw. The incisions were obvious, slashes that had sliced down through the windpipe almost to the hyoid, severing the main arteries and veins. The spray had mostly gone into the water, but some of it still marred the tiled floor beyond the brass tub. "They seem not to have struggled."

"They may have been insensible at the time," Holmes suggested. "We shall secure the remnants of the wine that they were drinking. If it is drugged, then we shall know why they put up no resistance." He confiscated bottles, glasses, and even the spirits in the tantalus for future consideration.

I went so far as to pinch the dead men's skin to estimate *rigor mortis* and *post mortem* decay.

Holmes had already done the calculations. "They died around two weeks back," he told me. "The cold weather has inhibited but not prevented the life-cycles of *muscidae* and *calliphoridae* which allow such an estimation."

"You are judging time of demise by the housefly and blowfly larvae," I translated.

"And by the putrefaction in the bloody bathwater. All most helpful. The killing cuts were administered from behind with a sharp straight razor with a small nick one-third of the way up the blade. I should know the weapon if I saw it. The murderer was left-handed."

Holmes carefully examined the corpses' hands. I knew from past experience that he could often discern a man's profession by merely reviewing the callosities and imprints that he observed there.

"This large fellow meets the description of Morrow," he told me. "His facial hair matches the tintype the nephew provided, of course, but additionally there are some old burns from metal-splash, such as I might expect from a silversmith's apprentice days, though he hasn't handled many crucibles in recent years. He has fleshed out considerably since his youth, as evidenced by the silver signet ring now embedded on his swollen finger."

Holmes turned to the second corpse, displaying the cadaver's right palm and digits. "This fellow regularly gripped a heavy bladed object and cut it downwards with significant force, as a man might with a cleaver on a carcass. There are additional indicators from thumb wear and an irritation of the wrist. From his posture, he probably suffered from back-strain from heavy carrying. I might postulate him a butcher."

"A successful one," I added, noting that this corpse also wore an expensive signet, this one of gold.

The last dead man's jaw had dropped open, so Holmes was also able to inspect the cadaver's dentition. "Our victim has several cavities – a sweet tooth – which still hold traces of the sugary baked goods which he has often sampled."

"There is an emptied tray of sweetmeats and chocolates beside the bath. Doubtless the scavengers that gnawed these bodies also ate up the delicacies that had been on this plate."

"This last man was a possibly a confectioner," Holmes revealed. "During his early career, he suffered several bad scaldings from sticky boiling liquids which have left their distinctive splash-marks on his person, and here are old burn indications where he brushed against some hot object such as an oven. This swelling on the wrist is from a repetitious stirring action – but long ago. Like the others, he has left behind manual labour and more recently enjoyed a supervisory role."

"These three men made themselves very at home here," I observed. "Were they poisoned and slaughtered by whoever else was in this bath with them?"

"It is too early to tell, Watson. But we shall know – We shall! This is a very gratifying scene."

By the time that Inspector Bradstreet arrived, Holmes had thoroughly examined the corpses and completed his check on every room of the hidden establishment. Bradstreet regarded Holmes and me with a kind of tired despair. It wasn't the first night's sleep that we had cost him.

Unlike other Scotland Yard detectives, Bradstreet wore a uniform, his regulation frogged jacket and peaked cap marking him as a former E-Street officer, a successor of the Bow Street Runners. [6] He rubbed his bristly black beard [7] and asked wearily, "What should I know?"

Holmes was pleased to give him the tour. "It appears as though Mr. Edwin Morrow, Angel Street silversmith, and two like-minded friends, prepared this hideaway to enjoy illicit activities with paid companions.

They lavished considerable attention and resources upon the site, dubbing it '*The Fayre*', presumably in homage to the nearby showground. It was a private establishment reserved for the three of them, not a public bawdy house."

"And the other two men?"

Holmes didn't bother to recite his inspection of the bodies and his conclusions from what he saw. He had since searched the three coats on the stand by the front door, discovering wallets with calling cards that identified the victims. "These are Gilbert Haydock, Specialist Charcutier, and Dromond Donnely, Confectioner and Pattisier. You understand why they associated with each other?"

"Presumably for immoral purposes with young women," I opined.

"Indubitably, but there is rather more to it than that."

"Then I would appreciate being informed," Bradstreet grumped.

Holmes took pity on the inspector. "They were men who shared particular amorous tastes. On the night of Friday, 7th June, these three men, Morrow, Haydock, and Donnely, arrived at The Fayre for a night of revels, or possibly for the weekend. Copious supplies of good fare and excellent drink were available, which, judging by the lading crates in the cellar, were delivered that morning."

"Someone must have received delivery," I objected.

"And someone must have seen it," Bradstreet insisted. He turned to P.C. Bagley. "There are always watchers in the alleys around places like this. Who will it be here?"

"The Mayhews and the Bucklands," the local bobby answered promptly and certainly. "They control this side of the showground and the streets this way as far as Duckett Street and Ben Jonson Road. Gamma Buckland is the head of the families."

"I believe that we encountered some of her kinsmen earlier tonight," Holmes mentioned. "The mud on their boots marked them as inhabitants of the waste ground where the horsefair used to be. I shall certainly wish to speak to Gamma Buckland presently. In the meantime . . . ."

Inspiration struck me. "I get it!" I gasped, interrupting because I had come to a discovery of my own. "The association that these three men had! They must have thought it a fine jest."

"A jest?" Holmes echoed, for once puzzled while I had my insight. "As I explained, they all had prurient interest in – "

"These fellows! Haydock was a charcutier, a producer of expensive pork products – ham, bacon, sausages, ballotines, pâtés, confits, terrines and suchlike – a *butcher*, in fact. Donnely was a pattisier, that is a licensed and accredited pastry chef – a kind of *baker*. And Morrow . . . ."

"Strewth!" Bradstreet cried. "Morrow was a silversmith – a *candlestick maker!*"

Holmes regarded me with furrowed brows. "You will have to explain further, Watson."

I was abruptly reminded of the strange gaps in Holmes's encyclopaedic knowledge. His eccentric upbringing and directed studies had left him strangely ignorant of certain common facts that were evident to the rest of us.

"There is an old nursery rhyme," I informed him. "Most children learn it in the crib:

> *"Rub-a-dub-dub, Three men in a tub,*
> *And who do you think they be?*
> *The butcher, the baker, the candlestick maker,*
> *And all of them out to sea."*

Holmes evinced a mild surprise. "Thank you for amending my ignorance, Doctor. I fear that childhood travels through Rotterdam, Cologne, Heidelberg, Berne, Lucerne, the Tyrol, Dresden, Mannheim, and many other locations fitted me with a good grasp of European languages and geography, but did nothing for my understanding of children's poetry. It is an interesting possibility that our three victims chose to associate because their professions matched those of an old saw."

P.C. Bagley swallowed hard and flushed red. Holmes recognised the signs of a young man unsure whether he should interject something into a conversation of his betters, and prompted the constable to say his piece.

"Well, begging Dr. Watson's pardon, but that rhyme's not the one as I was taught as a little 'un. I was told it as:

> *"Rub-a-dub dub, Three fools in a tub,*
> *And who do you think they be?*
> *The butcher, the baker, the candlestick maker.*
> *Turn them out, knaves all three."*

Now Bradstreet shook his head. "That isn't it neither. My old gran used to recite this to me as I sat on her knee, and later on she told me what it was about also. It originally went like this:

> *"Hey! Rub-a-dub, ho! rub-a-dub, three maids in a tub,*
> *And who do you think were there?*
> *The butcher, the baker, the candlestick-maker,*
> *And all of them gone to the fair."*

217

Bradstreet smoothed his beard in embarrassment. "On account of, back in the old days, I mean right back to the Middle Ages, them fairgrounds used to have a sort of sideshow tent where fellows would pay to peek through holes at young women a-taking their clothes off and splashing about together in a bath. '*The butcher, the baker, the candlestick maker*' was a way of saying '*Every Tom, Dick, and Harry*', all the respectable gentlemen sneaking off to ogle the girls. '*Rub-a-dub*' was an old fashioned way of saying '*Tsk-tsk!*'" [8]

I wondered if Holmes might resent having his deliberations and explanations interrupted by people whose expertise for once exceeded his own, but he accepted the instruction enthusiastically. "That helps to make sense of the activities of the house – which, you will note, was called '*The Fayre*' by its occupants."

He went back to his account. "The three men came to this establishment to partake of a particular practice. You will notice the curtain which bifurcates the room. Close inspection will reveal three small holes cut into the fabric at eye level – peepholes. It seems that our butcher, baker, and candlestick maker were also aware of the version of the nursery rhyme that the inspector has supplied. This chamber was set up for voyeuristic viewing of the bathing area, and for the owners of the establishment to later join the objects of their infatuation in the tub."

"Morrow had a wife, convalescing at the coast," I objected.

"He appears to have kept a mistress here," Holmes replied. "Or several. Although I note that the wardrobes upstairs have all been emptied."

"Those mistresses may well have cut their masters' throats," Bradstreet objected.

"Only one hand did the killing, Inspector. All the cuts were administered with the same force and, dare I venture, expertise. I doubt that this was the murderer's first slaughter."

"Still, we shall need to find those doxies. And whoever maintained the house and took deliveries on the morning of the seventh."

"There are a good number of facts yet to ascertain," Holmes assured us all. "What is the hour? I fear that we shall have to wake up Gamma Bucklands."

It wasn't an easy matter to call upon the travelling showfolk's matriarch. Her caravan was positioned so that it was invisible from any of the approaches to the old showground, ringed in as if fortified by humbler wagons and ride-transporters. The wagon wasn't large but amazingly detailed, a blend of the traditional Romany huts one often sees at fairs and a wood-carved Swiss chalet. It was painted in royal colours of red, purple, and gold, every groove and spur detail picked out in another hue.

And it was protected. There must have been forty burly fellows of the kind who had assailed us earlier in Scuddall Passage, who now simply oozed out of the shadows about the campsite. Several of them brought fierce dogs. Two or three of them even carried large blunderbuss shotguns.

Holmes spoke with their leader, using demotic terms that I didn't understand but which I gathered were *parlyari*, the patois of the travelling folk to which he had resorted earlier. He requested and eventually received an audience with the occupant of that significant caravan.

"The showmen are on edge," Holmes reported to me as he returned from his negotiation. "They know about the police going to Morrow's house, of course. That is in part why there are so many fellows up and about at this hour of the night. But they are also concerned about 'Docklands townies' – that is, the toughs who control the shoreward element of Wapping, the wharves and warehouses and the cheap lodgings for sailors and teamsters. It seems that there is presently an ongoing dispute over demarcation of territory, with regular nightly forays from the opposition to cause damage or other trouble."

"You have assured them that we aren't such 'townies'?" I asked, unnerved by the unmoving, unfriendly crowd that surrounded us. "You speak their language?"

"I understand their cant somewhat. It is similar to the Gypsy *Romani* and the *Shelta* or *Gammon* of Irish tinkers, with certain elements of Yiddish, Lingua Franca, and Cockney backslang added in. However, it is distinct from the *Polari* used by theatre and circus folk. [9] Speakers of *Parlyari* and *Polari* might understand the meaning of the other but would know the speakers to be rivals by their choice of dialect."

I was more concerned about the mob that closed about us. Holmes insisted that we should surrender our pistols and walking canes before we proceeded.

I was feeling decidedly nervous, then, as we were marched like prisoners towards that royal wagon. The skyline of London was hidden by night and by the high-sided caravans and trucks that formed the maze around Gamma Bucklands' centre of power.

Holmes evidently sensed my unease and filled the silence with more showground speech. "We are indeed 'flatties' here, Watson, which is to say, non-fairground people. We would prefer not to be 'jossers', who would be strangers, people suitable for conning or robbery. Since I 'rocker the jib' a little – understand the language – and since the locals don't wish attention from the 'Mingers' – the constabulary – at this time, we may

219

meet the 'Donah', which means 'Old Woman' – that very Gamma Bucklands whom we seek."

"It is as if we had entered another country, right here in East London," I considered. "A Gypsy nation."

"You shouldn't make such an identification," Holmes cautioned me. "There are Romanichal showmen, many of them, but there are more of other heritages. Calling these folks '*Gypsy*' would be considered as much an insult as if they termed you an Irishman. They are a distinct community. The Showman's Guild of Great Britain was established six years ago to resist attempts to pass the Moveable Dwellings Bill that would restrict their movement around the country. Four years ago it expanded as the Van Dwellers' Protection Association, [10] effectively a trade guild that emphasises the difference between those who tour the country with amusement attractions and shows from others who live a migratory existence for other purposes. There is sometimes considerable friction between the show-folk and the Romanys."

Holmes's lecture had brought us to the remarkable painted caravan. We were allowed past two even-larger sentries into the vehicle's cluttered interior.

My first impression of the claustrophobic wagon was of the sheer clutter. Every surface, including shelves on every wall, were crowded with plates and porcelain figurines. Statues and knick-knacks obscured all flat surfaces. Some of the items were beautiful, wasted within the overwhelming display. Others were tasteless tat, cheap souvenirs of wide travel.

My second perception was of the caravan's sole occupant. Painted by coloured lamplight, Gamma Bucklands sat in a heavy rocker regarding us with a suspicious eye. She was an immensely large woman, fat to obesity, with triple chins and meaty jowls, her lank grey hair plaited into long twin braids tied with thatched green ribbons. Her lower part was entirely covered by quilted rugs of many patterns. A dish of jellied eels was constantly by her left hand, and she dipped into it regularly.

"So, you'd be Sherlock Holmes," she greeted my companion. "And this is Doctor Watson."

"That is so," Holmes told her, allowing the matriarch a small respectful bob which I mimicked. "I am presently investigating the secret house of the late Edwin Morrow, a disguised property at the far end past Scuddall Passage."

"That's what all the fuss was about," Gamma sighed, chewing another eel.

"Your watchers have spotted the police," I assumed.

"No," Holmes corrected me. "Gamma means the she now comprehends what the recent disturbances and invasions of her territory were for. Outsiders were trying to access that house." He regarded the head of the Mayhews and the Bucklands carefully. "You were aware of Morrow's property, of course. He paid you a security fee."

"Perhaps he did," the old woman answered, confessing nothing. "Flatties around here often think it best to offer a little *gelt* to the Showfolk, as a sign of neighbourly respect. In return, we keeps an eye on their houses for them and sees that nothing ill happens."

"They pay you so that their homes aren't robbed," I interpreted.

"Are you calling my family *thieves*, Dr. Watson?" Gamma hissed, and for a moment I saw a deep roiling fury beneath her corpulent exterior, a murderous rage that made her the unquestioned ruler of these travelling people.

"We aren't here to discuss your business practices, Madam," Holmes went on smoothly, "except as they concern Mr. Morrow. Might we enquire as to when your care of the silversmith's 'store' began?"

Gamma Bucklands sniffed, eyed me for a moment longer, stuffed another eel into huge maw, and then answered. "It'd be the best part of a year ago. That house had been empty for some time, near as matters derelict, before the smith bought it. Morrow's builder came to me for permission to fix it up. An arrangement was made to allow it."

Holmes admired a handsome silver statue of a dancing showgirl but said nothing.

"Since then there have been monthly . . . *presents*," Gamma told us. "Morrow was a good neighbour."

"Until the trouble started," Holmes spurred her.

The matriarch's brows furrowed again. "Two weeks back now, we 'ad some swaggering dockers from The Neptune and Isis trying to come through, *kativa* bully boys with a wagon for movables. They didn't say as they were going to the Morrow house, and I didn't guess it. But I won't 'ave Georgie Wilson's muscle swaggering along *my* streets, *questra homa a vardring the slum*. [11] Not never! So we turned them back hard – and they've been trespassing ever since."

"Georgie Wilson?" I appealed to Holmes.

"He is the unpleasant proprietor of The Neptune hostelry, a sailor's bar down neat the water," my friend replied. "He is well-versed in the ecology of riverfront wrongdoers, and a prime mover in their organisation. His Thames-side wharf tavern is his base of operations, a den of vice, a receivers' market, gambling hell, and opium pit."

221

"Wilson is a notorious canary-trainer," Gamma informed us. "I'll not have him or his men walk these pavements!" She added a number of obscene epithets regarding the tavern-keeper.

"A canary-trainer?" I repeated, aware that I was again acting only as Holmes's echo, but unsure as to how a music-hall performer who bred and taught songbirds to perform actual tunes [12] might feature in our present discussions.

"In this case, 'canary-trainer' is a euphemism," Holmes interpreted for me. "We aren't speaking of the tuneful colourful avians of the genus *Serinus*. Here, the 'canary' is some hapless street-waif, and her training is in the trade of prostitution. Wilson is the worst procurer and pimp in the East End, the apex of a shameful system of deplorable exploitation and degradation."

Gamma Bucklands actually spat into one of four moulded spittoons that ringed the floor about her. "That ------ takes flower girls off the street, or snatches mudlarks, toshers, or pure finders, [13] or else buys *rakli* from orphanages. They'll be little *fiella* eight or ten years old maybe, and 'e breaks them into dollymops. There's a *chava* or two gone missing from our families, and I told that Georgie Wilson that if ever I finds as *he* took 'em, I'd have his chitlins for supper! [14] I won't have his men on our patch, not never!"

"Hence your barring Mr. Wilson's wagon two weeks ago, with all the consequent friction," Holmes surmised.

"I say, Holmes," I calculated, "if Wilson was trying to get to The Fayre to strip it of Morrow's rich trappings, then he must have known about the murders. Had it not been for Gamma Bucklands here barring Wilson's movers, we might well have found the whole place stripped."

The Showfolk matriarch possibly betrayed some angst that she had been unaware that a rich secret hideaway had remained unlooted after Morrow's murder. Or had the Showmen decided that Morrow's unofficial ground rend for protection wasn't as lucrative as more direct action?

Holmes quickly learned what else Gamma had to tell us: That a scrub-woman and her daughter from Scuddall Passage were allowed into the house twice a week to undertake domestic duties under the supervision of a young fellow from "up West". That the house took deliveries every Friday morning, permitted by the locals due to Morrow's regular gifts.The supplies were received by that same smart *homy*, who generally departed by lunchtime. That Morrow and his two friends arrived around seven that same evening and were soon joined by a trio of "nightingales". "Always three of 'em, young *chava* not old enough to ply that trade, but not al'us the same trio," Gamma informed us.

I bristled at the idea of youngsters being abused by three rich debauchees like that, but the practice is all too common. My sympathy for the butcher, the baker, and the candlestick maker, never very high, descended to a new low.

The girls and their patrons stayed overnight and sometimes for the whole weekend. What Holmes had termed the Scuddall Passage Mutual Benefit Association allowed the liaisons because of Morrow's gratuities. Other more-local harlots might have been offered except that Gamma didn't permit the sale of showground girls young enough to meet Morrow, Heydock, and Donnely's tastes.

At Holmes's request, Gamma Bucklands sent for the "*Rum Col*" that had last seen anyone at The Fayre. That turned out to mean the senior lurker who had "the watch" on that part of the Showmen's territory, to whom lesser spies, thieves, and pickpockets reported. This rather leery fellow showed Gamma extreme deference – I suspect that in his greener days this burly roustabout had often felt the back of her hand, and perhaps sometimes still did – and he racked his brain to recall details from the morning of June the Eighth.

Under Holmes's prompting he remembered the three child prostitutes vacating the premises. Their departure wouldn't ordinarily have been specially marked, since it was known that their visits to Morrow were allowed if not sanctioned by Gamma, but on that occasion each "*palone*" carried with her a heavy fabric bundle almost as large as herself. Without Gamma's established word of safe passage, the three waifs would undoubtedly have been parted from their parcels.

"The wardrobes of the three bedrooms were all emptied," Holmes reminded me. "Such clothes and outfits as were retained there for the girls' use were all removed, though nothing else had been distrained, even the victims' wallets. The clothing was the three girls' natural share, but they were permitted naught more."

"Three children were responsible for murdering Morrow and his fellows?" I gasped, appalled.

Holmes wasn't so sure. "They are the most likely candidates to have drugged any drink that was served to Morrow, Heydock, and Donnely, to render the three men insensible," Holmes considered. "After that, they may well have simply followed instructions to allow some other person into the house."

"And that was the murderer," I recognised. "This notorious Wilson?"

"Georgie Wilson wouldn't set foot upon these showgrounds!" Gamma insisted. "Not here, not in the Hodgekin's *gaff*, not with the Lovridges over at the other side of the field. Not if he ever wanted to walk out again." From this I gathered that other fairground families controlled different portions of the wasteground campsite, and none of them felt favourably towards the docklands operators.

"Then . . . three poor maids were taught to murder?" I objected unhappily.

"Our investigation continues," Holmes insisted. To Gamma Bucklands he proffered a bow and said, "Madam, thank you for your hospitality."

"Georgie Wilson is a plague-spot upon the East End!" Inspector Bradstreet almost exploded as we met him back at The Fayre house. "He is a venomous predator, more deserving of the gallows than any man still alive!"

"We haven't heard anything good of him," I admitted.

"Nor shall you. There is no good in him. There is no vice of the Docklands in which he doesn't have a part. He receives tribute for every drinking-hole and molly-shop, from any skinner or bad-man who preys on the sailors on the wharves, from the fences who take the stolen goods . . . He personally supervises the doxies, who regard him with mortal fear for the harm he inflicts upon those who fail him. And yet there is never proof to bring a case, never a witness who will testify, no victim who will press any charge against him."

P.C. Bagley, still required to be in attendance at the murder scene, and flushed with his earlier success in contributing nursery lore to our investigation, ventured another old saw:

"Georgie Porgie, pudding and pie, kissed the girls and made them cry . . . ."

I knew that one too, and completed the couplet:

"But when the boys came out to play, Georgie Porgie ran away." [15]

It was an apposite verse for a coward who abused women and children, but hardly furthered our researches.

"That'll do, Bagley," Bradstreet shut down his eager constable. "Georgie Wilson is no laughing matter. His possible involvement makes a serious case more dangerous yet."

"Surely such a fellow must be hunted by the police?" I enquired, glancing at Holmes.

"He is slick amongst rogues, both ruthless and organised," the detective admitted. "But he is only one of far too many purveyors of

224

unsavoury services. If he is removed, then a half-dozen other villains will step in and take his place before morning. Still . . . Mr. Wilson hadn't before come to my personal attention. He has it now."

"You believe him involved in this triple murder?" Bradstreet asked. "I should need to draft in many extra officers if I am to raid The Neptune and Isis. I'd need to speak with the Chief Inspector at the very least."

"There is insufficient evidence for any warrant of arrest at this stage," Holmes calmed Bradstreet. "The investigation proceeds. What information have you from the Heydock and Donnely residences?"

The inspector remembered his professional demeanour. He produced his notebook as if he was giving evidence at the bar of the Old Bailey and ran down his findings.

"Mr. Gilbert Haydock had a 'specialist charcutier' shop on Vere Street, off Oxford Street – that's a sort of fancy French butchers, as Dr. Watson said, that caters to the West End crowd – restaurants an' that. His wife lives in Bath with their three children, which is evidently a healthier place to raise them than smoky old London. Haydock was a well-to-do merchant, active in his guild, a freemason and a churchman."

"And he kept young girls in a private seraglio," I added, disgusted.

"Mr. Desmond Donnely's shop is on Regent Street near Oxford Circus, and is fitted with a gentleman's flat over it, at which Donnely spent most of his time rather than at his family townhouse at Sussex Gardens with his wife."

"All three men were somewhat estranged from their spouses," I noted. "Given their proclivities, I am not surprised."

"It either provoked or facilitated their life styles," Holmes considered. "Why had none of the households or businesses raised alarms about the men's absences?"

"Haydock's shop manager *had* actually contacted the police about his missing employer," Bradstreet reported. "No connection had been made to any other disappearance. Donnely was in the habit of making unannounced trips for which his staff had to cover, and didn't usually inform Mrs. Donnely in advance, so there was only mild concern over the length of his present disappearance. I must say that neither wife expressed overmuch grief at their widowhood." The inspector consulted his checklist. "I'll have someone from the Brighton Force inform Mrs. Morrow about her husband as soon as morning comes, and take a statement. This is going to be a long investigation."

"Not necessarily," Holmes told him. "We have a house full of useful data. We have some telling testimony. There are several witnesses yet to be interviewed whose accounts may be revealing. And of course, there is the unpleasant canary-trainer Wilson, whom I feel is now due my significant attention." Despite the lateness of the night, my friend seemed energised and enthusiastic. "There is much to do, Inspector, and time may be critical."

"Critical why?" Bradstreet objected. "The three men will still be dead come morning."

"But what of the three maids?" Holmes challenged us. "If they were made accomplices in a murder, and our investigation becomes known, how long will the murderer allow them to continue breathing to bear testimony to his deeds?"

I managed to snatch a few hours sleep before Holmes's clattering in our sitting room roused me from my slumbers. He had been out all night, as evidenced by the discarded rags and jumble-sale garments now scattered across our furniture, and the greasy cloths where he had wiped off theatrical make-up.

"You have had a night on the town," I surmised, knowing Holmes's habits and methods.

"A night on the docks, Watson," he corrected me. "Kindly ring and indicate to Mrs. Hudson that a rack of toast would be quite welcome, along with some strong tea. I must presently visit our washroom to detach myself from this sour alcohol smell, but first I must stoke my body for our day's programme of investigation!"

Holmes was still in fine spirits, I noticed. Grim deadlines tended to galvanise rather than oppress him, and this case also afforded him the excuse to disguise himself as one of his grotesque low-life characters and play the part of some docklands vagrant or down-on-his luck merchant seaman. "You have been to The Neptune, then," I mentioned, to demonstrate that I was keeping up.

"I have patronised a number of Wapping establishments," Holmes informed me, "not least of which was the rat-hole warren known as The Neptune and Isis. I have seldom seen a better subject for corrective arson than that grim venue. But my peregrinations have proved valuable, for I now know rather more about Georgie Wilson's business affairs and present status."

I saw the loathing in my friend's face. "The fellow needs whipping before he is hanged," I decided.

"He is one of the more unsavoury characters to come to criminal eminence since the departure of the late Professor Moriarty. Most of my information on Wilson came prefixed with a warning about not speaking further of him, or with some anecdote of dire punishment that was wreaked upon those that gossiped. Wilson appears to secure his hold over his people not by cleverness or cunning, but through sheer viciousness."

"Any man who exploits helpless children as Wilson does cannot be aught else. How can I assist to bring him low?"

"A strategy is forming, Watson, but there is more to discover before it's complete. We must use caution. I'm convinced that Wilson's brutal enforcers have deterred the river police from venturing too near to his establishments, granting him licence for his many crimes. His men are evidently not above threatening the families of the bobbies who patrol that patch. If any organised raid is prepared in advance, he will undoubtedly hear of it."

"But the three girls from The Fayre – ?"

"I believe I may have identified two of the most recent 'performers' who attended upon Morrow and his colleagues for their *tableaux*. Not all the girls who survive in the docklands are for sale, or are under Wilson's direct control. They naturally keep a sharp lookout for the 'canary-trainer' and his men, and know if any of their number are taken by these brutes. From these flower girls and hemp-pickers, I learned the name Hetty Slaithwaite, a country runaway who lived amongst them for four months before being 'recruited' by Wilson's agents. The girls have seen her since, painted and 'dolled', being escorted to the border between Wilson's territory and that of Gamma Buckland, in company with two other 'moppets'. Likewise, inmates of the workhouse on Artichoak Lane have recognised a girl named Susie Wattedyke, whose mother died there last February and who vanished soon after. The residents suspect that the beadle [16] sold her to Morrow, though there is no proof."

"Where are Hetty and Susie now?"

"Since some of the public house hangs over the river on groynes, the better to dispose of refuse and the occasional corpse, I have made what inspection I could from below and estimated the site's layout. There are dormitories within the sprawling Neptune establishment and the several adjoining properties – although cattle sheds might be a better term from what I can tell. If the three girls are at The Neptune, then they are likely confined in those quarters."

"You have taken a dinghy underneath the tavern and mapped the place?"

"As best I could in the time available at low tide. There are several trap-doors of a sinister nature where unwanted bodies might be flushed into the river, but they are sealed from the interior. The Neptune is something of a fortress."

"It will be difficult to siege, then? And Wilson will have many hostages."

"Indeed. But I am setting things in motion regarding Georgie Wilson. He isn't so secure as he imagines himself."

Our page arrived then with the required breakfast, and the detective applied himself to the stoking he required. Then Holmes and I set forth again, to interview the apprentices of the late Edwin Morrow.

Christoph Nuncier had no chance versus Sherlock Holmes. Within two minutes of his interrogation, Morrow's senior apprentice admitted that he knew of The Fayre. It was he who was sent there each Friday to receive deliveries for the debaucheries to come, and who ordered the cleaning women's visits. He was also the one who had taken the initiative at his master's absence to inform Mrs. Morrow of the problem, and to contact the Morrow nephew who had referred the matter to Holmes.

"I went back to the house to check, I swear," he told us, shaking with anxiety. "It was all locked up. I only have Mr. Morrow's key when I'm sent there, so I couldn't get in. The scrub-woman's hovel was empty too, abandoned. I didn't know what else to do, so I telegraphed master's wife and nephew."

Nuncier's Friday duties in the house off Scuddall's Passage were to stock the larder, to prepare and table covered dishes of various cold cuts and confections that had been previously sent from Haydock's and Donnely's shops, to set new candles in their sconces, and to lay fires if the weather required it. He was well aware of the uses to which his employer put the property and seemed envious rather than appalled. He had never been present to encounter any of the bathing maids.

"Master met Mr. Donnely at a gentleman's entertainment," he told us. "They were amused to find themselves to be a baker and a candlestick maker, and determined to seek out a like-minded butcher to form a league. They soon discovered Mr. Haydock, and between them set up their secret hideaway. They all thought it was a splendid jape."

Holmes had from Nuncier the name of the establishment where Morrow and Donnely had met, and where they had later recruited Haydock. "The bordello on Rosemary Lane in Aldgate is one of Wilson's properties," my friend instructed me. "It is a much better class of establishment than a stew like The Neptune, catering for wealthy men of low tastes who enjoy a *frisson* from venturing into the *demi-monde*. It caters for patrons of particular requirements, including those who especially enjoy the company of the inexperienced and the young."

Nuncier had perhaps hoped that his questioning was over, but Holmes had saved the best for last. "Now, young man, perhaps you will tell me who it was that gave you a thrashing about three weeks ago?"

The senior apprentice flinched and blanched. His denials meant nothing to Holmes, who had noticed faded bruising on Nuncier's left zygomatic arch, a still-unhealed *haematoma auris*, and a slight stiffness of the left middle phalanx where it had been dislocated – that is, a black eye, a cauliflower ear, and a dislocated middle finger.

At last Nuncier made his confession. Five days before his master's disappearance, the apprentice silversmith had been cornered by a rough stranger who had used considerable force to have the truth from him about activities at The Fayre. Christoph Nuncier had squealed out all that he knew then, and had nothing more to tell us now except a description of his assailant.

"You have no idea why you were beaten and interrogated?" I asked the effete apprentice disbelievingly.

"The brute told me to keep my tongue behind my teeth," he answered sullenly. "If I wanted to keep my teeth, that was. Well, I'm not paid enough to go against that."

I was in a bad mood, and I admit it. Bounders like Wilson raise my ire. They shouldn't be permitted in a civilised world.

For this reason, I was more than willing to go along with Holmes's proposed scheme, outlandish and unexpected as it was. Hence, at sunset of the night after we had discovered the three dead men, I was stood beside P.C. Bagley regarding a most unusual steam vessel.

The *S.S. Parsley* was a river dredger, one of those barges used to keep the Thames channels from silting and clogging. The busiest river in the world cannot be impeded by navigational hazards. The ship was fifty yards long but shallow-beamed, with a reinforced prow for breaking up jetsam tangles, a centrally-positioned boiler engine, side catamarans for buoyancy, and a counterbalanced digger arm for scooping up mud from the river bed. [17]

The *Parsley*'s captain greeted us with pleasure, beaming so widely that even his full white beard couldn't conceal it. "You're here to do God's work?" he asked us to confirm, indicating the collar-pin that marked him as a newly-converted temperancer and Salvationist. "Praise be!"

Bagley was quite nervous, either because he wasn't used to being on the water in a strange wheezing steaming contraption that scarcely resembled a boat, or since we were about to poke a hornet's nest and face the consequences. Still, he had his orders, confirmed by Inspector Bradstreet. All his fellow constables might be gathering for a raid upon the Rosemary Lane bordello, but the young constable was detached to observe another aspect of Holmes's investigation.

"Stout heart!" I encouraged him. "The odious Wilson may be willing to threaten officers of the law with reprisals against their families, but this is England. We don't countenance such behaviour here. You are sent along to bear witness of it!"

229

I signalled to Captain Sloan that we could depart the dock. Night was falling fast, but the steam dredger let out a cheery whistle, deployed its night lamps, and set off across the river.

The lights of The Neptune and Isis drew closer. I heard the noise of raucous revelry across the water. Someone was singing a bawdy ballad that I need not record, and there were all the other sounds of sailors and shoremen at their amusements.

"This is warranted?" Bagley checked again, asking both me and our enthusiastic captain.

I showed him again the magistrate's document that permitted our entry and search of The Neptune tavern for Hetty Slaithwaite and Susie Wattedyke, girls of the parish, who may have been distrained against their will for immoral purposes.

"Shall I go in?" Sloan asked, eyeing the low-slung sheds backing onto The Neptune where they overhung the water.

"Make it so, Captain," I requested, standing ready amidships for the furore that would follow.

Bagley eyed the windowless expanse of wooden sidings bleakly. "There's no way in from this side. What windows there are seem shuttered tight. Any water-doors will be fast pent."

"That warrant allows us to force entry if no other alternative is available," I pointed out. Holmes had been very specific in his instructions to Bradstreet about the magistrate's licence. "Captain Sloan, our police observer, has verified that no easy entrance is possible. You may make us another opening,"

"Aye-aye, sir!" the white-bearded dredger man cried with gusto. He turned and yelled instructions at his crew.

The steam barge's heavy rake-shovel hissed like a dragon, then pistoned out to port. Its steel bucket caught on the wall and roof of the nearest building, tearing through the wooden planking like an engine of destruction. Sloan whooped.

"What?" gasped Bagley, caught by surprise at this unusual tactic. I could only hope that Wilson and his henchmen would be similarly flummoxed.

Equipment that was designed to shift wreckage was quite as adept at causing it. We all ducked as splinters flew out across the water. The *Parsley* had momentum on her side, as well as a powerful turbine. The raking armature dragged the whole length of the property, shredding the riverside wall until the roof above collapsed.

Shrieks and oaths came from inside The Neptune. The patrons began to flee from the landward exits, flooding out into the darkened wharves and alleys beyond.

"Is this really allowed?" P.C. Bagley asked me nervously. "I mean, you don't have a demolition order!"

"The *Angels* of the *Lord* have come to *Sodom* and *Gomorrah!*" Captain Sloan boomed, laughing with delight as he directed his men with the steam shovel. "We are doing *God's* work!"

"We are being careful to damage only the rearmost parts of the buildings," I assured the worried constable. "We are warranted to use force to gain entry to make a search for the missing girls, and nothing says that force cannot be applied at the water-side of The Neptune, on those storehouse sheds where there will be nobody to harm."

I heard the *put-put-putting* of a pair of police river boats to starboard. The water patrol had finally been made aware that there was a major operation underway, and had received their written orders to cruise in and take up any felons who attempted to swim off. I knew that simultaneously Inspector Bradstreet would now have redirected those constables who had thought themselves assembled for a raid upon the exclusive Rosemary Lane bordello. The redirected constabulary would block the alleys and rat-runs about The Neptune to pick up what felons they encountered fleeing the demolition of their thieves' den.

A bullet thudded into the *Parsley*'s side. We all crouched low under the gunnels.

"That is a firearms offence!" Bagley cried, outraged at such a felony in London.

Holmes had anticipated such a response, so I had brought along my Lee-Enfield in case. I laid the long-barrelled rifle on the taff-rail and returned fire with better accuracy, scattering the would-be snipers from their partial cover.

The river police lit up their great limelight spotlamps, illuminating the damaged buildings as bright as day. From shore came Inspector Bradstreet's bull-horn-shouted warning that the police were declaring a riot and that they would use force if people didn't come along quietly.

"Wilson may have been able to intimidate local officers with personal threats," I told Bagley, "but when the institutions of Great Britain finally come to bear, a petty criminal such as he has no chance of victory."

Indeed, beat bobbies who had previously been intimidated were amongst the many officers of the law who were now assembled around The Neptune, and were amongst the most enthusiastic in subduing those enforcers of Wilson's will that attempted to resist detainment.

"Mr. Holmes did all of this?" the constable wondered, staring at the ruin that The Neptune and Isis was quickly becoming. "But where is he?"

"Inside," I revealed. "As confusion reigns, some scruffy longshoreman will be passing by the panicking denizens, making his way into the private back-rooms. His goals will be to liberate any women or girls who are confined there and to reach the office where Wilson keeps his ledgers."

"Ledgers?"

"No criminal enterprise as organised as this one could continue without such books. If Holmes can secure those, then there will be proof to dismantle Wilson's entire empire. Every property Wilson owns, every villain he employs, every enterprise he has set in place, every official he has corrupted to acquire his young victims will be known and exposed."

"Hallelujah!" called our Captain, resembling some demented Spirit of Christmas Past as he directed his vessel's armature at the crumbling tavern.

"Fire!" Bagley called urgently. He pointed at the centre of The Neptune, where a rose of flame suddenly bloomed from the wooden roofing plates. "The place is burning!"

It might have been a lamp overturned in the panic, but more likely Wilson had decided to destroy evidence that might otherwise incriminate him.

Bagley signalled to the police boats, which glided in to try and use their pump-hoses on the flames. Unfortunately, the fire was at the extreme reach of their sprays so there was little that the vessels could do to impede the spread of the blaze across the ramshackle edifice's rotted timbers.

I saw more movement in the shattered warehouses that we had broken open. I hefted my Lee-Enfield again but halted when a gawky scarecrow of a fellow waved in my direction – Holmes in his humble guise. Behind him trailed a string of girls, more than a score of them, in various states of undress. Some of them still had shackles attached to wrist or ankle.

"Bring the boat in!" I called to Captain Sloan. "The front parts of the tavern are too dangerous to escape through now because of the fire, and possibly since there are still felons fighting with policemen there. Those girls will be trapped on a blazing platform if we cannot rescue them!"

Sloan immediately reeled off orders to his faithful crew, slewing the *Parsley* about and heeling in to come alongside the walls we had sundered. The police barges stayed off, continuing their futile efforts to slow the fire, collecting the occasional fugitive from the chilly Thames flow. Only a shallow dredger might come in close enough between broken old groynes and accumulated river detritus.

"Hurry, Watson!" Holmes called to me. "The flames cannot now be far from the paraffin store!"

The *Parsley* bumped up against the rear of The Neptune. Our sailors hastily deployed long planks so that the girls could hurry aboard. We quickly made fast as Holmes chivvied the terrified former captives over to Bagley on the deck.

There were more young women and children than I had expected. My estimation of a score was out by sixty or so, far too many for a single rescue vessel. The small dredger sank uncomfortably low as they all came aboard.

"There!" came a shout from behind the escaping captives. "That boat! We c'n get away on that!"

Four large brutes elbowed their way through the last refugees. I didn't like the way that the girls shied away from them so quickly and completely. Their reactions told a story. The men carried guns, three pistols and a sawn-off shotgun, and they seemed intent on stealing the *Parsley*.

Holmes took the rear fellow quite by surprise with a boxing manoeuvre that wasn't in Queensbury's rules, folding the fellow over even as he relieved him of his firearm. Bagley leaped at the lead invader as he boarded the boat. The constable grappled the shotgun-wielder, driving the shortened barrel down so that it discharged into the deck.

The third intruder raised his snub-nosed revolver at me but discovered I had aimed my Lee-Enfield back at him, directly between his eyes. The bully halted, recognised his situation, saw my face, and then dropped his weapon overboard.

The fourth hopeful pirate got no further than Captain Sloan's massive ham-fist, which slammed into the fugitive's head like the *Parsley*'s steam-shovel. "Hoo!" he cried out in fierce exaltation. "Blow ye the *trumpet* in Zion, and sound an *alarm* in my holy mountain. Let all the inhabitants of the land *tremble*, for the *day* of the *Lord* cometh, for it is *nigh* at hand!" [18] The villain went down like the Philistines of old and didn't rise again.

P.C. Bagley brought his night-stick down hard on the wrist of the burly brute with whom he tussled. I heard the bone snap and the fellow howled. Bagley followed with a smack to the kneecap that sent the villain to the deck, then dropped atop him to pinion him for handcuffs.

"Georgie Wilson," the young constable who was soon to be a sergeant hissed triumphantly, "You are under arrest!"

"Get us away from here, Captain!" Holmes called urgently to Sloan. "We cannot have long now." To me he cried, "Watson, collect the documents that the girls are carrying! They are Wilson's files. Secure them safely."

As I did so, the ropes mooring the *Parsley* were hastily cast off or cut. The steam turbine churned. An alarming wash of river crested the deck, since we were so low in the water. The dredger swivelled about and pulled away from the blazing tavern.

"I'm making for the police launches!" Sloan shouted over the noise of the fire and the wailing of the girls. "We're too overladen to make it to shore. We must pass some of our passengers over to the other boats or we'll go down!"

Holmes nodded. He and I joined Bagley in securing our four prisoners. The fellow I had taken sat quietly, stunned at the reversals of his fortune. Two others weren't conscious. Wilson was in evident pain from his shattered wrist and knee, spewing obscenities until I jammed his hat in his mouth to shut him up.

The flames reached the fuel store. A great explosion lit the night. Sections of The Neptune flew into the sky, blazing, to drop down hissing into the Thames. The rear portion of the buildings descended into the river with a cloud of steam.

Whatever fight the fugitive denizens of the tavern still had went out of them at that blast.

The *Parsley* rocked unsteadily, water washing over our gunwales. We were only sustained by the air-filled catamarans affixed to the *Parley*'s hull. Hands urgently manned pumps to try and keep our dredger afloat. Sloan aimed us at the nearer of the river police boats, roaring over the distance between us to warn the vessel of the need for an urgent rendezvous.

We met with the first rescue craft. By ropes and pulleys we were able to winch in alongside the police boat so that some of our human cargo could be offloaded. With each rescued girl sent to safety, I felt a burden off my heart.

That reminded me of another priority. "Hetty Slaithwaite and Susie Wattedyke?" I prompted the detective worriedly. "Are they amongst the children we have recovered?"

"They aren't here," Holmes told me soberly. "These girls inform me that Hetty, Susie, and a third child called Jemima never returned to The Neptune after being dispatched to The Fayre two weeks ago."

So the case was still unresolved.

"Enquiries are proceeding," I informed Gamma Bucklands, sitting again in conference in her crowded trinket-decked caravan. "Prosecutions are ongoing."

"Those are official answers, about which you already know, Gamma," Holmes chided our corpulent hostess. "Georgie Wilson is fallen. His books are in the hands of the police. As the evidence is sifted, many arrests will follow. The Neptune and Isis is a charred smoking wreck marring the waterfront, yet still a cleaner place than it was yesterday. Close to a hundred girls have been handed on to charitable institutions for care and new accommodation. A great plague-spot has been erased from the city of London. And yet . . . ."

"What else is there?" the matriarch of the Mayhews and the Bucklands enquired. "Three *rakli* were sent to *jogger* three *omi*, and one time they was sent to drug 'em too, so that Wilson's murderer could slit three throats. If my family 'adn't closed the roads to Wilson's henchies, then they'd have stripped the house and taken all they could carry and there'd be naught left. As it is, you and the Mingers have taken a fine haul and all's well."

"You might perhaps have better luck with whoever takes over Wilson's patch," I suggested. "It might even be someone related to you."

"Too far from the Showground," Gamma sniffed. "We're for the road, not the river. But we'll see as if we might get on better with our new neighbours."

"There is still the matter of Hetty Slaithwaite, Susie Wattedyke, and Jemima Clover to resolve," Holmes mentioned. "I have studied Wilson's ledgers. They are horrifyingly comprehensive, as detailed as any slaver's books from a previous century. The three maids never returned to The Neptune after their visit to Scuddall Passage that night."

"Your lookout claimed that he saw them departing the next morning with packages of clothing," I reminded Gamma. "Yet it seems that the girls never went back to Wilson."

Gamma Bucklands paused to ingest another fried eel. At last she said, "I don't hold with girls that young plying that particular trade. I'm sure that if they wanted to find some other occupation, far off from London, where they could be happy and decent, there would be some way for them to just disappear and Wilson would never find them."

"Do you think that is what happened?" Holmes asked the Showground queen carefully.

"Yes. I reckon that's where they went. Mebbe they went off with that char-woman and 'er lass 'as also escaped. I doubt that anyone will ever catch them now."

"Fair enough. However, there are a few other matters that also hold my attention. A week before the murders, Mr. Morrow's apprentices were troubled by a rather brutal enquiry agent seeking information about their master's business. His name is Thompson, and he works from a rather seedy base near Covent Garden."

"And . . . ?" Gamma Bucklands asked indifferently.

"He was retained by Mrs. Morrow to discover if her husband was being unfaithful while she was convalescing at the seaside. He reported back with incontrovertible evidence about the butcher, the baker, and the candlestick maker's visits to their Fayre."

"Sufficient for Mrs. Morrow to institute divorce proceedings," I estimated.

Holmes had gone deeply into the agent Thompson's actions, knowing him of old as a ruthless "fixer" who played fast-and-loose with the law. "Thompson thereafter visited the spouses of Heydock and Donnelly, doubtless informing them too of their husbands' extramural activities. After that, he paid a visit to you here, I believe."

Gamma stirred wrathfully in her chair. "Who told you that?" she demanded.

"It was surmise," my friend told her. "I *said* that I believed it to be so. You have now helpfully confirmed my suspicion, Gamma."

The old woman glared at Holmes so balefully that I began to fear for our safety, for all that Holmes had taken precautions this time of having armed police officers with dogs within whistle range.

He went on. "There was always the question of *why* Morrow, Haydock, and Donnelly were drugged and murdered. They were good customers of the notorious 'canary-trainer'. Why should he have them eliminated for short-term gain? He didn't profit from it, unless he was paid to do it by one or more vengeful wives who will now inherit control of significant sums of money and of their husbands' businesses. Howsoever, though several murders may be laid upon Wilson from the documentation that we captured, there is no such transaction noted in his ledgers for these assassinations."

"Wilson was crafty," Gamma pointed out.

"Thompson's visit to you raises an alternative possibility: That someone else arranged The Fayre killings. It would have been an easy thing for one of the Showmen to intercept the three maids, to offer them a way from their sordid slavery in exchange for slipping a sedative into their patrons' cups and then unbolting a door – with the girls then transported far off where they might never be found to testify."

I followed Holmes's reasoning. "Three unpleasant fellows who chose to make this neighbourhood their wicked playground, who even called their seraglio '*The Fayre*', must have been quite offensive to your sensibilities, Gamma Bucklands. It would be easy to see such men erased and the girls liberated, and to pick up a fee for it as well."

"Perhaps it would," the Showground matriarch agreed. "If only there was evidence."

"If only there was," Sherlock Holmes agreed. "However, the girls have left London, most probably with the caravans that set off towards Hull twelve days ago, perhaps as wards of the Hawthorn family. The feud with Wilson and his Wapping dockland crew is decisively ended. Whatever testimony those criminals might have offered is now tainted beyond credulity. Morrow's hideaway was cleverly not looted, so there is no chain of stolen goods to trace back to any perpetrator. The locals here will doubtless be unanimous in their witness of what occurred."

"I'm certain of it, Mr. Holmes," Gamma assured the detective. She tensed, like a monster ready to strike. "So, what next?"

Holmes eyes her coolly, and I was suddenly certain as which of us in the crowded caravan was truly the most dangerous. "I have cautioned Thompson that I shall be reviewing his activities closely in the future," he mentioned. "As for the Showfolk, Gamma, I see little point in pursuing this case further. I was retained by Morrow's nephew to locate his missing uncle, which I have accomplished. I am pleased to have removed Georgie Wilson from the general population. I trust the public hangman will soon remove him from this life. It isn't my job to prevent neighbourhood reform and the elimination of antisocial elements.

"'*The butcher, the baker, the candlestick maker. Turn them out, knaves all three.*'"

"*Bona* riddance to *kativa* rubbish," Gamma Bucklands agreed.

"I shall be keeping an eye on Scuddall Passage, and the old fairground also," Holmes warned the matriarch.

She swallowed another eel and made no other reply.

In this memorable year '95 a curious and incongruous succession of cases had engaged his attention . . . his arrest of Wilson, the notorious canary-trainer, which removed a plague-spot from the East End of London.

– Dr. John Watson
"Black Peter"

NOTES

1. The Fairs Acts of 1868, 1871, and 1873 did much to diminish or eliminate the traditional fairs and fairgrounds that had survived since the time of their medieval charters. Annual gatherings that had once served as trading events (either Charter Fairs authorised by Royal Warrant or Prescriptive Fairs legitimised by ancient custom, or else agricultural Mop Fairs where seasonal labour was hired) had largely become sometimes-rowdy entertainment events. The controversial new legislation allowed landowners to petition for long-established rights to be legally revoked, freeing up prime "fairground" land for new housing construction. Wapping was amongst many London Boroughs that officially eliminated its "showground", but the undesirable neighbourhood in the shadow of the dockyard walls did not attract new development, so the derelict fair site continued to be unofficially used by migrant "showfolk" for many years.

2. These examples of the showmen's language were recorded by journalist Henry Mayhew in Volume 3 of his three-volume work, *London Labour and the London Poor* (1851, with a fourth volume added in the 1861 edition), from discussion with Punch-and-Judy show performers. Holmes would undoubtedly have found much of value in Mayhew's investigations.

3. This investigation is also mentioned in "The Adventure of the Sussex Vampire" (1924), collected in *The Case-Book of Sherlock Holmes* (1927).

4. That is, in The City of London proper, between the Barbican and St Paul's Cathedral, a prestige address.

5. "The Amateur Mendicant Society, who held a luxurious club in the lower vault of a furniture warehouse" was referenced in passing in "The Five Orange Pips", *The Adventures of Sherlock Holmes* (1891).

6. The law enforcement officers of the Bow Street Magistrates' Court in the City of Westminster were established in 1749 by magistrate Henry Fielding and are often described as London's first professional police force. They were colloquially but never officially called "The Bow Street Runners". When finally disbanded in 1839, the group's operatives were brought into the new Metropolitan Police force, forming the backbone of the Police Detective Agency that was thereafter based at Scotland Yard.

   Inspector Bradstreet's allegiance to E Division, one of 22 administrative geographical divisions in London policing, is established in "The Man With the Twisted Lip" (1891, collected in *The Adventures of Sherlock Holmes*, 1892), wherein Bradstreet also reveals that he has been a policeman since 1862. By the time of "The Adventure of the Blue Carbuncle" (first published in 1892, also collected in *The Adventures of Sherlock Holmes*), Bradstreet is attached to B Division. At his appearance in "The Adventure of the Engineer's Thumb" (first published in 1892, also collected in T*he Adventures of Sherlock Holmes*), Bradstreet appears to be peripatetic, leading *The Encyclopaedia Sherlockiana* author Jack Tracy to conclude that he was *"assigned most likely to the central headquarters staff"*.

7. Bradstreet's beardedness comes from Sidney Paget's *Strand Magazine* illustrations, and not from Canonical text.

8. The rhyme has been tentatively traced back to the Fourteenth Century. Bradstreet's version is similar to the earliest extant written version in the lengthily-titled *Second Volume of Christmas Box Containing the Following Bagatelles for Juvenile Amusement: High ding a ding, Christmas comes but once a Yr, Little Tom Tucker, Little Robin Red-breast, Rub a dub dub, I'll Sing a Song of Sixpence, Little Boy Blue, Gooseberrys, Grow on an Angry Tree, When I was a Little Boy, Robin a Bobin, a Bilberry Hen, There Was an Old Woman Living, There were Two Blackbirds. Set to Music by Mr. Hook* (London, 1798) and to *Mother Goose's Quarto or Melodies Complete* (Boston, Massachusetts, c1825). Scholarship since the middle of the Twentieth Century has favoured the peep-show interpretation of the original work [c.f. I. Opie and P. Opie, *The Oxford Dictionary of Nursery Rhymes* (1951, 1997) and Roberts, Chris (2003), *Heavy Words Lightly Thrown*.]

9. From the 1950's, *polari* also became the secret language of choice of Britain's gay community, at a time when homosexuality was a still a criminal act punishable by imprisonment. Some *parlyari* terms are still current amongst British seamen.

    It should also be noted that many of these traveller lingoes had regional or cultural variants that distinguished and separated the speakers from each other, and that all of these dialects have changed over time.

10. Recognised as a trade guild for the travelling fun-fair business in 1917, known today as the Showmen's Guild of Great Britain, this association promotes and protects the Showmen's way of life and preserves *"the unique cultural heritage of travelling fairs and circuses."* The 4,700-showpeople strong Guild has a Code of Rules and makes representations concerning proposed legislation about travellers.

11. *"Somebody looking at/spying on the patch."*

12. In the eighteenth and nineteenth century, there was considerable demand for canaries and other highly trained songbirds such as goldfinches, linnets, blackbirds, thrushes, and nightingales, which were bought for upper and middle-class homes to actually provide music. There were published song-sheets of "bird music" by which trainers could teach teams of canaries, bullfinches, linnets, and the like to simulate well-known popular tunes. So popular were such collections that conmen would paint up non-singing birds and try to sell them to unsuspecting buyers by simulating birdsong. The best-trained avian choirs were displayed as fairground or theatrical exhibits.

13. Mudlarks combed the sand and silt of riverbeds for flotsam and jetsam. Toshers or grubbers scavenged the sewers and drains for scrap metals and lost coins. Pure finders collected dog dung to sell to tanneries. All three occupations were work of last resort for the poorest people of Victorian London. Children were well-suited to the tasks because they were small, lightweight, and nimble, able to squeeze where adults could not go, to cross

sucking mud that would engulf a heavy adult, and to weave between horses' hooves and carriage wheels to claim fresh ordure.

14. *Fiella* are children. A *dollymop* is a child prostitute. *Rakli* are girls who are not from Showfolk families (and may therefore be fair game for robbery or seduction). A *chava* is a Showfolk girl. *Chitlins* or *chitterlings* are the small intestines, usually of domestic animals, sold as a food for the very poor.

15. A variant form of this children's rhyme is first recorded as "*an old ballad*" in *The Kentish Coronal* (1841). *National Nursery Rhymes* (1870) set the poem to music by James William Elliott. Rudyard Kipling quoted the poem in his short story "*Georgie Porgie*" in *Life's Handicap: Being Stories of Mine Own People* (1891). It appears in the *Roud Folk Song Index*, number 19532.

    The poem was often sung by children at some victim who was thought to be fat, effeminate, or a bully of girls. A gender-flipped variant, "Margie Pargie" was sometimes used to mock overweight or sexually-aggressive girls.

    The Oxford Dictionary of Nursery Rhymes (1951, Peter and Iona Opie), which used the 1880's version with the line "*when the boys came out to play*", reported and popularised some folklorists attributions that the rhyme as originally a satirical verse upon King George IV (1762-1830), whose fifty-inch waistline, rampant womanising, treatment of his wife (including banning her from his coronation), adversity to "manly" conflict, and huge debts (£630,000 by 1795, around $65-million today) occasioned public criticism in his lifetime, or that it was King Charles I's friend and possible lover George Villiers, the 1st Duke of Buckingham (1592-1628), a Knight of the King's Bedchamber, who was the poem's inspiration.

16. By Holmes's era, a beadle had come to refer to a parish constable who was often charged with running an orphanage or workhouse. Charles Dickens' *Oliver Twist* (1838) included the overbearing beadle Mr. Bumble as a minor antagonist.

17. An 1883 photograph of a similar if smaller such vessel may be viewed at:
    https://historicengland.org.uk/services-skills/education/educational-images/dredging-on-the-river-thames-at-culham-4135
    An even earlier drawing of steam-powered ballast dredger on the Thames from 1859 is online at:
    https://victorianweb.org/technology/ships/26.html

18. *The Book of Joel*, 2:1

The Adventure of the African Prospector
by Arthur Hall

I looked at my friend, Mr. Sherlock Holmes the consulting detective, curiously. He did not lift his eyes from the morning edition of *The Standard,* but adjusted his position in his armchair while blowing out a cloud of fragrant smoke. That didn't prevent him from noticing my interest, however.

"I take it that it's my new pipe that has attracted your attention, Watson?"

"I was certain that I hadn't seen it before now."

He looked up slowly, and from the other side of the empty fireplace I could see a glint in his eyes – or it could have been a reflection of the early summer sunlight?

"I received it in the first post, before you presented yourself for breakfast. It's a gift from someone who was of great assistance to me during my time in Montague Street. You may have seen mention of Sir James Saunders in the dailies from time to time."

"The famous dermatologist? I recall that he had some success with identifying that outbreak in the northern counties, several years ago. But why would he have sent you a gift? Has the pipe some special significance?"

Holmes smiled. "No, only that I once mentioned to him that I have a small collection. It was the accompanying letter that was of interest."

"He requires your services, then?"

"Precisely, and I shall be glad to aid him in any way that I can, to discharge the debt that I owe him. It is a case of double murder that he mentions." He extracted his pocket watch from his waistcoat and looked at it briefly. "I'm to catch the mid-morning train for Gorhampton Priors within the hour. Pray pack an overnight bag, if you would care to accompany me."

Having complied with this, I stood next to my friend on a rather crowded platform in Fenchurch Street Station. While in the hansom that had conveyed us from our lodgings, I had noted that, as often on such occasions, he had brought no visible baggage. His requirements, he stated on more than one occasion previously, were no more than a clean collar and a toothbrush.

241

Our wait was short. Holmes had no sooner purchased our tickets than the train came to rest before us with a squeal of brakes and surrounded by wreathes of smoke. We were fortunate in finding a compartment to ourselves in the first smoker we approached, and I contained my curiosity with difficulty until the outskirts of the capital were left behind.

"I think," I said then, "that there is time for you to tell me something of what we're about to undertake, before we reach our destination."

He settled himself in the seat opposite mine and produced his new pipe, which he lit. I refrained from doing likewise, as I was more interested in discovering the nature of the task before us.

"The letter from Sir James was quite extensive," he began as smoke swirled above him. "You may have wondered, Watson, why I didn't show it to you. The reason is that I was uncertain of your participation after your recent bout of influenza, which I know taxed your strength severely."

I have never doubted my friend's concern, but I couldn't help wondering whether the nature of Sir James' assistance, years ago, was a secondary reason why the letter had been withheld from me. Holmes had been unusually vague as to the specifics of it.

"Pray do not concern yourself. I am fully recovered."

"Excellent! My work would be of lesser satisfaction to me without my Boswell."

"Holmes," I said as the train rattled over the points and took a new direction, "what is it that has caused Sir James to consult you?"

"Two of his guests have been murdered. The local force is mystified, and have concluded that the perpetrator is a vagabond who has been seen in the surrounding villages. They have therefore concentrated their enquiries in that direction, and Sir James has indicated that he is grateful for that since he views the official detective, Inspector Winster Soames – I have never made his acquaintance – as an incompetent idiot. It was after forming this opinion that he recalled my profession."

"Were the visitors killed at the same time?" I asked after considering for a moment.

"The murders occurred on the same afternoon, at a garden party held by Sir James."

"When was this?"

"Three days past."

"How were they committed?"

"It was arsenic poisoning, according to the police pathologist, administered in the wine that was served."

"Did Sir James mention any additional features, or anything of peculiar significance?"

"He did indeed, and that is the reason why he couldn't confide completely with Inspector Soames."

I raised my eyebrows. "What was it, then?"

"The element that attracted me at once. You see, Watson, Sir James is an excellent fellow, but he has always been possessed of a strong fear of becoming the subject of ridicule. An event such as this occurring at his home is disturbing enough, but when the perpetrator appears to be a younger brother who has long been thought dead, the resulting scandal to the family seems to him unendurable."

"Did he actually see the murderer?"

"It appears that one of the victims saw the man looking down from a window. She spoke his name and pointed as she expired."

"Was he seen by any of the others present?"

"Apparently only by Sir James. Everyone else saw only a blank window."

"Possibly it was a reflection or an illusion. It is known that this happens to death-bed cases occasionally before they pass from this life, although that doesn't explain what Sir James saw. At any rate, this cannot be the truth of it. How often have you proved that so-called supernatural incidents are nothing but trickery?"

"Quite so, and I fully expect the result of this investigation to be similar. However, I see from my watch that we have scarcely ten minutes left before we arrive at Gorhampton Priors Station, so I suggest that we continue this discussion later."

He had made no mention of it, but Holmes must have telegraphed Sir James to indicate the time of our arrival, since a shining landau awaited us. The driver, who apparently had long been in service there, lost no time in cheerfully conveying us through a succession of leafy lanes until we came upon the open fields that surrounded Darkly Grange, Sir James' ancestral home.

We soon found ourselves upon a wide gravel path, with tall bushes on either side. Someone with extensive knowledge of the art of topiary had shaped them expertly into various animal species.

The house wasn't at all as I had imagined. Holmes had mentioned that it dated from the time of the Tudors, but it wasn't typical of that style. Both wings appeared to have succumbed to the ravages of time and been removed, with obvious repairs to the main structure. What remained was a building of three storeys, the upper two boasting fifteen windows each and the ground floor bisected by an arch that was the entrance to the courtyard.

The driver brought the landau to a halt and we alighted. Before it had disappeared beneath the arch, the massive iron-studded door swung open and a middle-aged man of average height descended the steps, obviously pleased to see us.

"Holmes!" he shook my friend's hand vigorously. "How good of you to come!"

"I am very glad to make your acquaintance once more, Sir James." Holmes disengaged himself and gestured in my direction. "Allow me to introduce my friend and colleague, Doctor John Watson."

Our host seemed equally glad of my presence, and quickly ushered us into the house. It was like many I had seen before, with oak-panelled walls surmounted by ancestral portraits and crossed swords. Suits of polished armour stood sentry-like in corners and niches. After being shown to our rooms by a butler who seemed unfamiliar with the configuration of the place, we joined Sir James for luncheon.

Our host proved to serve an excellent table, and he chatted enthusiastically throughout the meal. I could sense that Holmes was growing tired of this prevarication and had, as was usual for him, consumed little.

"I understand, Sir James," he said as our host paused to drink, "that you are experiencing some difficulty, the precise details of which you haven't yet informed me. If you would care to elaborate, Watson and myself will be pleased to render what assistance we can."

Sir James replaced his glass, suddenly more serious. "I have indeed found these last few days most trying, as has everyone here. Indeed, I can remember no time to compare."

"Your letter mentioned the murders of two of your guests."

"That was three days ago, at Lady Anne's garden party. I still call it that, though my good lady passed on five years past. Mrs. Margaret Feldeane, a widowed lady from the village, and her son, barely eighteen, keeled over and died near that bush you see there." He gestured through the high window, across the lawn to a topiary shape of a hen. "Poor young fellow, about to enter the army too. Would have made a great name for himself, I'm sure."

"It was arsenic poisoning, according to the police pathologist?"

"That was his conclusion. Fortunately, if I may put it so, only Mrs. Feldeane and her son drank from that bottle. The wine was an Alsace vintage, known to be a favourite of hers and ordered specially. It was a startling and sad affair, but the strangest thing occurred after the poor lady collapsed." He shook his head, incredulously. "You gentlemen cannot know it, but I had a younger brother, Gilbert, who was at one time engaged to Mrs. Feldeane before he embarked upon an expedition to prospect for gold in Africa. Apparently, she forced him to choose between her and the voyage and he chose, unwisely in my opinion, to depart. That was years ago, and he has long since been lost and given up for dead. The relevance is that she looked up at the house as she died and cried out, 'Oh, it is you, Gilbert!' as she expired."

"It isn't unusual, Sir James," I said then, "for the dying to experience visions of those they have known. I don't think we should place too much credence on the incident."

He appeared no less perplexed, and hesitated before continuing. "I could accept that, Doctor. Indeed, I heard as much from Inspector Soames, fool that he is. But I was with Mrs. Feldeane and immediately turned to where she stared in her last moments." He hesitated again. "It seems that I saw what no one else except she had noticed. For an instant, I perceived but faintly the face of my brother grimly observing us. Then it was gone."

Holmes nodded slowly. "Did this – Apparition, shall we call it? – appear to say anything. To gesticulate or move?"

"Not at all. It had vanished before I had realised what I was seeing."

"Do you recall the window where it appeared?"

"Later, when some of the shock had passed, I returned to the garden and looked again at the back of the house. I would swear that the window where I had seen the vision is the ninth from the left side, on the second floor. Together with the groom and my new butler, Melhuish, I examined every room on both the first and second stories. Most of that part of the house lies unused, and has done for a considerable time, but I can assure you that we discovered nothing out of the ordinary."

"Has anything else of an unusual nature occurred in your household?" Holmes asked after a moment. "Pray be precise as to details, however insignificant they may seem."

Sir James pushed away his empty plate. "Now that you mention it, Holmes, I suppose you could say that there has been rather a lot of activity at Darkly Grange recently. Usually, you know, we live quiet lives here, but I suppose everyone has their ups and downs."

"Kindly elaborate," my friend requested with a trace of impatience.

"Well, let me see. About two months ago, I acquired a magnificent Cezanne. It is a self-portrait of the artist, but quite different from the famous one, as it shows him as a younger man. I have always collected art, and I consider this my crowning achievement. My cousin, Mr. Erasmus Bartley, was rather jealous, but that wasn't unexpected. He is a collector also, somewhat more fanatically so than myself. When I invited him to view the picture, he offered to buy it, but it isn't for sale."

"I would be delighted to see it," Holmes said surprisingly.

"Of course. Shortly afterwards," our host continued, "Rowens died suddenly. He was my butler for many years, and our local doctor thought it was his heart since it had troubled him previously. I had another visit from Erasmus about then, to repeat his offer. He lives not far away, a couple of miles over the hill at Mortley Manor, and this time he did me a bit of good. Poor Rowens wasn't yet cold, if you will forgive me for putting it like that, before the new butler, Courtney, replaced him at my cousin's recommendation. It saved me the trouble of consulting an agency, references and all that. I was grateful to Erasmus at the time, but I'm not so sure now."

"Courtney proved unsatisfactory?" I presumed.

"Not in his work. The fact is, he left Darkly Grange just before the garden party. I recall that it was the night after Mrs. Feldeane and her son arrived. I intended them to stay for a day or two." He spread his hands in an incredulous gesture. "The fellow just let himself out and went in the early hours!"

"Curious," Holmes commented as the dessert arrived.

"I thought perhaps he had received word of a dying relative or something of the sort, but he could at least have informed me."

"One would have expected so," said I.

There was silence between us while we ate, my friend sparingly, until Sir James put down his spoon in conclusion.

"That, I believe, is all I can tell you. Except that Melhuish was subsequently supplied to me by the agency that I should have used in the first place. Oh, and there was the kitchen maid Alice, who I had to dismiss."

Holmes leaned forward in his seat, his interest aroused further. "May I ask why?"

"I cannot tolerate dishonesty. Food and wine was missing from the kitchen four or five times. It wasn't as if I didn't pay the girl enough."

My friend said little more as we drank our coffee.

"Sir James," he began when our cups were empty, "there are clear indications that whoever is responsible for the deaths of Mrs. Feldeane and her son is familiar with both your house and your visitors. Otherwise how, for example, did he know which window would best enable his victims to see him, and how was he able to identify the wine which Mrs. Feldeane preferred? There are also other indications. It would be as well, I think, if I examined the back of the house from the exact spot where you and she stood at the moment of her passing. But first, I would appreciate it if you would describe the other guests."

"Since my wife passed, fewer of our former guests have attended. They are mostly my own friends now, such as Captain Tebbitt and his wife, and Mr. Jonathan Strider. Mrs. Georgina Gough was also present, and Miss Crowther. Some of them brought friends with them who are unknown to me, as they have always been free to do. All of these reside either in the north of the country or, in the case of Mr. Strider, in Plymouth. They usually stay for a night after the party and then return to their homes. I fear that the tradition will not be continued henceforth."

We then adjourned to the garden as Holmes had suggested. Sir James indicated the place near the topiary hen where he had stood when he glimpsed the face at the window, and from there my friend examined the rear of the building. I saw the faintest smile pass over his face, but then he shook his head, and I knew he had reached no definite conclusion.

"Very well," he said then. "Perhaps, Sir James, you will now allow Watson and myself to see the Cezanne. I have always maintained an interest in art, at least since I was fortunate enough to see a Da Vinci when I travelled through Italy a few years ago."

"Of course!" Our host's face lit up at the mention of the subject that was so beloved to him. "Come this way, gentlemen."

He led us back into the house and along a ground-floor corridor that ran the entire length of the building. Before we had progressed halfway, he stopped before a sturdy door and produced a key. We entered a dark and spacious room.

Sir James lit an oil lamp near the door, and then another, and we saw that we were surrounded by portraits of unsmiling gentlemen in various styles of attire.

"Your ancestors, presumably?" Holmes asked.

"They are, though the exhibition is incomplete." Our host ushered us along the room until we were confronted by a large portrait that was unlike the others. "Here it is – my Cezanne. Magnificent, isn't it?"

Holmes scrutinized it for several minutes. "The brushwork is exquisite. The detail, both in the features and the background, is unmistakeably his work. Many a collector, and indeed public galleries, must envy you this, Sir James."

"Undoubtedly this is so, but while it remains in my possession it will not leave this room. I have considered leaving it to a museum upon my death, but for the moment the matter is undecided."

"A noble thought, indeed."

I, without Holmes's enthusiasm, examined the collection as we retraced our steps. I reflected that his knowledge of art was yet another side of my friend of which I had been unaware until now. Over the years I had learned something of many of the facets of his personality, but evidently, he could still surprise me.

"Are any of these portraits in the likeness of your brother Gilbert?" he enquired of our host as we returned along the aisle.

Sir James shook his head. "As far as I am aware, there is but one picture of him as an adult in existence, commissioned by Erasmus a few months before Gilbert undertook the African expedition. It is still part of

247

his collection."

"Excellent! Would it be possible for us to accompany you on a visit to your cousin tomorrow? I have a mind to also view his collection."

Our host looked rather taken aback at this unexpected request, but readily agreed. "You'll find him an interesting fellow, though rather boorish in some of his ways. Do you know, he ran away and joined a circus before he was seventeen years old? When he eventually returned to the family, it was as a man who had experienced many adventures. What a life he has had!"

I caught a glance that told me that my friend had formed a theory, but knew he would say nothing until he felt the time was right.

"I wonder from where his love of art developed."

"Perhaps it was inherited, as was mine. He used to tell us stories of his exploits. Once, when he had indulged in too many glasses of port, he related to Lady Anne and myself a saga of his involvement with a gang of art thieves in Paris during the circus's visit there, but of course we never took him seriously. I'm quite sure that many of his stories were exaggerated."

We remained in that room for a considerable time, so that I became depressed by the closeness of its windowless walls. My two companions seemed unaffected, and the discussion continued with my occasional contributions. At last we emerged into the corridor, and Sir James consulted his pocket watch remarking that, to his surprise, dinner would be served in little more than an hour.

"How time speeds by when you are absorbed," he observed.

"Will tomorrow afternoon be convenient for our visit to your cousin?" Holmes asked him then.

"Oh, there is no need to make an appointment. Erasmus turns up here whenever the mood takes him, so he can hardly complain if we do the same."

"Thank you, Sir James. I am confident that I will have some news for you afterwards." He ignored our host's look of pleasant surprise. "There is one more question I must ask you, if you would be so kind."

"I am at your service."

"It concerns Mrs. Feldeane. Since you mentioned that your brother was once engaged to her, I presume that she once lived near here."

"That is so. She grew up near the village. It could have been that she and Gilbert married in our local church on his return from Africa, but, as you know, it wasn't to be."

"And so, when he was declared dead, she married another?"

He nodded. "After a respectable time had passed, she wed Mr. Andrew Feldeane, and moved to his family home in Northumberland."

"But during her early life, did she have a close friend or confidante?"

Sir James looked puzzled for a moment. Then: "Yes, of course. Miss Janet Crenthorpe. She is unmarried, and still lives near the village."

"Then that is where me must go in the morning, if you will kindly furnish us with the address."

Dinner was an elaborate and, for me, very satisfying meal. Holmes, as was usual for him, ate only a small portion. This, I observed, wasn't only because of his poor appetite, but also because of his responses to Sir James' enquiries regarding our past adventures. My friend was polite, as always, but guarded in his revelations. This continued further into the evening, when we smoked and drank brandy with Sir James in the library. Earlier than was our custom, we left our host in a jovial mood and retired.

We breakfasted alone, Melhuish having informed us that his master had risen early in order to supervise the repairs to stock fencing in the north pasture. He hadn't returned as we finished our meal and set off for Miss Crenthorpe's house.

The village was near the edge of the estate, but easily within walking distance. Sir James had furnished us with precise directions, and we came upon a group of thatched cottages near the vicarage, as he had described. At the end of the long wall of the Reverend's garden stood a tiny house, white with black beams and a tall chimney. Holmes knocked lightly upon the door, which opened to reveal a woman of prim appearance with *pince-nez* perched on an aquiline nose.

"Good morning," he began cheerfully. "I hope you will forgive this intrusion. My name is Sherlock Holmes, I'm a consulting detective, and would be grateful for a few minutes of your time."

She gave us a worried look which softened quite suddenly.

"Why yes, I believe I have read of you."

"My friend," he indicated me, "Doctor John Watson, was fond of exaggerating my trifling successes in print."

"It's an honour to meet you, sir, but what brings you to me? Have I unknowingly committed a crime?"

"Nothing of the sort," Holmes smiled. "We're making enquiries on behalf of Sir James Saunders regarding the recent deaths at Darkly Grange. I believe you knew one of the victims – Mrs. Margaret Feldeane – and it is she about whom we are seeking information."

The *pince-nez* glinted as she nodded her bird-like head.

"My poor friend. We were close when she was Margaret Derrow, it is true, but I have seen little of her since her marriage. However, come in gentlemen, and I will try to assist you."

We thanked her and entered into a narrow corridor leading to a

249

spotless sitting room. I saw at once that the furniture was perfectly positioned around the fireplace, and the tiny desk in the corner shone from much polishing. I concluded that, being unmarried, she poured her energies into maintaining an immaculate home, and possibly into service at the nearby church also.

When we were seated, she offered refreshments, which we refused as we hadn't long eaten breakfast. She arranged herself upon a chair that faced us both with an expectant expression.

"Can you remember anything of Mrs. Feldeane that could aid us in our investigation?" Holmes began. "For example, do you know of anyone who had reason to dislike her, or harbour hatred? I understand that this is an unusual request but, as you will appreciate, whoever is responsible for her death didn't become so without reason."

Miss Crenthorpe spent a few seconds in thoughtful concentration before shaking her head slowly. "Throughout our childhood and after, I can recall but one occasion when Margaret was involved in a heated exchange. We had walked a long way into the countryside and realised quite late in the day that we wouldn't be able to return before dark. Margaret, after some thought, led us through the forest on Lord Northingham's estate because that would shorten the distance by a few miles. We had the misfortune to meet the gamekeeper, Grimforth, always an unpleasant fellow, who was quite rude. Margaret told him what she thought of his attitude in no uncertain terms, and apart from the oaths he directed at us, he troubled us no further. Apart from that incident, her disposition was always calm and placid, inviting no animosity from anyone."

"Was there anything about her behaviour that might have caused offence to her friends or neighbours, however accidentally?"

This time Miss Crenthorpe needed no time to consider.

"Nothing," she answered immediately, "and as she grew older, that became less likely still."

"Why do you say that, Miss Crenthorpe?"

"Because of her health. She became prone to seizures, which would strike when she grew anxious or excessively concerned."

"Was the cause ever identified?" I asked.

"Not with any certainty. She saw several physicians over the years. One concluded that her heart was defective, another that the blood supply to her brain was periodically interrupted. Still others put forward opinions that were less conventional."

I glanced at my friend and saw understanding written on his face. After several more questions and a short but friendly conversation, we thanked Miss Crenthorpe and left. We had walked almost to the edge of

Sir James' estate when I broke the silence between us.

"I cannot see that we learned much, except for a little of Mrs. Feldeane's life that seems unconnected to our investigation."

"Much to the contrary. Until now, the purpose of the apparition had eluded me, but no more. As each piece of the puzzle presents itself, the picture becomes clearer."

He then launched into a detailed description of some of the habits of the birds who flittered among the trees around us, which I knew was his way of deflecting more of my questions. When we reached Darkly Grange, we were ushered into the sitting room by Meluish to find Sir James awaiting us.

"Gentlemen," he said as we entered, "I have good news. A telegram from Inspector Soames has arrived, in advance of his intended visit tomorrow morning. It seems the fellow who killed poor Mrs. Feldeane and her son has been arrested in Braintree. Perhaps I misjudged the inspector, after all."

Holmes accepted a glass of port as I had done, and we settled ourselves in comfortable armchairs.

"I regret that I am unable to agree, Sir James. However, the inspector's visit will be most timely, since I expect to have the real villain in readiness for him by then."

"Are you certain, Holmes?" Our host put down his glass, wearing an incredulous expression.

"There can be no doubt of it."

"But that means that this poor fellow who Soames has arrested is innocent!"

Holmes nodded. "He is, in fact, the second innocent to suffer in this affair."

"Who is the other unfortunate then?" I enquired.

"The maid who you dismissed for stealing food. She was quite blameless."

The dermatologist appeared totally shocked. He attempted a few words, but then gave up and drained his glass before he was able to respond.

"I am not usually such a poor judge of character. Again, I ask if you are confident in your conclusions."

"They are simple enough to verify. I take it that your cook is at present engaged in preparing luncheon?"

"Of course. It will be served in less than an hour."

"If you will summon her, I will not detain her for long."

"Very well." Sir James rang for Melhuish, who was promptly despatched to the kitchen. After a few minutes, a stout but pleasant woman

251

appeared, with all the indications of one who is both hot and busy.

"You called for me, Sir James?" she asked, with respect.

"Yes, Martha. Pray answer a question or two from Mr. Holmes."

She turned to us, and Holmes spoke in a kindly voice.

"Pray do not be alarmed, Martha. You are aware that the maid, Alice, was dismissed for stealing food?"

"Yes sir."

"But since then, is food still disappearing?"

She looked nervously at Sir James, then at the carpet at her feet. "It is. Sir."

"Then why have you not reported this?"

"I did not wish to be blamed sir, as Alice was."

"You need have no fear, Martha," Sir James said then. "It appears I have some restitution to make, since I have punished an innocent girl."

Our host was unusually quiet during our meal, doubtless regretting his recent treatment of Alice or speculating who was likely the guilty party. When the meal was over, he called for the landau to take us to Mortley Manor. The conversation during the journey was almost exclusively between Sir James and myself. Holmes sat beside me brooding, or perhaps reviewing the facts he had gleaned from his observations. He was oblivious, I knew of old, to the beauty and freshness of the fields, flowers, and trees around us.

Quite suddenly, our driver turned our conveyance into a grove of tall oaks. These screened out the afternoon sunlight, so that the only illumination was from the remaining narrow strip of sky directly overhead. I saw deer watching us cautiously from concealment, and squirrels scampering along leafy branches. Further afield, sheep were dotted about the landscape.

The landau came to rest before a sturdy door that opened at once. A tall man, remarkably young, I thought, to occupy his position, stood waiting. We alighted and Sir James approached him.

"Good afternoon, Farquar. I have brought these gentlemen, who share the interest of your master and myself, here to see his collection. If you would be so good as to announce us."

The butler frowned. "I can do nothing but apologise, sir. The master is away."

"I am surprised. Do you know when he will return?"

"He didn't say. He indicated only that he could be away for a week at most."

I glanced at Holmes and saw an expression that told me that he had anticipated this.

"Did he mention his intended destination?" asked Sir James.

"Not to me, sir," Farquar adopted a mildly conspiratorial tone, "but I did chance to hear him mention to the cook that he had some legal business to attend to. However, he did not say where."

"I understand," our host said. "Look, will you allow us to see Erasmus' collection in his absence? I'm quite certain that he would raise no objection."

Farquar hesitated.

"It would be a pity to have come so far to see such splendid work, only to be disappointed," my friend remarked sadly.

The butler made his decision, smiling. "I am sure the master would be glad to accommodate you gentlemen. Please come in. I will take you to the gallery."

In contrast to Sir James' collection, the portraits here were displayed openly along a wide corridor. Holmes peered at each as we passed.

"Many of these are ancestral, as are your own, Sir James. Some of the subjects are the same." He reached the end of a long display and stood thoughtfully. "Others are unknown to me. Pray indicate the likeness of your brother, Gilbert."

Sir James stood back and looked along the wall and back, then did so again. "I cannot see it, Holmes. I imagine that Erasmus has sent it away for restoration or cleaning."

"Yes, of course. It must be that."

We spent a further forty minutes in the gallery, during which my friend surprised me by putting his face to the wall several times in order to see beneath the ornate frames. When we were once more aboard the landau, the driver, who was noticeably less talkative than on our arrival, set off at once.

Holmes said nothing, but I detected an air of satisfaction about him as the green fields sped by. I sensed Sir James' expectancy increase, as did my own, until he could bear the silence no longer.

"Well, Holmes, did you learn anything from our visit?"

"Nothing that I didn't expect to find, Sir James."

"Such a pity that your cousin was absent," I remarked to our host.

Holmes smiled faintly. "I would have been surprised to find him in residence."

"He didn't inform me of his intention to be away." Sir James looked perplexed at Holmes's remark, but did not pursue it. "What will you do now?"

Holmes consulted his pocket watch. "I must examine the second floor of Darkly Grange – with your permission. There is, I think, time enough for that before dinner."

So it was that, half-an-hour or so later, Holmes and I stood alone in a dusty corridor.

"You will see, Watson, that the floor tells us of recent habitation here, although some effort has been made to conceal the footprints in the dust. Now," he produced a measuring-tape from his pocket, "if we count nine rooms from the right, or the left as it was when viewed from the garden, we will see what can be learned."

He then sank to his knees and crawled four doors to the left of the selected position, and then four to the right, always measuring the distance between them. Finally, he got to his feet and put away the tape before brushing the dust from his clothes.

"What have you discovered?" I enquired, having noted that the open doors revealed that the rooms were empty.

"It really was most skilfully done," he said after a moment. "The intricate pattern all along the walls within is an effective additional concealment. I imagine the original intention was to hide priests from the wrath of reigning monarchs who disagreed with the religion of this household."

"You are referring to some concealed space?"

He pointed to the skirting-board. "You see, the width of every window is slightly less than that of its neighbour. This is so much so that, at this point, there is sufficient left-over space for another narrow room. There is no indication of that from here, but an additional window looks out upon the garden."

"If you are correct, then where is the entrance to this hidden chamber?"

He went into the rooms at either side of the chosen position and rapped upon the walls. After a moment he returned.

"Somewhere nearby is a sliding panel or trapdoor. It must be of substantial construction, since testing the walls brings no result. However, the time has arrived for dinner, I think. Sir James will be curious as to our absence."

In fact, both Sir James and I said very little throughout an excellent dinner of locally caught bream, and I considered that this was because some sort of explanation from Holmes was expected but not forthcoming. I knew that it was my friend's custom not to reveal his conclusions until he was ready, but Sir James had no such familiarity with him. Holmes seemed to sense this, and after the dessert of strawberries and cream was served, he spoke to our host in a calming voice.

"Have no fear, Sir James. I confidently expect to put this matter to rights before another day dawns. You may depend upon it."

Sir James nodded agreeably, doubtless remembering from his previous encounter that Holmes was invariably as good as his word. From

254

that moment the atmosphere seemed to lighten somewhat, and after coffee we sat for a while smoking cigarettes. The evening drew on until midnight was little more than an hour away, and it had long been dark before we finally rose to retire.

The servants had extinguished most of the lights as we approached our rooms. I had my hand on the door-handle, but Holmes shook his head.

"Not for us yet, Watson. We have work to do."

I followed him to the stairs and we crept to the second floor. Our footfalls made no noise as we groped our way to our earlier position and waited silently in the darkness.

On many of our previous adventures, I have accompanied my friend on a vigil such as faced us now. Because of the darkness and silence, and much against my will, these interludes are a constant fight against falling asleep. The cramp that sets into my war wound from long immobility is also a difficulty. Holmes, however, always appears immune from both. His stillness is that of a statue, and I cannot hear his breathing. When he speaks, it is in the lightest whisper, and very infrequently.

We were able to seat ourselves upon the long empty chest that stood opposite the yawning darkness of the open doors. I sensed that Holmes was fully alert and constantly shifting his attention from one room to the next. By my estimation at least an hour had passed, during which the only sounds had been the faint ringing of a bell that I presumed emanated from a distant monastery or convent, and an occasional scuttling of rats somewhere within the house. I found myself battling against a persistent drowsiness, until I was startled by words spoken so quietly that they were hardly more than an intake of breath.

"Did you hear it, Watson? It came from the room on your right."

I had heard nothing, but Holmes's sharp ears hadn't failed him. Seconds later, I heard a scraping noise, as of an ill-fitting door opening.

"Keep your hand on your weapon," he whispered then. He rose and entered the room like a shifting shadow, and I followed.

An entire section of the wall we faced moved slowly and horizontally out of sight. The cavity exposed was almost the height of the room, and the dim glow from within was extinguished immediately. We stood still and silent, our weapons drawn as a vague figure stepped out and moved unknowingly towards us. Holmes opened his dark lantern, startling the man who was revealed.

"Make no attempt to escape," my friend commanded. "We are both armed."

The figure was still at once, but made no sound.

"Watson, enter the secret room and light the oil lamp that our friend here extinguished a moment ago, then tell me what you see in there."

255

I complied at once. The lamp was easily found atop a stool near the entrance. I lit it with a vesper and was at once surprised, as the room was of much greater size than I had imagined.

"There is dust everywhere," I began, "but I see the remains of several meals scattered across the floor, together with wine bottles that appear to be full of water. A portrait is propped against the wall near the window." I held up the lamp. "The section of wall that formed the concealed entrance is of solid wood, and was manipulated by a system of pulleys. Oil has been applied recently."

"That will do. I seem to have been correct in my suppositions, although there is still much to learn from this man. Come out of there and we will find a more convenient place to question him."

I left that evil-smelling place and held our prisoner at gunpoint while Holmes secured his hands with police handcuffs. Descending to the ground floor was slow and uncertain, I preceded the restrained man and Holmes held his revolver at the ready behind him.

"In here." Holmes opened a heavy door in the corridor. It led into a small room that contained nothing but an ornate table and three chairs. I realised that he must have foreseen the situation and possibly described it to Sir James. I guarded our prisoner while Holmes lit two oil lamps and extinguished his dark lantern.

"Sit there, Mr. Erasmus Bartley." Holmes directed him to the single stiff-backed chair positioned on one side of the table, as we took our seats opposite. "My name is Sherlock Holmes. I am a consulting detective, and my friend is Doctor John Watson."

"He is Sir James' cousin?" I queried with astonishment.

"Who else could he be, when everything is considered? When I learn that the tormentor and murderer of Mrs. Feldeane is familiar with its history and her former engagement to Sir James' brother, and is in possession of a portrait of him, what other conclusion can there be?" He placed his weapon upon the table, but near his hand, and looked sternly at our prisoner.

"Since you have spoken not a word since we encountered you emerging from your hiding place, I presume you intend to maintain your silence?"

Mr. Bartley said nothing and avoided Holmes's steely stare, fixing his eyes upon the table-top.

"Very well then, since you will reveal nothing of this affair, I will relate it to you as I see it. You are at liberty to correct me, if I stray from the truth."

Holmes and I glanced at each other. Our prisoner did not move.

"First, you knew of the forthcoming garden party well in advance,"

Holmes began, "although it wasn't your custom to attend. You had made your plans. I'm aware that you were responsible for the death of Rowens, Sir James' butler, though I have yet to discover how. You then recommended Courtney, who was yourself in disguise, to replace him."

"How is that possible?" I asked.

Holmes allowed himself a brief smile. "Observe the traces of theatrical make-up remaining on Mr. Bartley's face, Watson. He has had no opportunity to remove them, and you have surely noticed that his clothes are those of a butler. You will recall Sir James mentioning that his cousin once joined a circus, where he doubtlessly learned the art of changing his facial appearance."

"He also impersonated Mrs. Feldeane's former fiancé, Mr. Gilbert Saunders, then?" I ventured.

"Not so. Having poisoned the wine that he knew she would drink, he realised that he had no means of determining *when* she would take it. The delicate balance of her health was known to him. He therefore arranged for an appearance of her former fiancé to induce a seizure such as she suffered when shocked or suddenly startled. This was achieved by a momentary display of Mr. Gilbert's portrait at the window, but he wasn't quite quick enough in removing it since Sir James also glimpsed the image."

I stared hard at Erasmus Bartley. "That was callous, sir. I hope you are now suitably ashamed." The obvious question then occurred to me. "But why was it necessary to kill Mrs. Feldeane and her son? What harm could they have done to you?"

He made no response, other than to lower his head further so that only his crown was visible to us.

"The answer to that question is a simple one," Holmes explained. "You will recall that Sir James stated that his guests were mostly from afar. Mrs. Feldeane and her son, then, were the only ones likely to recognise 'Courtney' as, in truth, his cousin."

"And the portrait was from his collection at Mortley Manor, and the true reason for our visit there," I realised.

"Precisely. He was careful enough not to leave an empty space among his pictures upon the wall, but by looking beneath them I saw marks suggesting that one had recently replaced a portrait of a slightly smaller size. That, and the fact that he had been absent for a while, confirmed the supposition that I had formed."

"But," I objected, "all this means that three people have died in order to allow and preserve this man's impersonation of a butler in his cousin's house. What can be the reason behind this?"

"Have you not realised yet? It is the Cezanne. Sir James wouldn't sell

257

it, so his cousin devised a rather elaborate means to obtain its possession."

Erasmus Bartley raised his head and stared at us with eyes that held a strange expression. His blunt, unshaven features held no hint of fear or regret, but a crafty smile lingered upon his lips.

"I have always known," he began in a hoarse and indifferent voice, "that it was likely that the hangman would end my life." He stared directly at Holmes. "You, sir, are a man of some ability, to have reconstructed my actions and intentions with such accuracy. As you may know, I never married, for that would have satisfied neither of the two passions that have always dominated me. The first, as you have deduced, is art. I crave for the exquisite works of the Masters as some men crave gold, and have pursued their possession with no less determination. In my home there are far more examples than those you have seen, and well hidden. Oh yes, I have stolen, blackmailed, and killed to acquire those sources of satisfaction and fulfilment that some would call an obsession. I consider it as of no account that my cousin is the owner of that wonderful portrait. Such an accident of birth in no way alters my intent. I would have taken the Cezanne without harm to him or the others hereabouts if that were possible, but otherwise . . . ."

"You would have murdered your cousin?" I asked as he paused.

"Is that not your second passion?" enquired Holmes. "Murder?"

The furtive expression intensified. "The killing of my fellow man, or woman, on occasion? Yes, it has always filled me with a joy and satisfaction that I couldn't describe to you. As a young man, I joined a circus because I felt the county police were getting close to discovering that I was responsible for several deaths that occurred in the area, and of course my travels as a clown or acrobat provided many opportunities abroad. As for Rowens, who you were concerned about, a fine needle inserted in the base of his skull produced his unexpected demise rather more quickly than I would have liked, but then it was experimental. I always enjoyed trying new methods, especially those of my own invention."

He raised his manacled hands to brush away a lock of lank hair. "But make no mistake, gentlemen, I have suffered for my extravagances. Awaiting my chance in that hidden room that I had known about since a childhood exploration – breathing the foul air and creeping about this place to take food from the kitchen in the early hours – wasn't the least of it. But it was necessary, and but for you I would have taken a prize to be the pinnacle of my collection."

I was about to remark that the future held for him, at best, the remainder of his life in an asylum, when the door opened. Our heads turned to see Sir James, wearing a dressing-gown over his nightshirt and holding a lantern, framed in the entrance.

"Holmes, I could not sleep so – " He stopped abruptly as he saw our prisoner. "Good Heavens! Erasmus, why are you restrained" Then the truth of the situation became obvious to him, and he groaned heavily. "Oh, my God, no!"

"I regret, Sir James, that this is indeed the outcome of my investigation," my friend replied. "When he arrives, Inspector Soames will have little to do, other than make the arrest and accompany Mr. Bartley to the local police station. As for the African prospector that Mrs. Feldeane and yourself glimpsed at the window that day, I am afraid that he remains lost to you."

". . . and I have brought with me a friend whose discretion may absolutely be trusted. I was able once to do him a professional service, and he is ready to advise as a friend rather than as a specialist. His name is Sir James Saunders. "

– Sherlock Holmes
"The Blanched Soldier"

259

The Unlikely Assassin
by Tim Newton Anderson

While I was used to Sherlock Holmes being recognised wherever he was in the world, it was highly unusual for him to be sought out by a client at anywhere other than his flat at 221b Baker Street.

I was therefore surprised when we were approached as we sat on the pavement outside Les Deux Magots in Paris by a tall man who entreated my friend's assistance.

Holmes had been sent to Paris by his brother, Mycroft, to assist the French authorities in their investigation of the catastrophic fire at the Bazar de la Charite. The initial conclusion of the Gendarmerie and fire brigade was that a faulty cinematograph which had been set up as part of a reconstruction of a medieval street had caught fire and caused a blaze in the *papier mâché* and wooden scenery. In the ensuing conflagration and panic, one-hundred-twenty-six people had been killed. Mycroft's interest was that a large number of foreign ambassadors and their relatives were killed in the blaze and he was concerned it was the result of nihilists or foreign agent provocateurs rather than an unfortunate accident.

Holmes had already scrutinised the scene and interviewed survivors and the authorities, and he and I were sitting with a *petit cafe* and *croissants* while he employed his deductive skills to the problem. He had filled his pipe with sweet smelling French tobacco and was leaning back, staring at the sky, while his mind assembled the facts and clues. I was happy to enjoy the early summer sunshine while gazing at the street scene of the Rive Gauche. The trees were in full bloom, and the smell of Holmes's tobacco failed to mask to perfume of their flowers. The cafe's clientele were an interesting mix of students, Bohemian artists, elegant bourgeoisie, and government office workers who had crossed from the Ile de Cite to have a leisurely lunch. Our own order had just been placed on the table along by the aproned waiter who wrote the total on the paper tablecloth, and I had swallowed a single sip of coffee when a tall young man came over.

"*Pardonez moi,*" he said. "*Parler vous Francais?*"

Holmes replied in his own perfect French and asked the man to speak in English if he could, for my benefit.

"Of course," the man said. "I am aware of your chronicler and associate, Monsieur Holmes, and would be happy for him to give his thoughts as well as yourself. The more people who can help free my friend from false imprisonment, the better."

The man was in his early twenties and conservatively dressed in frock coat, grey trousers, white shirt, and thin tie. He had short black hair with a clean shaven face and was thin, although I could see he had wiry muscles.

"It is always a pleasure to meet a gentleman of the Fourth Estate," said Holmes.

"How did you know I was a journalist?" the man asked.

"The ink stains on the fingers of your right hand," said Holmes, "show you are engaged in some kind of clerical work, but you do not have the bent back of an accountant. There is a notebook in the right hand pocket of your coat and this morning's newspaper in your left, so journalist is the obvious conclusion."

"You are right," the man said, sitting at another of the wrought-iron chairs by our table. "I write for *The Paris Herald*, as well as a number of revues. My name is Phillipe Roget."

"Did you cover the fire at the Bazar de la Charite?" asked Holmes.

"Not the fire itself, but I compiled some of the biographies of the victims," said Roget. "We already had biographies of the more famous among the deaths, but I wanted to add some of the ordinary people who lost their lives. In my eyes, they are just as important. Elise Blonska, a Russian immigrant who worked as a librarian, and Juilie Garivet, a nun. It was a tragedy – not just for the victims, but that an event which has done so much good for charitable causes will now be associated with disaster."

Holmes steepled his fingers and stared into space again.

"I presume that is not the reason you sought us out," he said.

"Not at all," said Roget. "My friend, Alfred Jarry, has been arrested on charges of terrorism. Charges of which he is totally innocent."

"The playwright, I assume," said Holmes. "I'm familiar with the *success de scandale* associated with his play, *Ubu Roi*. I had some small experience in the theatre myself when I was younger, and I try and keep up with developments. Please tell me the full story."

Unlike Holmes, I had heard of neither the play nor the playwright, and was often surprised at my friend's areas of interest outside of his profession as a consulting detective.

"He is indeed," said Roget. "Although he was only an aspiring author when we met at the Ecole and became friends. We have stayed close, even though we live in different worlds.

Roget drew out a pipe of his own – a briar in contrast to Holmes's clay pipe – and I took a cheroot from the packet I had bought. I offered him a light when he'd filled the pipe with tobacco.

"Alfred isn't always the most sensible person," Roget said. "He likes to be the centre of attention, and can dress and act outrageously. Since the success of the play, he has become even more so. Ubu's speech was based on his own eccentric way of talking, but it often seems that he is now impersonating his creation. That's what has gotten him into trouble. He carries a bull-nose revolver with him at all times, and when he has been drinking he will fire it in the streets. He has never harmed anything, apart from the occasional pigeon, but he has been reported to the police a few times and given warnings.

"This time was different. He hadn't even fired his weapon, but half-a-dozen gendarmes and two of the GDSP suddenly surrounded him at a cafe in Montmartre and arrested him. He was taken to Police Headquarters, and it was only at the insistence of my editor that they allowed me to see him. He had been interrogated, but not told on what charge he was taken into custody. Again, it was only though my editor and his contacts that I was able to find out he was suspected of plotting to assassinate Count Von und Zu Grafenstein – one of the top diplomats in the German Embassy."

"Do you know why your friend became a suspect?" asked Holmes.

"Apparently they had been tipped off by someone in another embassy who claimed to have heard it through their investigations into Anarchist and Nihilist organisations."

"Let me guess," said Holmes. "It was Pyotr Rachkovsky."

"How did you know?" asked Roget.

"Rachkovsky is well-known to the British Government," said Holmes. "Ostensibly he is part of the Embassy staff, but in fact is the head of the Russian Secret Police. While he is supposedly monitoring Russian dissidents in France and the rest of Europe, he has long been suspected of fomenting intrigues so he can then claim the credit for discovering them. He has even tried that tactic in my own country. If Rachkovsky has accused your friend, there must be a reason behind it."

"So, you will investigate, Mr. Holmes?"

"I believe this has a connection with a mission in which I'm already engaged," Holmes said, "and I'll be happy to clear your friend's name. I'll go with you to the Police Station and re-introduce myself to Prefect Lepine. I was able to be of some assistance to him concerning the assassination of President Carnot a few years ago, and I'm sure he'll be happy to allow me to assist him again."

We finished our smoking and coffees and set off for the Police Station. On the way, Philippe Roget told us more about his friend. Jarry was something of an *enfant terrible* on the artistic scene in Paris. As well as his play, he had written a number of strange books and poems, and was part of the banquet culture of the Symbolists and their supporters. As well as brandishing a pistol, he had caused gossip with his excessive drinking and regular feuds with other artists. It sounded to me as if he had been adopted as a sort of court jester.

As he had prophesied, Holmes was welcomed with open arms at the Prefecture. We was ushered in to see Lepine, who embraced Holmes in the French way, which clearly made my friend slightly uncomfortable. There was no small talk, however, as Holmes wanted to get straight down to business.

"I understand you have Alfred Jarry in custody on a charge of suspected conspiracy to murder," he said.

"Mr. Jarry is helping us with our inquiries," said Lepine. "We had received intelligence that he was planning an assassination and we are questioning him about that."

I hadn't met Lepine before, but he seemed embarrassed by the conversation. Holmes had clearly discerned this as well.

"You don't seem convinced of his guilt," said Holmes.

"Jarry can be a nuisance," said Lepine, "but it is hard to believe he is a dangerous Nihilist, however wild his behaviour. As you know, I have had considerable dealings with rioters and terrorists, and in my experience they tend to keep a low profile until they act. There are many people we keep under surveillance, and Jarry is not one of them. As far as we are aware, he has no links to any known group."

"And is your information source reliable?" asked Holmes.

"Rachkovsky has indeed proved useful in giving information on revolutionary groups – often led by his own countrymen – but I have always suspected he is *too* close to them. His information often comes just before some planned outrage – like the Landesen plot to kill the Tsar. I know your brother Mycroft has similar misgivings, as we have collaborated in tackling terrorists."

"Then why not simply release Jarry?" asked Holmes.

"Because I cannot afford to be wrong," said Lepine. "The Germans have been trying to improve their relationship with France. No doubt this is because they feel isolated by the Franco-Russian alliance, but we would like good relations with all of our neighbours. There are still many who remember the Franco-Prussian war and are aggrieved over the loss of Alsace Lorraine, but we must move on from the past if we are to preserve peace in Europe."

"Is it not odd that Rachkovsky should be so concerned about the health of a man whose nation is seen as a rival of his own?" Holmes asked.

"You may say that, Mr. Holmes. I couldn't possibly comment."

"I have a suggestion," Holmes said. "If you release Jarry into my custody, I will undertake to ensure he behaves himself. I will also come along with you to the German Embassy Ball this evening and see if there is any truth in the supposed assassination plot."

"I wish you good fortune in keeping Jarry out of trouble," said Lepine, "but I would be grateful for any intelligence you can gather. If I have your word you will keep him out of harm's way, I will allow you to take him on bail."

My friend exchanged some further pleasantries with Lepine as we waited for Jarry to be brought up from the cells. Holmes, Roget, Lepine, and I joined the playwright at the front desk.

I hadn't known what to expect of Jarry from the pictures Roget and Lepine had painted of him. My first impression was of someone in late adolescence rather than his twenties – apart from the goatee beard. He was very short – not much over five feet in height – and had long black hair brushing his shoulders. As Roget had said, he was eccentrically dressed in bicycle trousers, a woman's blouse and shoes, and a black pea jacket that looked some years older than he was. He was grinning broadly and demanding the return of his pistol, which the policeman on the desk understandably refused. He was given various papers, however, which he stuffed into his pockets.

"Ah," he said when he saw us. "*Il n'y a pas de police comme*, Holmes."

Holmes smiled thinly. It was a joke he had heard before.

Judging from their grim expressions, the police at the desk didn't share Lepine's view that Jarry was harmless, but had no choice about his release. Holmes, Roget, Jarry, and I walked out into the May sunshine and headed for Jarry's flat, which Roget told us was called his *Grand Chasublerie*.

The flat was as eccentric as Jarry himself. Religious artefacts were placed at random on tables and other surfaces and a racing bicycle was hung on one wall, while a skeleton dangled from the ceiling, and papers and books were scattered everywhere. Everything was covered in dust and the droppings of a pair of owls that perched on a chair at the table.

"Welcome to our home, Holmes," said Jarry. (I could only presume that "*our*" apparently referred to him and his owls.) "We will not offer you water, as that which flows is poisonous to our system, but there is wine and absinthe which you are welcome to share."

"I am afraid I will have to decline," said Holmes. "I have work to do and must leave you in the care of my colleague, Dr. Watson."

I would have preferred to accompany Holmes on his mission – especially as the room only had a single chair which hadn't had the attention of a maid for many years. Even the tolerant Mrs. Hudson would have shuddered to see the disarray.

"I can also stay here," said Roget.

"I have another mission for you," said Holmes. "I need you to go to the hotel where Watson and I are staying and bring our evening clothes. You should also get your own evening wear and buy or hire appropriate clothes for Jarry. I believe the case will come to a climax tonight at the Embassy Ball, and it's appropriate you and he attend, along with the doctor and myself."

"Won't that be dangerous?" I asked Holmes. "Surely bringing Jarry face to face with the man he is supposed to be about to kill is risky."

"It isn't without some risk," said Holmes, "but if I'm to prevent a human tragedy and a major diplomatic upset, having Jarry in plain sight is a necessary precaution."

After Holmes and Roget left, I was a little nervous about being alone with a supposed lunatic, but Jarry excused himself and sat down at his desk to write. His owls hopped from the back of the chair to sit on either side of his papers, and he devoted himself to furious scribbling on his papers. After a few minutes, Jarry's concierge arrived with a mug of coffee which Holmes had ordered for me, and I sat on the window ledge to drink it. Unlike the abomination that is French tea, the coffee was excellent and I busied myself with that and another cheroot and watched the bustle in the street below as Jarry wrote.

I kept a close eye on the passers-by in the street in case anyone was taking an unusual interest in our building. If Jarry was the subject of a plot, the person behind it could well have agents watching. However, everyone seemed to be going about his or her everyday business. Until, that is, I noticed that some men who were walking past and having a conversation at the corner. One would saunter along under our window, talk to a companion, who would then pass in the opposite direction. There were three of them in all, taking turns to pass us and then hand over to another. They didn't obviously stare at my station in the window, but certainly glanced up, taking care not to catch my eye. There was nothing unusual about them, apart from their activities.

It was about an hour before Roget arrived with the clothes that Holmes had requested, and another two hours before my friend arrived. Jarry hadn't looked up from his labours when his friend knocked and I let him in, and stayed intent on his task as Roget and I chatted while maintaining a watch on the street. As a fellow writer, Roget was interested in the stories I had published about Holmes, and I told him of other tales I was planning to write – especially how Holmes had escaped death at the hands of Professor Moriarty at the Reichenbach Falls.

I wanted to ask Holmes what he had discovered, but he placed a finger to his lips to indicate now wasn't the time. Instead he distributed the clothes Roget had brought and instructed us to dress for the ball. Even in an evening suit, Jarry looked dishevelled. The shirt and jacket fit well enough, but the trousers were two inches too long, and the only other shoes he possessed were a pair of rubber boots. Roget attempted to improve the look by folding the ends of the trousers inside the cuffs, but the playwright still looked like the eccentric artist he was.

The German Embassy was in the Hotel Beauharnais on the left bank of the Seine. Holmes had ordered us a carriage and we were greeted by an Embassy employee in the frock coat of a hotel concierge. Having examined our invitations (and casting more than a few suspicious glances at Jarry), he waved us up the marble stairs to the large double doors. Once inside, we were handed a glass of champagne and directed to the ballroom at the rear of the building. Most of the guests had already arrived, and the orchestra was playing a Strauss waltz, which had tempted many to take to the floor. I cautiously looked around the room and noticed that several of the waiters were stationed near entrances and exits rather than carrying around drinks and canapés. They were obviously policemen employed by Lepine to safeguard the Count. I assume their presence explained why Holmes hadn't requested me to bring my service revolver.

I was pleased that Jarry didn't have access to his gun, as he had headed straight for the buffet table and was drinking champagne with great gusto. He didn't seem to be eating, and I feared his behaviour might revert to his anarchic self.

Holmes and I walked across the room towards the Count Von und Zu Grafenstein, who was talking to a man of medium height with a thick moustache.

"Is this a thawing in German-Russian relations?" asked Holmes as we reached the pair. "Pyotr Rachkovsky, I believe? I am Sherlock Holmes, and this is my colleague Dr. Watson."

"A pleasure to meet you, Mr. Holmes," said the Count. He was nearly Holmes's height and had an impressive Prussian handlebar moustache. He was dressed in full military uniform with an impressive row of medals from the Franco-Prussian War, while Rachkovsky wore an unadorned dress suit. "I am pleased you are here, following the rumours of an attempted assassination. Rachkovsky has been detailing the information he has gleaned from his informants in the terrorist community. They are a problem we all share, but I fear France and Britain have given a refuge to quite a number of them."

"It is often hard to differentiate between those fleeing persecution to find a new home and those fleeing justice," said Holmes. "Rest assured my brother is active in determining which of our new citizens are which."

"I have given Mycroft Holmes the benefit of my council," said Rachkovsky. "We have a shared ambition to keep our citizens safe."

Holmes raised an eyebrow, but did not reply.

I turned to examine the room once again. As I had feared, Jarry now seemed intoxicated and was wandering around disturbing the other guests with insolent stares. His friend Roget was following at a discreet distance, doubtless to step in if the playwright became more obnoxious.

Then the crowd suddenly parted as one of the waiters started to run towards us brandishing a pistol. Lepine's men also grabbed for their weapons, but I feared they would be too late. Holmes and I stood in front of the ambassador to form a shield, but the waiter suddenly plunged to the floor and his weapon skittered out of his hand. Jarry had spun round and tripped the man as he ran and Roget pounced on top of him, pinning the would-be assassin to the ground. The police had now reached the man and knelt down to pinion his arms and legs, allowing Roget to stand up again. Lepine had moved forward from his position at the side of the room and picked up the gun.

"Well done, gentlemen," he said. "I believe this man is Ivan Klopman. I recognised him from our files and have been keeping him under close watch, but as you suggested Mr. Holmes, we had to be sure of his intentions before making an arrest. If we had taken him off the streets, there are dozens of his fellow Nihilists who would have taken his place."

The police had handcuffed the terrorist and were lifting him to his feet when his body began to violently shudder before collapsing in a dead weight. I swiftly went over to him and could smell the strong aroma of bitter almonds from his mouth.

"He has swallowed cyanide," I said.

"Doubtless so he couldn't be forced to betray his fellow conspirators," said Holmes. I saw he looked over at Rashkovsky as he said this.

"He will not stop us finding them," said Lepine. "Our surveillance has already identified some of his associates, and no doubt we will be able to bring more of them to justice." He also started at Rachkovsky, and the Count looked at the Russian with suspicion as he had had noticed the looks from Lepine and Holmes.

"Thank you all, gentlemen," the Count said. "I am sure my government would have had serious concerns about the relationship between our countries if he had succeeded. Who is the young gentleman who acted so promptly?"

Jarry stepped forward and gave an exaggerated bow. Unfortunately the gesture was spoiled as he almost tripped and stumbled into the Count. Roget grasped him by the shoulders and steadied him on his feet.

267

"Monsieur Jarry was the person who was originally suspected of the plan to kill you," said Holmes. "We should all be grateful he had the opportunity to prove his innocence. We should also be grateful that Klopman was caught, as my investigations show he was the person responsible for the fire at the Bazar de la Charite. His organisation has been going to great lengths to blacken the reputation of the French and make them more isolated on the international stage – apart from their growing alliances with Britain and Russia, of course."

He looked at Rachkovsky again.

"Despite our differences with some of our neighbours over territory in Asia and Africa, my brother Mycroft and the Prince of Wales have been working hard to establish harmony across the Continent, and they will be delighted a diplomatic incident has been averted."

"I am sure we understand who the people who bear the real responsibility for this near tragedy are," said the Count. "I mean, of course, Nihilist terrorists. My government will be made aware of this."

Rachkovsky was working hard to keep a neutral expression on his face.

After the terrorist's body was taken away, Holmes and I made our excuses and left with Jarry and Roget. Jarry had consumed even more wine after the incident and, having narrowly averted one major diplomatic incident, we wanted to make sure there wasn't another one.

"Do you think Lepine will uncover Rachkovsky's role in the plot?" I asked Holmes.

"I am sure he already knows," said Holmes. "However, I don't believe he'll ever face charges. As you are aware from previous cases, relations between the great European nations and Russia are finely balanced, and the Great Powers are all working hard to maintain that equilibrium, even if some of their agents are pursuing their own agendas which risk it. Rather, it is the pawns that are being swept from the board instead of the chess masters. There are many tyrants like Jarry's King Ubu who would relish war when the time is right, and we should be grateful we can play our small part in delaying that time as long as possible."

We had arrived back at Les Deux Magots, where we first met Roget, and settled at a table in the early summer's evening chill. I couldn't help wondering how many more years the summer of peace would last.

"It was I also who saved from murder, by the Nihilist Klopman, Count Von und Zu Grafenstein, who was your mother's elder brother."
– Sherlock Holmes
"His Last Bow"

The Two-Line Note
by Chris Chan

Shortly after I finished writing my account of the Charles Augustus Milverton case, I proofread my manuscript and realized that I had some unanswered questions about the background of the late blackmailer. When Holmes returned from an information-gathering assignment, I sat in the chair opposite his in front of the fire and asked him, "Holmes, do you remember during the Milverton case, you mentioned a footman who destroyed a prominent family by selling a very short note for seven-hundred pounds?"

A dark shadow passed over Holmes's face as he recalled the incident. "I do indeed. It isn't an occurrence that is likely to fade from my mind anytime soon."

"I can understand that. No doubt, you can understand my interest in the subject? Could you possibly see your way as to informing me about the details of this tragic story?"

Holmes sighed and tented his fingers together. "You realize, of course, that the details of this case aren't for general publication? If you choose to take notes on this matter, then I trust that your account of the case will remain locked in your dispatch-box at the bank for decades to come?"

"Absolutely. You know as well as I do that I've adhered to those restrictions many times in the past."

He nodded, adding, "Yes, but in no other case in recent memory have so many innocent people been humiliated by something that was in no way their fault. They were, quite simply, destroyed by circumstances beyond their control. Fate, it has often been said, is a cruel mistress, and this maliciousness was in full play in this sad incident. You will, of course, understand it if I refer to the unhappy family in question by an alias. I shall refer to the family as the 'Melpomenes' – you can see the significance of this false name, or course? Melpomene was the Greek Muse of Tragedy, and certainly this was a tragedy. In many cases, downfalls are brought about by hubris and personal failings. It is a particularly crushing fate to know that there was nothing you could possibly have done to save yourself – the seeds of your destruction were sown decades before some of the victims were even born."

"You intrigue me."

"Yes, it's an interesting, albeit upsetting story. The events in question took place one brisk autumn day a few years ago – you were away visiting a friend, and I was visited by Steven and Scott Sobotta, a pair of brothers who were solicitors with their own firm, catering to the wealthiest class of clients. I should clarify that Steven and Scott were identical twins." I was about to say something, but Holmes held up a hand. *"I will point out right away that the fact that the two men were twins and only distinguishable from each other after close scrutiny has nothing to do with the investigation, save for their hiring me. You need not wonder if there will be any twist about one pretending to be the other, or anything of the sort of cheap surprises that often pop up in popular fiction."*

"Understood."

"The Sobotta twins were both clearly upset, so I rang Mrs. Hudson for a pot of tea in the hopes that it would calm them, allowing us to discuss the matter that brought them to me. After a cuppa and a biscuit each, they began do tell me their story . . . ."

"You see, Mr. Holmes," Steven began, "I'm afraid we're dealing with a very tricky situation, one that – "

" – Could mean the ruin of a particularly respected family," Scott finished. I soon learned that the pair were in the habit of finishing each other's sentences.

"I'd appreciate it if you could please explain the situation thoroughly," I told them.

"Well, that's the problem," Steven sighed as he tugged at his collar. "There are certain issues here that require extreme delicacy. Doubtless, you understand that there is an issue of confidentiality here. It's a situation where we can see a disaster looming, but we are powerless – "

" – to stop it," finished Scott. "If I keep their names anonymous, I can tell you that I don't believe that these people don't wish to bring about their own ruin, but – "

" – they have no choice in the matter," Steven continued. "It seems as if they're being forced to destroy themselves against their will. Perhaps they're being – "

" – threatened or blackmailed," added Scott. "Though I don't believe that they could be blackmailed. They're not the sort of people who have anything to hide in the personal lives. I believe that they are a family of exemplary moral courage. No one is – "

" – more respectable," chimed in Steven. "I simply can't think of any reason why they would fold under pressure."

"Is there nothing you can tell me to identify the family in question?"

"No, not without breaching confidentiality," Scott shook his head mournfully. "But we believe that a man of your skills – "

" – and discretion," Steven hastily added, "is more than capable of figuring out who the family in question is without any help from us. A quick look at the newspapers and a little more investigation, and we feel certain that you'll know at once to whom we're referring, even if we can't confirm your suspicions."

I must confess to feeling a touch of frustration at the limited amount of information made available to me, but I was intrigued, so I agreed to investigate the situation. The brothers provided me with a bit of money for my initial expenses, shook hands with me enthusiastically, and left.

Recalling Steven's comment about "a quick look at the newspapers," I suspected that there had to be a news story in a recent edition that would point me in the right direction. I summoned a few members of the Irregulars, provided them with a handful of coins, and told them to bring me a copy of every newspaper they could find. I realized that there was a possibility that the story in question was from a previous day or an earlier edition, but I would wait until I had studied the crisp, clean papers before asking the Irregulars to locate older copies, which would likely be found in dustbins, or possibly in fish-and-chip shops, turned into cones to be filled with fried food.

Within the hour, my young friends presented me with a stack of assorted newspapers and I started poring through them, looking for the story that would launch my investigation. The first few papers provided me with nothing relevant, but when I reached the society pages of the fourth paper in the stack, I discovered an article about the cancellation of the Green Gala, just a week before it was set to be the social event of the season. As you know, the Green Gala was an annual event that had delighted the upper crust of London society for over thirty years. The Melpomene family hosted the event in the enormous ballroom of their family home.

The Gala derived its colorful name from the color that saturated the festivities. The ballroom itself was painted in various shades of green, with a malachite-tiled floor. Streamers and banners in the aforementioned hue were hung on all the walls, and the chandeliers were not composed of clear crystal, but instead were tinted so they looked like emeralds. All the guests were expected to wear at least a trace of green. A few of the men contented themselves with merely wearing a green tie or cummerbund, but some wore a fully green suit, purchased specially for this occasion. All of the women wore green gowns, and those who had emerald or jade jewelry wore it. The flowers were all naturally white, but they had been placed in vases of green dye until the coloring had been drawn up the stems through capillary action and had stained the petals. All of the food was green – the buffet was filled with salads, and the pale fish, chicken, and cheese had also been dyed. *Crème de menthe* was the liqueur of choice, but there were also many clear alcohols that had received their share of coloring.

It wasn't the sort of entertainment that I personally would subject myself to if I had any choice at all, but the titled nobility seemed to love it. Only the most perfunctory excuse had been given for the cancellation – that a family matter had called the Melpomenes away, and there was no indication of when they would return.

Naturally, I journeyed to the Melpomene residence at once, only to learn that the family had already boarded a ship bound for Canada. However, the house was still filled with servants who appeared to be giving the building a thorough cleaning. A few discreet inquiries led a maid to confide in me that one of the footman had departed from the house that morning, and had left most of his old, tattered possessions and clothing behind. Meanwhile, a team of movers were collecting antiques and works of art, placing them into crates, and shipping them to Canada.

I managed to obtain a set of coveralls matching those of the movers, and I was able to slip into the house unchallenged. It soon became clear to me that the residents of the house weren't planning to come back. Some of the nicer furniture was also being wrapped away and placed into crates, and the paintings that were left on the walls were clearly of inferior quality.

The butler was a man of sixty, obviously trained to be proper and unflappable, but at the moment, he was red in the face, and if his current state of aggravation worsened much, it seemed likely that he could be described as "flustered" in a short while. He was giving orders and advice to the movers, sharply informing them, "Take more care with that mirror – you'll scrape off the gilding on the wood!" and "Mind the brocade on that chair – your oily fingerprints will leave a stain!" I rather had the impression that the movers had no interest in gaining the butler's approval, and that the workmen rather enjoyed provoking him through their deliberately annoying questions and their occasional missteps.

The sound of a smash filled the entry hall as a two-foot tall red-and-pink enamel vase slipped through the fingers of one the workmen. The butler descended upon the erring workman, looking rather like a gigantic owl swooping down upon a mouse, and launched into a tirade of such fury that the two parlor maids on the landing, overlooking the incident, were both tittering with laughter and shaking with fear that such anger might later be directed towards them.

Deciding to take advantage of the distraction, I went up the stairwell, slipped into the nearest room, and began to search. I found nothing of note for several minutes, but eventually I found my way to the family bedrooms. It was clear that they weren't planning on returning anytime soon. Not so much as a sock remained in any of the cabinets or closets. When a family goes on a trip – even an extended vacation, they don't take everything they own with them. Indeed, a family with the wealth of the Melpomenes would very likely take the opportunity to buy more new clothing in Canada.

I continued to search the house. The library shelves were still filled with books, but a portrait of a woman in a silver dress was now propped against a wall. Based on the nail in the wall above it and the rectangle that was faded into the wallpaper, it seemed safe to assume that the picture was used to hide the safe built into the wall. The door to the safe was now open, and the safe was empty. Though it was possible that a robbery had occurred, I thought it far more likely that the safe had been opened by its owner.

I had a bit of a start when the foreman of the workers burst into the room and barked at me to hurry out to the dining room and to start gathering up chairs. I muttered gibberish in an obsequious manner and slipped away in the general direction of the dining room. Before reaching that destination, however, I managed to slip into the servants' stairwell, and I made my way to the room that until recently had been occupied by the now-disappeared footman.

It was obvious after a minute's investigation that I realized the footman hadn't simply disappeared and left his belongings behind him. There was no suitcase, and though several articles of clothing had been left in the wardrobe, everything that remained was either part of his footman's uniform, or so old and worn that it was practically unwearable. There was one pair of brown boots that looked like they had about a month's worth of use left before holes developed in the seams and soles. I also found no watch, money, or anything else of value, nor were there any photographs or anything else that could potentially hold sentimental value. There were several newspapers and magazines, all at least a few days old and well-thumbed. The general untidiness of the tiny room gave the impression that the previous occupant had left most of his possessions behind, but the reality was that he had taken away the useful items, and had abandoned the items in poor condition.

The shirts in the wardrobe had been mended several times, and some of the buttons had been resewn. Judging by the clumsiness of the stitchery, I thought it likely that the footman had done the sewing himself. That indicated that he had a long habit of thrift, undoubtedly imposed upon him due to a lifetime of living hand-to-mouth. A career filled with hard work, long hours, and scanty wages was likely to leave a man feeling embittered. Resentful employees are rarely loyal. Seeing as how the footman had left

273

behind a pair of boots that still had a bit of use left in them, I thought it probable that he had come into some money, enough that he was willing to abandon his job without a reference, or even waiting until his next payday. The speed with which he left was indicative of a guilty conscience. Had he stolen something from his employers? This was certainly possible. With the general chaos of the move, it was more than likely that a few stolen items, provided that they weren't the jewels of the collection, might go overlooked for weeks or even months, if their absence was ever discovered at all. Therefore, there was no real need to slip away so hastily. It would be far more prudent to stay for a while – unless there was some other reason for fleeing.

I realized had I hadn't yet searched the grate in the fireplace, so I sifted through the ashes with my fingers, and soon uncovered a small corner of an envelope. The edges of the paper fragment had been badly scorched, but a bit of the return address was still legible – I could read the words "*C.A. Mil*". Everything after the "*l*" had been burnt away. I understood immediately what the full name in question was: *Charles Augustus Milverton* had come to my attention not long before, and I knew that he made his living through blackmail.

This new knowledge solidified my theory behind the footman's disappearance. He was one of Milverton's many spies, and had somehow come across the information for which Milverton was willing to pay handsomely, almost certainly in the form of some sort of document. The nature of the incriminating paper was impossible to determine at this point, but it had to be something sufficiently scandalous to destroy the social standing of the Melpomene family. Not only that, but the threat of revelation had to be so pressing that the Melpomenes weren't willing to wait until after the Green Gala, when they would be able to play the roles of welcoming hosts to some of the most respected and prominent families in London.

My musings were interrupted by a voice behind me. "What are you doing here? You're supposed to be downstairs. Everything that's supposed to be boxed up in down there. There's nothing of value here."

I whirled around and saw a footman eying me suspiciously. "Answer me," the footman snapped, "or I'll call the police and have you arrested on suspicion of stealing!"

Adopting a cockney accent, I replied, "If I was looking for something to steal, while would I be poking around the servants' quarters? There's nothing worth steeling here. If I was a thief – and I'm not – wouldn't I be downstairs where all the silverware and pretty knickknacks are?"

"There's something in that," the footman grudgingly concurred. "But what are you doing here, then?"

"We need a bit of rope to keep the furniture from bouncing around in the crates where it could get damaged. I was told there might be some rope here. Haven't found anything yet, though."

"Oh. Well, you're in the wrong room. There's a storage space down the hall, and it's filled with all sorts of rubbish that I suppose might be useful someday. Here, follow me."

I had no choice but to walk behind him down the hall. He opened the door and entered, and I heard the sound of something moderately heavy being pushed to one side until I finally heard a satisfied groan. The footman emerged a moment later with a dusty coil of rope in his hand. "Here we are. Right where I thought it would be – on top of the bookshelf." He handed it to me, and I thanked him, wondering what I was going to do with it.

"I wasn't poking around your room, was I?"

He shook his head. "No, that room belonged to one of the other footmen. He seems to have left us without any warning. I shouldn't be surprised. He's had quite the windfall lately. I suspect that he must have made an extremely lucky and detailed bet on the ponies."

"Oh?" I tried to sound interested, but I took care not to overplay it. "Do you happen to know the horse's name? It's good to keep a successful horse's name handy for future reference."

"No idea," he told me, "but it must have been an incredible long shot. I saw him counting the money the day he left: Seven-hundred pounds! He was acting odd about it. He attached the envelope of boodle to his chest with a bandage, and he was looking at me funny, as if he expected me to attack him and steal it. Don't know why I didn't, really. I never liked him, and I could use the money."

"Did he say anything else interesting recently?"

"Nothing in particular. He did say something odd last week. I saw him holding a sheet of paper, and he was staring at it and laughing. I asked him about it, and he waved it front of me and told me that it was his meal ticket. I didn't get a very good look at it, but it was a handwritten note of about two lines in length. It was addressed to Mrs. Melpomene, and I could see it said that, '*I'm afraid your father's treatment isn't*'. That was all I could read before the bell rang and I had to hurry away. Why do you ask?"

"I'll be honest with you," I lied. "I played cards with your footman pal last week, and he owes me fifty quid. He's said nothing about exactly when he'd pay me, but he told me not to worry, he'd have the money soon. I hadn't a clue where he'd get that amount of cash, but it looks like he found it somehow. Still don't know if I'll see a farthing of it, though."

That seemed to satisfy my new acquaintance, and he left to continue his work.

I reasoned that I had found out everything that I needed to at the Melpomene house, and my continued presence would only lead to more questions I didn't feel like answering. I hurried down the back steps and left the rope hanging around the doorknob as I departed.

The rest of the day was spent inquiring into the details of Mrs. Melpomene's father. My initial inquires led me to learn that all of London society believed him to have passed away quietly in his sleep years earlier. I suspected that there was much more to the story, and I kept digging into the matter. By the end of the day, I had made a critical discovery, and I wrote to the Sobotta brothers to visit me that evening. When they arrived, I showed them to their chairs and explained the situation to them. "What do you know about Mrs. Melpomene's family?" I asked.

"They've passed away," Steven told me.

"Diphtheria, if I remember correctly," Scott added. "Mrs. Melpomene was orphaned at a very young age. She was taken in by two – "

" – maiden aunts," finished Steven.

"That's only half true," I told him. "Mrs. Melpomene's mother did indeed die thirty years ago, but the cause of death wasn't diphtheria. And her father is still alive." From the expressions on their faces, it was clear than neither sibling had any idea of this.

Scott stammered, "Why would she keep her father's existence a – "

" – secret?" the brothers said together.

"For a very good reason: Her father is a madman. He is incurably violent, and has been kept in an asylum for three decades."

"He's dangerous, then?" Scott asked.

"Yes. He has killed one person that we know of: His wife. Mrs. Melpomene's mother."

The jaws of the Sobotta twins headed in the general direction of the floor.

"What?" they asked simultaneously.

"He strangled her in a fit when Mrs. Melpomene was a girl. Luckily for her public reputation, at the time they lived in an isolated manor house in the countryside. The local authorities were sympathetic, and with the help of her aunts, the case was hushed up. Mrs. Melpomene's father was locked away in an asylum under an assumed name, and she hasn't seen him since the night her mother died. Every now and then, the doctors send her a note on her father's condition. Unfortunately, the most recent letter was intercepted and sold to a blackmailer."

"How did – "

" – this happen?" Scott completed his brother's sentence.

"A footman in their employment. If you like, I can provide you with his name, and you can look into tracking him down and seeing him punished, though I should warn you that if he were ever brought to trial, Mrs. Melpomene's secret would almost certainly be revealed to the world."

"Not an option," Steven replied, and Scott nodded vigorously.

"Very well. In any case, I suspect that the blackmailer demanded a massive sum of money, and threatened to reveal the true fate of Mrs. Melpomene's parents, possibly at the Green Gala, in front of all of London society. The Melpomenes had a choice: Either they could allow themselves to be extorted into penury, or their family secret could be exposed. No respectable family would allow their children to marry the grandchildren of a mad murderer. Mr. Melpomene clearly loves his wife, and he chose a third option: Flee the country, and start a new life overseas. They are in the process of shipping their possessions to Canada, and I strongly suspect that they will adopt a new name in their new country."

The brothers seemed utterly crushed by the news that their friends had been driven from their home for reasons beyond their control. They thanked me for my efforts, recompensed me for my time, and they decided to let the matter rest out of respect for their friends' reputations. As they left 221b, Steven said, "I hope that the blackmailer responsible for this gets –"

" – his just deserts," Scott finished.

Holmes turned towards me. "And as you know, Watson, Milverton has finally paid for his crimes."

"I happen to know that he paid seven-hundred pounds to a footman for a note two lines in length, and that the ruin of a noble family was the result."

– Sherlock Holmes
"Charles Augustus Milverton"

NOTE

Special thanks to Steven and Scott Sobotta, a real-life pair of twins who were kind enough to purchase the "*Have a character named after you*" option in my recent Kickstarter campaign for *Nessie's Nemesis* and asked to be Holmes's clients, with their real-life habit of finishing each other's sentences. Thanks so much, Steven and Scott! – C.C.

The Stolen Brougham
by Dan Rowley

Chapter I

"Mr. Holmes," exclaimed our hostess, her face writhing and her hand nervously plucking at her dress, "are you confident this will work?"

"Martha, please put your trust in Holmes." Our host looked fondly at his wife, patting her on the back in an attempt to sooth her. "I have known him almost as long as your brother, and he is one of the most reliable chaps there is. He is exactly what we need. And besides, these Home Office men are here to protect us."

"Lord Robert," my friend replied, "might I suggest that Her Ladyship take some laudanum and lie down on the davenport over by the fire to rest while we are gone. I assure you, Madam, Watson and I have everything under control. We'll resolve this fiendish plot within the next hour or so. Now, we must be off. Come, Watson, we don't wish to be late."

We exited the study and, as we proceeded down the hallway, I expostulated, "Holmes, I fully comprehend your plan and the need for these disguises. But why must I pose as Lady Martha, and not you?"

Holmes wryly smiled. "I quite understand your discomfort, old friend. But I did base this charade, as always, on facts and logic. You are of middle height, only slightly taller than Lady Martha, while I'm more similar in stature to Lord Robert. Also, I believe our opponent will come after me first, which will permit the two of us a far better chance of overcoming him. He'll be focused on me, which will lessen the chance that he will inspect you closely. You must concede that, with my makeup and padding, I look quite like our host. If you keep your veil down, the scarf high around your neck, and your hands inside the muffler, all should go well. And the muffler provides a convenient way to conceal your service revolver, making it more easily accessible than if I was required to reach inside a pocket while struggling with a marauder. Ah, here is our transportation, and a well turned-out brougham it is. Off we go, Watson!"

Somewhat mollified, I allowed my friend to assist me climbing into the brougham. I noticed that our luggage was already loaded, and the driver was seated, wearing a voluminous scarf against the cold air, which quite obscured his visage. Once we were settled, he gave rein to the horses and we pulled away.

* * * * *

I should pause here to explain how Sherlock Holmes and I had come to this rather unusual pass. It was late November of 1900, a rather cold, damp, and blustery month. He and I had been in Bishop's Stratford dealing with the rather puzzling matter of the local Vicar having acquired the habit of suddenly starting to speak Ancient Greek in the middle of his sermons, which Holmes had resolved after inspecting the local solicitor's collection of rare books. After that, Holmes remarked to me that he had a standing invitation to visit Sir James Saunders, an acquaintance, one might say almost a friend, from their days together at University. He had recently received a telegram from Sir James indicating that he was staying at Hounslow, his brother-in-law's country estate near Welwyn in Buckinghamshire.

Apparently Sir James had seen reports of our exploits with the Vicar and extended an invitation, and his telegram stated that his relatives would also be pleased to see us. I had met Sir James on several occasions both when he visited Holmes and at professional gatherings, as he was a rather renowned skin specialist, or *dermatologist* as they prefer to be called. From conversations with him and Holmes, I knew that Holmes had attended the wedding of Sir James's sister to Lord Robert Stevens, who was engaged in Government service and had met Holmes and his brother Mycroft on several occasions – although Holmes was markedly circumspect about those meetings. Perhaps someday I may persuade Holmes to recount them for me.

I readily agreed to the suggestion that we spend a few days at Hounslow. I wasn't particularly busy, and hoped that I might have an opportunity to explore the nearby Roman ruins in Welwyn. Little did I anticipate that wasn't to be.

During the train ride from Bishop's Stratford to Welwyn, I was watching the passing countryside when Holmes interrupted my reverie. "Yes, Watson, I'm sure you are gratified that the Conservatives triumphed over the Liberals in such a a resounding fashion."

"As always, you are correct. I'm confident you are now about to explain."

"You just finished reading the front page of the newspaper, and I note it is mostly devoted to the news from South Africa regarding our latest conflict, which I believe the press, with its penchant for colorful labels, is calling the 'Second Boer War' You are aware that our host at Hounslow is a principal secretary to Lord Salisbury, although my impression is that Lord Robert handles things more on the foreign affairs side of the good Lord's dual portfolio as Prime Minister and Foreign Secretary. That combination inevitably led you to reflect on the 'snap' election called by

Lord Salisbury, in which the electorate reaffirmed a resounding mandate for his war policy."

"Yes. As you noted, the inclination of the press to invent labels leads them to call it the 'Khaki Election'. In my view, that rather condescending attitude once again evinces the lesser press's underestimation of the British public's support for the Army, especially during an ongoing conflict."

"No doubt, my friend. Ah, I believe we are about there."

At the Welwyn station, we were met by a driver, whom Lord Robert had sent after receiving our telegram. He introduced himself as Geoff Banton, explaining he doubled as horse groom and driver. He apologized for bringing the open barouche in cold weather like this, but the enclosed brougham was being repaired. We assured him it was no problem, and left the station encased in warm blankets.

We arrived at Hounslow mid-afternoon. The central portion was a Queen Anne country house with three stories. There were four pillars inset in the dull red-brick front, spaced at each end and either side of the front entrance. An oddity was that, on the right side of the house, there were two additions of recent vintage that weren't smoothly joined, which offset the symmetry of the structure. The house sat in about forty acres of park and woodland.

We were met at the door by an imposing butler who I later learned was named Worthington, a tall, erect man in his mid-sixties who, despite his shock of white hair, otherwise showed little sign of aging. He bowed deeply and intoned, "Mr. Holmes and Doctor Watson, it is an honor to meet you both. If I may be permitted a familiarity, Doctor, I read all your recounting of your adventures, as His Lordship is kind enough to subscribe to *The Strand* for me and the other servants."

Ignoring Holmes's bemused expression, I replied, "Thank you so much. I'm gratified that I could add my small mite to the reading public's pleasure."

"Oh, indeed. Sir James and His Lordship are eagerly awaiting you. If you will leave your luggage here, Lord Robert has instructed me to bring you to the library, which also serves as his study. That tells me how much he anticipates your visit, as very few people are permitted to enter."

"Is that so?" queried Holmes, unable to curb his inveterate curiosity. "And why is that?"

"Well, sir, for several reasons. The room leads to His Lordship's private quarters and those of Lady Martha. And he keeps important government documents there, so the doors from the hallway and his rooms are always kept locked. Either Lord Robert or Lady Martha must be present when the maid cleans the room."

"That explains it. Please lead the way." With another bow, our guide led us up the central staircase to the first floor. Once there, we turned left and proceeded to the front of the house. The butler then knocked at a massive oak door, cautiously opened it, and looked inside. "Begging your pardon, my Lordship. Your visitors are here and anxious to see you, if that is convenient."

From inside the room, we heard a hearty voice. "By all means, Worthington! Show them in."

The room was large, paneled in the same oak as the door. The inner walls were covered with bookcases, and two windows at the front wall let in what light there was on that gloomy day. A fire blazed away in a fireplace opposite the door, and the room was filled with hunting prints, comfortable chairs and sofas, a side table with various decanters and a humidor, and other *accoutrements* of a male refuge from the cares of the world.

Our host rose from behind a large desk and made his way over to us. He was about Holmes's height, although stouter, with softened features. His lined face and greying hair gave his appearance an older look, although I knew him to be only a bit older than my friend.

"Holmes, what an absolute delight to see you! And a pleasure to meet you as well, Doctor Watson."

His brother-in-law had also risen and come over. Sir James was thin, a bit shorter than Holmes, and showing his age more than my friend. His hair, although fair, had signs of grey, but his blue eyes sparkled with delight. "Wonderful to see you! Robert didn't hesitate when I asked if I could invite you. And, Watson, it's always a pleasure. I trust you had a hand in persuading my old acquaintance to accept my offer to come to Hounslow. Doctor's orders, what?

Lord Robert smiled. "Here, come have a seat by the fire and take the chill off. May I offer you something to drink?"

After the four of us settled in with a delicious dry sherry, Holmes and Sir James caught up on what they had been doing since their last meeting. When Holmes modestly alluded to our recent matter, Lord Robert interjected. "So, Holmes, I would be delighted to hear about your adventures in Bishop's Stratford, but I suspect that would be even more enjoyable over brandy and cigars after dinner. Normally I would show you the gardens, as Martha and the gardener have created several delightful follies and grottoes, but it's too inclement today to offer that. And I do have a spot of work to do, so I apologize that we must cut short this pleasant time."

"Yes, I must admit I had wondered why you weren't in Town at this time of year, given that I've read there will be a special session of Parliament early next month."

Our host sighed. "Despite our resounding victory, the Prime Minister felt we should move the opening, including the Queen's Speech, up to December to deal with further funds for the Army. He and his politicos believe they can capitalize on the results of the election quickly before the Liberals latch onto something to use as a cudgel. He loves staying at Hatfield House, but wants to have his lieutenants close by. I decided it would be easier to come here in case I needed to make a quick jaunt over to Hertfordshire. We shall not be here much longer, though, as Salisbury has indicated he wants to return to London in the next few days."

"I thought you didn't involve yourself as much on the political side."

"Normally, no. But with this blasted Boer business and the Liberals, war and foreign policy become inextricably mixed with domestic issues – especially if they involve spending."

"That makes eminent sense. I trust we will not be a burden for you and Lady Martha."

"Nonsense. It will give me companions with whom I can relax and chat about things to take my mind off the 'cares of the Empire', as Martha likes to call it. Besides, we have a rather light house at the moment. Just me, James, Martha, and our children, Peter and Dorothy. Her fiancé, a solicitor chap named Ormquist, is here, as is Captain Thorpe, a friend of Peter's on leave from duty with Kitchener in South Africa. Oh, yes, and my secretary, Sauls, a bright and delightful Cornishman. That's the lot."

"Very well. Watson and I can use the opportunity to freshen up."

"Of course. Your rooms are on the next floor. I'll have Blunt, my valet, show you. I'm sure Worthington has taken your bags up. We have drinks at seven, so see you then, unless the blasted work requires more time than I anticipate. James, you mentioned you wanted to work on a paper, so perhaps you could do that now." His brother-in-law took his leave, and Lord Robert pulled a bell cord. Blunt, a short, glum man in his mid-forties with rabbity features and wispy hair, took us up to our rooms. Mine was next to that of Holmes. There was a pleasant fire going. The room sported floral wallpaper with complementary pictures, sturdy mahogany bed furniture, comfortable chair, washstand, and wardrobe. I wasn't surprised that the efficient Worthington, or perhaps Blunt, had unpacked and laid away my things. I read for a bit and then got ready for dinner. Shortly before seven, Holmes came to my door, and we went back down to the main entry hall. Worthington was standing there and escorted us to the drawing room to the right of the staircase.

The room was comfortably furnished in rose and gold, with ample seating and side tables. As we entered, Sir James immediately hurried over to us. "Excellent! There you are. Holmes, Martha is anxious to see you. Doctor, I don't believe you've met. Come over here."

We approached two women standing by the fireplace. The older one was in her mid-forties with auburn hair. It was obvious she worked hard to maintain her figure, although her facial features were softening and the hands that clutched the lace handkerchief were showing signs of age, as they always do no matter what the rest of the body looks like. The younger woman, about eighteen, was a prettier version of the other, slim with reddish hair and quite captivating eyes, nose, and mouth.

"Martha, you know Holmes. Doctor, allow me to introduce my sister, Martha, and her daughter, Dorothy."

Holmes and I both made our regards. Holmes then asked, "I do trust we aren't a burden."

"Ha, ha . . . er, that is to say no, no, no, no! We are always, er, pleased to have distinguished company. I apologize for Robert's absence, but he is still working upstairs. He hadn't begun to dress for dinner when I came down."

"Martha, why don't you and Holmes catch up. I'll be right back, but I want to introduce the Good Doctor to the rest of our company." As he led me away, he confided, "Martha is always anxious when entertaining new guests. She is a perfectionist. Ah, here we are." Three younger men were gathered in front of the drinks table. Sir James performed the formalities, we acknowledged one another, and a gin was procured for me. Sir James left us to rejoin Holmes and his sister and niece, and I had an opportunity to observe the three younger men while they continued their previous conversation, which apparently concerned the South African war. Richard Ormquist,, Dorothy's fiancé, was about twenty-five, blond, with strong, chiseled features. I could see that, once he was a full barrister, he would be effective in front of a jury, even if only on looks alone. Peter Stevens, the scion, was slightly older than his sister, and looked much like his father, although more wiry and athletic. Captain Mathew Thorpe, Peter's friend, was in his early twenties. He possessed a typical soldier's bearing, ramrod straight, cropped hair, and sharp features weathered by the sun. It was he who now was holding forth.

"Yes, I wish I could graduate from a staff position to one where I could experience action at the front. But Kitchener has been indifferent to my pleas. He contends that this isn't a real war because the blasted Boers will not 'play' by what he considers the proper methods of civilized combat. Doctor Watson, I believe you served, did you not?"

"Yes, I was in Afghanistan and India twenty years ago."

283

"I suspect life as an Army surgeon must be a bit like serving on the staff."

"Actually, I was at the front, and was wounded at the Battle of Maiwand. That led to complications during my recuperation in Peshawar."

"Sorry, old man. I didn't mean to imply any dishonor. Was merely trying to compare service in the two conflicts. I suspect the natives in your war engaged in irregular tactics like the Boers in mine."

"Thank you, no offense taken. In fact, there was some of that interspersed with more regular engagements."

"Just so. But at least twenty years ago the Government didn't engage in shameful conduct." At this, Peter began nodding vehemently. Ormquist spoke up, "At least back then, the Conservatives had a leader like Disraeli, who had a sense of honor. And of course he knew Gladstone was waiting in the wings to bring the Liberals to triumph again."

Before I could pursue this curious interchange further, we were called in to dinner. Holmes and I were seated at opposite ends of the table in the commodious dining room, which was situated across the hall. It was furnished with the usual accoutrements of mahogany furniture, exquisite china and silverware, and painted silk wallpaper with charming Chinese scenes. By this time, Lord Robert and his secretary, Daniel Sauls, had joined us. Sauls was a man of about thirty-five, although his hair was already turning white. He was of medium height, and his bright roving eyes belied the inconspicuousness of his features.

I was seated to Lady Martha's right, but could still hear the conversation at the other end of the table, where Holmes politely asked Dorothy whether there was any local news of note.

"Oh, Mister Holmes, nothing much occurs here, at least not like your various adventures."

"Come, Sister," said Peter Stevens, "you are neglecting our local mystery."

Lord Robert interrupted. "Don't bother our guest with such trivialities."

"But Father, it is the talk of everyone."

Holmes smiled. "Please enlighten us. Perhaps Doctor Watson can make use of it."

I disregarded his gibe, which no one but us understood. He believes that I embellish our cases for effect, but I don't agree with him on that. "Yes, please don't keep us in suspense."

Our host grimaced. "My children are exaggerating. In the past several weeks, three vehicles have been stolen in the surrounding area. In each case, the deed was carried out during the night, and no one heard a thing.

No one has seen the vehicles. None of the thefts were in Walwyn, but rather in the outlying areas."

"Is there any commonality to the thefts?"

"No, Holmes. The owners are quite varied: A local inn, the village doctor, and a farmer. Also a different type of vehicle each time, I believe: A trap, a barouche, and a hansom."

"Were horses stolen as well?"

"No. The local constable believes the thief or thieves may have been concerned about noise if a horse was startled by someone it didn't know."

"I assume the authorities have made attempts to locate the vehicles."

"Yes. I spoke yesterday to the Justice of the Peace. He says the police theorize the vehicles have been taken to London or some similar location where they will blend in. They're quite stymied."

"In my experience, that isn't an unusual occurrence. It doesn't appear to have anything of interest to me, as I normally don't pursue such matters."

"Quite so. Enough of this, children. Let us discuss something more interesting. How about the Hunt."

The conversation turned to that and other such matters. It was quite pleasant company, matching the delicious repast. We had beef with seasonal vegetables, fresh bread and butter, potatoes *au gratin*, a nicely dressed salad, cheese and fruit, all accompanied by excellent wines with each course. After the women retired, Lord Robert coaxed us to relate our recent outing over brandy and cigars, which Holmes did with some reluctance. Our host then held forth for a while on politics and the war, expressing his opinions in a manner that didn't brook interruption. I noticed that the younger members of the company didn't resume their earlier comments. At about midnight, we all turned in for a good night's sleep. On our way out, Sir James said to us, "I say, let us make sure we have more time tomorrow to visit. I admire my brother-in-law, but he can go on. Perhaps we can find time alone."

Chapter II

The next morning, Lord Robert, Sir James, Daniel Sauls, Holmes, and I were breakfasting in the dining room over eggs, rashers, toast, and coffee. Apparently the women had their breakfast in Lady Martha's room, and the young men had gone for an early hike. We were discussing a possible excursion to the Roman ruins when Worthington entered the room. He cleared his throat. "Begging your Lordship's pardon – I hesitated to interrupt, but I have some news that I thought you would wish to hear sooner rather than later."

"Go on then, man."

"Martin – Sorry, sirs, as Martin is the gardener – Martin went to the stables to have a chat with Banton. Sirs, he is – "

"Yes, yes, they met him yesterday. Get on with it."

"Sorry, your Lordship. When Martin arrived at the stable, he called out for Banton but received no answer. He went inside, discovered an overturned chair inside the door, and noticed what appeared to be some scuff marks and blood on the floor. It was then he noticed that the brougham, which normally sits in the center between the horse stalls, wasn't there. Martin immediately came to the back door and told the cook and housekeeper, who sent for me. I thought I should come here immediately. I told Martin to take one of the shotguns and wait at the stable."

"Good Lord, can this be another damnable theft? Worthington, go to town and fetch the constable. I'll go out and look the place over."

Sir James stood up. "Robert, I shall come with you. Holmes, would you accompany us? I know that, as you said last evening, you normally wouldn't be bothered by anything so trivial, but may I presume to base my request on our relationship. Frankly, the local constable isn't of the first water."

"Of course, Saunders, if that's acceptable to Lord Robert. You know I could never disappoint a friend, especially of your nature, if I could avoid it. Watson, I assume you'll come along."

Without bothering to don overcoats, we exited the dining room from double doors that let out onto a terrace. The briskness of our pace alleviated the cold and dampness, as Lord Robert led the way from the back to the house to a red-brick building, standing on the edge of a driveway and shielded by trees.

Holmes paused a moment. "Where does that driveway lead?"

"It goes to a tradesman entrance several hundred feet from the main entrance. There is a short extension that joins the main drive so that a cab can easily be brought to the front. As you can see, it also leads over to those extensions on the other side of the house, which is where the kitchen, pantries, and offices for the butler and housekeeper are located."

"Is there a locked gate at the trade entrance?"

"No. It would be a constant nuisance, especially in inclement weather. We take the precaution of locking the house at night. Banton sleeps over the stable to guard that building. All other out-buildings are locked when not in use."

"I see. Let us proceed to the stable, then."

We came to the building and entered the large, central doors. Inside was a middle-aged man, rather nondescript, holding his cap in one hand and a gun in the other, looking quite miserable.

"Martin, Worthington has told us what you found. Have you looked upstairs for Banton?"

"No, Your Worship. I thought it better to do as I were told."

"Hmmph. Quite right I suppose."

"Lord Robert, an excellent suggestion. Might Watson and I take a look upstairs. I suggest that you, Saunders, and Martin stay right here until we return. And when the constable arrives, please don't let him trample around before I can have a look."

"Very well, Holmes. Quite decent of you to help. You'll be a sight better than the locals, I would imagine."

We went upstairs to a small spare room, containing only an iron bedstead, washstand, chair, side table, oil lamp, and wardrobe. Holmes nonetheless made his usual painstaking inspection, looking in the wardrobe, rifling through the clothes, picking up the implements on the washstand, peering under the bed, feeling the floorboards, even lifting the pillow and bedclothes.

"Nothing out of the ordinary, Watson. Seems a simple man. No reading material or correspondence, no pictures, nothing to personalize him. Unless someone else has been up in here, there's no way of knowing if anything is missing. Let us go back downstairs."

We returned to find Lord Robert, Sir James, and Martin standing in silence as if they had never moved. Sir James spoke first, "Find anything?"

"If you will indulge me for a moment. Martin, have you ever been up in Banton's room?"

"No, sir."

"Did Banton often sit in that chair over there?"

"Aye. During the day he'd sit there working on patching leather or other parts. In fact, he finished fixing the brougham yesterday. At night, he'd relax in the chair with a pipe. Said it comforted the horses."

"I note those implements hanging on the walls – tools, pitch forks, shovels, and so forth. Anything missing or out of place?"

The gardener squinted and looked carefully, as if his very employment hung in the balance. "Sir, near as I can tell, she's all there."

To the equal puzzlement of Lord Robert and Martin, but apparently not to Sir James, Holmes began walking around the stable without another word, looking at the overturned chair, the area where the brougham had been parked, and into each of the horse stalls. Their confusion increased when he got down on his hands and knees to look over the scuff marks and the nearby blood stain.

He abruptly stood up. "Lord Robert, I'm done. Can you confirm that none of the horses are missing."

Lord Robert went down each side to the stalls. "No, they're all here."

"We may as well return to the house and let the constable trample at will. You go ahead of us. I wish to take in some of your grounds."

"Fine. Meet me in the library."

With instructions to Martin to remain at his post, we strolled along at a leisurely pace as Lord Robert and Sir James hurried ahead. "I say," I asked, "isn't it a bit brisk to be perusing the grounds?"

He smiled. "Actually, I wanted a few moments to think. There may be some items of interest in this theft after all." Not quite sure how to respond, I maintained my silence as my friend was lost in thought. I was accustomed to these periods where his mighty intellect was engaged in cogitation. As was normal during such a reverie, he was oblivious to all external stimulus, often not eating or, in this case, paying mind to the cold.

Eventually we returned to the house and went upstairs to the library, where Lord Robert and Sir James had come after our excursion. A fire had been readied, which our host had lit. Just as we were settling in, Holmes began to explain that he had noticed a few things that caught his attention, but before he could go further, there was a knock at the door.

"Come," said Lord Robert.

"Begging your Lordship's pardon," said Worthington, "I have two telegrams here that you'll want to see. One is for you, and one for Sir James."

"Let me have them." He then read through the one for him, and a momentary irritation passed over his face. Without a word, he handed it to Holmes. I was able to see the short note, which read:

Need to consult. Come tomorrow by yourself with Lady M. Stay overnight.

S

Holmes looked up at our host. "I assume this is a summons to Hatfield House."

"Yes. I was hoping to stay here with you, but duty calls. I'll have to alert Martha. Since the death of his wife last year, Lord Salisbury, who loved her greatly, often desires to have some female companionship. He often asks for Martha to accompany me. Bother! The brougham was our only enclosed vehicle. Worthington, it's too cold to drive Martha that far in a vehicle that isn't enclosed, and she would prefer that to the train, as it will not require packing and unpacking the luggage. Arrange with the livery service to have a cab and driver here tomorrow morning by ten. Preferably a brougham like ours."

"Certainly, your Lordship."

Upon his departure, Lord Robert turned to Sir James. "What is in your telegram, if I may ask?"

"I fear that I too must leave, if only for a day or so. One of my colleagues is scheduled to perform surgery tomorrow morning. The patient apparently has a terrible skin condition at the site of the proposed incision. The specialist with whom the surgeon was consulting has come down with influenza, and they have requested my presence to examine the patient, provide advice, and be present during surgery and initial recovery in the event something goes awry. I must leave at once, but hopefully will be back tomorrow. Robert, might I make a suggestion?"

"Of course."

"Holmes was about to explain to us what he had noticed. Given that I will hopefully be gone only slightly more than a day, perhaps he and Watson could remain here and pursue their inquiries further in the hope they can discover what is behind this series of thefts. While it isn't his normal type of case, I might once again presume on our long-standing acquaintance to persuade him to do so." He looked quizzically at my friend.

"I would never turn down this family in its time of need, so long as Lord Robert agrees."

"Of course, Holmes. That is most gracious of you. I apologize, but I must go talk to Martha, and then I'll need to talk with Sauls to ensure I'm up to date. I'll see you at dinner, but I'm afraid you'll need to amuse yourselves until then."

"Don't be concerned for a moment. I think I'll take a stroll into town to have a look, and Watson here has some professional reading to catch up on. We'll be fine."

Sir James smiled. "Thank you so much. If ever I can return the favor, please don't hesitate to call on me. I shall also leave now, but trust I'll be back tomorrow to renew our reminiscences."

After our host and his brother-in-law left, I turned to my friend. "I hope I didn't allow my astonishment to manifest itself. What reading are you talking about?"

"Watson, that was just an excuse so that we could divide forces. While I'm in town, I would like you to use your considerable charms on the female servants to learn what gossip they might impart about the household and neighborhood, especially as it might relate to Banton the groom. Recall that this is the first vehicle theft where a person has gone

289

missing. Just learn whatever you can. I leave it to your ingenuity as to how to accomplish this."

"Of course. I shall retire to my room for a bit to think through my strategy. I'm not sure what you're looking for, so I'll need to cast my net rather broadly."

"Capital, my good man. I knew I could count on you. When I return, let us meet in my room before dinner so that you can tell me what you've learned. Until then, good casting!"

I went to my room to make some notes. At noon, I went to the dining room where there was a cold collation of meats and cheeses with an excellent Rhône wine. Only the young men were there, and they were excitedly discussing their afternoon plans. I then returned to my room for further planning. I had partially formulated an idea, and wished to mull it over further. At mid-afternoon, I felt I was ready and started down the staircase. I had decided that the most likely avenue for the mission Holmes had set for me was the kitchen, so I made that my destination.

It was located in the extension on the right side of the main house. It apparently had been built to provide a larger space with all the modern cooking apparatus. I introduced myself to a plump woman in her mid-forties with black hair, grey eyes, and a ruddy complexion. As she was wearing an apron sprinkled with flour, it didn't require the deductive abilities of Sherlock Holmes to divine she was the cook.

"Hello, Madam. I'm John Watson, and I just came back to offer my complements on your culinary talents."

"As I live and breathe, I never thought I'd have the famous Doctor Watson in my kitchen! Mrs. Pierce, our housekeeper, and I both read all your stories. What an honor! If I could just meet Sherlock Holmes, my day would truly be made! Please – call me Lydia."

"It would be my pleasure. Last evening's meal was a true masterpiece."

"Oh, Doctor, would you like to have some tea? I was just brewing some. Please sit over here by the fire. And if it wouldn't be imposing on you, could I fetch Mrs. Pierce to join us?"

"I would love some tea, but only if you and Mrs. Pierce join me." She bustled off and soon returned with the housekeeper, a stately woman in her mid-fifties, rather thin with sharp features and red hair that hadn't yet lost its luster. Although she was trying to maintain her natural composure, I could sense she too was excited. I could only imagine the reaction of Holmes to my instantaneous celebrity. "How do you do, Mrs. Pierce? Please join us for what I'm sure will be a splendid spot of tea."

Once it was poured and a plate of fresh scones appeared, we settled in.

"You know, Doctor," said Mrs. Pierce, "I was just saying to Lydia the other day we haven't seen anything from your pen in a while. We do pray you'll continue to recount the adventures you and Mister Holmes have undertaken."

"As a matter of fact, I'm working on a longer tale of something that happened some time ago. It's about a mysterious hound in a most fantastic setting. It should be published next year, but I'll say no more so that you can enjoy it in full when it comes out."

We then discussed several of our more memorable cases and, just as I was trying to think of a way to get to the gossip Holmes wanted, Lydia the cook said, "I understand that you and Mister Holmes accompanied the Master out to the stable after Geoff and the brougham disappeared. That's probably not as exciting as what we were just discussing."

"Well, every case has its own peculiarities. We had heard last night about the other thefts, but this seems to be the only one where a person was abducted."

Lydia shuddered. "Martin told me there was blood and some overturned furniture."

"Now, Lydia," said the housekeeper, "you know he has a tendency to sensationalize things. I'm sure it wasn't that bad, was it, Doctor?"

"There were signs of a struggle. If you don't mind my asking, what was Banton's daily routine like?"

"Oh, Mrs. Pierce – just like in the stories! You tell the Doctor."

"Unless he has to take His Lordship somewhere, it's nothing special. He tends to the horses, keeping them groomed, watered, and fed. That is his primary responsibility. He also makes minor repairs to the horse trappings and vehicles as needed. Anything major might require assistance from the livery in town."

"Don't forget the dogs, Mrs. Pierce."

"I was just coming to that, Lydia. His Lordship keeps a pack of hunting dogs, which Banton cares for."

"So, Lord Robert is keen on hunting."

"Oh, yes. Miss Dorothy doesn't care for it, but the rest of the family goes out quite frequently. They will go by themselves, or in pairs, or all of them together. His Lordship felt the dogs and horses need exercise, so Banton rides them, and whichever family members want to go out, or if none of them do, he goes by himself, but often one or more joins him. It's quite fitting that they take advantage of the Christian virtues of being in God's fresh air and sunshine."

"What about Banton's arrangements here otherwise?"

"He takes his meals here in the kitchen like the other servants. He sleeps over the stables, as you probably know."

291

"What is he like?"

"A rather pleasant young man. He has a very quick wit, always ready with a joke or a quip."

Lydia interjected. "Now Mrs. Pierce, you're letting your religious views obscure some of it. Doctor, he enjoys a drink now and then, I believe down at the public house in town, as His Lordship doesn't permit alcohol consumption by the servants here on the property. And, if truth be told, he enjoys his time with the girls. I often believe that Sally thinks he's going to marry her."

"That would be just like that silly thing. Doctor, Sally is the parlor maid. Lydia is likely correct that Geoff turned her head." I had noticed Sally, a pert, pretty blonde in her mid-twenties. Mrs. Pierce continued. "Of course, I'll not have any foolishness in my household. I told Sally she will be given her papers if I think she is sneaking out at night to see him."

"Quite right. Does he have any family or relatives or friends?"

"No family that I know of. I believe he has a friend or two in town that he meets at the public house." We turned then to other matters about members of the staff, but I learned no more about the groom. I then thanked Lydia and Mrs. Pierce and went back into the main house.

As I walked along the corridor toward the front of the house on the side opposite from the dining room, I heard raised voices behind a heavy, closed door. I paused for a moment, attempting to ascertain what was going on, as I thought it might interest Holmes. The voices were those of Captain Thorpe and the secretary, Sauls. I couldn't make out what they were saying, other than to once hear Sauls loudly say, "Absolutely not!"

I moved to the staircase so as not to be found in a compromising position. Taking extra care to step softly, I reached the first floor landing where, to my astonishment, I saw Ormquist, Dorothy's fiancé, trying the door to the library. It obviously was locked, but he continued to jiggle and twist the knob. Luckily he didn't perceive my presence, so I silently went on up to my room. I assumed that Lord Robert wasn't in there. Otherwise he would have heard the noise. Perhaps he was taking a short rest in his own room, or was with Lady Martha in hers.

Chapter III

About an hour or so later, I was leaving for a walk when Holmes returned, so we adjourned to his room. I recounted my conversation in the kitchen. He sat for a few moments in silence, then looked at me.

"Excellent as always, Watson. I knew your charms with the ladies would bear fruit. That, combined with what I discovered in town, is beginning to make what was obscure much clearer."

292

"I should add a few other points as well, which go beyond the purview of my assignment."

"By all means, proceed."

"After I left the kitchen, I overheard Sauls and Thorpe arguing. I assume it was only the two of them. Obviously I didn't eavesdrop, but what I could make out was that Sauls was refusing something – "Absolutely not!" he cried. Then, when I came up to the landing, I saw Ormquist attempting to gain entrance to the library, clearly unaware that the door is locked when no one is in there. And last night before the meal, Thorpe made an obscure reference to something untoward occurring in the war. I'm wondering whether all those things are related, but I confess I cannot ascertain what they have to do with the theft of the brougham and the kidnapping of Banton."

"Very interesting, my friend. If you'll excuse me, I would like to have some time alone for a pipe or two to cogitate on all this."

Promising to return before we needed to go back downstairs, I left his room, whereupon I immediately encountered Sauls coming upstairs. Pulling him aside, I told him, "I couldn't help but overhear your argument with Captain Thorpe a while ago." Even as I did so, I thought that perhaps Holmes might have preferred to have this discussion, but now I was committed.

Sauls' face turned bright red. "This is an outrage. How dare you listen to a private conversation!"

"I did no such thing. One couldn't help but overhear, given the timbre and volume of your voice."

"Well, since you've already eavesdropped, I'll only say this: The Captain has learned that Emily Hobhouse is my relative."

"You mean the radical suffragette that is opposed to the war?"

"Yes. She's my mother's second cousin. The Captain presumptuously assumes I share her views. Nothing could be further from the truth. I'm utterly loyal to the Conservative viewpoint, and to Lord Robert. The Captain was attempting to worm very sensitive information from me, but I refused to speak with him about it in no uncertain terms."

"What information?"

"I cannot and will not tell you either. I have a sacred trust and will not breach it. Now if you will excuse me, I must take my leave."

After his departure, I realized that Holmes likely needed to know of this development, so I returned to his room, apologizing for disturbing him so soon, and also for asking questions that might have gone against his own effort.

He shook his head and smiled, stating that it would all work out. Then he resumed smoking his pipe, which I took that as a signal that I should leave. When I returned to his rooms later that afternoon to go down for drinks, he stated. "Watson, you have performed yeoman's service today. I've sent a note to our host asking that we see him alone after dinner in his library."

"So, you have solved this."

"I believe so. There are troubling matters here, but I have a plan, and you are a crucial part of it. Let us go down, but say no more until we can talk to Lord Robert in private.

The evening was uneventful, and no one touched upon any of the matters that were on my mind. Dorothy did ask about the theft and the upcoming trip to Hatfield House, but Lord Robert said he wanted to relax and talk about other things, so we focused on hunting, fishing, and the upcoming social season. The meal, as before, was excellent: Some very tender lamb, seasonal vegetables, and a delightful *soufflé*, accompanied again by selections from what was obviously a splendid cellar. When we finished, Lord Robert indicated that he, Holmes, and I would take cigars and port in his library so that we could reminisce about the past so as not to bore anyone.

Once Worthington had us ensconced by the fire, Lord Robert turned to my friend. "All right, Holmes, I have followed your instructions. Please enlighten me as to what is going on."

"I'll explain to you in more detail tomorrow, but I've concluded there will an attempt to kidnap you and Lady Martha."

"That is extraordinary! What on earth leads you to that conclusion?"

"A number of facts, but the most important is that the telegram purporting to be from Lord Salisbury is a forgery."

"How do you know that?"

"While in Walwyn today, I sent a message to my brother, Mycroft. Through his contacts, he confirmed that no such message was sent to you by the Prime Minister."

"But what led you to check with him?"

"As I said, I'll explain in more detail tomorrow. I must beg your indulgence, but I don't want to stay closeted in here for too long. Watson and I have to make some preparations. Also, I don't want to arouse the suspicion of any members of the household."

"What! My family and guests? Do you mean to imply one or more of them might be involved? That's preposterous."

I interrupted. "If you would allow me, Lord Robert." Holmes nodded for me to continue. "There have been several curious incidents in the last twenty-four hours. Last night, Captain Thorpe made an allusion to certain matters going on in the current war that he implied could damage the Government. Your son and Ormquist seemed to agree with him. Today, I saw Ormquist attempting to gain entrance to this room. And then I overheard Thorpe and Sauls arguing about something. When we confronted Sauls, he refused to tell us what Thorpe wanted and professed his loyalty to you. All that suggests to me that at least three of the young men are trying to obtain information, and the kidnapping might be a way to extract that from you. At this point, I don't know how to explain Banton's disappearance. Perhaps he recognized the thieves, or put up a struggle, and they concluded it was prudent to remove him."

Holmes resumed. "Allow me to continue, Lord Robert. Here is the telegram from Mycroft to which I referred. In it, he also authorizes you to reveal to Watson and me the nature of your secret."

Our host slumped in his chair, visibly shaken by the turn of events. After gazing at the fire for some minutes, he turned to Holmes. "I must admit that both of my children have Liberal sympathies. Dorothy has been influenced by Ormquist, and Peter has picked up some notions from people with whom he associates in the City. I believe I know what Thorpe was referring to, and Sauls, bless him, refused to tell you.

"As you probably know, this current war doesn't exactly follow conventional lines. At times, our foes use regular military formations. They also use irregular tactics, often terroristic. They are indistinguishable from the civilian population, and are able to invisibly merge back into their communities, where their compatriots provide aid and comfort. To combat this infernal situation, the Army has constructed camps in which to concentrate the civilians, thus isolating and neutralizing the threat.

"I fear that the Army doesn't have the resources or the experience to man and supply these so called concentration camps in the condition that one might wish. The War Office has received reports of food shortages, unsanitary conditions, and untreated medical problems. We have heard rumors that certain elements of the Liberals, particularly the Radicals led by Lloyd George, are attempting to discover what is going on in the camps.

"So far, this situation has been held in the tightest secrecy for obvious reasons, especially given the need for more funding for the Army. There are only a few documents with this information, all kept in a safe at the War Office. Lord Salisbury, and of course myself, have no papers. Only the smallest handful of people in the Government know. All discussions are oral, with no notes or minutes. If you are correct about the kidnapping of us, then it's likely to be what lies at the root of it. I suppose they plan on using Martha as a lever against me."

"I'm positive there will be an attempt," said Holmes. "I speculate that the other vehicle thefts in the vicinity are blinds, so that the theft of your own brougham wouldn't raise undue suspicion. Again, I'll explain more tomorrow, as we have already been here for a rather lengthy period of time.

"Allow me to suggest the following: Say nothing to anyone in the house about this, including any member of your family. Even if the listener is innocent, he or she might slip and tell someone else. Go about your normal routine tonight. Watson and I'll remain on guard. Mycroft is sending some help from the Home Office, and we'll let them in. Tomorrow morning, you and Lady Martha come here to the library, and I'll outline our plan. If you follow this course, we'll apprehend the scoundrels in the act."

"I still cannot believe this, but your brother's telegram is irrefutable. I'll say nothing to anyone. I'll turn in now, but sleep will likely elude me. Good night. And thank you, I suppose . . . ."

After Lord Robert left us alone, Holmes outlined his plan. I went upstairs to retrieve my service revolver and returned to the library, where we settled in with the door slightly ajar so that we could hear anyone in the hallway. At about two in the morning, Holmes consulted his pocket watch, left the room, and came back shortly with two impassive men, clearly well-fit and ready for the task at hand. Holmes then gave them detailed instructions, to which they assented. Clearly, Mycroft Holmes had told them to follow whatever his brother required.

Chapter IV

As dawn broke, Lord Robert opened the inner door from his chamber. "Would you gentlemen like something to eat?"

"No, thank you. Food for the four of us would arouse suspicion. We'll see you and Lady Martha shortly." Holmes moved to close the door to the hall.

Slightly over an hour later, our host and hostess entered by the inner door. She looked faint and grasped her husband's arm. "Robert, what is going on? Who are those two men with Mr. Holmes? Has something happened?"

"Lady Martha, I apologize for startling you. Please trust me this extraordinary situation is to ensure the safety of you and your husband. I have uncovered an attempt to kidnap you and Lord Robert."

"But why would someone want to kidnap us?"

"Darling, I fear it is an attempt to extract Government information from me, utilizing you to pressure me into compliance."

Tears were streaming down her face. "Oh, Robert, is it those horrid camps?"

His face contorted into a mask of agony. "It probably is. These men are from the Home Office. Holmes has a plan to catch the culprits. I was unable to sleep last night for thinking about this. I've come to the conclusion it is best for us to trust him. There, there, we'll be safe here. There's no need to carry on so."

"Yes, Lady Martha, these men will stay here to protect you. Watson and I are going to disguise ourselves as both of you on the journey today."

"This is ridiculous! Outlandish! Foolish . . . ." Lady Martha descended into sobs, with Lord Robert still attempting to placate her.

"With your permission, Lord Robert, Watson and I'll go to your room now and prepare." We left through the inner door. Luckily, there was a connecting door to Lady Martha's room, where I procured my disguise. I have already related what transpired when we went back to the library before descending to enter the hired cab. I'll recommence at that point.

We drove a mile or so from the house and through a secluded wooded area, when our vehicle abruptly stopped. Suddenly, the door next to Holmes flung open, and there stood a man with a scarf tied across his face holding a gun.

"Step out slowly . . . ."

Before he could finish, Holmes struck his wrist with the head of his walking stick, which he had designed himself by hollowing out the center and pouring in melted lead to fill the void. The intruder gave a howl of pain, dropped his gun, and was holding his wrist when Holmes jumped from the cab, locked his arms around him, and threw him to the ground.

As that was transpiring, I opened my own door and exited as quickly as my costume would permit. I hurried forward and saw the driver turned toward Holmes and his captive, apparently preparing to come to his confederate's aid.

"Don't move an inch! This revolver is loaded, and I'll not hesitate to use it." The man's back, which was to me, stiffened. He hesitated a moment, but realized by my voice that I wasn't who he expected. I didn't know him either. "Put your hands up and slowly climb down here toward me. That's good. Now lie on the ground face down and place your hands behind your head." He complied, and I reached inside a pocket and withdrew the handcuffs brought by the Home Office men. Assured that he was secure, I called out, "Everything under control, Holmes?"

"Capital, Watson! I've applied the handcuffs. Let's put these ruffians into the carriage. You may keep them under guard while I drive us back to Hounslow."

The return trip was swifter than the ride out. When we arrived, as we had discussed the night before, Holmes went inside. Meanwhile, my two prisoners glared at me but remained silent. Holmes shortly returned with one of the Home Office men, who took charge of our prisoners. Holmes and I went inside and up to the library.

"Well, Lord Robert, we have them."

297

"Holmes, that is marvelous! Martha, why don't you go lie down after all the excitement. You're looking pale, and that trembling will not stop."

"A good idea, Lady Martha," added Holmes. "This man will remain on guard in the hall just in case there's a third malefactor who tries something desperate."

After she left, Lord Robert shut the door. "Holmes, you promised me a more complete exposition once we reached this point. Please proceed."

"What initially struck me was the improbability of this whole matter, an impression that grew as yesterday wore on."

"Whatever do you mean?"

"Let us start with the thefts of the cabs. Why would thieves come out here to commit such acts? Local people notice anything unusual and, once there was one theft, people would be even more likely to notice. There also is the matter of disposing of the ill-gotten cabs. Someone local might recognize them, or see one being taken off somewhere else, because it's natural to assume they couldn't be used or sold in this vicinity. No horses were stolen, so they would have had to use local horses or bring some in, again increasing the risk of local detection. All in all, it would be far easier to do this in London, so I began to suspect the thefts were for the purpose of *distraction*. But distraction from what? When your brougham was stolen, my suspicions were heightened.

"The next thing that struck me was that only in your case was a person taken along with the brougham. If there was a struggle, why not knock Banton out and leave him behind? Of course, as Watson speculated, Banton may have recognized one or more of his assailants, but all the evidence indicated that the 'struggle' was contrived. The door to the stable creaks quite loudly, and it would have been closed against the chill, so no one could have sneaked up on Banton in that chair, which is some distance from the door.

"Martin said Banton liked to sit there and smoke to calm the horses, but there was no evidence of ashes or smoking implements such as a pipe or cigar or cigarette butts. According to Martin, implements hanging on the wall, which Banton could have used to defend himself, were undisturbed. You might then ask, what if the intruder had a gun? Why then the blood and scuff marks on the floor? I doubt that the blood was human – rather, perhaps from a pig or goat. And when there is a struggle, normally the heel marks left by boots aren't like the pattern here. There was only one set, all in a straight line, as if someone had taken a pair of boots and dragged them toward him across the floor. It was also odd that there wasn't a single personal item in Banton's room, as people normally have photographs, writing implements, or something that they cherish –

298

especially an outgoing and jovial person as was described to Watson. That suggests any such items were removed by the person who valued them."

"Are you saying Banton was involved?"

"I'll come to that. Perhaps these puerile attempts to create the impression of a struggle would have deceived the good constable, but the perpetrators didn't expect I would be here.

"I'll turn next to the purported rationale for the kidnapping. That too seemed improbable to me. Why try to extract information about these camps from you in such a clumsy way? The crime likely would be traced back to the perpetrators given their ineptness, and, if not, then certainly to those who used the information you gave them to damage the Government. The user of the information would be tainted by the crime, which certainly would blunt, if not completely counteract, the attack on the Government. What sensible or shrewd politician would take such a risk, as the information about the camps is bound to come out sooner or later? While only a few Government people here in England know, the knowledge isn't contained in South Africa, as evidenced by Captain Thorne's outrage. And after Winston Churchill's escape from captivity in Pretoria last year, and his sensational account of it, journalists are there in legions. Given all that, extracting information from you about the camps would seem to be just another misdirection."

"But are you saying that the camps and the activities of Thorpe, Ormquist, and Peter are just a coincidence?

"Not quite. Banton is involved, as I had deduced. I learned yesterday in town that he and the livery owner frequent the public house, where Watson learned he was a regular. The livery owner was our driver today, and Banton was the second kidnapper, who I disarmed and is now in the hands of the Home Office men. They are interrogating him . . . ." At that moment, there was a knock at the door. Holmes went to answer it. There was murmuring in the hall, and he shortly returned with a slight smile on his face.

"Banton says he and a friend were hired by an unknown man to kidnap you and Lady Martha and to use her to force you to tell them about some camps. He claims he doesn't know who the man was, or what camps he wants to know about."

"That corroborates the theory."

"It is yet another cover story," countered Holmes, "which Banton was instructed to spin if caught. It does, however, confirm that someone in the house is involved. How otherwise could Banton know about the camps?"

"I fear I'm at a total loss, Holmes. You yourself supported the theory."

"No, I never did. Watson laid the groundwork with you. Then you picked up the threads and wove them yourself."

"If you didn't believe it, why did you allow me to be deluded?"

"I trust you'll forgive me once I explain. Watson learned that Banton looks after the dogs and often goes riding with you, Lady Martha, and Peter, either singly or in groups. Think now who else could have known about the camps? Who would know there were no papers in here? Who could have listened at the inner door without attracting attention? Who has been exceedingly nervous, even though all measures for safety were taken? Who blurted out about the camps earlier this morning?

Lord Robert, ashen and with tears in his eyes, whispered. "No, no, no!"

"I'm afraid so. Lady Martha is the obvious conclusion. She realized the camps would divert attention from the fact that she and Banton were in this together. That's why I abjured you last night to tell no one in your family. That's also why the Home Office men were here in the library – to ensure she couldn't get away or warn anyone, and it's why one of them is on guard in the hall right now.

"Likely it was *she* who concocted the plan. She gave Banton the cover story about the camps if caught. I have suggested to the Home Office man some further lines of questioning. When faced with a possible charge of attempted murder, I expect Banton will crumple and confess." Lord Robert, staring at the floor, couldn't bring himself to utter the dread word.

"If the plan succeeded, Lady Martha would somehow 'escape' after your demise and tell the terrible story of your refusal to reveal anything about the camps in which the kidnappers were so interested, and your heroic death under extreme torture. I assume she will inherit at least a life interest, on which she and Banton could comfortably retire to the Continent."

"I . . . I don't know what to say. This is horrid."

"Indeed. If I might make a suggestion: Catch the earliest train to London and go immediately to see my brother. The two would-be kidnappers will be held *incognito* and the guard will remain until the two of you decide what to do. The Home Office also will do its utmost to locate your vehicle, so that its absence doesn't lead to local gossip."

Lord Robert nodded reluctantly. "May I impose on you once more? When James returns, could you be so kind as to explain all this to him" He'll need to know, as he'll undoubtedly notice Martha's state. Indeed, he likely can help, as the two of them are quite close, as you know." At Holmes's assent, Lord Robert shuffled from the room without looking at us, closing the door behind him.

A few hours later, Sir James returned from London. We retired to the library, at which time Holmes gave him a delicate summary of the last twenty-four hours, without, however, sparing him from the implications of his sister's involvement.

Sir James sat at the end of the recital, pale and silent. He finally straightened his back and looked forthrightly at us. "Holmes, might I be permitted to ask a question or two?"

"Of course."

"I understand that the conspirators didn't anticipate your presence. But once you were here, why didn't they postpone their scheme? Martha could have slipped out and warned Banton."

"An excellent question. As I just explained, I did take precautions this morning. That doesn't explain why they didn't call it off yesterday. It might have been pure arrogance, but I suspect there is a simpler reason. Recall that Lord Robert mentioned when we arrived that Lord Salisbury was planning on going back to London very soon. That would have unraveled their plans, as it would be simple to hire a cab in London, and their confederate at the livery wouldn't be available without arousing suspicion concerning his absence from here. And often criminals become so caught up in their plans that they don't pause to reconsider."

"I see. My second question is more delicate, and I trust you'll not take it amiss."

"You know me, Saunders. Proceed."

"What do you think will come of all this – especially as regards Martha?"

"The scandal would be tremendous, almost as damaging to the Government as the revelation of the camps. Imagine the press if it latched on to a plot against one of the Prime Minister's chief aides. What other official secrets might have been at risk? Mycroft will undoubtedly ensure that none of this ever becomes public, and Lady Martha likely will live a life of quiet seclusion due to an unnamed illness that has suddenly struck, or some similar stratagem. Your brother-in-law indicated that you might be of assistance in helping her come to grips with the situation, but he probably hadn't thought it through completely, given his shocked state. Perhaps it would better to wait until his return, when you can learn the plan."

"I understand. I'll go to check on her now, but I won't let on that I know. When I'm done, I'll seek you out. I believe a good drink and your company would be helpful."

After he left, I spoke up. "I also have a question. I would have hoped that you would trust me, and not keep me in the dark, allowing me to ramble on about the three young men."

"Trust has nothing to do with it. Your steadfastness is something I can always rely upon. Indeed, I often stake my life on it, as was the case this morning. I apologize for allowing you to go on about the young men and the War. But it did have an element of truth, even if it wasn't the real solution. The Captain must know about the camps, and be was enlisting the other two to assist him to find concrete evidence, even to the extent of trying to worm information from Sauls and gain entry to this room. Even though those efforts were futile, I shall have a word with Mycroft.

"I concede it suited my purposes to mislead our hosts, but I also know you're honest and forthright and might have struggled with my deception, which someone might have noticed. This matter had so many layers of deception – by the culprits, by the three young men – that I felt I needed to counter deception with deception."

"Thank you. I must admit that, if you're correct about what your brother will recommend, concealing this does bother me a bit."

"Unfortunately, you'll be a part of it. You obviously may not write of this, or at least not permit publication for a very long time."

"But is such concealment justice?"

"We prevented a serious crime, Watson. There are times when that must be enough."

"I foresaw this situation," I explained, "and I have brought with me a friend whose discretion may absolutely be trusted. I was once able to do him a professional service, and he is ready to advise as a friend rather than a specialist. His name is Sir James Saunders."

– Sherlock Holmes
"The Blanched Soldier"

The Theft at the Wallace Collection
by Barry Clay

Chapter I

The spring of 1901 in London was a rainy one, and that Thursday in April had been no exception. The skies had poured forth water with determination throughout the day, and I had been forced to make my rounds with my medical satchel in one hand and my raised umbrella in the other – not that it was a completely effective shield against the weather, blown by the wind as the torrent was. I had been pleased to return to the lodgings I shared with my friend, Sherlock Holmes, at 221b Baker Street, where our landlady, Mrs. Hudson, in anticipation of my arrival, had prepared hot tea that she had left in our sitting room. I was no sooner in my chair with a cup than I could hear the rain stop. Though the wind was still brisk, I felt it was rather unfair of the rain to wait until I was safe to abate.

Holmes, who had been working on particularly vile experiment on our dining table, said, "Is Mrs. Carlton improving?"

"Yes," I replied. "She seems to be – How on earth did you know I had been to see Mrs. Carlton? I hadn't planned to do so until I saw that I had the time."

"Cat hairs," my friend replied distractedly. "You told me that good woman has eight cats, and I can see cat hairs of at least six colors and varieties clinging to your trouser legs."

"Well, yes, I can see that," I admitted, and I stood to get a brush.

Still intent on his experiment, he informed me, "I told Mrs. Hudson we would be dining out." I could not but think how thoughtful he had been to her and to me, for the concoction bubbling over the burner on the dining room table, while it had no discernable odor, was an obnoxious and unappetizing green. I had no desire to share my meal with it taking a spot beside my dinner. As I brushed my pants leg, I looked up and saw the liquid turn a bright yellow.

"My goodness," said my friend. "That was unexpected."

And then the flask containing the liquid exploded, flinging a viscous, yellow liquid about the room and onto my friend. Fortunately, I was far enough away that I wasn't struck by it. After his initial astonishment,

Holmes burst into laughter. "Let that be a lesson to you, Watson: Be careful working with ammonium nitrate. I fear that this is no way to improve plaster casts for preserving footprints." After some thought he added, "Though I confess, I didn't expect such a reaction. I wonder if it was quite as pure as I had been led to believe."

I wasn't unaccustomed to my friend's experiments. Indeed, some of them were of such a nature that the results of this one were mild in comparison. Not surprisingly, shortly after the eruption, Mrs. Hudson was at our door, entering at Holmes's invitation.

"I thought I heard something, Mr. Holmes," she said, impassively taking stock of the condition of the room as she entered. Like me, she was used to her lodger's eccentricities.

"An experiment gone awry." He had the grace to look a trifle abashed. "I will set it to right."

"You will not!" she contradicted him. "I will – " But she didn't finish. The sound of the bell being rung, followed by loud banging at our front door, interrupted her. "I will see who that is. Excuse me." And she rushed as quickly as she could down the stairs.

Holmes had already begun picking up broken pieces of the flask and I joined him in the effort. "That was the sound of a prospective client who cannot wait."

Our landlady returned within minutes, ushering a tall, young man with light brown hair into our room. His face was oval and, I thought, handsome. He was so agitated, he barely took in the disarray of the room, but his eyes widened a little at the sight of the yellow substance on my friend's suit. He was breathing deeply, as if he had been exerting himself.

Mrs. Hudson, seeing how we were engaged, shooed us into the sitting portion of our main room. "I will see to this," she told us. "See to your guest."

We left the work of restoring the room to its original condition to the good woman, who made one or two inadvertent sounds of disgust as she did so. The young man looked between the two of us, not quite calmly. "Which of you is Sherlock Holmes?" he asked, his voice pitched high, I thought from agitation.

"I am Holmes," said my friend. "This is Dr. John Watson, who has been of great help to me in many of my cases. What brings you to our humble lodgings so desperately at this hour?"

He was still breathing heavily. "I beg your pardon to barge in so abruptly," he said, "but I have been sent by Mr. Fairdale Hobbs of the Wallace Collection. There has been a theft. The police are there, but they are intent on arresting the wrong man for the crime – a boy really. You must come!"

"Let me commend you on your fortitude," said Holmes. "It is no small feat to run all this way."

He goggled. "How did you know – ?"

"Your pants legs are quite wet, almost to your knees. That wouldn't have happened if you had merely been walking. You were running and taking no care to step around puddles. Had your speed been slower, the splashes of water wouldn't have reached so high. You are out of breath, but only slightly so. Hence, I commend you on your stamina. But here, let me quickly change, and then we will be on our way. Watson, if you would be so good to hail a cab. It is obvious the matter is urgent."

I descended to the street with our visitor, where I was able to flag a growler in short order, holding my coat against the wind. Soon, Holmes, having quickly donned a clean suit, joined us, and the three of us alighted.

"And now," Holmes asked our visitor, "who are you?"

"My name is Foster, Dominic Foster. I work at the Wallace Collection, restoring metals."

"And you say there has been a theft?"

"The payroll has been stolen from Mr. Hobbs's office."

"And the local constabulary has been called?"

"Yes, and they want to arrest Donny."

"And 'Donny' is?"

"Donald Smith – Mr. Smith's son. I'm afraid he is a little simple. They surely have the wrong person. He is only sixteen!"

"That age is hardly one that precludes him from theft."

"But you will see at once that he is innocent!" Mr. Foster was quite adamant, almost desperate, in his insistence. No doubt, Holmes would have questioned him further, but we had already arrived.

I had, of course, heard of the Wallace Collection, which was only a short ten-minute walk from our lodgings. Despite its proximity, I had never been. I had always intended to visit the museum, which was free, but one thing or another had always prevented me from doing so. I doubted if Holmes had the inclination. He appreciated the theatre and the concert hall, but I had never known him to show an interest in art, unless it were in relation to a crime. The cab deposited at the front door of the museum. It was a striking, three-story, red-brick building of immense size, with wood trim painted white. The ornately decorated white *porte-cochère* jutted from its front and reached over its drive and walkway, both of which had been laid in tan stone and stretched under it in an arc.

Holmes paid the fare and the three of us entered through the front doors. No sooner had we done so then it began to rain again, and with no little vigor.

The entryway was breathtakingly striking. The floor and steps were of white marble. A brilliant red carpet with an off-red leaf pattern ascended the steps, which had brown marble, fantastic carved animals, and railings of brown stone with sections overlayed in what I assumed was gold leaf. The combination of gold against the brown was both pleasing and arresting. So remarkable was my initial impression that I didn't at first notice the older man sitting beside the door at a small table, apparently a porter. "Back so soon, Mr. Foster?" he asked.

"Yes, Ryder. I ran."

"Not the whole way!" he exclaimed.

"It was only a couple of minutes," he stated – rather modestly I thought.

"Ah," said Ryder, removing his cap to show a head bereft of hair, "to be young again."

"Are they still in Mr. Hobbs's office?" asked Foster.

"That they are, except the ones in the conference room." His face darkened. "They've got the wrong end of the stick on this."

"We all think so. That's why Mr. Hobbs sent me for Mr. Holmes."

"Well, I hope he can keep young Donny out of gaol, for a finer, more-innocent lad one is unlikely to meet."

Leaving the watchman behind, we followed Foster up the stairs surrounded by a spectacle of paintings, statuary, furniture, and ceramic works of such beauty that I regretted that I had never taken the time to visit with my Mary when she had been alive, for I was certain that she would have appreciated it greatly. Such, I suppose, is the way of life when one is young. One always supposes that there will be time, only to find, perhaps, that there is less of it than one might have thought. *"Carpe Diem"* said the ancients. They weren't far wrong.

The stairway curved both to the right and the left, and we took the left turning, which took us past more rooms in which I caught glimpses of more paintings, statues, and furniture, but also, to my surprise, armour and weapons. One room had, as its focal point, a knight astride a horse, his right arm upraised. It was so prominent and so unexpected that Holmes broke his stride to admire it, forcing Foster to look back at us when he realized we were no longer following. "This way, Mr. Holmes," he urged.

He led us up another flight of stairs to the second story, and it was obvious to me that this section of the museum was, at least in part, reserved for the staff. While no less impressive, it wasn't quite as ostentatious. If there were rooms with exhibits, they couldn't be seen from the hallway. We passed several doors with brass knobs and dark wood that I took to be walnut. Plaques with names were affixed to them, but I only took notice of the richness of the plaques, and noticed none of the names until we reached our destination. Foster stopped at one of the doors on which the name of *F. Hobbs, Managing Director* stood in gold relief on the plaque. He knocked and entered without waiting for an answer.

"Ah, Foster," said an older, distinguished-looking man of medium height upon our entry. "You've made good time." His hair was white with streaks of a darker colour, but full, except for a slight receding at the forehead. His eyes were the grey of metal, but not forbidding. He was dressed in a dark blue suit, white shirt, and blue tie.

A light-skinned woman stood beside him. She had blond hair pulled into a bun over her head, fastened by an unusual brown hairpin, and was blessed with uncommon, pale-blue eyes. Her manner of dress was severe, but becomingly feminine. Glasses hung from a chain around her neck and rested upon her bosom. I was reminded of a school teacher, though she was much younger and far more attractive than any teacher I had ever known. I fancied that her eyes rested a little longer on Mr. Foster than I would have thought our entry warranted, but they quickly turned to look at Holmes and myself.

"Here now! Who is this?" A man wearing a sergeant's uniform was the one who spoke. He had his helmet resting in the crook of his arm. His dark brown hair lay in strips along his balding head, and a large brown mustache nearly obscured his mouth. His head was square. His brown eyes were severe, his mouth unsmiling.

But if his eyes could intimidate one of his subordinates, Hobbs was impervious to them. "This is Mr. Sherlock Holmes." The sergeant opened his mouth to speak – and if I had to judge from his expression – to protest, but Hobbs continued. "Mr. Holmes, Sergeant Peeples."

Peeples turned to Hobbs, indignant. "What is *he* doing here?"

Calmly, the managing director said, "I sent for him." He turned to Holmes. "You performed a great service for the son of a friend of mine. You come highly recommended."

"I hope to be of service." Holmes introduced me, and I took notice of the other men in the room, as well as the cabinet behind the desk, which had been shattered. An imprint of a hand was visibly on the wall beside it. The door had been ripped off the cabinet, and I thought it must have made quite a noise when it happened. Off to the side was a considerable amount of brown paper and string, as if from an opened package. Standing between two constables was a tall young man moving from foot to foot. He held a cap in his hand which he was turning nervously. Our entry must have increased his anxiety, for he was beginning to make pitiable noises.

"Leave off!" ordered the sergeant. "Stop making that noise!"

But instead of stopping, the sounds increased. "I want my Da!" he said. His voice increased in wild intensity. "I want my Da!" The two constables made ready to restrain him, and it looked to me like they had been forced to do so previously and found it no easy task. Both of their uniforms were in disarray, and the young man had the beginnings of a bruise on his forehead. The boy – for he looked no more than a boy for all his size – was a sturdy lad. It was obvious from the way he spoke that he didn't have all his wits. I had two patients of similar mental inability. I looked at Holmes, who nodded to me.

I approached the boy. "Hello," I said. "I am Doctor Watson." I held out my hand. "What is your name?"

He looked at me uncertainly for several moments, then extended his hand, engulfing mine in his. "My name is Donny." He said it shyly. The standard greeting had done much to calm him, and the constables looked relieved.

"Well, Donny, I am pleased to meet you." I could feel the eyes of the others in the room upon us.

He released my hand and began twisting his cap around in a circle between his hands. More calmly, he said, "I want my Da."

"Mr. Holmes and I are here to help," I told him. "Be brave, and Mr. Holmes will return you to your father."

Sergeant Peeples objected. "You have no cause to promise that."

Hobbs explained. "His father works here as a handyman. Donny helps with heavy lifting." I could well believe it. I am not a short man, but the boy towered over me.

Holmes asked, "Where is the boy's father?"

It was Sergeant Peeples who answered. "In the conference room with the others. I'm arresting the boy for theft, and as the father interfered with us in the course of our duties. I've half-a-mind to arrest him, too."

Hobbs interjected, "Arresting this boy is preposterous. He could no more rob my office than I could."

I gathered he and Sergeant Peeples had had this conversation before, for the sergeant said, "You know the facts." He pointed at the cabinet. "It took a strong man to rip that door off its hinges by hand. The print of his hand is right there, where he pressed upon the wall to give him more leverage when doing so." He pointed again, this time to the wall. "And we found the payroll in his lunch bag." He seemed both satisfied and implacable. "Part of it, anyway. That's enough to put him into Newgate, I would wager."

Holmes replied, caustically, "Then you would lose it."

"How's that?"

"The door wasn't ripped off its hinges by hand. I can see the marks of a crowbar on the wood from here."

But Peeples wasn't so easily diverted. "Then he used a crowbar."

"In which case, he wouldn't need to press his hand against the wall for leverage."

"The print is there," persisted Peeples. "And look at its size! No one but the boy could have left a handprint that size."

"The print is obviously false." Holmes turned to the boy. "Please, put your hand on the wall above that print."

He looked to me. "You can trust Mr. Holmes," I assured him. The boy went to the wall and put his palm on it. When he withdrew, he left no print on the wall. He stepped back between the two constables.

Holmes raised his eyebrows and looked at Peeples, who blustered, "That proves nothing."

"It proves that his hands are clean enough not to leave a print on the wall."

"He could have washed them!"

I knew Holmes well, and I could tell he was quickly developing nothing but disdain for Sergeant Peeples. He said, "Watson, I see some wood dust caused by the destruction of the cabinet. Would you be so good as to help the boy put his palm in it, ensure it is well spread about his hand, and then put his print on the wall?"

Donny looked apprehensive, and I did my best to reassure him again. "Mr. Holmes has a reason." He nodded his head, and the others watched as I did as Holmes had directed. This time, when we were finished, there was a dusty print left on the wall.

"There, you see!" crowed Peeples. "They are the same size!"

"But not the same," Holmes pointed out. "A human hand has creases and indentations on it. The second print shows those irregularities, as one would expect. The first print does not."

"Huh," said Peeples, visibly confounded as the proof of Holmes's words was before us.

Attempting to be patient, unsuccessfully I thought, for annoyance bordering on contempt could still be discerned in his voice, Holmes explained. "The first print wasn't left by a human hand. That is obvious by looking at it. It was left by some kind of stamp, perhaps of wood, cut in the shape of a human hand. Since the print is large, it was created to impeach the young man before us." And then he added, "A stratagem that has worked far better than it should have done."

I could see that the two constables were impressed with Holmes's deductions, and to judge from the sideways look he gave them, Peeples was as aware of that fact as I. He wasn't happy to so lose the respect of his subordinates, though I wondered how much of it he had previously. He continued to maintain his position. "That is all well and good, though a trifle out of the way, for we found the payroll in his lunch bag."

Peeples thought it conclusive, but Holmes asked, "And you didn't find that suspicious?"

"The boy is simple," the sergeant stated. I winced, for he spoke in front of the boy without any consideration of his feelings. The lad, however, didn't seem to mind the description. Perhaps he was used to hearing the word "simple" used in relation to him.

Yet I wasn't the only one who took exception with the sergeant's characterization of the boy, for the woman spoke for the first time. "That was unkind," she stated, sternly, but unexpectedly melodiously. "Donny has been employed here for over a year, and he's been doing excellent work. I wish everyone were like him."

The look the boy gave her was nothing short of worshipful.

"Miss Simington is quite correct," agreed Hobbs. "I expected better than this kind of inconsiderate rudeness from the London Police."

"I'm sorry, but it's the truth. The boy is simple. Bandying words will not change that fact. It explains why your so much of your payroll was found in his possession."

"So much?" echoed Holmes. "I gather the entire payroll wasn't recovered then?"

Impatiently, the sergeant returned, "Not yet."

With a voice that could have been used to scorch wood, Holmes said, "I presume you searched for it."

"Well, not yet. The museum is a big place, and we searched the people first."

"Let me summarize your theory as I understand it: The boy put some of the money in his lunch bag because he is simple, but he isn't so simple that he was unable to hide the remainder of the money where you cannot easily find it." Peeples's men looked at him fearfully. No doubt, they knew him better than I did and expected him to take umbrage at Holmes's words. Indeed, his face turned red and his face distorted in anger. Holmes feigned not to notice and continued. "You cannot have it both ways, Sergeant: Either the boy is simple, and you would have found all the money in his lunch bag, or the boy isn't simple, and you wouldn't have found any of it." Holmes's face was impassive, but I knew he, too, was angry, for he said, "If you arrest this boy, I will offer myself to the defense and bear witness on his behalf." And after a moment he added, "It will not go well for you if I do."

I struggled how to best intervene and lessen the rising animosity between the two, and was pleased I didn't have to do so, for Hobbs inserted himself verbally between them. "I think you have made a clear case for Donny's innocence, Mr. Holmes, and am I certain Sergeant Peeples, given time to reflect, will agree. Your reputation precedes you. Your observations and deductions were most impressive."

I wasn't convinced that Peeples considered the matter as settled as the managing director did, but he was intelligent enough to see that his was a losing proposition. When next he spoke, it was in a conciliatory tone. "Perhaps you can help us find the money then, Mr. Holmes."

"I believe we have a more pressing matter at hand. Where is the missing sword?"

The question took me thoroughly by surprise. If I had to judge from the looks of everyone around me, save perhaps the boy, they, too, found Holmes's words equally baffling.

Hobbs cleared his throat. "I don't understand you, Mr. Holmes."

"On our way here, we passed a room that housed armour and weapons. One suit of armour was mounted on a model of a horse, like a knight heading into battle. The arm of the knight was raised as if encouraging the men following him to charge, but it had no sword in its hand, as one would expect. Instead, the hand had been opened and, I suspect, the sword removed."

"I . . . I . . . ." Hobbs seemed at a loss for words, but then regained his composure. "Mr. Holmes, you are correct. That exhibit should have a sword. You say it is missing?"

"I do."

He turned to Foster. "Foster, this is your purview. Did you take the sword?"

He young man blanched. "No, sir! Why would I? Mr. Holmes must be mistaken."

"I assure you, I am not."

"Go check," said Hobbs to his employee. The young man nodded and left the room at a dash. And then the managing director, who had so far mastered his emotions, said, "I pray you are mistaken, Mr. Holmes. This will ruin the reputation of the museum."

Calmly, Holmes said, "Is everyone accounted for?"

"Yes, yes, of course," answered the sergeant.

"How many are here?"

It was Hobbs who answered. "Including those of us here, twelve."

"The others are guarded by two other constables," added Peeples. "They're in a conference room."

"But surely, a concern of this size has more than twelve employees."

"That it does, Mr. Holmes," agreed Fairdale Hobbs, who had seemed to regain his self-control, "but many left prior to the discovery that the payroll was missing."

"It might help if I have a fuller picture of what happened tonight."

311

We all watched as Hobbs gathered his thoughts. "The museum closes at five. The bank delivered the payroll shortly before closing, and I put it in this cabinet, which I locked."

"A safe would have been better," said Holmes, and I agreed.

"We have no safe."

"You should consider the purchase of one in the future," suggested my friend.

"I will do so. We have never had a problem before. The public isn't permitted in this wing of the museum, and we do not advertise our schedule."

"Why did you not distribute the payroll immediately?"

"Many of our staff, particularly those who cook and serve in the garden area outside – we serve meals there, and quite good meals – had already gone home. And I had yet to count it, which I never do alone. Having locked the payroll in the cabinet, I went to find Miss Simington to help me count and divide the pay into envelopes for distribution to the staff tomorrow morning."

"Leaving the room unguarded?"

"I locked the door."

"And does Miss Simington always assist you?"

"Invariably."

"And your entire staff would know this schedule?"

"Of course."

"Go on."

"Miss Simington wasn't in her office. This is not unusual. I roamed the museum for her. I found her in the basement area, where we have workshops and storage areas. She was with Mr. Hastings, our curator, in his workshop."

Miss Simington added, "Mr. Hastings had left a note on my desk, but I couldn't make out his handwriting."

"What had he wanted?"

"That was the odd thing, Mr. Holmes. He said he had left no note."

"Is leaving a note his normal procedure?"

"I can't recall that he had ever left one before, but I handle the scheduling. I thought he might be requesting a day off or a consideration. The note, I fear, was illegible. I could make out his signature, but only because he printed it."

Holmes eyebrows rose. "He handwrote his note but printed his signature."

"Yes."

"Who else has offices in this area of the building?"

Hobbs resumed his narration. "Other than Miss Simington and myself? Terrance Cotter, the Assistant Managing Director. We have a room for a head curator, but that position is currently vacant. We have three museum accountants."

"Were they in their offices?"

"As is their habit, the accountants left at four o'clock. Mr. Cotter is here, but he wasn't in his office. We were short a room attendant, and he was standing in his stead."

"A room attendant?"

"Many of our exhibits are locked in glass, but others are not. We place an attendant in each room. They are trained to answer questions about the exhibits, but they are also there to oversee the guests. We rarely have problems with them, but it happens. There are some – particularly those from eastern countries – who want to touch the paintings. You may not know that there is oil on our fingers that damages oil paintings."

"I have heard that."

"And, I'm afraid, we've had a few breakages. There are signs prohibiting handling of the exhibits, of course, but it happens. Mr. Hastings isn't only one of our curators, but a ceramist of no little skill. He repairs breakages if possible."

Miss Simington said, "He is very expert. He once rescued a piece that had shattered into so many bits I thought it impossible to salvage, but he did so."

"I remember it," said Hobbs. "It took him weeks, but when he was done, you had to examine it closely to see the repairs."

"So, this wing of the museum was unoccupied."

"Yes, I suppose it was."

"Which would explain why no one heard the sound of the cabinet being broken into."

"Yes, I suppose you're right there, too."

"In addition to the fine artwork, statues, furniture, weapons, ceramics, and armour, what else do you have in the museum that might be of value."

"Period chandeliers, but they are rather inaccessible. We also have Limoges enamels, glass, bronzes, and a small collection of gold snuff boxes."

"I assume the latter are kept under lock and key?"

"Of course. Behind glass where they can be admired but not touched. They are too valuable and too portable to be left easily accessible to the public."

"Very well. I have a clearer picture now. You located Miss Simington. What did you do next?"

313

"She and I ascended to my office. It was now past closing time, and our patrons and many of our staff had already left. Mr. Ryder had arrived and Mr. Owen, our day porter, was leaving. The attendants were seeing each to his room. When all is in order, they would sign out with Mr. Ryder."

"When did you and Miss Simington return to your office?"

"Perhaps fifteen minutes after the hour. I unlocked the door and we entered. We found the cabinet as you now see it. The payroll was gone."

"You say you unlocked the door. Who else has a key?"

"Miss Simington keeps all our spare keys."

"Where?"

It was the lady who answered. "In my office, Mr. Holmes."

"And are these spares under lock and key?"

I could see by the look on her face that she immediately understood the implications of the question. "The cabinet can be locked, but I rarely do so in case someone should need a key when I am not available."

"So, anyone could have procured a key from Miss Simington's office, entered your office, broke into the cabinet with a crowbar, absconded with the payroll, and thoughtfully locked your office after he was done."

"I suppose so," admitted Hobbs.

"A most haphazard arrangement, if you will permit me to say so," said my friend. "What did you do when you realized the payroll was gone?"

"I left Miss Simington here and descended to the ground floor. On the way, I saw Mr. Foster in the West Gallery and had him join Miss Simington. I thought it best to have more than one person in the room to prevent accusations later. Mr. Ryder and Mr. Owen were still at the porter's desk, and I sent Mr. Owen to get the police. I instructed Mr. Ryder to let no one else leave."

"That was clear thinking, Mr. Hobbs, but it might have already been too late. The thief might have left after planting some of the payroll in this young man's lunch bag."

"I don't see how someone would have had the time. I had only left the payroll alone for perhaps twenty minutes."

"And yet, someone did."

"Yes, you're quite right. Someone did."

"When did the police arrive?"

"Quite soon after that. Perhaps about half-past. By this time, though, the entire staff knew about the theft and had been informed by Mr. Ryder that they were unable to leave on my order, and they had congregated in the entranceway – except of course for Miss Simington and Mr. Foster, who were standing guard in my office. The police arrived and asked where

314

the staff could be comfortably put to wait. On my recommendation, the police herded everyone to the second-story conference room, and then the police began a search. They found the money in the boy's lunch bag and separated him from his father. I escorted them to my office, and when it became inarguable that they suspected the boy and would likely arrest him, I took Foster aside and asked him to fetch you, giving him a note for Ryder to let him pass. And I am thankful I did."

"Can I go to my Da now?" asked the boy. I was quite ashamed of myself. In listening to Hobbs's recital, I had quite forgotten him.

Hobbs looked at both Holmes and the sergeant. Holmes said, "I see no reason why he cannot rejoin his father." He looked at Peeples. "His father is with the others?"

"Yes. Very well. But I don't want anyone leaving the museum until we find the rest of the money."

"A reasonable precaution. Let us hope the remainder of the payroll hasn't left the building, or we should be here quite a long time."

"Pierce," commanded Peeples, "see that the boy is returned to his father."

One of the constables obeyed, and the boy followed him out, nearly colliding into Dominic Foster, who was returning. His face ashen, he said, "It's gone! I've looked everywhere. The sword is gone!"

Chapter II

His words were greeted with no little consternation.

"Who would have reason to remove the sword?" Holmes asked.

"No one," replied Foster.

"It is one of our finest exhibits and one of our most well known," stated Hobbs. "I can't recall the last time we moved it."

Foster said, "It was before my time, sir, and I've been here five years."

"I assume you have other weapons. Are they as easily accessible?"

It was Foster who answered. "Easily? No. They're all locked up for the protection of our visitors. One would need to break the glass."

"Except for this sword."

"It was twelve feet in the air! Possibly more! One would need a step-ladder to reach it."

"Presumably you have a step-ladder in the museum for hanging paintings?"

"Several actually. I have used them myself."

Peeples seemed uneasy. "Are we sure this matters?"

Holmes awarded the remark with a sharp look at the sergeant. "A sword is missing from an exhibit in a museum where a theft has taken place. Yes, it matters." He looked at Hobbs. "Are you sure your entire staff is accounted for?"

"Well . . . yes. I mean . . . I assume so . . . ." He looked helplessly at Peeples.

"You were told." the sergeant said. "We assembled them all in a conference room."

"Oh, Mr. Holmes," said Miss Simington, "you don't think someone has been harmed!"

"Let us hope not," returned my friend. "I think it would be wise to assure ourselves of that."

"This way," said Peeples, but as we followed him and left the office, the porter, Mr. Ryder, met us.

"Begging your pardon, sir," he began.

Hobbs admonished him. "Ryder, you should be at your post."

"I had no choice, sir," the watchman returned. "There is a boy here, Mr. Smith's son, sent by his mother to see why his father and brother haven't returned home. What should I tell him?"

Peeples exploded. "You're to make sure no one leaves the museum!" he barked.

"But the lad is there – "

"Go back to your post!"

Calmly, Fairdale Hobbs said, "Tell the boy . . . Tell the boy to tell his mother that her husband and son are well, but that there has been a theft at the museum and they are assisting the police. They will be home as soon as practical."

"Yes, sir," said the porter, his face troubled, "but I don't think it will be welcome news."

"I daresay it won't," he murmured. The watchman turned and started back to the stairway from which he had come. As a group, we followed Peeples to a room, outside of which stood a third constable. He opened the door for his superior and we entered.

It was a large, beautifully apportioned room with an oval table that looked to me it would easily seat twenty, and it was well that it could. A fourth constable was watching eight people seated at the table, or in other chairs that stood against the wall. The wallpaper was a luxurious, deep blue with flowered designs, with a wainscot of dark wood below. The boy, Donny, was there, sitting worriedly beside a man nearly as large as he was who I assumed was his father, based upon the obvious likeness between the two. He was dressed in workman's clothing, as was his son. The

316

stubble on his face showed the lateness of the hour. I assumed that at the beginning of his day he had been clean-shaven.

The most striking of the eight people, however, were the two men who I took to be identical twins, or at least brothers who were so alike it would take a mother to tell them apart. They were very blond and handsome, and dressed identically except for the cravats. One wore a navy cravat, the other a dark green. The lateness of the hour had worn upon them somewhat, for their ties were a trifle loose. They were otherwise impeccably dressed and had brass name tags hanging from their coat breast pockets.

Another man, perhaps in his forties, with black hair and swarthy skin, sat at the table, as did an older man dressed in a similar vein as the porter, Mr. Ryder. I assumed the latter to be the day porter, and this was confirmed no little time afterwards. Based upon his dress, I took the swarthy man to be Terrance Cotter, for he bore little resemblance in his clothing to the identical twins.

Two other staff members completed the eight. An older man with a lugubrious and unhappy mein and who appeared nearsighted to me sat at table. He was carelessly dressed, as if he simply didn't care how he appeared to others. An older woman wearing an apron, heavy unladylike shoes, and with a cloth holding back her graying hair was the other.

Hobbs made the introductions. As I had assumed from this dress, the older man, George Owen, was the day porter. Dalton and Devon Carrin were introduced as well, with the comment that they were asked to wear ties of different colours so the staff could tell them apart more easily. Baxter Smith was Donny's father. The older, nearsighted man was Wesley Abberton. He maintained and restored paintings. Upon his introduction, he seemed even sadder to me than he had at first. The swarthy man was indeed the Assistant Managing Director of the museum, Terrence Cotter, and the older woman with the apron was the night cleaning lady, Matilda Voss.

To his staff, Hobbs said, "You have met Sergeant Peeples and his men. This is Sherlock Holmes and his associate, Dr. John Watson, who I have engaged to assist the police in their investigation."

The restorer, Wesley Abberton, said, "But I thought the police had the thief in hand." To his credit, he didn't look at Donny Smith.

Peeples looked uncomfortable, but he admitted, "Mr. Holmes has convinced me that the boy didn't take the money."

Abberton was puzzled. "But I thought you found it with him."

'Yes, we did. But only some of it." He continued to look uncomfortable, and he steadfastly refused to look at Holmes as he spoke.

317

Nonetheless, I gave him credit for his honesty. "I'm afraid that we were meant to suspect the boy."

Baxter Smith responded, with an unfriendly look to Abberton, "I said all along my boy had nothing to do with it."

Disdainfully, Abberton replied, "So you did, but he is your son, and one might presume that you are hardly without bias in the matter."

Objections arose around the table, and I gathered that Mr. Abberton's view was the minority one among the staff.

Hobbs spoke sternly to his restorer. "The matter has now been sorted out, Abberton. The boy is innocent."

But he couldn't leave it alone. "How was one to know?"

Holmes cut into the discussion. "By examining the facts, observing the evidence, and deducing from them, as we have done."

"Quite." said Peeples. "Someone who was less clever than he thought has attempted to pull the wool over our eyes." It seemed to me that the sergeant was rather taking credit for Holmes's work, and yet he still wasn't looking at him. I hoped that he wouldn't be difficult later. I had seen official members of the Force resent Holmes's contributions in the past, and I feared that might occur here.

"When might we go home?" asked Terrence Cotter. "My wife will begin to worry."

Peeples said, "Not until we find the remainder of the payroll."

"We cannot stay here all night!" Cotter objected.

"You will stay here all night if need be!" insisted Peeples.

"Then I must send word."

Fairdale Hobbs added his voice to Mr. Cotter's. "I often work late, so my wife will not be alarmed yet, but she will eventually become so. Certainly, we can send word."

"I cannot spare the men," said Peeples. I thought that most inconsiderate, but I couldn't see how word could be sent without someone leaving the museum, and it was certainly impractical to do so.

"You said everyone was searched?" Holmes asked.

"That they were," returned Peeples. "And quite thoroughly. That was how we came upon the money in the boy's lunch bag."

"But I didn't take anything," the boy said, becoming agitated again, I thought. I wasn't certain he completely understood that he had been exonerated.

"There, there, son. No one thinks you did," comforted his father, though I wasn't certain Mr. Abberton had been convinced by our words. Mr. Smith must have concurred with my assessment, for he cast a look of annoyance, perhaps even of resentment, toward Abberton, as if daring him to say anything to the contrary. If Abberton noticed the look, he ignored

318

it. The boy still looked worried, and he shrank within himself as much as his large frame would permit.

Holmes turned to Hobbs. "One name wasn't mentioned in your introductions – that of Mr. Hastings."

"He isn't here," explained the Managing Director.

The day porter, George Owen spoke up. "Mr. Hastings left before all this hullaballoo began."

"Are you certain?" asked Holmes.

"That I am. Mr. Ryder will say the same. But you don't have to take our word for it. It will be in our log."

Hobbs explained, "The porter keeps a log of entrances and exits from the museum – staff and visitors both."

"You don't have a separate log for the staff?"

"Yes. I apologize that I wasn't clear. The porters maintain it, along with the visitor log."

"You mentioned earlier that Mr. Cotter was serving as a room attendant because one of your staff didn't come to work."

"Yes. Brian Willoughby, who oversees the Back State Room, sent word that he was ill. Mr. Cotter covered for him."

"Returning to Mr. Hastings: We will need to speak with him."

"Why?" Peeples asked. "He left before the theft."

Holmes corrected him. "He left before the theft was *discovered*. We don't know that he left before the theft."

"He couldn't have done it," said Peeples, rather truculently, I thought. "He was in the basement when Mr. Hobbs found Miss Simington there. The two ascended back to the room, leaving him in the basement, and it was only later they found the cabinet broken into and the payroll gone."

"He couldn't have executed the theft, but that doesn't mean he wasn't involved. The note that brought Miss Simington to his basement workroom was attributed to him. Mr. Hobbs, looking for her, met her there. Mr. Cotter was in the Back State Room. The accountants, as is their custom, had left for the day. This note enticed Miss Simington to the basement, and after her Mr. Hobbs, leaving the staff area unattended. It is germane to the theft. Without emptying that staff area of personnel, it couldn't have taken place."

"But he said he didn't write it," Miss Simington observed.

"I rather believe it," returned Holmes, "for it is unusual to write a note and then print the signature. Normally, if one wants to be understood and one's handwriting is difficult to read, one does it the other way around: Prints the note and writes the signature. Despite that, I want to speak with him. He seems to have left the museum at a most opportune time."

At this point, I found myself muddled. There were so many people, some of whom had obviously left, and so much that had happened, all of it unresolved, that I found it difficult to know what needed to be done next. Fortunately, Holmes wasn't similarly handicapped.

He turned to Sergeant Peeples. "If you will permit me to suggest our next steps?"

The policeman answered, I thought rather tartly, "It hasn't appeared to me that you've needed my permission up until now."

"You must begin a search of museum. We need to find the remaining payroll, which may still be here. We should look for the crowbar that was used to enter the cabinet. And there is the missing sword for which to account."

These words caused no little dismay among those who had been held in the conference room and didn't know if the sword's disappearance. "A sword is missing?" Mr. Cotter exclaimed. "From one of the cases?"

"No, from the knight on horseback," Holmes stated.

"From the primary European Armoury room," clarified Mr. Foster.

That Cotter was bewildered was evident. "But why?"

"It couldn't have been with innocent intent, I fear," answered Holmes.

"But no one is hurt. We are all well."

"Those here aren't the entire staff of this museum," Holmes pointed out.

It was then that Peeples spoke. "I don't have the men to search these premises, Mr. Holmes, not and guard these folks here."

"Then we need to get more, for this must be done."

"You ask much," complained Peeples.

"I ask only for what is needed," returned my friend.

They stared at each other, each looked unwilling to yield, until finally Peeples barked, "Myers!"

One of the constables smartly stood before him and saluted. "Yes, sir?"

Without taking his eyes off of Holmes, Peeples ordered, "Take the police cab. Go to the station. Gather as many of the lads as you can, and return."

"Yes, sir." And he saluted and left the room.

"Satisfied?" Peeples asked Holmes.

"Somewhat. I don't think we should wait until your men return. We should begin now."

"How do you propose we do that?"

"We leave these men and women here with instructions that no one leaves the room – "

"But," objected the day porter, Mr. Owen, "what if we need to . . . you know?"

"You didn't permit me to finish. No one is to leave unless there is no recourse, and no one will leave this room alone for any reason. I see paper and pen on that desk against the wall. If someone leaves, someone must record those who do, the time they leave, and the time they return. They will be accompanied by a constable. I suggest Mr. Cotter maintain that list. We then take your remaining men, Sergeant, along with yourself, Watson, and myself, and we begin the search, splitting the five of us between the floors. A crowbar and the sword will not be easily hidden."

"We have several crowbars for uncrating boxes in the receiving room," Hobbs interjected.

"We are looking for one that is out of place."

"I can help look," the Managing Director asserted.

"You cannot," said Holmes. "I'm afraid that you are also a suspect until this matter is resolved."

Hobbs's eyebrows raised in mild surprise. "It was I who brought you here, Mr. Holmes," he pointed out.

"And I hope to earn my fee, Mr. Hobbs. That is why you must stay until the payroll is found. There must be no suggestion that you yourself pilfered the payroll, for you certainly had the time alone to do so."

"Oh," he said, taken aback. He recovered quickly. "I see your point."

"The only ones who can be trusted not to be involved are the police, Watson, and myself." He turned to Peeples. "I would suggest you take one of your remaining constables to the story below and begin a search. Watson and I will go to the ground floor and do the same. The last constable will go through the rooms on this floor."

Hobbs pointed out, "Some of them will be locked."

Holmes nodded. "Miss Simington has told us that she has duplicate keys in her office. The constable searching this floor will escort Miss Simington to her office, obtain the keys, and escort her back. He will then search this story, including the offices. May I suggest that her departure and return with the constable be recorded."

"This will take an infernally long time," said Peeples.

"Then we had best be started."

We had turned to the door to the room, when it opened, and a boy of perhaps fourteen years entered, holding a sack. He was a handsome lad, with blond hair that wasn't quite tamed, and blue eyes.

"Who the devil are you, and how did you get in here?" barked Peeples, and for once, I couldn't blame him.

Chapter III

I would have expected a boy of his age to react with dismay at such an angry greeting, but he seemed singularly unaffected by the sergeant's angry tone. Instead, he spoke quite calmly and respectfully. "I beg pardon, sir. Abel Smith, at your service."

"Abbie!" shouted Donny gleefully, and he left his father's side, pushed past a constable in his excitement, and wrapped his arm around his brother, lifting him from the floor with ease, for Abel Smith, though perhaps tall for his age, had the slimness of youth. Still, given the older boy's size, I rather expected that Donny could have lifted any of us without particular effort. He set his brother down. "They think I stole money, Abbie," he said fearfully.

It was instructive watching them. Donny was clearly the elder of the two, and the larger, but he was the younger in maturity, for Abel unmistakably set about to reassure his older brother as if he had done so previously on other occasions and accustomed to doing so. "I'm sure that's all a mistake, Donny. You shouldn't worry. Right, Da?"

Baxter Smith said, "Right you are, son, but I must ask the same question the sergeant did: How did you get here?"

"Mother sent me with dinner," he said holding up the sack. "When I couldn't say how long you would be here, she said that there was no reason you should go without your supper."

"Ah, your mother is a good woman."

"And she had me bring extra when I told her I didn't know how many others might be detained here, too." He lifted the sack to demonstrate. Abel Smith's speech was clear and precise, beyond his age, and even more, I thought, beyond his station. His clothing was clean but worn, telling me that his family wasn't a wealthy one. And yet, his mother had packed a very full sack of food, showing no little consideration and generosity.

"You'll thank her for us, son."

"That I will, Da."

"Very touching, all of this," said Peeples, "but how did you get in?"

"Through the front door of the museum, sir," Abel answered.

"It wasn't locked?"

"No, sir."

"Where was the porter?"

"Beg pardon, sir, but I don't know."

I winced as Peeples angrily shouted oaths that shouldn't have been spoken in mixed company, much less in front of children. However, the cleaning lady, Matilda Voss, was only appreciative of the tirade when the

322

sergeant was finished. "That was a good run," she said. "I haven't heard the like since me husband up and died."

Peeples was not amused. "Pierce, go find him!" After saluting, the constable departed, leaving his superior visibly fuming. "This is all at sixes-and-sevens." He turned to Holmes. "We hardly have enough men to search now."

"But we must do so. Perhaps when Constable Pierce returns."

"But while we wait," asked Mr. Abberton, "might we distribute the food? I, for one, am famished."

Peeples assented with little grace, I thought, and the younger Smith boy brought the sack to his father, who began to distribute food. There was bread and cheese, and I thought I recognized currant cakes among the provisions. Donny brought some bread and cakes to both Holmes and me, walking past Sergeant Peeples as he did so. Recognizing that he was being snubbed, the sergeant made a face, but said nothing. We thanked the boy and ate quickly. The bread was fresh, and the cake was sweet. They weren't up to Mrs. Hudson's standards, perhaps, but they were very welcome.

When Constable Pierce returned with Mr. Ryder, Peeples vented his spleen at the night porter. "Where were you? This boy," he pointed at Abel Smith, "walked in without so much as a by-your-leave. Why weren't you at your post?"

"Well, sir, I had to use the facilities, and there weren't no one to tell."

Holmes's face was without emotion, but I knew he was amused when he said, "Apparently not even the local constabulary can preempt a call to nature."

"Is the door still open?" asked Peeples.

Constable Pierce answered, "I had him lock it before bringing him here."

"Well, then let's stick him here so he can't go wandering again!"

"If I may . . ." began Holmes.

"What!" returned Peeples with no little ire.

"You sent a constable to bring help to search the museum. They will be unable to enter if there is no one at the door to unlock it."

"What a morass this is!" Peeples exclaimed with vehemence, then added more calmly, "You are right."

"It isn't ideal, but I suggest you put both porters at the door. They can watch each other. We'll begin the search as we agreed. When the rest of your men arrive, they can be admitted. After that, a constable can relieve them and the two can return here."

And that was what we did. As Holmes had proposed, one constable searched the second story, Peeples and another constable searched the first, and Holmes and I had covered the ground floor. The museum, which I assumed had originally been a grand home because rooms were often labeled "*Dining Room*" or "*Breakfast Room*", was large, and I was pleased when we could hear the sound of help arriving. Five more constables were admitted by the porters. Since Holmes and I were on the ground floor, it was Holmes who directed a constable to remain at the door, the porters having provided one of their keys, another to escort the porters to join the others, and the rest he distributed to the different stories of the museum to search it.

Although the circumstances were dire and not given to dawdling or admiring the exhibits, I couldn't help but appreciate their beauty as we worked. It was an astounding, magnificent collection. I recognized paintings of the masters, some of which I had heard spoken of but had never seen. But our purpose prevented us from admiring them at leisure. There was statuary behind which to look, doors of resplendent cabinets to open, showcases that partially divided rooms, and a seeming endless number of rooms in which to search.

At one point, Holmes stopped before a glass in which were shelves displaying the gold snuff boxes to which Hobbs had alluded. Catching sight of him, I asked, "Have you found something?"

"Perhaps," he said. When he abandoned the shelving, I went to it. The boxes were beautifully polished, ornate works of gold. To my surprise, one was damaged. A small scratch left a dark wound on it, but outside of that, I saw nothing that could have attracted Holmes's interest.

It was after this that Peeples joined us at the ground floor, carrying a crowbar and a wrapped package that was bound by twine. "Where were they found?" asked Holmes.

"An empty office, or so I am told."

"The one left vacant until a new head curator is engaged?"

"Yes. The crowbar was behind curtains. The money was found on the floor. According to Constable Myers, there was no attempt to hide them."

"But the package you identify as the payroll is wrapped. How did the constable know what it was?"

"He didn't. He had taken Miss Simington to get the keys to all the rooms. He escorted Miss Simington to the conference room to join the others, then began to search as directed. When he found the crowbar and the package, he returned to the conference room and confirmed with Mr. Hobbs that the package appeared to be the payroll. Then he went to find me."

"Interesting, and extremely suggestive."

"Should I arrest her?" I couldn't help but notice the change in his manner to Holmes. He wasn't quite deferential, but it was obvious to me that he was beginning to appreciate that my friend had his uses.

"Miss Simington?"

"Yes. She had possession of the keys."

"By no means. It is obvious that her keys are hardly effectively secured. Surely, Sergeant, you perceive that this discovery puts an entirely new complexion on this theft."

"I . . . I don't know what to say. It makes no sense."

"Let me help you make sense of it. Why did you think the Smith boy had stolen the payroll?"

He struggled to answer before stuttering, "Because . . . because he had the money."

"And yet," Holmes pointed out, "you are holding the payroll in your hands, wrapped, and to all appearances, intact."

The sergeant's mouth opened with the realization of what this find meant. "But . . . but why? Why this tomfoolery?"

Grimly, Holmes said, "The missing sword concerns me even more now. There, I suspect, is the reason behind this tomfoolery."

"Shall I call off the search?"

"We have yet to find the sword, and we haven't even begun to look in the museum basement, where we are told workrooms and storage rooms are housed. I suspect they present quite a warren. No. We must continue the search until that sword is found. I'm fearful what may occur if we don't locate it. I am fearful it may be too late. It is now nearly eight o'clock, and the chaos of this evening may have been a charade with no other purpose than to obscure more sinister schemes." He paused. "Have this money counted to be certain, but I suspect that none of it is missing."

"Then where did the money in the boy's lunch bag come from?"

"That is an extremely germane question. If we can answer that, I suspect we'll know all – or at least be well on our way to the solution of this mystery. I would like to speak with Mr. Smith and his son. Bring both of the boys. The younger appears to have a calming influence on the older."

"I will bring them myself."

"And some of these men searching with us can begin the search of the lower level."

Peeples sent two of the three constables who had been helping us to do so, and he left us to bring Baxter Smith and his sons. Keeping my voice low, I said, "Holmes, I find this all most perplexing. I must agree with Sergeant Peeples. It makes no sense to steal a payroll and then leave it. This all seems very complicated."

325

"It is deviously complicated. Something is afoot here that has nothing to do with common thievery. My mind would be relieved considerably if we were to find that sword."

In short order, Sergeant Peeples returned with the Smiths. The older boy, Donny, still appeared worried and fearful. The younger boy, unusually self-possessed, looked to be more curious than anything.

"Mr. Smith, you and your sons have had a trying evening, for which I apologize."

"It weren't no fault of yours," returned the father.

"No, but I apologize that I must ask you further questions. Did you and your son lunch together?"

"We did."

"When?"

"At noon."

"Is that your normal hour?"

"It is."

"Did you eat with anyone of the staff?"

"Look at us, Mr. Holmes. We're workmen, Donny and me. It isn't for the likes of us to eat with the staff. We eat in the receiving room."

"Which is where?"

"In the basement. There is an entrance from the back alley to the museum. We receive deliveries and open them there."

"I wouldn't have thought there were so many that it would fully occupy the two of you."

"There aren't. We carry and help move. We fix things that need mending."

"So, you aren't always in this receiving room."

"No."

"And today?"

"We were out and about. We spent no little time in the Oriental Armoury Room, helping Mr. Hobbs rearrange it in expectation, he said, of an added shipment of armour from Japan, if I remember right."

"And that was in the afternoon?"

"It was that, sir."

"And where was your son's lunch bag during this time?"

"It was with our things."

"In the receiving room?"

"Aye, sir."

"Is this room kept locked?"

"Why would it be?"

"No reason. Then anyone in the staff could enter that room?"

"That they could, and, in fact, they do when there is need."

"Who was there today?"

"I saw no one, but then we were so little there. Oh, at one point, Mr. Hastings stuck his head in to ask if the delivery of ceramics he was expecting had arrived, but I told him 'No'. It was when we was eating."

"But other than him, no one?"

"That's a fact."

"I want more and more to speak with this Mr. Hastings," he said, almost to himself. Then, to Mr. Smith, "Do I assume correctly that it was only when you were leaving, and prevented from doing so, carrying your things including your son's lunch bag, that you were taken to the conference room and searched?'

"Yes, sir. That's correct."

Holmes turned to Donny, and the boy shrunk back a little from him, only gaining courage when Abel said, "It's all right Donny. Mr. Holmes only wants to ask you questions."

"And then I can go home?"

Abel glanced at Holmes and said, "Maybe not just yet, but soon, I hope."

Holmes asked the boy, "Did you see anyone in the receiving room?"

"I seen nobody."

"But your father said Mr. Hastings was there."

Donny's brow furrowed. "Then he was."

"But you don't remember?"

Before Donny could answer, Mr. Smith said, in a lowered voice, "You cannot count on Donny, Mr. Holmes. He confuses days." A pained expression spasmed across his face. "He don't have a good mind, Mr. Holmes. He's a good boy, and gentle, but . . . Once he was like Abel here. He spoke very young. But a spooked horse run him over when he was a-playin' on the street. He weren't more than four or five. He wasn't the same after." He repeated. "You can't trust him, Mr. Holmes."

"I understand, Mr. Smith, but I would be negligent in my duties if I didn't ask. He might know something of importance."

I was afraid that if the boy did, it would never be discovered.

Holmes must have had a similar thought, for he asked the father, "May I speak with your younger son?"

His brows furrowed. "You may, but he wasn't here and knows nothing."

"I have an idea, but it concerns your younger son, if you will trust me."

"You've kept my Donny out of Newgate, Mr. Holmes. You have my trust."

327

Holmes withdrew Abel aside and spoke in a low voice to him while we watched. The boy nodded several times, and then the two returned to us.

It was at this point that the constables who had been sent to search the lower level of the museum returned, nearly at a run. One of them said, "We have found the sword, and it is in a dead body."

Holmes expelled air from his lungs. "I feared as much."

Chapter IV

Holmes wasted no time. He said to one of the constables, "Fetch Sergeant Peeples and Mr. Hobbs. Bring them to the body." The constable obeyed, dashing up the main stairway as if Holmes had been a member of the Force. Holmes said to Mr. Smith, "Take your boys back to the conference room. This isn't a sight for them."

"Aye, Mr. Holmes. That it isn't." And he turned with his boys, following the constable more slowly up the stairway.

To the remaining constable, Holmes said, "Take us." The stout officer, perhaps my age or a little older, led us to the stairway from which the lowest level was accessed. As Holmes had predicted, it was a warren of rooms. I suspected them of having been, at one time, living quarters for servants, as the upper rooms we had seen I thought too capacious for that class, but these rooms appeared to me to be no better and no worse than one might reserve for a cadre of servants. Despite the twistings and turnings of the path, the constable didn't hesitate. He took us directly to the body of a man resting in a corridor that ended in front of us, then stood aside so we could examine the corpse.

"Watson," said Holmes, indicating that I should look first. I couched beside it.

A sword, no doubt the one for which we had been searching, impaled the body through the chest, but it wasn't the only thrust of the sword. Although the body was laying on its side, I could see another wound in the abdomen. I doubted it would have been fatal, or at least quickly fatal, but it would have been incapacitating. Another slice was obvious on the right arm, where the man and had attempted to defend himself. Both the sleeve and abdomen were liberally covered by blood, but it was the last thrust of the sword in the chest that had ended the man's life. A touch to his carotid artery and the lack of warmth assured me that he was quite dead, though perhaps not long so.

The man was a small one, somewhat portly, with a face that, even in death, reminded me of a rabbit. His eyes were small and partially opened, and one could see the unmistakable opaqueness of death in their dullness.

I had seen this too often in the war. *Pince-nez* spectacles lay on the floor beside the nondescript, puffy face. His hair was thinning to the point where any attempt to cover the baldness would have been ludicrous, and yet he had made the attempt, for strands of hair had been combed over the pate.

He was dressed conservatively, in a brown three-piece suit. His shoes were also brown. One trouser leg had hitched up, revealing both one sock and the pink flesh of his leg. A watch chain hung from his vest pocket, in which I assumed was a pocket watch, and it connected to a button on his vest. There was a red carnation in the lapel, somewhat damaged by his fall, I thought. To my mind, it was an affectation of a man whose life was solitary and grey, and yet who insisted on some beauty in it, a kind of weak rebellion against a world for which he was unprepared to handle. I told myself at the time that I was reading too much character into these details, but later words were to confirm my impressions.

I rose, and Holmes asked, "How long has he been dead?"

"I can only make a rough estimate, but I would say two hours. No more than three."

"Three would place the hour at five, and he is reported to have been seen alive then," said Holmes. He, in turn, knelt to examine the corpse. He didn't touch it. "Left-handed, as he attempted to protect himself with the right, an unconscious defensive maneuver to keep the dominant hand free to attack, not that he appears to be a man accustomed to physical struggle. He is dressed as a banker might, but I see marks of glue staining the cuffs, and I see burns such as one might have from sparks from a kiln. He was nearsighted, perhaps from many years of close work. The carnation was fresh this morning, but the heat surrounding his work has taken its toll on it. You can see from the scuffing on the floor that the struggle was minimal. He was taken by surprise, and his defense was ineffectual. The cuffs of his pants legs and his shoes are wet."

As Holmes spoke, I took stock of where we stood. It was more of a corridor than a room. There were shelves on one side, and a handful of small boxes on the other, and yet there was room to walk easily between them. The body lay on its side, its back to the shelves. A small folder lay beside the head, and I assumed it was knocked from the shelves during the struggle that Holmes had categorized as "ineffectual". It had several streaks of blood, and I thought the mark of fingers on it, though it was hard to be certain because the marks were smeared.

At the end of the corridor, on the right side, was a sturdy, wooden door, bolted from the inside of the corridor. On the left side, opposite the door, were leaves curled along the wall. Between the two was the bare block of the foundation. The floor in front of the door glistened with moisture, and I assumed some liquid had been spilled there, though I saw no container that might have held it.

In a short time, the second constable arrived, escorting Peeples and Hobbs. The Managing Director made a sound of dismay at the sight of the body.

"Do you recognize him, Mr. Hobbs?" Holmes asked.

"Of course I do. It's Hastings. Tucket Hastings, our curator."

"As I recall, you also said he is the man who repaired your ceramics."

"Yes. But why? Who would do such a thing? I would have said he hadn't an enemy in the world." His face was drawn in sorrow.

"But didn't the porters say he had left?" Sergeant Peeples asked.

"They did," affirmed Holmes.

"Then how did he get here?" Suddenly his face suffused in anger, and he answered his own question. "They let him back in and didn't mention it!"

"I think not," said Holmes, "but it would be prudent nonetheless to inquire. I would suggest we speak with them. Have them bring their log-book."

One of the constables went to fetch them, and Holmes spent the time waiting for them by carefully examining the area around the body. He had withdrawn his magnifying glass, and he used it to lift one edge of the folder, only to find it empty. He used it to coax out the pocket watch. "Unfortunate," he said. "It is still working. Had it broken in the fall, we would have known exactly when he was killed." He touched nothing directly, but used the magnifying glass to move those items. At one point, he commented, "Here the sword rested on its tip, waiting to be used." He then slowly made his way from the body to the bolted door, examining it and the bolt closely.

Holmes concluded his investigation only when the constable returned the night and day porters, Mr. Ryder and Mr. Owens. Both gawked at the corpse before them. Peeples immediately asserted himself, fixing his eyes on the two men. "You said Hastings had left."

"And he had," affirmed Ryder.

"What's he doing here?" asked Owen. "How did he get here?"

"When did Mr. Hastings leave the museum?" asked Holmes.

"I'd have to check me logs," said Ryder, and he opened the log book he had been carrying. "It was ten minutes after five."

"I was off duty," added Owen, "but I was there. Me and Ryder are mates. We always talk a bit before I goes home."

Peeples spoke accusingly. "While you were jawing, Mr. Hastings came back without you noticing!"

330

Holmes interrupted the pair before they could respond. "I have already said that I doubted that," he said, with a note of reproof in his voice."

"Oh? Then how did he get here?"

Holmes pointed. "Through that door."

"The door is bolted from this side," observed Peeples with emphasis, as if he needed to explain the obvious to someone who was dim-witted. I gathered he was enjoying obtaining some of his own back.

"But certainly, you noticed the green leaves there against the wall, quite wet. The flakes of rust on the floor before the door. The water pooling off to the side, and, not last nor least, the broken thread tied to the bolt."

"Eh?" Peeples seemed not to know what to make of what Holmes said.

"And the bolt has been recently oiled. You can see the sheen, and even smell the oil."

"But that makes no sense, Mr. Holmes," Hobbs said. "As far as I know, that door hasn't been opened in years – at least as long as I have been here. We have had no need of it. We receive shipments at the larger double doors on the other side of the lower level. I suspect this was used for the servants who lived in the basement, so they would have the ability to enter and leave with some privacy on their days off. It might have been a wall for all the use we made of it."

Holmes responded to Hobbs's assertion. "And yet, the bolt has been oiled, and recently."

"This is all well and good," stated Peeples, showing his frustration "but it doesn't get us any closer to knowing who has done all this."

"On the contrary," said Holmes diffidently. "It tells us everything."

"What?" Peeples actually blinked in astonishment.

Holmes repeated himself. "It tells us everything. I believe I know all."

"You know who did this?"

"Indeed. It can only be one person. I suspect I know why that person has acted in that manner, and I hope to confirm that next." He turned to Hobbs. "You said that there are workrooms here, and that Mr. Hastings was a ceramist. Is his workroom in this lower level?"

"It is."

"Please take us there."

Hobbs led all of us through the maze of rooms until he came to a larger room that had several worktables and a kiln, such as would be used for pottery or ceramics. Residual heat from the kiln kept the room warmer than the rest of the basement. Several pieces of ceramics were on the workbench. Holmes approached the bench on which they rested and looked at them. "As I thought," he said, obviously satisfied.

331

I looked at them and saw nothing, except some of them were streaked with dirt or paint.

"I see nothing," Sergeant Peeples said.

"Perhaps you are unaware that gold, being a soft metal, when scratched on ceramic, will leave a golden streak behind."

"Well, no. I had never heard that."

"But, Holmes," I pointed out, "only some of these streaks are golden."

"Precisely," said Holmes. He turned to the sergeant. "Let me congratulate you, Sergeant. You are about to arrest a most ingenious, ruthless, and clever thief, who vainly resorted to murder in an attempt to conceal his crimes." And he added, with a hint a twinkle in his eye, "It should be quite a feather for your cap."

Chapter V

As a group, we returned the second-story conference room, having first gathered all the constables who were still searching the museum. Combined, there were nine of them, and with their superior, the three members of the museum staff, Holmes, and me, we made a not-inconsiderable party. At Holmes's insistence, we stopped at the room with the armour. "It is good to be thorough," he told us. He examined the area around the knight on the horse. Satisfied, he observed, "As I expected: The faint marks of a step-ladder."

Our entrance to the room was met with a barrage of questions. Some were indignant, others concerned or weary. A few spoke timidly. No matter how it was voiced, they were all in agreement that they wanted to go home, and that they felt they had been detained at the museum long enough.

"I quite agree," Holmes said, "but if you will permit me half-an-hour, perhaps an hour if you delay me with questions and comments, I believe we can resolve this matter and bring the guilty party to justice."

Sergeant Peeples added his voice of authority to Holmes's statement. "This here isn't just theft now. It's murder." Sounds of shock and horror went around the room. More than one person asked who had been killed.

It was Hobbs who answered. "I am very sorry to inform you that one of our own, Mr. Tucket Hastings, has been murdered with the sword taken from the primary European Armoury room."

"Someone broke into the cabinets?" asked one of the twins, incredulous.

"No. The sword held by the knight on horseback had gone missing."

"How is that possible?" The other twin asked. "It's completely out of reach!"

"As one might expect," said Holmes, "a step-ladder was used. The marks it left on the floor are clearly visible."

The first twin spoke, as if the two were volleying the conversation between them. "But then someone would have seen it done."

Holmes, impassive, responded, "I'm sure someone did, and thought nothing of it."

Abberton said, "You're being very mysterious."

"Not at all. I'm confident that any number of people saw it happen, but because it was removed by a museum staff member, they assumed he was acting in the course of his duties."

Baxter Smith, the handyman, asked, "Are you saying one of us did it?"

Peeples was the one who answered instead of Holmes. "That's exactly what we're saying."

Holmes gave him a sharp look, but only added, "There are one or two facts that we must confirm before we arrest the murderer. May I request that you all stand against that wall."

There was some grumbling, but they all did so. Holmes slowly walked up and down, examining their shoes and trousers. When he had walked the length of them, he said, "You may all regain your seats. As I expected, none of you show the signs of having been outside, except for Mr. Foster, Mr, Owen, and Mr. Ryder. Your shoes and trousers are dry."

"What does that prove?" scoffed Abberton.

"It indicates that none of you, except Foster, Owen, or Ryder, could have killed Mr. Hastings."

All three men started, and Miss Simington exclaimed, "What?" Everyone else, including myself, was quite at a loss.

"Let us not be so hasty, Mr. Holmes," enjoined Peeples. "I don't follow that at all. Anyone here could have murdered the poor man."

Holmes contradicted him. "No, not anyone here, for the murderer clearly entered from outside the museum, through the door in the basement."

"You heard Mr. Hobbs," Peeples pointed out. "That door hasn't been opened for years."

"On the contrary, the indications are that it *was* opened recently. I had thought I was clear on that fact. Remember what we saw: There are flakes of rust lying in front of the door from the hinges that, until today, had been rusted shut. They fell to the floor when the door was opened. The bolt has been recently oiled. When one approached it, as I did, one could see the sheen of the newly applied oil, and even smell it. It's still wet outside because of the recent rain, and the leaves that were in the hallway opposite the door were green and damp. They hadn't been there long. They were opposite the door because they were blown by the wind that knocked them from the trees and into the basement when the door was opened. The floor was wet from their passage, that and the passage of Mr. Hastings."

"But he had left the museum."

"And he returned through that door. I had pointed out that his shoes and cuffs of his trousers were wet as well. Mr. Ryder and Mr. Owen did indeed see him leave, but he returned through that door." After a pause, he said, "And so did his murderer."

Sergeant Peeples seemed equally perplexed and unbelieving. "The door was bolted!" he blustered. "From the inside!"

"It was bolted," agreed Holmes, "but *not* from the inside."

"How can you possibly know?" the sergeant scoffed.

"Because of the broken thread hanging from the bolt."

Silence greeted this statement. In the past two hours, I had watched the sergeant veer from derision of my friend, to respect, and then back again. I could see he didn't understand Holmes's reasoning. For that matter, neither did I. But I could see Peeples hesitate, no doubt recalling Holmes's deductions in Hobbs's office that had deconstructed his intention of arresting the boy, Donny. I could see him grappling with the possibility that the broken thread hanging from the bolt had a meaning that escaped him, and he didn't want to appear foolish in front of his men and these witnesses by disputing with Holmes about it – and perhaps losing the argument again.

Finally, he asked, "What does that mean to you?"

"Have you never, as a boy, bolted a door by tying a thread to the bolt and then pulling it shut from the other side?"

"Never."

Holmes actually smiled. "It is quite a trick, and confounding to adults. A room locked from the outside in this manner is quite inaccessible. Entry to the room must be affected by a window, sometimes using a ladder, or if the windows are locked, the door must be removed from its hinges. Some children find this diverting." I couldn't help but wonder if Holmes hadn't been one of them. He rarely spoke of his childhood, nor of his youth, even to me. I rather thought I had been given a glimpse into what it might have been like to raise a very young Sherlock Holmes, who hadn't yet quite decided to confine his activities to the moral side of the equation.

And then I found myself wondering if his older brother, Mycroft, might also have participated in such devilment. As soon as the thought occurred to me, I dismissed it. I couldn't picture the elder Holmes engaged in such mischief. I could barely picture Holmes so occupied.

"This is – ?" Peeples asked. "Why would someone go to all that trouble?"

"I would have thought that was obvious."

Hobbs said, "Not to me. This is incredibly baffling. Are you certain of this, Mr. Holmes?"

"I am. You can even see where the thread rubbed against the door while the bolt was being drawn shut. It left a mark."

"Then I ask again," repeated Peeples, "why go to all that bother?"

"Because it gave the appearance that Mr. Hastings had been murdered by someone confined to the museum and not someone who had been outside."

Understanding flooded Peeples's face. "Ryder, who left his post! It was him. And his shoes are still wet!"

"But I told you," the porter exclaimed, "I had to step out!"

"It wasn't Mr. Ryder, Sergeant," clarified Holmes. "His shoes and trousers bore the unmistakable signs of moisture because he had arrived to work shortly before the rain ended. He and Mr. Owen watched Mr. Hasting leave the building. He was at his post when Watson and I arrived with Mr. Foster, and by that time, Mr. Hastings was dead."

"Are you certain?"

"Watson?" Holmes said, turning to me.

"As certain as I can be without investigation on the table by the medical examiner. His body was cooling, but not cold. The blood had congealed. He couldn't have been alive much past six o'clock, and I would have said earlier."

"Then it was Owen! He did it before he fetched us!"

The other porter made a noise of dismay, a look of fear washing over his face.

Holmes answered, "Possibly, but you are forgetting the sword."

"Eh?"

Holmes continued to explain. "As Mr. Hastings had been seen alive and well at ten-after-five, it rather narrows down the list of those who could have killed him. Most of those who are now here, outside of Watson, myself, the police, and Mr. Owen who ran to notify the police, had been confined to the museum by the discovery of what was thought to be the theft of the payroll, and after the police arrived, confined to the conference room on the second story. Mr. Ryder was the exception, and he had no need to leave the building to obtain access to the basement. There is only one person who was free to commit the murder and who had left the museum, and who could have re-entered the museum through the basement door, murdered Mr. Hastings, and then drew the bolt shut from the outside using the thread before running to 221b Baker Street to enlist my services."

Suddenly, Foster attempted to exit the room through one of the other doors, and was only prevented from doing so by the constable closest to him.

Forced to stay in the room, Foster cried, "How can you say such things, Mr. Holmes? I'm on your side!"

"You are on no one's side but your own," my friend declared.

"Here, now," Sergeant Peeples said, "I'm sure you know what you're about, but before I arrest a man, I have to know why I'm doing so, and moreover, how I can prove it."

Miss Simington seemed singularly affected by Holmes's revelation. "Why would Dominic want to murder Mr. Hastings?" Her voice was almost pleading. "Mr. Hastings was such an inoffensive man. What possible reason could he have?"

Holmes was sober. "Mr. Hastings suspected that someone had been replacing gold snuff boxes with forgeries, and he had the misfortune of confiding his suspicions to the very man who was responsible."

His words were met with astonishment. Those of us who had been with Holmes earlier, in Hastings' workshop, were only slightly less surprised.

My friend continued. By this time, no one was asking to leave. We were all hanging on his words.

"The Wallace Collection, from what I have seen, is a sprawling and eclectic collection of various forms of art: Paintings, porcelain, sculpture, ceramics, furniture, and even armour and weapons, though I would have thought the latter would qualify more as history than artwork. And as we were told and I observed myself, there is a collection of gold snuff boxes. It was while engaged in the search for the missing sword that I came upon a collection of these boxes, and, to my surprise, saw a golden snuff box that had been slightly damaged, showing a dark scratch along it edge."

Hobbs interrupted my friend. "But that can't be, Mr. Holmes! A scratch on gold would only reveal more gold."

"Precisely, Mr. Hobbs. I'm afraid that some of your gold snuff boxes have been replaced with imitations."

I watched as the Managing Director struggled with that information. He looked at Foster. I could see the realization dawn on him that his metal smith should have known of the substitutions, and the fact that he didn't was particularly damning.

Foster, under his gaze and the implied question, claimed, "I know nothing of this."

Peeples said, "Gold snuff boxes, Mr. Holmes?"

"Imitations, Sergeant."

"But we were called here for the missing payroll!"

"Indeed, but the cause of everything was the snuff boxes. We didn't know that at first, but we know it now."

Peeples was struggling manfully to keep up. "We do?"

"We do," Holmes affirmed. "The theft of the payroll, which you will recall wasn't actually stolen, was a diversion, concocted by Mr. Foster, to cover the thefts and substitutions of the golden snuff boxes. The gold alone made them extremely valuable, but they couldn't simply be stolen. They are kept in locked cases, and suspicion would immediately have fallen on those who had keys."

Hobbs said, "Myself and Mr. Cotter, you mean?"

"And on Miss Simington, who had duplicate keys in her office. In fact, she briefly came under suspicion for just that reason." I remembered Peeples asking Holmes if he should arrest her. "But I suspect there was one who was often in her office in the course of his duties at the museum, or perhaps, merely because she is an attractive young woman and he a handsome young man of the same age."

Everyone looked at Foster, and Wesley Abberton said, "Well, it's certainly true that Foster was in her office every chance he got."

"You're a snake, Abberton!" accused Foster.

He shot back, "Apparently not so reptilian as you are, if what Mr. Holmes says is true!" Foster winced at the acid in his tone.

Holmes was continuing. "Now that we know about the snuff boxes, everything becomes clear, including Mr. Foster's role in their substitution and the murder of Mr. Hastings. It would be impossible to know the exact incident that alerted Mr. Hastings to the substitutions, but as I myself concluded that simply from having seen, by chance, a snuff box that was obviously not gold displayed prominently as if it were valuable, a similar incident isn't unlikely. In his workroom, we saw that there were pieces of ceramic with streaks across them. Some were yellow streaks. Others were dark streaks. A gold snuff box, drawn over ceramic, will leave a yellow streak. A forgery would leave a dark streak. From this, we can deduce that he was methodically examining all the museum's exhibits of snuff boxes."

Miss Simington put a hand to her mouth. "Mr. Hastings kept borrowing the keys for the cabinets. I thought nothing of it, as there are ceramics protected from touch in some of the cases."

"But now we know he was testing the snuff boxes to ensure they were solid gold. I am certain he made notes about his discoveries which have now been destroyed by Mr. Foster, and this was why we found an empty folder beside his body. Once he suspected that some of the snuff boxes were forgeries, he should have gone to Hobbs and reported his suspicions.

337

Again, we cannot know why he didn't do so, or why he disclosed his suspicions to Mr. Foster and no one else. Did they work together often and share other confidences? We cannot know for sure. Once alerted to his colleague's suspicions, Foster realized he couldn't simply murder Mr. Hastings. He no doubt feared being seen and reported. He and Hastings worked in the basement, but so did Mr. Smith and his son, Danny. Upon learning what Hastings suspected, he no doubt suggested that they investigate together to see how widespread the forgeries were, perhaps convincing his co-worker to delay reporting their suspicions until they knew for certain how serious it was and, perhaps, uncover who was responsible.

"As I said, it was most imprudent to confide in Foster, who decided he needed a diversion if he was to murder his coworker and end the threat he presented. He invented the elaborate charade of the theft of the museum payroll as that diversion. He, of course, knew when the payroll was delivered. He worked out his timing. He created the handprint from a wooden carving, which I expect we will find somewhere in the top story of the museum if he hasn't already consigned it to the fire. He prepared the unused door by oiling its bolt, and he arranged with Hastings to meet him there after the theft was reported."

Hobbs said, "But why did Hastings agree to that?"

"Mr. Foster, would you care to explain?"

Foster's face twisted. "This is all make believe. I am not playing this game!"

"He agreed, I theorize," answered Holmes, "because he thought Foster had a plan to catch the thief stealing still another snuff box in the confusion. Hastings was to leave before the theft of the payroll was discovered – which he did – but he then returned by way of the newly opened door to aid Mr. Foster. His cue to leave was his visit from Miss Simington, and then by Mr. Hobbs searching for her, leaving the office area empty. Having spent much of his time in Miss Simington's office, Mr. Foster had already made duplicate keys of Mr. Hobbs's office, the cabinets in which the valuable snuff boxes were locked, and anything else he thought he might need.

"Shortly after the payroll had arrived and when the staff were beginning to leave, and when he knew both Miss Simington and Mr. Hobbs were in the basement with Mr. Hastings, he used his key to enter Mr. Hobbs's office, unwrapped the package in which he had been carrying a crowbar, used it to open the cabinet, left the mark of the handprint where it couldn't help but be seen, removed the payroll, and placed the crowbar and payroll in the empty office, from which he could extract both at his leisure."

"But the money the boy had!" objected Sergeant Peeples. "How did it get there?"

"Foster had placed it in his lunch bag earlier. For his plan to succeed, he needed an apparent thief. He knew he wouldn't have the time to remove the payroll and plant part of it in the boy's belongings, so he used his own money, a large enough sum that, when found in the boy's possession, he would be suspected of the theft."

"Where did he get the money?" asked Hobbs.

"From his illegal activities, of course. We don't know how long Foster has been substituting forgeries for the real gold, but we may assume that he had amassed quite a sum by his skullduggery. He chose the boy because he feared anyone else would discover the money too early. He reasoned that the boy, accompanying his father around the museum, wouldn't examine his lunch bag after the noon hour, or, if he did, wouldn't realize the import of his discovery. In all likelihood, after having consumed his lunch during the noon hour, he never looked in it again."

"He was willing to be out that sum! It wasn't insignificant."

"No doubt worth it to avoid suspicion of his betrayal of the museum's trust." Holmes added flatly, "and since he would have the payroll, he would recoup his money back with interest."

"That's dastardly!" It was one of the twins. I couldn't have told you which one. I had been watching the Smith family. I was uncertain that Donny understood any of what he heard, for his expression was puzzled, but that of his brother's was rapt. The father was listening intently to Holmes.

"Even more than you know. With everyone convinced that the boy stole the payroll, Foster no doubt expected him to be convicted of the murder of Mr. Hastings when his body was found. The assumption would have been that Hastings discovered what the boy had done, and the boy killed him before he could expose him."

"We would have gotten onto that, though," asserted Peeples, "when the payroll was found intact."

"Would you have? Or would it simply have been an unexplained mystery? Might you not have theorized that the bank had made a mistake in their sums? After all, the boy had more money than he should have in his possession. How did he get it? But even more to the point: Are you quite certain that you would have found the money without my insistence that a search be conducted for the remaining payroll and the sword? You thought you had your thief, and you were unaware the sword was missing. Given sufficient time, Mr. Foster would have assured himself that the payroll disappeared thoroughly. I have no doubt he would have found a way to smuggle it out of the museum when the boy had been arrested and the staff permitted to leave. I suspect it was only found so easily because Mr. Hobbs and Miss Simington returned to the office area too quickly for him to hide the money better – for he must have witnesses to account for all his time to ensure he himself wouldn't fall under suspicion."

"You have convinced me, Mr. Holmes," said Sergeant Peeples, "but this will be a devil to prove."

"Except for one thing: The sword. It was already missing when I arrived. Who could have removed it? As I have said, who but a member of the museum staff could hope to place a step-ladder against the form of the horse and remove the sword without it being remarked upon? And who, but Mr. Foster, the metal smith of the museum, could have answered the question, 'What are you doing?' He could have said that he was removing the sword for cleaning."

Holmes turned to Foster, "You should never have denied knowing anything about it. That lie alone will convict you."

Holmes turned to Peeples. "I suggest these lines of inquiry: Interview the museum staff who aren't here. Did anyone see Mr. Foster remove the sword? If not, interview today's visitors from the scrupulously kept log. Did any of them see him remove it? Examine his workbench, for there must be indications of his work. I expect his home will also show the materials used for the fabrication of the forgeries. I would scour known fences for gold snuff boxes and see from whom they acquired them. His bank may have recorded the withdrawal of an amount of money that corresponds to the money found in young Smith's bag. And one last thing: It's been raining all day, and certainly had been raining this morning, as I recall. Where is Mr. Smith's impermeable?" Holmes turned to Ryder. "When Foster left, did he have an impermeable?"

The poor man could only helplessly say, "I don't remember. He may have done."

Holmes turned back to Peeples. "It would only make sense, given what the day is like, that he would have worn one. I would suggest that you scour the dustbins from here to Baker Street for such an outer garment with blood stains on it, which might well account for the fact that Foster has none on him."

I could see Peeples jaw tighten as Holmes spoke. Finally, he nodded to his men. "Take him," he said, nodding towards Foster. "And thank you, Mr. Holmes."

Epilogue

In my experience, it isn't unusual for someone who has engaged Holmes's services to express his appreciation after he had concluded a case. At times, the thanks were expressed monetarily, and sometimes by other means. Following the aftermath of his work at the Wallace Collection, and to my surprise, we had three such.

The first came the next day and was quite ordinary. We were visited by Mr. Fairdale Hobbs, the managing director of the Wallace Collection. Mrs. Hudson showed him to our rooms.

"I shall not stay long," he told us. "I have brought your fee in person, rather than put it in the post. I greatly appreciated your work on the Collection's behalf. I fear that, without you, a miscarriage of justice might have occurred."

Holmes thanked the managing director, who added, "I have already begun the process of replacing the cabinet with a safe."

"You will not regret it," said my friend.

But Mr. Hobbs sighed and responded, "I regret the necessity. I wish it were not so. We have also begun a procedure to log the use of the museum keys and to keep them locked except when requested. I am embarrassed to think that a man in my employ, one I trusted and whose career I underwrote, could so betray my trust. It was also disturbing to see how easily an innocent child might be arrested for a crime he didn't commit. You have my thanks and appreciation. You are everything I was told you were."

The next visit came several days later, when Mrs. Hudson showed Sergeant Peeples to our rooms. Holmes welcomed him courteously. I was less sanguine, for although we had parted on good terms, he had so often appeared hostile to my friend that I wasn't able to convince myself his appearance in our rooms was a happy one. He soon set my mind to rest.

"To what do we owe the honour of your visit, Sergeant?"

"Two things I wanted to say to you, Mr. Holmes. The first is that you were right. We interviewed the patrons of the museum. No fewer than five of them, two couples and an older gent, saw Foster remove the sword in the early morning and have identified him to our satisfaction. We found what looked like gold pieces in his flat, but I am told they only *appear* to be gold: Pyrite, I was told. His bank affirms that he removed cash from his account matching the amount found in the boy's lunch sack, and further confirmed cash deposits of no small amount that have nothing to do with his pay. We found the fence he was using: The scoundrel was quite openly advertising the snuff boxes at exorbitant prices. He claims he didn't know they were stolen, but I have my doubts about that."

"As do I."

"But I can only prove what I can prove, and he quite cheerfully agreed to testify against Foster, so we can at least put Foster behind bars where he belongs, and perhaps help him to be hanged."

341

"And the impermeable?"

"Ah! We found that, too. As you said, with blood stains on it. There was a launderer's mark on it, and he confirms it is Foster's."

"Then I predict that a jury of his peers will send him to the gallows. He will not be able to account for the blood on the coat, or if he can, why it was disposed of so unceremoniously."

But the sergeant didn't leave after giving us his report. Instead, he looked increasingly uncomfortable.

"Is there more, Sergeant?" Holmes asked.

The policeman seemed to come to a decision. "Yes. There is. When I was relating what happened to Mrs. Peeples, she said to me that I owed you an apology. She told me, quite gently, for she is a good woman, that perhaps I was too quick to take exception with you being called, and acted quite ungentlemanly as a result." He took a deep breath as if intending to plunge into cold water. "And so, I want to offer you my apology."

"Which I accept without hesitation."

"I assure you that should our paths cross again, I will not be so boorish. You helped prevent me arresting the wrong man. Justice," he added, "is more important than my pride."

After he left, Holmes asked, "What did you think of that, Watson?"

"His apology? It was most gracious."

"If we all could only admit our wrongs so manfully, the world would be a better place."

But that wasn't the last visit in connection with the theft at the Wallace Collection. Three days later, Mrs. Hudson introduced Baxter Smith and his not-inconsiderable family to our lodgings. Mrs. Smith was a portly but comely woman holding a small boy in her arms. Donny and Abel were there, and no fewer than four other children, two girls and two boys. Holmes had the uncanny ability to foresee much, but I could tell he had no expectation that he would receive such a visit.

"We will only stay a minute," Baxter Smith said, "but Mrs. Smith and the entire family wanted to thank you for keeping Donny out of gaol, for I have no doubt but that he would have gone there but for you."

And the entire family thanked him, not quite one by one, but almost. The youngest girl presented him with a flower. "I picked it myself," she informed him.

Donny himself offered Holmes his gigantic hand. "I didn't understand everything, but Da says you kept me safe."

And last was Abel, who also shook hands with Holmes. "When I grow up, I'm going to be just like you."

I could see this bemused my friend. "I'm honoured," he replied, "but I think you would do better to be just like your father."

And I quite agreed. There is only one Sherlock Holmes, after all, and that is quite enough.

> *"You arranged an affair for a lodger of mine last year," she said. "Mr. Fairdale Hobbs."*
>
> *"Ah, yes – a simple matter."*
>
> *"But he would never cease talking of it – your kindness, sir, and the way in which you brought light into the darkness."*
>
> – Mrs. Warren and Sherlock Holmes
> "The Red Circle"

The St. Pancras Puzzle
by Susan Knight

"Is anyone a doctor? A doctor! We need a doctor!"

A frantic porter in the uniform of the Midlands Railway was accosting passengers arriving at St. Pancras Station, Holmes and myself among them. We had just returned from the smoky midland city of Birmingham, where my friend had been instrumental in foiling a vile blackmail plot: Mrs. N. need no longer fear that a girlhood indiscretion would ruin her life as a devoted wife and mother.

"I am a doctor!" I informed the porter.

"Thanks be to God, sir!" he replied, grabbing my arm. "It's a nasty business and no mistake."

He pulled me through the crowds to a distant and deserted platform where two others of his ilk – one short and fat, the other young and white with shock – were standing guard over a prone figure. As we approached, I saw that the man lying there, a burly individual of middle age, was wearing the uniform of a police constable. Blood that had flowed from a wound on his head, now pooled and congealed around him.

"I am very much afraid," I said, after examining the man, "that he is quite beyond my help."

The first porter must have been of the Catholic religion, for he made the sign of the cross over his breast.

"We thought as much, sir," he replied. "The poor fellow. Did he fall, do you think?"

I shook my head. "This was no accident."

Even a casual view of the injuries would indicate that someone had bludgeoned the man many times with some heavy object.

"Oh, Lawd!" the fat porter said, shaking his head, "Mr. Wright won't like that. Not one bit, he won't."

"Who is Mr. Wright?" I asked.

All three men looked at me with astonishment as if to ask had I really never heard of this illustrious personage?

"Mr. Nehemiah Wright. The director-in-chief of the Midland Railways!"

"I see. Well, before you inform anyone, even Mr. Nehemiah Wright, you had better alert the police."

344

"If *you* say so, sir," the first porter replied, placing the responsibility for bypassing the director on to my shoulders.

He headed off to make the call.

"And for the love of God," I said to the other two, "find something to cover this poor fellow." For the curious had started to gather as they always will at the scene of anything untoward.

The two porters looked at each other, rather stupidly, I thought, and stayed where they were.

"Or we can use this," I told them, lightly spreading the copy of *The Birmingham Daily Post* I had been reading on the train over the victim's upper body.

I then looked around for Holmes. He was standing a way off, a frown on his brow.

"What do you make of this, Watson?" he asked, indicating an object lying on the ground.

It was a long nightcap of white cloth, just like the one worn by Ebenezer Scrooge in illustrations to the famous story by Mr. Dickens.

"Curious, isn't it?" Holmes remarked.

"Most odd. I didn't think anyone wore such things these days, except perhaps for some of my more elderly patients."

Holmes sighed.

"The fashion element is hardly relevant. What is odd is that it should be lying discarded on a station platform instead of neatly folded in someone's bedroom."

He stared down at it as if it were a witness able to reveal exactly what had happened.

"What is also most telling," he continued, "is what is not here – what's missing."

"What?" I asked.

"Surely you don't need me to tell you?" he replied.

I ignored the jibe. I was tired after a very early start, was most anxious to get home after our trip – the Midland railway not being the most clean and comfortable mode of transport – and was not in the mood for one of his conundrums. However, leaving immediately was out of the question. The first porter, having returned, informed us that the police were on their way, but wished us all to stay put until they arrived. Sighing resignedly, I observed with a sinking heart, from Holmes's alert demeanour – bloodhound that he was – that he was as keen to linger as I was to leave the poor victim to the attention of the proper authorities.

In the meantime, a small, ball-shaped, choleric gentleman, with a shiny bald head, shiny forehead, and shiny cheeks and chins that hung down over a tight starched collar, was bouncing towards us as fast as his short legs would carry him. The porters shrank back.

"What exactly is going on here?" he barked at no one in particular. "Another old tramp has croaked, is it?"

He made to lift a corner of the newspaper.

"Better wait for the police," Holmes warned.

The man stared at him through piggy eyes. "And who are you, sir, to tell me what to do?"

"I am Sherlock Holmes, and this is my colleague, Dr. Watson, who has ascertained that the man has met a violent end. You, I presume, are Mr. Nehemiah Wright."

"You presume correctly, sir." He puffed himself up like a turkey cock.

I wondered who had informed him of the incident. Presumably the porter who had telephoned to the police, terrified to be found remiss, had also notified his superior at the same time.

The name of my friend seemed to have made no impression whatsoever on the director, who perhaps was one of those rare beings who had never heard of Sherlock Holmes. He spent the time waiting for the police impatiently tapping a highly polished boot on the platform, while casting venomous glances our way, as if it were we who were responsible for the corpse.

At long last, the familiar lanky figure of Inspector Merivale, together with a couple of constables, could be seen marching along the platform towards us.

"Ha!" he said, when he drew close. "Sherlock Holmes! How do you happen be involved in this business, might I ask?"

"Completely by chance, Merivale. Watson and I were arriving from Birmingham when this porter – " (indicating the man) " – called urgently for a doctor. Watson responded, only to find the poor fellow lying here as you can see him."

"Right you are." Merivale carefully lifted the newssheet. One of the constables gasped.

"It's . . . it's Jim Walters! From Islington Station."

The inspector turned to me.

"Was the man still alive when you first examined him, Doctor?"

I shook my head. "No. It was clear that life had let him some time earlier. Not long, mind. Maybe a half-hour or so, judging by the temperature of the body. And, as you see, *rigor mortis* hasn't yet set in."

Meanwhile, the director was hopping impatiently from one leg to another.

"Inspector," he shrilled, "I am Nehemiah Wright!"

346

"Are you indeed?" Merivale said. "And what have you to do with this sorry business?"

"Well . . . nothing. Nothing at all. I know nothing at all about it. Of course not. But I am director of the Midland Railway, do you see. To have a dead man, a policeman as I understand it, on my property – I have a certain responsibility, you understand, to the travelling public."

Merivale nodded. "It was clearly a frenzied attack," he said. "Have you any idea, sir, how the constable happened to be here on this particular platform?"

"None at all. This is a seldom-used branch line connecting to the lesser-inhabited regions of the Home Counties. I cannot comprehend what your man was doing here. Not at all. No, no, no." Mr. Wright shook his head so vigorously that all his chins wobbled.

"He was perhaps in pursuit of some felon," Merivale suggested, "when the man turned on him."

Wright nodded. "Yes, yes. That must be it. Assuredly."

"Which raises the question," said Holmes, "as to where this supposed-felon was heading."

We all cast our eyes to the limit of the platform, the empty rails stretching beyond it.

"Did any train leave from here in the past half-hour?" Merivale asked.

Nehemiah Wright took a large fob watch from his waistcoat pocket and proceeded to consult it, as if the answer lay within its silver case.

"No," said the first porter. "Last train – "

"Yes, yes, yes, Sullivan," the director interrupted. "As I was about to say, the last train from here was at a quarter-past-nine. It now being eleven-thirty . . . ."

"So that rules out the possibility that anyone escaped that way," I said, while Wright glared at me. "As I said, the man has only been dead around a half-hour."

"In any case," added Holmes drily, "if a dead body were lying on the platform when the train pulled in or out, someone might possibly have noticed."

"Then the assailant probably simply and coolly made his way back up the empty platform and out through the station," Merivale said. "I assume, if no train was due, there would be no one guarding the barrier."

"Of course not," Wright remarked. "That would be a sheer waste of manpower."

"So how come," Merivale addressed the porters, "you lot went onto that platform, if no trains were due in or out?"

The men shuffled, embarrassed, glancing at Wright.

"Did you hear an altercation?"

347

"I wish we did, sir," the first porter said. "Then this poor fellow might still be with us. No, me, Fred, and Garrick here just popped down to check . . . er – "

"You came for a quiet smoke," Holmes said.

The porter looked at him astonished. "How d'you figure that, sir?"

Holmes pointed to a large pillar. It provided a convenient hiding place for anyone not wishing to be observed. At its base, at the side facing away from the main station, was a heap of cigarette stubs, as well as an empty box that promoted a particularly noxious brand of the weed.

Nehemiah Wright looked about to explode with rage. Indeed, his face had turned to such an intense shade of purple that I quite feared a stroke might be imminent.

"Smoking on duty!" he roared. "That's cause for immediate dismissal!"

"Come now, sir," Holmes said. "We surely have more pressing matters demanding our attention. Had these men not left their duties for a five-minute break, this Jim Walters might not have been found for hours."

"It is against the rules, Mr. Shercock!" Nehemiah Wright retorted, still purple. "These men know that full well. No smoking at work!"

"Be a little flexible, sir," Holmes went on. "Have you never enjoyed a fine cigar in your office? In fact, I see from the light dusting of ash on your waistcoat that you have very recently smoked . . . What – ?" He approached Wright and, to that gentleman's amazement, sniffed at his jacket. "A *Flor de Cano*, if I'm not much mistaken."

The director fell back, his mouth open.

"What trickery is this, sir?" he exclaimed.

"Mr. Holmes has written a monograph on the subject of cigar ash," I explained, though I am afraid this didn't appease the man, who continued to gaze on my friend with superstitious horror.

"That's all well and good," Merivale said briskly, "but it hardly advances our investigation into poor Walters' demise. Thank you for your help, Dr. Watson. However, I think you and Mr. Holmes might now leave the rest to us."

I could hope for nothing better, but Holmes delayed.

"I should be inclined to agree with you," he said, "were it not for two or three odd elements to the case."

"Whatever are you talking about?" Merivale asked.

"First of all, the man's head has been caved in. Why was he not wearing his helmet, and where is it now? Moreover, where is his truncheon?"

"Hmm," Merivale said, scratching his jaw. "Well, I expect they'll turn up, once we start searching."

348

"And then," Holmes continued, "there's that."

He pointed to the nightcap, lying a little way off.

Merivale laughed. "Are you suggesting Constable Walters was wearing that instead of his helmet? Oh, Mr. Holmes, you'll be the death of me, you surely will."

"I am, of course, suggesting no such thing." Holmes retorted, rather huffily. "I just wonder how to account for its presence."

"All right. Let me borrow your deductive powers for a moment, Mr. Holmes." Merivale frowned thoughtfully. Then clicked his fingers. "How about this? An elderly gent – for only an elderly gent would wear such a thing – staying in the Midland Grand Hotel, wakes late and rushes for his morning train, quite forgetting in his haste that he is still wearing his nightcap. When he does, he tears it from his head, casting it from him, before jumping on the train."

"Really, Merivale?" Holmes shook his head. "A forgetful elderly gentleman? Is that the best you can come up with?"

"Well, or some other totally innocent explanation. Nothing to do with the matter in hand, anyway. Or perhaps," chuckling, "you reckon our felon was wearing it when chased by Walters here. Perhaps it's *Wee Willie Winkie* we should be looking for." He paused. "All right. It's curious, I'll grant you that. So if you really want to look into it, be my guest."

Holmes smiled. "Thank you. May I take the nightcap, then?"

Merivale nodded, smiling indulgently. However, for Nehemiah Wright, this would not do.

"It's lost property," he said. "Suppose the elderly gentleman comes back to ask for it? What then, sir? What then?"

"Then you notify me, sir, and I shall return it forthwith. But I don't imagine it will come to that." Holmes turned to the three porters. "I may have some further questions for you later. With Mr. Wright's permission, of course."

That personage nodding grudgingly, Holmes took the last names of the porters: Sullivan, Whalley, and Jessop. He then picked up the nightcap carefully and carried it away with him, while I followed, having nodded farewell to Inspector Merivale and the others.

"Did anything strike you as unusual about all this?" Holmes asked me, once we had settled in the hansom taking us back to Baker Street.

"Nothing at all," I replied. "I frequently trip over dead policemen when at main line railway stations."

He viewed me through narrowed lids.

"Facetiousness doesn't become you, Watson," he said. "Think, man!"

349

I knitted my brow in an attempt to satisfy my friend. However, apart from the presence of the nightcap, and the absence of the helmet and truncheon, I couldn't recall anything that jumped out at me. I said as much.

"Yes, this cap is most enlightening," he replied. "As for the helmet and truncheon, they are key, I think. But there is more."

"I'm afraid you must explain."

"What brought this Walters to a pillar on a deserted platform? He was hardly on a random patrol."

"Well, if he was chasing someone – "

"Surely people would have noticed a pursuit through the main body of the station. No one seems to have done so."

"Perhaps the constable also wanted a quiet smoke."

"Tut! There you go again, making light of it. No, Watson, I rather believe Walters had gone there for a specific purpose, even maybe to meet someone." Holmes sat back.

"The person who killed him?"

"Quite possibly. Moreover," he continued, "there was no forgetful elderly gentleman."

He held up the nightcap and, like Maskelyne performing a magic trick, turned it inside out, returning it, in fact, to its proper configuration, for now a ball formed of cut wool was revealed to be on the pointed tip of it. Holmes held it out for me to examine. There were bloodstains upon it.

"This was used as a weapon," Holmes said.

"Death by pompom," I commented.

"Really, Watson!"

"I'm sorry, but I still don't see – "

"Clearly some hard object, a rock or brick perhaps, was placed inside the cap, which was then swung with considerable force to hit the constable's head."

"Bludgeoning him to death."

"Hmm . . . ." Holmes considered the matter. "But in that case, surely there would be more blood on the thing. Rather more likely, isn't it, that the man's own truncheon was used to finish him off. Perhaps this was used to surprise him, knocking off his helmet and laying him flat."

He squeezed the fabric of the cap.

"Ha!" he exclaimed. "How very interesting!"

"What?"

He held out his hand on which a few tiny glistening particles lay.

"Glass? But what does it mean? That a paperweight was used?"

"As to that, at the present moment, we can only speculate – something, as you well know, I am not inclined to do, preferring to rationalise from hard evidence. In fact – Hello, what's this?" He scraped a few darker particles off the side of the cap, and examined them closely. "Glue, I think. I can't be sure until I examine this under the microscope. But meanwhile . . . Yes, I must go back immediately!"

He called to the driver to stop.

"Shall I accompany you?" I asked, somewhat aghast at this sudden change of mind.

"No," he said, climbing out of the vehicle. "I should like you to go to Islington Police Station forthwith, and make enquiries regarding Constable Walters – his family, friends, and so on. Find out if he was the sort of man likely to confront a suspect on his own."

Seeing my hopes of dozing at home over a restorative glass of tonic wine fading fast, I gave new instruction to the cab driver, and then settled back, musing on the case into which we had just fallen. I have to say that I wasn't inclined to accept Holmes's notion that Walters had gone to meet someone. Much more likely that he had seen something suspicious and, diligent in his duty to investigate, had walked to his doom.

The constable on the desk was a large man in his fifties, with ginger whiskers and a florid complexion. High blood pressure, for sure. He was suspicious of my enquiries at first, but when I mentioned Inspector Merivale and Sherlock Holmes, he became more forthcoming.

"Very shocked I was to 'ear what 'appened." he said. "Very shocked I was, sir."

"Yes, indeed. A sad business. But I'm hoping you can tell me more about Walters."

"What d'you mean, sir?"

"Family man, was he?"

The constable shook his head. "Not at all. A confirmed bachelor, 'im. Lived with his old mum. Invalid she is. It'll be a terrible shock to 'er, poor soul."

"Walters got on well with his colleagues, I suppose?"

"Well, now . . . ." There was a perceptible pause. "Don't get me wrong. Jim Walters was a decent enough chap." Another pause. I could almost hear "*Speak no ill of the dead*" going through the man's mind. "Decent enough, 'e was. Though to tell the truth, we got the feeling 'e thought 'isself a cut above the rest of us. Kept 'isself to 'isself, if you know what I mean."

"Did his job and then went home."

"That's exactly it, sir. Never any complaints about 'im doing what was asked for, though 'e never put 'isself out, neither. But no interest in coming for a pint after 'is shift with the rest of us lads. Always said 'e 'ad to get back to mum. Still, you'd think once in while, wouldn't you, sir?"

I nodded. "You would, indeed. It's only comradely."

"You've 'it on the 'ead again there, sir. *Comradely*. Yes, indeed."

"I suppose," I continued, "he was the sort of man likely to pursue a possibly violent criminal on his own."

The constable's jaw dropped open under his gingery moustache. Then he burst into a great wheezy laugh. "Jim Walters! An 'ero! Not at all, sir. Steered well clear of anything that might get 'is 'ands dirty, if you gets my meaning."

"Hmm."

"Walked 'is beat, and if anything looked dodgy, 'e was first to call in the troops."

"I see."

"Don't get me wrong, sir. I don't mean to put 'im down. It's just funny that Jim of all people should be kilt like that. They must 'ave jumped out at 'im, unexpected, like."

"Yes, it's very strange." I smiled at the constable, whose ruddy face suddenly looked almost comically downcast.

"Might I ask," I continued, "where does Walters's mother live? I'd like to pay my respects."

The obliging constable promptly gave me the address and directions and, the house being nearby, I set off on foot, soon reaching a road of modest little dwellings.

Inside Number Fifteen, I found Mrs. Walters, a very old and feeble person indeed, sitting in the small front parlour, a crocheted shawl in evil shades of purple and sulphur over her knees, even though the heat in the room from an open fire was already oppressive. The lady wasn't alone, but in the capable hands of a neighbour, one Mrs. Biggs, who took me aside and informed me, in a stage whisper, that must have reached the old lady if she wasn't deaf, that "She keeps askin' for Jim. Doesn't unnerstand when I tell 'er 'e's gorn. Poor old soul." Her ample bosom heaved with a deep sigh. "Don't know what she'll do now. 'E done everything for 'er, 'e did. I can 'elp out, o' course, but I've mine to mind, too. Unnerstand me, Doctor?"

"I do indeed, Mrs. Biggs," I replied, adding, "Do you think I might I have a quiet word with Mrs. Walters? Perhaps if I explain – "

"O' course. Though much good it'll do you, the way she is." She smiled briskly. "Keeps rambling on, she does. I can't make 'ead nor tail of it. Anyways, I'll put the kettle on. I'm sure we'd all like a nice cuppa tea."

"That would be most acceptable," I said and, as she left the room, I turned to Mrs. Walters.

She looked up at me with milky eyes that showed advanced signs of cataracts.

"Are you Mr. Chance?" she asked.

352

"No, I am Dr. Watson. How are you, Mrs. Walters?"

"I thought you was Mr. Chance," she said, her voice quavering. "Jim told me Mr. Chance would be coming our way soon."

"Do you understand what has happened to Jim, Mrs. Walters?"

"Jim. 'E's a good boy, 'e is. Said Mr. Chance would sort all our problems."

"I'm afraid Jim has had an accident." I took her hand, all bluish skin stretched over bone. "Jim won't be coming back, Mrs. Walters."

"Oh you," she said, with a toothless grin. "Mr. Chance. My Jim always comes back. 'E's a good boy, 'e is."

Mrs. Biggs returning with teacups on a tray with a big brown china teapot, milk jug, and sugar bowl, all mismatched and chipped, I sat with the ladies for a while, drinking my boiled and bitter beverage, and wondering what else I should do. Mrs. Biggs gave me a strange look when I asked to see Jim's room, though she raised no objections when Mrs. Walters nodded.

"You go on up, Mr. Chance," she said.

The room furnished no clues, unless you counted Walters's taste for rather fancy accessories. Thrust into the back of a drawer I found a quantity of rings and tie pins, as well as a fob watch complete with chain and stamp seal. I don't claim sufficient expertise to tell genuine from fake, but they looked rather too good to be mere gilded metal and coloured glass. However, if made of gold and precious stones, such objects would be quite beyond a constable's salary. Perhaps they were inherited. Otherwise, the room was somewhat lacking in personal effects, although a rather saucy picture of the musical hall performer Marie Lloyd was stuck to the inside of the wardrobe door.

I am afraid Mrs. Biggs surprised me as I was studying this.

"Are you quite done 'ere, Doctor?" she asked. Her face had hardened. "Only I 'ave to get back to the little 'uns."

"Of course," I said, blushing as I closed the wardrobe door. "But I am wondering what will happen to Mrs. Walters now. Clearly a busy woman like yourself cannot be imposed on any further. Is there any other family?"

My concerned tone caused Mrs. Biggs to relent a little.

"She 'as a niece, what lives in Lewisham. I'll write to 'er. Meantime, I'll be sure to keep an eye on the poor old soul."

"Maybe there will be some sort of pension for the dependants of a policeman killed in the line of duty. I'll make enquiries."

"God bless you, sir." She was utterly won over again.

"Nothing much to report, Watson?" Holmes exclaimed. "On the contrary, you have discovered a great deal."

"Have I?"

It was evening and we were both back in our Baker Street sitting room.

"Putting it together with my new information," Holmes rubbed his hands together, "I am happy to say we are making excellent progress.

"So, what exactly did you find out? The identity of the assassin, I suppose."

"Well, now. Not quite. I need to confirm more details." He leaned back in his chair, drawing on his pipe, emitting the usual clouds of rank smoke. Really, he was most aggravating.

"What?" I asked. "For the love of God, Holmes, can't you explain?"

"I decided to visit the Midland Grand Hotel – and very grand it is, too. Only those with exceedingly well-lined wallets can afford to stay there."

"I am fully aware of that fact. Now tell me something I don't know. Why you went there, for instance?"

"I suspected that a robbery had taken place."

"And had it?"

He waved long fingers in the air.

"They denied it, but I insisted. You know how persistent I can be,"

I did indeed.

No one had reported anything missing, he explained. However, the hotel possessed a strongroom where guests might leave their valuables.

"To the casual eye," Holmes explained, "the boxes were intact, but I examined each one closely and discovered that one of these had indeed been forced open. A quantity of priceless gems were gone, property of a Dutch diamond merchant." He sat back the familiar satisfied smile on his face of one proved right.

"The security must have been very lax," I said.

"Judge for yourself. On further investigation, and after rousing the night manager, I learned that an elderly person had descended to the hotel lobby in the early hours 'in a right state', as the man informed me, still in his night clothes, which included – please to note, Watson – a white nightcap. Waving the key to his strongbox in the air, he insisted on checking that it was still safely stowed, shouting out that he was sure he had been robbed. The manager, one Smithson by name, after trying to persuade him that all was well, eventually gave in and accompanied the old man to the strongroom. He unlocked its heavy door and then left the guest by himself, as was customary with keyholders. Smithson assured me that the man was alone for a few minutes at most. Soon enough, he reappeared, apparently reassured, and anxious to get back to bed. And no, he wasn't carrying anything that the manager could see."

"But he was presumably in a loose night shirt or dressing gown with pockets. Diamonds are easily concealed."

"Well reasoned." Holmes gave me a merry look.

"So, who was this anxious old man?"

"He gave his name as *L. Chance, Esquire*, when checking in."

"Good Lord!"

"Yes, indeed. The same that Mrs. Walters mentioned to you."

"The Mr. Chance who was about to change the fortunes of Walters and his mother! But assuming that Chance was the thief, that suggests – Does it not? – that Constable Walters was aware of the robbery. Could he even have been part of it?"

"Now we're perhaps getting somewhere. What you have told me about the man's tastes and habits suggest that Walters was a man dissatisfied with his lot in life. A man perhaps easily seduced into crime. Quite possibly the fob watch and so on that you found hidden away in the drawer weren't mere trinkets, but rather the fruit of earlier thefts." He sighed. "It is a shame, Watson, you don't share my ability in distinguishing fakes from the real thing."

I decided to ignore the barb.

"But by God!" I exclaimed. "If Walters was involved, that changes everything."

"We mustn't jump to conclusions. Let us give the man the benefit of the doubt, unless and until the facts prove otherwise. Meanwhile, tomorrow, we must return to the hotel. Part of the solution must lie there."

I was most gratified to hear that "we", since the case was starting to intrigue me considerably.

At that moment, however, before he could expatiate further, we were interrupted by a light tap on the door. It was Mrs. Hudson with supper. I suddenly realised that I was very hungry. It was, after all, only that same morning we had come from Birmingham before being plunged into this new adventure, and I had hardly broken my fast since an early breakfast. Our good landlady placed before us plates heaped with chops, potatoes, peas and carrots, enhanced with some home-made mustard. I set to with appetite.

"I am glad to see you have your priorities," Holmes remarked drily, picking up a pea on the tine of his fork.

"Sorry, but I find I am ravenous. And my brain works better when I am well-fed. Of course, I wish you to continue your discourse. What happened to Chance? Has he been apprehended?"

"Ah, the elusive Mr. Chance. I am afraid, upon checking his room, that the hotel found that he had quite vanished."

He popped the pea into his mouth.

"Vanished! Leaving the contents of his strong box?"

"Oh, Watson! Use what brains you have, man. There was nothing in his strong box."

"He had already emptied it, then."

"My friend, there was never anything in the box. It was simply a ploy to give him admission to the strongroom in order to rob the gems."

I clapped a hand to my forehead. "Of course! Forgive my slowness."

"Eat up your chops, Watson. They *may* help speed you up."

"Anyway – " I cut a juicy portion of meat from the bone. " – you were wrong to some extent. There is an elderly man in the story after all."

Holmes smiled patiently. "Mr. Chance vanished, as I said. Leaving behind a night shirt, false whiskers, and other bits and pieces. I am apparently not the only person to resort to disguises from time to time." He laughed. "By the way, that was indeed glue on the cap, as I informed Merrivale. Goodness knows what he will make of it all."

"I see." I chewed slowly, not really seeing anything at all. "So, the thief made his escape, but for some reason, still wearing his nightcap. That would surely make him stand out in a crowd."

Holmes sighed.

"Are you deliberately being obtuse tonight? Of course, the man wasn't wearing the cap at the time. No, I imagine it proved a handy receptacle for the fruit of his theft."

"Oh, yes. The diamonds, of course."

It was true. My brain wasn't working properly at that moment. The wine with the meal, along with a post-prandial glass of brandy left me, I am sorry to say, so sleepy that I dozed off in my chair. My only excuse: It had been a long and eventful day. When I roused myself, maybe half-an-hour later, it was to find Holmes staring out into the blackness of Baker Street, perhaps musing on the blackness of the human heart.

"Ah, you have returned to consciousness, Watson. Good. Well, let us hope we can finish with this sorry case soon enough."

"You think you have solved it already, then?"

"Hardly that, my dear fellow. There are too many unknowns as yet. Tomorrow: The hotel, and then the porters."

The following morning found Holmes and me entering the lobby of the Midland Grand Hotel, located at St. Pancras Station. Although I had visited this renowned establishment before – once, as I recall, to meet an Edinburgh surgeon come to the Middlesex Hospital to conduct a particularly complex operation – I was as always taken aback at the sight that greeted me.

356

The place catered to a wealthy clientele, as reflected in the lavishness of the architecture and interior ornamentation. Indeed, the design was more reminiscent of some medieval cathedral than a London railway hotel, with its vaulted ceiling, high pointed arches, and pillars surmounted by carvings of flowers, fruits, and fleurs-de-lis. But it was far as it could be from the gloomy Gothic piles with which we are familiar these days. Instead, it is as a cathedral would have been in the Middle Ages, all visible surfaces brightly coloured to dazzle the eye – reds, blues and greens predominating, with more gold leaf than I have ever seen in one place before. Rather too ornate for my taste, but undoubtedly impressive.

On this occasion, after we had made ourselves known to the receptionist, we were shown, not up the swooping staircase to the splendours of the coffee room where I had previously met my colleague, but to the altogether plainer office of the day manager. Holmes had interviewed the man, a shrunken elderly party by the name of Horrocks, on the previous day and, following the discovery of the theft, the manager had requested him return to investigate it.

"I trust you will be able to get to the bottom of this matter quickly, Mr. Holmes, and recover the stolen property," he enunciated gravely. "I assured Mr. van de Groot that he could ask for no better than yourself in solving this heinous crime. He awaits your visit." Holmes nodded, but the man continued. "So far only a few people know of it, and my hope is that we can recover the diamonds before the story leaks out. That's why both Mr. van de Groot and I have agreed not to involve the police. You understand how badly such a thing reflects on the reputation of the hotel, Mr. Holmes. We here at the Midland Grand pride ourselves on maintaining the very highest of standards. If our guests cannot trust the security of – "

"Quite," said Holmes, at which interruption the man raised thin grey eyebrows. He was not, I think, used to being stopped in mid-flow.

"I should like, if possible," Holmes went on, "to speak first to the maids who serviced the Dutchman's room, and that of Mr. Chance."

Mr. Horrocks, tight-lipped now, consulted a list.

"It is the one girl," he said finally. "Molly Bliss."

He rang a bell on his desk and a liveried page with a cheeky face who, from the speed of his arrival, must have been standing right outside the door awaiting the call, hopped in smartly. Mr. Horrocks gave the lad instructions to fetch this same Molly.

"She should be about her work on the third floor," he told him.

The page saluted and hopped out again.

"I wonder, Mr. Horrocks," Holmes asked, "is there a quiet room where we can speak to the girl?"

"You can stay here," he replied. "I have no objection."

357

"Thank you, but I should prefer somewhere more private."

That is to say, as we all understood his words: *Without* your *presence, sir.* The manager was clearly again put out, so I decided to intervene.

"You must understand, Mr. Horrocks," I said, "the girl is more likely to be frank and relaxed with us if her superiors are absent."

"But what can she possibly tell you?" he asked. "Unless – " He bristled. " – Unless you think Molly herself is part of this gang! Girls, these days – "

"No, no. Not at all," Holmes interrupted quickly, before Mr. Horrocks got started on another hobby horse. "It is just that she may have seen or heard something that can help us. Something she may not even know is important."

"Very well," the man grudgingly acquiesced. "You may still use this room, I suppose. I shall make myself scarce. I have, after all, many important duties to attend to."

"Thank you, sir," I said. "Most obliging of you." Holmes shot me a look.

While we waited for Molly to arrive, Mr. Horrocks sat frowning and silent, drumming bony fingers on a desk rather too large for such an undersized person.

"You have a magnificent establishment here," I said at last, to try and sweeten the atmosphere.

"Yes, indeed. I have a great responsibility in making sure everything runs like clockwork. This business has quite upset me, you understand."

"Of course. Rest assured, Mr. Holmes will do his utmost to catch the thieves and recover the diamonds."

"I pray so," Mr. Horrocks replied, at the same time casting a doubtful eye on the detective, who, his back to us, was studying a crudely executed portrait, affixed to the wall, of the manager himself.

After what seemed an unconscionably long time, the page returned with an undernourished girl, hardly more than a child, whose big eyes, moving from Horrocks to myself and finally to Holmes's back, were filled with terror. It seemed as if she had recently been crying, for her face was flushed and tear-stained.

"Now, Molly," the manager said, fixing her with a significant stare, "these men are going to ask you some questions. I hope you will be a good girl when you answer them, and tell them what they need to know."

She nodded, wide-eyed, hovering.

"Sit down, do," he went on impatiently, indicating an empty chair on which she gingerly perched herself. "Now, I am going to leave you for a little while. Don't be afraid."

"We don't bite," I added, smiling at her.

358

"Of course, you don't," the manager said tartly and left the room, followed by the page, who gave Molly a big wink.

Holmes spun around, making the girl jump.

"Be yous the po-lees, sirs?" the girl asked, looking from one of us to the other.

"No, Molly. Not the police. I am Sherlock Holmes, a private detective, and this is my colleague and friend, Dr. Watson."

"A doctor," the girl looked even more confused.

"Nothing to do with the matter in hand," I reassured her.

"Now, Molly," Holmes said briskly, "I believe you are responsible for cleaning the rooms belonging to both the Dutchman and the elderly gentleman, Mr. Chance."

The girl stared at him for a moment or two and then burst into an avalanche of tears.

"Now, now, Molly. What is it?" Holmes asked, put out, his voice become gentle for once.

"I din mean it!" she burst out. "I din mean anything! And now 'e's dead!"

"Do you mean Constable Walters, my dear?"

"Yessur. *Jim!* Oh, Lawd forgive me!"

Holmes sat down beside her.

"Just tell us everything. How you got to know Jim Walters."

"It'll make you feel better to get it off your chest," I added, and she gave me a grateful look.

"It will, sir. I 'ope so. I bin that fussed."

She poured it all out.

"'E come 'ere after all the robberies, d'you see."

"What robberies?"

"From the strongroom. The safes."

"Are you telling us there has been more than one?"

"Oh yes, sir. There's been a few." She grinned then, exposing teeth in dire need of attention. "I weren't supposed to know about it, but you can't help finding out, can you?"

"No, quite right."

"You won't say nothing to the old 'Orror, will yer, please? 'E'd kill me."

"Mr. Horrocks?"

The girl nodded.

Holmes shook his head, smiling. "Your secret is safe with us."

"Anyhow, since the robberies, Jim always called in to see me. Good to me, 'e was." She gave a wan little smile. "Ever so kind to me, Jim was. Give me this, 'e did."

She fished a locket out from under the blouse of her uniform.

"Can I see?"

She took it off and passed it to Holmes, who raised his eyebrows and then gave it to me. Gold or base metal, I wasn't sure.

"So then 'e tells me 'ow 'e's on the trail of a crimbinal mastermind." Her eyes glowed with excitement at the memory. "And 'e asks for my 'elp. Asked me to tell 'im if any of my guests had partic'lar valubles. So 'e could lay a trap for the villain, like."

"So, what did you tell him, Molly? About Mr. van de Groot."

"Oo?"

"The Dutchman."

"Oh yes, 'im. I told Jim all about the diamonds. "E asked me what number safe they were in, and all."

"I suppose you hardly knew that."

"Yes, I did, sir. I did, cos Groot left 'is key one time on the bedside table when I bought 'im clean towels. Snatched it up, 'e did, but not afore I saw the number: Unlucky thirteen."

"And you passed that information to Constable Walters."

"Yes, I did, sir. I reckoned it was all right, cos 'e was the po-lees, like – ? D'you think – ? Would Jim be alive today if I didn't of?"

Holmes shrugged his shoulders.

"Oh, Lawd." She looked to be on the verge of tears again.

"We don't know, Molly," I said, "but I doubt that you telling him made any difference." I didn't necessarily believe that, but the poor child was already upset enough. No need to make it worse.

With regard to her other gentleman, Mr. Chance, Molly could tell us nothing that we didn't already know. She had never seen him.

After we sent her away with further reassurances, Holmes stretched out in Mr. Horrocks's chair.

"Now, Watson, whyever do you suppose our esteemed manager failed to inform us of the previous thefts?"

"I don't know. To preserve the reputation of the hotel, perhaps."

"Hmm. Well, we can but ask him."

"What about the reputation of little Molly Bliss? He will know that it is she who has told us."

"You're right. We'll try and keep Molly out of it. But first of all, we should have a word with this Dutchman. Let us go to his room."

Joop van de Groot was a large fellow in all respects, over six foot tall with muscles running to fat, causing the silver buttons on his dark-blue jacket to stretch almost to bursting point. I put his age in the mid-thirties. A thatch of straw-coloured hair surmounted a ruddy complexion, deep lines marking a weather-coarsened face. After standing to receive us, he sat himself back at a paper-strewn desk, a small aquarium containing several small tropical fish providing an exotic touch.

"Harlequin rasbora and cherry barb!" Holmes exclaimed, peering at the little creatures. "A charming combination."

"If you say so," the Dutchman replied. "I know nothing of such things. They are pretty enough, I suppose. But I think we are hardly here to discuss fishes." His English was impeccable, but his tone was decidedly gruff and unfriendly.

"I apologise," Holmes said. "Ichthyology is a particular interest of mine, and these are fine specimens."

The Dutchman shrugged. "They come with the room," he said, turning away from the desk. "So, have you found my diamonds?"

"Alas, not yet. But I hope to have good news soon."

The other looked as if he very much doubted it.

"When are you planning to return to South Africa?" Holmes continued.

"What? How did you – ?" He gave a sharp laugh. "Oh, famous detective, you have been asking about me."

"Not at all. I knew nothing about you before entering this room. It is you who have told me."

The man almost leapt from his seat. "What the devil!"

"Nothing devilish about it," Holmes replied genially. "Your bleached hair, your ruddy complexion, the freckles on your hands, all speak of one who has worked under a hot sun. South Africa is known for its diamond mines, so that would be the obvious place for you to have visited. Moreover, there is a letter on your desk with the banner heading of one such mine."

"Ha!" The man smacked a big, red, and decidedly freckled hand on the desk. "Yes, sir. You are correct. I spent fifteen years at Jagersfontein, near Bloemfontein. But now I am back."

"In Amsterdam?"

"Where else? The centre of the diamond industry in Europe, Mynheer."

"So, what brings you to London?"

"There's a man in Hatton Garden I deal with. I prefer to do it face-to-face."

Holmes regarded him for a moment. The fellow stared back, unperturbed.

"The theft of the diamonds must be a great loss to you."

The man shrugged. "Of course."

"But I suppose they are insured."

361

"Naturally. I am not a fool, sir."

"Hmm."

I couldn't understand it. A hostility simmered between the two men. But why? Was not Mr. van de Groot the injured party here?

"Well," Holmes said after a while, with a smile, "I hope to be in a position to restore your losses, and avoid the necessity of involving your insurance company."

"Ah!" The Dutchman smiled back. A gold-capped tooth, a canine, twinkled at us. "But you see, I have already informed them."

"Of course, because you return to Amsterdam imminently."

"Yes, I do. There is no reason to stay here now."

"Or are you going back to Bloemfontein, perhaps?"

"Maybe. Not yet." He smiled again, and then provided Holmes with a detailed description of the gems. I almost whistled at the value placed upon them.

"You see, they include one of the biggest diamonds ever found – uncut of course," van de Groot explained. "Big as a woman's fist." He clenched his own. "Such a beauty, *Mynheeren*, with that characteristic pink tinge of the stones of the Jagerfontein Mine." He sighed. "It would be truly *wonderful* if you could track it down. In that event, I would reward you handsomely, of course. However, I fear the thieves are already far, far away."

"Perhaps," Holmes replied, regarding him steadily.

"If I had known then that the strongroom wasn't safe, I should have kept them hidden here in my room. Alas, it is easy to be wise after the event, is it not?"

Taking our leave of him, we rejoined Mr. Horrocks back in his office.

"Why did you not inform us, sir," Holmes asked, "that there had been other thefts?"

"Did *he* tell you? Ha! Never trust a foreigner to keep his mouth shut!"

Neither Holmes nor I contradicted him. Better to blame the Dutchman than poor Molly.

"Anyway," the manager continued, "the previous thefts were all insignificant ones, mere trifles, nothing of great value. And we of course reimbursed our guests for their losses."

"I see. But surely that should have alerted you."

Instead of looking discomforted, Mr. Horrocks, surprisingly, looked smug.

"As to that, we had good reason to suspect one of the caretakers here – an odd-job man – though nothing could be proved and he denied everything. We sent him packing anyway, with a flea in his ear."

"Together with the stolen items, assuming he was the guilty party"

362

"Well, yes. Unfortunately, it proved impossible to recover the 'loot', as I think such blackguards call it."

"What?" I couldn't help exclaiming. "You didn't think to involve the police?"

The manager gave me a disdainful glance.

"In point of fact, the police *were* involved, in the person of the sadly late Constable James Walters. However, he agreed with me when I insisted that the reputation of the hotel must remain paramount. It was certainly worth more than a few baubles, a few shillings."

"Presumably," Holmes said, "you rewarded Walters for his discretion."

Mr. Horrocks waved a hand in the air. "A trivial sum. In any case, the good constable was able to advise us on increased security after Garrick had been dismissed. Alas, of course, as it turned out, not well enough."

"Garrick?"

"That wasn't the wretch's real name, but it was the one we all called him – as a joke, d'you see."

We didn't see, and gave him a puzzled stare.

Mr. Horrocks sighed. "After David Garrick, don't you know. The great actor. This fellow was some sort of a failed thespian. Had to take up a menial job here, since he couldn't keep body and soul together on what he earned treading the boards, as I believe the expression goes. Quite a dab hand at the picture-framing, as well, in fact – " He indicated the painting on the wall. "Garrick's work. The frame, that is," he added with a false modesty. "The art work is mine. A self-portrait."

"Ah," Holmes sniffed, regarding the thing.

"Yes. Inspector Merrivale was very interested," the manager continued, "when I informed him about Garrick."

"I see," Holmes said. "And do you know," he asked, "where Garrick is now?"

"I have no idea." It was as if a lamp was suddenly lit in the manager's limited brain. "By God, do you think Garrick was behind this business?"

Holmes made a non-committal gesture, while I tried to remember where I had heard the name before – beyond the famous actor, of course.

"At last," Holmes remarked, with satisfaction, as we quitted the manager and made our way out through the hotel lobby. "The matter is coming together rather well, don't you agree, Watson?"

How could I? I was as puzzled as ever.

"Please explain," I said.

"You mean you really have no idea as yet?"

I knitted my brow with the effort of trying to make sense of the business.

"If Walters," I reasoned at last, "was, as he told Molly, in pursuit of a master criminal, discovered who he was, and confronted him, then the villain must have killed him to prevent exposure. But – ?" I shook my head. "Would Walters not have summoned 'the troops', as the station officer affirmed would be his way, rather than facing him alone? Hmm – unless . . . ."

"Yes?" Holmes's eager eyes flashed with amusement.

"You know all the answers," I said crossly, "so why not spare me?"

"No, no. Go on. Unless what?"

"Well, unless Walters knew about the robbery and wanted a pay-off. Maybe he was in on it from the start, and provided the thief with the necessary information as gleaned from Molly. Or maybe – " I gasped at the thought. "Maybe, he was Chance himself!"

Holmes burst out laughing and clapped his hands together, sorely alarming a passing dowager, whose little dog started yapping at us. "Capital reasoning, Watson! And so nearly right. However, you have gone rather too far down the road of speculation. Think about it: It is hardly likely that the constable, well-known in the hotel, would have had the skill or nerve to pass himself off as an elderly guest. No, it is high time for you to ask Inspector Merivale to summon the main actors in this drama, in order at last to get at the truth."

"*I* am to ask him?"

"Yes, Watson, if you would be so kind. I am afraid he is about to charge the wrong person with the murder. In fact, it took all my powers of persuasion to have him hold off already. Meanwhile, there there is just one last thing I have to do first. To make absolutely sure, do you see."

Thus it was that an hour or so later found a motley band of people – most of whom were puzzled to find themselves in such a place – assembled at St. Pancras Station in the rather fine, cigar-scented office of Mr. Nehemiah Wright. Present were Inspector Merivale and one of his sergeants, Mr. Horrocks, Mynheer Joop van de Groot, the three porters, and myself, awaiting the arrival of Holmes, who entered shortly after, accompanied by little Molly Bliss.

"In the interests of discretion," Holmes said, "I thought it more appropriate to meet here than in the hotel, to inform you of the results of my investigation."

"I hope it will be worth it," the director exclaimed. "It is all most inconvenient, you know."

"Apologies, Mr. Wright, but I assumed you would wish to hear an explanation of the sad event that took place on your premises," Holmes replied.

Wright nodded, though with something of a bad grace.

"It is a tale of insatiable greed," Holmes continued. "Constable Walters was killed because, as my colleague Dr. Watson so rightly surmised, he had discovered the identity – " Here he winked at Molly. " – of the criminal mastermind. However, instead of having him arrested, Walters craved a share of the loot, whereupon he let himself be lured to the empty and remote platform, where he met his end."

"That's quite an accusation against a member of His Majesty's police force," Merivale interrupted. "I hope you can prove what you say."

"Patience, my dear Inspector. All will very soon be revealed." Holmes made a steeple with the fingers of both hands, pressed them to his lips, and continued. "As you will recall, there were some strange but telling elements to the scene. The missing helmet and truncheon. The out-of-place nightcap. Now, we know from Molly – " Holmes smiling at her reassuringly. " – that Walters was well aware of the existence of Mynheer van de Groot's diamonds, and even knew into which box they had been deposited."

"What!" exclaimed the hotel manager, glaring at the girl. "You told him! You were part of – "

"Now, now, Mr. Horrocks," Holmes said soothingly. "Molly believed she was helping the police, not conniving at a robbery. Anyway, keep that fact of Walters's knowledge in mind for the moment, if you please. First, I wish to consider the mysterious Mr. Chance."

"Oh yes. Chance." Merivale shook his head "Well, I'm afraid we haven't been able to find hide nor hair of the man. He has completely disappeared, as if he were never there."

"On the contrary, Inspector, he is here with us now," Holmes said, his words inspiring not a little consternation as we looked about ourselves. Where the devil was the man?

"Mr. L. Chance," Holmes continued. "The 'L' standing for 'Lucky'. I suppose. A joke name – just like your own – Garrick."

One of the porters jumped at being so addressed. "What!

"Though in this case, as it turned out, not so lucky?"

I started at the name. Garrick! Of course! The third porter, who had lurked behind the others and said little. I studied him now: An insignificant-looking individual, medium build, fairish colouring, a perfect *tabula rasa* on which to write any number of characters.

"By God, it's him!" said Mr. Horrocks, like me staring at the man. "I didn't recognise the blackguard in that uniform."

"Interesting you should mention his uniform," Holmes said, "because that is also part of the story, which we shall come to in due course. First, what do you have to say for yourself, Garrick?"

"It's a lie! You can't lay this on me, just because . . . because Horrocks took against me."

"Do you deny that you entered the hotel in the guise of an elderly man, pretended to stow valuables in the strongroom in order to gain legitimate access to that place, and, on the night before last, entered that same strongroom and broke into box number thirteen, containing the diamonds belonging to Mynheer van de Groot here?"

"A lie!" repeated Garrick – or Frank Jessop, as his real name turned out to be. "I'd like to see you prove it."

"You will," Holmes replied calmly.

Inspector Merivale stepped forward. "Thank you, Mr Holmes. You have proved me right after all. Frank Jessop," he continued, "I arrest you – "

"Not so fast, Inspector. Do you not think that if Jessop had stolen the diamonds, he'd be long gone? Not still working as a railway porter."

"But you just said . . . ." Inspector Merrivale scratched his head in confusion.

"He's here," Holmes said, "because the box he was trying to rob was as empty as his own. Or rather, he found a heap of glass beads, which at the time he took to be the real thing."

"What!" the Dutchman cried out. "Glass beads? What are you talking about? Those diamonds were priceless."

"For the theft of which you are about to receive a huge sum in insurance money, while all the time the genuine gems haven't left your hotel room. As you said to me earlier, they are safer there than in the strongroom."

"*Nee*. What I said was, I *wished* I had kept them in my room, where they would have been safe."

"So, Inspector Merivale's man will find nothing during the search he is conducting at this very moment?"

"Of course not!" Van de Groot looked furious, a deep flush creeping over his already ruddy complexion.

"We shall see." Holmes tapped those steepled fingers together. "This is what I think happened: Constable Walters passes information to his partner in crime: Jessop, also known as Garrick. Remember, Walters investigated those earlier minor robberies, so he would come to know the suspect. Was it he or you, Garrick, who saw the possibilities for something much more ambitious?"

The porter scowled and shook his head.

"Those baubles you found in Walter's drawer, Watson," Holmes said, "quite possibly they indeed form part of the stash that Garrick stole, a pay-off to the policeman for turning a blind eye." He turned to Mr. Horrocks, who shifted uncomfortably. "It was Walters who persuaded you against having your employee arrested. Didn't he, sir? Not the other way round." The day manager nodded, subdued, and Holmes continued. "So, Garrick, disguised as Chance, robs the supposed diamonds, which he then stows in the nightcap he's wearing during his nocturnal foray. The glue I found on the cap, by the way, Merivale, was nothing to do with Garrick's picture-framing hobby as you surmised, but everything to do with affixing false whiskers." He glanced at the porter, whose head was bowed, and resumed his account. "Garrick thereupon quits the hotel – as a previous employee, he knows how to leave unseen, avoiding the front lobby – and goes to meet with Walters. However, the pair of them soon discover that the gems are worthless bits of glass. They figure out that van de Groot himself is perpetrating a gigantic fraud, and Walters contacts him with a view to blackmail, so that they will at least get something out of the business."

The Dutchman laughed.

"Such fantasies," he said.

Paying him no attention, Holmes continued. "An arrangement was made to meet away from prying eyes on a remote platform at St. Pancras at such-and-such a time to sort out the pay-off. Correct me if I am wrong, Mynheer, but I imagine you arrived early and positioned yourself behind the pillar." Van de Groot glowered and shook his head, muttering under his breath. "Walters comes to meet you while Garrick stands guard in the body of the station to stop anyone else venturing on to the platform. What happened then? Did Walters produce the fake diamonds hidden in the nightcap? I imagine you had a weapon with you already, a gun perhaps or a knife, but instead, took advantage of what was offered, swung the loaded nightcap at Walters, knocking his helmet off, and then used his own truncheon to bludgeon him to death. He then tipped out the lumps of glass that afterwards lay unnoticed until I found them there amid the general filth of the platform – " (Nehemiah Wright bristled at the imputation.) " – though shards remained in the nightcap, as Dr. Watson and I noticed when we examined it. Cool as a cucumber, you then donned the constable's helmet and wiped the truncheon on the nightcap, thereafter strolling out into the station as if a policeman on the beat."

"What the Dickens!" Merivale exclaimed.

"Note his garb, if you please, Inspector. For all the world the blue jacket and silver buttons of the London bobby. No one would have given him a second glance – except Garrick, of course. But he, only too aware of the attack and frightened near to death, took cover in the anonymity of his own uniform. After all, van de Groot didn't know who he was."

Holmes paused. No one said a word now, agog to hear more, while the Dutchman continued to stare at Holmes, a smirk twisting his lips.

"I imagine," Holmes continued, "from the nonchalance with which you took a life, it isn't the first murder you've committed, Mynheer."

That smirk broadened into a grin that chilled my heart. Then van de Groot started to applaud slowly.

"What a wonderful fairytale, Mr. Holmes! You have a great imagination. There is a large flaw, however, in your reasoning." His wolfish grin revealed that twinkling, gold-capped canine. "My supposed fraud depended on me knowing a theft was about to take place. But how could I know?

"He's right there, Holmes," Merivale said. "He's got you."

"Of course," Holmes remarked calmly, "he couldn't have known."

"He showed me the diamonds," Mr. Horrocks put in. "They looked real enough to me."

"Yes, indeed," Holmes continued. "I am sure van de Groot made a great point of displaying the diamonds – the real ones, I mean – before substituting them. He also left the key to his strongbox where anyone entering his room could see it. And elsewhere too, I imagine. Beside his dinner plate, perhaps. On the bar?" Van de Groot shook his great head. Holmes addressed him. "Learning of the previous petty thefts, you were quite ready to use that intelligence to stage the disappearance of your diamonds. How surprised and delighted you must have been when Garrick and Walters made that unnecessary."

"I have never in my life," the Dutchman said, rising to his feet, "heard anything so preposterous. So this man is London's Great Detective, is he? Ha! He is a joke. It is all a fancy. He has no proof whatsoever."

"The proof. Ah! I forgot." Holmes reached into his pocket and drew out a large stone, the size of a woman's fist. He held it up to the light while we all gazed upon it as if mesmerised. "Observe the characteristic pink tinge of the stones of the Jagerfontein Mine."

Van de Groot let out an angry yelp and tried to grab the stone.

"I should have thought you would be pleased to have it back," Holmes said. "But oh, I forgot, it never left you, did it?"

"*Godverdomme jij!*"

Van de Groot started to reach into his pocket.

"Stop him!" Holmes shouted. "He's armed!" Inspector Merivale and his constable jumped forward and, as they grabbed the Dutchman, a pistol clattered to the floor.

We stared at it, frozen with shock. Only Holmes remained unruffled.

"But how did you know where to find the diamonds?" Merivale asked. I was wondering the same thing myself.

"Oh, I knew all along," Holmes elongated himself in his chair with that arrogance of his that so often borders on the insufferable. "Well, at least from the moment I spied the harlequin rasbora and cherry barb in their habitat."

"What?"

"The fish tank," I told him.

"What a strange thing to find in a hotel bedroom. Van de Groot told me it came with the room, but that was of course rubbish. He requested it, and so the hotel provided it."

"We at the Midland Grand are pleased to indulge our guests," Mr. Horrocks remarked. "You wouldn't believe what some of them require. Why, on one occasion – "

"Quite," said Holmes. "On viewing it up close, I noticed the floor of the aquarium was covered with gleaming stones and rocks. What a place to hide diamonds, in plain sight. But I must thank Molly for this."

He held up the huge diamond again.

The girl's pale little face lit up.

"I did good, did I, sir?"

"You did indeed. You see," he told the rest of us, "I asked Molly, while cleaning the room, to pick the biggest stone out of the Dutchman's fish tank and bring it to me. And here it is. I imagine by now your constable will have recovered the rest, Inspector."

"He did it all right." Garrick, realising the game was up and perhaps reckoning after all that his crimes weren't very big ones – stealing non-existent gems and attempting to blackmail a murderer – now decided to tell all he knew. "He killed Jim. I saw him beat him to death, the animal. He didn't need to do it," he went on. "We'd have settled for a pay-off."

"Would you? Would you really?" the Dutchman spat at him. "How could I trust you? You miserable little man! Unlucky Chance! Although . . . ." He had the grin of a crocodile, "On the other hand, I suppose you are lucky, in that I didn't find you, too."

Soon enough, an unrepentant van de Groot, still grinning, was led off in chains to face the justice that would eventually see him go to the gallows for the murder of Walters and, as it emerged, for many other vicious crimes. Garrick, for his part, spent a mere few months in Wormwood Scrubs, a salutary experience which must have caused him to mend his ways, for subsequently, as we learned with amusement, he at last managed to find employment with a provincial theatre company that specialised in knockabout farce. Ironically, he particularly excelled in the role of a foolish policeman.

Young Molly was rewarded for her enterprise. No longer a lowly chambermaid in the Midland Grand Hotel, but nowadays, in a spruce black dress with a white cap and apron, she serves guests in that splendid coffee room. Indeed, I sometimes go there for the pleasure of seeing her so happy and rosy-cheeked. Moreover, van de Groot's insurance company provided a reward in recognition of the exposure of a serious fraud, and from that not inconsiderable sum, Holmes gave a portion to Molly, some of which she used to fix her teeth.

All in all, then, a happy outcome, although the next time I hear the cry, "Doctor! Doctor! Is there a doctor here?" I think I may just slip quietly away.

> *"In the St. Pancras case you may remember that a cap was found beside the dead policeman. The accused man denies that it is his. But he is a picture-frame maker who habitually handles glue."*
> *"Is it one of your cases?"*
> *"No; my friend, Merivale, of the Yard, asked me to look into the case."*
>
> – Sherlock Holmes and Dr. John H. Watson
> "Shoscombe Old Place"

The Impossible Adventure
of the Vanishing Murderer
by Barry Clay

It was December of 1902, and one of the coldest and snowiest in recent memory. Christmas was soon to be upon us. The frequent, heavy snows made my rounds all the more difficult and time-consuming, but that Monday I was working from my surgery. It had snowed heavily overnight, and the journey from Baker Street, where I had been staying while my wife was away, had taken longer than it normally would have as I was forced to walk through almost two feet of snow. I expected that the inclement weather, perhaps combined with the nearness of the holiday, would mean that I would have few patients. I had left early to get there, and I expected I would spend the majority of the day ensuring my records were up to date, taking inventory of my medical supplies, and making notes to order those for which I was running short.

After only an hour, I was considering shuttering the surgery early – for after all, Friday would be Christmas – when I heard the door to my front room open. Some hardy soul, I thought, or perhaps someone who was so ill he could not wait had come to my door. It was only a little past the hour of nine. I went to the waiting room to greet my visitor, only to discover that it was my friend, Sherlock Holmes.

He wasted no time in explaining why he was there. "We've had a wire from Inspector MacDonald. He's asking us to come most urgently. Pack a bag. I have a cab waiting. We can just catch the next train. The game is afoot!"

"I am at your disposal," I told him, grabbing my medical satchel.

"Splendid. Then let us be off."

On the way to the station, I asked, "What has happened?"

"Murder of a mathematics teacher at the Harlow Abbey School."

"I have never heard of it."

"Nor I, but it appears to be quite a select establishment. Lord Oswald Dillingston, Duke of Greyminster, sends his only son to the school. It is for that reason MacDonald's call had such urgency. The boy was on the premises when the murder occurred, and is in some way involved."

I had to confess to Holmes that I was also unfamiliar with the Duke.

371

"I had to look him up. He is quite highly placed in His Majesty's government. A member of the House of Lords, of course. A widower. He is often called to negotiate treaties with Continental heads of state."

"How is his son involved?"

"That is unclear."

We had arrived at the station, shouldered our belongings, and boarded the train. We had a half-hour ahead of us, which I attempted to use as an opportunity to learn more about the murder, only to discover that Holmes knew little more than he had already told me. "Mac said in his telegram that it was quite a puzzle, and that the murderer has somehow vanished." Holmes lapsed into one of his characteristic silences, and I was forced to resort to a copy of *The Times* that some other passenger had left behind to occupy my time.

MacDonald met us at the station. Holmes and MacDonald were friends, and Holmes had assisted MacDonald several times in the past. He was a dour, almost-forbidding man with a thick accent that proclaimed him not only Scottish, but from Aberdeen. His long face, normally set in disapproval due to the misdeeds of his fellow man which he was often called to navigate, became a little less forbidding when he saw Holmes.

"Mr. Holmes. Doctor," he greeted us laconically. "I thank ye for coming to quickly."

"Mr. Mac," said Holmes. "I only wish we were meeting under more pleasant circumstances. How can Watson and I assist?"

"Well, ye can find the missing murderer and how he got spirited away, but ye'll see that soon enough. I have a cab waiting."

Once in the cab, Holmes asked, "How is the Duke of Greyminster's son involved in this?"

"He all but saw the murderer – he and the Latin teacher, Professor Coghill."

"Then you have a description?"

MacDonald snorted. "Not much of one. He was wearing a tan coat, had brown hair, and was a man. They aren't sure of much else. It could be you or me for all the description they gave. They only saw him for a minute before he jumped out of the window."

"He jumped out of a window?" I asked, not more than a little surprised.

"Aye. From the first story, and two stories down into the snow."

"Then I should have thought he would have been easy to track," Holmes thought.

"Aye. I would have thought that, too." His tone was dismal and cheerless. "But here we are."

We had driven through Harlow Town. There was a decided nip in the air. The countryside had that fresh, bright look that new-fallen snow gives the world, and the roads through which we traveled had the expected impediments that a large snowfall brings. Had the situation not been so serious, I could have admired the beauty of both town and country. As it was, I could see that the Abbey School was equally covered by the blanket of snow, except that the building in front of which we stopped. It had a pathway shoveled from the front doors to the street, a gash in the unbroken snow that lay on each side of it. The building itself was of brown stone. It was a solid, distinguished edifice four storys high with dormers that bore witness to a fifth story under the dark grey, slate roof. The windows were painted a gleaming white as if they, too, were made of snow. The door was a waxed, deep brown.

"This is Eddingsford Hall," MacDonald told us. "I've asked the headmaster to wait for us."

"I am surprised he is here," I said. "Isn't the school closed for the holidays?"

"Aye, but it appears that they leave this building open for those students and staff that have nowhere to go for Christmas and Boxing Day." Gloomily, he murmured, "Poor lads, they. Not that Mrs. MacDonald was happy when I was called here." He fixed Holmes with one of his stark stares. "I have hopes you can clear this up before the day is out so I can spend my time with the missus and the little ones." And then he added, "But how you will do it is beyond me."

"I will do my best."

"I have no doubt of it. But whether or not your best is enough, I have no ken."

There was a constable standing at the door to the hall, and he opened it for us. We walked into a large entryway, decorated for the holidays. A pine tree festooned with ornaments and candles, now unlit, stood in one corner, with a smattering of presents under it. Our entrance interrupted a conversation between a tall man dressed in a tweed suit and a short, plump woman wearing an apron. She seemed distressed, as well she might be given that there had been a murder at the school. The two were being watched with a dollop of amusement by a third man who was sitting at a desk just inside the door, and who managed to look a little like a vulture because of an unfortunately long neck, prominent Adam's apple and beak-like nose. His face was weathered and covered with fine wrinkles.

The man wearing the tweed suit broke away from the woman. "Ah, Inspector. I am at your disposal."

MacDonald introduced the man as the headmaster of school, Doctor Hezekiah Hunniford.

"Your reputation precedes you, Mr. Holmes. Inspector MacDonald speaks highly of you. A horrible business this. Horrible. Poor Thorebourne. I can't imagine why anyone would want to kill him."

"But we have disturbed your conversation with this good woman," Holmes pointed out.

He beckoned to her and she approached us, appearing not more than a little uncomfortable. "This is Mrs. Howlett. She was understandably upset, informing me that some items were missing from the kitchen."

"How do you do, Mrs. Howlett. I am Sherlock Holmes. This is my associate, Dr. John Watson."

"I am pleased to meet your Lordships," she said in a voice roughed by age and, I suspected, hard work throughout her life.

"What is missing?"

"Oh, it's nothing to bother your Lordships about," she said. "With such goings on, I don't know why I'm bothering about this."

But I knew why. I had seen it before, more than once. When faced by tragedy and unexpected heartbreak, we retreat to the familiar. Unwilling to face the worse, we complain about the mundane. I remember one woman whose infant, despite all my best efforts, was dying. She continued to fuss over a spot on her kitchen floor that would not come clean. I thought that was what was happening to Mrs. Howlett.

Holmes encouraged her. "If there is anything out of the ordinary, even if it seems inconsequential, it may prove to be important."

"If you say so, Mr. Holmes," said Dr. Hunniford. "Go ahead, Mrs. Howlett."

She grew even more uncomfortable. "Well, it's a trifle, I suppose, but the Christmas pudding is gone. I'll have to make another." She made a face. "It happens. The boys get hungry, and they ransack the larder at night when I am away. But what I don't understand is my stock pot! It's up and vanished! I've looked everywhere! Now, I know boys will be boys, but there will be no stew without that pot!" And then she made a motion of frustration. "And what does it matter with poor Master Thorebourne lying dead in his rooms!" She burst into tears, burying her face in her apron.

Hunniford didn't seem certain how to react to this. Awkwardly, he patted her on the shoulder. "There, there, Mrs. Howlett. This has upset us all."

She regained control over herself. "I'm sorry, Dr. Hunniford. It's just so sad."

"Yes," he responded, seeming to consider. "Would you like to go home?"

MacDonald interrupted immediately. "I'm sorry, Dr. Hunniford, but no one can leave until we have interviewed everyone."

"Oh! Of course. I'm sorry."

"And who will feed this lot if I don't?" Mrs. Howlett asked. "The boys will be hungry soon, murder or no murder. I'd bet my life on it."

Hunniford seemed to brighten at her words. "Yes, you're absolutely right. Would you be able to make sandwiches for everyone, do you think?"

"Can I make sandwiches? Of course I can make sandwiches! There is no trouble that can stop me from making sandwiches! Lunch at noon," she declared and bustled off.

There was a moment of silence, and Holmes said, "It might be helpful to understand the events that led to the discovery of the murder."

"I did the preliminary interviews," MacDonald said. "Let me give ye the setting."

"Please, do."

He gathered his thoughts. "Living in this hall are seven boys, two masters, and Mr. Bates here." He pointed out the man at the desk beside the door. "Bates does the handywork and makes sure the doors are locked at night."

"I have a room right here in the hall."

"I should explain," offered Hunniford. "Most of our boys and instructors went home for the holidays at the beginning of the week. But many of our charity boys have nowhere to go. Some of them are invited to the homes of friends, and we have some townspeople who open their home to a boy for Christmas. But it always leaves a few boys with nowhere to go. We consolidate all our boys and staff here in Eddingsford Hall to save the expense of keeping more than one building open. It has rooms for boys and masters. Mrs. Howlett comes in to cook and clean. Mr. Bates does the heavy work and whatever else is needed."

"And Mr. Bates lives here?"

"It's part of his pay. He has rooms here, rent-free."

"I'm always on call," Bates said cheerfully. "And being around the young'uns keeps me young." He didn't look it.

"Did you shovel the walk to the street?"

"That I did. I was up early, knowing that Mrs. Howlett would be coming to fix breakfast for this lot."

"Did you see anyone?"

"I saw Master Hunniford. He and I are on the same floor. 'You are up early,' I says. 'Couldn't sleep,' says he, and it showed, too. Something on his mind, if you ask me, though what it might be with school out for the holidays, I don't know."

"Anyone else?"

"Well, the twins were up and about. Surprised me, it did. Most of the boys sleep late when school is out."

"Do they share the same floor with you?"

"No. All the students are on the second story. They were down here, on the ground floor, just off the library, which I didn't know until I came down myself. 'Here now,' I says, 'what are you doing up and about, Elisha?' 'I'm Elias,' he says, rather cheeky I thought. 'Where is your brother?' I asks, for they are almost always together. 'Right here,' he says and calls for him through the open door, but he don't come. 'He's reading. I'll get him.' And he goes and gets him. Elisha sticks his head out and asks what I want. 'Just to see you boys aren't up to no good.' 'We're just reading, Mr. Bates' says Elisha, like butter wouldn't melt in his mouth. 'See that's all you do,' I tells him."

"Is this usual?"

"Them in the library so early in the morning? I'd say not. Rapscallions, those boys are. Smart as a pair of whips, but not to be trusted with your eye-teeth. Not like the Lewis boy. Now, him, I wouldn't be surprised to find him in the library. Hard worker, that boy is."

"Benton Lewis is one of our charity boys," Dr. Hunniford explained, "and an orphan. The Abbey began in 1703 as schooling for boys of families who had need, or boys without families. A century later, it expanded to accept students in all walks of life by reason of the high academic standards set by the school. Charity boys must maintain a certain grade level to keep their scholarships."

"And non-charity boys?"

"They must maintain the same level or be dismissed from the school – but charity boys have no other recourse but the scholarship, and they aren't guaranteed to obtain one elsewhere if they have failed here. Our boys from wealthy families may go somewhere else, or their parents may pay for a private tutor. A charity boy has fewer options." I could see where that might instill a greater degree of diligence among the charity boys. He thought for a moment. "All the boys here now, except Hayward Dillingston, are charity boys."

"I see." Holmes looked at Bates. "And after you spoke to the twins?"

"I went to shovel a path for Mrs. Howlett."

"That must have taken some time."

"A good hour. You saw it. It's a long path, and it was a deep snow. Took me time. I'm not as young as I used to be. Finished just as Mrs. Howlett made her way here."

"What time was that?"

"I was done at seven, or close enough that makes no difference."

"So, your conversation with the twins was at six? And your conversation with Mr. Thorebourne even earlier?"

"Around five-thirty, that were," affirmed Bates.

"When was the body discovered?"

"I was here," Mr. Hunniford answered. "I had come about seven-thirty to see to the boys and professors. And I had brought Christmas presents for all of them and the masters, as well as Mr. Bates and Mrs. Howlett. I had placed my presents under the tree when Dillingston and Coghill rushed together down the stairs, shouting that Mr. Thorebourne had been murdered, and they had seen the murderer leap out the window of his room. The sound of their shouts brought the rest of the boys after them. I told Lewis, who is on our track and field team, to run to the police station, and I instructed Bates to lock the doors and open them only for the police."

"That was quick thinking," said Holmes.

"It seemed self-evident," the headmaster replied. "I told the boys to go to the library and remain there. I had Coghill take me to Mr. Thorebourne's room."

"Before you show us, when did the police arrive?"

"Quarter-to-eight, I thought."

"And I was here an hour after that," said MacDonald. "They called me straight away."

"May we see the body now?"

We followed the headmaster up the stairs to the first story, and then down the hall to a door, in front of which stood another constable who opened it for us.

We entered a comfortable room with a fireplace and chairs. It wasn't overly large, but more than sufficient for one person. A door led to a room I assumed was a bedroom. One wall had a bookcase heavy with books, most of which I saw were mathematical in nature. Farther from us was a desk used for working. Perhaps at one point it had been ordered, but papers were now scattered on its surface with some on the floor. The stand near the fireplace, which held pokers and a shovel, had been upset, and one poker was lying athwart the body of a young man, perhaps in his late twenties. Even at a distance, I could see he had been struck several times. His head was bloodied, and the marks of the poker (or an instrument like it) creased his skull. His hair was thinning. He was dressed conservatively, but in slippers, and had no ascot or cravat. His shirt was open at the collar. Behind the desk, the window was open.

"We've touched nothing, Mr. Holmes," said Inspector MacDonald. "I know your methods."

"I'm afraid that we did, Mr. Holmes," said Dr. Hunniford. "Touch things, I mean. We thought he might be alive."

"Did you touch anything besides the body?" Holmes asked.

"We went to the window and looked down. You can see where Thorebourne's assailant landed."

Holmes glanced at MacDonald. "There doesn't seem to be much of a mystery."

"Ah, just you wait, Mr. Holmes. Just you wait."

Holmes gave him a sharp glance, then removed a magnifying glass from his coat pocket and went to work. He spent a good deal of time around the fireplace examining the stand, which was lying on its side. He spent even more time around the body and around the desk, finally looking at the papers on top of it. He moved nothing, but at one point, he made a noise, almost a grunt. I recognized its meaning. He had found something. He then moved to the window and looked down from it. After several moments, he withdrew his head back to the room. "I see the problem," said Holmes.

"I've never seen anything like it," agreed MacDonald. "We're fortunate that the first officers on the scene realized that they should leave it alone."

"What is it?" I asked.

"Come and look, Watson. I'm quite done here."

I went to the window and looked down. I could see the depression in the snow where the killer had landed after leaping from the window. The impact of his landing was such that I could actually see some of the hard ground that normally would have been hidden by the snow. But there was no sign of him having made his way from where he landed! His body wasn't there, and there was no way he could have left the spot where he landed without leaving a trail through the snow. And yet, he was gone, and around where he had landed, the snow was undisturbed.

"But that's impossible!" I exclaimed.

"I quite agree."

"You see the problem, Mr. Holmes?" asked the inspector.

"I do."

"There is no way he could have run off without leaving a trail, and yet he isn't there!"

"Could he have brushed the snow back after running away?" I asked.

"Not without showing signs of it," said Holmes. "And there are no such signs. They would be evident even from this distance."

"Could he have burrowed under the snow?"

"Without leaving humps or depressions in the snow marking his passing? I think not."

"Then where did he go?"

"That is the question. Is there a window on the ground floor underneath this one?" Holmes asked MacDonald.

"Yes," the inspector said, "but it's locked. Did you want to examine it?"

"Later, for verification. I would like to speak with the master and boy who found the body – Mr. Coghill and young Dillingston."

"Here?"

"No. Is there another room where I can interview them?"

"I will have them brought to Mr. Coghill's rooms."

"Splendid."

"Have you learned anything, Mr. Holmes?" asked MacDonald when the headmaster had left.

"Very little. The poker came from the stand, as its design matches the other pokers. Mr. Thorebourne was struck five times, once when he was standing, and four more times when lying on the floor. Any of the blows might have killed him, and five assured his assailant that he was dead. You can see the marks of the poker as it struck the floor when striking him or when his assailant missed. He hadn't been working at his desk. The chair hasn't been moved, which you can see because there is blood on it and around it on the floor. But there are several interesting things to be gleaned."

"What are they?"

He took us to the window. "What marks do you see here on the ledge?" he asked us.

"Why, none," MacDonald said.

"Precisely. And down below?"

"Nothing but the snow where the murderer fell while escaping."

"But did you notice that you can actually see the ground at one point?"

"I did."

"Don't you consider that odd? Why can we see the ground? Why wasn't the snow packed by his fall instead?"

"I don't know, Mr. Holmes. Perhaps he scratched the snow away as he righted himself."

"And then there is this." He took us to papers that lay on the floor and pointed a fragment of a book. "Did you see this?"

"I did. It looks like it's from the cover of a notebook."

"I agree. And this?" He was now pointing to a paper on the floor.

"I did. It looked to me like an answer key."

"It is indeed. But look here." He pointed to another paper, with the top quarter visible from under a disturbed pile. "What does that look to you?"

MacDonald said, "Another answer key?"

Holmes extracted it from under the disordered heap. "Look at it and compare it to the one on the floor."

We did so. "Why, they are the same!" I observed.

"Not quite," said Holmes, "for the first is obviously different."

"I'm sorry, Mr. Holmes, but what does that mean?"

"They were written by two different hands. I believe we have here a motive for Mr. Thorebourne's murder." Holmes added, "This has made one thing clear: We must find Mrs. Howlett's missing stock pot."

I could tell that MacDonald was surprised, as I was, for I could see no reason for it to be important, but the inspector offered no objection. "I'll have this door locked and the constable search for it."

"Have him start on this floor. I suspect that it will be close by."

The headmaster returned and interrupted us. "Mr. Coghill and young Dillingston are waiting for you."

"Lead the way," said Holmes.

MacDonald gave instructions to the constable, after which we followed the headmaster to Mr. Coghill's rooms, which were much the same as Mr. Thorebourne's. He, too, had a desk, but it was tidy, as perhaps the mathematics teacher's desk had been before his murder. The window behind it was closed, and a fire was alive in the fireplace. Mr. Coghill was a tall, athletic-appearing man, handsome, with blond hair and blue eyes. Beside him was a youth of perhaps sixteen or seventeen years of age, with dark hair. He was fully as tall as the teacher, though slimmer of build. He, too, could be described as handsome, aristocratically so, with an aquiline nose not so different from Holmes's.

Inspector MacDonald instructed the pair, "Tell Mr. Holmes what you told me."

I had expected the teacher to speak, but it was the student who said, "I had gone to Mr. Coghill's room to ask him some questions about a Latin translation."

"He is your language master, I assume?"

"Yes, sir."

"Do you do that often?"

The boy seemed uncomfortable. "More of late. I'm afraid my grades weren't the best when I began this term." He then faced Holmes resolutely. "I am trying to improve them."

The headmaster explained, "We encourage the boys to seek help whenever they feel they are falling behind."

"Even on holiday?"

"Even then."

"And it isn't much of a holiday when one can't go home," the boy said. "Father is . . . busy with important matters. He is in France at the moment, I understand." He shrugged, I thought attempting to appear unconcerned, but I detected a suspicion of unhappiness in his manner. "I decided to work."

"Very commendable."

"Thank you, sir."

"So, you and Mr. Coghill were discussing Latin. Then what?"

The boy looked at his teacher, and it was the latter who spoke. "We heard a shout and a struggle."

"You were in this room?"

"No. I had been leaving my room when young master Dillingston approached me. We were in the hallway."

"No doubt why you heard the sounds."

"Yes. They seemed to be coming from Thorebourne's room. We rushed to it. I could hear movement. I knocked. I called out. When I got no response, I tried the door, which was open, and entered, just in time to see a man perched on the window ledge, the window open."

"You both saw this man?"

The student answered, "Yes, sir. You couldn't miss him. But it was for only a second. He seemed to glance back, and then he leaped."

The teacher picked up the thread of the narrative. "We could see poor Thorebourne, his head bloody. I ran to him."

Holmes turned to the boy, who did his best to stand bravely under the detective's piercing gaze, which I knew could be formidable. "And what did you do?"

Again, he looked uncomfortable. "I'm afraid I just stood there, sir." He looked down. "I'm ashamed to say it. It was so . . . I mean . . . there was so much blood." I felt for the boy. I had seen more than my share of dead bodies over the years, and I had myself thought it a grisly sight.

Coghill continued. "There was nothing that could be done for Thorebourne. He was quite dead."

"And then?"

"I went to the window. I'm not sure why. I thought I'd see which direction the man went, but there was nothing."

"There was no depression in the snow?"

"That, of course. I meant the man was gone."

"Are you sure, quite sure, that he leaped out of the window?"

"There can be no mistake about it," Coghill replied.

Holmes turned to Dillingston, who said, "It's just as Mr. Coghill says, sir."

"What did this man look like?"

Both looked a little lost. "It happened so fast," Coghill said. "He was wearing a tan coat. His hair was brown."

381

The boy interrupted. "I thought his hair was darker. Black like mine, perhaps."

"And then?"

"We rushed down the stairs to sound the alarm."

Holmes thought for a moment, then asked MacDonald, "How did this man get into the hall?"

MacDonald started. "I hadn't thought of that."

Dr. Hunniford asked, "Is that important?"

"It is certainly as unexplained as his departure. Except for the depression beneath Mr. Thorebourne's window, there are no tracks to or from the hall."

Holmes addressed his next question to the headmaster. "You mentioned that Bates locks the doors to the hall. When does he do that?"

"Ten o'clock."

"We must verify that he did so." He nodded to Coghill and the boy. "You have been most helpful. You may return to the others."

When they were gone, I asked, "Could he have come inside before last night's snow?"

Instead of answering, Holmes left the room, the rest of us following him. "Where are you off to, Mr. Holmes?" asked the inspector.

"To ask Mr. Bates two questions, and to examine the place from which our assailant disappeared so impossibly."

We found Bates at his desk beside the front door.

"Mr. Bates, I have two questions for you."

"I hope to have two answers," he returned.

"When did you lock the doors to the hall last night?"

"Ten on the dot, same as always. I checked all the windows on the ground floor – they's all common rooms – to make sure they were shut and locked. I checked the kitchen and door to the back."

"And they were all locked?"

"The hall was tight as a drum."

"And when you shoveled the walk this morning, were there any tracks leading up to the door."

This question seemed to puzzle the handyman. "Tracks? What do you mean?"

"Was the snow undisturbed?"

This seemed to puzzle him even more. "Well, of course it was! That was why I shoveled it."

"Quite. And now, I'd like to see the place where the murderer fell. Can you show us the way, Dr. Hunniford? Only take us part way there, then stand back. I want to examine the place he landed."

We followed the headmaster outside and around the building. The air was still, but bitterly cold, with the fresh tang that follows a snow. "There it is, Mr. Holmes."

"Stand here, everyone, until I have had a chance to examine the area."

Very slowly, Holmes made his way to the spot in the snow where the murderer had landed. Reaching his goal, he then examined that for a short time, then the wall and window beside it, before motioning us to join him. It was then I noticed the drain pipe beside the depression.

"Holmes, could our murderer have climbed this pipe and gained entry?" And then I pointed out, "He might still be inside!"

"He is most assuredly inside," my friend returned, "but not by way of that pipe." His eyes twinkled. "Try it, Watson."

With a glance to him, I tried to climb the pipe. I had only just begun when I felt it move. I stopped, stepping down. "It will not hold my weight."

"No. An agile youth might scale the wall by way of that drainpipe, but no man of normal size could hope to do so without pulling the pipe away from the wall. That was obvious from the way it is affixed in the stone."

But MacDonald interrupted him. "Then were did he go?"

"That window?" asked the headmaster, for there was a window in the wall above the depression.

Holmes shook his head. "Any entry from here through that window would leave the marks of his passing. There are none."

MacDonald asked, "Then how the devil did he escape?"

"Surely you aren't saying one of the students – " began the headmaster.

"It was someone who was in the school last night."

The headmaster paled. "Not one of the boys!"

Holmes didn't allay his concern. "Look at the ground where he fell. Do you see the ice?"

The inspector looked, as did I. There was a thin sheet of ice covering a portion of the ground. "I see it," admitted MacDonald.

"What does that suggest to you?"

"That it is very cold out."

Holmes chuckled. "It is that. But combined with the place where the snow has been disturbed? Does that suggest nothing in relation to the ice?"

"I'm afraid not, Mr. Holmes. Not to me. I don't see what you're getting at. It's a puzzle."

He straightened. "Well, we are almost done here. We needn't have packed our bags, Watson. We'll be on the afternoon train and home in time for the holidays."

"You know how it was done, Mr. Holmes?" MacDonald seemed more astonished than I was.

"There are one or two little things I must clear up. Dr. Hunniford, you said that everyone was in the library?"

"Those were my instructions."

"Then let's join them."

When we entered the hall, we were met by the constable who had been instructed to search for Mrs. Howlett's pot. He was holding a large, metal pot in his hands.

"Where did you find it?" Holmes asked him.

"In a closet near Mr. Thorebourne's rooms."

"That's one question answered. You may return it to Mrs. Howlett. I wouldn't want to prevent her from cooking her stew. Mr. Bates, please come with us."

"But Holmes," I objected, "you said the murderer was inside. Shouldn't we leave someone here at the door?"

"The constable will see to it. I have need of Mr. Bates. Dr. Hunniford, take us to the library."

The library was a very large room with rows of tables surrounded by three chairs on each side. As is any library, it was floor-to-ceiling books on each wall, with more stacks shelved with books. It was quite an impressive collection. Sitting at the tables were seven boys, Hayward Dillingston one of them. There were two boys of about the same age, obviously twins, and two other boys, perhaps slightly younger. One was a thin, short lad, with glasses. The other was tow-headed and more robust in appearance. Two other boys, even younger than they were, sitting together. I could see a resemblance between them. One was clearly older than the other. I thought the youngest was no more than twelve. He looked fearful, as well he might, but I couldn't prevent myself from remembering Holmes's words that an agile youth might have climbed the drain pipe. I hoped it wasn't this child. Surely he was too young to commit such a heinous crime, and what reason could he have? And our two witnesses had said it was a man. They would have recognized any of the students. Mr. Coghill was sitting off to the side, away from the boys.

"Is Mr. Thorebourne really dead then?" asked one of the older boys.

The headmaster answered, "I'm afraid so, Wareham."

One of the twins asked, "Who done it?"

"That is what we are trying to determine. You must be brave. You have already met Inspector MacDonald. This is Mr. Holmes and Dr. Watson, who have been called by the inspector to help us get to the bottom of this horrible crime. Please, answer their questions completely."

"I won't hold most of you for long," said Holmes. "First, did any of you chance to talk with Mr. Thorebourne this morning?"

The boy with the glasses raised his hand. "I did, sir."

"And you are?"

"Benton Lewis, sir."

"What did he want?"

"He was carrying a notebook. He wanted to know whose it was."

"Did you know?"

"Yes, sir." Stricken, he looked at the headmaster. "Do I have to tell, Dr. Hunniford?"

Before the headmaster could respond, Holmes said, "It was Hayward Dillingston's, was it not?"

"Yes, sir."

"And did he ask you to get Mr. Dillingston?"

"Yes, sir."

"What did you do?"

"I went to Hay's room, sir, and woke him and told him that Mr. Thorebourne wanted to see him right away."

"And then?"

"I had intended to go to the library, but I decided to go to my room and read." He added, "Mr. Thorebourne was very upset, and so was Hay."

"Thank you. And now, Mr. Bates, which of the twins is Elisha?"

Bates looked uncomfortable. "I don't rightly know, Mr. Holmes.

"I'm Elisha," announced one of the boys. "Elisha Sullivan, sir, and this is my brother, Elias," he concluded, motioning to this twin.

"Which one of you pilfered Mrs. Howlett's Christmas pudding?" Holmes asked.

"Beg pardon, sir," said Elisha. "We neither of us stole the pudding."

"Come, come," admonished Holmes. "Do not waste my time. Which of you was it?" They both looked so innocent that I was certain one of them had stolen the pudding with the other's connivance.

MacDonald said, "Why are we wasting time on a missing pudding when we have a dead body upstairs?"

"Because the pudding is the only mystery remaining, and it may shed light on the murder."

Bates interrupted. "They couldn't have taken the pudding, Mr. Holmes. They were in the library. I saw them."

"You saw one of them," Holmes said. "Which one was it?"

"I saw them both, sir," insisted Bates.

"Together?" asked Holmes.

Bates's face was first uncomprehending, and then assumed a comical expression. "No! One boy went to get his brother – "

385

"Precisely. It is obvious that you cannot tell them apart, though the slight depression on the right cheek of Elias, no doubt from a childhood misadventure, makes it quite clear which is which. I'm sure they take no little pleasure in correcting you when you misname them, or even when you get their names correct. You saw one boy in the hallway, who claimed that his brother was in the library. He went to get his brother, then returned, pretending to be his brother, which suggests the other one was engaged some untoward activity and unavailable." Holmes fixed his eyes on the two of them. "Which of you stole the pudding?"

Neither spoke.

"Unless one of you wishes to be suspected of the murder of Mr. Thorebourne, I suggest you become more forthcoming immediately."

One of the boys squeaked, "We didn't kill Mr. Thorebourne!"

"Then which of you stole the pudding?"

As one, the boys pointed to each other and said, "It was him."

"Did you eat it?"

Both of them assumed a sullen expression. "Didn't get the chance, did we?" Elisha said.

"And while you were stealing the Christmas pudding, did you, by chance, see Mrs. Howlett's stock pot?"

The eyes of the twin called Elisha widened. "Hay took it. He said it was for a lark."

"Thank you. If you return the pudding to Mrs. Howlett – uneaten – we will say no more about it. You may all go," my friend continued, " – except for Mr. Coghill and Mr. Dillingston."

When no one moved, the headmaster said, "All but those two may leave."

When we were alone with the two, Holmes asked, "Which of you killed Mr. Thorebourne?"

The language teacher was indignant. "How dare you! We told you! It was that man who jumped from the window!"

Holmes expression hardened. "I expect it was Mr. Dillingston, but I cannot be certain. What I am certain of is this: One of you killed Mr. Thorebourne, and the other is covering for him."

"That's . . . ridiculous! It was the man we saw."

"There was no man," declared Holmes.

"But we saw him!"

"You are lying, and rather obviously at that."

Inspector MacDonald said, "How can you be sure of this, Mr. Holmes?"

Holmes began to explain. "A man couldn't have leaped from that window without scuffing the sill. It isn't possible. And yet, the sill was

386

unmarked. Further, if a man leaped from the window, he would leave a depression farther from the wall then the one we found. To land at that spot could only have happened if he hung by the window with his hands and then let go. Lastly, if a man leaped from the window, he couldn't possibly vanish without leaving a trail through the snow. *Ergo*, there was no man."

MacDonald asked, "But the depression from when he jumped?"

"Ah! Remember that that the snow wasn't packed from the landing, but actually showed the ground covered with ice? Water was poured out the window, which melted the snow and, in contact with the ground, began to freeze. And this was why Mrs. Howlett's stock pot was missing. It was used to carry the water, which was then poured onto the snow."

He looked at the teacher and student. "Since there was no man, it was obvious he was an invention. So I return to my question: Which of you killed Mr. Thorebourne?"

Coghill seemed in anguish. "This is all incredible! Why would either of us kill Thorebourne? He was a friend! A colleague!"

"Because he had discovered that someone was copying his answer keys, and because he now knew why young Dillingston's grades had improved so dramatically. It wasn't because he hadn't been applying himself to his studies. Rather, he was obtaining the answer keys to his tests."

"That's preposterous!"

"Is it? I submit comparing your own handwriting to the answer keys found in Mr. Thorebourne's room will make it clear that you have been providing copies of your colleague's tests, and perhaps others, to young Dillingston here. I'm confident that a search of his rooms will turn up many such keys. What do you think?"

The boy suddenly broke. "It was him! He did it! He forced me!"

The teacher turned on him. "You swine!"

The boy ignored him. "He made me take the papers!"

"That won't do, Mr. Dillingston. How did he make you do anything? You either participated in the cheating, or you did not. In fact, I rather believe it was *you* who killed your mathematics teacher and then forced Mr. Coghill to lie for you. You had leverage to force him to lie, for if he were exposed for helping you cheat, he would never work again, at least not as a teacher. But if Coghill killed Mr. Thorebourne, what leverage did he use on you? That you were cheating? It's possible, but I rather consider it an unlikely motive."

The two looked at him, their faces transfixed by hatred of my friend. "Arrest them," Holmes told Inspector MacDonald. "I believe you can take it from here and be home for Christmas."

* * * * *

It was after the holidays when a cable arrived from MacDonald, thanking Holmes for his work in solving what, to him, had been an impossible case. To Holmes's consternation, Coghill had been arrested for murder, and Hayward Dillingston dismissed from the school in disgrace.

"What was Mac thinking?" Holmes asked me, and then answered his own questions. "I see the hand of his superiors in this."

"When did you first know they were lying?" I asked my friend, as much to distract him as to learn the answer.

"Almost from the first. As you said, it was impossible. A close examination of the clues made it clear that the man who jumped from the window never existed. After that became obvious, one could only conclude that the two must have been in collusion. And once we found the copied answer key, the motive became equally evident."

"Well, Mr. Coghill will be in jail where he belongs."

Slowly, Holmes said, "I am not certain jail is where he belongs, Watson."

"Why not? It was a horrible thing to do!"

"I do not believe he committed the murder. Remember what we learned from Benton Lewis? He was sent to get Hayward Dillingston by Mr. Thorebourne. I suspect Thorebourne knew from the notebook he found that Dillingston was guilty of cheating on his exams. He must have found his own answer key in it. But did he know who had copied his answer key? He had to suspect it was a fellow teacher, but I doubt he knew who it was."

"What do you mean?"

"There are two ways this could have happened. Dillingston is faced with proof of his cheating by his mathematics teacher. He is the son of a Lord, facing expulsion and scandal. He attempts to snatch back his notebook. Thorebourne resists, and part of the cover is torn off. Inflamed by the struggle, frustrated, Dillingston takes the poker, there at hand, and hits his teacher with it repeatedly. Realizing belatedly that he has killed his teacher, he wakes Coghill, explains what he has done, and tells him he will expose him if he doesn't help him. Faced with the financial ruin losing his job would mean as well as the shame, Coghill submits to the blackmail. Dillingston removes the stockpot from the kitchen and they pour water from it onto the snow to provide evidence to support their story.

"The second way is less satisfying. Thorebourne has spoken with Dillingston. We knew he must have done so, for Lewis roused his classmate with the message that the mathematics teacher wanted to see

388

him. Thorebourne learns from Dillingston that Coghill is supplying him with the answer keys, presumably for money. Armed with this information, what does he do?"

"I assume he confronts Coghill."

"And invites him to his rooms to do so? Why? What does he hope to gain?"

"Perhaps to give Coghill a chance to explain?"

"What explanation is there? No, Watson. The more likely course is that he would take the evidence he has to his headmaster. Even if he is imprudent enough to face Coghill, what then? How does Coghill force Dillingston to lie for him?"

"To prevent his expulsion?"

"It is possible, Watson, just possible. But I think not," he added bitterly. "I doubt it occurred that way."

"But you said Coghill had been arrested for the murder!"

"Indeed I did. Mr. Mac does not say it in his telegram, but I suspect his superiors – not to mention a British jury – would more likely believe a man guilty of murder than a sixteen- or seventeen-year-old boy, the scion of a Lord. It is even possible Mac agrees. He has children, Watson. No doubt, his could never do such a thing."

"Holmes, that's terrible!"

"It is indeed. A man guilty only of moral weakness may be convicted of a capital offense. But this boy?" said Holmes. "I fear we may see him again. He has gotten away with murder once. He may try it another time." After a moment, he said, "I will cable Mac with my suspicions. Failing that, I will offer to give evidence for the defense, for I fear, otherwise, he will be found guilty. Our system of justice is not infallible."

It was a sobering thought, and one I found I chose not to entertain long. I decided to put it out of my mind and hope that my friend was wrong.

I feared, however, that he was not.

It happened that at the moment I was clearing up the case which my friend Watson has described as that of the Abbey School, in which the Duke of Greyminster was so deeply involved.

– Sherlock Holmes
"The Blanched Soldier"

Mr. Phillimore's Umbrella
by Paul Hiscock

I was sitting at my desk, trying to write down an account of one of the extraordinary mysteries solved by Sherlock Holmes, when I heard the doorbell ring. I sighed and waited for the inevitable arrival of the maid. She was quite new, and a pleasant girl, but she seemed to lack the initiative to handle any unexpected occurrences on her own. Not for the first time, I missed the formidable Mrs. Hudson who had always guarded us against trivial interruptions when I had lived at 221b Baker Street.

As predicted, after a few moments the maid knocked on the door to my study and then opened the door.

"I am sorry to disturb you, sir, but you have a visitor."

"Who is it?" I asked.

Her cheeks flushed with embarrassment. "I'm sorry, sir. I forgot to find out. Should I go back and ask?"

I groaned quietly. It was not the first time this had happened, and I began to suspect that I would be seeking out a replacement before too long.

"Never mind, Milly. I'll see who it is for myself."

"Very good, sir," she said, and then ran off.

My back cracked as I stood up to see who it was and I realised that I had been sitting there all morning. It would probably be good for me to take a short break. Still, I hoped that I would be able to deal with this visitor quickly, as I was eager to continue with my writing.

However, when I entered the hall, all thoughts of work fled my mind as I saw that, far from being a stranger, my visitor was actually my dear friend, Holmes.

"Watson," he said, "it's good to see you."

"You too, but this is quite a surprise. Surely it is next weekend that we're meeting for dinner, not today?"

"No, you're quite correct. This visit wasn't planned, but I hoped that you might be available to join me for a few hours."

"Of course. I can always make time for you. What is it that brings you back into London, away from your cottage and your bees?"

"I've been summoned to the Diogenes Club by Mycroft. All I know is that he requires my assistance with a grave matter of national importance."

"Then let me fetch my coat at once. I know your brother doesn't like to be kept waiting."

As usual, upon our arrival at the Diogenes Club, we were escorted in silence to the Stranger's Room, where Mycroft Holmes was waiting for us.

"Thank you for coming, Brother," he said, once the door was firmly closed. "And Dr. Watson – I assumed that Sherlock would bring you, and so as you will see, took the precaution of having tea prepared for three."

I looked down at the table, where three cups were indeed waiting next to a steaming teapot – and a photograph of a middle-aged man and a young woman.

"The gentleman is Mr. James Phillimore," said Mycroft. "Two days ago, he went missing from his home, and no one has seen or heard from him since then."

I studied the portrait. The man had a thin face, a feature that was accentuated by the pointed Van Dyke beard on his chin. He wore a pair of small, round metal-rimmed glasses.

"What about his wife?" I asked, pointing at the woman who stood next to him. "Does she know anything?"

"I believe that is his daughter," said Holmes. "If you study the image closely, you will note the similarity of their features, particularly that distinctive bump in the nose."

When I looked at the photograph again, I wondered how I could have missed it. Now that Holmes had drawn it to my attention, the resemblance between them was obvious.

"Since it would be an unusual choice to exclude one's wife from a family portrait like this," Holmes continued, "I also deduce that Phillimore is a widower."

Mycroft nodded. "That is correct. He lives with his daughter, Julia, in Hammersmith. They both set off for work together on Monday, as was their habit, but he had forgotten something and returned home. He stepped back into his house and that was the last time he was seen."

"He never arrived at the laboratory?" asked Holmes.

Mycroft shook his head.

"What laboratory?" I asked

"Phillimore is a scientist employed by the government on an important project," said Holmes.

"Have you heard of him before then?"

"No, Watson, but it's obvious. That my brother is the one asking for help, rather than the daughter, tells me that the interest in Phillimore is due to his work, not his personal life. As for his profession, you can see that he has dressed smartly for the photograph, yet there are unsightly marks on his hands that he hasn't been able to wash off. Such stains can linger

391

for days. You might have noticed similar ones on my hands in the past, as they come from spilling certain substances used to conduct chemical experiments. The obvious conclusion is that he is a scientist, and that his disappearance is of concern because he has been conducting experiments deemed to be of national importance."

"I sometimes wonder if Dr. Watson feigns ignorance to humour you, Sherlock," said Mycroft. "Your deductions are correct, but glaringly obvious."

I had noticed none of the details that Mycroft deemed to be obvious, but one depressing fact dawned upon me. "The only time the government takes such a keen interest in scientific work is when it has a military application. Was he developing some kind of weapon?"

Mycroft nodded and smiled, like a schoolmaster whose pupil has finally grasped their lesson. "I'm led to believe it is some type of gas. The details remain a closely guarded secret, but the War Office seems especially excited about its potential applications."

"So they want him brought back to finish his work?" I asked.

"No, Watson," replied Holmes. "I believe this weapon already exists. Their concern is that Phillimore has been taken by agents of another power that wants it."

"Actually, we think it more likely that he is acting of his own volition. This project, and his involvement with it, were a closely guarded secret until yesterday, when his disappearance forced the War Office to share some details more widely. They believe that Phillimore stole materials related to his discovery and plans to sell them to another country. They aren't sure what was taken, as he destroyed everything he left behind, but he and his work must be recovered, at any cost."

"It isn't just foreign countries that we should be concerned about," said Holmes. "There are many criminals who have no scruples about taking lives and would happily use such a substance to deadly effect in order to further their schemes. You shouldn't have waited so long to summon me, Mycroft. If you would provide the addresses of Phillimore's residence and place of employment, we will begin our investigation at once, before the trail grows any colder."

James Phillimore and his daughter lived in a narrow three-floor house on Hammersmith Terrace, a quiet residential street that runs alongside the river. I immediately recognised the young woman from the photograph when she answered the door. Her eyes were red and puffy, and it was obvious that she had been crying. However, her voice was calm and steady when she greeted us.

"Can I help you gentlemen?"

392

"Miss Phillimore, I am Sherlock Holmes, and this is my associate, Dr. Watson. We are here to investigate your father's disappearance."

I had expected that she would be grateful that we were offering our assistance, and so was quite unprepared for the vehemence of her reply.

"If you're here to make more baseless accusations like the other 'gentlemen' who came to search our house, you can leave now. I've only just finished clearing up the mess that they left behind. I'll tell you what I told them: My father isn't hiding in the cellar or the attic, and he is neither a thief nor a spy. There are no secret formulas concealed behind the picture frames, fragments of messages from foreign agents in the fireplace, or dangerous substances hidden in the drinks cabinet!"

"I am sorry," I said. "I know that the police can often be tactless and heavy-handed when they investigate."

"It wasn't the police. These two men claiming to be from the War Office turned up early yesterday morning, just as I was wondering if I should go to the police station. They told me that my father had never made it to work the day before, and demanded to come into the house. Despite my assurances that he wasn't here, they seemed convinced that he was hiding somewhere inside."

"That must have been very distressing," I said, "but I can assure you that we have nothing to do with those men, and certainly don't condone their actions."

"We know that all you want is to find your father," said Holmes. "We want that too, and if you could tell us, in your own words, exactly what happened on Monday morning, I'm certain we'll be able to help you."

Miss Phillimore nodded hesitantly. "Very well," she said, before reluctantly letting us into her home. She led us past the kitchen and stairs to the cosy parlour at the rear of the house.

I accepted a seat in one of two well-worn chairs while Holmes stood, looking out of the back window. Without turning around, he repeated his request for Miss Phillimore to describe the events of the morning her father disappeared.

"I've thought it through time and time again," she began, "but I can honestly say that I remember nothing out of the ordinary. We have a very regular routine. I rise first and come down to make our breakfast: Eggs and toast. I like my eggs runny, but father prefers them hard and with the yolk just slightly sticky. He cuts them up into neat little circles and lays them out on his toast, always in the same neat pattern. That is what you need to understand about my father: He loves order, precision, and routine. That is what makes him a great scientist, and why it is so unlike him to have disappeared like this. The men who came seemed convinced that he has

393

chosen to disappear, but I cannot believe that. Someone must have done something to prevent him from returning home."

She began to sob gently, taking a rumpled lacy handkerchief from her sleeve that had clearly seen plenty of use already that day.

"What happened after breakfast?" asked Holmes.

"We headed into the hall, picked up our coats and bags, and set off for work, just the same as always. Father always walks with me to the tram stop before we part ways. He then heads to his laboratory, while I catch the tram to Kew Gardens, where I work in the Tea House. However, on Monday, when we reached the end of the road, he realised that he had forgotten his umbrella, and went back home to fetch it."

"You didn't go with him or wait?"

"No, I offered to, but he insisted that I go on ahead. Like all of our morning routine, our walk to the tram stop is planned very carefully. I have just the right amount of time to reach it comfortably before the tram arrives. However, it does mean that if I delay for any reason, I'm in danger of missing it."

"It has been bright and sunny all week," I said. "Surely he could have left his umbrella at home? He wouldn't have needed it?"

"If you had ever met my father, you wouldn't be surprised. He never leaves home without it. He is adamant that one should always be prepared for the worst that might happen."

"Why do you think the men from the government were so convinced that your father was hiding in the house?" I asked.

"I'm not sure. I saw him opening the front door, just as I turned the corner by the Black Lion. He waved to me before he stepped inside. That was the last time I saw him, but he could have left the house easily at any time after that."

"I suppose they might have asked your neighbours," I said, "but even if he wasn't seen in the street at the front of the house, he still could have left through the back door."

Miss Phillimore shook her head. "Why would he do such a thing? Besides, it's impossible."

"Not impossible," replied Holmes, "but certainly unlikely. You should come and see for yourself, Watson. There is a nice little garden back here, and beyond that the river. I'm sure it makes for a stunning view from the upper floors, but the river wall is too high to jump from without risking serious injury."

I went over to the window to stand next to Holmes and saw what he meant. The house did indeed look out upon a lovely view, but it wasn't a practical way to leave the building.

"Do you know what your father was working on?" asked Holmes

"No. He never talks about such things. He always says it's far too boring. In the evenings, he prefers to hear me tell him stories about the customers I serve at the Tea House.

"Can you think of anyone who might want to hurt him?" I asked.

"No, of course not. Outside work, he barely speaks to anyone apart from me. Certainly he never spends enough time with anyone to make them his enemy."

"Very well," said Holmes. "I think that you've told me everything that I need to know, for now. I promise that I will do all that I can to locate your father and bring him home safely."

"Thank you, Mr. Holmes – and you, Dr. Watson. I'm sorry for the way I greeted you. I'm relieved to learn that someone cares what happened to my father, and not just about his work."

She stood up and led us out of the house.

As we were leaving, I noticed that the stand at the bottom of the stairs still held a gentleman's black umbrella with a curved bamboo handle. Once we were outside and the door was closed, I turned to mention it to Holmes, but as always he was ahead of me.

"I saw the umbrella too, Watson. It certainly adds credibility to Miss Phillimore's assertion that someone took her father against his will. Perhaps we will learn more from his colleagues."

We were lucky, and swiftly managed to procure a cab from outside the Black Lion public house at the end of the street, to take us to Phillimore's laboratory, which was located in nearby Kensington, at the Imperial Institute.

Like many Londoners, I had visited the Institute when it first opened to see the British Empire Exhibition. Although I knew it contained offices and laboratories belonging to University College, this grand building, with its elaborate neo-Renaissance towers, seemed to me to be an unlikely place to conduct research into dangerous weapons. Indeed, there was nothing to indicate the nature of Phillimore's work until we reached the corridor outside his laboratory, where a soldier stood guarding the door. Luckily, Mycroft had prepared the way for us with the War Office, and once we had identified ourselves, we were immediately admitted.

Upon entering the laboratory, I was immediately reminded of our old rooms in Baker Street, where Holmes would set up all manner of elaborate experiments that would emit strange fumes and noxious smells, to the annoyance of both myself and Mrs. Hudson. Here, however, there was plenty of space for the scientists to carry out their work without the risk of contaminating anyone's breakfast or burning holes in the carpet.

There were two men in the room, each standing behind a workbench covered in equipment. There was a third workbench at the back of the room, but this one was covered in shards of glass from broken test tubes and beakers, and fallen, twisted metal armatures that had once held everything in place. I remembered being told that Phillimore had destroyed his work, and this was obviously the result of that action.

One of the scientists looked up when we entered and quickly stepped out from behind his bench to stop us from progressing any further.

"I'm sorry, gentlemen, but this is a restricted area. We're handling very dangerous materials. I'm afraid you cannot be here."

"I can assure you that we are authorised," I said. "We're here investigating the disappearance of your colleague, Mr. James Phillimore."

The scientist groaned. "Not more of you! Look, we don't know where he has gone, or why he destroyed everything after everyone else left on Friday? And yes, we could tell you what he was working on, but you would never understand us, so let's just say that it was very dangerous, and we need to find whatever materials he took as soon as possible."

The government men who had intimidated Miss Phillimore had obviously been here before us as well, and left just as favourable an impression.

"Please, may we have just a moment?" I said. "Mr. Holmes and I aren't with the War Office. We've been asked to help – "

The second scientist suddenly looked up from his work and interrupted me.

"Mr. Holmes? Do you mean *Sherlock* Holmes?"

"Yes, the consulting detective. That is correct."

"No, I mean the *scientist*. You wrote 'The Comparative Effects of Various Acidic Solutions on Human Tissue', and dozens of other seminal papers."

Holmes nodded. "That was one of mine, although it has since been overtaken in the field by Humphries' work."

"Nevertheless, you provided the groundwork. Let them come in, Lansdale. I'm sure they won't knock over any of your test tubes. I'm Dr. Archer. It's a pleasure to meet you, Mr. Holmes."

"Likewise. This is my colleague, Dr. Watson."

"Another chemist?"

"No," I replied. "Physician."

"Oh well. Someone has to do it, I guess. Never had the desire to deal with patients myself. We prefer research, don't we Lansdale?"

"That's *Professor* Lansdale," the first scientist replied. "Or are you forgetting that I'm your superior, and the one who decides who enters this laboratory."

396

Despite his protestations, however, *Professor* Lansdale stepped back and allowed us to approach their benches.

"What was Phillimore's position in the laboratory?" I asked. "I don't recall anyone mentioning that he had a doctorate."

"That is because he didn't," replied Lansdale. "He was the most junior member of the team."

"Junior, but brilliant," added Archer. "He was the cleverest one in the room, and could have passed his doctorate easily, but it simply didn't interest him."

"So he was working for you?"

"Technically, yes, but we all have our own projects. Phillimore was doing work on poisons, whereas I'm more interested in corrosives. A few months ago, he told us that he had made an important discovery – something to do with insecticides – but didn't want to say much until he had experimented further."

"It was a complete breach of protocols," said Lansdale, "and so I reported him to the Director. All work undertaken here is meant to be subject to rigorous supervision and peer review. However, Phillimore has had a few successes in the past, and the decision was taken to give him a little space to work."

"We were patient with him," said Archer, "but I must admit that I was curious to learn what he was working on. Finally, the week before last, he shared his secret. It seems that last year he had an accident in the lab. He spilled some liquid insecticide that he had modified, and it created a gas that left him seriously unwell for weeks."

"An accident which he should have reported," complained Lansdale. "Once again he managed to get away with flouting the rules."

"Anyway," continued Archer, "he discovered just a small amount of this liquid could be used to cover a large area with an odourless, colourless gas cloud that would incapacitate or kill anyone who came into contact with it."

"I recognised the military applications of this discovery immediately, and contacted the War Office," said Lansdale. "They were very excited by it, and immediately sent men to secure the lab."

The military uses for such a discovery were clear to me as well. However, while Lansdale appeared excited, I found the idea terrifying. I knew how to fight men, and how to treat wounds caused by bullets and knives, but how could one hope to defeat an invisible cloud?

"It was agreed that Phillimore would share his research," continued Lansdale, "and that we would begin a properly supervised program of experimentation and development. We were given a week to wrap up our other projects and were due to start working on Phillimore's formula on Monday, but that morning he never arrived."

"What of his workbench?" asked Holmes. "Did he leave any clue that might point to his whereabouts or his intentions?"

"You can see for yourself," said Archer. "We were instructed to leave everything as we found it, in case something could be salvaged, but his destructive efforts were very thorough."

He led us over to the bench at the back of the room, so that we could inspect the damage. Upon closer inspection, I could see that the metal mixed in with the broken glass had been melted in places. Even the wooden worktop was damaged, its surface pitted and discoloured.

"What happened?" I asked.

"Phillimore stole some of my acid samples and used them to destroy all his equipment. Whatever substances he was working on, there isn't a trace of them left."

"What about his notes?" asked Holmes.

"There is evidence that he destroyed some papers," replied Professor Lansdale, "but as I told the men from the War Office, we cannot be certain if he took anything with him. The guard outside has been checking the bags of anyone leaving the laboratory ever since they arrived last week. However, I know from personal experience that they aren't always very thorough. They're more concerned about intruders than those of us who work here. All we know for certain is that he left nothing behind that we can use."

"Do you think he took a sample of the substance?" I asked nervously.

"He's a fool if he tried. It is dangerous enough within the controlled conditions of the laboratory. Outside, any accident would be fatal. The tiniest spillage could kill dozens of people – maybe even more in crowded part of the city.

"And you're sure that he is the one responsible for this damage?"

"Absolutely!" said Archer. "As Lansdale already told you, he stayed late on Friday evening, and aside from the dean, the three of us are the only ones with keys to this laboratory. Even before Phillimore's discovery, we had to ensure the highest levels of security to ensure that none of our experiments are contaminated or tampered with. Besides, only someone intimately acquainted with my research could have known how to use my store of acids to destroy everything this effectively."

"What will happen to his project now?" I asked.

"There is no project," replied Lansdale bitterly. "Without Phillimore's notes, we don't even have a place to start. Not only that, but as his supervisor, I'm being blamed for the loss by the university, even though we repeatedly warned them that he needed to be brought back into line."

"The War Office seems to think that he is planning to sell his formula to a hostile country," said Holmes. "Do you agree with them?"

"I'm not certain this gas of his is even real," said Lansdale. "He wasn't as clever as people thought, and it cannot be coincidental that all of the evidence that it existed disappeared as soon as he was ordered to share it."

"I'm sure it's real," replied Archer, "but as to whether he would sell it, I'm not sure. A week ago I would have told you it was impossible. Neurotic old Phillimore, with his silly habits and those stupid umbrellas could never do a thing like that. However, now I'm not so sure. Maybe he is some type of master spy and he has been playing us for fools all this time."

"Umbrellas?" asked Holmes. "He had more than one?"

"Not really," said Archer. "Week after week, month after month, he has always come into work with that same umbrella of his, even on the hottest day of the year. However, last Tuesday, he came in carrying a different one. Most people probably didn't even realise, but I have had to look at that umbrella with its bamboo handle every day for the last three years. I spotted the difference immediately. This one had a smooth dark-wooden handle. I admit I might have teased him about it a bit – Old Phillimore finally making a change – but he told me his old one was simply being repaired, and sure enough, by Friday everything was back to normal. At the time it seemed like some great drama, but it pales into insignificance compared to what he did this week."

"This has been most illuminating," said Holmes. "Thank you, gentlemen for your assistance."

"If you find Phillimore's notes," said Lansdale, "make sure you return them to me. If he really did achieve what he claimed, it will take a skilled scientist to recreate his work."

"What about Mr. Phillimore?" I asked. "Are you not at all concerned about his well-being?"

"Phillimore is a disgrace to the scientific community. If you find him, you should hand him over to the police to answer for the damage he's caused. He is certainly not welcome back here."

When we left the laboratory, the guard stopped us to check our bags, just as Dr. Archer had said. When he saw that we weren't carrying anything, he quickly patted us down before letting us go. It wasn't the most thorough of searches, and he might not have noticed someone passing through with a few sheets of paper, but I would not have wanted to try to smuggle a whole file past him.

"Should we speak to Miss Phillimore again?" I asked as we walked through the Institute towards the gate. "She was convinced that her father was taken by force, but that clearly isn't what happened. Perhaps if we confront her with the truth, she'll remember something else that could help us find him."

"There is more than one type of force," replied Holmes. "He might have been responsible for the destruction in the laboratory, but acting under duress. If someone threatened his daughter, I imagine he would follow whatever instructions he was given."

"Still, I think we should tell her what we have learned."

"We will, but there is somewhere else I want to stop first. I have a feeling that there is some deeper significance to Phillimore's decision to return home for his umbrella. Of all his actions over the last few days, leaving his umbrella in the house seems the most out of character."

"More out of character than destroying his work?"

"Yes. That was a conscious and deliberate act, but a fastidious creature of habit like the man that everyone has described to us doesn't just forget his umbrella one day. The habit of picking it up would be so ingrained within him that he would do it instinctively, without giving the action a single thought."

Upon stepping outside, I signalled to the drivers waiting at the nearby rank. A cab pulled out from near the back and headed towards us. There was some shouting as he passed the cabs that had been waiting in front of him. They were meant to take fares in order, but it wasn't the first time that I had seen a driver jump the queue, and I wasn't particularly concerned which one we used.

"Where are we going?" I asked as the cab pulled up in front of us.

At first he didn't reply. I looked around and saw that he was staring at the vehicle as though it had reminded him of something. Then, a moment later, he snapped out of his reverie.

"Take us to New Oxford Street."

"Very good, Guv'nor," replied the cabbie.

"Did you have any idea that the gas Phillimore was working on was something so deadly," I asked, once we had set off. "I imagined some sort of thick cloud that could be used to hide our soldiers from the enemy. Certainly nothing like the substance his colleagues described."

"It is a terrifying development," agreed Holmes. "We must do everything we can to prevent the formula from falling into the wrong hands."

"Do you think Phillimore is just planning to sell any notes he managed to steal, or is he going to recreate the formula himself?"

"From what Professor Lansdale and Dr. Archer told us, it sounds as though it will be difficult to replicate, even with Phillimore's notes. Scientists rarely think of others when jotting down their notes. They may well be incomprehensible to anyone else. Still, it isn't the notes that worry me most. It will take him time to reproduce his work."

He seemed to be about to say something else, but he paused for a moment before resuming in a tone so quiet that I had trouble hearing him.

"I still worry that he might have taken a sample of his formula. It would strengthen his negotiating position if he is trying to sell his work, and would almost certainly have been among the demands if someone is coercing him."

"I hope you're wrong," I replied. "I hate to think how many people would die if this gas were released on the streets of London. But why are we whispering? We often discuss our cases while travelling in hansom cabs."

"True, but we're now talking about a life-or-death situation. It isn't just reputations at risk if we're overheard."

Then, as though to underscore his point, he sat back in his seat and didn't speak again until we reached our destination.

When Holmes instructed the driver to stop at the corner of New Oxford Street and Shaftesbury Avenue, I immediately saw what had drawn him there: The windows of James Smith and Sons were filled with umbrellas of every size, shape, style, and colour imaginable.

"Why are we here?" I asked, when we had alighted on to the pavement outside the shop. "I realise that this is an excellent establishment from which to buy an umbrella or walking stick. Indeed, I own one of their umbrellas, and the stick I gave to you for Christmas a few years ago came from here. However, I don't see how they can help us find Phillimore."

"I only glanced briefly at Phillimore's umbrella, but it was obvious that it wasn't a cheap, mass-produced item, and I recognised the workmanship immediately. I'm hoping that the family who made it can help me understand its significance."

"By all accounts, he has owned his umbrella for years. They must have sold hundreds more since then. Surely they aren't going to remember one customer from so long ago."

"Let us see," said Holmes.

The shop bell rang as we pushed open the door, and the proprietor looked up from behind the counter.

"Good afternoon, gentlemen. How can I be of assistance? It's been a few years since we last saw you, Dr. Watson. Is your umbrella still in good working order? I would be happy to look it over and make sure it's working smoothly."

"It is working very well. I have no complaints, but I'm surprised you remember me. I am hardly one of your most regular customers."

"I make a point of trying to remember our clients – particularly the more notable members of society such as yourself and Mr. Holmes here. Now, if your umbrella is in good working order, what can I interest you in today? Maybe something in a different style, or a parasol of your wife?"

"We aren't here to make a purchase," explained Holmes. "We were hoping that you could assist us with a case."

The proprietor was about to reply, when the shop bell rang again.

"Please come in. I'll be with you in just a few moments. In the meantime, why don't you browse through our stock? There is a selection of umbrellas which might suit you just over there on the left."

The newcomer behind us must have nodded in agreement, because the proprietor then returned his attention to us.

"We were hoping to talk to you about one of your customers," said Holmes softly. "Mr. James Phillimore."

"Ah, yes. A classic solid maple stick with a whangee cane crook and brass fittings. I believe he purchased it almost twenty years ago."

"However did you remember that?" I asked in astonishment. "Surely you aren't old enough to have sold it to him?"

"No, I imagine it was my father who served him. However, he is one of those select clients who chooses to bring his umbrella back to the shop once a year to be cleaned and serviced. He comes in regularly, every September, in preparation for the autumn and winter ahead."

"So you haven't seen him since last year?" I said.

"On the contrary, he was here just last week."

"Mr. Phillimore went into work last week with a different umbrella, while his was being repaired."

"Yes, I lent him one of our basic models for a few days. However, you are incorrect, Mr. Holmes. His umbrella didn't need to be repaired. It was in fine working order. Instead, he asked if we could *modify* his umbrella. I have to admit I was surprised. His umbrella wasn't ideally suited to the changes he wanted made, and would make it far more vulnerable to damage in windy weather. I suggested that he could purchase another of more suitable construction for his purposes, but he insisted that we use his umbrella."

"What did he ask you to do?" asked Holmes.

"His main request was that we install a small glass flask within the handle."

"Is that not a rather strange request?" I asked.

"Not especially, although it is more common in canes rather than umbrellas. They're commonly known as tippling sticks, as the vial is intended to hold a small measure of one's preferred libation. We have a few over here."

He went over to one of the displays and took down a wooden cane with a horizontal brass handle which he turned a few times and then removed to reveal a small glass container.

"So you installed one of these in Mr. Phillimore's umbrella?" asked Holmes.

"Almost. It wasn't quite the same, as he insisted on providing the vial himself. I couldn't really see the difference, but he was was insistent."

"And you completed the modifications in time for him to collect it on Thursday afternoon?" said Holmes.

"Correct. You seem remarkably well informed."

I was confused by this revelation. From all that I had heard, I hadn't imagined Phillimore to be a heavy drinker, and couldn't imagine him indulging in a covert draft from his umbrella handle in the middle of the day.

Then a terrifying thought crossed my mind, and I must have visibly blanched, because Holmes noticed the change in me. He took me by the shoulder and led me away from the counter so that we could talk privately.

"You understand the significance of the umbrella now, Watson?"

"Yes, I'm afraid I do. A flask like that could easily hold a small amount of the substance he was working on in its liquid form."

"Indeed. So now it is imperative that we find Phillimore's umbrella before it falls into the wrong hands."

I looked at him in confusion. "But we know where it is!" I exclaimed. "We saw it in his hallway earlier today. Do you think the poison is still inside?"

I heard someone moving behind me, and a moment later the shop bell rang as the door opened and closed.

"Watson!" Holmes shouted. "Didn't I warn you earlier that we needed to be careful not to be overheard speaking about this case? Now he has a head start!"

"Who does?" I asked.

"The customer who came into the shop just after us, and who has been stalking us all day in the guise of our cab driver. Hurry! We know he already has a vehicle. We must procure one of our own if we're to catch up with him."

403

Hearing the urgency in Holmes's voice, I turned to open the door.

"I am sorry," Holmes said to the proprietor, "but we must hurry away."

"Just a moment!" was the reply. "There's something else I think you should know."

"You'll need to be quick! Watson – go find us another cab. I'll be right behind you."

I followed his instructions and stepped out into the street. Luckily, we were in one of the busiest parts of London, and the nearest cab rank was full. I procured the first vehicle and instructed the driver to pull up in front of the umbrella shop. As we approached the curb, Holmes came rushing out. He leapt into the cab before we could stop and shouted, "Hammersmith Terrace – as fast as you can!"

The driver whipped the horse into motion, and Holmes stumbled back, falling into the seat next to me.

"I'm sorry," I said, once he was settled. "I had completely forgotten there was anyone else in the shop."

"It isn't your fault. This spy has clearly been trained to observe without being noticed, taking on the roles of people that we would naturally ignore. He even went so far as to change his outfit between journeys. However, that was the mistake that raised my suspicions, because I recognised a distinctive set of scratches on the paintwork by the cab's door. If our original cab might well have stayed in the area after dropping us off, but it would still have been driven by the same man. I realised then that our luck in finding cabs today wasn't luck at all."

"Do you think we can make it back to Hammersmith Terrace before him?"

"I hope so, but I'm more worried that we might already be too late. If Miss Phillimore has meddled with that umbrella in our absence, she could very well have released the gas."

"Let us hope it doesn't come to that," I said, and then I banged on the roof. "Hurry!" I shouted at the driver. "Every second counts!"

I have rarely travelled across London so fast, yet when we arrived I was alarmed to see that the hansom cab in which we had travelled earlier was already standing outside the Phillimore house.

I paid our driver as quickly as possible and then followed Holmes, who was already rushing inside. When I reached the door, I saw that it had been forced open, splintering the wood around the latch.

As I entered, I heard Holmes shout, "Leave it alone! You mustn't open it here!"

I came close enough to see over Holmes's shoulder and saw that the fake cabbie had already unscrewed the umbrella handle. He removed the glass vial, held it up to the light, and squinted at it.

Taking the opportunity while the man was distracted, Holmes rushed over and grabbed him by the wrist. I shouted in alarm as the vial fell from his hand, but Holmes had obviously planned for this and was already holding out his other hand to catch it safely.

Recovering from his initial shock, the cabbie twisted free of Holmes's grip. The two men stood facing each other for a moment before starting to fight. Although it was clear from the outset that his opponent had been trained in hand-to-hand combat, under normal circumstances I would have expected Holmes to quickly prevail in such an encounter. However, he was handicapped by the need to prevent the glass vial in his left hand from smashing.

The hallway was narrow, leaving the two men little space to manoeuvre. Holmes dodged the first few punches, but was then forced to duck to avoid a particularly brutal blow, and I worried that he might be in trouble. However, he bobbed back up with a smile on his face and Phillimore's furled umbrella in his hand. Then he unleashed a flurry of blows upon his opponent, incapacitating the man in moments.

He turned and handed me the umbrella. "I must return to James Smith and Sons and complement them on their craftsmanship. A lesser umbrella would have broken at the first blow, but this served as acceptable substitute for my short stick."

Then Holmes opened his left hand to reveal the vial of deadly poison. I breathed a sigh of relief.

"At least it isn't broken," I said. "It's hard to believe that such a small item could be so dangerous."

Holmes held it up to the light and examined it carefully. Then he laughed.

"You can relax, Watson," he said. "The vial is empty."

"Are you certain?" I asked. "Dr. Archer told us that the gas is odourless and colourless."

"No, it is definitely empty."

"What if it was damaged during the fight and the substance leaked out? We could start to feel its effects at any moment."

"No," said Holmes, "I don't think we're in any danger. There are no cracks, or even the slightest residue in the vial. I don't think that Phillimore ever used it."

I was still nervous, but since I wasn't feeling ill, I hoped that Holmes was correct.

"We should tie this man up and call for the police," I said, and had started to look through the coat rack for a scarf that might serve when I was interrupted by the voice of Miss Phillimore, coming from upstairs.

"Is it safe now? Has that man gone?"

"We've secured the intruder," I replied, "and the danger has passed."

"Thank God you're here! When that man broke in, I feared for my life and ran up here and hid in the wardrobe. I thought he would pursue me, but after a while, when I had heard nothing, I crept out to the landing. That's when I heard the reassuring sound of your voices."

"Just give me a moment to restrain him, and then you can come downstairs," I said, but then was interrupted once more by someone knocking at the broken door.

"Is there anyone in here?" the newcomer said, pushing the broken door open.

"Can we help you?" asked Holmes.

"Inspector Brown of the Yard. I gather there has been a break-in here."

"Thank goodness, Inspector!" cried Miss Phillimore. "A man broke into my house, and if it hadn't been for the timely arrival of these two gentlemen, I don't know what might have happened."

"Yes," I said, "it's good that you're here, but how did you know to come? We haven't yet had a chance to call the police."

"One of the neighbours called us," he said. It was a perfectly plausible answer, as we had made quite a commotion. Yet somehow it didn't ring true. "Now, is this the miscreant?"

He went over to the man on the floor, who was just stirring, and knelt down beside him. There was a brief exchange of words between them, but although I tried hard to listen, I couldn't make out what was said. Then our fake cabbie was dragged to his feet by the inspector. I expected him to resist, but he accepted his arrest with surprisingly good grace.

As they were walking past us, the inspector suddenly stopped in front of Holmes.

"What do you have there?" he asked.

"Nothing of consequence. Just an empty glass vial." He held it up for the inspector to study. "This man was trying to steal it from Miss Phillimore."

"Was he really? In that case, I think I should take it with me as evidence. It will of course be returned in due course."

I thought Holmes would object, but instead he meekly dropped the vial into the inspector's open hand.

"Thank you, sir, "said the inspector and hurried out of the house with his prisoner. "Good day to you all."

"Holmes, there was something not quite right about that man. Did you not see it?"

"'Inspector' Brown is no more a police officer than Miss Phillimore here. I may have retired to Sussex, but I still make it my business to know the name and face of every detective at Scotland Yard."

"Then why did you give him the vial?" I asked. "We must get it back."

I hurried to the door to see if I could stop the fake policeman and his prisoner, and was just in time to see the hansom cab that had been parked outside pulling away, the inspector seated inside and the fake cabbie back at the reins.

"They were working together all along," I said upon returning inside. "And what's worse, I realised something was wrong. I should have stopped them while I had the chance."

"I suspected as much immediately," replied Holmes, "but it was confirmed when Brown asked me for the vial. He couldn't have known it was in my hand, let alone realised its significance, if our fake cabbie hadn't told him."

"Why did you let him take it then?"

"I didn't wish to risk Miss Phillimore's safety. These men have already demonstrated a willingness to employ violence to achieve their ends. Besides, now that we know the vial is empty, it is of no concern. They can do what they like with it."

"I still don't like it," I replied. "Those were undoubtedly the people who coerced or persuaded Phillimore to steal the formula. We should have arrested them and taken them to the real police."

"Who would have then released them within the hour. Those men weren't foreign spys, or members of a criminal gang. They are agents of our own government, and they've been watching this house ever since Phillimore destroyed his research on Friday.

"You mean they are working for Mycroft too?"

"No – at least I don't think so. I believe he trusts me to act on his behalf without needing to send someone to shadow my movements. He would also send far more skilful operatives. I'm sure that they are agents commissioned by the War Office."

"Why do you think they've been here since Friday? Phillimore only went missing on Monday."

"They were watching when Phillimore stepped back into the house that morning. That's why the government agents who searched the house were convinced that he was still inside, and why his disappearance was deemed so mysterious that they had to ask Mycroft to involve me.

"Then why didn't they just arrest him on Friday? They knew where he was all weekend."

"They knew his location, but they didn't know who was buying the formula. I suspect they hoped to catch them all at once."

Miss Phillimore started to cry. I had almost forgotten that she was there with us, and immediately regretted the tone of our conversation.

"Did my father really steal from the government?" she sobbed.

"He certainly deprived them of some research that they would dearly love to recover," said Holmes, "but his motive for doing so still remains a mystery. However, the answer may have been right in front of us all along. Come, let us sit down comfortably in the parlour and find out what your father left behind.

We did as Holmes instructed and sat down in the parlour. He followed us through and placed Phillimore's umbrella on the table in front of us. I noticed that at some point he had reattached the handle.

"Miss Phillimore, last year your father had an accident at work which made him very ill for a while."

"I remember. I spent weeks nursing him back to health. At one point, I feared that he might never fully recover."

"It led him to discover a very dangerous substance," continued Holmes. "One that would have been of great value to the War Office. However, on Friday, before returning home to spend the weekend with you, he destroyed all his work. The War Office believes that he did it in order to sell his research to agents from another country. It would be a lot more valuable if he was offering exclusive access to his work."

"I just can't believe it!" cried Miss Phillimore. "My father wouldn't have done such a thing."

"Sometimes even the ones closest to us can act in ways that we just cannot imagine," I said to her, trying to soften the blow of what Holmes was saying. "I'm sure that, whatever he did, he never meant to hurt you."

"Last week," Holmes continued, "he took his precious umbrella to be modified. It had to be the same umbrella he had carried every day for years, so not as to arouse suspicion on the day that he left the laboratory for the last time. We know that it was noticed when he went in with a different one a few days before."

"He didn't like having to use it, but he told me that there was a small tear in the canopy that needed to be fixed. It left him upset and distracted all week."

"I wonder if that had more to do with what he was planning," I said. "He had the umbrella shop install a small vial in the handle of his umbrella so that he could smuggle some of his formula out of the laboratory. That's what the intruder was searching for when he broke in. However, I still don't understand why the vial was empty."

"I think the explanation might lie in here," said Holmes. He unfurled the umbrella and then started to feel around the canopy, panel by panel. I wondered what he was doing, but then he pulled a sheet of paper from a pocket concealed within the fabric.

"The shop made a *second* modification to the umbrella while it was at the shop. The proprietor called me back in order to tell me about it. There is a hidden compartment in each panel, capable of concealing two or three sheets of paper each without being visibly obvious. I assumed that Mr. Phillimore intended to use them to smuggle his notes out of the laboratory, and perhaps he did. However, he also used one of them to leave this letter for you."

He handed the piece of paper over to Miss Phillimore. For a moment she held it in silence, before she said, "This is my father's writing."

Then she started to read:

My dearest Julia,

I deeply regret leaving you in this way, but a life on the run is no life at all for a young woman such as yourself.

By accident, I have created something terrible. At first, I thought that it might be something beneficial to mankind: A weapon that resulted in no destruction of buildings and no loss of life. However, the results of my experiments soon proved that I was tragically incorrect. I had discovered a monstrous substance that could indiscriminately kill dozens of people with a single drop.

I spoke to my superiors, telling them that I wanted to shut down my experiments and that my works should be confined to the deepest vaults, never to be used. However, to my horror, they wanted to develop my discovery further, making it more powerful and more deadly. I realised then that I couldn't let them have it.

I devised a plan to destroy my work, taking only a small sample and a few notes. It was my intention to use these to develop an antidote, against the inevitable day when someone replicated my discovery. However, at the last minute I realised I couldn't do it. Every drop had to be destroyed lest it fall into the wrong hands.

I should have started running as soon as I left the laboratory, but I couldn't bear not to see you again. It was a

409

great risk to come home, but I would not trade the last two days for anything. I only wish there could have been more.

However, by now they will be discovering what I have done, and they will come to arrest me. So I must disappear, lest they force me to share the knowledge that now only exists in my mind.

I have left my umbrella to protect you, now that I cannot. Please use it, and remember me fondly every time it rains.

With all my love,

Father

We sat in silence for a minute after she finished reading, until I asked, "Will you show this letter to Mycroft?"

"There is no need. I'll tell him what he needs to know: That Mr. Phillimore destroyed his formula rather than see it used to end countless lives."

"He'll still want to know how Mr. Phillimore disappeared from this house, and where he is now."

"I'm sure that I could find multiple ways that a man might leave this house unseen. However, I don't intend to investigate any of them. I am sorry, Miss Phillimore, but I must break my promise to you. I will not be continuing the search for your father."

"Thank you, Mr. Holmes. I'm sorry that you won't be able to clear my father's name, but I'm grateful to you for honouring his wishes."

"The War Office will send others to look for him," I said.

"I have no doubt that they will," replied Holmes, "but I don't think they'll discover anything. The fate of James Phillimore, after he stepped back into his house to get his umbrella, will forever remain a mystery."

A problem without a solution may interest the student, but can hardly fail to annoy the casual reader. Among these unfinished tales is that of Mr. James Phillimore, who, stepping back into his own house to get his umbrella, was never more seen in this world.
– Dr. John H. Watson
"The Problem of Thor Bridge"

Trouble at Emberly
by Kevin P. Thornton

It had been some time since I had last seen Sherlock Holmes. He had mentioned on more than one occasion that his bees kept him busy down in Sussex, so we met whenever he came to London on business or when I found either the time or the inclination to visit him. I missed my old friend dearly – some of the best times of my life emanated from our shared rooms in Baker Street – but age and decrepitude had caught up to me and dragged me ever slower towards grumpy old age. The litany of aches and pains that visited me every morning, reminders of wounds from wars and bruising from pastimes, bore testament to a life well yet harshly lived.

I found it easier every year to postpone visiting Holmes in Sussex, just as he used his apiaries to avoid London. In truth, I believed the excuse of the bees was an aide to perpetuate his solitude. I had read enough about their industriousness to know that one could leave their hives alone for extended periods without fear. Indeed, they had survived for thousands of years without human help, and likely would do so for thousands more. Holmes liked to be alone, and that was that.

Regardless, I for one was always glad to hear from him, so when a telegram arrived inviting me to meet him in Whitehall, the complex of buildings that defined the heart of our Government, I was delighted. Not only would I see my friend, but the venue suggested more than one member of the Holmes family might be in attendance. Although Mycroft was in his seventy-fifth year and must have retired according to Civil Service mandate, Holmes had mentioned on more than one occasion that people like his brother never quite went away. "His mind is a national treasure," he'd said, "They will always find a way to utilize it."

Holmes was waiting for me at the grand entrance to the Horse Guards building. Although it was ostensibly a barracks and stables for the Household Cavalry, it was such a dramatic entrance to the Halls of Power that it was often used as a means to impress visitors to the labyrinthine buildings that housed the machinations of the Empire.

Holmes mentioned as much as we walked. "This is not Mycroft's idea, to shuffle us through the corridors of incompetence. Whoever we are meeting is important enough to force my brother back to these offices, and our manner of ingress speaks volumes about the personage and his self-inflated opinion."

Indeed it did. While Mycroft greeted his brother in as warm a manner as stultified siblings can, he seemed delighted to see me.

"Doctor Watson!" he said ominously. "Good to have a man who can staunch the blood."

He guided us to the tea table and we sat. The room was most un-Mycroft-like. He'd never, in all the time I'd known him, stood on ceremony or hid behind the trappings of power, yet this office was a corner suite with windows overlooking the parade ground outside. There was ornate woodwork on the walls, with detailed panelling, and gloss finishes and tables around the room that, if moved, that would take six men to carry. As if in answer, Holmes laughed once sharply. "What must they need of you, to loan you such rooms? Ah, wait – it is not *you*. The man we await has pretensions of power."

"And, though running late, will be here momentarily. Give portent to his words, if not his manner, else we will get nowhere."

As if on cue, the subject of the conversation arrived in a harried walk, as if blown in from Parliament between the bells. He didn't introduce himself – maybe he felt he didn't need to – yet even I knew of him. I had read his opinions in *The Times*. He followed the pattern and content of much of his ilk, clamouring for change, all while hoping things would stay the same.

"Gentlemen," said Mycroft, "may I present – "

"No names please," said the latecomer. Holmes seemed amused by this and raising a quizzical eyebrow to his brother let out another short laugh and leaped out of his chair.

"Ha! Of course not. No names it shall be." He waved his hand vaguely around the room. "Meanwhile, there are a thousand civil servants who already know that you are meeting with Sherlock Holmes in this 'discreet' set of chambers. We will use no names for I will not stay. Whatever news leak you planned from this, I will not be a part of it."

He started to walk towards the door when his brother stepped in front of him and said, "Sherlock, please?"

The two brothers faced each other, then Mycroft leaned in and said something so softly only Sherlock Holmes could hear. He paused for one more second then turned on the balls of his feet and sat down again.

"Very well," he said. "I will listen, Mister Anonymous MP from Birmingham-Ladywood."

There was a look of thunder on the MP's face as he spoke to Mycroft. "I ordered you keep my name out of this, yet you disobeyed me!"

Mycroft seemed amused at the reaction. "You can hardly be surprised that a detective will detect an anonymous client, especially one in the public eye. And I don't work for you or feel the need to obey. I am here as a favour to the King. My brother is here as a favour to me, and Doctor Watson is here to lend an air of sanity to the meeting. If you feel you have been compromised, you may take your questions elsewhere and we will repair to the tables of the Diogenes Club." In an aside to me he continued, "I hear the members are saying our Dover sole to be the equivalent of the Savoy this year. If we are brief here, we may find out. I would value your thoughts, Doctor."

My inept comparison of fish dishes was going to have to wait, as out anonymous/not-anonymous reason to be here stepped towards us with his hands slightly outstretched, as if he wished to beg forgiveness, but hadn't been taught how. Revisiting my memories of the day much later, I thought his attempts at appeasement to be indicative of his entire career – indecisive and half-hearted. Nevertheless, he had the floor.

Our MP stood two inches over fix feet and was dressed in London formal: Grey pinstripes with a darker, longer, morning suit jacket. He had been elected for less than four years, having been, like his Father before him, the Mayor of his hometown, and with the Government of Lloyd George wobbling, he was seen as a man of the future. *O tempora, o mores.*

As he spoke, he portrayed the manner of one who wished to appear imposing. He failed. He wore a mustache to add *gravitas*, which it didn't, and while he stood as tall as possible – as if there were vanity risers in his shoes – he seemed diminished by the very surrounds he thought would impress. I hoped at least for grandeur from his voice, but like everything else about him I was disappointed. Instead, he spoke in a clipped Belgravia tone, as if he had translated the image of a stiff upper lip into sound.

"A former constituent of mine, and a very dear family friend, moved recently to become the Headmaster of Emberly. It is a small school in Surrey, not far from Eton. Indeed, in manner and tone it aspires to be one of the country's best educational institutions, and Doctor Chilvers, for that is his name, delights in telling me all about the work he has done with the school. There have been new lawns laid, rose gardens set out, and even a cricket pitch to county standard. He is so industrious he also has a greenhouse for the boys where they grow cane, to refurbish the masters' needs when required."

"Ah, it is a bastion of educational enlightenment," said Holmes, to Mycroft's displeasure and our host's puzzlement.

"'Er yes, quite," he said, continuing. "Emberly has fine traditions, and one of those is its own House football competition. Like Eton's wall game or Harrow's own peculiar brand of team sport, Emberly's is only played by the school at the school grounds. During the course of these games, that is when it happened."

He paused as if all was understood. I waited. Mycroft seemed distracted, as if he would rather be at his club, yet I know he heard all and observed all. Holmes had his eyes closed, yet for all I could tell he heard all and saw all as well.

"You need to elucidate," said Mycroft.

"But these are top secrets."

"And you have asked for my help. My brother has a knack for these puzzles. Please continue."

"Very well then. There has been talk among the boys of the cormorants. And the lighthouse."

Holmes opened his eyes only to facilitate the narrowing of his brows. My friend the grand detective of yore would have dismissed such a client out of hand. The only reason he had stayed at all was for his brother, who also seemed keen to move things along.

"My esteemed colleague," Mycroft said in a way that made one sure he was neither, "is worried because not too far south of the school, in the Channel, there are the beginnings of a War Office experiment. As new lighthouses are built along the coast, they are being fitted with advanced optical equipment to pre-empt an attempt at invasion. It is a highly secret project. The government can't be seen to be preparing for another war so soon after the last one. It will look cowardly and ineffective."

"And what of the cormorants?" asked Holmes.

"They are being trained as message birds, like carrier pigeons in the war. In the event of loss of radio or undersea cable, it is felt on high that a back-up system is needed."

"Why not pigeons then," I said. "They proved successful in the last ding-dong."

"They don't like lighthouses. More specifically, they aren't suited to life at sea. Apparently, they pine and are ineffective."

The Politician in the Corner, as I was already naming him in the story I would write one day, was uncomfortable at being usurped as the centre of attention. "We need to know if there's a leak." He turned to Holmes the Elder and said, "See to it. The cabinet meets next week." Then he left the room.

The room seemed warmer with his departure. Both the brothers declined to fill the vacuum with sound, as if they waited for me. I did not disappoint.

"That was outrageous!" I said to Holmes. "He shouldn't treat Mycroft as a . . . as a . . . ." Words failed me.

"A *servant*?" said Holmes. "Calm yourself, Watson. Your apoplexy threatens you. Mycroft is here of his own volition and is inured to the rudeness of the chattering classes. He is also the only reason we are both here."

"For which my thanks," murmured his brother.

"What of the man who just left? He seems a prime candidate for idiocy, which means he will likely be Prime Minister one day."

"He brought his story to a man I know who is level-headed," said Mycroft. "There are also a few other level-headed people within these corridors who were sufficiently concerned to ask me for help. It is likely a coincidence that two of the main components of a top-secret project, cormorants and lighthouses, are mentioned on a school playground. What are the chances that such a thing were to happen in such a way the headmaster would remember it and relay the story to his friend, the up-and-coming Member of Parliament?"

"They would give long odds indeed," said Holmes. "And yet, we are none of us a fan of coincidence. The Universe rarely serves up such laziness. So you volunteered me?"

"I know you are bored with your bees, so I assumed you would have the time. That you brought the Doctor with you will add some dignity to your school visit."

"There is more, is there not?"

"There is always more," said Mycroft with a hint of asperity, "else you would never have made a living all those years ago."

Holmes acknowledged the comment with a wave of his hand. "Is this the part where you tell me the Government will fall if we don't find the link behind a secret spy program and a second-class school in Surrey?"

"Pah!" said Mycroft, "Governments are always about to topple, yet the great machine of state moves ever forward. The lighthouse lookouts aren't the worst idea in the world, although I suspect if there is another war the invasion will be by aeroplane. If we learned anything from trench warfare, it was that soldiers as cannon fodder is senseless."

"In addition," he continued, "it isn't all flim-flam. Cormorants can actually be trained. I took the time to find out, and they are used for fishing in the East. The real issue, and the one with which I am concerned, is how do schoolboys know of such a thing? If there a leak in the War Office, if someone is talking about secret projects, they must be stopped. Doctor Chilvers has guest rooms at the school for parents travelling from afar, and he expects you soonest. The staff dining room, so I hear, serves excellent food, unlike the swill they give to the boarders. See to it please, Sherlock. We are four years past the war to end all wars. Let us see if we can reach five."

* * * * *

Dr. Chilvers sent the school shooting brake to the railway station to fetch us and was waiting in the entrance hall himself when we arrived – most un-headmaster-like behaviour. Many of the little autocrats who aspire to run schools, or hospitals, have flunkies at their beck-and-call. Dr. Leslie Chilvers seemed to be cut from a different cloth.

He was an affable man who nevertheless looked like he hadn't slept in a year.

"We have a newborn," he said, "our first, and she doesn't sleep. At all. I have been trying to help Ariadne, but," he shrugged, "I am a mere man."

"Keep trying," I said to him. "She will remember your efforts."

"Thank you, Doctor. That is kind of you."

We were interrupted by a *"Harrumph"* from Holmes. "Do you think we could move on to the salient details of the case?"

"Of course," said Chilvers. "Please follow me."

With tea served, Chilvers started with a brief history. Normally, when Holmes was in his *Harrumphing* mood, this would have irked. However, the Headmaster spoke with economy and clarity.

"Emberly is a little over fifty years from its creation, and came out of the educational reforms of the early part of Queen Victoria's reign. Eton was full, so other schools were needed to create more good Englishmen to go out and conquer the world. In fact, we were founded by Old Etonians to be the equal of their *alma mater*, and many of the quirks of that grand old school were borrowed, including the wall game. Are either of you familiar with it?"

"Treat us as if we are not," said Holmes.

"It is a game with a peculiar set of rules. Part rugby, part football, with a varied number of players per team, the whole being played against a large and long wall that is the boundary of one side of the playing field. While the rules are written in a laudable manner, talking of striving towards goals and teamwork, it is, I believe just another means of institutionalized violence. When I first arrived, I was horrified at the game. Nearly three-quarters of all the injuries our boys sustain during the course of a school year are from Emberly's wall game."

"Why don't you stop it?" I asked.

Doctor Chilvers shook his head gently. "I would like to, and I may. The Board of Governors, however, will not have it, and I am new enough in charge to know how to pick my fights. The wall game is not one of them, not just yet. Besides, even though there are a lot of injuries, until recently they have all been minor. Scratches, scrapes, bruises, bumps, the occasional sprain or strain. There is nothing different from any other

416

schoolboy activity save the frequency, much of which is because it is a wall game. The wall is all that remains of an ancient Cistercian Abbey – rough-hewn, angled, and capable of tearing skin off quicker than a slide into the crease on a dry wicket. It's like applying sanding paper to a rugby match."

"You said," said Holmes, "until recently."

"Yes," said Chilvers. "This season, in addition to the expected traumas, we are seeing more vigorous damage. Six boys have had arms or legs reset from breaks. There have been a multitude of re-settings of dislocated fingers, and there has even been a worrying concussion where the boy was bedridden for four days. There also seems to have been a change in tactics."

"In what manner?" said Holmes. He lent forward as the sleuth of old, and for a moment I didn't see his grey hair and wrinkled visage. He was once again *Sherlock Holmes*, the finest detective of his age, no longer the pedantic beekeeper.

"The destructive part of the game seems more structured. It's as if these injuries are caused on command. On the sidelines we hear a call, an order almost, and not too many minutes later there is an injury."

"And those calls are the words *cormorant* and *lighthouse*," said Holmes.

"Yes," said Chilvers.

"Have you asked the boys about the change in tactics?"

"Yes. The long tradition of not snitching is still prevalent. Admirable, but annoying."

"And what does the boy giving the orders have to say?"

"We have yet to identify him," said Chilvers. He saw the look of puzzlement on my face. "I think it would be best to show you."

The walk from the school to the old abbey grounds was a gentle one. As we strolled, I took the time to look back. The buildings were far older than the school, and in answer to my question, Chilvers said, "The monastery and abbey were destroyed by Henry VIII. Then it was rebuilt in parts, and has since served as a private residence, a hospital, farm storage, and even, I believe, a bawdy house, although the Governors will not thank me for remembering that."

As we approached the field of play, the noise grew louder and the hum and roar of the game captured my heart.

"Have you played a game such as this, Doctor?" asked the headmaster.

"Only rugby," I said. "More years ago than I care to remember."

417

"Forty-seven," said Holmes. "You've stated that your last game for Barts was in 1875. You may have played other games later, but not formally. "

"Thank you, old friend," I said, to Doctor Chilvers' amusement. We had arrived at the field. There seemed to be more people playing than not. I estimated more than twenty per side, blues versus greens, all scrumming against each other, holding on, pushing against the wall as much as the opponent. Every now and then there was a shout, and I'm sure I heard the word "Cormorant" uttered gutturally, as if in command.

"It is an ugly game," said Chilvers. "There are no elegant cover drives to the boundary, no side-steps past the wing three-quarter on the way to the try line. The game challenges nothing in the making of a boy to a man except fear and pain. I will put a stop to it one day. I will." I could see the fiery determination in him as he said this. Emberly would do well with this man at the helm.

There was sharp cry out on the field, followed by a cessation in play. I watched as a trainer ran out, followed by a man in a suit with a bag. "Do you always have a doctor present for the games?" I asked.

"I have had Doctor Waters here this season, since the nature of the injuries have intensified. He is an Old Boy and a local practitioner. It works out well, as I believe he enjoys being here, It gets him out of the practice in such a way his partners can't complain about."

As if he could hear us, the doctor called the stretcher bearers on and then came over to talk to Chilvers. "It looks like the ankle," he said. "I'll have to take him to the infirmary."

"Doctor Watson, why don't you go with Doctor Waters," said Holmes. "The increase in injuries is troublesome. Maybe the two of you could theorize as to why it is so."

"I would be delighted," said the young *locum*. "I read your stories, you know. Fascinating stuff. Tell me, this character of yours – '*Holmes*' or something. He isn't real, is he? He seems to be too good to be true."

"Sadly, he is anything but," I said, and out of the corner of my eye I could see Chilvers fighting a laugh, while even Holmes seemed amused.

As Doctor Waters and I looked back at the field. The boys seemed to be taking a break, blues gathered on one side, greens on the other, chewing on orange wedges and gulping down water. One player stood apart. He seemed to be of adult size already, He was over six feet in height and was bulky without running to fat. As he stretched himself, he appeared light on his feet, and his movements were agile despite his cumbersome build.

Although he wore a blue shirt, he seemed separate from the others until one of the smaller boys brought him an orange and water and waited, subserviently, until the bigger boy was done. His image stayed with me all the way back to the infirmary. A boy not yet a man, alone, and possibly lonely.

We met again for dinner. Mycroft was right. The food at the staff table was simple but excellent. "We have an arrangement with some of the women of the village," said Chilvers. "They cook local food for us. I'm trying to get the school cooks to do the same, but the house kitchen is entrenched in its ways, and the slop that they serve is worthy of a Dickens novel."

"Surely that is the way of public schools," said Holmes. "The experience is so bad it toughens up the boys and they go on to conquer the world. Was it not 'Chinese' Gordon who said, while dining on insects in the desert, that after surviving the kitchen at Taunton there was nothing no more frightening food anywhere, locusts included."

"That once may have been the way," said Chilvers, "but I believe firmly in what Juvenal wrote: '*Mens sana in corpore sano*' – 'A healthy mind in a healthy body'. If the Good Lord gives us all this nutritious food to eat, should we not do our best to pass that nutrition onto the charges in our care?" He sighed and rubbed the top of his head. "I shouldn't grumble. We are making much headway. Already some of my ideas are reaching the ears of other, bigger schools. People will listen to reason, but not from a school where what is supposed to be a pastime has become a source of serious injury." Chilvers turned to me. "Is it true, Doctor? Our latest injury today is a broken ankle?"

"It would appear so. Doctor Waters seems very capable, and the young man will no doubt recover, but it was a strange injury."

"In what way?" said Holmes.

"Well, if we hadn't been there when it happened and saw the accident on the playing field, I would almost have thought it was deliberate. As if the boy was targeted."

"But surely such a thing would be noticed?" said Doctor Chilvers

"I don't know," I replied. "In my time playing rugby, I was witness to one or two acts of retribution that were not noticed off field. Those took place in scrums with less than half the players your wall game has, so it is entirely possible that today's act was deliberate, although you wouldn't wish to believe it so."

"The sweet flowers of youth," observed Holmes, "may not be as sweet as one would hope. Tell me, Doctor Chilvers, would you be able to enquire whether this boy who was injured today had recently fallen out with anyone? Maybe even the previous two injured boys as well?"

"I don't wish to believe that possible," replied Chilvers.

"Nevertheless," Holmes countered, "We must know all possibilities. As to the code words you heard, how did that come about, and how did you know they were significant."

"I didn't, at first. I noticed the frequency of their usage. 'Lighthouse' and 'cormorant' are perfectly normal words that wouldn't register as significant in day-to-day conversation. It was, however, unusual how often I heard them in the week before my visit to London. Apart from reports of their use during the wall game, there were incongruous calls in the schoolyard, and accidental usages of either word in class, slightly out of context. They even appeared once or twice in homework assignments. Look, I have one with me". He reached for his valise and took out a notebook, turned to a page. "Read that," he said.

Early to rise, early to rouse
With shotguns for our armament
We'll hunt for grouse
Near the old lighthouse
And try not to hit a cormorant.

"It's unusual for this boy to be even this ambitious," said Chilvers. "There is a hint of scansion and even a passing attempt at a rhyme scheme. I was going to ask him about it, but there seems now to be no doubt he was put up to it."

"You should ask anyway," said Holmes. "One of them will eventually let something slip. It might be our aspiring poet is the one to give up the answers we need."

"I will," said Chilvers. "As soon as he gets out of the infirmary. He's the boy with the broken ankle."

Holmes sat still for a moment, as if replaying the conversation in his head. "You said the references to the lighthouse and the cormorant were noted in the week before you went to London. Tell me Doctor Chilvers: Is it not unusual for the headmaster to leave his school during term."

"Normally, yes, but this was a special invitation to give a report on education to a House of Commons committee. It was quite an honour to be invited and the Board insisted I go. They even stood me the costs, and the story made the local papers."

"So, it was common knowledge you would be in London, and also when you be in London and where you would be when you were there. Did you ever mention your special friendship with the Member from your old hometown?"

"I'm sure I have. I am proud to know and hope one day to call him Prime Minister. I remember all too well the horrors of the last war. My friend believes in peace at all costs. One day, if he is indeed destined to run the country, he will never take us into the madness of war."

"Quite" said Holmes and the look on his face showed, to me at least, his differing view on the subject. I'll not say that Holmes never changed his opinion about a man, bur he rarely needed to. "To sum up: The entire school knew you would be in London. A week before you go, top secret code words are being bandied about at your school. You mention them to your friend, and he panics and sends us to find out the why's and wherefore's."

"You have solved it then?" I asked.

"Not yet," said Holmes. "We are missing two vital bits of information: How did a schoolboy get hold of those code words, and why did he start spreading them across the school like gold doubloons in a harbour bar? What was the point?"

I knew better than to answer. "This must stop before someone is hurt badly," continued Holmes, "or even killed. Watson, what did you and Doctor Waters discover about the injuries?"

"The serious injuries seem to be of a type," I said. "They appear to have been caused by a hard object and applied to joints: Knees, shoulders, fingers. In two instances where an arm was broken, Doctor Waters wrote in his notes that the arm was badly scraped."

"As if the boy was dragged?" asked Chilvers.

"Or as if the perpetrator missed his target instead of hitting an elbow or a wrist."

"Were any toes damaged?"

"No, the boots they wear would protect against that."

"And are the boots uniform in nature, or could they be modified."

"There are precious few regulations to the entire contest," said Chilvers, "and none about boots. You could even wear cricket spikes for added purchase." He stopped as he heard what he'd just said. "No. I cannot believe what you are thinking."

"Not cricket spikes," said Holmes, "but some form of modified boot capable of causing a crushing injury. When did they start, Watson? These serious injuries?"

"Just before Michaelmas."

"And how many new students have you had in that period?" said Holmes. "I would talk to all of them separately."

"There is only one," said Chilvers. I was surprised at his immediate knowledge, and Chilvers must have seen my reaction. "We discourage boys starting part way through the year, as we find it puts them under even more pressure, with all the other changes going on in their lives. The only new entry into our school since the term started is a boy from Poland. His father is working for the League of Nations in London, and we were persuaded to take him."

"How has he fit in?" I asked.

"I don't think he has fit so much as changed his surrounds to suit him. He is polite and he stays out of trouble, but there is something about the boy, a . . . ." Chilvers paused. "You'll see what I mean. I shall send someone to fetch him."

"Do so," said Holmes, "and immediately thereafter send someone else to fetch his boots."

There are no official naming rules for public schools. Boys are normally known by their last name. Two members of the same family are often known, by way of example, as Smith Major, and Smith Minor. A third brother causes naming confusion and the boy can sometimes be ignored for years until the oldest brother leaves the school. Some boys are given nicknames that can stay until manhood. Boys named White are almost always "Chalky". Those with acne or freckles are usually cursed with "Spotty". I knew a doctor from Lincolnshire who, having been taught Mathematics one year by an Irish priest, was forever known as "*36*" – "*Dublin accent and the twelve times table,*" he explained once. He was in his forties at the time, but the name still stuck.

And then there are those who are known by their first name, a singular honour bestowed by the other boys out of either admiration or fear. Our diplomat's son was introduced as Ernie, and there was no hint admiration on the part of the sixth-former who showed him in.

It was the boy who had stood alone on the playing field, and somehow, I had known that would be the case.

"What is your actual first name, Ernie?" asked Holmes.

"Ernie is fine, thank you."

Chilvers handed Holmes a piece of paper and Holmes, glancing at it briefly, seemed about to use the information to gain the ascendancy over the boy. Then he looked at him. Ernie seemed bland, even wholesome at first, but Holmes saw something different.

"You are assessed as being one of the smartest boys in the school, despite only being in the third form. Does this surprise you?"

"No," said the boy. "I am aware of my capabilities."

"Are you also aware that if your father is deemed to have given away secrets, he will be gaoled for the rest of his life."

"I'm sure I have no idea what you are talking about," said the boy.

"Don't presume to insult me again," said Holmes. "The only way you could have known the importance of the words 'Cormorant' and 'Lighthouse' was if you had heard them, in the correct context, from your father."

Ernie was about to lie again. Then he replied, "My father works for the League of Nations. As such, he has the same diplomatic protections as an ambassador. You are bluffing."

"Maybe," said Holmes, "but we'll be able to make a case of espionage against you at least."

I thought Holmes had gone too far as the boy turned and brought a handkerchief up to his face. And then the most astonishing event happened. Ernie wasn't crying in fear, he was laughing. "In your words, sir, don't presume to insult me. I am afforded the same protections as my father. You have nothing, sir. Now, if you'll excuse me.

"Sit down now," said Chilvers. He had been standing at the door behind the boy when the door opened, and a parcel was handed in.

The boy, who was such in age only, towered over Chilvers, yet there was something in the steel of the headmaster's tone that made him obey. Chilvers threw the bag to the floor, and it fell open as it landed. There were steel plates attached to the bottom of the boots and I shivered as I looked at them. What manner of evil possessed this child?

Chilvers contained his anger, barely. "I shall have you expelled," he said, "and I shall write to all the schools I know in England to make sure none of them accept you. What you have done is evil. It is beyond the pale. How could you?"

Ernie seemed delighted, and Holmes noted his behaviour. "No," he said, "we shall make a recommendation to the Board of Governors to keep you here at the school, as well as during the holidays. Your punishment will be to stay back a year and be forced to relearn the same lessons again and again." He got no further as the boy lunged at Holmes, who was more than up to the task and sidestepped Ernie as he attacked, tripping him and twisting his arm back up into the boy's shoulder blade.

"What else?" said Holmes. "There were the injuries and the code words. What else have you done?"

For a moment I though Holmes would break his arm. The boy was strong and stubborn, and seemed impervious to pain. Then he gasped once and said, "The gas pipes in the kitchen. There is a slow leak."

Chilvers was already running.

Some hours later, after the gas was turned off and the boy was safely locked in the root vegetable store, Holmes telephoned Mycroft, who promised to send out some Special Branch Police to fetch the child and deal with the diplomatic fallout.

"The gas would have filled the pantry," said Chilvers. "That's where he had damaged it."

"Surely that's off limits to the boys?" I said.

423

The headmaster looked abashed. "I don't like the idea of corporal punishment," he said, "so when Ernie was caught bullying a younger boy with a potato in a sock – " He saw my puzzlement. "It makes for a delicate weapon, or so I'm told. A cosh with a conscience. Anyway, yesterday, to make the punishment fit the crime, he spent two hours in the kitchen, peeling potatoes for the supper. I gave him his chance, and he could have killed us all in an explosion." He looked at Holmes and said, "What did we do wrong, and how did you know there was something else?"

"When you threatened to expel him, he was delighted," said Holmes, "as if that was the goal. He was taking any opportunity he had to create an untenable situation. He heard the code words at home, and hoped that they would get back to the Government by word of mouth through you to your friend. Maybe his Father would be asked to leave his work at the League of Nations. If that didn't work, he knew eventually he would be discovered as the instigator of the injuries to the boys and you would have to expel him. The gas leak was opportunistic. I don't think her thought that one through.

"But why," asked Chilvers. "His behaviour was excessive. Why didn't he simply ask to be transferred to a school he liked?"

"I suspect his parents are not sympathetic," said Holmes. "And his behaviour, although abnormal to us, is normal to him. He wanted to leave the school and he was presented with three opportunities to effect such an escape. There are psychiatric studies being done about men whose brains work differently, and I suspect young Ernie fits the bill. Psychopathic behaviour is the latest turn of phrase."

We slept well. Chilvers, however, looked exhausted at breakfast, though whether it was the baby or the events of the evening, I didn't ask.

"You seem fairly enlightened, Doctor," said Holmes. "I am impressed, and your attitude towards choices other than corporal punishment is laudatory. Why then do you cultivate weaponry in your greenhouse."

"I am sure I have no idea what you are talking about."

"You friend the politician. He told us you grew your own cane to keep the teachers supplied. You seem enlightened, yet such a practice is a continuation of the acts of barbarism that I thought you disapproved of."

There was a look of absolute astonishment on Chilvers' face. "Oh dear," he said. "We do try to grow cane – not very successfully, I might add, but it is not to provide the swishes of corporal punishment. They are for the vegetable garden to build lattices to support the vine tomatoes and to take the runner beans off the ground."

Special Branch arrived to escort the "diplomatic flippin' nuisance back to Belgravia", as the sergeant-in-charge said when he called on us.

"Begging your pardon, Mister Holmes, but the boy would like a word."

We walked out to the wagon. Ernie was sitting between two policemen who looked as if they uprooted trees for a living.

"I will tell you who it was that told my father, if you promise you do everything in your power to get me and my mother out of this country."

"I am already doing that," said Holmes.

"Do you promise?" said the boy.

"I do," said Holmes, at which the boy leaned over and whispered to Holmes.

As the wagon startled away, Holmes began to laugh. He laughed so hard that when he stopped laughing, he laughed some more. He tried to tell me what he knew, but he was unable.

It didn't matter. I knew.

The next day we went calling on Mycroft in Whitehall, this time in an office of his choosing. It had room for four chairs and a table. We three were all there on time. The politician was late, and when he came in he played the same as before, busily blustering. Holmes interrupted him.

"We found the leak of the top-secret information, and we are in the final stages of tidying up the last pieces of the puzzle."

"I have seen naught of an arrest," said the man. "What has happened? Will there be a trial? I demand to know what steps you've taken."

"I have taken the following steps," said Holmes. "Based on information received, I traced the leak to a small dinner party at the League of Nations encampment. The person who leaked it wasn't a spy, or a traitor. He was a Member of Parliament with one too many glasses under his belt. He told the tale to his opposite number, a Polish representative of the League, to the man's wife, and to their fourteen-year-old, who I believe you managed to get into Emberly, did you not? The leak was *you*, Mister Chamberlain."

The Honourable Member for Birmingham-Ladywood looked shocked as Holmes filled in the details. Then I saw the politician change as he realized he was in a quiet private room and there was no one waiting outside to arrest him.

"I shall deny everything," he said. "You cannot prove it."

"We have statements from the father and mother of the boy," said Mycroft. At this Chamberlain paled and he looked as if he would lash out. Before he could utter another empty threat, Mycroft held up his hands. "Enough," he said. "I tire of all politicians, and I am most notably tired of

425

you. I shall keep the evidence. Learn from this and try to do better. We caught this one this time. We may not be able to help you with your next mistake."

"Try to do better?" said Chamberlain.

"A novel concept, I'm sure. Go now, Mister Chamberlain. Remember who you serve, and try to do better."

The man left in a daze, forgetting even to strut importantly.

"Will he listen?" I asked.

"Likely not," said Holmes. "But he is a nincompoop, not a traitor. And if we rid the government of all of them, who would be left?"

We arranged to meet Mycroft for lunch at the Diogenes Club. As we walked out, I said to Holmes, "What was the boy's name?"

"What does it matter?"

"I need to know, in case I ever write about this. If I know the name, I'll know whether I can use it or need a pseudonym."

"Blofeld," said Holmes. "Ernie Blofeld. We'll probably never hear of him again."

The source of these outrages is known, and if they are repeated I have Mr. Holmes's authority for saying that the whole story concerning the politician, the lighthouse, and the trained cormorant will be given to the public.

– Dr. John H. Watson
"The Veiled Lodger"

Appendix:
The Untold Cases

The following has been assembled from several sources, including lists compiled by Phil Jones and Randall Stock, as well as some internet resources and my own research. I cannot promise that it's complete – some Untold Cases may be missing – after all, there's a great deal of Sherlockian Scholarship that involves interpretation and rationalizing – and there are some listed here that certain readers may believe shouldn't be listed at all.

As a fanatical supporter and collector of pastiches since I was a ten-year-old boy in 1975, reading Nicholas Meyer's *The Seven-Per-Cent Solution* and *The West End Horror* before I'd even read all of The Canon, I can attest that serious and legitimate versions of all of these Untold Cases exist out there – some of them occurring with much greater frequency than others – and I hope to collect, read, and chronologicize them all.

There's so much more to The Adventures of Sherlock Holmes than the pitifully few sixty stories that were fixed up by the First Literary Agent. I highly recommend that you find and read all of the rest of them as well, including those relating these Untold Cases. You won't regret it.

David Marcum

A Study in Scarlet

- Mr. Lestrade . . . got himself in a fog recently over a forgery case
- A young girl called, fashionably dressed
- A gray-headed, seedy visitor, looking like a Jew pedlar who appeared to be very much excited
- A slipshod elderly woman
- An old, white-haired gentleman had an interview
- A railway porter in his velveteen uniform

The Sign of Four

- The consultation last week by Francois le Villard
- The most winning woman Holmes ever knew was hanged for poisoning three little children for their insurance money

429

- The most repellent man of Holmes's acquaintance was a philanthropist who has spent nearly a quarter of a million upon the London poor
- Holmes once enabled Mrs. Cecil Forrester to unravel a little domestic complication. She was much impressed by his kindness and skill
- Holmes lectured the police on causes and inferences and effects in the Bishopgate jewel case

The Adventures of Sherlock Holmes

"A Scandal in Bohemia"
- The summons to Odessa in the case of the Trepoff murder
- The singular tragedy of the Atkinson brothers at Trincomalee
- The mission which Holmes had accomplished so delicately and successfully for the reigning family of Holland. (He also received a remarkably brilliant ring)
- The Darlington substitution scandal, and . . .
- The Arnsworth castle business. (When a woman thinks that her house is on fire, her instinct is at once to rush to the thing which she values most. It is a perfectly overpowering impulse, and Holmes has more than once taken advantage of it

"The Red-Headed League"
- The previous skirmishes with John Clay

"A Case of Identity"
- The Dundas separation case, where Holmes was engaged in clearing up some small points in connection with it. The husband was a teetotaler, there was no other woman, and the conduct complained of was that he had drifted into the habit of winding up every meal by taking out his false teeth and hurling them at his wife, which is not an action likely to occur to the imagination of the average story-teller.
- The rather intricate matter from Marseilles
- Mrs. Etherege, whose husband Holmes found so easy when the police and everyone had given him up for dead
- Windibank, who will rise from crime to crime until he does something very bad, and ends on a gallows. *(An Untold Case previously unlisted and newly identified for this volume by David Marcum.)*

"The Boscombe Valley Mystery"
NONE LISTED

"The Five Orange Pips"
- The adventure of the Paradol Chamber
- The Amateur Mendicant Society, who held a luxurious club in the lower vault of a furniture warehouse
- The facts connected with the disappearance of the British barque *Sophy Anderson*
- The singular adventures of the Grice-Patersons in the island of Uffa
- The Camberwell poisoning case, in which, as may be remembered, Holmes was able, by winding up the dead man's watch, to prove that it had been wound up two hours before, and that therefore the deceased had gone to bed within that time – a deduction which was of the greatest importance in clearing up the case
- Holmes saved Major Prendergast in the Tankerville Club scandal. He was wrongfully accused of cheating at cards
- Holmes has been beaten four times – three times by men and once by a woman

"The Man with the Twisted Lip"
- The rascally Lascar who runs The Bar of Gold in Upper Swandam Lane has sworn to have vengeance upon Holmes

"The Adventure of the Blue Carbuncle"
NONE LISTED

"The Adventure of the Speckled Band"
- Mrs. Farintosh and an opal tiara. (It was before Watson's time)

"The Adventure of the Engineer's Thumb"
- Colonel Warburton's madness

"The Adventure of the Noble Bachelor"
- The letter from a fishmonger
- The letter a tide-waiter
- The service for Lord Backwater

- The little problem of the Grosvenor Square furniture van
- The service for the King of Scandinavia

"The Adventure of the Beryl Coronet"
NONE LISTED

"The Adventure of the Copper Beeches"
NONE LISTED

The Memoirs of Sherlock Holmes

"Silver Blaze"
NONE LISTED

"The Cardboard Box"
- Aldridge, who helped in the bogus laundry affair

"The Yellow Face"
- The (First) Adventure of the Second Stain was a failure which present[s] the strongest features of interest

'The Stockbroker's Clerk"
NONE LISTED

"The "Gloria Scott"
NONE LISTED

"The Musgrave Ritual"
- The Tarleton murders
- The case of Vamberry, the wine merchant
- The adventure of the old Russian woman
- The singular affair of the aluminum crutch
- A full account of Ricoletti of the club foot and his abominable wife
- The two cases before the Musgrave Ritual from Holmes's fellow students

"The Reigate Squires"
- The whole question of the Netherland-Sumatra Company and of the colossal schemes of Baron Maupertuis

The Crooked Man"
NONE LISTED

The Resident Patient"
- [Catalepsy] is a very easy complaint to imitate. Holmes has done it himself.

"The Greek Interpreter"
- Mycroft expected to see Holmes round last week to consult me over that Manor House case. It was Adams, of course
- Some of Holmes's most interesting cases have come to him through Mycroft

"The Naval Treaty"
- The (Second) adventure of the Second Stain, which dealt with interest of such importance and implicated so many of the first families in the kingdom that for many years it would be impossible to make it public. No case, however, in which Holmes was engaged had ever illustrated the value of his analytical methods so clearly or had impressed those who were associated with him so deeply. Watson still retained an almost verbatim report of the interview in which Holmes demonstrated the true facts of the case to Monsieur Dubugue of the Paris police, and Fritz von Waldbaum, the well-known specialist of Dantzig, both of whom had wasted their energies upon what proved to be side-issues. The new century will have come, however, before the story could be safely told.
- The Adventure of the Tired Captain
- A very commonplace little murder. If it [this paper] turns red, it means a man's life . . . .

"The Final Problem"
- The engagement for the French Government upon a matter of supreme importance
- The assistance to the Royal Family of Scandinavia

The Return of Sherlock Holmes

"The Adventure of the Empty House"

- Holmes traveled for two years in Tibet (as) a Norwegian named Sigerson, amusing himself by visiting Lhassa [*sic*] and spending some days with the head Llama [*sic*]
- Holmes traveled in Persia
- . . . looked in at Mecca . . .
- . . . and paid a short but interesting visit to the Khalifa at Khartoum
- Returning to France, Holmes spent some months in a research into the coal-tar derivatives, which he conducted in a laboratory at Montpelier [*sic*], in the South of France
- Mathews, who knocked out Holmes's left canine in the waiting room at Charing Cross
- The death of Mrs. Stewart, of Lauder, in 1887
- Morgan the poisoner
- Merridew of abominable memory
- The Molesey Mystery (Inspector Lestrade's Case. He handled it fairly well.)
- Three undetected murders in one year. Lestrade wants want a little unofficial help. *(An Untold Case previously unlisted and newly identified for this volume by Alan Dimes.)*

"The Adventure of the Norwood Builder"
- The case of the papers of ex-President Murillo
- The shocking affair of the Dutch steamship, *Friesland*, which so nearly cost both Holmes and Watson their lives
- That terrible murderer, Bert Stevens, who wanted Holmes and Watson to get him off in '87

"The Adventure of the Dancing Men"
   NONE LISTED

"The Adventure of the Solitary Cyclist"
- The peculiar persecution of John Vincent Harden, the well-known tobacco millionaire
- It was near Farnham that Holmes and Watson took Archie Stamford, the forger

"The Adventure of the Priory School"
- Holmes was retained in the case of the Ferrers Documents
- The Abergavenny murder, which is coming up for trial

"The Adventure of Black Peter"
- The sudden death of Cardinal Tosca – an inquiry which was carried out by him at the express desire of His Holiness the Pope
- The arrest of Wilson, the notorious canary-trainer, which removed a plague-spot from the East-End of London.

"The Adventure of Charles Augustus Milverton"
- Milverton paid seven hundred pounds to a footman for a note two lines in length, and that the ruin of a noble family was the result. *(An Untold Case previously unlisted and newly identified for this volume by Chris Chan.)*

"The Adventure of the Six Napoleons"
- The dreadful business of the Abernetty family, which was first brought to Holmes's attention by the depth which the parsley had sunk into the butter upon a hot day
- The Conk-Singleton forgery case
- Holmes was consulted upon the case of the disappearance of the black pearl of the Borgias, but was unable to throw any light upon it

"The Adventure of the Three Students"
- Some laborious researches in Early English charters

"The Adventure of the Golden Pince-Nez"
- The repulsive story of the red leech
- . . . and the terrible death of Crosby, the banker
- The Addleton tragedy
- . . . and the singular contents of the ancient British barrow
- The famous Smith-Mortimer succession case
- The tracking and arrest of Huret, the boulevard assassin

"The Adventure of the Missing Three-Quarter"
- Henry Staunton, whom Holmes helped to hang
- Arthur H. Staunton, the rising young forger

"The Adventure of the Abbey Grange"
- Hopkins called Holmes in seven times, and on each occasion his summons was entirely justified

- The woman at Margate. No powder on her nose – that proved to be the correct solution. How can one build on such a quicksand? A woman's most trivial action may mean volumes, or their most extraordinary conduct may depend upon a hairpin or a curling-tong

The Hound of the Baskervilles

- That little affair of the Vatican cameos, in which Holmes obliged the Pope
- The little case in which Holmes had the good fortune to help Messenger Manager Wilson
- One of the most revered names in England is being besmirched by a blackmailer, and only Holmes can stop a disastrous scandal
- The atrocious conduct of Colonel Upwood in connection with the famous card scandal at the Nonpareil Club
- Holmes defended the unfortunate Mme. Montpensier from the charge of murder that hung over her in connection with the death of her stepdaughter Mlle. Carere, the young lady who, as it will be remembered, was found six months later alive and married in New York

The Valley of Fear

- Twice already Holmes had helped Inspector Macdonald

His Last Bow

"The Adventure of Wisteria Lodge"
- The locking-up Colonel Carruthers

"The Adventure of the Red Circle"
- The affair last year for Mr. Fairdale Hobbs
- The Long Island cave mystery

"The Adventure of the Bruce-Partington Plans"
- Brooks . . .

- ... or Woodhouse, or any of the fifty men who have good reason for taking Holmes's life

"The Adventure of the Dying Detective"
  NONE LISTED

"The Disappearance of Lady Frances Carfax"
- Holmes cannot possibly leave London while old Abrahams is in such mortal terror of his life

"The Adventure of the Devil's Foot"
- Holmes's dramatic introduction to Dr. Moore Agar, of Harley Street

"His Last Bow"
- Holmes started his pilgrimage at Chicago ...
- ... graduated in an Irish secret society at Buffalo
- ... gave serious trouble to the constabulary at Skibbareen
- Holmes saves Count Von und Zu Grafenstein from murder by the Nihilist Klopman

The Case-Book of Sherlock Holmes

"The Adventure of the Illustrious Client"
- Negotiations with Sir George Lewis over the Hammerford Will case

"The Adventure of the Blanched Soldier"
- The Abbey School in which the Duke of Greyminster was so deeply involved
- The commission from the Sultan of Turkey which required immediate action
- The professional service for Sir James Saunders

"The Adventure of the Mazarin Stone"
- Old Baron Dowson said the night before he was hanged that in Holmes's case what the law had gained the stage had lost
- The death of old Mrs. Harold, who left Count Sylvius the Blymer estate
- The compete life history of Miss Minnie Warrender

- The robbery in the train de-luxe to the Riviera on February 13, 1892

"The Adventure of the Three Gables"
- The killing of young Perkins outside the Holborn Bar
- Mortimer Maberly, was one of Holmes's early clients

"The Adventure of the Sussex Vampire"
- *Matilda Briggs*, a ship which is associated with the giant rat of Sumatra, a story for which the world is not yet prepared
- Victor Lynch, the forger
- Venomous lizard, or Gila. Remarkable case, that!
- Vittoria the circus belle
- Vanderbilt and the Yeggman
- Vigor, the Hammersmith wonder

"The Adventure of the Three Garridebs"
- Holmes refused a knighthood for services which may, someday, be described

"The Problem of Thor Bridge"
- Mr. James Phillimore who, stepping back into his own house to get his umbrella, was never more seen in this world
- The cutter *Alicia*, which sailed one spring morning into a patch of mist from where she never again emerged, nor was anything further ever heard of herself and her crew.
- Isadora Persano, the well-known journalist and duelist who was found stark staring mad with a match box in front of him which contained a remarkable worm said to be unknown to science

"The Adventure of the Creeping Man"
NONE LISTED

"The Adventure of the Lion's Mane"
NONE LISTED

"The Adventure of the Veiled Lodger"
- The whole story concerning the politician, the lighthouse, and the trained cormorant

438

"The Adventure of Shoscombe Old Place"
- Holmes ran down that coiner by the zinc and copper filings in the seam of his cuff
- The St. Pancras case, where a cap was found beside the dead policeman. The accused man denied that it is his. But he was a picture-frame maker who habitually handled glue.
  - "Is it one of your cases?" Merivale of the Yard asked Holmes to look into it

"The Adventure of the Retired Colourman"
- The case of the two Coptic Patriarchs

About the Contributors

The following contributors appear in this volume:
The MX Book of New Sherlock Holmes Stories
Part XLII – Further Untold Cases (1894-1922)

Tim Newton Anderson is a former senior daily newspaper journalist and PR manager who has recently started writing fiction. In the past six months, he has placed fourteen stories in publications including *Parsec Magazine*, *Tales of the Shadowmen*, *SF Writers Guild*, *Zoetic Press*, *Dark Lane Books*, *Dark Horses Magazine*, *Emanations*, and *Planet Bizarro*.

Deanna Baran lives in a remote part of Texas where cowboys may still be seen in their natural habitat. A librarian and former museum curator, she writes in between cups of tea, playing *Go*, and trading postcards with people around the world.

Donald I. Baxter has practiced medicine for over forty years. He resides in Erie Pennsylvania with his wife and their dog. His family and his friends are for the most part lawyers who have given him the ability to make stuff up just as they do.

Brian Belanger, PSI, is a publisher, illustrator, graphic designer, editor, and author. In 2015, he co-founded Belanger Books publishing company along with his brother, author Derrick Belanger. His illustrations have appeared in *The Essential Sherlock Holmes* and *Sherlock Holmes: A Three-Pipe Christmas*, and in children's books such as *The MacDougall Twins with Sherlock Holmes* series, *Dragonella*, and *Scones and Bones on Baker Street*. Brian has published a number of Sherlock Holmes anthologies and novels through Belanger Books, as well as new editions of August Derleth's classic Solar Pons mysteries. Brian continues to design all of the covers for Belanger Books, and since 2016 he has designed the majority of book covers for MX Publishing. In 2019, Brian received his investiture in the PSI as "Sir Ronald Duveen." More recently, he illustrated a comic book featuring the band The Moonlight Initiative, created the logo for the Arthur Conan Doyle Society and designed *The Great Game of Sherlock Holmes* card game. Find him online at:
www.belangerbooks.com and
www.redbubble.com/people/zhahadun and
zhahadun.wixsite.com/221b

Thomas A. Burns Jr. writes *The Natalie McMasters Mysteries* from the small town of Wendell, North Carolina, where he lives with his wife and son, four cats, and a Cardigan Welsh Corgi. He was born and grew up in New Jersey, attended Xavier High School in Manhattan, earned B.S degrees in Zoology and Microbiology at Michigan State University, and a M.S. in Microbiology at North Carolina State University. As a kid, Tom started reading mysteries with The Hardy Boys, Ken Holt, and Rick Brant, then graduated to the classic stories by authors such as A. Conan Doyle, Dorothy Sayers, John Dickson Carr, Erle Stanley Gardner, and Rex Stout, to name a few. Tom has written fiction as a hobby all of his life, starting with *The Man from U.N.C.L.E.* stories in marble-backed copybooks in grade school. He built a career as technical, science, and medical writer and editor for nearly thirty years in industry and government. Now that he's a full-time novelist, he's excited to publish his own mystery series, as well as to write stories about his second most favorite detective, Sherlock Holmes. His Holmes story, "The Camberwell Poisoner",

441

appeared in the March-June 2021 issue of *The Strand Magazine*. Tom has also written a Lovecraftian horror novel, *The Legacy of the Unborn*, under the pen name of Silas K. Henderson – a sequel to H.P. Lovecraft's masterpiece *At the Mountains of Madness*. His Natalie McMasters novel *Killers!* won the Killer Nashville Silver Falchion Award for Best Book of 2021.

Chris Chan is a writer, educator, and historian. He works as a researcher and "International Goodwill Ambassador" for Agatha Christie Ltd. His true crime articles, reviews, and short fiction have appeared (or will soon appear) in *The Strand*, *The Wisconsin Magazine of History*, *Mystery Weekly*, *Gilbert!*, *Nerd HQ*, Akashic Books' *Mondays are Murder* web series, *The Baker Street Journal*, *The MX Book of New Sherlock Holmes Stories*, *Masthead: The Best New England Crime Stories*, *Sherlock Holmes Mystery Magazine*, and multiple Belanger Books anthologies. He is the creator of the Funderburke mysteries, a series featuring a private investigator who works for a school and helps students during times of crisis. The Funderburke short story "The Six-Year-Old Serial Killer" was nominated for a Derringer Award. His first book, *Sherlock & Irene: The Secret Truth Behind "A Scandal in Bohemia"*, was published in 2020 by MX Publishing. His second book, *Murder Most Grotesque: The Comedic Crime Fiction of Joyce Porter* will be released by Level Best Books in 2021, and his first novel, *Sherlock's Secretary*, was published by MX Publishing in 2021. *Murder Most Grotesque* was nominated for the Agatha and Silver Falchion Awards for Nonfiction Writing, and *Sherlock's Secretary* was nominated for the Silver Falchion for Best Comedy. He is also the author of the anthology of Sherlock Holmes stories *Of Course He Pushed Him*.

Barry Clay is a graduate of Shippensburg University with a BA in English. He's dug ditches, stocked grocery shelves, tutored for room and board, cleaned restrooms, mopped floors, taught cartooning, worked in a bank, asked if you'd like fries with that (and cooked the fries to boot), ordered carpet for cars, and worked commission sales at Sears, and most recently a long-time veteran of the Federal employee workforce. He has been writing all his life, in different genres, and he has written thirteen books ranging from Christian theology, anthologies, speculative fiction, horror, science fiction, and humor. He volunteers as conductor of a local student orchestra and has been commissioned to write music. His first two musicals were locally produced. He is the husband of one wife, father of four children, and "Opa" to one granddaughter.

Alan Dimes was born in Northwest London and graduated from Sussex University with a BA in English Literature. He has spent most of his working life teaching English. Living in the Czech Republic since 2003, he is now semi-retired and divides his time between Prague and his country cottage. He has also written some fifty stories of horror and fantasy and thirty stories about his husband-and-wife detectives, Peter and Deirdre Creighton, set in the 1930's.

Sir Arthur Conan Doyle (1859-1930) *Holmes Chronicler Emeritus*. If not for him, this anthology would not exist. Author, physician, patriot, sportsman, spiritualist, husband and father, and advocate for the oppressed. He is remembered and honored for the purposes of this collection by being the man who introduced Sherlock Holmes to the world. Through fifty-six Holmes short stories, four novels, and additional Apocryphal entries, Doyle revolutionized mystery stories and also greatly influenced and improved police forensic methods and techniques for the betterment of all. *Steel True Blade Straight.*

Steve Emecz's main field is technology, in which he has been working for about twenty-five years. Steve is a regular speaker at trade shows and his tech career has taken him to more than fifty countries – so he's no stranger to planes and airports. In 2008, MX published its first Sherlock Holmes book, and MX has gone on to become the largest specialist Holmes publisher in the world with over 500 books. MX is a social enterprise and supports three main causes. The first is Happy Life, a children's rescue project in Nairobi, Kenya, where he and his wife, Sharon, spend every Christmas at the rescue centre in Kasarani. They have written two editions of a short book about the project, *The Happy Life Story*. The second is Undershaw, Sir Arthur Conan Doyle's former home, which is a school for children with learning disabilities for which Steve is a patron. Steve has been a mentor for the World Food Programme for several years, and was part of the Nobel Peace Prize winning team in 2020.

Mark A. Gagen BSI is co-founder of Wessex Press, sponsor of the popular *From Gillette to Brett* conferences, and publisher of *The Sherlock Holmes Reference Library* and many other fine Sherlockian titles. A life-long Holmes enthusiast, he is a member of *The Baker Street Irregulars* and *The Illustrious Clients of Indianapolis*. A graphic artist by profession, his work is often seen on the covers of *The Baker Street Journal* and various BSI books.

John Atkinson Grimshaw (1836-1893) was born in Leeds, England. His amazing paintings, usually featuring twilight or night scenes illuminated by gas-lamps or moonlight, are easily recognizable, and are often used on the covers of books about The Great Detective to set the mood, as shadowy figures move in the distance through misty mysterious settings and over rain-slicked streets.

Arthur Hall was born in Aston, Birmingham, UK, in 1944. He discovered his interest in writing during his schooldays, along with a love of fictional adventure and suspense. His first novel, *Sole Contact*, was an espionage story about an ultra-secret government department known as "Sector Three", and was followed, to date, by three sequels. Other works include seven Sherlock Holmes novels, *The Demon of the Dusk*, *The One Hundred Percent Society*, *The Secret Assassin*, *The Phantom Killer*, *In Pursuit of the Dead*, *The Justice Master*, and *The Experience Club* as well as three collections of Holmes *Further Little-Known Cases of Sherlock* Holmes, *Tales from the Annals of Sherlock* Holmes, and *The Additional Investigations of Sherlock Holmes.* He has also written other short stories and a modern detective novel. He lives in the West Midlands, United Kingdom.

Paul Hiscock is an author of crime, fantasy, horror, and science fiction tales. His short stories have appeared in a variety of anthologies, and include a seventeenth-century whodunnit, a science fiction western, a clockpunk fairytale, and numerous Sherlock Holmes pastiches. He lives with his family in Kent (England) and spends his days taking care of his two children. He mainly does his writing in coffee shops with members of the local NaNoWriMo group, or in the middle of the night when his family has gone to sleep. Consequently, his stories tend to be fuelled by large amounts of black coffee. You can find out more about Paul's writing at *www.detectivesanddragons.uk.*

Roger Johnson, BSI, ASH, PSI, etc, is a member of more Holmesian societies than he can remember, thanks to his (so far) 16 years as editor of *The Sherlock Holmes Journal*, and thirty-two years as editor of *The District Messenger*. The latter, the newsletter of *The Sherlock Holmes Society of London*, is now in the safe hands of Jean Upton, with whom he collaborated on the well-received book, *The Sherlock Holmes Miscellany*. Roger is resigned to the fact that he will never match the Du ke of Holdernesse, whose name was followed by *"half the alphabet"*.

Kelvin I. Jones is the author of six books about Sherlock Holmes and the definitive biography of Conan Doyle as a spiritualist, *Conan Doyle and The Spirits*. A member of *The Sherlock Holmes Society of London*, he has published numerous short occult and ghost stories in British anthologies over the last thirty years. His work has appeared on BBC Radio, and in 1984 he won the Mason Hall Literary Award for his poem cycle about the survivors of Hiroshima and Nagasaki, recently reprinted as "Omega". (Oakmagic Publications) A one-time teacher of creative writing at the University of East Anglia, he is also the author of four crime novels featuring his ex-met sleuth John Bottrell, who first appeared in *Stone Dead*. He has over fifty titles on Kindle, and is also the author of several novellas and short story collections featuring a Norwich based detective, DCI Ketch, an intrepid sleuth who investigates East Anglian murder cases. He also published a series of short stories about an Edwardian psychic detective, Dr. John Carter (*Carter's Occult Casebook*). Ramsey Campbell, the British horror writer, and Francis King, the renowned novelist, have both compared his supernatural stories to those of M. R. James. He has also published children's fiction, namely *Odin's Eye*, and, in collaboration with his wife Debbie, *The Dark Entry*. Since 1995, he has been the proprietor of Oakmagic Publications, publishers of British folklore and of his fiction titles.

Susan Knight's newest novel, *Death in the Garden of England* (2023) from MX publishing, is the latest in a series which began with her collection of stories, *Mrs. Hudson Investigates* (2019), the novel *Mrs. Hudson goes to Ireland* (2020), and *Mrs. Hudson Goes to Paris* (2022). She has contributed to many recent MX anthologies of new Sherlock Holmes short stories and enjoys writing as Dr. Watson as much as she does Mrs. Hudson. Nine of these stories comprise a new collection of hers, *The Strange Case of the Pale Boy and Other Mysteries* (2023). Susan is the author of two other non-Sherlockian story collections, as well as three novels, a book of non-fiction, and several plays, and has won several prizes for her writing. Susan lives in Dublin.

David Marcum plays *The Game* with deadly seriousness. He first discovered Sherlock Holmes in 1975 at the age of ten, and since that time, he has collected, read, and chronologicized literally thousands of traditional Holmes pastiches in the form of novels, short stories, radio and television episodes, movies and scripts, comics, fan-fiction, and unpublished manuscripts. He is the author of over one-hundred Sherlockian pastiches, some published in anthologies and magazines such as *The Best Mystery Stories of the Year 2021* and *The Strand*, and others collected in his own books, *The Papers of Sherlock Holmes, Sherlock Holmes and A Quantity of Debt, Sherlock Holmes – Tangled Skeins, Sherlock Holmes and The Eye of Heka*, and *The Collected Papers of Sherlock Holmes*. He has won first place fiction awards from *The Arthur Conan Doyle Society* and the Nero Wolfe *Wolfe Pack*. He has edited over eighty books, including several dozen traditional Sherlockian anthologies, such as the ongoing series *The MX Book of New Sherlock Holmes Stories*, which he created in 2015. This collection is now at forty-two volumes, with more in preparation. He was responsible for bringing back August Derleth's Solar Pons for a new generation with his collection of authorized Pons stories, *The Papers of Solar Pons* and *The Further Papers of Solar Pons*. Pons's return was further assisted by his editing of the reissued authorized versions of the original Pons books, and then several volumes of new Pons adventures. He has done the same for the adventures of Dr. Thorndyke, and has plans for similar projects in the future. He has contributed numerous essays to various publications, and is a member of a number of Sherlockian groups and Scions, as well as *The Mystery Writers of America*. His irregular Sherlockian blog, *A Seventeen Step*

Program, addresses various topics related to his favorite book friends (as his son used to call them when he was small), and can be found at *http://17stepprogram.blogspot.com/* He is a licensed Civil Engineer, living in Tennessee with his wife and son. Since the age of nineteen, he has worn a deerstalker as his regular-and-only hat. In 2013, he and his deerstalker were finally able make his first trip-of-a-lifetime Holmes Pilgrimage to England, with return Pilgrimages in 2015 and 2016, where you may have spotted him. If you ever run into him and his deerstalker out and about, feel free to say hello!

Tom Mead is a UK-based author and Golden Age Mystery aficionado. His debut novel, *Death and the Conjuror*, was an international bestseller, and named one of the best mysteries of 2022 by *Publishers Weekly*. The sequel, *The Murder Wheel*, was published in July 2023, and described as "compelling" by *Crimereads* and "pure nostalgic pleasure" by the *Wall Street Journal*. His short fiction has appeared in *Ellery Queen's Mystery Magazine*, *Alfred Hitchcock Mystery Magazine*, and *The Best Mystery Stories of the Year*, edited by Lee Child.

Sidney Paget (1860-1908), a few of whose illustrations are used within this anthology, was born in London, and like his two older brothers, became a famed illustrator and painter. He completed over three-hundred-and-fifty drawings for the Sherlock Holmes stories that were first published in *The Strand* magazine, defining Holmes's image forever after in the public mind.

Tracy J. Revels, a Sherlockian from the age of eleven, is a professor of history at Wofford College in Spartanburg, South Carolina. She is a member of *The Survivors of the Gloria Scott* and *The Studious Scarlets Society*, and is a past recipient of the Beacon Society Award. Almost every semester, she teaches a class that covers The Canon, either to college students or to senior citizens. She is also the author of three supernatural Sherlockian pastiches with MX (*Shadowfall*, *Shadowblood*, and *Shadowwraith*), and a regular contributor to her scion's newsletter. She also has some notoriety as an author of very silly skits: For proof, see "The Adventure of the Adversarial Adventuress" and "Occupy Baker Street" on YouTube. When not studying Sherlock, she can be found researching the history of her native state, and has written books on Florida in the Civil War and on the development of Florida's tourism industry.

Dan Rowley practiced law for over forty years in private practice and with a large international corporation. He is retired and lives in Erie, Pennsylvania, with his wife Judy, who puts her artistic eye to his transcription of Watson's manuscripts. He inherited his writing ability and creativity from his children, Jim and Katy, and his love of mysteries from his parents, Jim and Ruth.

Fifteen of **Brenda Seabrooke**'s Sherlock Holmes pastiches have been anthologized in MX Publishing and Belanger Books, six in *Best Crime Stories of New England*, one in *Destination: Mystery* and *Mystery Tribune*, and twelve in literary reviews such as *Yemassee*, *Confrontation*, and one in *Redbook*. Twenty-two of her books for young readers have been published at Penguin, Clarion, etc., and won awards such as a Notable from the National Council of Social Studies, Junior Literary Guild, Hornbook Honor, an Edgar finalist, etc. She received a grant from the National Endowment for the Arts, and The Robie Macauley Award from Emerson College. In 2022, MX published her collection, *Sherlock Holmes: The Persian Slipper and Other Stories*.

Kevin P. Thornton was shortlisted six times for the Crime Writers of Canada best unpublished novel. He never won – they are all still unpublished, and now he writes short stories. He lives in Canada, north enough that ringing Santa Claus is a local call and winter is a way of life. He has contributed numerous short stories to The MX Book of New Sherlock Holmes Stories. By the time you next hear from him, he hopes to have written more.

DJ Tyrer is the person behind Atlantean Publishing and has had fiction featuring Sherlock Holmes published in volumes from MX Publishing and Belanger Books, and an issue of *Awesome Tales*, and has a forthcoming story in *Sherlock Holmes Mystery Magazine*. DJ's non-Sherlockian mysteries can be found in anthologies such as *Mardi Gras Mysteries* (Mystery and Horror LLC) and *The Trench Coat Chronicles* (Celestial Echo Press), and on *Mystery Tribune*.
DJ Tyrer's website is at *https://djtyrer.blogspot.co.uk/*
DJ's Facebook page is at *https://www.facebook.com/DJTyrerwriter/*
The Atlantean Publishing website is at *https://atlanteanpublishing.wordpress.com/*

I.A. Watson great-grand-nephew of Dr. John H. Watson, has been intrigued by the notorious "black sheep" of the family since childhood, and was fascinated to inherit from his grandmother a number of unedited manuscripts removed circa 1956 from a rather larger collection reposing at Lloyds Bank Ltd (which acquired Cox & Co Bank in 1923). Upon discovering the published corpus of accounts regarding the detective Sherlock Holmes from which a censorious upbringing had shielded him, he felt obliged to allow an interested public access to these additional memoranda, and is gradually undertaking the task of transcribing them for admirers of Mr. Holmes and Dr. Watson's works. In the meantime, I.A. Watson continues to pen other books, the latest of which is *The Incunabulum of Sherlock Holmes*. A full list of his seventy or so published works are available at: *http://www.chillwater.org.uk/writing/iawatsonhome.htm*

Emma West joined Undershaw in April 2021 as the Director of Education with a brief to ensure that qualifications formed the bedrock of our provision, whilst facilitating a positive balance between academia, pastoral care, and well-being. She quickly took on the role of Acting Headteacher from early summer 2021. Under her leadership, Undershaw has embraced its new name, new vision, and consequently we have seen an exponential increase in demand for places. There is a buzz in the air as we invite prospective students and families through the doors. Emma has overseen a strategic review, re-cemented relationships with Local Authorities, and positioned Undershaw at the helm of SEND education in Surrey and beyond. Undershaw has a wide appeal: Our students present to us with mild to moderate learning needs and therefore may have some very recent memories of poor experiences in their previous schools. Emma's background as a senior leader within the independent school sector has meant she is well-versed in brokering relationships between the key stakeholders, our many interdependences, local businesses, families, and staff, and all this while ensuring Undershaw remains relentlessly child-centric in its approach. Emma's energetic smile and boundless enthusiasm for Undershaw is inspiring.

*The following contributors appear
in the companion volumes:*
The MX Book of New Sherlock Holmes Stories
Part XL – Further Untold Cases (1879-1886)
Part XLI – Further Untold Cases (1887-1892)

Mike Adamson holds a Doctoral degree from Flinders University of South Australia. After early aspirations in art and writing, Mike secured qualifications in both marine biology and archaeology. Mike has been a university educator since 2006, has worked in the replication of convincing ancient fossils, is a passionate photographer, master-level hobbyist, and journalist for international magazines. Short fiction sales include to *Metastellar, Strand Magazine, Little Blue Marble, Abyss,* and *Apex, Daily Science Fiction, Compelling Science Fiction,* and *Nature Futures.* Mike has placed some two-hundred stories to date, totaling over a million words. Mike has completed his first Sherlock Holmes novel with Belanger Books, and will be appearing in translation in European magazines. You can catch up with his journey at his blog "The View From the Keyboard"
http://mike-adamson.blogspot.com

Tim Newton Anderson *also has stories in Parts XL and XLI*

Hugh Ashton was born in the U.K., and moved to Japan in 1988, where he remained until 2016, living with his wife Yoshiko in the historic city of Kamakura, a little to the south of Yokohama. He and Yoshiko have now moved to Lichfield, a small cathedral city in the Midlands of the U.K., the birthplace of Samuel Johnson, and one-time home of Erasmus Darwin. In the past, he has worked in the technology and financial services industries, which have provided him with material for some of his books set in the 21st century. He currently works as a writer: Novelist, freelance editor, and copywriter, (his work for large Japanese corporations has appeared in international business journals), and journalist, as well as producing industry reports on various aspects of the financial services industry. However, his lifelong interest in Sherlock Holmes has developed into an acclaimed series of adventures featuring the world's most famous detective, written in the style of the originals. In addition to these, he has also published historical and alternate historical novels, short stories, and thrillers. Together with artist Andy Boerger, he has produced the *Sherlock Ferret* series of stories for children, featuring the world's cutest detective.

Mike Chinn's first-ever Sherlock Holmes fiction was a steampunk mashup of *The Valley of Fear*, entitled *Vallis Timoris* (Fringeworks 2015). Since then he has written about Holmes's archenemy in *The Mammoth Book of the Adventures of Moriarty* (Robinson 2015), appeared in three volumes of *The MX Book of New Sherlock Holmes Stories*, and faced the retired detective with cross-dimensional magic in the second volume of *Sherlock Holmes and the Occult Detectives* (Belanger Books 2020).

Barry Clay *also has a story in Part XLI*

Martin Daley was born in Carlisle, Cumbria in 1964. His thirty-year writing career has seen over twenty books and numerous short stories published. Inevitably, Holmes and Watson remain his favourite literary characters, and they continue to inspire his own detective writing. In 2010, Martin created Inspector Cornelius Armstrong, who carries out his police work against the backdrop of Edwardian Carlisle. With the publication of the first Inspector Armstrong Casebook (published by MX Publishing), Martin became a

447

member of the Crime Writers' Association. He lives with his wife Wendy, in Kirkcudbrightshire, in Southwest.

Alan Dimes *also has a story in Part XL*

Brett Fawcett is a humanities and Latin teacher at the Chesterton Academy of St. Isidore in Sherwood Park, Alberta. He lives with his wife and son in Edmonton, where he is a member of The Wisteria Lodgers (The Sherlock Holmes Society of Edmonton). He vividly remembers the first time he finished reading the Sherlock Holmes stories in Grade 6, and has been a student of Holmesian literature and scholarship since then. He is also a frequent author of columns and articles on topics like theology, education, and mental health, as well as the occasional mystery story.

Paul D. Gilbert was born in 1954 and has lived in and around London all of his life. His wife Jackie is a Holmes expert who keeps him on the straight and narrow! He has two sons, one of whom now lives in Spain. His interests include literature, ancient history, all religions, most sports, and movies. He is currently employed full-time as a funeral director. His books so far include *The Lost Files of Sherlock Holmes* (2007), *The Chronicles of Sherlock Holmes* (2008), *Sherlock Holmes and the Giant Rat of Sumatra* (2010), *The Annals of Sherlock Holmes* (2012), *Sherlock Holmes and the Unholy Trinity* (2015), *Sherlock Holmes: The Four Handed Game* (2017), *The Illumination of Sherlock Holmes* (2019), and *The Treasure of the Poison King* (2021).

Arthur Hall *also has stories in Parts XL and XLI*

Paula Hammond has written over sixty fiction and non-fiction books, as well as short stories, comics, poetry, and scripts for educational DVD's. When not glued to the keyboard, she can usually be found prowling round second-hand books shops or hunkered down in a hide, soaking up the joys of the natural world.

Stephen Herczeg is an IT Geek, writer, actor, and film-maker based in Canberra Australia. He has been writing for over twenty years and has completed a couple of dodgy novels, sixteen feature-length screenplays, and numerous short stories and scripts. Stephen was very successful in 2017's International Horror Hotel screenplay competition, with his scripts *TITAN* winning the Sci-Fi category and *Dark are the Woods* placing second in the horror category. His three-volume short story collection, *The Curious Cases of Sherlock Holmes*, will be published in 2021. His work has featured in *Sproutlings – A Compendium of Little Fictions* from Hunter Anthologies, the *Hells Bells* Christmas horror anthology published by the Australasian Horror Writers Association, and the *Below the Stairs*, *Trickster's Treats*, *Shades of Santa*, *Behind the Mask*, and *Beyond the Infinite* anthologies from *OzHorror.Con*, *The Body Horror Book*, *Anemone Enemy*, and *Petrified Punks* from Oscillate Wildly Press, and *Sherlock Holmes In the Realms of H.G. Wells* and *Sherlock Holmes: Adventures Beyond the Canon* from Belanger Books.

Naching T. Kassa is a wife, mother, and writer. She's created short stories, novellas, poems, and co-created three children. She resides in Eastern Washington State with her husband, Dan Kassa. Naching is a member of *The Horror Writers Association, Mystery Writers of America, The Sound of the Baskervilles, The ACD Society, The Crew of the Barque Lone Star*, and *The Sherlock Holmes Society of London*. She works in Talent Relations at Crystal Lake Publishing and was a recipient of the 2022 HWA Diversity Grant. You can find her work on Amazon.

Susan Knight *also has a story in Part XL*

Gordon Linzner is founder and former editor of *Space and Time Magazine*, and author of four published novels and dozens of short stories in *F&SF*, *Twilight Zone*, *Sherlock Holmes Mystery Magazine*, and numerous other magazines and anthologies. He is a full member of the *Horror Writers Association* and a lifetime member of *Science Fiction and Fantasy Writers Association.*

David MacGregor is a playwright, screenwriter, novelist, and nonfiction writer. He is a resident artist at The Purple Rose Theatre in Michigan, where a number of his plays have been produced. His plays have been performed from New York to Tasmania, and his work has been published by Dramatic Publishing, Playscripts, Smith & Kraus, Applause, Heuer Publishing, and Theatrical Rights Worldwide (TRW). He adapted his dark comedy, *Vino Veritas*, for the silver screen, and it stars Carrie Preston (Emmy-winner for *The Good Wife*). Several of his short plays have also been adapted into films. He is the author of three Sherlock Holmes plays: *Sherlock Holmes and the Adventure of the Elusive Ear*, *Sherlock Holmes and the Adventure of the Fallen Soufflé*, and *Sherlock Holmes and the Adventure of the Ghost Machine*. He adapted all three plays into novels for Orange Pip Books, and also wrote the two-volume nonfiction *Sherlock Holmes: The Hero with a Thousand Faces* for MX Publishing. He teaches writing at Wayne State University in Detroit and is inordinately fond of cheese and terriers.

David Marcum *also has stories in Parts XL and XLI*

Kevin Patrick McCann has published eight collections of poems for adults, one for children (*Diary of a Shapeshifter*, Beul Aithris), a book of ghost stories (*It's Gone Dark*, The Otherside Books), *Teach Yourself Self-Publishing* (Hodder) co-written with the playwright Tom Green, and *Ov* (Beul Aithris Publications) a fantasy novel for children.

Adrian Middleton is a Staffordshire-born independent publisher. The son of a real-world detective, he is a former civil servant and policy adviser who now writes and edits science fiction, fantasy, and a popular series of steampunked Sherlock Holmes stories.

Will Murray is the author of some 75 novels, including some 20 posthumous Doc Savage collaborations with Lester Dent, and 40 books in the long-running Destroyer series. Other Murray novels star the Executioner, Tarzan of the Apes, The Spider, Pat Savage and the Mars Attacks characters. His book, *Nick Fury, Agent of S.H.I.E.L.D.: Empyre* (2000) foreshadowed the 9/11 terrorist attacks. Murray has penned more than 45 Sherlock Holmes short stories. Twenty of Murray's Holmes short stories have been collected as *The Wild Adventures of Sherlock Holmes*, Vols 1 and 2. His novelette, "The Adventure of the Vengeful Viscount", in which Tarzan of the Apes, otherwise Lord Greystoke, hires Sherlock Holmes to solve a mystery, was approved by both the Estate of Sir Arthur Conan Doyle and Edgar Rice Burroughs, Inc. Murray is the author of the non-fiction book, *Master of Mystery: The Rise of The Shadow*, which is an exploration of the famous radio and magazine character, and a sequel, *Dark Avenger: The Strange Saga of The Shadow*. *The Wild Adventures of Cthulhu* Vols 1 & 2 collect Murray's Lovecraftian short stories. For Marvel Comics, Murray created the Unbeatable Squirrel Girl with legendary artist Steve Ditko. Website:
www.adventuresinbronze.com

Ember Pepper was born and raised in San Diego, CA. She has an M.F.A. degree in Creative Fiction Writing. She has been a fan of The Great Detective since she was a pre-teen and her greatest artistic enjoyment is challenging herself to write quality pastiches of Sherlock Holmes and his stalwart biographer and friend, John Watson.

Tracy J. Revels *also has a story in Part XL*

Roger Riccard's family history has Scottish roots, which trace his lineage back to Highland Scotland. This British Isles ancestry encouraged his interest in the writings of Sir Arthur Conan Doyle at an early age. He has authored the novels, *Sherlock Holmes & The Case of the Poisoned Lilly*, and *Sherlock Holmes & The Case of the Twain Papers*. In addition he has produced several short stories in *Sherlock Holmes Adventures for the Twelve Days of Christmas* and the series *A Sherlock Holmes Alphabet of Cases*. A new series will begin publishing in the Autumn of 2022, and his has another novel in the works. All of his books have been published by Baker Street Studios. His Bachelor of Arts Degrees in both Journalism and History from California State University, Northridge, have proven valuable to his writing historical fiction, as well as the encouragement of his wife/editor/inspiration and Sherlock Holmes fan, Rosilyn. She passed in 2021, and it is in her memory that he continues to contribute to the legacy of the "*man who never lived and will never die*".

Jane Rubino is the author of *A Jersey Shore* mystery series, featuring a Jane Austen-loving amateur sleuth and a Sherlock Holmes-quoting detective, *Knight Errant, Lady Vernon and Her Daughter*, (a novel-length adaptation of Jane Austen's novella *Lady Susan*, co-authored with her daughter Caitlen Rubino-Bradway, *What Would Austen Do?*, also co-authored with her daughter, a short story in the anthology *Jane Austen Made Me Do It, The Rucastles' Pawn, The Copper Beeches from Violet Turner's POV*, and, of course, there's the Sherlockian novel in the drawer – who doesn't have one? Jane lives on a barrier island at the New Jersey shore.

Brenda Seabrooke *also has stories in Part XL*

Liese Sherwood-Fabre knew she was destined to write when she got an A+ in the second grade for her story about Dick, Jane, and Sally's ruined picnic. After obtaining her PhD, she joined the federal government and worked and lived internationally for more than fifteen years. Returning to the states, she seriously pursued her writing career, garnering such awards as a finalist in the Romance Writers of America's Golden Heart contest and a Pushcart Prize nomination. A recognized Sherlockian scholar, her essays have appeared in newsletters, *The Baker Street Journal*, and *Canadian Holmes*. She has recently turned to a childhood passion: Sherlock Holmes. *The Adventure of the Murdered Midwife*, the first book in *The Early Case Files of Sherlock Holmes* series, was the CIBA Mystery and Mayhem 2020 first-place winner. *Her latest book is a young adult fantasy Wilhelmina Quigley: Magic School Dropout*, which is available through all major booksellers. More about her writing can be found at *www.liesesherwoodfabre.com*.

Robert V. Stapleton was born and brought up in Leeds, Yorkshire, England, and studied at Durham University. After working in various parts of the country as an Anglican parish priest, he is now retired and lives with his wife in North Yorkshire. As a member of his local writing group, he now has time to develop his other life as a writer of adventure

450

stories. He has published a number of short stories, and he is hoping to have a couple of completed novels published at some time in the future.

Award winning poet and author **Joseph W. Svec III** enjoys writing, poetry, and stories, and creating new adventures for Holmes and Watson that take them into the worlds of famous literary authors and scientists. His *Missing Authors* trilogy introduced Holmes to Lewis Carroll, Jules Verne, H.G. Wells, and Alfred Lord Tennyson, as well as many of their characters. His transitional story *Sherlock Holmes and the Mystery of the First Unicorn* involved several historical figures, besides a Unicorn or two. He has also written the rhymed and metered Sherlock Holmes Christmas adventure, *The Night Before Christmas in 221b*, sure to be a delight for Sherlock Holmes enthusiasts of all ages. Joseph won the Amador Arts Council 2021 Original Poetry Contest, with his Rhymed and metered story poem, "The Homecoming". Joseph has presented a literary paper on Sherlock Holmes/Alice in Wonderland crossover literature to the Lewis Carroll Society of North America, as well as given several presentations to the Amador County Holmes Hounds, Sherlockian Society. He is currently working on his first book in the *Missing Scientist Trilogy, Sherlock Holmes and the Adventure of the Demonstrative Dinosaur*, in which Sherlock meets Professor George Edward Challenger. Joseph has Masters Degrees in Systems Engineering and Human Organization Management, and has written numerous technical papers on Aerospace Testing. In addition to writing, Joseph enjoys creating miniature dioramas based on music, literature, and history from many different eras. His dioramas have been featured in magazine articles and many different blogs, including the North American Jules Verne society newsletter. He currently has 57 dioramas set up in his display area, and has written a reference book on toy castles and knights from around the world. An avid tea enthusiast, his tea cabinet contains over five-hundred different varieties, and he delights in sharing afternoon tea with his childhood sweetheart and wonderful wife, who has inspired and coauthored several books with him.

Margaret Walsh was born Auckland, New Zealand and now lives in Melbourne, Australia. She is the author of *Sherlock Holmes and the Molly-Boy Murders, Sherlock Holmes and the Case of the Perplexed Politician, Sherlock Holmes and the Case of the London Dock Deaths, The Adventure of the Bloody Duck and Other Tales of Sherlock Holmes, Sherlock Holmes and the Curse of Neb-Heka-Ra*, and *Sherlock Holmes and the Hellfire Heirs*, all published by MX Publishing. She is currently working on her seventh book, *Sherlock Holmes and the Deathly Clairvoyant*. Margaret has been a devotee of Sherlock Holmes since childhood and has had several Holmesian related essays printed in anthologies, and is a member of the online society *Doyle's Rotary Coffin, as well as being a member of Sisters of Crime Australia*. She has an ongoing love affair with the city of London. When she's not working or planning trips to London. Margaret can be found frequenting the many and varied bookshops of Melbourne.

The MX Book of New Sherlock Holmes Stories
Edited by David Marcum
((MX Publishing, 2015-   )

"This is the finest volume of Sherlockian fiction I have ever read, and I have read, literally, thousands." – Philip K. Jones

"Beyond Impressive . . . This is a splendid venture for a great cause!"
– Roger Johnson, Editor, *The Sherlock Holmes Journal,*
The Sherlock Holmes Society of London

Part I: 1881-1889; Part II: 1890-1895; Part III: 1896-1929

Part IV: 2016 Annual

Part V: Christmas Adventures

Part VI: 2017 Annual

Eliminate the Impossible
Part VII: (1880-1891); Part VIII: (1892-1905)

2018 Annual
Part IX: (1879-1895); Part X: (1896-1916)

Some Untold Cases
Part XI: (1880-1891); Part XII: (1894-1902)

2019 Annual
Part XIII: (1881-1890); Part XIV: (1891-1897); Part XV: (1898-1917)

Whatever Remains . . . Must be the Truth
Part XVI: (1881-1890); Part XVII: (1891-1898); Part XVIII: (1898-1925)

2020 Annual
Part XIX: (1882-1890); Part XX: (1891-1897); Part XXI: (1898-1923)·

Some More Untold Cases
Part XXII: (1877-1887); Part XXIII: (1888-1894); Part XXIV: (1895-1903)

2021 Annual
Part XXV: (1881-1888); Part XXVI: (1889-1897); Part XXVII: (1898-1928)

More Christmas Adventures
Part XXVIII: (1869-1888); Part XXIX: (1889-1896); Part XXX: (1897-1928)

2022 Annual
Part XXXI: (1875-1887); Part XXXII: (1888-1895); Part XXXIII: (1896-1919)

"However Improbable . . . ."
Part XXXIV: (1878-1888); Part XXXV: (1889-1896); Part XXXVI: (1897-1919)

2023 Annual
Parts XXXVII (1875-1889), XXXVIII (1889-1896), and XXXIX (1897-1923)

Further Untold Cases
Part XL: (1879-1886), Part XLI: (1887-1892) and Part XLII: (1894-1922)

In Preparation *. . . Part XLIII (and XLIV and XLV as well?)*
and more to come!

The MX Book of New Sherlock Holmes Stories
Edited by David Marcum
(MX Publishing, 2015-)

<u>*Publishers Weekly* says:</u>

Part VI: *The traditional pastiche is alive and well . . . .*

Part VII: *Sherlockians eager for faithful-to-the-canon plots and characters will be delighted.*

Part VIII: *The imagination of the contributors in coming up with variations on the volume's theme is matched by their ingenious resolutions.*

Part IX: *The 18 stories . . . will satisfy fans of Conan Doyle's originals. Sherlockians will rejoice that more volumes are on the way.*

Part X: *. . . new Sherlock Holmes adventures of consistently high quality.*

Part XI: *. . . an essential volume for Sherlock Holmes fans.*

Part XII: *. . . continues to amaze with the number of high-quality pastiches.*

Part XIII: *. . . Amazingly, Marcum has found 22 superb pastiches . . . his is more catnip for fans of stories faithful to Conan Doyle's original*

Part XIV: *. . . this standout anthology of 21 short stories written in the spirit of Conan Doyle's originals.*

Part XV: *Stories pitting Sherlock Holmes against seemingly supernatural phenomena highlight Marcum's 15th anthology of superior short pastiches.*

Part XVI: *Marcum has once again done fans of Conan Doyle's originals a service.*

Part XVII: *This is yet another impressive array of new but traditional Holmes stories.*

Part XVIII: *Sherlockians will again be grateful to Marcum and MX for high-quality new Holmes tales.*

Part XIX: *Inventive plots and intriguing explorations of aspects of Dr. Watson's life and beliefs lift the 24 pastiches in Marcum's impressive 19th Sherlock Holmes anthology*

Part XX: *Marcum's reserve of high-quality new Holmes exploits seems endless.*

Part XXI: *This is another must-have for Sherlockians.*

Part XXII: *Marcum's superlative 22nd Sherlock Holmes pastiche anthology features 21 short stories that successfully emulate the spirit of Conan Doyle's originals while expanding on the canon's tantalizing references to mysteries Dr. Watson never got around to chronicling.*

Part XXIII: *Marcum's well of talented authors able to mimic the feel of The Canon seems bottomless.*

Part XXIV: *Marcum's expertise at selecting high-quality pastiches remains impressive.*

Part XXVIII: *All entries adhere to the spirit, language, and characterizations of Conan Doyle's originals, evincing the deep pool of talent Marcum has access to. Against the odds, this series remains strong, hundreds of stories in.*

Part XXXI: *. . . yet another stellar anthology of 21 short pastiches that effectively mimic the originals . . . Marcum's diligent searches for high-quality stories has again paid off for Sherlockians.*

Part XXXIV: *Mind-bending puzzles are the highlight of Marcum's fully satisfying 34th anthology, which again demonstrates that multiple authors are capable of giving Sherlock Holmes and Watson innovative mysteries to tackle while staying in character. Marcum's inventory of canonical pastiches shows no signs of being exhausted any time soon.*

The MX Book of New Sherlock Holmes Stories
Edited by David Marcum
(MX Publishing, 2015-   )

An Investees' Anthology
Edited by David Marcum
(MX Publishing, 2022)

Selected Contributions to
The MX Book of New Sherlock Holmes Stories
by Members of
The Baker Street Irregulars

*All royalties from this collection are being donated
for the benefit of the preservation of Undershaw,
a school for special needs students located at
one of the former homes of Sir Arthur Conan Doyle*

Stories, Forewords, and Poems in this volume
have previously appeared in Parts I – XXXVI of
The MX Book of New Sherlock Holmes Stories

Featuring Contributions by:

Mark Alberstat, Marino C. Alvarez, Peter Calamai, Catherine Cooke, Carla Coupe, David Stuart Davies, John Farrell, Lyndsay Faye, Sonia Fetherston, Jayantika Ganguly, Jeffrey Hatcher, Roger Johnson, Leslie S. Klinger, Ann Margaret Lewis, Bonnie MacBird, Stephen Mason, Julie McKuras Nicholas Meyer, Jacquelynn Morris, Otto Penzler, Christopher Redmond, Tracy J. Revels, Steven Rothman, Nancy Holder, Mark Levy (and Arlene Mantin Levy), Nicholas Utechin, and Sean M. Wright (and DeForeest B. Wright, III)

MX Publishing

MX Publishing is the world's largest specialist Sherlock Holmes publisher, with over five-hundred titles and over two-hundred authors creating the latest in Sherlock Holmes fiction and non-fiction

The catalogue includes several award winning books, and over two-hundred-and-fifty have been converted into audio.

MX Publishing also has one of the largest communities of Holmes fans on Facebook, with regular contributions from dozens of authors.

www.mxpublishing.com

@mxpublishing on Facebook, Twitter, and Instagram

www.ingramcontent.com/pod-product-compliance
Lightning Source LLC
Chambersburg PA
CBHW032301020726
47495CB00001B/206